THE ARBOR HOUSE
TREASURY OF MYSTERY
AND SUSPENSE

THE ARBOR HOUSE TREASURY OF
MYSTERY AND SUSPENSE

Compiled by BILL PRONZINI,
BARRY N. MALZBERG
and MARTIN H. GREENBERG

With an Introduction by JOHN D. MACDONALD

ARBOR HOUSE   *New York*

ACKNOWLEDGMENTS

The following pages constitute an extension of the copyright page.

"Ransom," by Pearl S. Buck, reprinted by permission of Harold Ober Associates, Inc. Copyright © 1938 by Hearst Magazines, Inc. Renewed 1965 by Pearl S. Buck.

"The Adventure of the Glass-Domed Clock," by Ellery Queen is from *The Adventures of Ellery Queen.* Copyright © 1933 by Ellery Queen. Renewed 1961 by Frederic Dannay and Manfred B. Lee. Reprinted by permission of the author and his agents, Scott Meredith Literary Agency, Inc., 845 Third Avenue, New York, N.Y. 10022.

"The Arrow of God," by Leslie Charteris, copyright © 1954 by Leslie Charteris. Reprinted by permission of the author.

"A Passage to Benares," by T.S. Stribling is reprinted from *Clues of the Caribbees,* by T.S. Stribling. Copyright © 1929 by Doubleday and Co., Inc. Renewed 1957 by T.S. Stribling. Reprinted by permission of Mrs. Ella Stribling.

"The Case of the Emerald Sky," by Eric Ambler, copyright © Eric Ambler 1939. Reprinted by permission of the author.

"The Other Hangman," by John Dickson Carr, reprinted from *The Department of Queer Complaints* by Carter Dickson. Copyright © 1940 by William Morrow & Company, Inc.; renewed 1968 by John Dickson Carr. By permission of William Morrow & Company, Inc.

"The Couple Next Door," by Margaret Millar, reprinted by permission of Harold Ober Associates, Inc. Copyright © 1954 by Mercury Publications, Inc. First appeared in *Ellery Queen's Mystery Magazine.*

"Danger Out of the Past," by Erle Stanley Gardner, copyright © 1955 by Erle Stanley Gardner; originally titled "Protection." Reprinted by permission of the estate of Erle Stanley Gardner and Curtis Brown, Ltd.

"A Matter of Public Notice," by Dorothy Salisbury Davis, copyright © 1957 by Dorothy Salisbury Davis. Reprinted by permission of McIntosh and Otis, Inc.

"The Cat's-Paw," by Stanley Ellin, copyright © *Ellery Queen's Mystery Magazine,* June, 1949. Copyright renewed June, 1977. Reprinted by permission of the author.

"The Road to Damascus," by Michael Gilbert, copyright © Michael Gilbert 1963. Reprinted by permission of the author.

"Midnight Blue," by Ross Macdonald, reprinted by permission of Harold Ober Associates, Inc. Copyright © 1960 by Ross Macdonald.

"I'll Die Tomorrow," by Mickey Spillane, copyright © 1960 by Mickey Spillane. First published in *Cavalier* and reprinted by permission of the author.

"For All the Rude People," by Jack Ritchie, from June, 1961 *Alfred Hitchcock's*

6 ACKNOWLEDGMENTS

Mystery Magazine. Copyright © 1961 by H.S.D. Publications. Reprinted by permission of Larry Sternig Literary Agency.

"Hangover," by John D. MacDonald, copyright © 1956 by John D. MacDonald Publishing, Inc. Reprinted by permission of the author.

"The Santa Claus Club," by Julian Symons, is from *How to Trap a Crook* by Julian Symons. Davis Publications, copyright © 1977. Reprinted by permission of the author.

"The Wager," by Robert L. Fish, copyright © 1974 by Robert L. Fish. First published in *Playboy.* Reprinted by permission of Robert P. Mills, Ltd., agents for the estate of Robert L. Fish.

"A Fool About Money," by Ngaio Marsh, reprinted by permission of Harold Ober Associates, Inc. Copyright © 1974, Ngaio Marsh Limited. First appeared in *Ellery Queen's Mystery Magazine.*

"And Three to Get Ready . . . ," by H.L. Gold, copyright © 1952 by Ziff-Davis Publishing Company. First published in *Fantastic.* Reprinted by permission of the author.

"J," by Ed McBain, reprinted by permission of William Morris Agency, Inc. on behalf of the author. Copyright © 1961 by Ed McBain.

"Burial Monuments Three," by Edward D. Hoch, copyright © 1972 by H.S.D. Publications, Inc. First published in *Alfred Hitchcock's Mystery Magazine.* Reprinted by permission of the author.

"The Murder" and "Fatal Woman," by Joyce Carol Oates. Copyright © 1977 by Joyce Carol Oates. Appeared in *Night-Side.* Reprinted by permission of the author.

"Last Rendezvous," by Jean L. Backus, copyright © 1977 by Jean L. Backus. First published in *Ellery Queen's Mystery Magazine.* Reprinted by permission of the author.

"The Real Shape of the Coast," by John Lutz, copyright © 1971 by John Lutz. First published in *Ellery Queen's Mystery Magazine.* Reprinted by permission of the author.

"Hercule Poirot in the Year 2010," by Jon L. Breen, copyright © 1975 by Jon L. Breen. First published in *Ellery Queen's Mystery Magazine.* Reprinted by permission of the author.

"Merrill-Go-Round," by Marcia Muller, copyright © 1981 by Marcia Muller. An original story published by permission of the author.

"Tranquillity Base," by Asa Baber, copyright © 1979 by Fiction International. Reprinted by permission of the author.

"The Cabin in the Hollow," by Joyce Harrington. Copyright © 1974 by Davis Publications, Inc. Originally published in *Ellery Queen's Mystery Magazine;*

reprinted by permission of the author and her agents, Scott Meredith Literary Agency, Inc., 845 Third Avenue, New York, N.Y. 10022.

"Peckerman," by Robert S. Phillips, copyright © 1981 by Robert Phillips. Published by arrangement with the author.

"A Simple, Willing Attempt," by Elizabeth Morton, copyright © 1981 by Elizabeth Morton and published by arrangement with the author.

"Crime Wave in Pinhole," by Julie Smith, copyright © 1980 by Davis Publications, Inc. First published in *Alfred Hitchcock's Mystery Magazine*. Reprinted by permission of the author.

"Watching Marcia," by Michael D. Resnick. Copyright © 1981 by Michael D. Resnick; published by arrangement with the author.

"Somebody Cares," by Talmage Powell, copyright © 1962 by Davis Publications, Inc. First published in *Ellery Queen's Mystery Magazine*. Reprinted by permission of the author.

"Jode's Last Hunt," by Brian Garfield, copyright © 1976 by Brian Garfield. First published in the January, 1977 issue of *Ellery Queen's Mystery Magazine*. Reprinted by permission of the author.

"Many Mansions," by Robert Silverberg. Copyright © 1973 by Robert Silverberg; originally appeared in *Universe,* edited by Terry Carr and reprinted by permission of the author.

"My Son the Murderer," by Bernard Malamud, from *Rembrandt's Hat* by Bernard Malamud. Copyright © 1968, 1973 by Bernard Malamud. Reprinted by permission of Farrar, Straus and Giroux, Inc.

"A Craving for Originality," by Bill Pronzini, copyright © 1979 by Bill Pronzini. First published in *Ellery Queen's Mystery Magazine*. Reprinted by permission of the author.

"Agony Column," by Barry N. Malzberg, copyright © 1971 by Barry N. Malzberg. First published in *Ellery Queen's Mystery Magazine*. Reprinted by permission of the author.

Contents

Introduction

JOHN D. MACDONALD

Because I wrote one of the forty-two stories herein, and because several of the others were written by friends and acquaintances, it would be tacky to say anything other than that they are all of an equal, unsurpassable merit.

Twenty-five years ago the Macmillan Company published a symposium called *The Living Novel.* In the section written by Wright Morris, he said, in part, "Life, raw life, the kind we lead every day, whether it leads us into the past or the future, has the curious property of not seeming real *enough.* We have a need, however illusive, for a life that is more real than life. It lies in the imagination. Fiction would seem to be the way it is processed into reality. If this were not so we should have little excuse for art. Life, raw life, would be more than satisfactory in itself. But it seems to be the nature of man to transform—himself, if possible, and then the world around him—and the technique of this transformation is what we call art. When man fails to transform, he loses consciousness, he stops living."

I would have changed the word "consciousness" in the last sentence of the excerpt to "awareness."

Each of these stories, to be successful, must take us into its own reality, must make us accept its premise, believe in its people, yearn for the solutions to their dilemmas.

In stories as short as these, the writer must trust you, just as I am trusting you now, to turn these arbitrary little marks the printer has made on white paper into scenes and images and emotions. The reader, in a creative act in concert with the writer, must draw upon his own store-house, his own rich legacy of life experience and build an acceptable reality on the inferences within the prose style.

Let's play a game. First I will write an off-the-cuff description of a room:

"It was a high-ceilinged room paneled in a dark wood. When he walked in, he saw the heavy furniture, the desk with ornate carved legs, the grandfather clock, the long bookshelves, the gleam of small ivory figures behind the glass of a corner cabinet. Night was coming. The french doors were ajar."

That moves very slowly. I have not trusted you. I have told you more than you care to know or have to know. And so here is another way to do it:

"When he walked into the old man's den a white cat squalled and leapt from a high bookshelf down to the corner of the desk and to the floor, then trotted out the narrow opening of the french doors into the dusk of the garden, just as the grandfather clock began to strike."

I do not present the second version as any triumph of style, but merely to illustrate that kind of compression which advances a short story quickly because it trusts the reader to fill in static details from his own life experience.

In a novel there is more room for a leisurely pace, for more explicit description of environment and movement. In the short story the writer must trust the reader to help him achieve, quickly, "a life more real than life."

As must be obvious to you, the writer can pick the pockets of your mind most readily if the story relates to aspects of living which are familiar to you. Technological unemployment in a frabbis factory on the second largest moon of Neptune is going to require a lot more volume of words to establish than would a breakdown in a neighborhood laundromat. Percentage deals for foreign exploitation of winners from the film festival at Cannes is a situation far more difficult to handle in a short story than a ripoff on a used car. There is no more drama inherent in one situation than in the other. What is important to the people in the story becomes important to you. If a lot of establishing detail is required, it takes just that much longer to get to the action. If it takes too long, you, the reader, will go over and turn on the television set.

The able writer makes you build pictures in your head. Because those pictures are composed of bits and pieces of your human knowledge and experience, they are far more personal and far more satisfying and vivid than anything a producer, director and cluster of stars can show you on the big or the little screen. Those are pictures other people have made up. Your own personal private pictures are better and, curiously enough, more lasting.

This leads into another aspect of trust-the-reader. These are stories of mystery and suspense. People get involved with one another. People get killed. The reader knows what death is. The reader knows what sex is. The reader knows what a Christmas tree is, and so it is enough to say "There was a Christmas tree in the corner of the living room." One need not describe the tree, ornament by ornament, *unless* there is something totally unique about one ornament. Or unique about a death, or about a physical encounter. *Unique* in this context refers to what Hemingway said about all fiction—there should not be a word in it which does not either illuminate character or advance the story.

Trust the reader to become very quickly bored when the writer starts showing off a special knowledge which does not advance the story, be it about philately, dirt bikes, autopsies or tax shelters. Compression requires the imparting of esoteric knowledge only when it is directly involved with the story, or with a significant aspect of the character of one of the people in the story.

Also, dwelling upon gore in loving detail not only wastes time, space and momentum, but is far less effective than the showing of someone backing away from it in total horror, eyes bugging, fist pressed to the lips, color ashen. Then you, the reader, build your own little scene of dreadfulness instead of having the writer try to invent it for you.

If this sounds like a series of instructions to the writers of stories of mystery and suspense, I am not getting my point across. It is exactly that, but it is also, and more importantly, a guide to the reader who wonders why a certain story or novel seems flat.

Take a ridiculous aspect of a story such as the names of the characters. If it is about four people named Williamson, Jackson, Thompson and Johnson, the confusion is like a persistent knock in an engine. It spoils the trip.

Another trip-spoiler that can jump out at you without warning is the inadvertant grotesquerie, the image that jolts you out of the spell. My favorite of all time is, "He rolled his eyes down the front of her dress."

The writer I will not name who committed that little gem to paper was tone deaf. A writer—and that includes every professional I know—reads endlessly, and through reading learns the subtle nuances of meaning, learns the color and tone of words by themselves and in combination with other words. The writer who does not read is tone deaf. He clumps along humming his deadly monotone, not even hearing the thud of his wooden shoes on the floor of his little shed.

Tone deafness can afflict the reader as well, and in the case of the writer and the reader it is not as much a matter of a lack of sensitivity as it is too little lifetime reading. The creative reader takes these strange little black marks and turns them into bright convincing pictures.

The last aspect of trust I am going to mention—that trust which lets the reader process fiction into a kind of reality—is that degree of trust of the reader's intelligence and imagination which rules out needless reiteration. As with bad movie scripts, some stories insist upon telling the reader what you are going to tell him, then telling him, then telling him what you told him. That way lies madness—and a considerable impatience.

This is a pretty dumb introduction to these forty-two stories. I have told you a lot of the ways the writer can fail to hold up his end of the cooperative creative reader/writer relationship. But the people in this collection don't do these things. At least not very often. They have learned the arts of compression, illusion, honest misdirection and the discipline of how much to leave out.

Perhaps by my telling you about a few things they shouldn't do, you will appreciate all the better the good things they do. Each of us has our own way of processing the imagination into a kind of reality you will accept for the duration of the story. A different word for that is style.

Enough of this. I am writing about writing, and you are reading about reading. An incestuous arrangement. So turn to the real stuff.

John D. MacDonald

THE ARBOR HOUSE TREASURY OF MYSTERY AND SUSPENSE

The Gold-Bug

EDGAR ALLAN POE

It has been said that Edgar Allan Poe, that tortured genius who is considered the father of the modern detective story, foretold the entire evolution of the form in his handful of brilliant detective tales. Deduction, ratiocination, suspense, mystery—all of these elements and more were pioneered by Poe. "The Murders in the Rue Morgue" is the first locked room story; "The Mystery of Marie Roget" is the first psychological detective story. And "The Gold-Bug" is both the first cipher story and a masterpiece of mystery and detective analysis.

> What ho! what ho! this fellow is dancing mad!
> He hath been bitten by the Tarantula.
> *—All in the Wrong*

Many years ago, I contracted an intimacy with a Mr. William Legrand. He was of an ancient Huguenot family, and had once been wealthy; but a series of misfortunes had reduced him to want. To avoid the mortification consequent upon his disasters, he left New Orleans, the city of his forefathers, and took up his residence at Sullivan's Island, near Charleston, South Carolina.

This island is a very singular one. It consists of little else than the sea sand, and is about three miles long. Its breadth at no point exceeds a quarter of a mile. It is separated from the mainland by a scarcely perceptible creek, oozing its way through a wilderness of reeds and slime, a favorite resort of the marsh-hen. The vegetation, as might be supposed, is scant, or at least dwarfish. No trees of any magnitude are to be seen. Near the western extremity, where Fort Moultrie stands, and where are some miserable frame buildings, tenanted, during summer, by the fugitives from Charleston dust and fever, may be found, indeed, the bristly palmetto; but the whole island, with the exception of this western point, and a line of hard, white beach on the seacoast, is covered with a dense undergrowth of the sweet myrtle so much prized by the horticulturists of England. The shrub here often attains the height of fifteen or twenty feet, and forms an almost impenetrable coppice, burdening the air with its fragrance.

In the inmost recesses of this coppice, not far from the eastern or more remote end of the island, Legrand had built himself a small hut, which he occupied when I first, by mere accident, made his acquaintance. This soon ripened into friendship—for there was much in the recluse to excite interest and esteem. I found him well educated, with unusual powers of mind, but infected with misanthropy, and subject to perverse moods of alternate enthusiasm and melancholy. He had with him many books, but rarely employed them. His chief amusements were gunning and fishing, or sauntering along the beach and through the myrtles, in quest of shells or entomological specimens—his collection of the latter might have been envied by a Swammerdamm. In these excursions he was usually accompanied by an old Negro, called Jupiter, who had been manumitted before the reverses of the family, but who could be induced, neither by threats nor by promises, to abandon what he considered his right of attendance upon the footsteps of his young "Massa Will." It is not improbable that the relatives of Legrand, conceiving him to be somewhat unsettled in intellect, had contrived to instill this obstinancy into Jupiter, with a view to the supervision and guardianship of the wanderer.

The winters in the latitude of Sullivan's Island are seldom very severe, and in the fall of the year it is a rare event indeed when a fire is considered necessary. About the middle of October 18——, there occurred, however, a day of remarkable chilliness. Just before sunset I scrambled my way through the evergreens to the hut of my friend, whom I had not visited for several weeks—my residence being, at that time, in Charleston, a distance of nine miles from the island, while the facilities of passage and repassage were very far behind those of the present day. Upon reaching the hut I rapped, as was my custom, and getting no reply, sought for the key where I knew it was secreted, unlocked the door, and went in. A fine fire was blazing upon the hearth. It was a novelty, and by no means an ungrateful one. I threw off an overcoat, took an armchair by the crackling logs, and awaited patiently the arrival of my hosts.

Soon after dark they arrived, and gave me a most cordial welcome. Jupiter, grinning from ear to ear, bustled about to prepare some marshhens for supper. Legrand was in one of his fits—how else shall I term them?—of enthusiasm. He had found an unknown bivalve, forming a new genus, and, more than this, he had hunted down and secured, with Jupiter's assistance, a *scarabaeus* which he believed to be totally new, but in respect to which he wished to have my opinion on the morrow.

"And why not tonight?" I asked, rubbing my hands over the blaze, and wishing the whole tribe of *scarabaei* at the devil.

"Ah, if I had only known you were here!" said Legrand, "but it's so long since I saw you; and how could I foresee that you would pay me a visit this very night, of all others? As I was coming home I met Lieutenant G———, from the fort, and, very foolishly, I lent him the bug; so it will be impossible for you to see it until the morning. Stay here tonight, and I will send Jup down for it at sunrise. It is the loveliest thing in creation!"

"What?—sunrise?"

"Nonsense! No!—the bug. It is of a brilliant gold color—about the size of a large hickory-nut—with two jet-black spots near one extremity of the back, and another, somewhat longer, at the other. The antennae are—"

"Dey aint no tin in him, Massa Will, I keep a tellin on you," here interrupted Jupiter; "de bug is a goole-bug, solid, ebery bit of him, inside and all, sep him wing—neber feel half so hebby a bug in my life."

"Well, suppose it is, Jup," replied Legrand, somewhat more earnestly, it seemed to me, than the case demanded; "is that any reason for your letting the birds burn? The color—" here he turned to me—"is really almost enough to warrant Jupiter's idea. You never saw a more brilliant metallic luster than the scales emit—but of this you cannot judge till tomorrow. In the meantime I can give you some idea of the shape." Saying this, he seated himself at a small table, on which were a pen and ink, but no paper. He looked for some in a drawer, but found none.

"Never mind," he said at length, "this will answer"; and he drew from his waistcoat pocket a scrap of what I took to be very dirty foolscap, and made upon it a rough drawing with the pen. While he did this, I retained my seat by the fire, for I was still chilly. When the design was complete, he handed it to me without rising. As I received it, a loud growl was heard, succeeded by a scratching at the door. Jupiter opened it, and a large Newfoundland, belonging to Legrand, rushed in, leaped upon my shoulders, and loaded me with caresses; for I had shown him much attention during previous visits. When his gambols were over, I looked at the paper, and, to speak the truth, found myself not a little puzzled at what my friend had depicted.

"Well!" I said, after contemplating it for some minutes, "this *is* a strange *scarabaeus*, I must confess; new to me; never saw anything like it before—unless it was a skull, or a death's-head, which it more nearly resembles than anything else that has come under *my* observation."

"A death's-head!" echoed Legrand. "Oh—yes, well, it has something of that appearance upon paper, no doubt. The two upper black spots look like eyes, eh? And the longer one at the bottom like a mouth—and then the shape of the whole is oval."

"Perhaps so," said I; "but, Legrand, I fear you are no artist. I must wait until I see the beetle itself, if I am to form any idea of its personal appearance."

"Well, I don't know," said he, a little nettled, "I draw tolerably—*should* do it at least—have had good masters, and flatter myself that I am not quite a blockhead."

"But, my dear fellow, you are joking, then," said I; "this is a very passable *skull*—indeed, I may say that it is a very *excellent* skull, according to the vulgar notions about such specimens of physiology—and your *scarabaeus* must be the queerest *scarabaeus* in the world if it resembles it. Why, we may get up a very thrilling bit of superstition upon this hint. I presume you will call the bug *Scarabaeus caput hominis,* or something of that kind—there are many similar titles in the natural histories. But where are the antennae you spoke of?"

"The antennae?" said Legrand, who seemed to be getting unaccountably warm upon the subject; "I am sure you must see the antennae. I made them as distinct as they are in the original insect, and I presume that is sufficient."

"Well, well," I said, "perhaps you have—still I don't see them"; and I handed him the paper without additional remark, not wishing to ruffle his temper; but I was much surprised at the turn affairs had taken; his ill humor puzzled me—and, as for the drawing of the beetle, there were positively *no* antennae visible, and the whole *did* bear a very close resemblance to the ordinary cuts of a death's-head.

He received the paper very peevishly, and was about to crumple it, apparently to throw it in the fire, when a casual glance at the design seemed suddenly to rivet his attention. In an instant his face grew violently red—in another excessively pale. For some minutes he continued to scrutinize the drawing minutely where he sat. At length he arose, took a candle from the table, and proceeded to seat himself upon a sea-chest in the furthest corner of the room. Here again he made an anxious examination of the paper; turning it in all directions. He said nothing, however, and his conduct greatly astonished me; yet I thought it prudent not to exacerbate the growing moodiness of his temper by any comment. Presently he took from his coat pocket a wallet, placed the paper carefully in it, and deposited both in a writing desk, which he locked. He now grew more composed in his demeanor; but his original air of enthusiasm had quite disappeared. Yet he seemed not so much sulky as abstracted. As the evening wore away he became more and more absorbed in reverie, from which no sallies of mine could arouse him. It had been my intention to pass the night at the hut, as I had frequently done before, but, seeing my host in this mood, I deemed it proper to take leave. He did not press me to remain, but, as I departed, he shook my hand with even more than his usual cordiality.

It was about a month after this (and during the interval I had seen nothing of Legrand) when I received a visit, at Charleston, from his man, Jupiter. I had never seen the good old Negro look so dispirited, and I feared that some serious disaster had befallen my friend.

"Well, Jup," said I, "what is the matter now?—how is your master?"

"Why, to speak de troof, massa, him not so berry well as mought be."

"Not well! I am truly sorry to hear it. What does he complain of?"

"Dar! Dat's it!—him neber plain of notin—but him berry sick for all dat."

"*Very* sick, Jupiter!—why didn't you say so at once? Is he confined to bed?"

"No, dat he aint!—he aint fin'd nowhar—dat's just whar de shoe pinch —my mind is got to be berry hebby bout poor Massa Will."

"Jupiter, I should like to understand what it is you are talking about. You say your master is sick. Hasn't he told you what ails him?"

"Why, massa, taint worf while for to git mad about de matter—Massa Will say noffin at all aint de matter wid him—but den what make him go about looking dis here way, wid he head down and he soldiers up, and as white as a gose? And den he keep a syphon all de time—"

"Keeps a what, Jupiter?"

"Keeps a syphon wid de figgurs on de slate—de queerest figgurs I ebber did see. Ise gittin to be skeered, I tell you. Hab for to keep mighty tight eye pon him noovers. Todder day he gib me slip fore de sun up and was gone de whole ob de blessed day. I had a big stick ready cut for to gib him deuced good beating when he did come—but Ise sich a fool dat I hadn't de heart arter all—he looked so berry poorly."

"Eh?—what?—ah yes!—upon the whole I think you had better not be too severe with the poor fellow—don't flog him, Jupiter—he can't very well stand it—but can you form no idea of what has occasioned this illness, or rather this change of conduct? Has anything unpleasant happened since I saw you?"

"No, massa, dey aint bin noffin onpleasant *since* den—'twas *fore* den I'm feared—'twas de berry day you was dare."

"How? what do you mean?"

"Why, massa, I mean de bug—dare now."

"The what?"

"De bug—I'm berry sartin dat Massa Will bin bit somewhere bout de head by dat goole-bug."

"And what cause have you, Jupiter, for such a supposition?"

"Claws enuff, massa, and mouff, too. I nebber did see sich a deuced bug —he kick and he bite ebery ting what cum near him. Massa Will cotch him fuss, but had for to let him go gin mighty quick, I tell you—den was de time he must ha got de bite. I didn't like de look ob de bug mouff, myself, nohow, so I wouldn't take hold ob him wid my finger, but I cotch him wid a piece ob paper dat I found. I rap him up in de paper and stuff a piece of it in he mouff—dat was de way."

"And you think, then, that your master was really bitten by the beetle, and that the bite made him sick?"

"I don't tink noffin about it—I nose it. What make him dream bout de goole so much, if taint cause he bit by the goole-bug? Ise heerd bout dem goole-bugs fore dis."

"But how do you know he dreams about gold?"

"How I know? why, cause he talk about it in he sleep—dat's how I nose."

"Well, Jup, perhaps you are right; but to what fortunate circumstance am I to attribute the honor of a visit from you today?"

"What de matter, massa?"

"Did you bring any message from Mr. Legrand?"

"No, massa, I bring dis here pissel"; and here Jupiter handed me a note which ran thus:

My Dear————:

Why have I not seen you for so long a time? I hope you have not been so foolish as to take offense at any little brusquerie of mine; but no, that is improbable.

Since I saw you I have had great cause for anxiety. I have something to tell you, yet scarcely know how to tell it, or whether I should tell it at all.

I have not been quite well for some days past, and poor old Jup annoys me, almost beyond endurance, by his well-meant attentions. Would you believe it? —he had prepared a huge stick, the other day, with which to chastise me for giving him the slip, and spending the day, solus, among the hills on the mainland. I verily believe that my ill looks alone saved me a flogging.

I have made no addition to my cabinet since we met.

If you can, in any way, make it convenient, come over with Jupiter. Do come. I wish to see you tonight, upon business of importance. I assure you that it is of the highest importance.

Ever yours,
William Legrand

There was something in the tone of this note which gave me great uneasiness. Its whole style differed materially from that of Legrand. What could he be dreaming of? What new crotchet possessed his excitable brain? What "business of the highest importance," could *he* possibly have to transact? Jupiter's account of him boded no good. I dreaded lest the continued pressure of misfortune had, at length, fairly unsettled the reason of my friend. Without a moment's hesitation, therefore, I prepared to accompany the Negro.

Upon reaching the wharf, I noticed a scythe and three spades, all apparently new, lying in the bottom of the boat in which we were to embark.

"What is the meaning of all this, Jup?" I inquired.

"Him syfe, massa, and spade."

"Very true; but what are they doing here?"

"Him de syfe and de spade what Massa Will sis pon my buying for him in de town, and de debbil's own lot of money I had to gib for em."

"But what, in the name of all that is mysterious, is your 'Massa Will' going to do with scythes and spades?"

"Dat's more dan *I* know, and debbil take me if I don't blieve 'tis more dan he know, too. But it's all cum ob de bug."

Finding that no satisfaction was to be obtained of Jupiter, whose whole intellect seemed to be absorbed by "de bug," I now stepped into the boat, and made sail. With a fair and strong breeze we soon ran into the little cove to the northward of Fort Moultrie, and a walk of some two miles brought us to the hut. It was about three in the afternoon when we arrived. Legrand had been awaiting us in eager expectation. He grasped my hand with a nervous *empressement* which alarmed me and strengthened the suspicions already entertained. His countenance was pale even to ghastliness, and his deep-set eyes glared with unnatural luster. After some inquiries respecting his health, I asked him, not knowing what better to say, if he had yet obtained the *scarabaeus* from Lieutenant G———.

"Oh, yes," he replied, coloring violently, "I got it from him the next morning. Nothing should tempt me to part with that *scarabaeus*. Do you know that Jupiter is quite right about it?"

"In what way?" I asked, with a sad foreboding at heart.

"In supposing it to be a bug of *real gold.*" He said this with an air of profound seriousness, and I felt inexpressibly shocked.

"This bug is to make my fortune," he continued, with a triumphant smile; "to reinstate me in my family possessions. Is it any wonder, then, that I prize it? Since fortune has thought fit to bestow it upon me, I have only to use it properly, and I shall arrive at the gold of which it is the index. Jupiter, bring me that *scarabaeus!*"

"What! De bug, massa? I'd rudder not go fer trubble dat bug; you mus git him for your own self." Hereupon Legrand arose, with a grave and stately air, and brought me the beetle from a glass case in which it was enclosed. It was a beautiful *scarabaeus,* and, at that time, unknown to naturalists—of course a great prize in a scientific point of view. There were two round black spots near one extremity of the back, and a long one near the other. The scales were exceedingly hard and glossy, with all the appearance of burnished gold. The weight of the insect was very remarkable, and, taking all things into consideration, I could hardly blame Jupiter for his opinion respecting it; but what to make of Legrand's concordance with that opinion, I could not, for the life of me, tell.

"I sent for you," said he, in a grandiloquent tone, when I had completed my examination of the beetle, "I sent for you that I might have your counsel and assistance in furthering the views of fate and of the bug—"

"My dear Legrand," I cried, interrupting him, "you are certainly unwell, and had better use some little precautions. You shall go to bed, and I will remain with you a few days, until you get over this. You are feverish and—"

"Feel my pulse," said he.

I felt it, and, to say the truth, found not the slightest indication of fever.

"But you may be ill and yet have no fever. Allow me this once to prescribe for you. In the first place, go to bed. In the next—"

"You are mistaken," he interposed, "I am as well as I can expect to be under the excitement which I suffer. If you really wish me well, you will relieve this excitement."

"And how is this to be done?"

"Very easily. Jupiter and myself are going upon an expedition into the hills, upon the mainland, and, in this expedition, we shall need the aid of some person in whom we can confide. You are the only one we can trust. Whether we succeed or fail, the excitement which you now perceive in me will be equally allayed."

"I am anxious to oblige you in any way," I replied; "but do you mean to say that this infernal beetle has any connection with your expedition into the hills?"

"It has."

"Then, Legrand, I can become a party to no such absurd proceeding."

"I am sorry—very sorry—for we shall have to try it by ourselves."

"Try it by yourselves! The man is surely mad!—but stay!—how long do you propose to be absent?"

"Probably all night. We shall start immediately, and be back, at all events, by sunrise."

"And will you promise me, upon your honor, that when this freak of yours is over, and the bug business (good God!) settled to your satisfaction, you will then return home and follow my advice implicitly, as that of your physician?"

"Yes; I promise; and now let us be off, for we have no time to lose."

With a heavy heart I accompanied my friend. We started about four o'clock—Legrand, Jupiter, the dog, and myself. Jupiter had with him the scythe and spades—the whole of which he insisted upon carrying—more through fear, it seemed to me, of trusting either of the implements within reach of his master, than from any excess of industry or complaisance. His demeanor was dogged in the extreme, and "dat deuced bug" were the sole words which escaped his lips during the journey. For my own part, I had charge of a couple of dark lanterns, while Legrand contented himself with the *scarabaeus,* which he carried attached to the end of a bit of whip-cord; twirling it to and fro, with the air of a conjuror, as he went. When I observed this last, plain evidence of my friend's aberration of mind, I could scarcely refrain from tears. I thought it best, however, to humor his fancy, at least for the present, or until I could adopt some more energetic measures with a chance of success. In the meantime I endeavored, but all in vain, to sound him in regard to the object of the expedition. Having succeeded in inducing me to accompany him, he seemed unwilling to hold conversation upon any topic of minor importance, and to all my questions vouchsafed no other reply than "we shall see!"

We crossed the creek at the head of the island by means of a skiff, and, ascending the high grounds on the shore of the mainland, proceeded in a northwesterly direction, through a tract of country excessively wild and desolate, where no trace of a human footstep was to be seen. Legrand led the way with decision; pausing only for an instant, here and there, to consult what appeared to be certain landmarks of his own contrivance upon a former occasion.

In this manner we journeyed for about two hours, and the sun was just setting when we entered a region infinitely more dreary than any yet seen. It was a species of tableland, near the summit of an almost inaccessible hill, densely wooded from base to pinnacle, and interspersed with huge crags that appeared to lie loosely upon the soil, and in many cases were prevented from precipitating themselves into the valleys below, merely by the support of the trees against which they reclined. Deep ravines, in various directions, gave an air of still sterner solemnity to the scene.

The natural platform to which we had clambered was thickly over-grown with brambles, through which we soon discovered that it would have been impossible to force our way but for the scythe; and Jupiter, by direction of his master, proceeded to clear for us a path to the foot of an enormously tall tulip-tree, which stood, with some eight or ten oaks, upon the level, and far surpassed them all, and all other trees which I had then ever seen, in the beauty of its foliage and form, in the wide spread of its branches, and in the general majesty of its appearance. When we reached this tree, Legrand turned to Jupiter, and asked him if he thought he could climb it. The old man seemed a little staggered by the question, and for some moments made no reply. At length he approached the huge trunk, walked slowly around it and examined it with minute attention. When he had completed his scrutiny, he merely said:

"Yes, massa, Jup climb any tree he ebber see in he life."

"Then up with you as soon as possible, for it will soon be too dark to see what we are about."

"How far mus go up, massa?" inquired Jupiter.

"Get up the main trunk first, and then I will tell you which way to go —and here—stop! take this beetle with you."

"De bug, Massa Will!—de goole-bug!" cried the Negro, drawing back in dismay—"what for mus tote de bug way up de tree?—d——n if I do!"

"If you are afraid, Jup, a great big Negro like you, to take hold of a harmless little dead beetle, why you can carry it up by this string—but, if you do not take it up with you in some way, I shall be under the necessity of breaking your head with this shovel."

"What de matter now, massa?" said Jup, evidently shamed into compli-ance; "always want for to raise fuss wid old nigger. Was only funnin, anyhow. *Me* feered de bug! what I keer for de bug?" Here he took cautiously hold of the extreme end of the string, and, maintaining the insect as far from his person as circumstances would permit, prepared to ascend the tree.

In youth, the tulip-tree, or *Liriodendron tulipiferum*, the most magnificent of American foresters, has a trunk peculiarly smooth, and often rises to a great height without lateral branches; but, in its riper age, the bark becomes gnarled and uneven, while many short limbs make their appearance on the stem. Thus the difficulty of ascension, in the present case, lay more in semblance than in reality. Embracing the huge cylinder, as closely as possible with his arms and knees, seizing with his hands some projections, and resting his naked toes upon others, Jupiter, after one or two narrow escapes from falling, at length wriggled himself into the first great fork, and seemed to consider the whole business as virtually accomplished. The *risk* of the achievement was, in fact, now over, although the climber was some sixty or seventy feet from the ground.

"Which way mus go now, Massa Will?" he asked.

"Keep up the largest branch—the one on this side," said Legrand. The Negro obeyed him promptly, and apparently with but little trouble; ascending higher and higher, until no glimpse of his squat figure could be obtained through the dense foliage which enveloped it. Presently his voice was heard in a sort of halloo.

"How much fudder is got for go?"

"How high up are you?" asked Legrand.

"Ebber so fur," replied the Negro; "can see de sky fru de top ob de tree."

"Never mind the sky, but attend to what I say. Look down the trunk and count the limbs below you on this side. How many limbs have you passed?"

"One, two, tree, four, fibe—I done pass fibe big limb, massa, pon dis side."

"Then go one limb higher."

In a few minutes the voice was heard again, announcing that the seventh limb was attained.

"Now, Jup," cried Legrand, evidently much excited, "I want you to work your way out upon that limb as far as you can. If you see anything strange let me know."

By this time what little doubt I might have entertained of my poor friend's insanity was put finally at rest. I had no alternative but to conclude him stricken with lunacy, and I became seriously anxious about getting him home. While I was pondering upon what was best to be done, Jupiter's voice was again heard.

"Mos feered for to venture pon dis limb berry far—tis dead limb putty much all de way."

"Did you say it was a *dead* limb, Jupiter?" cried Legrand in a quavering voice.

"Yes, massa, him dead as de door-nail—done up for sartin—done departed dis here life."

"What in the name of heaven shall I do?" asked Legrand, seemingly in the greatest distress.

"Do!" said I, glad of an opportunity to interpose a word, "why, come home and go to bed. Come now!—that's a fine fellow. It's getting late, and, besides, you remember your promise."

"Jupiter," cried he, without heeding me in the least, "do you hear me?"

"Yes, Massa Will, hear you ebber so plain."

"Try the wood well, then, with your knife, and see if you think it *very* rotten."

"Him rotten, massa, sure nuff," replied the Negro in a few moments, "but not so berry rotten as mought be. Mought venture out lettle way pon de limb by myself, dat's true."

"By yourself!—what do you mean?"

"Why, I mean de bug. Tis *berry* hebby bug. Spose I drop him down fuss, and den de limb won't break wid just de weight ob one nigger."

"You infernal scoundrel!" cried Legrand, apparently much relieved, "what do you mean by telling me such nonsense as that? As sure as you drop that beetle I'll break your neck. Look here, Jupiter, do you hear me?"

"Yes, massa, needn't hollo at poor nigger dat style."

"Well! Now listen!—if you will venture out on the limb as far as you think safe, and not let go the beetle, I'll make you a present of a silver dollar as soon as you get down."

"I'm gwine, Massa Will—deed I is," replied the Negro very promptly —"mos out to the eend now."

"Out to the end!" here fairly screamed Legrand; "do you say you are out to the end of that limb?"

"Soon be to the eend, massa—o-o-o-o-oh! Lor-gol-a-mercy! What *is* dis here pon de tree?"

"Well!" cried Legrand, highly delighted, "what is it?"

"Why, taint noffin but a skull—somebody bin lef him head up de tree, and de crows done gobble ebery bit ob de meat off."

"A skull, you say!—very well—how is it fastened to the limb?—what holds it on?"

'Sure nuff, massa; mus look. Why dis berry curious sarcumstance, pon my word—dare's a great big nail in de skull, what fastens ob it on to de tree."

"Well now, Jupiter, do exactly as I tell you—do you hear?"

"Yes, massa."

"Pay attention, then—find the left eye of the skull."

"Hum! Hoo! Dat's good! Why dey aint no lef eye at all."

"Curse your stupidity! Do you know your right hand from your left?"

"Yes, I nose dat—nose all about dat—tis my lef hand what I chops de wood wid."

"To be sure! You are left-handed; and your left eye is on the same side as your left hand. Now, I suppose, you can find the left eye of the skull, or the place where the left eye has been. Have you found it?"

Here was a long pause. At length the Negro asked:

"Is de lef eye of de skull pon de same side as de lef hand of de skull, too?—cause de skull aint got not a bit ob a hand at all—nebber mind! I got de lef eye now—here de lef eye! what mus do wid it?"

"Let the beetle drop through it, as far as the string will reach—but be careful and not let go your hold of the string."

"All dat done, Massa Will; mighty easy ting for to put de bug fru de hole—look out for him dare below!"

During this colloquy no portion of Jupiter's person could be seen; but the beetle, which he had suffered to descend, was now visible at the end of the string, and glistened, like a globe of burnished gold, in the last rays of the setting sun, some of which still faintly illumined the eminence upon which we stood. The *scarabaeus* hung quite clear of any branches, and, if allowed to fall, would have fallen at our feet. Legrand immediately took the scythe, and cleared with it a circular space, three or four yards in diameter, just beneath the insect, and, having accomplished this, ordered Jupiter to let go the string and come down from the tree.

Driving a peg, with great nicety, into the ground, at the precise spot where the beetle fell, my friend now produced from his pocket a tape-measure. Fastening one end of this at that point of the trunk of the tree which was nearest the peg, he unrolled it till it reached the peg and thence further unrolled it, in the direction already established by the two points of the tree and the peg, for the distance of fifty feet—Jupiter clearing away the brambles with the scythe. At the spot thus attained a second peg was driven, and about this, as a center, a rude circle, about four feet in diameter, described. Taking now a spade himself, and giving one to

Jupiter and one to me, Legrand begged us to set about digging as quickly as possible.

To speak the truth, I had no especial relish for such amusement at any time, and, at that particular moment, would willingly have declined it; for the night was coming on, and I felt much fatigued with the exercise already taken; but I saw no mode of escape, and was fearful of disturbing my poor friend's equanimity by a refusal. Could I have depended, indeed, upon Jupiter's aid, I would have had no hesitation in attempting to get the lunatic home by force; but I was too well assured of the old Negro's disposition to hope that he would assist me, under any circumstances, in a personal contest with his master. I made no doubt that the latter had been infected with some of the innumerable Southern superstitions about money buried, and that his fantasy had received confirmation by the finding of the *scarabaeus*, or, perhaps, by Jupiter's obstinancy in maintaining it to be "a bug of real gold." A mind disposed to lunacy would readily be led away by such suggestions—especially if chiming in with favorite preconceived ideas—and then I called to mind the poor fellow's speech about the beetle's being "the index of his fortune." Upon the whole, I was sadly vexed and puzzled, but, at length, I concluded to make a virtue of necessity—to dig with a good will, and thus the sooner to convince the visionary, by ocular demonstration, of the fallacy of the opinion he entertained.

The lanterns having been lit, we all fell to work with a zeal worthy a more rational cause; and, as the glare fell upon our persons and implements, I could not help thinking how picturesque a group we composed, and how strange and suspicious our labors must have appeared to any interloper who, by chance, might have stumbled upon our whereabouts.

We dug very steadily for two hours. Little was said; and our chief embarrassment lay in the yelping of the dog, who took exceeding interest in our proceedings. He, at length, became so obstreperous that we grew fearful of his giving the alarm to some stragglers in the vicinity—or, rather, this was the apprehension of Legrand—for myself, I should have rejoiced at any interruption which might have enabled me to get the wanderer home. The noise was, at length, very effectually silenced by Jupiter, who, getting out of the hole with a dogged air of deliberation, tied the brute's mouth up with one of his suspenders, and then returned, with a grave chuckle, to his task.

When the time mentioned had expired, we had reached a depth of five feet, and yet no signs of any treasure became manifest. A general pause ensued, and I began to hope that the farce was at an end. Legrand, however, although evidently much disconcerted, wiped his brow thoughtfully and recommenced. We had excavated the entire circle of four feet diameter, and now we slightly enlarged the limit, and went to the further depth of two feet. Still nothing appeared. The gold-seeker, whom I sincerely pitied, at length clambered from the pit, with the bitterest disappointment imprinted upon every feature, and proceeded, slowly and reluctantly, to put on his coat, which he had thrown off at the beginning of his labor. In the meantime I made no remark. Jupiter, at a signal from his master, began to gather up his tools. This done, and the dog having been unmuzzled, we turned in profound silence toward home.

We had taken, perhaps, a dozen steps in this direction, when, with a loud oath, Legrand strode up to Jupiter, and seized him by the collar. The astonished Negro opened his eyes and mouth to the fullest extent, let fall the spades, and fell upon his knees.

"You scoundrel!" said Legrand, hissing out the syllables from between his clinched teeth—"you infernal black villain!—speak, I tell you!—answer me this instant, without prevarication!—which—which is your left eye?"

"Oh, my golly, Massa Will! aint dis here my lef eye for sartain?" roared the terrified Jupiter, placing his hand upon his *right* organ of vision, and holding it there with a desperate pertinacity, as if in immediate dread of his master's attempt at a gouge.

"I thought so!—I knew it! Hurrah!" vociferated Legrand, letting the Negro go and executing a series of curvets and caracols, much to the astonishment of his valet, who, arising from his knees, looked, mutely, from his master to myself, and then from myself to his master.

"Come! We must go back," said the latter, "the game's not up yet"; and he again led the way to the tulip-tree.

"Jupiter," said he, when we reached its foot, "come here! was the skull nailed to the limb with the face outward, or with the face to the limb?"

"De face was out, massa, so dat de crows could gt at de eyes good, widout any trouble."

"Well, then, was it this eye or that through which you dropped the beetle?" her Legrand touched each of Jupiter's eyes.

" 'Twas dis eye, massa—de lef eye—jis as you tell me," and here it was his right eye that the negro indicated.

"That will do—we must try it again."

Here my friend, about whose madness I now saw, or fancied that I saw, certain indications of method, removed the peg which marked the spot where the beetle fell, to a spot about three inches to the westward of its former position. Taking, now, the tape measure from the nearest point of the trunk to the peg, as before, and continuing the extension in a straight line to the distance of fifty feet, a spot was indicated, removed, by several yards, from the point at which we had been digging.

Around the new position a circle, somewhat larger than in the former instance, was now described, and we again set to work with the spade. I was dreadfully weary, but, scarcely understanding what had occasioned the change in my thoughts, I felt no longer any great aversion from the labor imposed. I had become most unaccountably interested—nay, even excited. Perhaps there was something, amid all the extravagant demeanor of Legrand—some air of forethought, or of deliberation, which impressed me. I dug eagerly, and now and then caught myself actually looking, with something that very much resembled expectation, for the fancied treasure, the vision of which had demented my unfortunate companion. At a period when such vagaries of thought most fully possessed me, and when we had been at work perhaps an hour and a half, we were again interrupted by the violent howlings of the dog. His uneasiness, in the first instance, had been, evidently, but the result of playfulness or caprice, but he now assumed a bitter and serious tone. Upon Jupiter's again attempting to muzzle him, he made furious resistance, and, leaping into the hole, tore up the mould frantically with his claws. In a few seconds he had uncovered a mass of human bones, forming two complete skeletons, intermingled with several buttons of metal, and what appeared to be the dust of decayed woolen. One or two strokes of a spade upturned the blade of a large Spanish knife, and, as we dug further, three or four loose pieces of gold and silver coin came to light.

At sight of these the joy of Jupiter could scarcely be restrained, but the countenance of his master wore an air of extreme disappointment. He urged us, however, to continue our exertions, and the words were hardly uttered when I stumbled and fell forward, having caught the toe of my boot in a large ring of iron that lay half buried in the loose earth.

We now worked in earnest, and never did I pass ten minutes of more intense excitement. During this interval we had fairly unearthed an oblong chest of wood, which, from its perfect preservation and wonderful hardness, had plainly been subjected to some mineralizing process—perhaps that of the bichloride of mercury. This box was three feet and a half long, three feet broad, and two and a half feet deep. It was firmly

secured by bands of wrought iron, riveted, and forming a kind of open
trellis-work over the whole. On each side of the chest, near the top, were
three rings of iron—six in all—by means of which a firm hold could be
obtained by six persons. Our utmost united endeavors served only to
disturb the coffer very slightly in its bed. We at once saw the impossibility
of removing so great a weight. Luckily, the sole fastenings of the lid
consisted of two sliding bolts. These we drew back—trembling and panting with anxiety. In an instant, a treasure of incalculable value lay gleaming before us. As the rays of the lanterns fell within the pit, there flashed
upward a glow and a glare, from a confused heap of gold and jewels, that
absolutely dazzled our eyes.

I shall not pretend to describe the feelings with which I gazed. Amazement was, of course, predominant. Legrand appeared exhausted with
excitement, and spoke very few words. Jupiter's countenance wore, for
some minutes, as deadly a pallor as it is possible, in the nature of things,
for any Negro's visage to assume. He seemed stupefied—thunderstricken.
Presently he fell upon his knees in the pit, and burying his naked arms
up to the elbows in gold, let them there remain, as if enjoying the luxury
of a bath. At length, with a deep sigh, he exclaimed, as if in a soliloquy:

"And dis all cum ob de goole-bug! De putty goole-bug! De poor little
goole-bug, what I boosed in that sabage kind ob style! Aint you shamed
ob yourself, nigger?—answer me dat!"

It became necessary, at last, that I should arouse both master and valet
to the expediency of removing the treasure. It was growing late, and it
behooved us to make exertion, that we might get everything housed
before daylight. It was difficult to say what should be done, and much time
was spent in deliberation—so confused were the ideas of all. We, finally,
lightened the box by removing two-thirds of its contents, when we were
enabled, with some trouble, to raise it from the hole. The articles taken
out were deposited among the brambles, and the dog left to guard them,
with strict orders from Jupiter neither, upon any pretense, to stir from the
spot, nor to open his mouth until our return. We then hurriedly made
for home with the chest; reaching the hut in safety, but after excessive
toil, at one o'clock in the morning. Worn out as we were, it was not in
human nature to do more immediately. We rested until two, and had
supper; starting for the hills immediately afterward, armed with three
stout sacks, which, by good luck, were upon the premises. A little before
four we arrived at the pit, divided the remainder of the booty, as equally
as might be, among us, and, leaving the holes unfilled, again set out for

the hut, at which, for the second time, we deposited our golden burdens, just as the first faint streaks of the dawn gleamed from over the treetops in the east.

We were now thoroughly broken down; but the intense excitement of the time denied us repose. After an unquiet slumber of some three or four hours' duration, we arose, as if by preconcert, to make examination of our treasure.

The chest had been full to the brim, and we spent the whole day, and the greater part of the next night, in a scrutiny of its contents. There had been nothing like order or arrangement. Everything had been heaped in promiscuously. Having assorted all with care, we found ourselves possessed of even vaster wealth than we had at first supposed. In coin, there was rather more than four hundred and fifty thousand dollars—estimating the value of the pieces, as accurately as we could, by the tables of the period. There was not a particle of silver. All was gold of antique date and of great variety—French, Spanish, and German money, with a few English guineas, and some counters, of which we had never seen specimens before. There were several very large and heavy coins, so worn that we could make nothing of their inscriptions. There was no American money. The value of the jewels we found more difficulty in estimating. There were diamonds —some of them exceedingly large and fine—a hundred and ten in all, and not one of them small; eighteen rubies of remarkable brilliancy; three hundred and ten emeralds, all very beautiful; and twenty-one sapphires, with an opal. These stones had all been broken from their settings and thrown loose in the chest. The settings themselves, which we picked out from among the other gold, appeared to have been beaten up with hammers, as if to prevent identification. Besides all this, there was a vast quantity of solid gold ornaments; nearly two hundred massive finger and ear rings; rich chains—thirty of these, if I remember; eighty-three very large and heavy crucifixes; five gold censers of great value; a prodigious golden punch-bowl, ornamented with richly chased vine-leaves and Bacchanalian figures; with two sword-handles exquisitely embossed, and many other smaller articles which I can not recollect. The weight of these valuables exceeded three hundred and fifty pounds avoirdupois; and in this estimate I have not included one hundred and ninety-seven superb gold watches; three of the number being worth each five hundred dollars, if one. Many of them were very old, and as timekeepers, valueless; the works having suffered, more or less, from corrosion—but all were richly jeweled and in cases of great worth. We estimated the entire contents of the chest, that night, at a million and a half of dollars; and upon the subsequent disposal of the trinkets and jewels (a few being retained for our own use), it was found that we had greatly undervalued the treasure.

When, at length, we had concluded our examination, and the intense excitement of the time had, in some measure, subsided, Legrand, who saw that I was dying with impatience for a solution of this most extraordinary riddle, entered into a full detail of all the circumstances connected with it.

"You remember," said he, "the night when I handed you the rough sketch I had made of the *scarabaeus.* You recollect, also, that I became quite vexed at you for insisting that my drawing resembled a death's-head. When you first made this assertion I thought you were jesting; but afterward I called to mind the peculiar spots on the back of the insect, and admitted to myself that your remark ahd some little foundation in fact. Still, the sneer at my graphic powers irritated me—for I am considered a good artist—and, therefore, when you handed me the scrap of parchment, I was about to crumple it up and throw it angrily into the fire."

"The scrap of paper, you mean," said I.

"No; it had much of the appearance of paper, and at first I supposed it to be such, but when I came to draw upon it, I discovered it at once to be a piece of very thin parchment. It was quite dirty, you remember. Well, as I was in the very act of crumpling it up, my glance fell upon the sketch at which you had been looking, and you may imagine my astonishment when I perceived, in fact, the figure of a death's-head just where, it seemed to me, I had made the drawing of the beetle. For a moment I was too much amazed to think with accuracy. I knew that my design was very different in detail from this—although there was a certain similarity in general outline. Presently I took a candle, and seating myself at the other end of the room, proceeded to scrutinize the parchment more closely. Upon turning it over, I saw my own sketch upon the reverse, just as I had made it. My first idea, now, was mere surprise at the really remarkable similarity of outline—at the singular coincidence involved in the fact that, unknown to me, there should have been a skull upon the other side of the parchment, immediately beneath my figure of the *scarabaeus,* and that this skull, not only in outline, but in size should so closely resemble my drawing. I say the singularity of this coincidence absolutely stupefied me for a time. This is the usual effect of such coincidences. The mind struggles to establish a connection—a sequence of cause and effect—and, being unable to do so, suffers a species of temporary paralysis. But, when I recovered from this stupor, there dawned upon me gradually a conviction which startled me even far more than the coincidence. I began distinctly, positively, to remember that there had been *no* drawing upon the parchment when I made my sketch of the *scarabaeus.* I became perfectly certain of this; for I recollected turning up first one side and then the other, in search of the cleanest spot. Had the skull been then there, of course, I could not have failed to notice it. Here was indeed a mystery which I felt it impossible to explain; but, even at that early moment, there seemed to glimmer, faintly, within the most remote and secret chambers of my intellect, a glowwormlike conception of that truth which last night's adventure brought to so magnificent a demonstration. I arose at once, and, putting the parchment securely away, dismissed all further reflection until I should be alone.

"When you had gone, and when Jupiter was fast asleep, I betook myself to a more methodical investigation of the affair. In the first place, I considered the manner in which the parchment had come into my possession. The spot where we discovered the *scarabaeus* was on the coast of the mainland, about a mile eastward of the island, and but a short distance over high-water mark. Upon my taking hold of it, it gave me a sharp bite, which caused me to let it drop. Jupiter, with his accustomed caution, before seizing the insect, which had flown toward him, looked about him for a leaf, or something of that nature, by which to take hold of it. It was at this moment that his eyes, and mine also, fell upon the scrap of parchment, which I then supposed to be paper. It was lying half buried in the sand, a corner sticking up. Near the spot where we found it, I observed the remnants of the hull of what appeared to have been a ship's long-boat. The wreck seemed to have been there for a very great while; for the resemblance to boat timbers could scarcely be traced.

"Well, Jupiter picked up the parchment, wrapped the beetle in it, and gave it to me. Soon afterward we turned to go home, and on the way met Lieutenant G———. I showed him the insect, and he begged me to let him take it to the fort. Upon my consenting, he thrust it forthwith into his waistcoat pocket, without the parchment in which it had been wrapped, and which I had continued to hold in my hand during his inspection. Perhaps he dreaded my changing my mind, and thought it best to make sure of the prize at once—you know how enthusiastic he is on all subjects connected with natural history. At the same time, without being conscious of it, I must have deposited the parchment in my own pocket.

"You remember that when I went to the table for the purpose of making a sketch of the beetle, I found no paper where it was usually kept. I looked in the drawer, and found none there. I searched my pockets, hoping to find an old letter, when my hand fell upon the parchment. I thus detail the precise mode in which it came into my possession; for the circumstances impressed me with peculiar force.

"No doubt you will think me fanciful—but I had already established a kind of *connection.* I had put together two links of a great chain. There was a boat lying upon a seacoast, and not far from the boat was a parchment—*not a paper*—with a skull depicted upon it. You will, of course, ask 'where is the connection?' I reply that the skull, or death's-head, is the well-known emblem of the pirate. The flag of the death's-head is hoisted in all engagements.

"I have said that the scrap was parchment, and not paper. Parchment is durable—almost imperishable. Matters of little moment are rarely consigned to parchment; since, for the mere ordinary purposes of drawing or writing, it is not nearly so well adapted as paper. This reflection suggested some meaning—some relevancy—in the death's-head. I did not fail to observe, also the *form* of the parchment. Although one of its corners had been, by some accident, destroyed, it could be seen that the original form was oblong. It was just such a slip, indeed, as might have been chosen for a memorandum—for a record of something to be long remembered and carefully preserved."

"But," I interposed, "you say that the skull was *not* upon the parchment when you made the drawing of the beetle. How then do you trace any connection between the boat and the skull—since this latter, according to your own admission, must have been designed (God only knows how or by whom) at some period subsequent to your sketching the *scarabaeus?*"

"Ah, hereupon turns the whole mystery; although the secret, at this point, I had comparatively little difficulty in solving. My steps were sure, and could afford but a single result. I reasoned, for example, thus: when I drew the *scarabaeus,* there was no skull apparent upon the parchment. When I had completed the drawing I gave it to you, and observed you narrowly until you returned it. *You,* therefore, did not design the skull, and no one else was present to do it. Then it was not done by human agency. And nevertheless it was done.

"At this stage of my reflections I endeavored to remember, and *did* remember, with entire distinctiveness, every incident which occurred about the period in question. The weather was chilly (oh, rare and happy accident!), and a fire was blazing upon the hearth. I was heated with exercise and sat near the table. You, however, had drawn a chair close to the chimney. Just as I placed the parchment in your hand, and as you were in the act of inspecting it, Wolf, the Newfoundland, entered, and leaped upon your shoulders. With your left hand you caressed him and kept him off, while your right, holding the parchment, was permitted to fall list-lessly between your knees, and in close proximity to the fire. At one moment I thought the blaze had caught it, and was about to caution you, but, before I could speak, you had withdrawn it, and were engaged in its examination. When I considered all these particulars, I doubted not for a moment that *heat* had been the agent in bringing to light, upon the parchment, the skull which I saw designed upon it. You are well aware that chemical preparations exist, and have existed time out of mind, by means of which it is possible to write upon either paper or vellum, so that the characters shall become visible only when subjected to the action of fire. Zaffre, digested in *aqua regia,* and diluted with four times its weight of water, is sometimes employed; a green tint results. The regulus of cobalt, dissolved in spirit of nitre, gives a red. These colors disappear at longer or shorter intervals after the material written upon cools, but again becomes apparent upon the reapplication of heat.

"I now scrutinized the death's-head with care. Its outer edges—the edges of the drawing nearest the edge of the vellum—were far more *distinct* than the others. It was clear that the action of the caloric had been imperfect or unequal. I immediately kindled a fire, and subjected every portion of the parchment to a glowing heat. At first, the only effect was the strengthening of the faint lines in the skull; but, upon persevering in the experiment, there became visible, at the corner of the slip, diagon-ally opposite to the spot in which the death's-head was delineated, the figure of what I at first supposed to be a goat. A closer scrutiny, however, satisfied me that it was intended for a kid."

"Ha! Ha!" said I, "to be sure I have no right to laugh at you—a million and a half of money is too serious a matter for mirth—but you are not about to establish a third link in your chain—you will not find any especial connection between your pirates and a goat—pirates, you know, have nothing to do with goats; they appertain to the farming interest."

"But I have just said that the figure was *not* that of a goat."

"Well, a kid, then—pretty much the same thing."

"Pretty much, but not altogether," said Legrand. "You may have heard of one *Captain* Kidd. I at once looked upon the figure of the animal as a kind of punning or hieroglyphical signature. I say signature, because its position upon the vellum suggested this idea. The death's-head at the corner diagonally opposite, had, in the same manner, the air of a stamp, or seal. But I was sorely put out by the absence of all else—of the body to my imagined instrument—of the text for my context."

"I presume you expected to find a letter between the stamp and the signature."

"Something of that kind. The fact is, I felt irresistibly impressed with a presentiment of some vast good fortune impending. I can scarcely say why. Perhaps, after all, it was rather a desire than an actual belief—but do you know that Jupiter's silly words, about the bug being of solid gold, had a remarkable effect upon my fancy? And then the series of accidents and coincidents—there were so *very* extraordinary. Do you observe how mere an accident it was that these events should have occurred upon the *sole* day of all the year in which it has been, or may be sufficiently cool for fire, and that without the fire, or without the intervention of the dog at the precise moment in which he appeared, I should never have become aware of the death's-head, and so never the possessor of the treasure?"

"But proceed—I am all impatience."

"Well; you have heard, of course, the many stories current—the thousand vague rumors afloat about money buried, somewhere upon the Atlantic coast, by Kidd and his associates. These rumors must have had some foundation in fact. And that the rumors have existed so long and so continuously, could have resulted, it appeared to me, only from the circumstance of the buried treasures still *remaining* entombed. Had Kidd concealed his plunder for a time, and afterward reclaimed it, the rumors would scarcely have reached us in their present unvarying form. You will observe that the stories told are all about money-seekers, not about money-finders. Had the pirate recovered his money, there the affair would have dropped. It seemed to me that some accident—say the loss of a memorandum indicating its locality—had deprived him of the means of recovering it, and that this accident had become known to his followers, who otherwise might never have heard that the treasure had been concealed at all, and who, busying themselves in vain, because unguided, attempts to regain it, had given first birth, and then universal currency, to the reports which are now so common. Have you ever heard of any important treasure being unearthed along the coast?"

"Never."

"But that Kidd's accumulations were immense is well known. I took it for granted, therefore, that the earth still held them; and you will scarcely be surprised when I tell you that I felt a hope, nearly amounting to certainty, that the parchment so strangely found involved a lost record of the place of deposit."

"But how did you proceed?"

"I held the vellum again to the fire, after increasing the heat, but nothing appeared. I now thought it possible that the coating of dirt might have something to do with the failure: so I carefully rinsed the parchment by pouring warm water over it, and having done this, I placed it in a tin pan, with the skull downward, and put the pan upon a furnace of lighted charcoal. In a few minutes, the pan having become thoroughly heated, I removed the slip, and, to my inexpressible joy, found it spotted, in several places, with what appeared to be figures arranged in lines. Again I placed it in the pan, and suffered it to remain another minute. Upon taking it off, the whole was just as you see it now.

Here Legrand, having reheated the parchment, submitted it to my inspection. The following characters were rudely traced, in a a red tint, between the death's-head and the goat:

53‡‡†305))6*;4826)4‡(4‡.;806*;48†8¶(60))85;1‡(;:‡*8†83(88)5*†;46(;88*96*?;
8)*‡(;485);5*†2:*‡(;4956*2(5*—4)8¶[8*;4069285);)6†8)4‡‡;1(‡9;48081;8:8‡1;
48†85;4)485†528806*81(‡9;48;(88;4(‡?34;48)4‡;161;:188;‡?;

"But," said I, returning him the slip, "I am as much in the dark as ever. Were all the jewels of Golconda awaiting me upon my solution of this enigma, I am quite sure that I should be unable to earn them."

"And yet," said Legrand, "the solution is by no means so difficult as you might be led to imagine from the first hasty inspection of the characters. These characters, as anyone might readily guess, form a cipher—that is to say, they convey a meaning; but then from what is known of Kidd, I could not suppose him capable of constructing any of the more abstruse cryptographs. I made up my mind, at once, that this was of a simple species—such, however, as would appear, to the crude intellect of the sailor, absolutely insoluble without the key."

"And you really solved it?"

"Readily; I have solved others of an abstruseness ten thousand times greater. Circumstances, and a certain bias of mind, have led me to take interest in such riddles, and it may well be doubted whether human ingenuity can construct an enigma of the kind which human ingenuity may not, by proper application, resolve. In fact, having once established connected and legible characters, I scarcely gave a thought to the mere difficulty of developing their import.

"In the present case—indeed, in all cases of secret writing—the first question regards the *language* of the cipher; for the principles of solution, so far, especially, as the more simple ciphers are concerned, depend upon, and are varied by, the genius of the particular idiom. In general, there is no alternative but experiment (directed by probabilities) of every tongue known to him who attempts the solution, until the true one be attained. But, with the cipher now before us all difficulty was removed by the signature. The pun upon the word 'Kidd' is appreciable in no other language than the English. But for this consideration I should have begun my attempts with Spanish and French, as the tongues in which a secret of this kind would most naturally have been written by a pirate of the Spanish main. As it was, I assumed the cryptograph to be English.

"You observe there are no divisions between the words. Had there been divisions the task would have been comparatively easy. In such cases I should have commenced with a collation and analysis of the shorter words, and, had a word of a single letter occurred, as is most likely (*a* or *I*, for example), I should have considered the solution as assured. But, there being no division, my first step was to ascertain the predominant letters, as well as the least frequent. Counting all, I constructed a table thus:

Of the characters 8 there are		33.
;	"	26.
4	"	19.
‡)	"	16.
*	"	13.
5	"	12.
6	"	11.
†1	"	8.
o	"	6.
92	"	5.
:3	"	4.
?	"	3.
¶	"	2.
—.	"	1.

"Now, in English, the letter which most frequently occurs is *e*. Afterward, the succession runs thus: *a o i d h n r s t u y c f g l m w b k p q x z*. *E* predominates so remarkably, that an individual sentence of any length is rarely seen, in which it is not the prevailing character.

"Here, then, we have, in the very beginning, the groundwork for something more than a mere guess. The general use which may be made of the table is obvious—but, in this particular cipher, we shall only very partially require its aid. As our predominant character is 8, we will commence by assuming it as the *e* of the natural alphabet. To verify the supposition, let us observe if the 8 be seen often in couples—for *e* is doubled with great frequency in English—in such words, for example, as 'meet,' 'fleet,' 'speed,' 'seen,' 'been,' 'agree,' etc. In the presence instance we see it doubled no less than five times, although the cryptograph is brief.

"Let us assume 8, then, as *e*. Now, of all *words* in the language, 'the' is most usual; let us see, therefore, whether there are not repetitions of any three characters, in the same order of collocation, the last of them being 8. If we discover repetitions of such letters, so arranged, they will most probably represent the word 'the.' Upon inspection, we find no less than seven such arrangements, the characters being ;48. We may, therefore, assume that ; represents *t*, 4 represents *h*, and 8 represents *e*—the last being now well confirmed. Thus a great step has been taken.

"But, having established a single word, we are enabled to establish a vastly important point; that is to say, several commencements and terminations of other words. Let us refer, for example, to the last instance but one, in which the combination ;48 occurs—not far from the end of the cipher. We know that the ; immediately ensuing is the commencement of a word, and, of six characters succeeding this 'the,' we are cognizant of no less than five. Let us set these characters down, thus, by the letters we know them to represent, leaving a space for the unknown—

t eeth.

"Here we are enabled, at once, to discard the *th*, as forming no portion of the word commencing with the first *t*; since, by experiment of the entire alphabet for a letter adapted to the vacancy, we perceive that no word can be formed of which this *th* can be a part. We are thus narrowed into

t ee,

and, going through the alphabet, if necessary, as before, we arrive at the word 'tree,' as the sole possible reading. We thus gain another letter, *r*, represented by (, with the words 'the tree' in juxtaposition.

"Looking beyond these words, for a short distance, we again see the combination ;48, and employ it by way of termination to what immediately precedes. We have thus this arrangement:

the tree ;4(‡?34 the,

or, substituting the natural letters, where known, it reads thus:

the tree thr‡?3h the.

"Now, if, in the palce of the unknown characters, we leave blank spaces, or substitute dots, we read thus:

the tree thr...h the,

when the word *'through'* makes itself evident at once. But this discovery gives us three new letters, *o, u,* and *g,* represented by ‡, ?, and 3.

"Looking now, narrowly, through the cipher for combinations of known characters, we find, not very far from the beginning, this arrangement,

83(88, or egree,

which plainly, is the conclusion of the word 'degree,' and gives us another letter, *d,* represented by †.

"Four letters beyond the word 'degree,' we perceive the combination

;46(;88

"Translating the known characters, and representing the unknown by dots, as before, we read thus:

th.rtee,

an arrangement immediately suggestive of the word 'thirteen,' and again furnishing us with two new characters, *i* and *n,* represented by 6 and *.

"Referring, now, to the beginning of the cryptograph, we find the combination,

53‡‡†.

"Translating as before, we obtain

.good,

which assures us that the first letter is *A,* and that the first two words are 'A good.'

"It is now time that we arrange our key, as far as discovered, in a tabular form, to avoid confusion. It will stand thus:

5	represents	a
†	"	d
8	"	e
3	"	g
4	"	h
6	"	i
*	"	n
‡	"	o
(	"	r
;	"	t
?	"	u

"We have, therefore, no less than eleven of the most important letters represented, and it will be unnecessary to proceed with the details of the solution. I have said enough to convince you that ciphers of this nature are readily soluable, and to give you some insight into the *rationale* of their development. But be assured that the specimen before us appertains to the very simplest species of cryptograph. It now only remains to give you the full translation of the characters upon the parchment as unriddled. Here it is:

A good glass in the bishop's hostel in the devil's seat forty-one degrees and thirteen minutes northeast and by north main branch seventh limb east side shoot from the left eye of the death's-head a bee-line from the tree through the shot fifty feet out.

"But," said I, "the enigma seems still in as bad a condition as ever. How is it possible to extort a meaning from all this jargon about 'devil's seats,' 'death's-head,' and 'bishop's hostels?' "

"I confess," replied Legrand, "that the matter still wears a serious aspect, when regarded with a casual glance. My first endeavor was to divide the sentence into the natural division intended by the cryptograph-ist."

"You mean, to puncutate it?"

"Something of that kind."

"But how was it possible to effect this?"

"I reflected that it had been a *point* with the writer to run his words together without division, so as to increase the difficulty of solution. Now, a not overacute man, in pursuing such an object, would be nearly certain to overdo the matter. When, in the course of his composition, he arrived at a break in his subject which would naturally require a pause, or a point, he would be exceedingly apt to run his characters, at this place, more than usually close together. If you will observe the MS., in the present instance, you will easily detect five such cases of unusual crowding. Acting upon this hint, I made the division thus:

A good glass in the Bishop's hostel in the Devil's seat—forty-one degrees and thirteen minutes—northeast and by north—main branch seventh limb east side—shoot from the left eye of the death's-head—a bee-line from the tree through the shot fifty feet out.

"Even this division," said I, "leaves me still in the dark."

"It left me also in the dark," replied Legrand, "for a few days; during which I made diligent inquiry in the neighborhood of Sullivan's Island, for any building which went by name of the 'Bishop's Hotel'; for, of course, I dropped the obsolete word 'hostel.' Gaining no information on the subject, I was on the point of extending my sphere of search and proceeding in a more systematic manner, when, one morning, it entered into my head, quite suddenly, that this 'Bishop's Hostel' might have some reference to an old family, of the name of Bessop, which, time out of mind, had held possession of an ancient manor-house, about four miles to the northward of the island. I accordingly went over to the plantation, and reinstituted my inquiries among the older Negroes of the place. At length one of the most aged of the women said that she had heard of such a place as *Bessop's Castle,* and thought that she could guide me to it, but that it was not a castle, nor a tavern, but a high rock.

"I offered to pay her well for her trouble, and, after some demur, she consented to accompany me to the spot. We found it without much difficulty, when, dismissing her, I proceeded to examine the place. The 'castle' consisted of an irregular assemblage of cliffs and rocks—one of the latter being quite remarkable for its height as well as for its insulated and artificial appearance. I clambered to its apex, and then felt much at a loss as to what should be next done.

"While I was busied in reflection, my eyes fell upon a narrow ledge in the eastern face of the rock, perhaps a yard below the summit upon which I stood. This ledge projected about eighteen inches, and was not more than a foot wide, while a niche in the cliff just above it gave it a rude resemblance to one of the hollow-backed chairs used by our ancestors. I made no doubt that here was the 'devil's seat' alluded to in the MS., and now I seemed to grasp the full secret of the riddle.

"The 'good glass,' I knew, could have reference to nothing but a telescope; for the word 'glass' is rarely employed in any other sense by seamen. Now here, I at once saw, was a telescope to be used, and a definite point of view, *admitting no variation,* from which to use it. Nor did I hesitate to believe that the phrases, 'forty-one degrees and thirteen minutes,' and 'northeast and by north,' were intended as directions for the leveling of the glass. Greatly exicted by these discoveries, I hurried home, procured a telescope, and returned to the rock.

"I let myself down to the ledge, and found that it was impossible to retain a seat upon it except in one particular position. This fact confirmed my preconceived idea. I proceeded to use the glass. Of course, the 'forty-one degrees and thirteen minutes' could allude to nothing but elevation above the visible horizon, since the horizontal direction was clearly indicated by the words, 'northeast and by north.' This latter direction I at once established by means of a pocket-compass; then, pointing the glass as nearly at an angle of forty-one degrees of elevation as I could do it by guess, I moved it cautiously up or down, until my attention was arrested by a circular rift or opening in the foliage of a large tree that overtopped its fellows in the distance. In the center of this rift I perceived a white spot, but could not, at first, distinguish what it was. Adjusting the focus of the telescope, I again looked, and now made it out to be a human skull.

"Upon this discovery I was so sanguine as to consider the enigma solved; for the phrase 'main branch, seventh limb, east side,' could refer only to the position of the skull upon the tree, while 'shoot for the left eye of the death's-head' admitted, also, of but one interpretation, in regard to a search for buried treasure. I perceived that the design was to drop a bullet from the left eye of the skull, and that a bee-line, or, in other words, a straight line, drawn from the nearest point of the trunk through the shot (or the spot where the bullet fell), and thence extended to a distance of fifty feet, would indicate a definite point—and beneath this point I thought it at least *possible* that a deposit of value lay concealed."

"All this," I said, "is exceedingly clear, and, although ingenious, still simple and explicit. When you left the Bishop's Hotel, what then?"

"Why, having carefully taken the bearings of the tree, I turned homeward. The instant that I left 'the devil's seat,' however, the circular rift vanished; nor could I get a glimpse of it afterward, turn as I would. What seems to me the chief ingenuity in this whole business, is the fact (for repeated experiment has convinced me it *is* a fact) that the circular opening in question is visible from no other attainable point of view than that afforded by the narrow ledge upon the face of the rock.

"In this expedition to the 'Bishop's Hotel' I had been attended by Jupiter, who had, no doubt, observed, for some weeks past, the abstraction of my demeanor, and took especial care not to leave me alone. But, on the next day, getting up very early, I contrived to give him the slip, and went into the hills in search of the tree. After much toil I found it. When I came home at night my valet proposed to give me a flogging. With the rest of the adventure I believe you are as well acquainted as myself."

"I suppose," said I, "you missed the spot, in the first attempt at digging, through Jupiter's stupidity in letting the bug fall through the right instead of through the left eye of the skull."

"Precisely. This mistake made a difference of about two inches and a half in the 'shot'—that is to say, in the position of the peg nearest the tree; and had the treasure been *beneath* the 'shot,' the error would have been of little moment; but 'the shot,' together with the nearest point of the tree, were merely two points for the establishment of a line of direction; of course, the error, however trivial in the beginning, increased as we proceeded with the line, and by the time we had gone fifty feet threw us quite off the scent. But for my deep-seated impressions that treasure was here somewhere actually buried, we might have had all our labor in vain."

"But your grandiloquence, and your conduct in swinging the beetle—how excessively odd! I was sure you were mad. And why did you insist upon letting fall the bug, instead of a bullet, from the skull?"

"Why, to be frank, I felt somewhat annoyed by your evident suspicions touching my sanity, and so resolved to punish you quietly, in my own way, by a little bit of sober mystification. For this reason I swung the beetle, and for this reason I let it fall from the tree. An observation of yours about its great weight suggested the latter idea."

"Yes, I perceive; and now there is only one point which puzzles me. What are we to make of the skeletons found in the hole?"

"That is a question I am no more able to answer than yourself. There seems, however, only one plausible way of accounting for them—and yet it is dreadful to believe in such atrocity as my suggestion would imply. It is clear that Kidd—if Kidd indeed secreted this treasure, which I doubt not—it is clear that he must have had assistance in the labor. But this labor concluded, he may have thought it expedient to remove all participants in his secret. Perhaps a couple of blows with a mattock were sufficient, while his coadjutors were busy in the pit; perhaps it required a dozen—who shall tell?"

Hunted Down

CHARLES DICKENS

The careful pace, the slow and gathering contrivance, the inching rhythms of gathering monomania, will not put the reader off the point of "Hunted Down" which, like the museum piece in Bram Stoker's "The Squaw" is a lunging, closing vise of a story, all steel and teeth. The remorselessness of Dickens's vision, even in this elegant, low-pitched short story, is the remorselessness of all circumstance. The author of Great Expectations *and* Bleak House *knew more than enough about the machineries of thrall.*

The partition which separated my own office from our general outer office in the city was of thick plate glass. I could see through it what passed in the outer office, without hearing a word. I had it put up in place of a wall that had been there for years—ever since the house was built. It is no matter whether I did or did not make the change in order that I might derive my first impression of strangers, who came to us on business, from their faces alone, without being influenced by anything they said. Enough to mention that I turned my glass partition to that account, and that a life assurance office is at all times exposed to be practiced upon by the most crafty and cruel of the human race.

It was through my glass partition that I first saw the gentleman whose story I am going to tell.

He had come in without my observing it, and had put his hat and umbrella on the broad counter, and was bending over it to take some papers from one of the clerks. He was about forty or so, dark, exceedingly well dressed in black—being in mourning—and the hand he extended with a polite air had a particularly well-fitting black kid glove upon it. His hair, which was elaborately brushed and oiled, was parted straight up the middle; and he presented this parting to the clerk, exactly (to my thinking) as if he had said, in so many words: "You must take me, if you please, my friend, just as I show myself. Come straight up here, follow the gravel path, keep off the grass, I allow no trespassing."

I conceived a very great aversion to that man the moment I thus saw him.

He had asked for some of our printed forms, and the clerk was giving them to him and explaining them. An obliged and agreeable smile was on his face, and his eyes met those of the clerk with a sprightly look. (I have known a vast quantity of nonsense talked about bad men not looking you in the face. Don't trust that conventional idea. Dishonesty will stare honesty out of countenance, any day in the week, if there is anything to be got by it.)

I saw, in the corner of his eyelash, that he became aware of my looking at him. Immediately he turned the parting in his hair toward the glass partition, as if he said to me with a sweet smile, "Straight up here, if you please. Off the grass!"

In a few moments he had put on his hat and taken up his umbrella, and was gone.

I beckoned the clerk into my room, and asked, "Who was that?"

He had the gentleman's card in his hand. "Mr. Julius Slinkton, Middle Temple."

"A barrister, Mr. Adams?"

"I think not, sir."

"I should have thought him a clergyman, but for his having no Reverend here," said I.

"Probably, from his appearance," Mr. Adams replied, "he is reading for orders."

I should mention that he wore a dainty white cravat, and dainty linen altogether.

"What did he want, Mr. Adams?"

"Merely a form of proposal, sir, and form of reference."

"Recommended here? Did he say?"

"Yes, he said he was recommended here by a friend of yours. He noticed you, but said that as he had not the pleasure of your personal acquaintance he would not trouble you."

"Did he know my name?"

"Oh, yes, sir! He said, 'There *is* Mr. Sampson, I see!' "

"A well-spoken gentleman, apparently?"

"Remarkably so, sir."

"Insinuating manners, apparently?"

"Very much so, indeed, sir."

"Hah!" said I. "I want nothing at present, Mr. Adams."

Within a fortnight of that day I went to dine with a friend of mine, a merchant, a man of taste, who buys pictures and books, and the first man I saw among the company was Mr. Julius Slinkton. There he was, standing before the fire, with good large eyes and an open expression of face; but still (I thought) requiring everybody to come at him by the prepared way he offered, and by no other.

I noticed him ask my friend to introduce him to Mr. Sampson, and my friend did so. Mr. Slinkton was very happy to see me. Not too happy; there was no overdoing of the matter; happy in a thoroughly well-bred, perfectly unmeaning way.

"I thought you had met," our host observed.

"No," said Mr. Slinkton. "I did look in at Mr. Sampson's office, on your recommendation; but I really did not feel justified in troubling Mr. Sampson himself, on a point in the everyday routine of a clerk."

I said I should have been glad to show him any attention on our friend's introduction.

"I am sure of that," said he, "and am much obliged. At another time, perhaps, I may be less delicate. Only, however, if I have real business; for I know, Mr. Sampson, how precious business time is, and what a vast number of impertinent people there are in the world."

I acknowledged his consideration with a slight bow. "You were thinking," said I, "of effecting a policy on your life."

"Oh dear no! I am afraid I am not so prudent as you pay me the compliment of supposing me to be, Mr. Sampson. I merely inquired for a friend. But you know what friends are in such matters. Nothing may ever come of it. I have the greatest reluctance to trouble men of business with inquiries for friends, knowing the probabilities to be a thousand to one that the friends will never follow them up. People are so fickle, so selfish, so inconsiderate. Don't you, in your business, find them so every day?"

I was going to give a qualified answer; but he turned his smooth, white parting on me with its "Straight up here, if you please!" and I answered, "Yes."

"I hear, Mr. Sampson," he resumed presently, for our friend had a new cook, and dinner was not so punctual as usual, "that your profession has recently suffered a great loss."

"In money?" said I.

"No, in talent and vigor."

Not at once following out his allusion, I considered for a moment.

"*Has* it sustained a loss of that kind?" said I. "I was not aware of it."

"Understand me, Mr. Sampson. I don't imagine that you have retired.

It is not so bad as that. But Mr. Meltham—"

"Oh, to be sure!" said I. "Yes! Mr. Meltham, the young actuary of the 'Inestimable.' "

"Just so," he returned in a consoling way.

"He is a great loss. He was at once the most profound, the most original, and the most energetic man I have ever known connected with life assurance."

I spoke strongly; for I had a high esteem and admiration for Meltham; and my gentleman had indefinitely conveyed to me some suspicion that he wanted to sneer at him. He recalled me to my guard by presenting that trim pathway up his head, with its infernal "Not on the grass, if you please —the gravel."

"You knew him, Mr. Slinkton?"

"Only by reputation. To have known him as an acquaintance or as a friend, is an honor I should have sought if he had remained in society, though I might never have had the good fortune to attain it, being a man of far inferior mark. He was scarcely above thirty, I suppose?"

"About thirty."

"Ah!" he sighed in his former consoling way. "What creatures we are! To break up, Mr. Sampson, and become incapable of business at that time of life!—any reason assigned for the melancholy fact?"

("Humph!" thought I, as I looked at him. "But I *won't* go up the track, and I *will* go on the grass.")

"What reason have you heard assigned, Mr. Slinkton?" I asked, point-blank.

"Most likely a false one. You know what rumor is, Mr. Sampson. I never repeat what I hear; it is the only way of paring the nails and shaving the head of rumor. But when *you* ask me what reason I have heard assigned for Mr. Meltham's passing away from among men, it is another thing. I am not gratifying idle gossip then. I was told, Mr. Sampson, that Mr. Meltham had relinquished all his avocations and all his prospects, because he was, in fact, brokenhearted. A disappointed attachment, I heard— though it hardly seems probable, in the case of a man so distinguished and so attractive."

"Attractions and distinctions are no armor against death," said I.

"Oh, she died? Pray pardon me. I did not hear that. That, indeed, makes it very, very sad. Poor Mr. Meltham! Ah, dear me! Lamentable, lamentable!"

I still thought his pity was not quite genuine, and I still suspected an unaccountable sneer under all this, until he said, as we were parted, like the other knots of talkers, by the announcement of dinner:

"Mr. Sampson, you are surprised to see me so moved on behalf of a man whom I have never known. I am not so disinterested as you may suppose. I have suffered, and recently too, from death myself. I have lost one of two charming nieces, who were my constant companions. She died young—barely three-and-twenty; and even her remaining sister is far from strong. The world is a grave!"

He said this with deep feeling, and I felt reproached for the coldness of my manner. Coldness and distrust had been engendered in me, I knew, by my bad experiences; they were not natural to me; and I often thought how much I had lost in life, losing trustfulness, and how little I had gained, gaining hard caution. This state of mind being habitual to me, I troubled myself more about this conversation than I might have troubled myself about a greater matter. I listened to his talk at dinner, and observed how readily other men responded to it, and with what a graceful instinct he adapted his subjects to the knowledge and habits of those he talked with. As, in talking with me, he had easily started the subject I might be supposed to understand best, and to be the most interested in, so, in talking with others, he guided himself by the same rule. The company was of a varied character; but he was not at fault, that I could discover, with any member of it. He knew just as much of each man's pursuit as made him agreeable to that man in reference to it, and just as little as made it natural in him to seek modestly for information when the theme was broached.

As he talked and talked—but really not too much, for the rest of us seemed to force it upon him—I became quite angry with myself. I took his face to pieces in my mind, like a watch, and examined it in detail. I could not say much against any of his features separately; I could say even less against them when they were put together. "Then is it not monstrous," I asked myself, "that because a man happens to part his hair straight up the middle of his head, I should permit myself to suspect, and even to detest him?"

(I may stop to remark that this was no proof of my sense. An observer of men who finds himself steadily repelled by some apparently trifling thing in a stranger is right to give it great weight. It may be the clue to the whole mystery. A hair or two will show where a lion is hidden. A very little key will open a very heavy door.)

I took my part in the conversation with him after a time, and we got on remarkably well. In the drawing room I asked the host how long he had known Mr. Slinkton. He answered, not many months; he had met him at the house of a celebrated painter then present, who had known him well when he was traveling with his nieces in Italy for their health. His plans in life being broken by the death of one of them, he was reading with the intention of going back to college as a matter of form, taking his degree, and going into orders. I could not but argue with myself that here was the true explanation of his interest in poor Meltham, and that I had been almost brutal in my distrust on that simple head.

On the very next day but one I was sitting behind my glass partition, as before, when he came into the outer office, as before. The moment I saw him again without hearing him, I hated him worse than ever.

It was only for a moment that I had this opportunity; for he waved his tight-fitting black glove the instant I looked at him, and came straight in.

"Mr. Sampson, good day! I presume, you see, upon your kind permission to intrude upon you. I don't keep my word in being justified by business, for my business here—if I may so abuse the word—is of the slightest nature."

I asked, was it anything I could assist him in?

"I thank you, no. I merely called to inquire outside whether my dilatory friend had been so false to himself as to be practical and sensible. But, of course, he has done nothing. I gave him your papers with my own hand, and he was hot upon the intention, but of course he has done nothing. Apart from the general human disinclination to do anything that ought to be done, I dare say there is a specialty about assuring one's life. You find it like will making. People are so superstitious, and take it for granted they will die soon afterwards."

"Up here, if you please; straight up here, Mr. Sampson. Neither to the right nor to the left." I almost fancied I could hear him breathe the words as he sat smiling at me, with that intolerable parting exactly opposite the bridge of my nose.

"There is such a feeling sometimes, no doubt," I replied; "but I don't think it obtains to any great extent."

"Well," said he, with a shrug and a smile, "I wish some good angel would influence my friend in the right direction. I rashly promised his mother and sister in Norfolk to see it done, and he promised them that he would do it. But I suppose he never will."

He spoke for a minute or two on indifferent topics, and went away.

I had scarcely unlocked the drawers of my writing table next morning, when he reappeared. I noticed that he came straight to the door in the glass partition, and did not pause a single moment outside.

"Can you spare me two minutes, my dear Mr. Sampson?"

"By all means."

"Much obliged," laying his hat and umbrella on the table; "I came early, not to interrupt you. The fact is, I am taken by surprise in reference to this proposal my friend has made."

"Has he made one?" said I.

"Ye-es," he answered, deliberately looking at me; and then a bright idea seemed to strike him— "or he only tells me he has. Perhaps that may be a new way of evading the matter. By Jupiter, I never thought of that!"

Mr. Adams was opening the morning's letters in the outer office. "What is the name, Mr. Slinkton?" I asked.

"Beckwith."

I looked out at the door and requested Mr. Adams, if there were a proposal in that name, to bring it in. He had already laid it out of his hand on the counter. It was easily selected from the rest, and he gave it me. Alfred Beckwith. Proposal to effect a policy with us for two thousand pounds. Dated yesterday.

"From the Middle Temple, I see, Mr. Slinkton."

"Yes. He lives on the same staircase with me; his door is opposite. I never thought he would make me his reference though."

"It seems natural enough that he should."

"Quite so, Mr. Sampson; but I never thought of it. Let me see." He took the printed paper from his pocket. "How am I to answer all these questions?"

"According to the truth, of course," said I.

"Oh, of course!" he answered, looking up from the paper with a smile; "I meant they were so many. But you do right to be particular. It stands to reason that you must be particular. Will you allow me to use your pen and ink?"

"Certainly."

"And your desk?"

"Certainly."

He had been hovering about between his hat and his umbrella for a place to write on. He now sat down in my chair, at my blotting paper and inkstand, with the long walk up his head in accurate perspective before me, as I stood with my back to the fire.

Before answering each question he ran over it aloud, and discussed it. How long had he known Mr. Alfred Beckwith? That he had to calculate by years upon his fingers. What were his habits? No difficulty about them; temperate in the last degree, and took a little too much exercise, if anything. All the answers were satisfactory. When he had written them all, he looked them over, and finally signed them in a very pretty hand. He supposed he had now done with the business. I told him he was not likely to be troubled any further. Should he leave the papers there? If he pleased. Much obliged. Good morning.

I had had one other visitor before him; not at the office, but at my own house. That visitor had come to my bedside when it was not yet daylight, and had been seen by no one else but my faithful confidential servant.

A second reference paper (for we required always two) was sent down into Norfolk, and was duly received back by post. This, likewise, was satisfactorily answered in every respect. Our forms were all complied with; we accepted the proposal, and the premium for one year was paid.

For six or seven months I saw no more of Mr. Slinkton. He called once at my house, but I was not at home; and he once asked me to dine with him in the Temple, but I was engaged. His friend's assurance was effected in March. Late in September or early in October I was down at Scarborough for a breath of sea air, where I met him on the beach. It was a hot evening; he came toward me with his hat in his hand; and there was the walk I had felt so strongly disinclined to take in perfect order again, exactly in front of the bridge of my nose.

He was not alone, but had a young lady on his arm.

She was dressed in mourning, and I looked at her with great interest. She had the appearance of being extremely delicate, and her face was remarkably pale and melancholy; but she was very pretty. He introduced her as his niece, Miss Niner.

"Are you strolling, Mr. Sampson? Is it possible you can be idle?"

It *was* possible, and I *was* strolling.

"Shall we stroll together?"

"With pleasure."

The young lady walked between us, and we walked on the cool sea sand, in the direction of Filey.

"There have been wheels here," said Mr. Slinkton. "And now I look again, the wheels of a hand-carriage! Margaret, my love, your shadow without doubt!"

"Miss Niner's shadow?" I repeated, looking down at it on the sand.

"Not that one," Mr. Slinkton returned, laughing. "Margaret, my dear, tell Mr. Sampson."

"Indeed," said the young lady, turning to me, "there is nothing to tell —except that I constantly see the same invalid old gentleman at all times, wherever I go. I have mentioned it to my uncle, and he calls the gentleman my shadow."

"Does he live in Scarborough?" I asked.

"He is staying here."

"Do you live in Scarborough?"

"No, I am staying here. My uncle has placed me with a family here, for my health."

"And your shadow?" said I, smiling.

"My shadow," she answered, smiling too, "is—like myself—not very robust, I fear; for I lose my shadow sometimes, as my shadow loses me at other times. We both seem liable to confinement to the house. I have not seen my shadow for days and days; but it does oddly happen, occasionally, that wherever I go, for many days together, this gentleman goes. We have come together in the most unfrequented nooks on this shore."

"Is this he?" said I, pointing before us.

The wheels had swept down to the water's edge, and described a great loop on the sand in turning. Bringing the loop back towards us, and spinning it out as it came, was a hand-carriage, drawn by a man.

"Yes," said Miss Niner, "this really is my shadow, uncle."

As the carriage approached us and we approached the carriage, I saw within it an old man, whose head was sunk on his breast, and who was enveloped in a variety of wrappers. He was drawn by a very quiet but very keen-looking man, with iron-gray hair, who was slightly lame. They had passed us, when the carriage stopped, and the old gentleman within, putting out his arm, called to me by my name. I went back, and was absent from Mr. Slinkton and his niece for about five minutes.

When I rejoined them, Mr. Slinkton was the first to speak. Indeed, he said to me in a raised voice before I came up with him:

"It is well you have not been longer, or my niece might have died of curiosity to know who her shadow is, Mr. Sampson."

"An old East India director," said I. "An intimate friend of our friend's, at whose house I first had the pleasure of meeting you. A certain Major Banks. You have heard of him?"

"Never."

"Very rich, Miss Niner; but very old, and very crippled. An amiable man, sensible—much interested in you. He has just been expatiating on the affection that he has observed to exist between you and your uncle."

Mr. Slinkton was holding his hat again, and he passed his hand up the straight walk, as if he himself went up it serenely, after me.

"Mr. Sampson," he said, tenderly pressing his niece's arm in his, "our affection was always a strong one, for we have had but few near ties. We have still fewer now. We have associations to bring us together, that are not of this world, Margaret."

"Dear uncle!" murmured the young lady, and turned her face aside to hide her tears.

"My niece and I have such remembrances and regrets in common, Mr. Sampson," he feelingly pursued, "that it would be strange indeed if the relations between us were cold or indifferent. If I remember a conversation we once had together, you will understand the reference I make. Cheer up, dear Margaret. Don't droop, don't droop. My Margaret! I cannot bear to see you droop!"

The poor young lady was very much affected, but controlled herself. His feelings, too, were very acute. In a word, he found himself under such great need of a restorative, that he presently went away, to take a bath of sea water, leaving the young lady and me sitting by a point of rock, and probably presuming—but that you will say was a pardonable indulgence in a luxury—that she would praise him with all her heart.

She did, poor thing! With all her confiding heart, she praised him to me, for his care of her dead sister, and for his untiring devotion in her last illness. The sister had wasted away very slowly, and wild and terrible fantasies had come over her toward the end, but he had never been impatient with her, or at a loss; had always been gentle, watchful, and self-possessed. The sister had known him, as she had known him, to be the best of men, the kindest of men, and yet a man of such admirable strength of character, as to be a very tower for the support of their weak natures while their poor lives endured.

"I shall leave him, Mr. Sampson, very soon," said the young lady; "I know my life is drawing to an end; and when I am gone, I hope he will marry and be happy. I am sure he has lived single so long, only for my sake, and for my poor, poor sister's."

The little hand-carriage had made another great loop on the damp sand, and was coming back again, gradually spinning out a slim figure eight, half a mile long.

"Young lady," said I, looking around, laying my hand upon her arm, and speaking in a low voice, "time presses. You hear the gentle murmur of that sea?"

She looked at me with the utmost wonder and alarm, saying, "Yes!"

"And you know what a voice is in it when the storm comes?"

"Yes!"

"You see how quiet and peaceful it lies before us, and you know what an awful sight of power without pity it might be, this very night!"

"Yes!"

"But if you had never heard or seen it, or heard of it in its cruelty, could you believe that it beats every inanimate thing in its way to pieces, without mercy, and destroys life without remorse?"

"You terrify me, sir, by these questions!"

"To save you, young lady, to save you! For God's sake, collect your strength and collect your firmness! If you were here alone, and hemmed in by the rising tide on the flow to fifty feet above your head, you could not be in greater danger than the danger you are now to be saved from."

The figure on the sand was spun out, and straggled off into a crooked little jerk that ended at the cliff very near us.

"As I am, before heaven and the Judge of all mankind, your friend, and your dead sister's friend, I solemnly entreat you, Miss Niner, without one moment's loss of time, to come to this gentleman with me!"

If the little carriage had been less near to us, I doubt if I could have got her away; but it was so near that we were there before she had recovered the hurry of being urged from the rock. I did not remain there with her two minutes. Certainly within five, I had the inexpressible satisfaction of seeing her—from the point we had sat on, and to which I had returned—half supported and half carried up some rude steps notched in the cliff, by the figure of an active man. With that figure beside her, I knew she was safe anywhere.

I sat alone on the rock, awaiting Mr. Slinkton's return. The twilight was deepening and the shadows were heavy, when he came round the point, with his hat hanging at his buttonhole, smoothing his wet hair with one of his hands, and picking out the old path with the other and a pocket-comb.

"My niece not here, Mr. Sampson?" he said, looking about.

"Miss Niner seemed to feel a chill in the air after the sun was down, and has gone home."

He looked surprised, as though she were not accustomed to do anything without him.

"I persuaded Miss Niner," I explained.

"Ah!" said he. "She is easily persuaded—for her good. Thank you, Mr. Sampson; she is better within doors. The bathing place was farther than I thought, to say the truth."

"Miss Niner is very delicate," I observed.

He shook his head and drew a deep sigh. "Very, very, very. You may recollect my saying so. The time that has since intervened has not strengthened her. The gloomy shadow that fell upon her sister so early in life seems, in my anxious eyes, to gather over her, ever darker, ever darker. Dear Margaret, dear Margaret! But we must hope."

The hand-carriage was spinning away before us at a most indecorous pace for an invalid vehicle, and was making most irregular curves upon the sand. Mr. Slinkton, noticing it, said:

"If I may judge from appearances, your friend will be upset, Mr. Sampson."

"It looks probable, certainly," said I.

"The servants must be drunk."

"The servants of old gentlemen will get drunk sometimes," said I.

"The major draws very light, Mr. Sampson."

"The major does draw light," said I.

By this time the carriage, much to my relief, was lost in the darkness. We walked on for a little, side by side over the sand, in silence. After a short while he said, in a voice still affected by the emotion that his niece's state of health had awakened in him,

"Do you stay here long, Mr. Sampson?"

"Why, no. I am going away tonight."

"So soon? But business always holds you in request. Men like Mr. Sampson are too important to others, to be spared to their own need of relaxation and enjoyment."

"I don't know about that," said I. "However, I am going back. To London."

"I shall be there too, soon after you."

I knew that as well as he did. But I did not tell him so. Any more than I told him what defensive weapon my right hand rested on in my pocket, as I walked by his side. Any more than I told him why I did not walk on the sea side of him with the night closing in.

We left the beach, and our ways diverged. We exchanged good night, and had parted indeed, when he said, returning,

"Mr. Sampson, *may* I ask? Poor Meltham whom we spoke of—dead yet?"

"Not when I last heard of him; but too broken a man to live long, and hopelessly lost to his old calling."

"Dear, dear, dear!" said he, with great feeling. "Sad, sad, sad! The world is a grave!" And so went his way.

It was not his fault if the world were not a grave; but I did not call that observation after him, any more than I had mentioned those other things just now enumerated. He went his way, and I went mine with all expedition. This happened, as I have said, either at the end of September or beginning of October. The next time I saw him, and the last, was late in November.

I had a very particular engagement to breakfast in the Temple. It was a bitter northeasterly morning, and the sleet and slush lay inches deep in the streets. I could get no conveyance, and was soon wet to the knees; but I should have been true to that appointment, though I had to wade to it up to my neck in the same impediments.

The appointment took me to some chambers in the Temple. They were at the top of a lonely corner house overlooking the river. The name, MR. ALFRED BECKWITH, was painted on the outer door. On the door opposite, on the same landing, the name MR. JULIUS SLINKTON. The doors of both sets of chambers stood open, so that anything said aloud in one set could be heard in the other.

I had never been in those chambers before. They were dismal, close, unwholesome, and oppressive; the furniture, originally good, and not yet old, was faded and dirty—the rooms were in great disorder; there was a strong prevailing smell of opium, brandy, and tobacco; the grate and fire irons were splashed all over with unsightly blotches of rust; and on a sofa by the fire, in the room where breakfast had been prepared, lay the host, Mr. Beckwith, a man with all the appearances of the worst kind of drunkard, very far advanced upon his shameful way to death.

"Slinkton is not come yet," said this creature, staggering up when I went in; "I'll call him—Halloa! Julius Caesar! Come and drink!" As he hoarsely roared this out, he beat the poker and tongs together in a mad way, as if that were his usual manner of summoning his associate.

The voice of Mr. Slinkton was heard through the clatter from the opposite side of the staircase, and he came in. He had not expected the pleasure of meeting me. I have seen several artful men brought to a stand, but I never saw a man so aghast as he was when his eyes rested on mine.

"Julius Caesar," cried Beckwith, staggering between us, "Mist' Sampson! Mist' Sampson, Julius Caesar! Julius, Mist' Sampson, is the friend of my soul. Julius keeps me plied with liquor, morning, noon, and night. Julius is a real benefactor. Julius threw the tea and coffee out of window when I used to have any. Julius empties all the water jugs of their contents, and fills 'em with spirits. Julius winds me up and keeps me going—Boil the brandy, Julius!"

There was a rusty and furred saucepan in the ashes—the ashes looked like the accumulation of weeks—and Beckwith, rolling and staggering between us as if he were going to plunge headlong into the fire, got the saucepan out, and tried to force it into Slinkton's hand.

"Boil the brandy, Julius Caesar! Come! Do your usual office. Boil the brandy!"

He became so fierce in his gesticulations with the saucepan, that I expected to see him lay open Slinkton's head with it. I therefore put out my hand to check him. He reeled back to the sofa, and sat there panting, shaking, and red-eyed, in his rags of dressing gown, looking at us both. I noticed then that there was nothing to drink on the table but brandy, and nothing to eat but salted herrings, and a hot, sickly, highly peppered stew.

"At all events, Mr. Sampson," said Slinkton, offering me the smooth gravel path for the last time, "I thank you for interfering between me and this unfortunate man's violence. However you came here, Mr. Sampson, or with whatever motive you came here, at least I thank you for that."

Without gratifying his desire to know how I came there, I said, quietly, "How is your niece, Mr. Slinkton?"

He looked hard at me, and I looked hard at him.

"I am sorry to say, Mr. Sampson, that my niece has proved treacherous and ungrateful to her best friend. She left me without a word of notice or explanation. She was misled, no doubt, by some designing rascal. Perhaps you may have heard of it."

"I did hear that she was misled by a designing rascal. In fact, I have proof of it."

"Are you sure of that?" said he.

"Quite."

"Boil the brandy," muttered Beckwith. "Company to breakfast, Julius

Caesar. Do your usual office—provide the usual breakfast, dinner, tea, and supper. Boil the brandy!"

The eyes of Slinkton looked from him to me, and he said, after a moment's consideration,

"Mr. Sampson, you are a man of the world, and so am I. I will be plain with you."

"And I tell you you will not," said I. "I know all about you. *You* plain with anyone? Nonsense, nonsense!"

"I plainly tell you, Mr. Sampson," he went on, with a manner almost composed, "that I understand your object. You want to save your funds, and escape from your liabilities; these are old tricks of trade with you office gentlemen. But you will not do it, sir; you will not succeed. You have not an easy adversary to play against, when you play against me. We shall have to inquire, in due time, when and how Mr. Beckwith fell into his present habits. With that remark, sir, I put this poor creature, and his incoherent wanderings of speech, aside, and wish you a good morning and a better case next time."

While he was saying this, Beckwith had filled a half-pint glass with brandy. At this moment, he threw the brandy at his face, and threw the glass after it. Slinkton put his hands up, half blinded with the spirit, and cut with the glass across the forehead. At the sound of the breakage, a fourth person came into the room, closed the door, and stood at it; he was a very quiet but very keen-looking man, with iron-gray hair, and slightly lame.

Slinkton pulled out his handkerchief, assuaged the pain in his smarting eyes, and dabbled the blood on his forehead. He was a long time about it, and I saw that in the doing of it, a tremendous change came over him, occasioned by the change in Beckwith—who ceased to pant and tremble, sat upright, and never took his eyes off him. I never in my life saw a face in which abhorrence and determination were so forcibly painted as in Beckwith's then.

"Look at me, you villain," said Beckwith, "and see me as I really am. I took these rooms, to make them a trap for you. I came into them as a drunkard, to bait the trap for you. You fell into the trap, and you will never leave it alive. On the morning when you last went to Mr. Sampson's office, I had seen him first. Your plot has been known to both of us, all along, and you have been counterplotted all along. What? Having been cajoled into putting that prize of two thousands pounds in your power, I was to be done to death with brandy, and, brandy not proving quick enough, with something quicker? Have I never seen you, when you thought my senses gone, pouring from your little bottle into my glass? Why, you murderer and forger, alone here with you in the dead of night, as I have so often been, I have had my hand upon the trigger of a pistol, twenty times, to blow your brains out!"

This sudden starting up of the thing that he had supposed to be his imbecile victim into a determined man, with a settled resolution to hunt him down and be the death of him, mercilessly expressed from head to foot, was, in the first shock, too much for him. Without any figure of speech, he staggered under it. But there is no greater mistake than to suppose that a man who is a calculating criminal, is, in any phase of his guilt, otherwise than true to himself, and perfectly consistent with his whole character. Such a man commits murder, and murder is the natural culmination of his course; such a man has to outface murder, and will do it with hardihood and effrontery. It is a sort of fashion to express surprise that any notorious criminal, having such crime upon his conscience, can so brave it out. Do you think that if he had it on his conscience at all, or had a conscience to have it upon, he would ever have committed the crime?

Perfectly consistent with himself, as I believe all such monsters to be, this Slinkton recovered himself, and showed a defiance that was sufficiently cold and quiet. He was white, he was haggard, he was changed; but only as a sharper who had played for a great stake and had been outwitted.

"Listen to me, you villain," said Beckwith, "and let every word you hear me say be a stab in your wicked heart. When I took these rooms, to throw myself in your way and lead you on to the scheme that I knew my appearance and supposed character and habits would suggest to such a devil, how did I know that? Because you were no stranger to me. I knew you well. And I knew you to be the cruel wretch who, for so much money, had killed one innocent girl while she trusted him implicitly, and who was by inches killing another."

Slinkton took out a snuff-box, took a pinch of snuff, and laughed.

"But see here," said Beckwith, never looking away, never raising his voice, never relaxing his face, never unclenching his hand. "See what a dull wolf you have been, after all! The infatuated drunkard who never drank a fiftieth part of the liquor you plied him with, but poured it away, here, there, everywhere—almost before your eyes; who brought over the fellow you set to watch him and to ply him, by outbidding you in his bribe, before he had been at his work three days—with whom you have observed no caution, yet who was so bent on ridding the earth of you as a wild beast, that he should have defeated you if you had been ever so prudent—that drunkard whom you have, many a time, left on the floor of this room, and who has even let you go out of it, alive and undeceived, when you have turned him over with your foot—has, almost as often, on the same night, within an hour, within a few minutes, watched you awake, had his hand at your pillow when you were asleep, turned over your papers, taken samples from your bottles and packets of powder, changed their contents, rifled every secret of your life!"

He had had another pinch of snuff in his hand, but had gradually let it drop from between his fingers to the floor; where he now smoothed it out with his foot, looking down at it the while.

"That drunkard," said Beckwith, "who had free access to your rooms at all times, that he might drink the strong drinks that you left in his way and be the sooner ended, holding no more terms with you than he would hold with a tiger, has had his master key for all your locks, his test for all your poisons, his clue to your cipher writing. He can tell you, as well as you can tell him, how long it took to complete that deed, what doses there were, what intervals, what signs of gradual decay upon mind and body; what distempered fancies were produced, what observable changes, what physical pain. He can tell you, as well as you can tell him, that all this was recorded day by day, as a lesson of experience for future service. He can tell you, better than you can tell him, where that journal is now."

Slinkton stopped the action of his foot, and looked at Beckwith.

"No," said the latter, as if answering a question from him. "Not in the drawer of the writing desk that opens with a spring; it is not there, and it never will be there again."

"Then you are a thief!" said Slinkton.

Without any change whatever in the inflexible purpose, which it was quite terrific even to me to contemplate, and from the power of which I had always felt convinced it was impossible for this wretch to escape, Beckwith returned.

"I am your niece's shadow, too."

With an imprecation Slinkton put his hand to his head, tore out some hair, and flung it to the ground. It was the end of the smooth walk; he destroyed it in the action, and it will soon be seen that his use for it was past.

Beckwith went on: "Whenever you left here, I left here. Although I understood that you found it necessary to pause in the completion of that purpose, to avert suspicion, still I watched you close, with the poor confiding girl. When I had the diary, and could read it word by word—it was only about the night before your last visit to Scarborough—you remember the night? you slept with a small flat vial tied to your wrist—I sent to Mr. Sampson, who was kept out of view. This is Mr. Sampson's trusty servant standing by the door. We three saved your niece among us."

Slinkton looked at us all, took an uncertain step or two from the place where he stood, returned to it, and glanced about him in a very curious way—as one of the meaner reptiles might, looking for a hole to hide in. I noticed at the same time, that a singular change took place in the figure of the man—as if it collapsed within his clothes, and they consequently became ill-shapen and ill-fitting.

"You shall know," said Beckwith, "for I hope the knowledge will be bitter and terrible to you, why you have been pursued by one man, and why, when the whole interest that Mr. Sampson represents would have expended any money in hunting you down, you have been tracked to death at a single individual's charge. I hear you have had the name of Meltham on your lips sometimes?"

I saw, in addition to those other changes, a sudden stoppage come upon his breathing.

"When you sent the sweet girl whom you murdered (you know with what artfully made-out surroundings and probabilities you sent her) to Meltham's office, before taking her abroad to originate the transaction that doomed her to the grave, it fell to Meltham's lot to see her and to speak with her. It did not fall to his lot to save her, though I know he would freely give his own life to have done it. He admired her—I would say he loved her deeply, if I thought it possible that you could understand the word. When she was sacrificed, he was thoroughly assured of your guilt. Having lost her, he had but one object left in life, and that was to avenge her and destroy you.

"That man Meltham," Beckwith steadily pursued, "was as absolutely certain that you could never elude him in this world, if he devoted himself to your destruction with his utmost fidelity and earnestness, and if he divided the sacred duty with no other duty in life, as he was certain that in achieving it he would be a poor instrument in the hands of Providence, and would do well before heaven in striking you out from among living men. I am that man, and I thank God I have done my work!"

If Slinkton had been running for his life from swift-footed savages, a dozen miles, he could not have shown more emphatic signs of being oppressed at heart and laboring for breath, than he showed now, when he looked at the pursuer who had so relentlessly hunted him down.

"You never saw me under my right name before; you see me under my right name now. You shall see me once again in the body, when you are tried for your life. You shall see me once again in the spirit, when the cord is round your neck, and the crowd are crying against you!"

When Meltham had spoken these last words, the miscreant suddenly turned away his face, and seemed to strike his mouth with his open hand. At the same instant, the room was filled with a new and powerful odor, and, almost at the same instant, he broke into a crooked run, leap, start —I have no name for the spasm—and fell, with a dull weight that shook the heavy old doors and windows.

That was the fitting end of him.

When we saw that he was dead, we drew away from the room, and Meltham, giving me his hand, said, wearily, "I have no more work on earth, my friend. But I shall see her again elsewhere."

It was in vain that I tried to rally him. He might have saved her, he said; he had not saved her, and he reproached himself; he had lost her, and he was brokenhearted.

"The purpose that sustained me is over, Sampson, and there is nothing now to hold me to life. I am not fit for life; I am weak and spiritless; I have no hope and no object."

In truth, I could hardly have believed that the broken man who then spoke to me was the man who had so strongly and so differently impressed me when his purpose was before him. I used such entreaties with him as I could; but he still said, and always said, in a patient, undemonstrative way—nothing could avail him—he was brokenhearted.

He died early in the next spring. He was buried by the side of the poor young lady for whom he had cherished those tender and unhappy regrets; and he left all he had to her sister. She lived to be a happy wife and mother; she married my sister's son, who succeeded poor Meltham; she is living now, and her children ride about the garden on my walking stick when I go to see her.

The Stolen White Elephant

MARK TWAIN

Conceived in bitterness, executed with satiric force and great control, resolved in tempered fury, "The Stolen White Elephant" is absolutely characteristic of Twain working in the center of his vision, at the height of his technique—it is also a story of purloined goods, of a strange and unsedentary metier and probably the funniest piece in this collection.

The following curious history was related to me by a chance railway acquaintance. He was a gentleman more than seventy years of age, and his thoroughly good and gentle face and earnest and sincere manner imprinted the unmistakable stamp of truth upon every statement which fell from his lips. He said:

You know in what reverence the royal white elephant of Siam is held by the people of that country. You know it is sacred to kings, only kings may possess it, and that it is indeed in a measure even superior to kings, since it receives not merely honor but worship. Very well; five years ago, when the troubles concerning the frontier line arose between Great Britain and Siam, it was presently manifest that Siam had been in the wrong. Therefore every reparation was quickly made, and the British representative stated that he was satisfied and the past should be forgotten. This greatly relieved the king of Siam, and partly as a token of gratitude, but partly also, perhaps, to wipe out any little remaining vestige of unpleasantness which England might feel toward him, he wished to send the queen a present—the sole sure way of propitiating an enemy, according to Oriental ideas. This present ought not only to be a royal one, but transcendently royal. Wherefore, what offering could be so meet as that of a white elephant? My position in the Indian civil service was such that I was deemed peculiarly worthy of the honor of conveying the present to her majesty. A ship was fitted out for me and my servants and the officers and attendants of the elephant, and in due time I arrived in New York harbor and placed my royal charge in admirable quarters in Jersey City. It was necessary to remain a while in order to recruit the animal's health before resuming the voyage.

All went well during a fortnight—then my calamities began. The white elephant was stolen! I was called up at dead of night and informed of this fearful misfortune. For some moments I was beside myself with terror and anxiety; I was helpless. Then I grew calmer and collected my faculties. I soon saw my course—for indeed there was but the one course for an intelligent man to pursue. Late as it was, I flew to New York and got a policeman to conduct me to the headquarters of the detective force. Fortunately I arrived in time, though the chief of the force, the celebrated Inspector Blunt, was just on the point of leaving for his home. He was a man of middle size and compact frame, and when he was thinking deeply he had a way of knitting his brows and tapping his forehead reflectively with his finger, which impressed you at once with the conviction that you stood in the presence of a person of no common order. The very sight of him gave me confidence and made me hopeful. I stated my errand. It did not flurry him in the least; it had no more visible effect upon his iron self-possession than if I had told him somebody had stolen my dog. He motioned me to a seat, and said calmly—

"Allow me to think a moment, please."

So saying, he sat down at his office table and leaned his head upon his hand. Several clerks were at work at the other end of the room; the scratching of their pens was all the sound I heard during the next six or seven minutes. Meantime the inspector sat there, buried in thought. Finally he raised his head, and there was that in the firm lines of his face which showed me that his brain had done its work and his plan was made. Said he—and his voice was low and impressive—

"This is no ordinary case. Every step must be warily taken; each step must be made sure before the next is ventured. And secrecy must be observed—secrecy profound and absolute. Speak to no one about the matter, not even the reporters. I will take care of *them;* I will see that they get only what it may suit my ends to let them know." He touched a bell; a youth appeared. "Alaric, tell the reporters to remain for the present." The boy retired. "Now let us proceed to business—and systematically. Nothing can be accomplished in this trade of mine without strict and minute method."

He took a pen and some paper. "Now—name of the elephant?"

"Hassan Ben Ali Ben Selim Abdallah Mohammed Moisé Alhammal Jamsetjejeebhoy Dhuleep Sultan Ebu Bhudpoor."

"Very well. Given name?"

"Jumbo."

"Very well. Place of birth?"

"The capital city of Siam."

"Parents living?"

"No—dead."

"Had they any other issue besides this one?"

"None. He was an only child."

"Very well. These matters are sufficient under that head. Now please describe the elephant, and leave out no particular, however insignificant —that is, insignificant from *your* point of view. To men in my profession there *are* no insignificant particulars; they do not exist."

I described—he wrote. When I was done, he said—

"Now listen. If I have made any mistakes, correct me."

He read as follows:

"Height, nineteen feet; length from apex of forehead to insertion of tail, twenty-six feet; length of trunk, sixteen feet; length of tail, six feet; total length, including trunk and tail, forty-eight feet; length of tusks, nine and a half feet; ears in keeping with these dimensions; footprint resembles the mark left when one upends a barrel in the snow; color of the elephant, a dull white; has a hole the size of a plate in each ear for the insertion of jewelry, and possesses the habit in a remarkable degree of squirting water upon spectators and of maltreating with his trunk not only such persons as he is acquainted with, but even entire strangers; limps slightly with his right hind leg, and has a small scar in his left armpit caused by a former boil; had on, when stolen, a castle containing seats for fifteen persons, and a gold-cloth saddleblanket the size of an ordinary carpet."

There were no mistakes. The inspector touched the bell, handed the description to Alaric, and said—

"Have fifty thousand copies of this printed at once and mailed to every detective office and pawnbroker's shop on the continent." Alaric retired. "There—so far, so good. Next, I must have a photograph of the property."

I gave him one. He examined it critically, and said—

"It must do, since we can do no better; but he has his trunk curled up and tucked into his mouth. That is unfortunate, and is calculated to mislead, for of course he does not usually have it in that position." He touched his bell.

"Alaric, have fifty thousand copies of this photograph made, the first thing in the morning, and mail them with the descriptive circulars."

Alaric retired to execute his orders. The inspector said—

"It will be necessary to offer a reward, of course. Now as to the amount?"

"What sum would you suggest?"

"To *begin* with, I should say—well, twenty-five thousand dollars. It is an intricate and difficult business; there are a thousand avenues of escape and opportunities of concealment. These thieves have friends and pals everywhere—"

"Bless me, do you know who they are?"

The wary face, practiced in concealing the thoughts and feelings within, gave me no token, nor yet the replying words, so quietly uttered:

"Never mind about that. I may, and I may not. We generally gather a pretty shrewd inkling of who our man is by the manner of his work and the size of the game he goes after. We are not dealing with a pickpocket or a hall thief, now, make up your mind to that. This property was not 'lifted' by a novice. But, as I was saying, considering the amount of travel which will have to be done, and the diligence with which the thieves will cover up their traces as they move along, twenty-five thousand may be too small a sum to offer, yet I think it worth while to start with that."

So we determined upon that figure, as a beginning. Then this man, whom nothing escaped which could by any possibility be made to serve as a clue, said:

"There are cases in detective history to show that criminals have been detected through peculiarities in their appetites. Now, what does this elephant eat, and how much?"

"Well, as to *what* he eats, he will eat *anything*. He will eat a man, he will eat a Bible, he will eat anything *between* a man and a Bible."

"Good, very good indeed, but too general. Details are necessary—details are the only valuable things in our trade. Very well—as to men. At one meal—or, if you prefer, during one day—how many men will he eat, if fresh?"

"He would not care whether they were fresh or not; at a single meal he would eat five ordinary men."

"Very good; five men; we will put that down. What nationalities would he prefer?"

"He is indifferent about nationalities. He prefers acquaintances, but is not prejudiced against strangers."

"Very good. Now, as to Bibles. How many Bibles would he eat at a meal?"

"He would eat an entire edition."

"It is hardly succinct enough. Do you mean the ordinary octavo, or the family illustrated?"

"I think he would be indifferent to illustrations; that is, I think he would not value illustrations above simple letter-press."

"No, you do not get my idea. I refer to bulk. The ordinary octavo Bible weighs about two pounds and a half, while the great quarto with the illustrations weighs ten or twelve. How many Doré Bibles would he eat at a meal?"

"If you knew this elephant, you could not ask. He would take what they had."

"Well, put it in dollars and cents, then. We must get at it somehow. The Doré costs a hundred dollars a copy, Russia leather, beveled."

"He would require about fifty thousand dollars' worth—say an edition of five hundred copies."

"Now that is more exact. I will put that down. Very well; he likes men and Bibles; so far, so good. What else will he eat? I want particulars."

"He will leaves Bibles to eat bricks, he will leave bricks to eat bottles, he will leave bottles to eat clothing, he will leave clothing to eat cats, he will leave cats to eat oysters, he will leave oysters to eat ham, he will leave ham to eat sugar, he will leave sugar to eat pie, he will leave pie to eat potatoes, he will leave potatoes to eat bran, he will leave bran to eat hay, he will leave hay to eat oats, he will leave oats to eat rice, for he was mainly raised on it. There is nothing whatever that he will not eat but European butter, and he would eat that if he could taste it."

"Very good. General quantity at a meal—say about—"

"Well, anywhere from a quarter to half a ton."

"And he drinks—"

"Everything that is fluid. Milk, water, whiskey, molasses, castor oil, camphene, carbolic acid—it is no use to go into particulars; whatever fluid occurs to you set it down. He will drink anything that is fluid, except European coffee."

"Very good. As to quantity?"

"Put it down five to fifteen barrels—his thirst varies; his other appetites do not."

"These things are unusual. They ought to furnish quite good clues toward tracing him."

He touched the bell.

"Alaric, summon Captain Burns."

Burns appeared. Inspector Blunt unfolded the whole matter to him, detail by detail. Then he said in the clear, decisive tones of a man whose plans are clearly defined in his head, and who is accustomed to command—"Captain Burns, detail Detectives Jones, Davis, Halsey, Bates, and Hackett to shadow the elephant."

"Yes, sir."

"Detail Detectives Moses, Dakin, Murphy, Rogers, Tupper, Higgins, and Bartholomew to shadow the thieves."

"Yes, sir."

"Place a strong guard—a guard of thirty picked men, with a relief of thirty—over the place from whence the elephant was stolen, to keep strict watch there night and day, and allow none to approach—except reporters —without written authority from me."

"Yes, sir."

"Place detectives in plainclothes in the railway, steamship, and ferry depots, and upon all roadways leading out of Jersey City, with orders to search all suspicious persons."

"Yes, sir."

"Furnish all these men with photograph and accompanying description of the elephant, and instruct them to search all trains and outgoing ferry boats and other vessels."

"Yes, sir."

"If the elephant should be found, let him be seized, and the information forwarded to me by telegraph."

"Yes, sir."

"Let me be informed at once if any clues should be found—footprints of the animal, or anything of that kind."

"Yes, sir."

"Get an order commanding the harbor police to patrol the frontages vigilantly."

"Yes, sir."

"Dispatch detectives in plainclothes over all the railways, north as far as Canada, west as far as Ohio, south as far as Washington."

"Yes, sir."

"Place experts in all the telegraph offices to listen to all messages; and let them require that all cipher dispatches be interpreted to them."

"Yes, sir."

"Let all these things be done with the utmost secrecy—mind, the most impenetrable secrecy."

"Yes, sir."

"Report to me promptly at the usual hour."

"Yes, sir."

"Go!"

"Yes, sir."

He was gone.

Inspector Blunt was silent and thoughtful a moment, while the fire in his eye cooled down and faded out. Then he turned to me and said in a placid voice—

"I am not given to boasting, it is not my habit; but—we shall find the elephant."

I shook him warmly by the hand and thanked him; and I *felt* my thanks, too. The more I had seen of the man the more I liked him, and the more I admired him and marveled over the mysterious wonders of his profession. Then we parted for the night, and I went home with a far happier heart than I had carried with me to his office.

Next morning it was all in the newspapers, in the minutest detail. It even had additions—consisting of Detective This, Detective That, and Detective The Other's "theory" as to how the robbery was done, who the robbers were, and whither they had flown with their booty. There were eleven of these theories, and they covered all the possibilities; and this single fact shows what independent thinkers detectives are. No two theories were alike, or even much resembled each other, save in one striking particular, and in that one all the eleven theories were absolutely agreed. That was, that although the rear of my building was torn out and the only door remained locked, the elephant had not been removed through the rent, but by some other (undiscovered) outlet. All agreed that the robbers had made that rent only to mislead the detectives. That never would have occurred to me or to any other layman, perhaps, but it had not deceived the detectives for a moment. Thus, what I had supposed was the only thing that had no mystery about it was in fact the very thing I had gone furthest astray in. The eleven theories all named the supposed robbers, but no two named the same robbers; the total number of suspected persons was thirty-seven. The various newspaper accounts all closed with the most important opinion of all—that of Chief Inspector Blunt. A portion of this statement read as follows:

The chief knows who the two principals are, namely, "Brick" Duffy and "Red" McFadden. Ten days before the robbery was achieved he was already aware that it was to be attempted, and had quietly proceeded to shadow these two noted villains; but unfortunately on the night in question their track was lost, and before it could be found again the bird was flown—that is, the elephant.

Duffy and McFadden are the boldest scoundrels in the profession; the chief has reasons for believing that they are the men who stole the stove out of the detective headquarters on a bitter night last winter—in consequence of which the chief and every detective present were in the hands of the physicians before morning, some with frozen feet, others with frozen fingers, ears, and other members.

When I read the first half of that I was more astonished than ever at the wonderful sagacity of this strange man. He not only saw everything in the present with a clear eye, but even the future could not be hidden from him. I was soon at his office, and said I could not help wishing he had had those men arrested, and so prevented the trouble and loss; but his reply was simple and unanswerable:

"It is not our province to prevent crime, but to punish it. We cannot punish it until it is committed."

I remarked that the secrecy with which we had begun had been marred by the newspapers; not only all our facts but all our plans and purposes had been revealed; even all the suspected persons had been named; these would doubtless disguise themselves now, or go into hiding.

"Let them. They will find that when I am ready for them my hand will descend upon them, in their secret places, as unerringly as the hand of fate. As to the newspapers, we *must* keep in with them. Fame, reputation, constant public mention—these are the detective's bread and butter. He must publish his facts, else he will be supposed to have none; he must publish his theory, for nothing is so strange or striking as a detective's theory, or brings him so much wondering respect; we must publish our plans, for these the journals insist upon having, and we could not deny them without offending. We must constantly show the public what we are doing, or they will believe we are doing nothing. It is much pleasanter to have a newspaper say, 'Inspector Blunt's ingenious and extraordinary theory is as follows,' than to have it say some harsh thing, or, worse still, some sarcastic one."

"I see the force of what you say. But I noticed that in one part of your remarks in the papers this morning you refused to reveal your opinion upon a certain minor point."

"Yes, we always do that; it has a good effect. Besides, I had not formed any opinion on that point, anyway."

I deposited a considerable sum of money with the inspector, to meet current expenses, and sat down to wait for news. We were expecting the telegrams to begin to arrive at any moment now. Meantime I reread the newspapers and also our descriptive circular, and observed that our twenty-five-thousand-dollar reward seemed to be offered only to detectives. I said I thought it ought to be offered to anybody who would catch the elephant. The inspector said:

"It is the detectives who will find the elephant, hence the reward will go to the right place. If other people found the animal, it would only be by watching the detectives and taking advantage of clues and indications stolen from them, and that would entitle the detectives to the reward, after all. The proper office of a reward is to stimulate the men who deliver up their time and their trained sagacities to this sort of work, and not to confer benefits upon chance citizens who stumble upon a capture without having earned the benefits by their own merits and labors."

This was reasonable enough, certainly. Now the telegraphic machine in the corner began to click, and the following dispatch was the result:

> Flower Station, N.Y., 7:30 A.M.
> Have got a clue. Found a succession of deep tracks across a farm near here. Followed them two miles east without result; think elephant went west. Shall now shadow him in that direction.
> Darley, Detective

"Darley's one of the best men on the force," said the inspector. "We shall hear from him again before long."

Telegram number two came:

> Barker's, N.J., 7:40 A.M.
> Just arrived. Glass factory broken open here during night, and eight hundred bottles taken. Only water in large quantity near here is five miles distant. Shall strike for there. Elephant will be thirsty. Bottles were empty.
> Baker, Detective

"That promises well, too," said the inspector. "I told you the creature's appetites would not be bad clues."

Telegram number three:

> Taylorville, L.I., 8:15 A.M.
> A haystack near here disappeared during night. Probably eaten. Have got a clue, and am off.
> Hubbard, Detective

"How he does move around!" said the inspector. "I knew we had a difficult job on hand, but we shall catch him yet."

Flower Station, N.Y., 9 A.M.

Shadowed the tracks three miles westward. Large, deep, and ragged. Have just met a farmer who says they are not elephant tracks. Says they are holes where he dug up saplings for shade-trees when ground was frozen last winter. Give me orders how to proceed.

Darley, Detective

"Aha! a confederate of the thieves! The thing grows warm," said the inspector.

He dictated the following telegram to Darley:

Arrest the man and force him to name his pals. Continue to follow the tracks —to the Pacific, if necessary.

Chief Blunt

Next telegram:

Coney Point, Pa., 8:45 A.M.

Gas office broken open here during night and three months' unpaid gas bills taken. Have got a clue and am away.

Murphy, Detective

"Heavens!" said the inspector; "would he eat gas bills?"

"Through ignorance, yes; but they cannot support life. At least, unassisted."

Now came this exciting telegram:

Ironville, N.Y., 9:30 A.M.

Just arrived. This village in consternation. Elephant passed through here at five this morning. Some say he went east, some say west, some north, some south— but all say they did not wait to notice particularly. He killed a horse; have secured a piece of it for a clue. Killed it with his trunk; from style of blow, think he struck it left-handed. From position in which horse lies, think elephant traveled northward along line of Berkley railway. Has four and a half hours' start, but I move on his track at once.

Hawes, Detective

I uttered exclamations of joy. The inspector was as self-contained as a graven image. He clamly touched his bell.

"Alaric, send Captain Burns here."

Burns appeared.

"How many men are ready for instant orders?"

"Ninety-six, sir."

"Send them north at once. Let them concentrate along the line of the Berkley road north of Ironville."

"Yes, sir."

"Let them conduct their movements with the utmost secrecy. As fast as others are at liberty, hold them for orders."

"Yes, sir."

"Go!"

"Yes, sir."

Presently came another telegram:

> Sage Corners, N.Y., 10:30
>
> Just arrived. Elephant passed through here at 8:15. All escaped from the town but a policeman. Apparently elephant did not strike at policeman, but at the lamp-post. Got both. I have secured a portion of the policeman as clue.
>
> Stumm, Detective

"So the elephant has turned westward," said the inspector. "However, he will not escape, for my men are scattered all over that region."

The next telegram said:

> Glover's, 11:15
>
> Just arrived. Village deserted, except sick and aged. Elephant passed through three-quarters of an hour ago. The antitemperance mass meeting was in session; he put his trunk in at a window and washed it out with water from cistern. Some swallowed it—since dead; several drowned. Detective Cross and O'Shaughnessy were passing through town, but going south—so missed elephant. Whole region for many miles around in terror—people flying from their homes. Wherever they turn they meet elephant, and many are killed.
>
> Brant, Detective

I could have shed tears, this havoc so distressed me. But the inspector only said—

"You see—we are closing in on him. He feels our presence; he has turned eastward again."

Yet further troublous news was in store for us. The telegraph brought this:

> Hoganport, 12:19
>
> Just arrived. Elephant passed through half an hour ago, creating wildest fright and excitement. Elephant raged around streets; two plumbers going by, killed one —other escaped. Regret general.
>
> O'Flaherty, Detective

"Now he is right in the midst of my men," said the inspector. "Nothing can save him."

A succession of telegrams came from detectives who were scattered through New Jersey and Pennsylvania, and who were following clues consisting of ravaged barns, factories, and Sunday school libraries, with high hopes—hopes amounting to certainties, indeed. The inspector said—"I wish I could communicate with them and order them north, but that is impossible. A detective only visits a telegraph office to send his report; then he is off again, and you don't know where to put your hand on him."

Now came this dispatch:

> Bridgeport, Ct., 12:15
> Barnum offers rate of $4000 a year for exclusive privilege of using elephant as traveling advertising medium from now till detectives find him. Wants to paste circus posters on him. Desires immediate answer.
>
> Boggs, Detective

"That is perfectly absurd!" I exclaimed.

"Of course it is," said the inspector. "Evidently Mr. Barnum, who thinks he is so sharp, does not know me—but I know him."

Then he dictated this answer to the dispatch:

> Mr. Barnum's offer declined. Make it $7,000 or nothing.
>
> Chief Blunt

"There. We shall not have to wait long for an answer. Mr. Barnum is not at home; he is in the telegraph office—it is his way when he has business on hand. Inside of three—"

> Done.—P.T. Barnum

So interrupted the clicking telegraphic instrument. Before I could make a comment upon this extraordinary episode, the following dispatch carried my thoughts into another and very distressing channel:

> Bolivia, N.Y., 12:50
> Elephant arrived here from the south and passed through toward the forest at 11:50, dispersing a funeral on the way, and diminishing the mourners by two. Citizens fired some small cannonballs into him, and then fled. Detective Burke and I arrived ten minutes later, from the north, but mistook some excavations for footprints, and so lost a good deal of time; but at last we struck the right trail and followed it to the woods. We then got down on our hands and knees and continued to keep a sharp eye on the track, and so shadowed it into the brush. Burke was in advance. Unfortunately the animal had stopped to rest; therefore, Burke having his head down, intent upon the track, butted up against the elephant's hind legs before he was aware of his vicinity. Burke instantly rose to

his feet, seized the tail, and exclaimed joyfully, "I claim the re——" but got no further, for a single blow of the huge trunk laid the brave fellow's fragments low in death. I fled rearward, and the elephant turned and shadowed me to the edge of the wood, making tremendous speed, and I should inevitably have been lost, but that the remains of the funeral providentially intervened again and diverted his attention. I have just learned that nothing of that funeral is now left; but this is no loss, for there is an abundance of material for another. Meantime, the elephant has disappeared again.

Mulrooney, Detective

We heard no news except from the diligent and confident detectives scattered about New Jersey, Pennsylvania, Delaware, and Virginia—who were all following fresh and encouraging clues—until shortly after 2 P.M., when this telegram came:

Baxter Center, 2:15

Elephant been here, plastered over with circus bills, and broke up a revival, striking down and damaging many who were on the point of entering upon a better life. Citizens penned him up, and established a guard. When Detective Brown and I arrived, some time after, we entered enclosure and proceeded to identify elephant by photograph and description. All marks tallied exactly except one, which we could not see—the boil scar under armpit. To make sure, Brown crept under to look, and was immediately brained—that is, head crushed and destroyed, though nothing issued from debris. All fled; so did elephant, striking right and left with much effect. Has escaped, but left bold blood track from cannon wounds. Rediscovery certain. He broke southward, through a dense forest.

Brent, Detective

That was the last telegram. At nightfall a fog shut down which was so dense that objects but three feet away could not be discerned. This lasted all night. The ferry boats and even the omnibuses had to stop running.

Next morning the papers were as full of detective theories as before; they had all our tragic facts in detail also, and a great many more which they had received from their telegraphic correspondents. Column after column was occupied, a third of its way down, with glaring headlines, which it made my heart sick to read. Their general tone was like this:

THE WHITE ELEPHANT AT LARGE! HE MOVES UPON HIS FATAL MARCH! WHOLE VILLAGES DESERTED BY THEIR FRIGHT-STRICKEN OCCUPANTS! PALE TERROR GOES BEFORE HIM, DEATH AND DEVASTATION FOLLOW AFTER! AFTER THESE, THE DETEC-

TIVES. BARNS DESTROYED, FACTORIES GUTTED, HARVESTS DEVOURED, PUBLIC AS-
SEMBLAGES DISPERSED, ACCOMPANIED BY SCENES OF CARNAGE IMPOSSIBLE TO
DESCRIBE! THEORIES OF THIRTY-FOUR OF THE MOST DISTINGUISHED DETECTIVES ON
THE FORCE! THEORY OF CHIEF BLUNT!

"There!" said Inspector Blunt, almost betrayed into excitement, "this
is magnificent! This is the greatest windfall that any detective organization ever had. The fame of it will travel to the ends of the earth, and
endure to the end of time, and my name with it."

But there was no joy for me. I felt as if I had committed all those red
crimes, and that the elephant was only my irresponsible agent. And how
the list had grown! In one place he had "interfered with an election and
killed five repeaters." He had followed this act with the destruction of two
poor fellows, named O'Donohue and McFlannigan, who had "found a
refuge in the home of the oppressed of all lands only the day before, and
were in the act of exercising for the first time the noble right of American
citizens at the polls, when stricken down by the relentless hand of the
Scourge of Siam." In another, he had "found a crazy sensation-preacher
preparing his next season's heroic attacks on the dance, the theater, and
other things which can't strike back, and had stepped on him." And in
still another place he had "killed a lightning-rod agent." And so the list
went on, growing redder and redder, and more and more heartbreaking.
Sixty persons had been killed, and two hundred and forty wounded. All
the accounts bore just testimony to the activity and devotion of the
detectives, and all closed with the remark that "three hundred thousand
citizens and four detectives saw the dread creature, and two of the latter
he destroyed."

I dreaded to hear the telegraphic instrument begin to click again. By
and by the messages began to pour in, but I was happily disappointed in
their nature. It was soon apparent that all trace of the elephant was lost.
The fog had enabled him to search out a good hiding place unobserved.
Telegrams from the most absurdly distant points reported that a dim vast
mass had been glimpsed there through the fog at such and such an hour,
and was "undoubtedly the elephant." This dim vast mass had been
glimpsed in New Haven, in New Jersey, in Pennsylvania, in interior New
York, in Brooklyn, and even in the city of New York itself! But in all cases
the dim vast mass had vanished quickly and left no trace. Every detective
of the large force scattered over this huge extent of country sent his hourly
report, and each and every one of them had a clue, and was shadowing

something, and was hot upon the heels of it.

But the day passed without other result.

The next day the same.

The next just the same.

The newspaper reports began to grow monotonous with facts that amounted to nothing, clues which led to nothing, and theories which had nearly exhausted the elements which surprise and delight and dazzle.

By advice of the inspector I doubled the reward.

Four more dull days followed. Then came a bitter blow to the poor, hard-working detectives—the journalists declined to print their theories, and coldly said, "Give us a rest."

Two weeks after the elephant's disappearance I raised the reward to seventy-five thousand dollars by the inspector's advice. It was a great sum, but I felt that I would rather sacrifice my whole private fortune than lose my credit with my government. Now that the detectives were in adversity, the newspapers turned upon them, and began to fling the most stinging sarcasms at them. This gave the minstrels an idea, and they dressed themselves as detectives and hunted the elephant on the stage in the most extravagant way. The caricaturists made pictures of detectives scanning the country with spyglasses, while the elephant, at their back, stole apples out of their pockets. And they made all sorts of ridiculous pictures of the detective badge—you have seen that badge printed in gold on the back of detective novels, no doubt—it is a wide-staring eye, with the legend, WE NEVER SLEEP. When detectives called for a drink, the would-be facetious barkeeper resurrected an obsolete form of expression and said, "Will you have an eye-opener?" All the air was thick with sarcasms.

But there was one man who moved calm, untouched, unaffected, through it all. It was that heart of oak, the chief inspector. His brave eye never drooped, his serene confidence never wavered. He always said—

"Let them rail on; he laughs best who laughs last."

My admiration for the man grew into a species of worship. I was at his side always. His office had become an unpleasant place to me, and now became daily more and more so. Yet if he could endure it I meant to do so also; at least, as long as I could. So I came regularly, and stayed—the only outsider who seemed to be capable of it. Everybody wondered how I could; and often it seemed to me that I must desert, but at such times I looked into that calm and apparently unconscious face, and held my ground.

About three weeks after the elephant's disappearance I was about to say, one morning, that I should *have* to strike my colors and retire, when the great detective arrested the thought by proposing one more superb and masterly move.

This was to compromise with the robbers. The fertility of this man's invention exceeded anything I have ever seen, and I have had a wide intercourse with the world's finest minds. He said he was confident he could compromise for one hundred thousand dollars and recover the elephant. I said I believed I could scrape the amount together, but what would become of the poor detectives who had worked so faithfully? He said—

"In compromises they always get half."

This removed my only objection. So the inspector wrote two notes, in this form:

Dear Madam,
Your husband can make a large sum of money (and be entirely protected from the law) by making an immediate appointment with me.

Chief Blunt

He sent one of these by his confidential messenger to the "reputed wife" of Brick Duffy, and the other to the reputed wife of Red McFadden.

Within the hour these offensive answers came:

Ye owld fool:
brick McDuffys bin ded 2 yere.

Bridget Mahoney

Chief Bat,
Red McFadden is hung and in heving 18 month. Any Ass but a detective knose that.

Mary O'Hooligan

"I had long suspected these facts," said the inspector; "this testimony proves the unerring accuracy of my instinct."

The moment one resource failed him he was ready with another. He immediately wrote an advertisement for the morning papers, and I kept a copy of it:

A.—xwblv. 242 N. Tjnd—fz328wmlg. Ozpo,—; 2 m! ogw. Mum.

He said that if the thief was alive this would bring him to the usual rendezvous. He further explained that the usual rendezvous was a place where all business affairs between detectives and criminals were conducted. This meeting would take place at twelve the next night.

We could do nothing till then, and I lost no time in getting out of the office, and was grateful indeed for the privilege.

At eleven the next night I brought one hundred thousand dollars in banknotes and put them into the chief's hands, and shortly afterward he took his leave, with the brave old undimmed confidence in his eye. An almost intolerable hour dragged to a close; then I heard his welcome tread, and rose gasping and tottered to meet him. How his fine eyes flamed with triumph! He said—

"We've compromised! The jokers will sing a different tune tomorrow! Follow me!"

He took a lighted candle and strode down into the vast vaulted basement where sixty detectives always slept, and where a score were now playing cards to while the time. I followed close after him. He walked swiftly down to the dim remote end of the place, and just as I succumbed to the pangs of suffocation and was swooning away he stumbled and fell over the outlying members of a mighty object, and I heard him exclaim as he went down—

"Our noble profession is vindicated. Here is your elephant!"

I was carried to the office above and restored with carbolic acid. The whole detective force swarmed in, and such another season of triumphant rejoicing ensued as I had never witnessed before. The reporters were called, baskets of champagne were opened, toasts were drunk, the handshakings and congratulations were continuous and enthusiastic. Naturally the chief was the hero of the hour, and his happiness was so complete and had been so patiently and worthily and bravely won that it made me happy to see it, though I stood there a homeless beggar, my priceless charge dead, and my position in my country's service lost to me through what would always seem my fatally careless execution of a great trust. Many an eloquent eye testified its deep admiration for the chief, and many a detective's voice murmured, "Look at him—just the king of the profession—only give him a clue, it's all he wants, and there ain't anything hid that he can't find." The dividing of the fifty thousand dollars made great pleasure; when it was finished the chief made a little speech while he put his share in his pocket, in which he said, "Enjoy it, boys, for you've earned it; and more than that you've earned for the detective profession undying fame."

A telegram arrived, which read:

Monroe, Mich., 10 P.M.

First time I've struck a telegraph office in over three weeks. Have followed those footprints, horseback, through the woods, a thousand miles to here, and they get stronger and bigger and fresher every day. Don't worry—inside of another week I'll have the elephant. This is dead sure.

Darley, Detective

The chief ordered three cheers for "Darley, one of the finest minds on the force," and then commanded that he be telegraphed to come home and receive his share of the reward.

So ended that marvelous episode of the stolen elephant. The newspapers were pleasant with praises once more, the next day, with one contemptible exception. This sheet said, "Great is the detective! He may be a little slow in finding a little thing like a mislaid elephant—he may hunt him all day and sleep with his rotting carcass all night for three weeks, but he will find him at last—if he can get the man who mislaid him to show him the place!"

Poor Hassan was lost to me forever. The cannon shots had wounded him fatally, he had crept to that unfriendly place in the fog, and there, surrounded by his enemies and in constant danger of detection, he had wasted away with hunger and suffering till death gave him peace.

The compromise cost me one hundred thousand dollars; my detective expenses were forty-two thousand dollars more; I never applied for a place again under my government; I am a ruined man and a wanderer in the earth—but my admiration for that man, whom I believe to be the greatest detective the world has ever produced, remains undimmed to this day, and will so remain unto the end.

Ransom

PEARL S. BUCK

The intermixture of the common and the terrible, the routine and the inescapable dread which is its circumference, has rarely been accomplished as well as in this story of kidnapping by the second American and first woman to win the Nobel Prize (in 1936) for literature. The slow fading of Pearl S. Buck's reputation in her last decades will make this story an astonishing revelation to those unfamiliar with her work; in its careful and controlled dealing with terror and the uncontrollable it approaches the work of Cornell Woolrich, a contemporaneous writer who would have admired this story (and could have done it no better himself).

The Beethoven symphony stopped abruptly. A clear metallic voice broke across the melody of the third movement.

"Press radio news. The body of Jimmie Lane, kidnapped son of Mr. Headley Lane, has been found on the bank of the Hudson River near his home this afternoon. This ends the search of—"

"Kent, turn it off, please!" Allin exclaimed.

Kent Crothers hesitated a second. Then he turned off the radio.

In the silence Allin sat biting her lower lip. "That poor mother!" she exclaimed. "All these days—not giving up hope."

"I suppose it is better to know something definite," he said quietly, "even though it is the worst."

Perhaps this would be a good time to talk with her, to warn her that she was letting this kidnapping business grow into an obsession. After all, children did grow up in the United States, even in well-to-do families like theirs. The trouble was that they were not quite rich enough and still too rich—not rich enough to hire guards for their children, but rich enough, because his father owned the paper mill, to make them known in the neighborhood, at least.

The thing was to take it for granted that they did not belong to the millionaire class and therefore were not prize for kidnappers. They should do this for Bruce's sake. He would be starting to school next autumn. Bruce would have to walk back and forth on the streets like millions of other American children. Kent wouldn't have his son driven three blocks, even by Peter the outdoor man; it would do him more harm than . . . after all, it was a democracy they lived in, and Bruce had to grow up with the crowd.

"I'll go and see that the children are covered," Allin said. "Betsy throws off the covers whenever she can."

Kent knew that she simply wanted to make sure they were there. But he rose with her, lighting his pipe, thinking how to begin. They walked up the stairs together, their fingers interlaced. Softly she opened the nursery door. It was ridiculous how even he was being affected by her fears. Whenever the door opened his heart stood cold for a second, until he saw the two beds, each with a little head on the pillow.

They were there now, of course. He stood beside Bruce's bed and looked down at his son. Handsome little devil. He was sleeping so soundly that when his mother leaned over him he did not move. His black hair was a tousle; his red lips pouted. He was dark, but he had Allin's blue eyes.

They did not speak. Allin drew the cover gently over his outflung arm, and they stood a moment longer, hand in hand, gazing at the child. Then Allin looked up at Kent and smiled, and he kissed her. He put his arm about her shoulder, and they went to Betsy's bed.

Here was his secret obsession. He could say firmly that Bruce must take his chances with the other children, because a boy had to learn to be brave. But this baby—such a tiny feminine creature, his little daughter. She had Allin's auburn coloring, but by some miracle she had his dark eyes, so that when he looked into them he seemed to be looking into himself.

She was breathing now, a little unevenly, through her tiny nose.

"How's her cold?" he whispered.

"It doesn't seem worse," Allin whispered back. "I put stuff on her chest."

He was always angry when anything happened to this baby. He didn't trust her nurse, Mollie, too much. She was good-hearted, maybe, but easygoing.

The baby stirred and opened her eyes. She blinked, smiled and put up her arms to him.

"Don't pick her up, darling," Allin counseled. "She'll only want it every time."

So he did not take her. Instead, he put her arms down, one and then the other, playfully, under the cover.

"Go to sleep-bye, honey," he said. And she lay, sleepily smiling. She was a good little thing.

"Come—let's put out the light," Allin whispered. They tiptoed out and went back to the living room.

Kent sat down, puffed on his pipe, his mind full of what he wanted to say to Allin. It was essential to their life to believe that nothing could happen to their children.

"Kidnapping's like lightning," he began abruptly. "It happens, of course—once in a million. What you have to remember is all the rest of the children who are perfectly safe."

She had sat down on the ottoman before the fire, but she turned to him when he said this. "What would you do, honestly, Kent, if some night when we went upstairs—"

"Nonsense!" he broke in. "That's what I've been trying to tell you. It's so unlikely as to be—it's these damned newspapers! When a thing happens in one part of the country, every little hamlet hears of it."

"Jane Eliot told me there are three times as many kidnappings as ever get into the newspapers," Allin said.

"Jane's a newspaperwoman," Kent said. "You mustn't let her sense of drama—"

"Still, she's been on a lot of kidnapping cases," Allin replied. "She was telling me about the Wyeth case—"

This was the time to speak, now when all Allin's secret anxiety was quivering in her voice. Kent took her hand and fondled it as he spoke. He must remember how deeply she felt everything, and this thing had haunted her before Bruce was born. He had not even thought of it until one night in the darkness she had asked him the same question, "What would we do, Kent, if—" Only then he had not known what she meant.

"If what?" he had asked.

"If our baby were ever kidnapped."

He had answered what he had felt then and believed now to be true. "Why worry about what will never happen?" he had said. Nevertheless, he had followed all the cases since Bruce was born.

He kissed her palm now. "I can't bear having you afraid," he said. "It isn't necessary, you know, darling. We can't live under the shadow of this thing," he went on. "We have to come to some rational position on it."

"That's what I want, Kent. I'd be glad not to be afraid—if I knew how."

"After all," he went on again, "most people bring up their families without thinking about it."

"Most mothers think of it," she said. "Most of the women I know have said something about it to me—some time or other—enough to make me know they think about it all the time."

"You'd be better off not talking about it," he said.

But she said, "We keep wondering what we would do, Kent."

"That's just it!" he exclaimed. "That's why I think if we decided now what we would do—always bearing in mind that it's only the remotest possibility—"

"What *would* we do, Kent?" she asked.

He answered half playfully, "Promise to remember it's as remote as— an airplane attack on our home?"

She nodded.

"I've always thought that if one of the children were kidnapped I'd simply turn the whole thing over to the police at once."

"What police?" she asked instantly. "Gossipy old Mike O'Brien, who'd tell the newspapers the first thing? It's fatal to let it get into the papers, Jane says."

"Well, the federal police, then—the G-men."

"How does one get in touch with them?"

He had to confess he did not know. "I'll find out," he promised. "Anyway, it's the principle, darling, that we want to determine. Once we know what we'll do, we can put it out of our minds. No ransom, Allin— that I feel sure about. As long as we keep on paying ransoms, we're going to have kidnappings. Somebody has to be strong enough to take the stand. Then maybe other people will see what they ought to do."

But she did not look convinced. When she spoke, her voice was low and full of dread. "The thing is, Kent, if we decided not to pay ransom, we just couldn't stick to it—not really, I mean. Suppose it were Bruce— suppose he had a cold and it was winter—and he was taken out of his warm bed in his pajamas, we'd do anything. You know we would!" She rushed on. "We wouldn't care about other children, Kent. We would only be thinking of our own little Bruce—and no one else. How to get him back again, at whatever cost."

"Hush, darling," he said. "If you're going to be like this we can't talk about it, after all."

"No, Kent, please. I do want to talk. I want to know what we ought to do. If only I could be not afraid!" she whispered.

"Come here by me," he said. He drew her to the couch beside him. "First of all, you know I love the children as well as you do, don't you?" She nodded, and he went on, "Then, darling, I'd do anything I thought would be best for our children, wouldn't I?"

"You'd do the best you knew, Kent. The question is, do any of us know what to do?"

"I do know," he said gravely, "that until we make the giving and taking of ransoms unlawful we shall have kidnappers. And until somebody begins it, it will never be done. That's the law of democratic government. The people have to begin action before government takes a stand."

"What if they said not to tell the police?" she asked.

Her concreteness confounded him. It was not as if the thing could happen!

"It all depends," he retorted, "on whether you want to give in to rascals or stand on your principle."

"But if it were our own child?" she persisted. "Be honest, Kent. Please don't retire into principles."

"I am trying to be honest," he said slowly. "I think I would stick by principle and trust somehow to think of some way—" He looked waveringly into her unbelieving eyes.

"Try to remember exactly what happened!" he was shouting at the silly nurse. "Where did you leave her?"

Allin was quieter than he, but Allin's voice on the telephone half an hour ago had been like a scream: "Kent, we can't find Betsy!"

He had been in the mill directors' meeting, but he'd risen instantly. "Sorry," he'd said sharply. "I have to leave at once."

"Nothing serious, Kent?" His father's white eyebrows had lifted.

"I think not," he'd answered. He had sense enough not to say what Allin had screamed. "I'll let you know if it is."

He had leaped into his car and driven home like a crazy man. He'd drawn up in a spray of gravel at his own gate. Allin was there, and Mollie, the silly nurse. Mollie was sobbing.

"We was at the gate, sir, watchin' for Brucie to come home from school, like we do every day, and I put 'er down—she's heavy to carry— while I went in to get a clean hankie to wipe her little hands. She'd stooped into a puddle from the rain this morning. When I came back, she wasn't there. I ran around the shrubs, sir, lookin'—and then I screamed for the madam."

"Kent, I've combed the place," Allin whispered.

"The gate!" he gasped.

"It was shut, and the bar across," Mollie wailed. "I'd sense enough to see to that before I went in."

"How long were you gone?" he shouted at her.

"I don't know, sir," Mollie sobbed. "It didn't seem a minute!"

He rushed into the yard. "Betsy, Betsy!" he cried. "Come to daddy! Here's daddy!" He stooped under the big lilac bushes. "Have you looked in the garage?" he demanded of Allin.

"Peter's been through it twice," she answered.

"I'll see for myself," he said. "Go into the house, Allin. She may have got inside, somehow."

He tore into the garage. Peter crawled out from under the small car.

"She ain't hyah, suh," he whispered. "Ah done looked ev'ywheah."

But Kent looked again, Peter following him like a dog. In the back of his mind was a telephone number, National 7117. He had found out about that number the year before, after he and Allin had talked that evening. Only he wouldn't call yet. Betsy was sure to be somewhere.

The gate clicked, and he rushed out. But it was only Bruce.

"Why, what's the matter with you, daddy?" Bruce asked.

Kent swallowed—no use scaring Bruce. "Bruce, did you—you didn't see Betsy on the way home, did you?"

"No, daddy. I didn't see anybody except Mike to help me across the square 'cause there was a notomobile."

"Wha' dat?" Peter was pointing at something. It was a bit of white paper, held down by a stone.

As well as he knew anything, Kent knew what it was. He had read that note a dozen times in the newspaper accounts. He stooped and picked it up. There it was—the scrawled handwriting.

"We been waiting this chanse." The handwriting was there, illiterate, disguised. "Fifty grand is the price. Your dads got it if you aint. Youll hear where to put it. If you tell the police we kill the kid."

"Daddy, what's—" Bruce began.

"Bring him indoors," he ordered Peter.

Where was Allin? He had to—he had promised her it would not happen! The telephone number was—but—

"Allin!" he shouted.

He heard her running down from the attic.

"Allin!" he gasped. She was there, white and piteous with terror—and so helpless. God, they were both so helpless! He had to have help; he had to know what to do. But had not he—he had decided long ago what he must do, because what did he know about crooks and kidnappers? People gave the ransom and lost their children, too. He had to have advice he could trust.

"I'm going to call National 7117!" he blurted at her.

"No, Kent—wait!" she cried.

"I've got to," he insisted. Before she could move, he ran to the telephone and took up the receiver. "I want National 7117!" he shouted.

Her face went white. He held out his hand with the crumpled note. She read it and snatched at the receiver.

"No, Kent—wait. We don't know. Wait and see what they say!"

But a calm voice was already speaking at the other end of the wire: "This is National 7117." And Kent was shouting hoarsely, "I want to report a kidnapping. It's our baby girl. Kent Crothers, 134 Eastwood Avenue, Greenvale, New York."

He listened while the voice was telling him to do nothing, to wait until tomorrow, and then at a certain village inn, fifty miles away, to meet a certain man who would wear a plain gray suit.

And all the time Allin was whispering, "They'll kill her—they'll kill her, Kent."

"They won't know," he whispered back. "Nobody will know." When he put the receiver down he cried at her angrily, "They won't tell anybody —those fellows in Washington! Besides, I've got to have help, I tell you!"

She stood staring at him with horrified eyes. "They'll kill her," she repeated.

He wanted to get somewhere to weep, only men could not weep. But Allin was not weeping, either. Then suddenly they flung their arms about each other, and together broke into silent terrible tears.

He was not used to waiting, but he had to wait. And he had to help Allin wait. Men were supposed to be stronger.

At first it had been a comfort to have the directions to follow. First, everybody in the house—that was easy: simply the cook Sarah, the maid Rose, and Mollie and Peter. They of course were beyond blame, except Mollie. Perhaps Mollie was more than just a fool. They all had to be told they were to say absolutely nothing.

"Get everybody together in the dining room," Kent had told Allin. He had gone into the dining room.

"Daddy!" He saw Bruce's terrified figure in the doorway. "What's the matter? Where's Betsy?"

"We can't find her, son," Kent said, trying to make his voice calm. "Of course we will, but just now nobody must know she isn't here."

"Shall I go out in the yard?" Bruce asked. "Maybe I could find her."

"No," Kent said sharply. "I'd rather you went upstairs to your own room. I'll be up—in a minute."

The servants were coming in, Allin behind them.

"I'll go with Bruce," she said.

She was so still and so controlled, but he could tell by the quiver about her lips that she was only waiting for him.

"I'll be up in a very few minutes," he promised her. He stood until she had gone, Bruce's hand in hers. Then he turned to the four waiting figures. Mollie was still crying. He could tell by their faces that they all knew about the note.

"I see you know what has happened," he said. Strange how all these familiar faces looked sinister to him! Peter and Sarah had been in his mother's household. They had known him for years. And Rose was Sarah's niece. But they all looked hostile, or he imagined they did. "And I want not one word said of this to anyone in the town," he said harshly. "Remember, Betsy's life depends on no one outside knowing."

He paused, setting his jaws. He would not have believed he could cry as easily as a woman, but he could.

He cleared his throat. "Her life depends on how we behave now—in the next few hours." Mollie's sobbing burst out into wails. He rose. "That's all," he said. "We must simply wait."

The telephone rang, and he hurried to it. There was no way of knowing how the next message would come. But it was his father's peremptory voice: "Anything wrong over there, Kent?"

He knew now it would never do for his father to know what had happened. His father could keep nothing to himself.

"Everything is all right, dad," he answered. "Allin's not feeling very well, that's all."

"Have you had the doctor?" his father shouted.

"We will if it is necessary, dad," he answered and put up the receiver abruptly. He could not go on with that.

He thought of Bruce and went to find him. He was eating his supper in the nursery, and Allin was with him. She had told Mollie to stay downstairs. She could not bear to see the girl any more than he could.

But the nursery was unbearable, too. This was the time when Betsy, fresh from her bath . . .

"I'm—I'll be downstairs in the library," he told Allin hurriedly, and she nodded.

In the library the silence was torture. There was nothing to do but wait.

And all the time who knew what was happening to the child? Tomorrow, the man had said an hour ago. Wait, he had said. But what about tonight? In what sort of place would the child be sleeping?

Kent leaped to his feet. Something had to be done. He would have a look around the yard. There might be another letter.

He went out into the early autumn twilight. He had to hold himself together to keep from breaking into foolish shouts and curses. It was the agony of not being able to do anything. Then he controlled himself. The thing was to go on following a rational plan. He had come out to see if he could find anything.

He searched every inch of the yard. There was no message of any sort.

Then in the gathering darkness he saw a man at the gate. "Mist' Crothers!" it was Peter's voice. "Fo' God, Mist' Crothers, Ah don't know why they should pick on mah ole 'ooman. When Ah come home fo' suppah, she give it to me—she cain't read, so she don't know what wuz in it. Ah run all de way."

Kent snatched a paper from Peter's shaking hand and ran to the house. In the lighted hall he read:

Get the dough ready all banknotes dont mark any or well get the other kid too. Dont try double-crossing us. You cant get away with nothing. Put it in a box by the dead oak at the mill creek. You know where. At twelve o'clock tomorrow night.

He knew where, indeed. He had fished there from the time he was a little boy. The lightning had struck that oak tree one summer when he had been only a hundred yards away, standing in the doorway of the mill during a thunderstorm. How did they know he knew?

He turned on Peter. "Who brought this?" he demanded.

"Ah don' know, suh," Peter stammered. "She couldn't tell me nothin' 'cep'n' it wuz a white man. He chuck it at 'er and say, 'Give it to yo' ole man.' So she give it to me, and Ah come a-runnin'."

Kent stared at Peter, trying to ferret into that dark brain. Was Peter being used by someone; bribed, perhaps, to take a part? Did he know anything?

"If I thought you knew anything about Betsy, I'd kill you myself," he said.

"Fo' God, Ah don', Mist' Crothers—you know me, suh! Ah done gyardened for yo' since yo' and Miss Allin got mah'ied. 'Sides, whut Ah want in such devilment? Ah got all Ah want—mah house and a sal'ry. Ah don' want nuthin'."

It was all true, of course. The thing was, you suspected everybody.

"You tell Flossie to tell no one," he commanded Peter.

"Ah done tole 'er," Peter replied fervently. "Ah tole 'er Ah'd split 'er open if she tole anybody 'bout dat white man."

"Get along, then," said Kent. "And remember what I told you."

"Yassuh," Peter replied.

"Of course we'll pay the ransom!" Allin was insisting.

They were in their own room, the door open into the narrow passage, and beyond that the door into the nursery was open, too. They sat where, in the shadowy light of a night lamp, they could see Bruce's dark head on the pillow. Impossible, of course, to sleep. Sarah had sent up some cold chicken and they had eaten it here, and later Kent had made Allin take a hot bath and get into a warm robe and lie down on the chaise longue. He did not undress. Someone might call.

"I'll have to see what the man says tomorrow," he answered.

Terrifying to think how he was pinning everything on that fellow tomorrow—a man whose name, even, he did not know. All he knew was he'd wear a plain gray suit and he'd have a blue handkerchief in his pocket. That was all he had to save Betsy's life. No, that wasn't true. Behind that one man were hundreds of others, alert, strong, and ready to help him.

"We've got to pay it," Allin was saying hysterically. "What's money now?"

"Allin!" he cried. "You don't think I'm trying to save the money, in God's name!"

"We have about twenty thousand, haven't we, in the bank?" she said hurriedly. "Your father would have the rest, though, and we could give him the securities. It isn't as if we didn't have it."

"Allin, you're being absurd! The thing is to know how to—"

But she flew at him fiercely. "The thing is to save Betsy—that's all; there's nothing else—absolutely nothing. I don't care if it takes everything your father has."

"Allin, be quiet!" he shouted at her. "Do you mean my father would begrudge anything—?"

"You're afraid of him, Kent," she retorted. "Well, I'm not! If you don't go to him, I will."

They were quarreling now, like two insane people. They were both stretched beyond normal reason.

Suddenly Allin was sobbing. "I can't forget what you said that night," she cried. "All that standing on principle! Oh, Kent, she's with strangers, horrible people, crying her little heart out; perhaps they're even—hurting her, trying to make her keep quiet. Oh, Kent, Kent!"

He took her in his arms. They must not draw apart now. He must think of her.

"I'll do anything, darling," he said. "The first thing in the morning I'll get hold of dad and have the money ready."

"If they could only *know* it," she said.

"I could put something in the paper, perhaps," he said. "I believe I could word something that no one else would understand."

"Let's try, Kent!"

He took a pencil and envelope from his pocket and wrote. "How's this?" he asked. "Fifty agreed by dead oak at twelve."

"I can't see how it could do any harm," she said eagerly. "And if they see it, they'll understand we're willing to do anything."

"I'll go around to the newspaper office and pay for this in cash," he said. "Then I won't have to give names."

"Yes, yes!" she urged him. "It's something more than just sitting here!"

He drove through the darkness the two miles to the small town and parked in front of the ramshackle newspaper office. A red-eyed night clerk took his advertisement and read it off.

"This is a funny one," he said. "We get some, now and then. That'll be a dollar, Mr.—"

Kent did not answer. He put a dollar bill on the desk.

"I don't know what I've done, even so," he groaned to himself.

He drove back quietly through the intense darkness. The storm had not yet come, and the air was strangely silent. He kept his motor at its most noiseless, expecting somehow to hear through the sleeping stillness, Betsy's voice, crying.

They scarcely slept, and yet when they looked at each other the next morning the miracle was that they had slept at all. But he had made Allin go to bed at last, and then, still dressed, he had lain down on his own bed near her. It was Bruce who waked them. He stood hesitatingly between their beds. They heard his voice.

"Betsy hasn't come back yet, mommy."

The name waked them. And they looked at each other.

"How could we!" Allin whispered.

"It may be a long pull, dearest," he said, trying to be steady. He got up, feeling exhausted.

"Will she come back today?" Bruce asked.

"I think so, son."

At least it was Saturday, and Bruce need not go to school today.

"I'm going to get her tonight," Kent said after a moment.

Instantly he felt better. They must not give up hope—not by a great deal. There was too much to do: his father to see and the money to get. Secretly, he still reserved his own judgment about the ransom. If the man in gray was against it, he would tell Allin nothing—he simply would not give it. The responsibility would be his.

"You and mommy will have to get Betsy's things ready for her tonight," he said cheerfully. He would take a bath and get into a fresh suit. He had to have all his wits about him today, every moment—listen to everybody, and use his own judgment finally. In an emergency, one person had to act.

He paused at the sight of himself in the mirror. Would he be able to keep it from Allin if he made a mistake? Suppose they never got Betsy back. Suppose she just—disappeared. Or suppose they found her little body somewhere.

This was the way all those other parents had felt—this sickness and faintness. If he did not pay the ransom and *that* happened, would he be able *not* to tell Allin—or to tell her it was his fault? Both were impossible.

"I'll just have to go on from one thing to the next," he decided.

The chief thing was to try to be hopeful. He dressed and went back into the bedroom. Bruce had come in to dress in their room. But Allin was still in bed, lying against the pillows, white and exhausted.

He bent over her and kissed her. "I'll send your breakfast up," he said. "I'm going to see father first. If any message comes through, I'll be there —then at the bank."

She nodded, glanced up at him and closed her eyes. He stood looking down into her tortured face. Every nerve in it was quivering under the set stillness.

"Can't break yet," he said sharply. "The crisis is ahead."

"I know," she whispered. Then she sat up. "I can't lie here!" she exclaimed. "It's like lying on a bed of swords, being tortured. I'll be down, Kent—Bruce and I."

She flew into the bathroom. He heard the shower turned on instantly and strongly. But he could wait for no one.

"Come down with mother, son," he said. And he went on alone.

"If you could let me have thirty thousand today," he said to his father, "I can give it back as soon as I sell some stock."

"I don't care when I get it back," his father said irritably. "Good God, Kent, it's not that. It's just that I—it's none of my business, of course, but thirty thousand in cold cash! I'd like to ask what on earth you've been doing, but I won't."

Kent had made up his mind at the breakfast table when he picked up the paper that if he could keep the thing out of the papers, he would keep it from his father and mother. He'd turned to the personals. There it was, his answer to those scoundrels. Well, he wouldn't stick to it unless it were best for Betsy. Meanwhile, silence!

To Rose, bringing in the toast, he'd said sharply, "Tell everybody to come in now before your mistress comes down."

They had filed in, subdued and drooping, looking at him with frightened eyes.

"Oh, sir!" Mollie had cried hysterically.

"Please!" he'd exclaimed, glancing at her. Maybe the man in gray ought to see her. But last night he had distrusted Peter. This morning Peter looked like a faithful old dog, and as incapable of evil.

"I only want to thank you for obeying me so far," he said wearily. "If we can keep our trouble out of the papers, perhaps we can get Betsy back. At least, it's the only hope. If you succeed in letting no one know until we know—the end, I shall give each of you a hundred dollars as a token of my gratitude."

"Thank you, sir," Sarah and Rose had said. Mollie only sobbed. Peter was murmuring, "Ah don' wan' no hundred dollahs, Mist' Crothers. All Ah wan' is dat little chile back."

How could Peter be distrusted? Kent had wrung his hand. "That's all I want, too, Peter," he'd said fervently.

Strange how shaky and emotional he had felt!

Now, under his father's penetrating eyes, he held himself calm. "I know it sounds outrageous, father," he admitted, "but I simply ask you to trust me for a few days."

"You're not speculating, I hope. It's no time for that. The market's crazy."

It was, Kent thought grimly, the wildest kind of speculation—with his own child's life.

"It's not ordinary speculation, certainly," he said. "I can manage through the bank, dad," he said. "Never mind. I'll mortgage the house."

"Oh, nonsense!" his father retorted. He had his checkbook out and was writing. "I'm not going to have it get around that my son had to go mortgaging his place."

"Thanks," Kent said briefly.

Now for the bank!

Step by step the day went. It was amazing how quickly the hours passed. It was noon before he knew it, and in an hour he must start for the inn. He went home and found Allin on the front porch in the sunshine. She had a book in her hand, and Bruce was playing with his red truck out in the yard. Anyone passing would never dream there was tragedy here.

"Do you have it?" she asked him.

He touched his breast pocket. "All ready," he answered.

They sat through a silent meal, listening to Bruce's chatter. Allin ate nothing and he very little, but he was grateful to her for being there, for keeping the outward shape of the day usual.

"Good sport!" he said to her across the table in the midst of Bruce's conversation. She smiled faintly. "Thank you, no more coffee," he said to Rose. "I must be going, Allin."

"Yes," she said, and added, "I wish it were I—instead of waiting."

"I know," he replied, and kissed her.

Yesterday, waiting had seemed intolerable to him, too. But now that he was going toward the hour for which he had been waiting, he clung to the hopefulness of uncertainty.

He drove alone to the inn. The well-paved roads, the tended fields and comfortable farmhouses were not different from the landscape any day. He would have said, only yesterday, that it was impossible that underneath all this peace and plenty there could be men so evil as to take a child out of its home, away from its parents, for money.

There was, he pondered, driving steadily west, no other possible reason. He had no enemies; none, that is, whom he knew. There were always discontented people, of course, who hated anyone who seemed successful. There was, of course, too, the chance that his father had enemies—he was ruthless with idle workers.

"I can't blame a man if he is born a fool," Kent had heard his father maintain stoutly, "but I can blame even a fool for being lazy." It might be one of these. If only it were not some perverted mind!

He drove into the yard of the inn and parked his car. His heart was thudding in his breast, but he said casually to the woman at the door, "Have you a bar?"

"To the right," she answered quickly. It was Saturday afternoon, and business was good. She did not even look at him as he sauntered away.

The moment he entered the door of the bar he saw the man. He stood at the end of the bar, small, inconspicuous, in a gray suit and a blue-striped shirt. He wore a solid blue tie, and in his pocket was the blue handkerchief. Kent walked slowly to his side.

"Whiskey and soda, please," he ordered the bartender. The room was full of people at tables, drinking and talking noisily. He turned to the man in gray and smiled. "Rather unusual to find a bar like this in a village inn," he said.

"Yes, it is," the little man agreed. He had a kind, brisk voice, and he was drinking a tall glass of something clear, which he finished. "Give me another of the same," he remarked to the bartender. "London Washerwoman's Treat, it's called," he explained to Kent.

It was hard to imagine that this small hatchet-faced man had any importance.

"Going my way?" Kent asked suddenly.

"If you'll give me a lift," the little man replied.

Kent's heart subsided. The man knew him, then. He nodded. They paid for their drinks and went out to the car.

"Drive due north into a country road," the little man said with sudden sharpness. All his dreaminess was gone. He sat beside Kent, his arms folded. "Please tell me exactly what's happened, Mr. Crothers."

And Kent, driving along, told him.

He was grateful for the man's coldness; for the distrust of everything and everybody. He was like a lean hound in a life-and-death chase. Because of his coldness, Kent could talk without fear of breaking.

"I don't know your name," Kent said.

"Don't matter," said the man. "I'm detailed for the job."

"As I was saying," Kent went on, "we have no enemies—at least, none I know."

"Fellow always has enemies," the little man murmured.

"It hardly seems like a ganster would—" Kent began again.

"No, gangsters don't kidnap children," the little man told him.

"Adults, yes. But they don't monkey with kids. It's too dangerous, for one thing. Kidnapping children's the most dangerous job there is in crime, and the smart ones know it. It's always some little fellow does it—him and a couple of friends, maybe."

"Why dangerous?" Kent demanded.

"Always get caught," the little man said, shrugging. "Always!"

There was something so reassuring about this strange sharp creature that Kent said abruptly, "My wife wants to pay the ransom. I suppose you think that's wrong, don't you?"

"Perfectly *right*," the man said. "Absolutely! We aren't magicians, Mr. Crothers. We got to get in touch somehow. The only two cases I ever knew where nothing was solved was where the parents wouldn't pay. So we couldn't get a clue."

Kent set his lips. "Children killed?"

"Who knows?" the little man said, shrugging again. "Anyway, one of them was. And the other never came back."

There might be comfort, then, in death, Kent thought. He had infinitely rather hold Betsy's dead body in his arms than never know . . .

"Tell me what to do, and I'll do it," he said.

The little man lighted a cigarette. "Go on just as though you'd never told us. Go on and pay your ransom. Make a note of the numbers of the notes, of course—no matter what that letter says. How's he going to know? But pay it over—and do what he says next. You can call me up here." He took a paper out of his coat pocket and put it in Kent's pocket. "I maybe ought to tell you, though, we'll tap your telephone wire."

"Do anything you like," Kent said.

"That's all I need!" the man exclaimed. "That's our orders—to do what the parents want. You're a sensible one. Fellow I knew once walked around with a shotgun to keep off the police. Said he'd handle things himself."

"Did he get his child back?"

"Nope—paid the ransom, too. Paying the ransom's all right—that's the way we get 'em. But he went roarin' around the neighborhood trying to be his own law. We didn't get a chance."

Kent thought of one more thing. "I don't want anything spared— money or trouble. I'll pay anything, of course."

"Oh, sure," the man said. "Well, I guess that'll be all. You might let me off near the inn. I'll go in and get another drink."

He lapsed into dreaminess again, and in silence Kent drove back to the village.

"All right," the little man said. "So long. Good luck to you." He leaped out and disappeared into the bar.

And Kent, driving home through the early sunset, thought how little there was to tell Allin—really nothing at all, except that he liked and trusted the man in gray. No, it was much more than that: the fellow stood for something far greater than himself—he stood for all the power of the government organized against crimes like this. That was the comfort of the thing. Behind that man was the nation's police, all for him, Kent Crothers, helping him find his child.

When he reached home, Allin was in the hall waiting.

"He really said nothing, darling," Kent said, kissing her, "except you were right about the ransom. We have to pay that. Still, he was extraordinary. Somehow I feel—if she's still alive, we'll get her back. He's that sort of fellow." He did not let her break, though he felt her trembling against him. He said very practically, "We must check these banknotes, Allin."

And then, when they were checking them upstairs in their bedroom with doors locked, he kept insisting that what they were doing was right.

At a quarter to twelve he was bumping down the rutted road to the forks. He knew every turn the road made, having traveled it on foot from the time he was a little boy. But that boy out on holiday had nothing to do with himself as he was tonight, an anxious, harried man.

He drew up beneath the dead oak and took the cardboard box in which he and Allin had packed the money and stepped out of the car. There was not a sound in the dark night, yet he knew that somewhere not far away were the men who had his child.

He listened, suddenly swept again with the conviction he had had the night before, that she would cry out. She might even be this moment in the old mill. But there was not a sound. He stooped and put the box at the root of the tree.

And as he did this, he stumbled over a string raised from the ground about a foot. What was this? He followed it with his hands. It encircled the tree—a common piece of twine. Then it went under a stone, and under the stone was a piece of paper. He seized it, snapped on his cigarette lighter, read the clumsy printing.

If everything turns out like we told you to do, go to your hired mans house at twelve tomorrow night for the kid. If you double-cross us you get it back dead.

He snapped off the light. He'd get her back dead! It all depended on what he did. And what he did, he would have to do alone. He would not go home to Allin until he had decided every step.

He drove steadily away. If he did not call the man in gray, Betsy might be at Peter's alive. If he called, and they did not find out, she might be alive anyway. But if the man fumbled and they did find out, she would be dead.

He knew what Allin would say: "Just so we get her home, Kent, nothing else! People have to think for themselves, first." Yes, she was right. He would keep quiet; anyway, he would give the kidnappers a chance. If she were safe and alive, that would be justification for anything. If she were dead . . .

Then he remembered that there was something courageous and reassuring about that little man. Only he had seemed to know what to do. And anyway, what about those parents who had tried to manage it all themselves? Their children had never come back, either. No, he had better do what he knew he ought to do.

He tramped into the house. Allin was lying upstairs on her bed, her eyes closed.

"Darling," he said gently. Instantly she opened her eyes and sat up. He handed her the paper and sat down on her bed. She lifted miserable eyes to him.

"Twenty-four more hours!" she whispered. "I can't do it, Kent."

"Yes, you can," he said harshly. "You'll do it because you damned well have to." He thought, She can't break now, if I have to whip her! "We've got to wait," he went on. "Is there anything else we can do? Tell Mike O'Brien? Let the newspapers get it and ruin everything?"

She shook her head. "No," she said.

He got up. He longed to take her in his arms, but he did not dare. If this was ever over, he would tell her what he thought of her—how wonderful she was; how brave and game—but he could not now. It was better for them both to stay away from that edge of breaking.

"Get up," he said. "Let's have something to eat. I haven't really eaten all day."

It would be good for her to get up and busy herself. She had not eaten either.

"All right, Kent," she said. "I'll wash my face in cold water and be down."

"I'll be waiting," he replied.

This gave him the moment he had made up his mind he would use— damned if he wouldn't use it! The scoundrels had his money now, and he would take the chance on that queer fellow. He called the number the man had put into his pocket. And almost instantly he heard the fellow's drawl.

"Hello?" the man said.

"This is Kent Crothers," he answered. "I've had that invitation!"

"Yes?" The voice was suddenly alert.

"Twelve tomorrow!"

"Yes? Where? Midnight, of course. They always make it midnight."

"My gardener's house."

"Okay, Mr. Crothers. Go right ahead as if you hadn't told us." The phone clicked.

Kent listened, but there was nothing more. Everything seemed exactly the same, but nothing was the same. This very telephone wire was cut somewhere, by someone. Someone was listening to every word anyone spoke to and from his house. It was sinister and yet reassuring—sinister if you were the criminal.

He heard Allin's step on the stair and went out to meet her. "I have a hunch," he told her, smiling.

"What?" She tried to smile back.

He drew her toward the dining room. "We're going to win," he said.

Within himself he added, If she were still alive, that little heart of his life. Then he put the memory of Betsy's face away from him resolutely.

"I'm going to eat," he declared. "And so must you. We'll beat them tomorrow."

But tomorrow very nearly beat them. Time stood still—there was no making it pass. They filled it full of a score of odd jobs about the house. Lucky for them it was Sunday; luckier that Kent's mother had a cold and telephoned that she and Kent's father would not be over for their usual visit.

They stayed together, a little band of three. By midafternoon Kent had cleaned up everything—a year's odd jobs—and there were hours to go.

They played games with Bruce, and at last it was his suppertime and they put him to bed. Then they sat upstairs in their bedroom again, near the nursery, each with a book.

Sometimes, after these hours were over, he would have to think about a lot of things again. But everything had to wait now, until this life ended at midnight. Beyond that no thought could reach.

At eleven he rose. "I'm going now," he said, and stooped to kiss her. She clung to him, and then in an instant they drew apart. In strong accord they knew it was not yet time to give way.

He ran the car as noiselessly as he could and left it at the end of the street, six blocks away. Then he walked past the few tumble-down bungalows, past two empty lots, to Peter's rickety gate. There was no light in the house. He went to the door and knocked softly. He heard Peter's mumble: "Who dat?"

"Let me in, Peter," he called in a low voice. The door opened. "It's I, Peter—Kent Crothers. Let me in. Peter, they're bringing the baby here."

"To mah house? Lemme git de light on."

"No, Peter, no light. I'll just sit down here in the darkness, like this. Only don't lock the door, see? I'll sit by the door. Where's a chair? That's it." He was trembling so that he stumbled into the chair Peter pushed forward.

"Mist' Crothers, suh, will yo' have a drink? Ah got some corn likker."

"Thanks, Peter."

He heard Peter's footsteps shuffling away, and in a moment a tin cup was thrust into his hand. He drank the reeking stuff down. It burned him like indrawn flame, but he felt steadier for it.

"Ain't a thing Ah can do, Mist' Crothers?" Peter's whisper came ghostly out of the darkness.

"Not a thing. Just wait."

"Ah'll wait here, then. Mah ole 'ooman's asleep. Ah'll jest git thrashin' round if Ah go back to bed."

"Yes, only we mustn't talk." Kent whispered back.

"Nosuh."

This was the supremest agony of waiting in all the long agony that this day had been. To sit perfectly still, straining to hear, knowing nothing, wondering . . .

Suppose something went wrong with the man in gray, and they fumbled, and frightened the man who brought Betsy back. Suppose he just sat here waiting and waiting until dawn came. And at home Allin was waiting.

The long day had been nothing to this. He sat reviewing all his life, pondering on the horror of this monstrous situation in which he and Allin now were. A free country, was it? No one was free when his lips were locked against crime, because he dared not speak lest his child be murdered. If Betsy were dead, if they didn't bring her back, he'd never tell Allin he had telephoned the man in gray. He was still glad he had done

it. After all, were respectable men and women to be at the mercy of—
but if Betsy were dead, he'd wish he had killed himself before he had
anything to do with the fellow!

He sat, his hands interlocked so tightly he felt them grow cold and
bloodless and stinging, but he could not move. Someone came down the
street roaring out a song.

"Thass a drunk man," Peter whispered.

Kent did not answer. The street grew still again.

And then in the darkness—hours after midnight, it seemed to him—
he heard a car come up to the gate and stop. The gate creaked open and
then shut, and the car drove away.

"Guide me down the steps," he told Peter.

It was the blackest night he had ever seen. But the stars were shining
when he stepped out. Peter pulled him along the path. Then, by the gate,
Peter stooped.

"She's here," he said.

And Kent, wavering and dizzy, felt her in his arms again, limp and
heavy. "She's warm," he muttered. "That's something."

He carried her into the house, and Peter lighted a candle and held it
up. It was she—his little Betsy, her white dress filthy and a man's sweater
drawn over her. She was breathing heavily.

"Look lak she done got a dose of sumpin," Peter muttered.

"I must get her home," Kent whispered frantically. "Help me to the
car, Peter."

"Yassuh," Peter said, and blew out the candle.

They walked silently down the street, Peter's hand on Kent's arm.
When he got Betsy home, he—he—

"Want I should drive you?" Peter was asking him.

"I—maybe you'd better," he replied.

He climbed into the seat with her. She was so fearfully limp. Thank
God he could hear her breathing! In a few minutes he would put Betsy
into her mother's arms.

"Don't stay, Peter," he said.

"Nosuh," Peter answered.

Allin was at the door, waiting. She opened it and without a word
reached for the child. He closed the door behind them.

Then he felt himself grow sick. "I was going to tell you," he gasped,
"I didn't know whether to tell you—" He swayed and felt himself fall
upon the floor.

Allin was a miracle; Allin was wonderful, a rock of a woman. This tender thing who had endured the torture of these days was at his bedside when he woke next day, smiling, and only a little pale.

"The doctor says you're not to go to work, darling," she told him.

"The doctor?" he repeated.

"I had him last night for both of you—you and Betsy. He won't tell anyone."

"I've been crazy," he said, dazed. "Where is she? How—"

"She's going to be all right," Allin said.

"No, but—you're not telling me!"

"Come in here and see," she replied.

He got up, staggering a little. Funny how his legs had collapsed under him last night! His withers still felt all unstrung.

They went into the nursery. There in her bed she lay, his beloved child. She was more naturally asleep now, and her face bore no other mark than pallor.

"She won't even remember it," Allin said. "I'm glad it wasn't Bruce."

He did not answer. He couldn't think—nothing had to be thought about now.

"Come back to bed, Kent," Allin was saying. "I'm going to bring your breakfast up. Bruce is having his downstairs."

He climbed back into bed, shamefaced at his weakness. "I'll be all right after a little coffee. I'll get up then, maybe."

But his bed felt wonderfully good. He lay back, profoundly grateful to it—to everything. But as long as he lived he would wake up to sweat in the night with memory.

The telephone by his bed rang, and he picked it up. "Hello?" he called.

"Hello, Mr. Crothers," a voice answered. It was the voice of the man in gray. "Say, was the little girl hurt?"

"No!" Kent cried. "She's all right!"

"Fine. Well, I just wanted to tell you we caught the fellow last night."

"You *did!*" Kent leaped up. "No! Why, that's—that's extraordinary."

"We had a cordon around the place for blocks and got him. You'll get your money back, too."

"That—it doesn't seem to matter. Who was he?"

"Fellow named Harry Brown—a young chap in a drugstore."

"I never heard of him!"

"No, he says you don't know him—but his dad went to school with yours, and he's heard a lot of talk about you. His dad's a poor stick, I guess, and got jealous of yours. That's about it, probably. Fellow says he figured you sort of owed him something. Crazy, of course.

"Well, it was an easy case—he wasn't smart, and scared to death, besides. You were sensible about it. Most people ruin their chances with their own fuss. So long, Mr. Crothers. Mighty glad."

The telephone clicked. That was all. Everything was incredible, impossible. Kent gazed around the familiar room. Had this all happened? It had happened, and it was over. This was one of those cases of kidnapping that went on in this mad country, unheard of until they were all over and the criminals arrested.

When he went downstairs he would give the servants their hundred dollars apiece. Mollie had had nothing to do with it, after all. The mystery had dissolved like a mist at morning.

Allin was at the door with his tray. Behind her came Bruce, ready for school. She said, so casually Kent could hardly catch the tremor underneath her voice, "What would you say, darling, if we let Peter walk to school with Bruce today?"

Her eyes pleaded with him: "No? Oughtn't we to? What shall we do?"

Then he thought of something else that indomitable man in gray had said, that man whose name he would never know, one among all those other men trying to keep the law for the nation. "We're a lawless people," the little man had said that day in the car. "If we made a law against paying ransoms, nobody would obey it any more than they did Prohibition. No, when the Americans don't like a law, they break it. And so we still have kidnappers. It's the price you pay for a democracy."

Yes, it was the price. Everybody paid—he and Allin; the child they had so nearly lost; that boy locked up in prison.

"Bruce has to live in his own country," he said. "I guess you can go alone, can't you, son?"

"Course I can," Bruce said sturdily.

The Adventure of the Glass-Domed Clock

ELLERY QUEEN

Ellery Queen, both the character and the collaborative pseudonym of Frederic Dannay and Manfred B. Lee, has been at the top of the mystery field for over half a century. (And Ellery Queen's Mystery Magazine, *edited by Dannay, has been the premier crime-fiction periodical since its inception in 1941.) "The Adventure of the Glass-Domed Clock" is one of the early EQ stories and offers a solution "so simple," Ellery himself says, "that a sophomore student in high school with the most elementary knowledge of algebraic mathematics would find it as easy to solve as the merest equation." Beware such statements, however, for things are never quite as simple as they might seem in an EQ story . . .*

Of all the hundreds of criminal cases in the solution of which Mr. Ellery Queen participated by virtue of his self-imposed authority as son of the famous Inspector Queen of the New York Detective Bureau, he has steadfastly maintained that none offered a simpler diagnosis than the case which he has designated as "The Adventure of the Glass-Domed Clock." "So simple," he likes to say—sincerely!—"that a sophomore student in high school with the most elementary knowledge of algebraic mathematics would find it as easy to solve as the merest equation." He has been asked, as a result of such remarks, what a poor untutored first-grade detective on the regular police force—whose training in algebra might be something less than elementary—could be expected to make of such a "simple" case. His invariably serious response has been: "Amendment accepted. The resolution now reads: Anybody with common sense could have solved that crime. It's as basic as five minus four leaves one."

This was a little cruel, when it is noted that among those who had opportunity—and certainly wishfulness—to solve the crime was Mr. Ellery Queen's own father, the inspector, certainly not the most stupid of criminal investigators. But then Mr. Ellery Queen, for all his mental prowess, is sometimes prone to confuse his definitions: *viz.,* his uncanny capacity for strict logic is far from the average citizen's common sense.

Certainly one would not be inclined to term elementary a problem in which such components as the following figured: a pure purple amethyst, a somewhat bedraggled expatriate from Czarist Russia, a silver loving-cup, a poker game, five birthday encomiums, and of course that peculiarly ugly relic of early Americana catalogued as "the glass-domed clock"—among others! On the surface the thing seems too utterly fantastic, a maniac's howling nightmare. Anybody with Ellery's cherished "common sense" would have said so. Yet when he arranged those weird elements in their proper order and pointed out the "obvious" answer to the riddle—with that almost monastic intellectual innocence of his, as if everybody possessed his genius for piercing the veil of complexities!—Inspector Queen, good Sergeant Velie, and the others figuratively rubbed their eyes, the thing was so clear.

It began, as murders do, with a corpse. From the first the eeriness of the whole business struck those who stood about in the faintly musked atmosphere of Martin Orr's curio shop and stared down at the shambles that had been Martin Orr. Inspector Queen, for one, refused to credit the evidence of his old senses; and it was not the gory nature of the crime that gave him pause, for he was as familiar with scenes of carnage as a butcher and blood no longer made him squeamish. That Martin Orr, the celebrated little Fifth Avenue curio dealer whose establishment was a treasure-house of authentic rarities, had had his shiny little bald head bashed to red ruin—this was an indifferent if practical detail; the bludgeon, a heavy paperweight spattered with blood but wiped clean of fingerprints, lay not far from the body; so *that* much was clear. No, it was not the assault on Orr that opened their eyes, but what Orr had apparently done, as he lay gasping out his life on the cold cement floor of his shop, *after* the assault.

The reconstruction of events after Orr's assailant had fled the shop, leaving the curio dealer for dead, seemed perfectly legible: having been struck down in the main chamber of his establishment, toward the rear, Martin Orr had dragged his broken body six feet along a counter—the red trail told the story plainly—had by superhuman effort raised himself to a case of precious and semiprecious stones, had smashed the thin glass with a feeble fist, had groped about among the gem-trays, grasped a large unset amethyst, fallen back to the floor with the stone tightly clutched in his left hand, had then crawled on a tangent five feet past a table of antique clocks to a stone pedestal, raised himself again, and deliberately dragged off the pedestal the object it supported—an old clock with a glass dome over it—so that the clock fell to the floor by his side, shattering its fragile case into a thousand pieces. And there Martin Orr had died, in his left fist the amethyst, his bleeding right hand resting on the clock as if in benediction. By some miracle the clock's machinery had not been injured by the fall; it had been one of Martin Orr's fetishes to keep all his magnificent timepieces running; and to the bewildered ears of the little knot of men surrounding Martin Orr's corpse that gray Sunday morning came the pleasant *tick-tick-tick* of the no longer glass-domed clock.

Weird? It was insane!

"There ought to be a law against it," growled Sergeant Velie.

Dr. Samuel Prouty, assistant medical examiner of New York County, rose from his examination of the body and prodded Martin Orr's dead buttocks—the curio dealer was lying face down—with his foot.

"Now here's an old coot," he said grumpily, "sixty if he's a day, with more real stamina than many a youngster. Marvelous powers of resistance! He took a fearful beating about the head and shoulders, his assailant left him for dead, and the old monkey clung to life long enough to make a tour about the place! Many a younger man would have died in his tracks."

"Your professional admiration leaves me cold," said Ellery. He had been awakened out of a pleasantly warm bed not a half hour before to find Djuna, the Queens' gypsy boy-of-all-work, shaking him. The inspector had already gone, leaving word for Ellery, if he should be so minded, to follow. Ellery was always so minded when his nose sniffed crime, but he had not had breakfast and he was thoroughly out of temper. So his taxicab had rushed through Fifth Avenue to Martin Orr's shop, and he had found the inspector and Sergeant Velie already on the cluttered scene interrogating a grief-stunned old woman—Martin Orr's aged widow—and a badly frightened Slavic giant who introduced himself in garbled English as the "ex-Duke Paul." The ex-Duke Paul, it developed, had been one of the Nicholas Romanov's innumerable cousins caught in the whirlpool of the Russian revolution who had managed to flee the homeland and was eking out a none-too-fastidious living in New York as a sort of social curiosity. This was in 1926, when royal Russian expatriates were still something of a novelty in the land of democracy. As Ellery pointed out much later, this was not only 1926, but precisely Sunday, March the seventh, 1926, although at the time it seemed ridiculous to consider the specific date of any importance whatever.

"Who found the body?" demanded Ellery, puffing at his first cigarette of the day.

"His nibs here," said Sergeant Velie, hunching his colossal shoulders. "*And* the lady. Seems like the dook or whatever he is has been workin' a racket—been a kind of stooge for the old duck that was murdered. Orr used to give him commissions on the customers he brought in—and I understand he brought in plenty. Anyway, Mrs. Orr here got sort of worried when her hubby didn't come home last night from the poker game. . . ."

"Poker game?"

The Russian's dark face lighted up. "Yuss. Yuss. It is remarkable game. I have learned it since my sojourn in your so amazing country. Meester Orr, myself, and some others here play each week. Yuss." His face fell, and some of his fright returned. He looked fleetingly at the corpse and began to edge away.

"You played last night?" asked Ellery in a savage voice.

The Russian nodded. Inspector Queen said: "We're rounding 'em up. It seems that Orr, the duke, and four other men had a sort of poker club, and met in Orr's back room there every Saturday night and played till all hours. Looked over that back room, but there's nothing there except the cards and chips. When Orr didn't come home Mrs. Orr got frightened and called up the duke—he lives at some squirty little hotel in the Forties —the duke called for her, they came down here this morning. . . . This is what they found." The inspector eyed Martin Orr's corpse and the debris of glass surrounding him with gloom, almost with resentment. "Crazy, isn't it?"

Ellery glanced at Mrs. Orr; she was leaning against a counter, frozen-faced, tearless, staring down at her husband's body as if she could not believe her eyes. Actually, there was little to see: for Dr. Prouty had flung outspread sheets of a Sunday newspaper over the body, and only the left hand—still clutching the amethyst—was visible.

"Unbelievably so," said Ellery dryly. "I suppose there's a desk in the back room where Orr kept his accounts?"

"Sure."

"Any paper on Orr's body?"

"Paper?" repeated the inspector in bewilderment, "Why, no."

"Pencil or pen?"

"No. Why, for heaven's sake?"

Before Ellery could reply, a little old man with a face like wrinkled brown papyrus pushed past a detective at the front door; he walked like a man in a dream. His gaze fixed on the shapeless bulk and the bloodstains. Then, incredibly, he blinked four times and began to cry. His weazened frame jerked with sobs. Mrs. Orr awoke from her trance; she cried: "Oh, Sam, Sam!" and, putting her arms around the newcomer's racked shoulders, began to weep with him.

Ellery and the inspector looked at each other, and Sergeant Velie belched his disgust. Then the inspector grasped the crying man's little arm and shook him. "Here, stop that!" he said gruffly. "Who are you?"

The man raised his tear-stained face from Mrs. Orr's shoulder; he blubbered: "S-Sam Mingo, S-Sam Mingo, Mr. Orr's assistant. Who— who—Oh, I can't believe it!" and he buried his face in Mrs. Orr's shoulder again.

"Got to let him cry himself out, I guess," said the inspector, shrugging. "Ellery, what the deuce do you make of it? I'm stymied."

Ellery raised his eyebrows eloquently. A detective appeared in the street-door escorting a pale, trembling man. "Here's Arnold Pike, chief. Dug him out of bed just now."

Pike was a man of powerful physique and jutting jaw; but he was thoroughly unnerved and, somehow, bewildered. He fastened his eyes on the heap which represented Martin Orr's mortal remains and kept mechanically buttoning and unbuttoning his overcoat. The inspector said: "I understand you and a few others played poker in the back room here last night. With Orr. What time did you break up?"

"Twelve-thirty." Pike's voice wabbled drunkenly.

"What time did you start?"

"Around eleven."

"Cripes," said Inspector Queen, "that's not a poker game, that's a game of tiddledywinks. . . . Who killed Orr, Mr. Pike?"

Arnold Pike tore his eyes from the corpse. "God, sir, I don't know."

"You don't, hey? All friends, were you?"

"Yes. Oh, yes."

"What's your business, Mr. Pike?"

"I'm a stockbroker."

"Why—" began Ellery, and stopped. Under the urging of two detectives, three men advanced into the shop—all frightened, all exhibiting evidences of hasty awakening and hasty dressing, all fixing their eyes at once on the paper-covered bundle on the floor, the streaks of blood, the shattered glass. The three, like the incredible ex-Duke Paul, who was straight and stiff and somehow ridiculous, seemed petrified; men crushed by a sudden blow.

A small fat man with brilliant eyes muttered that he was Stanley Oxman, jeweler. Martin Orr's oldest, closest friend. He could not believe it. It was frightful, unheard of. Martin murdered! No, he could offer no explanation, Martin had been a peculiar man, perhaps, but as far as he, Oxman, knew the curio dealer had not had an enemy in the world. And so on, and so on, as the other two stood by, frozen, waiting their turn.

One was a lean, debauched fellow with the mark of the ex-athlete about him. His slight paunch and yellowed eyeballs could not conceal the signs of a vigorous prime. This was, said Oxman, their mutual friend, Leo Gurney, the newspaper feature writer. The other was J.D. Vincent, said Oxman—developing an unexpected streak of talkativeness which the inspector fanned gently—who, like Arnold Pike, was in Wall Street—"a manipulator," whatever that was. Vincent, a stocky man with the gambler's tight face, seemed incapable of speech, as for Gurney, he seemed glad that Oxman had constituted himself spokesman and kept staring at the body on the cement floor.

Ellery sighed, thought of his warm bed, put down the rebellion in his breakfastless stomach, and went to work—keeping an ear cocked for the inspector's sharp questions and the halting replies. Ellery followed the streaks of blood to the spot where Orr had ravished the case of gems. The case, its glass front smashed, little frazzled splinters framing the orifice, contained more than a dozen metal trays floored with black velvet, set in two rows. Each held scores of gems—a brilliant array of semiprecious and precious stones beautifully variegated in color. Two trays in the center of the front row attracted his eye particularly—one containing highly polished stones of red, brown, yellow, and green; the other a single variety, all of a subtranslucent quality, leek-green in color, and covered with small red spots. Ellery noted that both these trays were in direct line with the place where Orr's hand had smashed the glass case.

He went over to the trembling little assistant, Sam Mingo, who had quieted down and was standing by Mrs. Orr, clutching her hand like a child. "Mingo," he said, touching the man. Mingo started with a leap of his stringy muscles. "Don't be alarmed, Mingo. Just step over here with me for a moment." Ellery smiled reassuringly, took the man's arm, and led him to the shattered case.

And Ellery said: "How is it that Martin Orr bothered with such trifles as these? I see rubies here, and emeralds, but the others. . . . Was he a jeweler as well as a curio dealer?"

Orr's assistant mumbled: "No. N-No, he was not. But he always liked the baubles. The baubles, he called them. Kept them for love. Most of them are birthstones. He sold a few. This is a complete line."

"What are those green stones with the red spots?"

"Bloodstones."

"And this tray of red, brown, yellow, and green ones?"

"All jaspers. The common ones are red, brown, and yellow. The few green ones in the tray are more valuable. . . . The bloodstone is itself a variety of jasper. Beautiful! And . . ."

"Yes, yes," said Ellery hastily. "From which tray did the amethyst in Orr's hand come, Mingo?"

Mingo shivered and pointed a crinkled forefinger to a tray in the rear row, at the corner of the case.

"*All* the amethysts are kept in this one tray?"

"Yes. You can see for yourself—"

"Here!" growled the inspector, approaching. "Mingo! I want you to look over the stock. Check everything. See if anything's been stolen."

"Yes, sir," said Orr's assistant timidly, and began to potter about the shop with lagging steps. Ellery looked about. The door to the back room was twenty-five feet from the spot where Orr had been assaulted. No desk in the shop itself, he observed, no paper about. . . .

"Well, son," said the inspector in troubled tones, "it looks as if we're on the trail of something. I don't like it. . . . Finally dragged it out of these birds. I *thought* it was funny, this business of breaking up a weekly Saturday night poker game at half past twelve. They had a fight!"

"Who engaged in fisticuffs with whom?"

"Oh, don't be funny. It's this Pike feller, the stockbroker. Seems they all had something to drink during the game. They played stud, and Orr, with an ace-king-queen-jack showing, raised the roof off the play. Everybody dropped out except Pike; he had three sixes. Well, Orr gave it everything he had and when Pike threw his cards away on a big overraise, Orr cackled, showed his hole card—a deuce!—and raked in the pot. Pike, who'd lost his pile on the hand, began to grumble; he and Orr had words —you know how those things start. They were all pie-eyed, anyway, says the duke. Almost a fistfight. The others interfered, but it broke up the game."

"They all left together?"

"Yes. Orr stayed behind to clean up the mess in the back room. The five others went out together and separated a few blocks away. Any one of 'em could have come back and pulled off the job before Orr shut up shop!"

"And what does Pike say?"

"What the deuce would you expect him to say? That he went right home and to bed, of course."

"The others?"

"They deny any knowledge of what happened after they left here last night. . . . Well, Mingo? Anything missing?"

Mingo said helplessly: "Everything seems all right."

"I thought so," said the inspector with satisfaction. "This is a grudge kill, son. Well, I want to talk to these fellers some more. . . . What's eating you?"

Ellery lighted a cigarette. "A few random thoughts. Have you decided in your own mind why Orr dragged himself about the shop when he was three-quarters dead, broke the glass-domed clock, pulled an amethyst out of the gem case?"

"That," said the inspector, the troubled look returning, "is what I'm all foggy about. I can't—'Scuse me." He returned hastily to the waiting group of men.

Ellery took Mingo's lax arm. "Get a grip on yourself, man. I want you to look at that smashed clock for a moment. Don't be afraid of Orr—dead men don't bite, Mingo." He pushed the little assistant toward the paper-covered corpse. "Now tell me something about the clock. Has it a history?"

"Not much of one. It's a h-hundred and sixty-nine years old. Not especially valuable. Curious piece because of the glass dome over it. Happens to be the only glass-domed clock we have. That's all."

Ellery polished the lenses of his pince-nez, set the glasses firmly on his nose, and bent over to examine the fallen clock. It had a black wooden base, circular, about nine inches deep, and scarified with age. On this the clock was set—ticking away cozily. The dome of glass had fitted into a groove around the top of the black base, sheathing the clock completely. With the dome unshattered, the entire piece must have stood about two feet high.

Ellery rose, and his lean face was thoughtful. Mingo looked at him in a sort of stupid anxiety. "Did Pike, Oxman, Vincent, Gurney, or Paul ever own this piece?"

Mingo shook his head. "No, sir. We've had it for many years. We couldn't get rid of it. Certainly *those* gentlemen didn't want it."

"Then none of the five ever tried to purchase the clock?"

"Of course not."

"Admirable," said Ellery. "Thank you." Mingo felt that he had been dismissed; he hesitated, shuffled his feet, and finally went over to the silent widow and stood by her side. Ellery knelt on the cement floor and with difficulty loosened the grip of the dead man's fingers about the amethyst. He saw that the stone was a clear glowing purple in color, shook his head as if in perplexity, and rose.

Vincent, the stocky Wall Street gambler with the tight face, was saying to the inspector in a rusty voice: "—can't see why you suspect any of us. Pike particularly. What's in a little quarrel? We've always been good friends, all of us. Last night we were pickled—"

"Sure," said the inspector gently. "Last night you were pickled. A drunk sort of forgets himself at times, Vincent. Liquor affects a man's morals as well as his head."

"Nuts!" said the yellow-eyeballed Gurney suddenly. "Stop sleuthing, inspector. You're barking up the wrong tree. Vincent's right. We're all friends. It was Pike's birthday last week." Ellery stood very still. "We all sent him gifts. Had a celebration, and Orr was the cockiest of us all. Does that look like the preparation for a pay-off?"

Ellery stepped forward, and his eyes were shining. All his temper had fled by now, and his nostrils were quivering with the scent of the chase. "And when was this celebration held, gentlemen?" he asked softly.

Stanley Oxman puffed out his cheeks. "Now they're going to suspect a birthday blowout! Last Monday, mister. This past Monday. What of it?"

"This past Monday," said Ellery. "How nice. Mr. Pike, your gifts—."

"For God's sake. . . ." Pike's eyes were tortured.

"When did you receive them?"

"After the party, during the week. Boys sent them up to me. I didn't see any of them until last night, at the poker game."

The others nodded their heads in concert; the inspector was looking at Ellery with puzzlement. Ellery grinned, adjusted his pince-nez, and spoke to his father aside. The weight of the inspector's puzzlement, if his face was a scale, increased. But he said quietly to the white-haired broker: "Mr. Pike, you're going to take a little trip with Mr. Queen and Sergeant Velie. Just for a few moments. The others of you stay here with me. Mr. Pike, please remember not to try anything—foolish."

Pike was incapable of speech; his head twitched sidewise and he buttoned his coat for the twentieth time. Nobody said anything. Sergeant Velie took Pike's arm, and Ellery preceded them into the early morning peace of Fifth Avenue. On the sidewalk he asked Pike his address, the broker dreamily gave him a street and number, Ellery hailed a taxicab, and the three men were driven in silence to an apartment building a mile farther uptown. They took a self-service elevator to the seventh floor, marched a few steps to a door, Pike fumbled with a key, and they went into his apartment.

"Let me see your gifts, please," said Ellery without expression—the first words uttered since they had stepped into the taxicab. Pike led them to a denlike room. On a table stood four boxes of different shapes, and a handsome silver cup. "There," he said in a cracked voice.

Ellery went swiftly to the table. He picked up the silver cup. On it was engraved the sentimental legend:

> *To a True Friend*
> ARNOLD PIKE
> *March 1, 1876, to* ———
> *J. D. Vincent*

"Rather macabre humor, Mr. Pike," said Ellery, setting the cup down, "since Vincent has had space left for the date of your demise." Pike began to speak, then shivered and clamped his pale lips together.

Ellery removed the lid of a tiny black box. Inside, imbedded in a cleft between two pieces of purple velvet, there was a man's signet ring, a magnificent and heavy circlet the signet of which revealed the coat-of-arms of royalist Russia. "The tattered old eagle," murmured Ellery. "Let's see what our friend the ex-duke has to say." On a card in the box, inscribed in minute script, the following was written in French:

To my good friend Arnold Pike on his fiftieth birthday. March the first ever makes me sad. I remember that day in 1917—two weeks before the czar's abdication—the quiet, then the storm. . . . But be merry, Arnold! Accept this signet-ring, given to me by my royal cousin, as a token of my esteem. Long life!
Paul

Ellery did not comment. He restored ring and card to the box, and picked up another, a large flat packet. Inside there was a gold-tipped Morocco-leather wallet. The card tucked into one of the pockets said:

Twenty-one years of life's rattle
And men are no longer boys,
They gird their loins for the battle
And throw away their toys—

But here's a cheerful plaything
For a white-haired old mooncalf,
Who may act like any May-thing
For nine years more and a half!"

"Charming verse," chuckled Ellery. "Another misbegotten poet. Only a newspaperman would indite such nonsense. This is Gurney's?"

"Yes," muttered Pike. "It's nice, isn't it?"

"If you'll pardon me," said Ellery, "it's rotten." He threw aside the wallet and seized a larger carton. Inside there was a glittering pair of patent-leather carpet slippers; the card attached read:

Happy Birthday, Arnold! May We Be All Together On as Pleasant a March First to Celebrate Your Hundredth Anniversary!

Martin

"A poor prophet," said Ellery dryly. "And what's this?" He laid the shoebox down and picked up a small flat box. In it he saw a gold-plated cigarette case, with the initials A. P. engraved on the lid. The accompanying card read:

Good luck on your fiftieth birthday. I look forward to your sixtieth on March first, 1936, for another bout of whoopee!

Stanley Oxman

"And Mr. Stanley Oxman," remarked Ellery, putting down the cigarette case, "was a little less sanguine than Martin Orr. His imagination reached no farther than sixty, Mr. Pike. A significant point."

"I can't see—" began the broker in a stubborn little mutter, "why you have to bring my friends into it—"

Sergeant Velie gripped his elbow, and he winced. Ellery shook his head disapprovingly at the man-mountain. "And now, Mr. Pike, I think we may return to Martin Orr's shop. Or, as the sergeant might fastidiously phrase it, the scene of the crime. . . . Very interesting. *Very* interesting. It almost compensates for an empty belly."

"You got something?" whispered Sergeant Velie hoarsely as Pike preceded them into a taxicab downstairs.

"Cyclops," said Ellery, "all God's chillun got something. But *I* got everything."

Sergeant Velie disappeared somewhere en route to the curio shop, and Arnold Pike's spirits lifted at once. Ellery eyed him quizzically. "One thing, Mr. Pike," he said as the taxicab turned into Fifth Avenue, "before we disembark. How long have you six men been acquainted?"

The broker sighed. "It's complicated. *My* only friend of considerable duration is Leo; Gurney, you know. Known each other for fifteen years. But then Orr and the duke have been friends since 1918, I understand, and of course Stan Oxman and Orr have known each other—knew each other—for many years. I met Vincent about a year ago through my business affiliations and introduced him into our little clique."

"Had you yourself and the others—Oxman, Orr, Paul—been acquainted before this time two years ago?"

Pike looked puzzled. "I don't see . . . Why, no. I met Oxman and the duke a year and a half ago through Orr."

"And that," murmured Ellery, "is so perfect that I don't care if I *never* have breakfast. Here we are, Mr. Pike."

They found a glum group awaiting their return—nothing had changed, except that Orr's body had disappeared, Dr. Prouty was gone, and some attempts at sweeping up the glass fragments of the doomed clock had been made. The inspector was in a fever of impatience, demanded to know where Sergeant Velie was, what Ellery had sought in Pike's apartment. . . . Ellery whispered something to him, and the old man looked startled. Then he dipped his fingers into his brown snuff-box and partook with grim relish.

The regal expatriate cleared his bull throat. "You have mystery resolved?" he mumbled. "Yuss?"

"Your highness," said Ellery gravely, "I have indeed mystery resolved." He whirled and clapped his palms together; they jumped. "Attention, please! Piggott," he said to a detective, "stand at that door and don't let any one in but Sergeant Velie."

The detective nodded. Ellery studied the faces about him. If one of them was apprehensive, he had ample control of his physiognomy. They all seemed merely interested, now that the first shock of the tragedy had passed them by. Mrs. Orr clung to Mingo's fragile hand; her eyes did not once leave Ellery's face. The fat little jeweler, the journalist, the two Wall Street men, the Russian ex-duke . . .

"An absorbing affair," grinned Ellery, "and quite elementary, despite its points of interest. Follow me closely." He went over to the counter and picked up the purple amethyst which had been clutched in the dead man's hand. He looked at it and smiled. Then he glanced at the other object on the counter—the round-based clock, with the fragments of its glass dome protruding from the circular groove.

"Consider the situation. Martin Orr, brutally beaten about the head, manages in a last desperate living action to crawl to the jewel case on the counter, pick out this gem, then go to the stone pedestal and pull the glass-doomed clock from it. Whereupon, his mysterious mission accomplished, he dies.

"Why should a dying man engage in such a baffling procedure? There can be only one general explanation. He knows his assailant and is endeavoring to leave clues to his assailant's identity." At this point the inspector nodded, and Ellery grinned again behind the curling smoke of his cigarette. "But such clues! Why? Well, what would you expect a dying man to do if he wished to leave behind him the name of his murderer? The answer is obvious: he would write it. But on Orr's body we find no paper, pen or pencil; and no paper in the immediate vicinity. Where else might he secure writing materials? Well, you will observe that Martin Orr was assaulted at a spot twenty-five feet from the door of the back room. The distance, Orr must have felt, was too great for his failing strength. Then Orr couldn't write the name of his murderer except by the somewhat fantastic method of dipping his finger into his own blood and using the floor as a slate. Such an expedient probably didn't occur to him.

"He must have reasoned with rapidity, life ebbing out of him at every breath. Then—he crawled to the case, broke the glass, took out the amethyst. Then—he crawled to the pedestal and dragged off the glass-doomed clock. Then—he died. So the amethyst and the clock were Martin Orr's bequest to the police. You can almost hear him say: 'Don't fail me. This is clear, simple, easy. Punish my murderer.' "

Mrs. Orr gasped, but the expression on her wrinkled face did not alter. Mingo began to sniffle. The others waited in total silence.

"The clock first," said Ellery lazily. "The first thing one thinks of in connection with a timepiece is time. Was Orr trying, then, by dragging the clock off the pedestal, to smash the works and, stopping the clock, so fix the time of his murder? Offhand a possibility, it is true; but if this was his purpose, it failed, because the clock didn't stop running after all. While this circumstance does not invalidate the time interpretation, further consideration of the whole problem does. For you five gentlemen had left Orr in a body. The time of the assault could not possibly be so checked against your return to your several residences as to point inescapably to one of you as the murderer. Orr must have realized this, if he thought of it at all; in other words, there wouldn't be any particular *point* to such a purpose on Orr's part.

"And there is still another—and more conclusive—consideration that invalidates the time interpretation; and that is, that Orr crawled *past* a table full of running clocks to get to this glass-doomed one. If it had been time he was intending to indicate, he could have preserved his energies by stopping at this table and pulling down one of the many clocks upon it. But no—he deliberately passed that table to get to the *glass-domed* clock. So it wasn't time.

"Very well. Now since the glass-domed clock is *the only one* of its kind in the shop, it must have been not time in the general sense but this particular timepiece in the specific sense by which Martin Orr was motivated. But what could this particular timepiece possibly indicate? In itself, as Mr. Mingo has informed me, it has no personal connotation with any one connected with Orr. The idea that Orr was leaving a clue to a clock-maker is unsound; none of you gentlemen follows that delightful craft, and certainly Mr. Oxman, the jeweler, could not have been indicated when so many things in the gem-case would have served."

Oxman began to perspire; he fixed his eyes on the jewel in Ellery's hand.

"Then it wasn't a professional meaning from the clock, as a clock," continued Ellery equably, "that Orr was trying to convey. But what is there about this particular clock which is different from the other clocks in the shop?" Ellery shot his forefinger forward. "This particular clock has a glass dome over it!" He straightened slowly. "Can any of you gentlemen think of a fairly common object almost perfectly suggested by a glass-domed clock?"

No one answered, but Vincent and Pike began to lick their lips. "I see signs of intelligence," said Ellery. "Let me be more specific. What is it —I feel like Sam Lloyd!—that has a base, a glass dome, and ticking machinery inside the dome?" Still no answer. "Well," said Ellery, "I suppose I should have expected reticence. Of course, *it's a stock-ticker!*"

They stared at him, and then all eyes turned to examine the whitening faces of J.D. Vincent and Arnold Pike. "Yes," said Ellery, "you may well gaze upon the countenances of the Messieurs Vincent and Pike. For they are the only two of our little cast who are connected with stock-tickers:

Mr. Vincent is a Wall Street operator, Mr. Pike is a broker." Quietly two
detectives left a wall and approached the two men.

"Whereupon," said Ellery, "we lay aside the glass-domed clock and
take up this very fascinating little bauble in my hand." He held up the
amethyst. "A purple amethyst—there are bluish violet ones, you know.
What could this purple amethyst have signified to Martin Orr's frantic
brain? The obvious thing is that it is a jewel. Mr. Oxman looked disturbed
a moment ago; you needn't be, sir. The jewelry significance of this amethyst is eliminated on two counts. The first is that the tray on which the
amethysts lie is in a corner at the rear of the shattered case. It was
necessary for Orr to reach far into the case. If it was a jewel he sought,
why didn't he pick any one of the stones nearer to his palsied hand? For
any single one of them would connote 'jeweler.' But no; Orr went to the
excruciating trouble of ignoring what was close at hand—as in the business of the clock—and deliberately selected something from an inconven-
ient place. Then the amethyst did not signify a jeweler, but something
else.

"The second is this, Mr. Oxman: certainly Orr knew that the stock-
ticker clue would not fix guilt on *one* person; for two of his cronies are
connected with stocks. On the other hand, did Orr have two assailants,
rather than one? Not likely. For if by the amethyst he meant to connote
you, Mr. Oxman, and by the glass-domed clock he meant to connote
either Mr. Pike or Mr. Vincent, he was still leaving a wabbly trail; for we
still would not know whether Mr. Pike or Mr. Vincent was meant. Did
he have *three* assailants, then? You see, we are already in the realm of
fantasy. No, the major probability is that, since the glass-domed clock cut
the possibilities down to two persons, the amethyst was meant to single
out one of those two.

"How does the amethyst pin one of these gentlemen down? What
significance besides the obvious one of jewelry does the amethyst suggest?
Well, it is a rich purple in color. Ah, but one your coterie fits here: his
highness the ex-duke is certainly one born to the royal purple, even if it
is an ex-ducal purple, as it were. . . ."

The soldierly Russian growled: "I am *not* highness. You know nothing
of royal address!" His dark face became suffused with blood, and he broke
into a volley of guttural Russian.

Ellery grinned. "Don't excite yourself—your grace, is it? *You* weren't
meant. For if we postulate you, we again drag in a third person and leave
unsettled the question of which Wall Street man Orr meant to accuse;

we're no better off than before. Avaunt, royalty!

"Other possible significances? Yes. There is a species of hummingbird, for instance, known as the amethyst. Out! We have no aviarists here. For another thing, the amethyst was connected with ancient Hebrew ritual —an Orientalist told me this once—breastplate decoration of the high priest, or some such thing. Obviously inapplicable here. No, there is only one other possible application." Ellery turned to the stocky gambler. "Mr. Vincent, what is your birth date?"

Vincent stammered: "November s-second."

"Splendid. That eliminates *you.*" Ellery stopped abruptly. There was a stir at the door and Sergeant Velie barged in with very grim face. Ellery smiled. "Well, sergeant, was my hunch about motive correct?"

Velie said: "And how. He forged Orr's signature to a big check. Money trouble, all right. Orr hushed the matter up, paid, and said he'd collect from the forger. The banker doesn't even know who the forger is."

"Congratulations are in order, sergeant. Our murderer evidently wished to evade repayment. Murders have been committed for less vital reasons." Ellery flourished his pince-nez. "I said, Mr. Vincent, that you are eliminated. Eliminated because the only other significance of the amethyst left to us is that it is a *birthstone.* But the November birthstone is a topaz. On the other hand, Mr. Pike has just celebrated a birthday which . . ."

And with these words, as Pike gagged and the others broke into excited gabble, Ellery made a little sign to Sergeant Velie, and himself leaped forward. But it was not Arnold Pike who found himself in the crushing grip of Velie and staring into Ellery's amused eyes.

It was the newspaperman, Leo Gurney.

"As I said," explained Ellery later, in the privacy of the Queens' living room and after his belly had been comfortably filled with food, "this has been a ridiculously elementary problem." The inspector toasted his stockinged feet before the fire, and grunted. Sergeant Velie scratched his head. "You don't think so?

"But look. It was evident, when I decided what the clues of the clock and the amethyst were intended to convey, that Arnold Pike was the man meant to be indicated. For what is the month of which the amethyst is the birthstone? *February*—in both the Polish and Jewish birthstone systems, the two almost universally recognized. Of the two men indicated by the clock clue, Vincent was eliminated because his birthstone is a topaz. Was Pike's birthday then in February? Seemingly not, for he celebrated it—this year, 1926—in March! March first, observe. What could this mean? Only one thing: since Pike was the sole remaining possibility, then his birthday *was* in February, but on the *twenty-ninth,* on Leap Day, as it's called, and 1926 not being a leap year, Pike chose to celebrate his birthday on the day on which it would ordinarily fall, March first.

"But this meant that Martin Orr, to have left the amethyst, must have known Pike's birthday to be in February, since he seemingly left the February birthstone as a clue. Yet what did I find on the card accompanying Orr's gift of carpet slippers to Pike last week? 'May we all be together on as pleasant a *March first* to celebrate your hundredth anniversary.' But if Pike is fifty years old in 1926, he was born in 1876—a leap year—and his hundredth anniversary would be 1976, also a leap year. They wouldn't celebrate Pike's birthday on his hundredth anniversary on March first! Then Orr *didn't* know Pike's real birthday was February twenty-ninth, or he would have said so on the card. He thought it was March.

"But the person who left the amethyst sign *did* know Pike's birth month was February, since he left February's birthstone. We've just established that Martin Orr didn't know Pike's birth month was February, but thought it was March. Therefore Martin Orr was not the one who selected the amethyst.

"Any confirmation? Yes. The birthstone for March in the Polish system is the bloodstone; in the Jewish it's the jasper. But both these stones were nearer a grouping hand than the amethyst, which lay in a tray at the back of the case. In other words, whoever selected the amethyst deliberately ignored the March stone in favor of the February stone, and therefore knew that Pike was born in February, not in March. But had Orr selected a stone, it would have been bloodstone or jasper, since he believed Pike *was* born in March. Orr eliminated again.

"But if Orr did not select the amethyst, as I've shown, then what have we? Palpably, a frame-up. Some one arranged matters to make us believe that Orr himself had selected the amethyst and smashed the clock. You can see the murderer dragging poor old Orr's dead body around, leaving the blood trail on purpose. . . ."

Ellery sighed. "I never did believe Orr left those signs. It was all too pat, too slick, too weirdly unreal. It is conceivable that a dying man will leave one clue to his murderer's identity, but *two*. . . ." Ellery shook his head.

"If Orr didn't leave the clues, who did? Obviously the murderer. But the clues deliberately led to Arnold Pike. Then Pike couldn't be the murderer, for certainly he would not leave a trail to himself had he killed Orr.

"Who else? Well, one thing stood out. Whoever killed Orr, framed Pike, and really selected that amethyst, knew Pike's birthday to be in February. Orr and Pike we have eliminated. Vincent didn't know Pike's birthday was in February, as witness his inscription on the silver cup. Nor did our friend the ex-duke, who also wrote 'March the first,' on his card. Oxman didn't—he said they'd celebrate Pike's sixtieth birthday on March first, 1936—a leap year, observe, when Pike's birthday would be celebrated on February twenty-ninth. . . . Don't forget that we may accept these cards' evidence as valid; the cards were sent before the crime, and the crime would have no connection in the murderer's mind with Pike's five birthday cards. The flaw in the murderer's plot was that he assumed —a natural error—that Orr and perhaps the others, too, knew Pike's birthday really fell on Leap Day. And he never did see the cards which proved the others didn't know, because Pike himself told us that after the party Monday night he did not see any of the others until last night, the night of the murder."

"I'll be fried in lard," muttered Sergeant Velie, shaking his head.

"No doubt," grinned Ellery. "But we've left some one out. How about Leo Gurney, the newspaper feature writer? His stick o' doggerel said that Pike wouldn't reach the age of twenty-one for another nine and a half years. Interesting? Yes, and damning. For this means he considered facetiously that Pike was at the time of writing eleven and a half years old. But how is this possible, even in humorous verse? It's possible only if Gurney knew that Pike's birthday falls on February twenty-ninth, which occurs only once in four years! Fifty divided by four is twelve and a half. But since the year 1900 for some reason I've never been able to discover, was not a leap year, Gurney was right, and actually Pike had celebrated only 'eleven and a half' birthdays."

And Ellery drawled: "Being the only one who knew Pike's birthday to be in February, then Gurney was the only one who could have selected the amethyst. Then Gurney arranged matters to make it seem that Orr was accusing Pike. Then Gurney was the murderer of Orr. . . .

"Simple? As a child's sum!"

The Arrow of God

LESLIE CHARTERIS

*Mystery fiction thrives on the series detective (or investigator, for some of the finest have no license), and Leslie Charteris's Simon Templar (better known as the Saint) is certainly one of the three or four best known and loved. He has starred in films and a television series which rescued the career of Roger Moore; he has been translated into dozens of languages and dialects, and he had a magazine (*The Saint Mystery Magazine*) named after him. What deserves greater recognition is the fact that the Saint's adventures in novelette and short-story lengths are even better than the novels—"The Arrow of God" is arguably the best of a fine group.*

One of Simon Templar's stock criticisms of the classic type of detective story is that the victim of the murder, the reluctant spark plug of all the entertaining mystery and strife, is usually a mere nonentity who wanders vaguely through the first few pages with the sole purpose of becoming a convenient body in the library by the end of chapter one. But what his own feelings and problems may have been, the personality which has to provide so many people with adequate motives for desiring him to drop dead, is largely a matter of hearsay, retrospectively brought out in the conventional process of drawing attention to one suspect after another.

"You could almost," Simon has said, "call him a *corpus derelicti.* . . . Actually, the physical murder should only be the midpoint of the story: the things that led up to it are at least as interesting as the mechanical solution of who done it. . . . Personally, I've killed very few people that I didn't know plenty about first."

Coming from a man who is generally regarded as almost a detective-story character himself, this comment is at least worth recording for reference; but it certainly did not apply to the shuffling off of Mr. Floyd Vosper, which caused a brief commotion on the island of New Providence in the early spring of that year.

2

Why Simon Templar should have been in Nassau (which, for the benefit of the untraveled, is the city of New Providence, which is an island

126

in the Bahamas) at the time is one of those questions which always arise in stories about him, and which can only be answered by repeating that he liked to travel and was just as likely to show up there as in Nova Zembla or Namaqualand. As for why he should have been invited to the house of Mrs. Herbert H. Wexall, that is another irrelevancy which is hardly covered by the fact that he could just as well have shown up at the house of Joe Wallenski (of the arsonist Wallenskis) or the White House—he had friends in many places, legitimate and otherwise. But Mrs. Wexall had some international renown as a lion hunter, even if her stalking had been confined to the variety which roars loudest in plush drawing rooms; and it was not to be expected that the advent of such a creature as Simon Templar would have escaped the attention of her salon safari.

Thus one noontime Simon found himself strolling up the driveway and into what little was left of the life of Floyd Vosper. Naturally he did not know this at the time; nor did he know Floyd Vosper, except by name. In this he was no different from at least fifty million other people in that hemisphere; for Floyd Vosper was not only one of the most widely syndicated pundits of the day, but his books *(Feet of Clay; As I Saw Them;* and *The Twenty Worst Men in the World)* had all been the selections of one book club or another and still sold by the million in reprints. For Mr. Vosper specialized in the ever-popular sport of shattering reputations. In his journalistic years he had met, and apparently had unique opportunities to study, practically every great name in the national and international scene, and could unerringly remember everything in their biographies that they would prefer forgotten, and could impale and epitomize all their weaknesses with devastatingly pinpoint precision, leaving them naked and squirming on the operating table of his vocabulary. But what this merciless professional iconoclast was like as a person, Simon had never heard or bothered much to wonder about.

So the first impression that Vosper made on him was a voice, a still unidentified voice, a dry and deliberate and peculiarly needling voice, which came from behind a bank of riotous hibiscus and oleander.

"My dear Janet," it said, "you must not let your innocent admiration for Reggie's bulging biceps color your estimate of his perspicacity in world affairs. The title of All-American, I hate to disillusion you, has no reference to statesmanship."

There was a rather strained laugh that must have come from Reggie, and a girl's clear young voice said: "That isn't fair, Mr. Vosper. Reggie doesn't pretend to be a genius, but he's bright enough to have a wonderful job waiting for him on Wall Street."

"I don't doubt that he will make an excellent contact man for the more stupid clients," conceded the voice with the measured nasal gripe. "And I'm sure that his education can cope with the simple arithmetic of the Stock Exchange, just as I'm sure it can grasp the basic figures of your father's Dun and Bradstreet. This should not dazzle you with his brilliance, any more than it should make you believe that you have some spiritual fascination that lured him to your feet."

At this point Simon rounded a curve in the driveway and caught his first sight of the speakers, all of whom looked up at him with reserved curiosity and two-thirds of them with a certain hint of relief.

There was no difficulty in assigning them to their lines—the young red-headed giant with the pleasantly rugged face and the slim pretty blond girl, who sat at a wrought-iron table on the terrace in front of the house with a broken deck of cards in front of them which established an interrupted game of gin rummy, and the thin stringy man reclining in a long cane chair with a cigarette-holder in one hand and a highball glass in the other.

Simon smiled and said: "Hello. This is Mrs. Wexall's house, is it?"

The girl said "Yes," and he said: "My name's Templar, and I was invited here."

The girl jumped up and said: "Oh, yes. Lucy told me. I'm her sister, Janet Blaise. This is my fiancé, Reg Herrick. And Mr. Vosper."

Simon shook hands with the two men, and Janet said: "I think Lucy's on the beach. I'll take you around."

Vosper unwound his bony length from the long chair, looking like a slightly dissolute and acidulated mahatma in his white shorts and burnt-chocolate tan.

"Let me do it," he said. "I'm sure you two ingenues would rather be alone together. And I need another drink."

He led the way, not into the house but around it, by a flagged path which struck off to the side and meandered through a bower of scarlet poinciana. A breeze rustled in the leaves and mixed flower scents with the sweetness of the sea. Vosper smoothed down his sparse gray hair; and Simon was aware that the man's beady eyes and sharp thin nose were cocked towards him with brash speculation, as if he were already measuring another target for his tongue.

"Templar," he said. "Of course, you must be the Saint—the fellow they call the Robin Hood of modern crime."

"I see you read the right papers," said the Saint pleasantly.

"I read all the papers," Vosper said, "in order to keep in touch with the vagaries of vulgar taste. I've often wondered why the Robin Hood legend should have so much romantic appeal. Robin Hood, as I understand it, was a bandit who indulged in some well-publicized charity—but not, as I recall, at the expense of his own stomach. A good many unscrupulous promoters have also become generous—and with as much shrewd publicity—when their ill-gotten gains exceeded their personal spending capacity, but I don't remember that they succeeded in being glamorized for it."

"There may be some difference," Simon suggested, "in who was robbed to provide the surplus spoils."

"Then," Vosper said challengingly, "you consider yourself an infallible judge of who should be penalized and who should be rewarded."

"Oh, no," said the Saint modestly. "Not at all. No more, I'm sure, than you would call yourself the infallible judge of all the people that you dissect so definitively in print."

He felt the other's probing glance stab at him suspiciously and almost with puzzled incredulity, as if Vosper couldn't quite accept the idea that anyone had actually dared to cross swords with him, and moreover might have scored at least even on the riposte—or if it had happened at all, that it had been anything but a semantic accident. But the Saint's easily inscrutable poise gave no clue to the answer at all; and before anything further could develop there was a paragraphic distraction.

This took the form of a man seated on top of a truncated column which for reasons best known to the architect had been incorporated into the design of a wall which curved out from the house to encircle a portion of the shore like a possessive arm. The man had long curly hair that fell to his shoulders, which with his delicate ascetic features would have made him look more like a woman if it had not been complemented with an equally curly and silken beard. He sat cross-legged and upright, his hands folded symmetrically in his lap, staring straight out into the blue sky a little above the horizon, so motionless and almost rigid that he might easily have been taken for a tinted statue except for the fluttering of the long flowing white robe he wore.

After rolling with the first reasonable shock of the apparition, Simon would have passed on politely without comment, but the opportunity was irresistible for Vosper to display his virtuosity again, and perhaps also to recover from his momentary confusion.

"That fugitive from a Turkish bath," Vosper said, in the manner of a tired guide to a geek show, "calls himself Astron. He's a nature boy from the Dardanelles who just concluded a very successful season in Hollywood. He wears a beard to cover a receding chin, and long hair to cover a hole in the head. He purifies his soul with a diet of boiled grass and prune juice. Whenever this diet lets him off the pot, he meditates. After he was brought to the attention of the Western world by some engineers of the Anglo-Mongolian Oil Company, whom he cures of stomach ulcers by persuading them not to spike their ration of sacramental wine with rubbing alcohol, he began to meditate about the evils of earthly riches."

"Another member of our club?" Simon prompted innocuously.

"Astron maintains," Vosper said, leaning against the pillar and giving out as oracularly as if the object of his dissertation were not sitting on it at all, "that the only way for the holders of worldly wealth to purify themselves is to get rid of as much of it as they can spare. Being himself so pure that it hurts, he is unselfishly ready to become the custodian of as much corrupting cabbage as they would like to get rid of. Of course, he would have no part of it himself, but he will take the responsibility of parking it in a shrine in the Sea of Marmora which he plans to build as soon as there is enough kraut in the kitty."

The figure on the column finally moved. Without any waste motion, it simply expanded its crossed legs like a lazy tongs until it towered at its full height over them.

"You have heard the blasphemer," it said. "But I say to you that his words are dust in the wind, as he himself is dust among the stars that I see."

"I'm a blasphemer," Vosper repeated to the Saint, with a sort of derisive pride combined with the ponderous bonhomie of a vaudeville old-timer in a routine with a talking dog. He looked back up at the figure of the white-robed mystic towering above him, and said: "So if you have this direct pipeline to the Almighty, why don't you strike me dead?"

"Life and death are not in my hands," Astron said, in a calm and confident voice. "Death can only come from the hands of the Giver of all life. In His own good time He will strike you down, and the arrow of God will silence your mockeries. This I have seen in the stars."

"Quaint, isn't he?" Vosper said, and opened the gate between the wall and the beach.

Beyond the wall a few steps led down to a kind of Grecian courtyard open on the seaward side, where the paving merged directly into the white sand of the beach. The courtyard was furnished with gaily colored lounging chairs and a well-stocked pushcart bar, to which Vosper immediately directed himself.

"You have visitors, Lucy," he said, without letting it interfere with the important work of reviving his highball.

Out on the sand, on a towel spread under an enormous beach umbrella, Mrs. Herbert Wexall rolled over and said: "Oh, Mr. Templar."

Simon went over and shook hands with her as she stood up. It was hard to think of her as Janet Blaise's sister, for there were at least twenty years between them and hardly any physical resemblances. She was a big woman with an open homely face and patchily sun-bleached hair and a sloppy figure, but she made a virtue of those disadvantages by the cheerfulness with which she ignored them. She was what is rather inadequately known as "a person," which means that she had the personality to dispense with appearances and the money to back it up.

"Good to see you," she said, and turned to the man who had been sitting beside her, as he struggled to his feet. "Do you know Arthur Gresson?"

Mr. Gresson was a full head shorter than the Saint's six foot two, but he weighed a good deal more. Unlike anyone else that Simon had encountered on the premises so far, his skin looked as if it was unaccustomed to exposure. His round body and his round balding brow, under a liberal sheen of oil, had the hot rosy blush which the kiss of the sun evokes in virgin epidermis.

"Glad to meet you, Mr. Templar." His hand was soft and earnestly adhesive.

"I expect you'd like a drink," Lucy Wexall said. "Let's keep Floyd working."

They joined Vosper at the bar wagon, and after he had started to work on the orders she turned back to the Saint and said: "After this formal service, just make yourself at home. I'm so glad you could come."

"I'm sure Mr. Templar will be happy," Vosper said. "He's a man of the world like I am. We enjoy Lucy's food and liquor, and in return we give her the pleasure of hitting the society columns with our names. A perfectly businesslike exchange."

"That's progress for you," Lucy Wexall said breezily. "In the old days I'd have had a court jester. Now all I get is a professional stinker."

"That's no way to refer to Arthur," Vosper said, handing Simon a long cold glass. "For your information, Templar, Mr. Gresson—Mr. Arthur *Granville* Gresson—is a promoter. He has a long history of selling phony oil stock behind him. He is just about to take Herb Wexall for another sucker; but since Herb married Lucy he can afford it. Unless you're sure you can take Janet away from Reggie, I advise you not to listen to him."

Arthur Gresson's elbow nudged Simon's ribs.

"What a character!" he said, almost proudly.

"I only give out with facts," Vosper said. "My advice to you, Templar, is, never be an elephant. Resist all inducements. Because when you reach back into that memory, you will only be laughed at, and the people who should thank you will call you a stinker."

Gresson giggled, deep from his round pink stomach.

"Would you like to get in a swim before lunch?" Lucy Wexall said. "Floyd, show him where he can change."

"A pleasure," Vosper said. "And probably a legitimate part of the bargain."

He thoughtfully refilled his glass before he steered Simon by way of the verandah into the beachward side of the house, and into a bedroom. He sat on the bed and watched unblinkingly while Simon stripped down and pulled on the trunks he had brought with him.

"It must be nice to have the Body Beautiful," he observed. "Of course, in your business it almost ranks with plant and machinery, doesn't it?"

The Saint's blue eyes twinkled.

"The main difference," he agreed good-humoredly, "is that if I get a screw loose it may not be so noticeable."

As they were starting back through the living room, a small birdlike man in a dark and (for the setting outside the broad picture window) incongruous business suit bustled in by another door. He had the bright baggy eyes behind rimless glasses, the slack but fleshless jowls, and the wide tight mouth which may not be common to all lawyers, bankers, and business executives, but which is certainly found in very few other vocations; and he was followed by a statuesque brunette whose severe tailoring failed to disguise an outstanding combination of curves, who carried a notebook and a sheaf of papers.

"Herb!" Vosper said. "I want you to meet Lucy's latest addition to the menagerie which already contains Astron and me—Mr. Simon Templar, known as the Saint. Templar—your host, Mr. Wexall."

"Pleased to meet you," said Herbert Wexall, shaking hands briskly.

"And this is Pauline Stone," Vosper went on, indicating the nubile brunette. "The tired businessman's consolation. Whatever Lucy can't supply, she can."

"How do you do," said the girl stoically.

Her dark eyes lingered momentarily on the Saint's torso, and he noticed that her mouth was very full and soft.

"Going for a swim?" Wexall said, as if he had heard nothing. "Good. Then I'll see you at lunch, in a few minutes."

He trotted busily on his way, and Vosper ushered the Saint to the beach by another flight of steps that led directly down from the verandah. The house commanded a small half-moon bay, and both ends of the crescent of sand were naturally guarded by abrupt rises of jagged coral rock.

"Herbert is the living example of how really stupid a successful businessman can be," Vosper said tirelessly. "He was just an office boy of some kind in the Blaise outfit when he got smart enough to woo and win the boss's daughter. And from that flying start, he was clever enough to really pay his way by making Blaise Industries twice as big as even the old man himself had been able to do. And yet he's dumb enough to think that Lucy won't catch on to the extracurricular functions of that busty secretary sooner or later—or that when she does he won't be out on a cold doorstep in the rain. . . . No, I'm not going in. I'll hold your drink for you."

Simon ran down into the surf and churned seawards for a couple of hundred yards, then turned over and paddled lazily back, coordinating his impressions with idle amusement. The balmy water was still refreshing after the heat of the morning, and when he came out the breeze had become brisk enough to give him the luxury of a fleeting shiver as the wetness started to evaporate from his tanned skin.

He crossed the sand to the Greek patio, where Floyd Vosper was on duty again at the bar in a strategic position to keep his own needs supplied with a minimum of effort. Discreet servants were setting up a buffet table. Janet Blaise and Reg Herrick had transferred their gin rummy game and were playing at a table right under the column where Astron had resumed his seat and his cataleptic meditations—a weird juxtaposition of which the three members all seemed equally unconscious.

Simon took Lucy Wexall a martini and said with another glance at the tableau: "Where did you find him?"

"The people who brought him to California sent him to me when he had to leave the States. They gave me such a good time when I was out there, I couldn't refuse to do something for them. He's writing a book, you know, and of course he can't go back to that dreadful place he came from, wherever it is, before he has a chance to finish it in reasonable comfort."

Simon avoided discussing this assumption, but he said: "What's it like, having a resident prophet in the house?"

"He's very interesting. And quite as drastic as Floyd, in his own way, in summing up people. You ought to talk to him."

Arthur Gresson came over with an hors d'oeuvre plate of smoked salmon and stuffed eggs from the buffet. He said: "Anyone you meet at Lucy's is interesting, Mr. Templar. But if you don't mind my saying so, you have it all over the rest of 'em. Who'd ever think we'd find the Saint looking for crime in the Bahamas?"

"I hope no one will think I'm looking for crime," Simon said deprecatingly, "any more than I take it for granted that you're looking for oil."

"That's where you'd be wrong," Gresson said. "As a matter of fact, I am."

The Saint raised an eyebrow.

"Well, I can always learn something. I'd never heard of oil in the Bahamas."

"I'm not a bit surprised. But you will, Mr. Templar, you will." Gresson sat down, pillowing his round stomach on his thighs. "Just think for a moment about some of the places you have heard of, where there is certainly oil. Let me mention them in a certain order. Mexico, Texas, Louisiana, and the recent strike in the Florida Everglades. We might even include Venezuela in the south. Does that suggest anything to you?"

"Hm-mm," said the Saint thoughtfully.

"A pattern," Gresson said. "A vast central pool of oil somewhere under the Gulf of Mexico, with oil wells dipping into it from the edges of the bowl, where the geological strata have also been forced up. Now think of the islands of the Caribbean as the eastern edge of the same bowl. Why not?"

"It's a hell of an interesting theory," said the Saint.

"Mr. Wexall thinks so too, and I hope he's going into partnership with me."

"Herbert can afford it," intruded the metallic sneering voice of Floyd Vosper. "But before you decide to buy in, Templar, you'd better check with New York about the time when Mr. Gresson thought he could dig gold in the Catskills."

"Shut up, Floyd," said Mrs. Wexall, "and get me another martini."

Arthur Granville Gresson chuckled in his paunch like a happy Buddha.

"What a guy!" he said. "What a ribber. And he gets everyone mad. He kills me!"

Herbert Wexall came down from the verandah and beamed around. As a sort of tacit announcement that he had put aside his work for the day, he had changed into a sport shirt on which various exotic animals were depicted wandering through an idealized jungle, but he retained his business trousers and business shoes and business face.

"Well," he said, inspecting the buffet and addressing the world at large. "Let's come and get it whenever we're hungry."

As if a spell had been snapped, Astron removed himself from the contemplation of the infinite, descended from his pillar, and began to help himself to cottage cheese and caviar on a foundation of lettuce leaves.

Simon drifted in the same direction, and found Pauline Stone beside him, saying: "What do you feel like, Mr. Templar?"

Her indication of having come off duty was a good deal more radical than her employer's. In fact, the bathing suit which she had changed into seemed to be based more on the French minimums of the period than on any British tradition. There was no doubt that she filled it opulently; and her question amplified its suggestiveness with undertones which the Saint felt it wiser not to challenge at that moment.

"There's so much to drool over," he said, referring studiously to the buffet table. "But that green turtle aspic looks pretty good to me."

She stayed with him when he carried his plate to a table as thoughtfully diametric as possible from the berth chosen by Floyd Vosper, even though Astron had already settled there in temporary solitude. They were promptly joined by Reg Herrick and Janet Blaise, and slipped at once into an easy exchange of banalities.

But even then it was impossible to escape Vosper's tongue. It was not many minutes before his saw-edged voice whined across the patio above the general level of harmless chatter:

"When are you going to tell the Saint's fortune, Astron? That ought to be worth hearing."

There was a slightly embarrassed lull, and then everyone went on talking again; but Astron looked at the Saint with a gentle smile and said quietly: "You are a seeker after truth, Mr. Templar, as I am. But when instead of truth you find falsehood, you will destroy it with a sword. I only say 'This is falsehood, and God will destroy it. Do not come too close, lest you be destroyed with it.'"

"Okay," Herrick growled, just as quietly. "But if you're talking about Vosper, it's about time someone destroyed it."

"Sometimes," Astron said, "God places His arrow in the hand of a man."

For a few moments that seemed unconscionably long nobody said anything; and then before the silence spread beyond their small group the Saint said casually: "Talking of arrows—I hear that the sport this season is to go hunting sharks with a bow and arrow."

Herrick nodded with a healthy grin.

"It's a lot of fun. Would you like to try it?"

"Reggie's terrific," Janet Blaise said. "He shoots like a regular Howard Hill, but of course he uses a bow that nobody else can pull."

"I'd like to try," said the Saint, and the conversation slid harmlessly along the tangent he had provided.

After lunch everyone went back to the beach, with the exception of Astron, who retired to put his morning's meditations on paper. Chatter surrendered to an afternoon torpor which even subdued Vosper.

An indefinite while later, Herrick aroused with a yell and plunged roaring into the sea, followed by Janet Blaise. They were followed by others, including the Saint. An interlude of aquatic brawling developed somehow into a pick-up game of touch football on the beach, which was delightfully confused by recurrent arguments about who was supposed to be on which of the unequal sides. This boisterous nonsense churned up so much sand for the still freshening breeze to spray over Floyd Vosper, who by that time had drunk enough to be trying to sleep under the big beach umbrella, that the misanthropic oracle finally got back on his feet.

"Perhaps," he said witheringly, "I had better get out of the way of you perennial juveniles before you convert me into a dune."

He stalked off along the beach and lay down again about a hundred yards away. Simon noticed him still there, flat on his face and presumably unconscious, when the game eventually broke up through a confused water polo phase to leave everyone gasping and laughing and dripping on the patio with no immediate resurge of inspiration. It was the last time he saw the unpopular Mr. Vosper alive.

"Well," Arthur Gresson observed, mopping his short round body with a towel, "at least one of us seems to have enough sense to know when to lie down."

"And to choose the only partner who'd do it with him," Pauline added vaguely.

Herbert Wexall glanced along the beach in the direction that they both referred to, then glanced for further inspiration at the waterproof watch he was still wearing.

"It's almost cocktail time," he said. "How about it, anyone?"

His wife shivered, and said: "I'm starting to freeze my tail off. It's going to blow like a son-of-a-gun any minute. Let's all go in and get some clothes on first—then we'll be set for the evening. You'll stay for supper of course, Mr. Templar?"

"I hadn't planned to make a day of it," Simon protested diffidently, and was promptly overwhelmed from all quarters.

He found his way back to the room where he had left his clothes without the benefit of Floyd Vosper's chatty courier service, and made leisured and satisfactory use of the fresh-water shower and monogrammed towels. Even so, when he sauntered back into the living room, he almost had the feeling of being lost in a strange and empty house, for all the varied individuals who had peopled the stage so vividly and vigorously a short time before had vanished into other and unknown seclusions and had not yet returned.

He lighted a cigarette and strolled idly towards the picture window that overlooked the verandah and the sea. Everything around his solitude was so still, excepting the subsonic suggestion of distant movements within the house, that he was tempted to walk on tiptoe; and yet outside the broad pane of plate glass the fronds of coconut palms were fluttering in a thin febrile frenzy, and there were lacings of white cream on the incredible jade of the short waves simmering on the beach.

He noticed, first, in what should have been a lazily sensual survey of the panorama, that the big beach umbrella was no longer where he had first seen it, down to his right outside the pseudo-Grecian patio. He saw, as his eye wandered on, that it had been moved a hundred yards or so to his left—in fact, to the very place where Floyd Vosper was still lying. It occurred to him first that Vosper must have moved it himself, except that no shade was needed in the brief and darkening twilight. After that he noticed that Vosper seemed to have turned over on his back; and then at last as the Saint focused his eyes he saw with a weird thrill that the shaft of the umbrella stood straight up out of the left side of Vosper's scrawny brown chest, not in the sand beside him at all, but like a gigantic pin that had impaled a strange and inelegant insect—or, in a fantastic phrase that was not Simon's at all, like the arrow of God.

3

Major Rupert Fanshire, the senior superintendent of police, which made him third in the local hierarchy after the commissioner and deputy commissioner, paid tribute to the importance of the case by taking personal charge of it. He was a slight pinkish blond man with rather large and very bright blue eyes and such a discreetly modulated voice that it commanded rapt attention through the basic effort of trying to hear what it was saying. He sat at an ordinary writing desk in the living room, with a Bahamian sergeant standing stiffly beside him, and contrived to turn the whole room into an office in which seven previously happy-go-lucky adults wriggled like guilty schoolchildren whose teacher has been found libelously caricatured on their blackboard.

He said, with wholly impersonal conciseness: "Of course, you all know by now that Mr. Vosper was found on the beach with the steel spike of an umbrella through his chest. My job is to find out how it happened. So to start with, if anyone did it to him, the topography suggests that that person came from, or through, this house. I've heard all your statements, and all they seem to amount to is that each of you was going about his own business at the time when this might have happened."

"All I know," Herbert Wexall said, "is that I was in my study, reading and signing the letters that I dictated this morning."

"And I was getting dressed," said his wife.

"So was I," said Janet Blaise.

"I guess I was in the shower," said Reginald Herrick.

"I was having a bubble bath," said Pauline Stone.

"I was still working," said Astron. "This morning I started a new chapter of my book—in my mind, you understand. I do not write by putting everything on paper. For me it is necessary to meditate, to feel, to open floodgates in my mind, so that I can receive the wisdom that comes from beyond the—"

"Quite," Major Fanshire assented politely. "The point is that none of you have alibis, if you need them. You were all going about your own business, in your own rooms. Mr. Templar was changing in the late Mr. Vosper's room—"

"I wasn't here," Arthur Gresson said recklessly. "I drove back to my own place—I'm staying at the Fort Montagu Beach Hotel. I wanted a clean shirt. I drove back there, and when I came back here all this had happened."

"There's not much difference," Major Fanshire said. "Dr. Horan tells me we couldn't establish the time of death within an hour or two, anyway. . . . So the next thing we come to is the question of motive. Did anyone here," Fanshire said almost innocently, "have any really serious trouble with Mr. Vosper?"

There was an uncomfortable silence, which the Saint finally broke by saying: "I'm on the outside here, so I'll take the rap. I'll answer for everyone."

The superintendent cocked his bright eyes.

"Very well, sir. What would you say?"

"My answer," said the Saint, "is—everybody."

There was another silence, but a very different one, in which it seemed, surprisingly, as if all of them relaxed as unanimously as they had stiffened before. And yet, in its own way, this relaxation was as self-conscious and uncomfortable as the preceding tension had been. Only the Saint, who had every attitude of the completely careless onlooker, and Major Fanshire, whose deferential patience was impregnably correct, seemed immune to the interplay of hidden strains.

"Would you care to go any further?" Fanshire asked.

"Certainly," said the Saint. "I'll go anywhere. I can say what I like, and I don't have to care whether anyone is on speaking terms with me tomorrow. I'll go on record with my opinion that the late Mr. Vosper was one of the most unpleasant characters I've ever met. I'll make the statement, if it isn't already general knowledge, that he made a specialty of needling everyone he spoke to or about. He goaded everyone with nasty little things that he knew, or thought he knew, about them. I wouldn't blame anyone here for wanting, at least theoretically, to kill him."

"I'm not exactly concerned with your interpretation of blame," Fanshire said detachedly. "But if you have any facts, I'd like to hear them."

"I have no facts," said the Saint coolly. "I only know that in the few hours I've been here, Vosper made statements to me, a stranger, about everyone here, any one of which could be called fighting words."

"You will have to be more specific," Fanshire said.

"Okay," said the Saint. "I apologize in advance to anyone it hurts. Remember, I'm only repeating the kind of thing that made Vosper a good murder candidate. . . . I am now specific. In my hearing, he called Reg Herrick a dumb athlete who was trying to marry Janet Blaise for her money. He suggested that Janet was a stupid juvenile for taking him seriously. He called Astron a commercial charlatan. He implied that Lucy Wexall was a dope and a snob. He inferred that Herb Wexall had more use for his secretary's sex than for her stenography, and he thought out loud that Pauline was amenable. He called Mr. Gresson a crook to his face."

"And during all this," Fanshire said, with an inoffensiveness that had to be heard to be believed, "he said nothing about you?"

"He did indeed," said the Saint. "He analyzed me, more or less, as a flamboyant phony."

"And you didn't object to that?"

"I hardly could," Simon replied blandly, "after I'd hinted to him that I thought he was even phonier."

It was a line on which a stage audience could have tittered, but the tensions of the moment let it sink with a slow thud.

Fanshire drew down his upper lip with one forefinger and nibbled it inscrutably.

"I expect this bores you as much as it does me, but this is the job I'm paid for. I've got to say that all of you had the opportunity, and from what Mr. Templar says you could all have had some sort of motive. Well, now I've got to look into what you might call the problem of physical possibility."

Simon Templar lighted a cigarette. It was the only movement that anyone made, and after that he was the most intent listener of them all as Fanshire went on: "Dr. Horan says, and I must say I agree with him, that to drive that umbrella shaft clean through a man's chest must have taken quite exceptional strength. It seems to be something that no woman, and probably no ordinary man, could have done."

His pale bright eyes came to rest on Herrick as he finished speaking, and the Saint found his own eyes following others in the same direction.

The picture formed in his mind, the young giant towering over a prostrate Vosper, the umbrella raised in his mighty arms like a fantastic spear and the setting sun flaming on his red head, like an avenging angel, and the thrust downwards with all the power of those herculean shoulders . . . and then, as Herrick's face began to flush under the awareness of so many stares, Janet Blaise suddenly cried out: "No! No—it couldn't have been Reggie!"

Fanshire's gaze transferred itself to her curiously, and she said in a stammering rush: "You see, it's silly, but we didn't quite tell the truth, I mean about being in our own rooms. As a matter of fact, Reggie was in my room most of the time. We were—talking."

The superintendent cleared his throat and continued to gaze at her stolidly for a while. He didn't make any comment. But presently he looked at the Saint in the same dispassionately thoughtful way that he had first looked at Herrick.

Simon said calmly: "Yes, I was just wondering myself whether I could have done it. And I had a rather interesting thought."

"Yes, Mr. Templar?"

"Certainly it must take quite a lot of strength to drive a spike through a man's chest with one blow. But now remember that this wasn't just a spike, or a spear. It had an enormous great umbrella on top of it. Now think what would happen if you were stabbing down with a thing like that?"

"Well, what would happen?"

"The umbrella would be like a parachute. It would be like a sort of sky anchor holding the shaft back. The air resistance would be so great that I'm wondering how anyone, even a very strong man, could get much momentum into the thrust. And the more force he put into it, the more likely he'd be to lift himself off the ground, rather than drive the spike down."

Fanshire digested this, blinking, and took his full time to do it.

"That certainly is a thought," he admitted. "But damn it," he exploded, "we know it was done. So it must have been possible."

"There's something entirely backwards about that logic," said the Saint. "Suppose we say, if it was impossible, maybe it wasn't done."

"Now you're being a little ridiculous," Fanshire snapped. "We saw—"

"We saw a man with the sharp iron-tipped shaft of a beach umbrella through his chest. We jumped to the natural conclusion that somebody stuck it into him like a sword. And that may be just what a clever murderer meant us to think."

Then it was Arthur Gresson who shattered the fragile silence by leaping out of his chair like a bouncing ball.

"I've got it!" he yelped. "Believe me, everybody, I've got it! This'll kill you!"

"I hope not," Major Fanshire said dryly. "But what is it?"

"Listen," Gresson said. "I knew something rang a bell somewhere, but I couldn't place it. Now it all comes back to me. This is something I only heard at the hotel the other day, but some of you must have heard it before. It happened about a year ago, when Gregory Peck was visiting here. He stayed at the same hotel where I am, and one afternoon he was on the beach, and the wind came up, just like it did today, and it picked up one of those beach umbrellas and carried it right to where he was lying, and the point just grazed his ribs and gave him a nasty gash, but what the people who saw it happen were saying was that if it'd been just a few inches the other way, it could have gone smack into his heart, and you'd've had a film star killed in the most sensational way that ever was. Didn't you ever hear about that, major?"

"Now you mention it," Fanshire said slowly, "I think I did hear something about it."

"Well," Gresson said, *"what if it happened again this afternoon, to someone who wasn't as lucky as Peck?"*

There was another of those electric silences of assimilation, out of which Lucy Wexall said: "Yes, I heard about that." And Janet said: "Remember, I told you about it! I was visiting some friends at the hotel that day, and I didn't see it happen, but I was there for the commotion."

Gresson spread out his arms, his round face gleaming with excitement and perspiration.

"That's got to be it!" he said. "You remember how Vosper was lying under the umbrella outside the patio when we started playing touch football, and he got sore because we were kicking sand over him, and he went off to the other end of the beach? But he didn't take the umbrella with him. The wind did that, after we all went off to change. And this time it didn't miss!"

Suddenly Astron stood up beside him; but where Gresson had risen like a jumping bean, this was like the growth and unfolding of a tree.

"I have heard many words," Astron said, in his firm gentle voice, "but now at last I think I am hearing truth. No man struck the blasphemer down. The arrow of God smote him, in his wickedness and his pride, as it was written long ago in the stars."

"You can say that again," Gresson proclaimed triumphantly. "He sure had it coming."

Again the Saint drew at his cigarette and created his own vision behind half-closed eyes. He saw the huge umbrella plucked from the sand by the invisible fingers of the wind, picked up and hurled spinning along the deserted twilight beach, its great mushroom spread of gaudy canvas no longer a drag now but a sail for the wind to get behind, the whole thing transformed into a huge unearthly dart flung with literally superhuman power, the arrow of God indeed. A fantastic, an almost unimaginable solution; and yet it did not have to be imagined because there were witnesses that it had actually almost happened once before. . . .

Fanshire was saying: "By Jove, that's the best suggestion I've heard yet—without any religious implication, of course. It sounds as if it could be the right answer!"

Simon's eyes opened on him fully for an instant, almost pityingly, and then closed completely as the true and right and complete answer rolled through the Saint's mind like a long peaceful wave.

"I have one question to ask," said the Saint.

"What's that?" Fanshire said, too politely to be irritable, yet with a trace of impatience, as if he hated the inconvenience of even defending such a divinely tailored theory.

"Does anyone here have a gun?" asked the Saint.

There was an almost audible creaking of knitted brows, and Fanshire said: "Really, Mr. Templar, I don't quite follow you."

"I only asked," said the Saint imperturbably, "if anyone here had a gun. I'd sort of like to know the answer before I explain why."

"I have a revolver," Wexall said with some perplexity. "What about it?"

"Could we see it, please?" said the Saint.

"I'll get it," said Pauline Stone.

She got up and left the room.

"You know I have a gun, Fanshire," Wexall said. "You gave me my permit. But I don't see—"

"Neither do I," Fanshire said.

The Saint said nothing. He devoted himself to his cigarette, with impregnable detachment, until the voluptuous secretary came back. Then he put out the cigarette and extended his hand.

Pauline looked at Wexall, hesitantly, and at Fanshire. The superintendent nodded a sort of grudging acquiescence. Simon took the gun and broke it expertly.

"A Colt .38 Detective Special," he said. "Unloaded." He sniffed the barrel. "But fired quite recently," he said, and handed the gun to Fanshire.

"I used it myself this morning," Lucy Wexall said cheerfully. "Janet and Reg and I were shooting at the Portuguese men-of-war. There were quite a lot of them around before the breeze came up."

"I wondered what the noise was," Wexall said vaguely.

"I was coming up the drive when I heard it first," Gresson said, "and I thought the next war had started."

"This is all very int'resting," Fanshire said, removing the revolver barrel from the proximity of his nostrils with a trace of exasperation, "but I don't see what it has to do with the case. Nobody has been shot—"

"Major Fanshire," said the Saint quietly, "may I have a word with you, outside? And will you keep that gun in your pocket so that at least we can hope there will be no more shooting?"

The superintendent stared at him for several seconds, and at last unwillingly got up.

"Very well, Mr. Templar." He stuffed the revolver into the side pocket of his rumpled white jacket, and glanced back at his impassive chocolate sentinel. "Sergeant, see that nobody leaves here, will you?"

He followed Simon out on to the verandah and said almost peremptorily: "Come on now, what's this all about?"

It was so much like a flash of a faraway Scotland Yard inspector that the Saint had to control a smile. But he took Fanshire's arm and led him persuasively down the front steps to the beach. Off to their left a tiny red glowworm blinked low down under the silver stars.

"You still have somebody watching the place where the body was found," Simon said.

"Of course," Fanshire grumbled. "As a matter of routine. But the sand's much too soft to show any footprints, and—"

"Will you walk over there with me?"

Fanshire sighed briefly, and trudged beside him. His politeness was dogged but unfailing. He was a type that had been schooled from adolescence never to give up, even to the ultimate in ennui. In the interests of total fairness, he would be game to the last yawn.

He did go so far as to say: "I don't know what you're getting at, but why *couldn't* it have been an accident?"

"I never heard a better theory in my life," said the Saint equably, "with one insuperable flaw."

"What's that?"

"Only," said the Saint, very gently, "that the wind wasn't blowing the right way."

Major Fanshire kept his face straight ahead to the wind and said nothing more after that until they reached the glowworm that they were making for and it became a cigarette end that a constable dropped as he came to attention.

The place where Floyd Vosper had been lying was marked off in a square of tape, but there was nothing out of the ordinary about it except some small stains that showed almost black under the flashlight which the constable produced.

"May I mess up the scene a bit?" Simon asked.

"I don't see why not," Fanshire said doubtfully. "It doesn't show anything, really."

Simon went down on his knees and began to dig with his hands, around and under the place where the stains were. Minutes later he stood up, with sand trickling through his fingers, and showed Fanshire the mushroomed scrap of metal that he had found.

"A .38 bullet," Fanshire said, and whistled.

"And I think you'll be able to prove it was fired from the gun you have in your pocket," said the Saint. "Also you'd better have a sack of sand picked up from where I was digging. I think a laboratory examination will find that it also contains fragments of bone and human flesh."

"You'll have to explain this to me," Fanshire said quite humbly.

Simon dusted his hands and lighted a cigarette.

"Vosper was lying on his face when I last saw him," he said, "and I think he was as much passed out as sleeping. With the wind and the surf and the soft sand, it was easy for the murderer to creep up on him and shoot him in the back where he lay. But the murderer didn't want you looking for guns and comparing bullets. The umbrella was the inspiration. I don't have to remind you that the exit hole of a bullet is much larger than the entrance. By turning Vosper's body over, the murderer found a hole in his chest that it can't have been too difficult to force the umbrella shaft through—obliterating the original wound and confusing everybody in one simple operation."

"Let's get back to the house," said the superintendent abruptly.

After a while, as they walked, Fanshire said: "It's going to feel awfully funny, having to arrest Herbert Wexall."

"Good God!" said the Saint, in honest astonishment. "You weren't thinking of doing that?"

Fanshire stopped and blinked at him under the still distant light of the uncurtained windows.

"Why not?"

"Did Herbert seem at all guilty when he admitted he had a gun? Did he seem at all uncomfortable—I don't mean just puzzled, like you were —about having it produced? Was he ready with the explanation of why it still smelled of being fired?"

"But if anyone else used Wexall's gun," Fanshire pondered laboriously, "why should they go to such lengths to make it look as if no gun was used at all, when Wexall would obviously have been suspected?"

"Because it was somebody who didn't want Wexall to take the rap," said the Saint. "Because Wexall is the goose who could still lay golden eggs —but he wouldn't do much laying on the end of a rope, or whatever you do to murderers here."

The superintendent pulled out a handkerchief and wiped his face.

"My God," he said, "you mean you think Lucy—"

"I think we have to go all the way back to the prime question of motive," said the Saint. "Floyd Vosper was a nasty man who made dirty cracks about everyone here. But his cracks were dirtiest because he always had a wickedly good idea what he was talking about. Nevertheless, very few people become murderers because of a dirty crack. Very few people except me kill other people on points of principle. Vosper called us all variously dupes, phonies, cheaters and fools. But since he had roughly the same description for all of us, we could all laugh it off. There was only one person about whom he made the unforgivable accusation. . . . Now shall we rejoin the mob?"

"You'd better do this your own way," Fanshire muttered.

Simon Templar took him up the steps to the verandah and back through the french doors into the living room, where all eyes turned to them in deathly silence.

"A paraffin test will prove who fired that revolver in the last twenty-four hours, aside from those who have already admitted it," Simon said, as if there had been no interruption. "And you'll remember, I'm sure, who supplied that very handy theory about the arrow of God."

"Astron!" Fanshire gasped.

"Oh, no," said the Saint, a little tiredly. "He only said that God sometimes places His arrow in the hands of a man. And I feel quite sure that a wire to New York will establish that there is actually a criminal file under the name of Granville, with fingerprints and photos that should match Mr. Gresson's—as Vosper's fatally elephantine memory remembered. . . . That was the one crack he shouldn't have made, because it was the only one that was more than gossip or shrewd insult, the only one that could be easily proved, and the only one that had a chance of upsetting an operation which was all set—if you'll excuse the phrase—to make a big killing."

Major Fanshire fingered his upper lip.

"I don't know," he began; and then, as Arthur Granville Gresson began to rise like a floating balloon from his chair, and the ebony-faced sergeant moved to intercept him like a well-disciplined automaton, he knew.

A Passage to Benares

T.S. STRIBLING

*Writing about T.S. Stribling, the Pulitzer Prize-winning creator of
Henry Poggioli, Anthony Boucher once said that "he is the only detective-
story writer who ever succeeded in viewing his detective with complete
objectivity. No sleuth has ever been limned with such merciless accuracy
as Henry Poggioli, nor so skillfully portrayed as that mixture of pettiness
and sublimity which is Man." A unique and stunning Poggioli story is "A
Passage to Benares," for a reason which will become clear at its climax—
an ending which has justifiably been called "positively thunderous."*

In Port of Spain, Trinidad, at half past five in the morning, Mr. Henry
Poggioli, the American psychologist, stirred uneasily, became conscious of
a splitting headache, opened his eyes in bewilderment, and then slowly
reconstructed his surroundings. He recognized the dome of the Hindu
temple seen dimly above him, the jute rug on which he lay; the blur of
the image of Krishna sitting cross-legged on the altar. The American had
a dim impression that the figure had not sat thus on the altar all night
long—a dream, no doubt; he had a faint memory of lurid nightmares. The
psychologist allowed the thought to lose itself as he got up slowly from
the sleeping rug which the cicerone had spread for him the preceding
evening.

In the circular temple everything was still in deep shadow, but the gray
light of dawn filled the arched entrance. The white man moved carefully
to the door so as not to jar his aching head. A little distance from him
he saw another sleeper, a coolie beggar stretched out on a rug, and he
thought he saw still another farther away. As he passed out of the entrance
the cool freshness of the tropical morning caressed his face like the cool
fingers of a woman. Kiskadee birds were calling from palms and saman
trees, and there was a wide sound of dripping dew. Not far from the
temple a coolie woman stood on a seesaw with a great stone attached to
the other end of the plank, and by stepping to and fro she swung the stone
up and down and pounded some rice in a mortar.

Poggioli stood looking at her a moment, then felt in his pocket for the
key to his friend Lowe's garden gate. He found it and moved off up

147

Tragarette Road to where the squalid East Indian village gave way to the high garden walls and ornamental shrubbery of the English suburb of Port of Spain. He walked on more briskly as the fresh air eased his head, and presently he stopped and unlocked a gate in one of the bordering walls. He began to smile as he let himself in; his good humor increased as he walked across a green lawn to a stone cottage which had a lower window still standing open. This was his own room. He reached up to the sill and drew himself inside, which gave his head one last pang. He shook this away, however, and began undressing for his morning shower.

Mr. Poggioli was rather pleased with his exploit, although he had not forwarded the experiment which had induced him to sleep in the temple. It had come about in this way: on the foregoing evening the American and his host in Port of Spain, a Mr. Lowe, a bank clerk, had watched a Hindu wedding procession enter the same temple in which Poggioli had just spent the night. They had watched the dark-skinned white-robed musicians smiting their drums and skirling their pipes with bouffant cheeks. Behind them marched a procession of coolies. The bride was a little cream-colored girl who wore a breastplate of linked gold coins over her childish bosom, while anklets and bracelets almost covered her arms and legs. The groom, a tall, dark coolie, was the only man in the procession who wore European clothes, and he, oddly enough, was attired in a full evening dress suit. At the incongruous sight Poggioli burst out laughing, but Lowe touched his arm and said in an undertone:

"Don't take offense, old man, but if you didn't laugh it might help me somewhat."

Poggioli straightened his face.

"Certainly, but how's that?"

"The groom, Boodman Lal, owns one of the best curio shops in town and carries an account at my bank. That fifth man in the procession, the skeleton wearing the yellow *kapra,* is old Hira Dass. He is worth something near a million in pounds sterling."

The psychologist became sober enough, out of his American respect for money.

"Hira Dass," went on Lowe, "built this temple and rest house. He gives rice and tea to any traveler who comes in for the night. It's an Indian custom to help mendicant pilgrims to the different shrines. A rich Indian will build a temple and a rest house just as your American millionaires erect libraries."

The American nodded again, watching now the old man with the length of yellow silk wrapped around him. And just at this point Poggioli received the very queer impression which led to his night's adventure.

When the wedding procession entered the temple the harsh music stopped abruptly. Then, as the line of robed coolies disappeared into the dark interior the psychologist had a strange feeling that the procession had been swallowed up and had ceased to exist. The bizarre red-and-gold building stood in the glare of sunshine, a solid reality, while its devotees had been dissipated into nothingness.

So peculiar, so startling was the impression, that Poggioli blinked and wondered how he ever came by it. The temple had somehow suggested the Hindu theory of nirvana. Was it possible that the Hindu architect had caught some association of ideas between the doctrine of obliteration and these curves and planes and colors glowing before him? Had he done it by contrast or simile? The fact that Poggioli was a psychologist made the problem all the more intriguing to him—the psychologic influence of architecture. There must be some rationale behind it. An idea how he might pursue this problem came into his head. He turned to his friend and exclaimed:

"Lowe, how about staying all night in old Hira Dass's temple?"

"Doing what?" with a stare of amazement.

"Staying a night in the temple. I had an impression just then, a—"

"Why, my dear fellow!" ejaculated Lowe, "no white man ever stayed all night in a coolie temple. It simply isn't done!"

The American argued his case a moment:

"You and I had a wonderful night aboard the *Trevemore* when we became acquainted."

"That was a matter of necessity," said the bank clerk. "There were no first-class cabin accommodations left on the *Trevemore,* so we had to make the voyage on deck."

Here the psychologist gave up his bid for companionship. Late that night he slipped out of Lowe's cottage, walked back to the grotesque temple, was given a cup of tea, a plate of rice, and a sleeping rug. The only further impression the investigator obtained was a series of fantastic and highly colored dreams, of which he could not recall a detail. Then he waked with a miserable headache and came home.

Mr. Poggioli finished his dressing and in a few minutes the breakfast bell rang. He went to the dining room to find the bank clerk unfolding the damp pages of the Port of Spain *Inquirer.* This was a typical English sheet using small, solidly set columns without flaming headlines. Poggioli glanced at it and wondered mildly if nothing worth featuring ever happened in Trinidad.

Ram Jon, Lowe's Hindu servant, slipped in and out of the breakfast room with peeled oranges, tea, toast, and a custard fruit flanked by a half lemon to squeeze over it.

"Pound sterling advanced a point," droned Lowe from his paper.

"It'll reach par," said the American, smiling faintly and wondering what Lowe would say if he knew of his escapade.

"Our new governor general will arrive in Trinidad on the twelfth."

"Surely that deserved a headline," said the psychologist.

"Don't try to debauch me with your American yellow journalism," smiled the bank clerk.

"Go your own way if you prefer doing research work every morning for breakfast."

The bank clerk laughed again at this, continued his perusal, then said:

"Hello, another coolie kills his wife. Tell me, Poggioli, as a psychologist, why do coolies kill their wives?"

"For various reasons, I fancy, or perhaps this one didn't kill her at all. Surely now and then some other person—"

"Positively no! It's always the husband, and instead of having various reasons, they have none at all. They say their heads are hot, and so to cool their own they cut off their wives'!"

The psychologist was amused in a dull sort of way.

"Lowe, you Englishmen are a nation with fixed ideas. You genuinely believe that every coolie woman who is murdered is killed by her husband without any motive whatever."

"Sure, that's right," nodded Lowe, looking up from his paper.

"That simply shows me you English have no actual sympathy with your subordinate races. And that may be the reason your empire is great. Your aloofness, your unsympathy—by becoming automatic you become absolutely dependable. The idea, that every coolie woman is murdered by her husband without a motive!"

"That's correct," repeated Lowe with English imperturbability.

The conversation was interrupted by a ring at the garden-gate bell. A few moments later the two men saw through the shadow Ram Jon unlock the wall door, open it a few inches, parley a moment, and receive a letter. Then he came back with his limber, gliding gait.

Lowe received the note through the open window, broke the envelope, and fished out two notes instead of one. The clerk looked at the enclosures and began to read with a growing bewilderment in his face.

"What is it?" asked Poggioli at last.

"This is from Hira Dass to Jeffries, the vice-president of our bank. He says his nephew Boodman Lal has been arrested and he wants Jeffries to help get him out."

"What's he arrested for?"

"Er—for murdering his wife," said Lowe with a long face.

Poggioli stared.

"Wasn't he the man we saw in the procession yesterday?"

"Damn it, yes!" cried Lowe in sudden disturbance, "and he's a sensible fellow, too, one of our best patrons." He sat staring at the American over the letter, and then suddenly recalling a point, drove it home English fashion.

"That proves my contention, Poggioli—a groom of only six or eight hours' standing killing his wife. They simply commit uxoricide without any reason at all, the damned irrational rotters!"

"What's the other letter?" probed the American, leaning across the table.

"It's from Jeffries. He says he wants me to take this case and get the best talent in Trinidad to clear Mr. Hira Dass's house and consult with him." The clerk replaced the letters in the envelope. "Say, you've had some experience in this sort of thing. Won't you come with me?"

"Glad to."

The two men arose promptly from the table, got their hats, and went out into Tragarette Road once more. As they stood in the increasing heat waiting for a car, it occurred to Poggioli that the details of the murder ought to be in the morning's paper. He took the *Inquirer* from his friend and began a search through its closely printed columns. Presently he found a paragraph without any heading at all:

Boodman Lal, nephew of Mr. Hira Dass, was arrested early this morning at his home in Peru, the East Indian suburb, for the alleged murder of his wife, whom he married yesterday at the Hindu temple in Peru. The body was found at six o'clock this morning in the temple. The attendant gave the alarm. Mrs. Boodman Lal's head was severed completely from her body and she lay in front of the Buddhist altar in her bridal dress. All of her jewelry was gone. Five coolie beggars who were asleep in the temple when the body was discovered were arrested. They claimed to know nothing of the crime, but a search of their persons revealed that each beggar had a piece of the young bride's jewelry and a coin from her necklace.

Mr. Boodman Lal and his wife were seen to enter the temple at about eleven o'clock last night for the Krishnian rite of purification. Mr. Boodman, who is a prominent curio dealer in this city, declines to say anything further than that he thought his wife had gone back to her mother's home for the night after her prayers in the temple. The young bride, formerly a Miss Maila Ran, was thirteen years old. Mr. Boodman is the nephew of Mr. Hira Dass, one of the wealthiest men in Trinidad.

The paragraph following this contained a notice of a tea given at Queen's Park Hotel by Lady Henley-Hoads, and the names of her guests.

The psychologist spent a painful moment pondering the kind of editor who would run a millionaire murder mystery, without any caption whatever, in between a legal notice and a society note. Then he turned his attention to the gruesome and mysterious details the paragraph contained.

"Lowe, what do you make out of those beggars, each with a coin and a piece of jewelry?"

"Simple enough. The rotters laid in wait in the temple till the husband went out and left his wife, then they murdered her and divided the spoil."

"But that child had enough bangles to give a dozen to each man."

"Ye-es, that's a fact," admitted Lowe.

"And why should they continue sleeping in the temple?"

"Why shouldn't they? They knew they would be suspected, and they couldn't get off the island without capture, so they thought they might as well lie back down and go to sleep."

Here the streetcar approached and Mr. Poggioli nodded, apparently in agreement.

"Yes, I am satisfied that is how it occurred."

"You mean the beggars killed her?"

"No, I fancy the actual murderer took the girl's jewelry and went about the temple thrusting a bangle and a coin in the pockets of each of the sleeping beggars to lay a false scent."

"Aw, come now!" cried the bank clerk, "that's laying it on a bit too thick, Poggioli!"

"My dear fellow, that's the only possible explanation for the coins in the beggars' pockets."

By this time the men were on the tramcar and were clattering off down Tragarette Road. As they dashed along toward the Hindu village Poggioli remembered suddenly that he had walked this same distance the preceding night and had slept in this same temple. A certain sharp impulse caused the American to run a hand swiftly into his own pockets. In one side he felt the keys of his trunk and of Lowe's cottage; in the other he touched several coins and a round hard ring. With a little thrill he drew these to the edge of his pocket and took a covert glance at them. One showed the curve of a gold bangle; the other the face of an old English gold coin which evidently had been soldered to something.

With a little sinking sensation Poggioli eased them back into his pocket and stared ahead at the coolie village which they were approaching. He moistened his lips and thought what he would better do. The only notion that came into his head was to pack his trunk and take passage on the first steamer out of Trinidad, no matter to what port it was bound.

In his flurry of uneasiness the psychologist was tempted to drop the gold pieces then and there, but as the street car rattled into Peru he reflected that no other person in Trinidad knew that he had these things, except indeed the person who slipped them into his pocket, but that person was not likely to mention the matter. Then, too, it was such an odd occurrence, so piquing to his analytic instinct, that he decided he would go on with the inquiry.

Two minutes later Lowe rang down the motorman and the two companions got off in the Hindu settlement. By this time the street was full of coolies, greasy men and women gliding about with bundles on their heads or coiled down in the sunshine in pairs where they took turns in examining each other's head for vermin. Lowe glanced about, oriented himself, then started walking briskly past the temple, when Poggioli stopped him and asked him where he was going.

"To report to old Hira Dass, according to my instructions from Jeffries," said the Englishman.

"Suppose we stop in the temple a moment. We ought not to go to the old fellow without at least a working knowledge of the scene of the murder."

The clerk slowed up uncertainly, but at that moment they glanced through the temple door and saw five coolies sitting inside. A policeman at the entrance was evidently guarding these men as prisoners. Lowe approached the guard, made his mission known, and a little later he and his guest were admitted into the temple.

The coolie prisoners were as repulsive as are all of their kind. Four were as thin as cadavers, the fifth one greasily fat. All five wore cheesecloth around their bodies, which left them as exposed as if they had worn nothing at all. One of the emaciated men held his mouth open all the time with an expression of suffering caused by a chronic lack of food. The five squatted on their rugs and looked at the white men with their beadlike eyes. The fat one said in a low tone to his companions:

"The sahib."

This whispered ejaculation disquieted Poggioli somewhat, and he reflected again that it would have been discretion to withdraw from the murder of little Maila Ran as quietly as possible. Still he could explain his presence in the temple simply enough. And besides, the veiled face of the mystery seduced him. He stood studying the five beggars: the greasy one, the lean ones, the one with the suffering face.

"Boys," he said to the group, for all coolies are boys, "did any of you hear any noises in this temple last night?"

"Much sleep, sahib, no noise. Police-y-man punch us 'wake this morning make sit still here."

"What's your name?" asked the American of the loquacious fat mendicant.

"Chuder Chand, sahib."

"When did you go to sleep last night?"

"When I ate rice and tea, sahib."

"Do you remember seeing Boodman Lal and his wife enter this building last night?"

Here their evidence became divided. The fat man remembered; two of the cadavers remembered only the wife, one only Boodman Lal, and one nothing at all.

Poggioli confined himself to the fat man.

"Did you see them go out?"

All five shook their heads.

"You were all asleep then?"

A general nodding.

"Did you have any impressions during your sleep, any disturbance, any half rousing, any noises?"

The horror-struck man said in a ghastly tone:

"I dream bad dream, sahib. When police-y-man punch me awake this morning I think my dream is come to me."

"And me, sahib."

"Me, sahib."

"Me."

"Did you all have bad dreams?"

A general nodding.

"What did you dream, Chuder Chand?" inquired the psychologist with a certain growth of interest.

"Dream me a big fat pig, but still I starved, sahib."

"And you?" at a lean man.

"That I be mashed under a great bowl of rice, sahib, but hungry."

"And you?" asked Poggioli of the horror-struck coolie.

The coolie wet his dry lips and whispered in his ghastly tones:

"Sahib, I dreamed I was Siva, and I held the world in my hands and bit it and it tasted bitter, like the rind of a mammy apple. And I said to Vishnu, 'Let me be a dog in the streets, rather than taste the bitterness of this world,' and then the policeman punched me, sahib, and asked if I had murdered Maila Ran."

The psychologist stood staring at the sunken temples and withered chaps of the beggar, amazed at the enormous vision of godhood which had visited the old mendicant's head. No doubt this grandiloquent dream was a sort of compensation for the starved and wretched existence the beggar led.

Here the bank clerk intervened to say that they would better go on around to old Hira Dass's house according to instructions.

Poggioli turned and followed his friend out of the temple.

"Lowe, I think we can now entirely discard the theory that the beggars murdered the girl."

"On what grounds?" asked the clerk in surprise. "They told you nothing but their dreams."

"That is the reason. All five had wild, fantastic dreams. That suggests they were given some sort of opiate in their rice or tea last night. It is very improbable that five ignorant coolies would have wit enough to concoct such a piece of evidence as that."

"That's a fact," admitted the Englishman, a trifle surprised, "but I don't believe a Trinidad court would admit such evidence."

"We are not looking for legal evidence; we are after some indication of the real criminal."

By this time the two men were walking down a hot, malodorous alley which emptied into the square a little east of the temple. Lowe jerked a bell-pull in a high adobe wall, and Poggioli was surprised that this could be the home of a millionaire Hindu. Presently the shutter opened and Mr. Hira Dass himself stood in the opening. The old Hindu was still draped in yellow silk which revealed his emaciated form almost as completely as if he had been naked. But his face was alert with hooked nose and brilliant black eyes, and his wrinkles did not so much suggest great age as they did shrewdness and acumen.

The old coolie immediately led his callers into an open court surrounded by marble columns with a fountain in its center and white doves fluttering up to the frieze or floating back down again.

The Hindu began talking immediately of the murder and his anxiety to clear his unhappy nephew. The old man's English was very good, no doubt owing to the business association of his latter years.

"A most mysterious murder," he deplored, shaking his head, "and the life of my poor nephew will depend upon your exertions, gentlemen. What do you think of those beggars that were found in the temple with the bangles and coins?"

Mr. Hira Dass seated his guests on a white marble bench, and now walked nervously in front of them, like some fantastic old scarecrow draped in yellow silk.

"I am afraid my judgment of the beggars will disappoint you, Mr. Hira Dass," answered Poggioli. "My theory is they are innocent of the crime."

"Why do you say that?" queried Hira Dass, looking sharply at the American.

The psychologist explained his deduction from their dreams.

"You are not English, sir," exclaimed the old man. "No Englishman would have thought of that."

"No, I'm half Italian and half American."

The old Indian nodded.

"Your Latin blood has subtlety, Mr. Poggioli, but you base your proof on the mechanical cause of the dreams, not upon the dreams themselves."

The psychologist looked at the old man's cunning face and gnomelike figure and smiled.

"I could hardly use the dreams themselves, although they were fantastic enough."

"Oh, you did inquire into the actual dreams?"

"Yes, by the way of professional interest."

"What is your profession? Aren't you a detective?"

"No, I'm a psychologist."

Old Hira Dass paused in his rickety walking up and down the marble pavement to stare at the American and then burst into the most wrinkled cachinnation Poggioli had ever seen.

"A psychologist, and inquired into a suspected criminal's dreams out of mere curiosity!" the old gnome cackled again, then became serious. He held up a thin finger at the American. "I must not laugh. Your oversoul, your *atman,* is at least groping after knowledge as the blindworm gropes. But enough of that, Mr. Poggioli. Our problem is to find the criminal who committed this crime and restore my nephew Boodman Lal to liberty. You can imagine what a blow this is to me. I arranged this marriage for my nephew."

The American looked at the old man with new ground for deduction.

"You did—arranged a marriage for a nephew who is in the thirties?"

"Yes, I wanted him to avoid the pitfalls into which I fell," replied old Hira Dass seriously. "He was unmarried, and had already begun to add dollars to dollars. I did the same thing, Mr. Poggioli, and now look at me —an empty old man in a foreign land. What good is this marble court where men of my own kind cannot come and sit with me, and when I have no grandchildren to feed the doves? No, I have piled up dollars and pounds. I have eaten the world, Mr. Poggioli, and found it bitter; now here I am, an outcast."

There was a passion in this outburst which moved the American, and at the same time the old Hindu's phraseology was sharply reminiscent of the dreams told him by the beggars in the temple. The psychologist noted the point hurriedly and curiously in the flow of the conversation, and at the same moment some other part of his brain was inquiring tritely:

"Then why don't you go back to India, Mr. Hira Dass?"

"With this worn-out body," the old Hindu made a contemptuous gesture toward himself, "and with this face, wrinkled with pence! Why, Mr. Poggioli, my mind is half English. If I should return to Benares I would walk about thinking what the temples cost, what was the value of the stones set in the eyes of Krishna's image. That is why we Hindus lose our caste if we travel abroad and settle in a foreign land, because we do indeed lose caste. We become neither Hindus nor English. Our minds are divided, so if I would ever be one with my own people again, Mr. Poggioli, I must leave this Western mind and body here in Trinidad."

Old Hira Dass's speech brought to the American that fleeting credulity in transmigration of the soul which an ardent believer always inspires. The old Hindu made the theory of palingenesis appear almost matter-of-fact. A man died here and reappeared as a babe in India. There was nothing so unbelievable in that. A man's basic energy, which has loved, hated, aspired, and grieved here, must go somewhere, while matter itself was a mere dance of atoms. Which was the most permanent, Hira Dass's passion or his marble court? Both were mere forms of force. The psychologist drew himself out of his reverie.

"That is very interesting, or I should say moving, Hira Dass. You have strange griefs. But we were discussing your nephew, Boodman Lal. I think

I have a theory which may liberate him."

"And what is that?"

"As I have explained to you, I believe the beggars in the temple were given a sleeping potion. I suspect the temple attendant doped the rice and later murdered your nephew's wife."

The millionaire became thoughtful.

"That is good Gooka. I employ him. He is a miserably poor man, Mr. Poggioli, so I cannot believe he committed this murder."

"Pardon me, but I don't follow your reasoning. If he is poor he would have a strong motive for the robbery."

"That's true, but a very poor man would never have dropped the ten pieces of gold into the pockets of the beggars to lay a false scent. The man who did this deed must have been a well-to-do person accustomed to using money to forward his purposes. Therefore, in searching for the criminal I would look for a moneyed man."

"But, Mr. Hira Dass," protested the psychologist, "that swings suspicion back to your nephew."

"My nephew!" cried the old man, growing excited again. "What motive would my nephew have to slay his bride of a few hours!"

"But what motive," retorted Poggioli with academic curtness, "would a well-to-do man have to murder a child? And what chance would he have to place an opiate in the rice?"

The old Hindu lifted a finger and came closer.

"I'll tell you my suspicions," he said in a lowered voice, "and you can work out the details."

"Yes, what are they?" asked Poggioli, becoming attentive again.

"I went down to the temple this morning to have the body of my poor murdered niece brought here to my villa for burial. I talked to the five beggars and they told me that there was a sixth sleeper in the temple last night." The old coolie shook his finger, lifted his eyebrows, and assumed a very gnomish appearance indeed.

A certain trickle of dismay went through the American. He tried to keep from moistening his lips and perhaps he did, but all he could think to do was to lift his eyebrows and say:

"Was there, indeed?"

"Yes—and a white man!"

Lowe, the bank clerk, who had been sitting silent through all this, interrupted. "Surely not, Mr. Hira Dass, not a white man!"

"All five of the coolies and my man Gooka told me it was true," reiterated the old man, "and I have always found Gooka a truthful man. And besides, such a man would fill the role of assailant exactly. He would be well-to-do, accustomed to using money to forward his purposes."

The psychologist made a sort of mental lunge to refute this rapid array of evidence old Hira Dass was piling up against him.

"But, Mr. Hira Dass, decapitation is not an American mode of murder."

"American!"

"I—I was speaking generally," stammered the psychologist, "I mean a white man's method of murder."

"That is indicative in itself," returned the Hindu promptly. "I meant to call your attention to that point. It shows the white man was a highly educated man, who had studied the mental habit of other peoples than his own, so he was enabled to give the crime an extraordinary resemblance to a Hindu crime. I would suggest, gentlemen, that you begin your search for an intellectual white man."

"What motive could such a man have?" cried the American.

"Robbery, possibly, or if he were a very intellectual man indeed he might have murdered the poor child by way of experiment. I read not long ago in an American paper of two youths who committed such a crime."

"A murder for experiment!" cried Lowe, aghast.

"Yes, to record the psychological reaction."

Poggioli suddenly got to his feet.

"I can't agree with such a theory as that, Mr. Hira Dass," he said in a shaken voice.

"No, it's too far-fetched," declared the clerk at once.

"However, it is worth while investigating," persisted the Hindu.

"Yes, yes," agreed the American, evidently about to depart, "but I shall begin my investigations, gentlemen, with the man Gooka."

"As you will," agreed Hira Dass, "and in your investigations, gentlemen, hire any assistants you need, draw on me for any amount. I want my nephew exonerated, and above all things, I want the real criminal apprehended and brought to the gallows."

Lowe nodded.

"We'll do our best, sir," he answered in his thorough-going English manner.

The old man followed his guests to the gate and bowed them out into the malodorous alleyway again.

As the two friends set off through the hot sunshine once more the bank clerk laughed.

"A white man in that temple! That sounds like pure fiction to me to shield Boodman Lal. You know these coolies hang together like thieves."

He walked on a little way pondering, then added, "Jolly good thing we didn't decide to sleep in the temple last night, isn't it, Poggioli?"

A sickish feeling went over the American. For a moment he was tempted to tell his host frankly what he had done and ask his advice in the matter, but finally he said:

"In my opinion the actual criminal is Boodman Lal."

Lowe glanced around sidewise at his guest and nodded faintly.

"Same here. I thought it ever since I first saw the account in the *Inquirer.* Somehow these coolies will chop their wives to pieces for no reason at all."

"I know a very good reason in this instance," retorted the American warmly, taking out his uneasiness in this manner. "It's these damned child marriages! When a man marries some child he doesn't care a tuppence for—what do you know about Boodman Lal anyway?"

"All there is to know. He was born here and has always been a figure here in Port of Spain because of his rich uncle."

"Lived here all his life?"

"Except when he was in Oxford for six years."

"Oh, he's an Oxford man!"

"Yes."

"There you are, there's the trouble."

"What do you mean?"

"No doubt he fell in love with some English girl. But when his wealthy uncle, Hira Dass, chose a Hindu child for his wife, Boodman could not refuse the marriage. No man is going to quarrel with a million-pound legacy, but he chose this ghastly method of getting rid of the child."

"I venture you are right," declared the bank clerk. "I felt sure Boodman Lal had killed the girl."

"Likely as not he was engaged to some English girl and was waiting for his uncle's death to make him wealthy."

"Quite possible, in fact probable."

Here a cab came angling across the square toward the two men as they stood in front of the grotesque temple. The Negro driver waved his whip interrogatively. The clerk beckoned him in. The cab drew up at the curb. Lowe climbed in but Poggioli remained on the pavement.

"Aren't you coming?"

"You know, Lowe," said Poggioli seriously, "I don't feel that I can conscientiously continue this investigation, trying to clear a person whom I have every reason to believe guilty."

The bank clerk was disturbed.

"But, man, don't leave me like this! At least come on to the police headquarters and explain your theory about the temple keeper, Gooka, and the rice. That seems to hang together pretty well. It is possible Boodman Lal didn't do this thing after all. We owe it to him to do all we can."

As Poggioli still hung back on the curb, Lowe asked:

"What do you want to do?"

"Well, I—er—thought I would go back to the cottage and pack my things."

The bank clerk was amazed.

"Pack your things—your boat doesn't sail until Friday!"

"Yes, I know, but there is a daily service to Curaçao. It struck me to go—"

"Aw, come!" cried Lowe in hospitable astonishment, "you can't run off like that, just when I've stirred up an interesting murder mystery for you to unravel. You ought to appreciate my efforts as a host more than that."

"Well, I do," hesitated Poggioli seriously. At that moment his excess of caution took one of those odd, instantaneous shifts that come so unaccountably to men, and he thought to himself, "Well, damn it, this is an interesting situation. It's a shame to leave it, and nothing will happen to me."

So he swung into the cab with decision and ordered briskly: "All right, to the police station, Sambo!"

"Sounds more like it," declared the clerk, as the cab horses set out a brisk trot through the sunshine.

Mr. Lowe, the bank clerk, was not without a certain flair for making the most of a house guest, and when he reached the police station he introduced his companion to the chief of police as "Mr. Poggioli a professor in an American university and a research student in criminal psychology."

The chief of police, a Mr. Vickers, was a short, thick man with a tropic-browned face and eyes habitually squinted against the sun. He seemed not greatly impressed with the titles Lowe gave his friend but merely remarked that if Mr. Poggioli was hunting crimes, Trinidad was a good place to find them.

The bank clerk proceeded with a certain importance in his manner.

"I have asked his counsel in the Boodman Lal murder case. He has developed a theory, Mr. Vickers, as to who is the actual murderer of Mrs. Boodman Lal."

"So have I," replied Vickers with a dry smile.

"Of course you think Boodman Lal did it," said Lowe in a more commonplace manner.

Vickers did not answer this but continued looking at the two taller men in a listening attitude which caused Lowe to go on.

"Now in this matter, Mr. Vickers, I want to be perfectly frank with you. I'll admit we are in this case in the employ of Mr. Hira Dass, and are making an effort to clear Boodman Lal. We felt confident you would use the well-known skill of the police department of Port of Spain to work out a theory to clear Boodman Lal just as readily as you would to convict him."

"Our department usually devotes its time to conviction and not to clearing criminals."

"Yes, I know that, but if our theory will point out the actual murderer—"

"What is your theory?" inquired Vickers without enthusiasim.

The bank clerk began explaining the dream of the five beggars and the probability that they had been given sleeping potions.

The short man smiled faintly.

"So Mr. Poggioli's theory is based on the dreams of these men?"

Poggioli had a pedagogue's brevity of temper when his theories were questioned.

"It would be a remarkable coincidence, Mr. Vickers, if five men had lurid dreams simultaneously without some physical cause. It suggests strongly that their tea or rice was doped."

As Vickers continued looking at Poggioli the American continued with less acerbity:

"I should say that Gooka, the temple keeper, either doped the rice himself or he knows who did it."

"Possibly he does."

"My idea is that you send a man for the ricepot and teapot, have their contents analyzed, find out what soporific was used, then have your men search the sales records of the drugstores in the city to see who has lately bought such a drug."

Mr. Vickers grunted a noncommittal uh-huh, and then began in the livelier tones of a man who meets a stranger socially:

"How do you like Trinidad, Mr. Poggioli?"

"Remarkably luxuriant country—oranges and grapefruit growing wild."

"You've just arrived?"

"Yes."

"In what university do you teach?"

"Ohio State."

Mr. Vickers's eyes took on a humorous twinkle.

"A chair of criminal psychology in an ordinary state university—is that the result of your American Prohibition laws, professor?"

Poggioli smiled at this thrust.

"Mr. Lowe misstated my work a little. I am not a professor, I am simply a docent. And I have not specialized on criminal psychology. I quiz on general psychology."

"You are not teaching now?"

"No; this is my sabbatical year."

Mr. Vickers glanced up and down the American.

"You look young to have taught in a university six years."

There was something not altogether agreeable in this observation, but the officer rectified it a moment later by saying, "But you Americans start young—land of specialists. Now you, Mr. Poggioli—I suppose you are wrapped up heart and soul in your psychology?"

"I am," agreed the American positively.

"Do anything in the world to advance yourself in the science?"

"I rather think so," asserted Poggioli, with his enthusiasm mounting in his voice.

"Especially keen on original research work—"

Lowe interrupted, laughing.

"That's what he is, chief. Do you know what he asked me to do yesterday afternoon?"

"No, what?"

The American turned abruptly on his friend.

"Now, Lowe, don't let's burden Mr. Vickers with household anecdotes."

"But I am really curious," declared the police chief. "Just what did Professor Poggioli ask you to do yesterday afternoon, Mr. Lowe?"

The bank clerk looked from one to the other, hardly knowing whether to go on or not. Mr. Vickers was smiling; Poggioli was very serious as he prohibited anecdotes about himself. The bank clerk thought: "This is real modesty." He said aloud: "It was just a little psychological experiment he wanted to do."

"Did he do it?" smiled the chief.

"Oh, no, I wouldn't hear of it."

"As unconventional as that!" cried Mr. Vickers, lifting sandy brows.

"It was really nothing," said Lowe, looking at his guest's rigid face and then at the police captain.

Suddenly Mr. Vickers dropped his quizzical attitude.

"I think I could guess your anecdote if I tried, Lowe. About a half hour ago I received a telephone message from my man stationed at the Hindu temple to keep a lookout for you and Mr. Poggioli."

The American felt a tautening of his muscles at this frontal attack. He had suspected something of the sort from the policeman's manner. The bank clerk stared at the officer in amazement.

"What was your bobby telephoning about us for?"

"Because one of the coolies under arrest told him that Mr. Poggioli slept in the temple last night."

"My word, that's not true!" cried the bank clerk. "That is exactly what he did not do. He suggested it to me but I said no. You remember, Poggioli—"

Mr. Lowe turned for corroboration, but the look on his friend's face amazed him.

"You didn't do it, did you Poggioli?" he gasped.

"You see he did," said Vickers dryly.

"But, Poggioli—in God's name—"

The American braced himself for an attempt to explain. He lifted his hand with a certain pedagogic mannerism.

"Gentlemen, I—I had a perfectly valid, an important reason for sleeping in the temple last night."

"I told you," nodded Vickers.

"In coolie town, in a coolie temple!" ejaculated Lowe.

"Gentlemen, I—can only ask your—your sympathetic attention to what I am about to say."

"Go on," said Vickers.

"You remember, Lowe, you and I were down there watching a wedding procession. Well, just as the music stopped and the line of coolies entered the building, suddenly it seemed to me as if—as if—they had—" Poggioli swallowed at nothing and then added the odd word, "vanished."

Vickers looked at him.

"Naturally, they had gone into the building."

"I don't mean that. I'm afraid you won't understand what I do mean

—that the whole procession had ceased to exist, melted into nothingness."

Even Mr. Vickers blinked. Then he drew out a memorandum book and stolidly made a note.

"Is that all?"

"No, then I began speculating on what had given me such a strange impression. You see that is really the idea on which the Hindus base their notion of heaven—oblivion, nothingness."

"Yes, I've heard that before."

"Well, our medieval Gothic architecture was a conception of our Western heaven; and I thought perhaps the Indian architecture had somehow caught the motif of the Indian religion; you know, suggested nirvana. That was what amazed and intrigued me. That was why I wanted to sleep in the place. I wanted to see if I could further my shred of impression. Does this make any sense to you, Mr. Vickers?"

"I daresay it will, sir, to the criminal judge," opined the police chief cheerfully.

The psychologist felt a sinking of heart.

Mr. Vickers proceeded in the same matter-of-fact tone: "But no matter why you went in, what you did afterward is what counts. Here in Trinidad nobody is allowed to go around chopping off heads to see how it feels."

Poggioli looked at the officer with a ghastly sensation in his midriff.

"You don't think I did such a horrible thing as an experiment?"

Mr. Vickers drew out the makings of a cigarette.

"You Americans, especially you intellectual Americans, do some pretty stiff things, Mr. Poggioli. I was reading about two young intellectuals—"

"Good Lord!" quivered the psychologist with this particular reference beginning to grate on his nerves.

"These fellows I read about also tried to turn an honest penny by their murder—I don't suppose you happened to notice yesterday that the little girl, Maila Ran, was almost covered over with gold bangles and coins?"

"Of course I noticed it!" cried the psychologist, growing white, "but I had nothing whatever to do with the child. Your insinuations are brutal and repulsive. I did sleep in the temple—"

"By the way," interrupted Vickers suddenly, "you say you slept on a rug just as the coolies did?"

"Yes, I did."

"You didn't wake up either?"

"No."

"Then did the murderer of the child happen to put a coin and a bangle in your pockets, just as he did the other sleepers in the temple?"

"That's exactly what he did!" cried Poggioli, with the first ray of hope breaking upon him. "When I found them in my pocket on the tram this morning I came pretty near throwing them away, but fortunately I didn't. Here they are."

And gladly enough now he drew the trinkets out and showed them to the chief of police.

Mr. Vickers looked at the gold pieces, then at the psychologist.

"You don't happen to have any more, do you?"

The American said no, but it was with a certain thrill of anxiety that he began turning out his other pockets. If the mysterious criminal had placed more than two gold pieces in his pockets he would be in a very difficult position. However, the remainder of his belongings were quite legitimate.

"Well, that's something," admitted Vickers slowly. "Of course, you might have expected just such a questioning as this and provided yourself with these two pieces of gold, but I doubt it. Somehow, I don't believe you are a bright enough man to think of such a thing." He paused, pondering, and finally said, "I suppose you have no objection to my sending a man to search your baggage in Mr. Lowe's cottage?"

"Instead of objecting, I invite it, I request it."

Mr. Vickers nodded agreeably.

"Who can I telegraph to in America to learn something about your standing as a university man?"

"Dean Ingram, Ohio State, Columbus, Ohio, U.S.A."

Vickers made this note, then turned to Lowe.

"I suppose you've known Mr. Poggioli for a long time, Mr. Lowe?"

"Why n-no, I haven't," admitted the clerk.

"Where did you meet him?"

"Sailing from Barbuda to Antigua. On the *Trevemore.*"

"Did he seem to have respectable American friends aboard?"

Lowe hesitated and flushed faintly.

"I—can hardly say."

"Why?"

"If I tell you Mr. Poggioli's mode of travel I am afraid you would hold it to his disadvantage."

"How did he travel?" queried the officer in surprise.

"The fact is he traveled as a deck passenger."

"You mean he had no cabin, shipped along on deck with the Negroes!"

"I did it myself!" cried Lowe, growing ruddy. "We couldn't get a cabin —they were all occupied."

The American reflected rapidly, and realized that Vickers could easily find out the real state of things from the ship's agents up the islands.

"Chief," said the psychologist with a tongue that felt thick, "I boarded the *Trevemore* at St. Kitts. There were cabins available. I chose deck passage deliberately. I wanted to study the natives."

"Then you are broke, just as I thought," ejaculated Mr. Vickers, "and I'll bet pounds to pence we'll find the jewelry around your place somewhere."

The chief hailed a passing cab, called a plainclothesman, put the three in the vehicle and started them briskly back up Prince Edward's Street, toward Tragarette Road, and thence to Lowe's cottage beyond the Indian village and its ill-starred temple.

The three men and the Negro driver trotted back up Tragarette, each lost in his own thoughts. The plainclothesman rode on the front seat with the cabman, but occasionally he glanced back to look at his prisoner. Lowe evidently was reflecting how this contretemps would affect his social and business standing in the city. The Negro also kept peering back under the hood of his cab, and finally he ejaculated:

"Killum jess to see 'em die. I declah, dese 'Mericans—" and he shook his kinky head.

A hot resentment rose up in the psychologist at this continued recurrence of that detestable crime. He realized with deep resentment that the crimes of particular Americans were held tentatively against all American citizens, while their great national charities and humanities were forgotten with the breath that told them. In the midst of these angry thoughts the cab drew up before the clerk's garden gate.

All got out. Lowe let them in with a key and then the three walked in a kind of grave haste across the lawn. The door was opened by Ram Jon, who took their hats and then followed them into the room Lowe had set apart for his guest.

This room, like all Trinidad chambers, was furnished in the sparest and coolest manner possible; a table, three chairs, a bed with sheets, and Poggioli's trunk. It was so open to inspection nothing could have been concealed in it. The plainclothesman opened the table drawer.

"Would you mind opening your trunk, Mr. Poggioli?"

The American got out his keys, knelt and undid the hasp of his wardrobe trunk, then swung the two halves apart. One side held containers, the other suits. Poggioli opened the drawers casually; collar and handkerchief box at the top, hat box, shirt box. As he did this came a faint clinking sound. The detective stepped forward and lifted out the shirts. Beneath them lay a mass of coins and bangles flung into the tray helter-skelter.

The American stared with an open mouth, unable to say a word.

The plainclothesman snapped with a certain indignant admiration in his voice: "Your nerve almost got you by!"

The thing seemed unreal to the American. He had the same uncanny feeling that he had experienced when the procession entered the temple. Materiality seemed to have slipped a cog. A wild thought came to him that somehow the Hindus had dematerialized the gold and caused it to reappear in his trunk. Then there came a terrifying fancy that he had committed the crime in his sleep. This last clung to his mind. After all, he had murdered the little girl bride, Maila Ran!

The plainclothesman spoke to Lowe:

"Have your man bring me a sack to take this stuff back to headquarters."

Ram Jon slithered from the room and presently returned with a sack. The inspector took his handkerchief, lifted the pieces out with it, one by one, and placed them in the sack.

"Lowe," said Poggioli pitifully, "you don't believe I did this, do you?"

The bank clerk wiped his face with his handkerchief.

"In your trunk, Poggioli—"

"If I did it I was sleepwalking!" cried the unhappy man. "My God, to think it is possible—but right here in my own trunk—" he stood staring at the bag, at the shirt box.

The plainclothesman said dryly: "We might as well start back, I suppose. This is all."

Lowe suddenly cast in his lot with his guest.

"I'll go back with you, Poggioli. I'll see you through this pinch. Somehow I can't, I won't believe you did it!"

"Thanks! Thanks!"

The bank clerk masked his emotion under a certain grim facetiousness.

"You know, Poggioli, you set out to clear Boodman Lal—it looks as if you've done it."

"No, he didn't," denied the plainclothesman. "Boodman Lal was out of jail at least an hour before you fellows drove up a while ago."

"Out—had you turned him out?"

"Yes."

"How was that?"

"Because he didn't go to the temple at all last night with his wife. He went down to Queen's Park Hotel and played billiards till one o'clock. He called up some friends and proved that easily enough."

Lowe stared at his friend, aghast.

"My word, Poggioli, that leaves nobody but—you." The psychologist lost all semblance of resistance.

"I don't know anything about it. If I did it I was asleep. That's all I can say. The coolies—" He had a dim notion of accusing them again, but he recalled that he had proved to himself clearly and logically that they were innocent. "I don't know anything about it," he repeated helplessly.

Half an hour later the three men were at police headquarters once more, and the plainclothesman and the turnkey, a humble, gray sort of man, took the American back to a cell. The turnkey unlocked one in a long row of cells and swung it open for Poggioli.

The bank clerk gave him what encouragement he could.

"Don't be too downhearted. I'll do everything I can. Somehow I believe you are innocent. I'll hire your lawyers, cable your friends—"

Poggioli was repeating a stunned "Thanks! Thanks!" as the cell door shut between them. The bolt clashed home and was locked. And the men were tramping down the iron corridor. Poggioli was alone.

There was a chair and a bunk in the cell. The psychologist looked at these with an irrational feeling that he would not stay in the prison long enough to warrant his sitting down. Presently he did sit down on the bunk.

He sat perfectly still and tried to assemble his thoughts against the mountain of adverse evidence which suddenly had been piled against him. His sleep in the temple, the murder, the coins in his shirt box—after all he must have committed the crime in his sleep.

As he sat with his head in his hands pondering this theory, it grew more and more incredible. To commit the murder in his sleep, to put the coins in the pockets of the beggars in a clever effort to divert suspicion, to bring the gold to Lowe's cottage, and then to go back and lie down on the mat, all while he was asleep—that was impossible. He could not believe any human being could perform so fantastic, so complicated a feat.

On the other hand, no other criminal would place the whole booty in Poggioli's trunk and so lose it. That too was irrational. He was forced back to his dream theory.

When he accepted this hypothesis he wondered just what he had dreamed. If he had really murdered the girl in a nightmare, then the murder was stamped somewhere in his subconscious, divided from his day memories by the nebulous associations of sleep. He wondered if he could reproduce them.

To recall a lost dream is perhaps one of the nicest tasks that ever a human brain was driven to. Poggioli, being a psychologist, had had a certain amount of experience with such attempts. Now he lay down on his bunk and began the effort in a mechanical way.

He recalled as vividly as possible his covert exit from Lowe's cottage, his walk down Tragarette Road between perfumed gardens, the lights of Peru, and finally his entrance into the temple. He imagined again the temple attendant, Gooka, looking curiously at him, but giving him tea and rice and pointing out his rug. Poggioli remembered that he lay down on the rug on his back with his hands under his head exactly as he was now lying on his cell bunk. For a while he had stared at the illuminated image of Krishna, then at the dark spring of the dome over his head.

And as he lay there, gazing thus, his thoughts had begun to waver, to lose beat with his senses, to make misinterpretations. He had thought that the Krishna moved slightly, then settled back and became a statue again —here some tenuous connection in his thoughts snapped, and he lost his whole picture in the hard bars of his cell again.

Poggioli lay relaxed a while, then began once more. He reached the point where the Krishna moved, seemed about to speak, and then—there he was back in his cell.

It was nerve-racking, tantalizing, this fishing for the gossamers of a dream which continually broke; this pursuing the grotesqueries of a nightmare and trying to connect it with his solid everyday life of thought and action. What had he dreamed?

Minutes dragged out as Poggioli pursued the vanished visions of his head. Yes, it had seemed to him that the image of the Buddha moved, that it had even risen from its attitude of meditation, and suddenly, with a little thrill, Poggioli remembered that the dome of the Hindu temple was opened and this left him staring upward into a vast abyss. It seemed to the psychologist that he stared upward, and the Krishna stared upward, both gazing into an unending space, and presently he realized that he and the great upward-staring Krishna were one; that they had always been one; and that their oneness filled all space with enormous, with infinite power. But this oneness which was Poggioli was alone in an endless, featureless space. No other thing existed, because nothing had ever been created; there was only a Creator. All the creatures and matter which had ever been or ever would be were wrapped up in him, Poggioli, or Buddha. And then Poggioli saw that space and time had ceased to be, for space and time are the offspring of division. And at last Krishna or Poggioli was losing all entity or being in this tranced immobility.

And Poggioli began struggling desperately against nothingness. He writhed at his deadened muscles, he willed in torture to retain some vestige of being, and at last after what seemed millenniums of effort he formed the thought:

"I would rather lose my oneness with Krishna and become the vilest and poorest of creatures—to mate, fight, love, lust, kill, and be killed than to be lost in this terrible trance of the universal!"

And when he had formed this tortured thought Poggioli remembered that he had awakened and it was five o'clock in the morning. He had arisen with a throbbing headache and had gone home.

That was his dream.

The American arose from his bunk filled with the deepest satisfaction from his accomplishment. Then he recalled with surprise that all five of the coolies had much the same dream; grandiloquence and power accompanied by great unhappiness.

"That was an odd thing," thought the psychologist, "six men dreaming the same dream in different terms. There must have been some physical cause for such a phenomenon."

Then he remembered that he had heard the same story from another source. Old Hira Dass in his marble court had expressed the same sentiment, complaining of the emptiness of his riches and power. However— and this was crucial—Hira Dass's grief was not a mere passing nightmare, it was his settled condition.

With this a queer idea popped into Poggioli's mind. Could not these six dreams have been a transference of an idea? While he and the coolies lay sleeping with passive minds, suppose old Hira Dass had entered the temple with his great unhappiness in his mind, and suppose he had committed some terrible deed which wrought his emotions to a monsoon of passion. Would not his horrid thoughts have registered themselves in different forms on the minds of the sleeping men!

Here Poggioli's ideas danced about like the molecules of a crystal in solution, each one rushing of its own accord to take its appointed place in a complicated crystalline design. And so a complete understanding of the murder of little Maila Ran rushed in upon him.

Poggioli leaped to his feet and halloed his triumph.

"Here, Vickers! Lowe! Turnkey! I have it! I've solved it! Turn me out! I know who killed the girl!"

After he had shouted for several minutes Poggioli saw the form of a man coming up the dark aisle with a lamp. He was surprised at the lamp but passed over it.

"Turnkey!" he cried, "I know who murdered the child—old Hira Dass! Now listen—" He was about to relate his dream, but realized that would avail nothing in an English court, so he leaped to the physical end of the crime, matter with which the English juggle so expertly. His thoughts danced into shape.

"Listen, turnkey, go tell Vickers to take that gold and develop all the fingerprints on it—he'll find Hira Dass's prints! Also, tell him to follow out that opiate clue I gave him—he'll find Hira Dass's servant bought the opiate. Also, Hira Dass sent a man to put the gold in my trunk. See if you can't find brass or steel filings in my room where the scoundrel sat and filed a new key. Also, give Ram Jon the third degree; he knows who brought the gold."

The one with the lamp made a gesture.

"They've done all that, sir, long ago."

"They did!"

"Certainly, sir, and old Hira Dass confessed everything, though why a rich old man like him should have murdered a pretty child is more than I can see. These Hindus are unaccountable, sir, even the millionaires."

Poggioli passed over so simple a query.

"But why did the old devil pick on me for a scapegoat?" he cried, puzzled.

"Oh, he explained that to the police, sir. He said he picked on a white man so the police would make a thorough investigation and be sure to catch him. In fact, he said, sir, that he had willed that you should come and sleep in the temple that night."

Poggioli stared with a little prickling sensation at this touch of the occult world.

"What I can't see, sir," went on the man with the lamp, "was why the old coolie wanted to be caught and hanged—why didn't he commit suicide?"

"Because then his soul would have returned in the form of some beast.

He wanted to be slain. He expects to be reborn instantly in Benares with little Maila Ran. He hopes to be a great man with wife and children."

"Nutty idea!" cried the fellow.

But the psychologist sat staring at the lamp with a queer feeling that possibly such a fantastic idea might be true after all. For what goes with this passionate, uneasy force in man when he dies? May not the dead struggle to reanimate themselves as he had done in his dream? Perhaps the numberless dead still will to live and be divided; and perhaps living things are a result of the struggles of the dead, and not the dead of the living.

His thoughts suddenly shifted back to the present.

"Turnkey," he snapped with academic sharpness, "why didn't you come and tell me of old Hira Dass's confession the moment it occurred? What did you mean, keeping me locked up here when you knew I was an innocent man?"

"Because I couldn't," said the form with the lamp sorrowfully, "Old Hira Dass didn't confess until a month and ten days after you were hanged, sir."

And the lamp went out.

The Case of the Emerald Sky

ERIC AMBLER

Few people realize that Eric Ambler, the author of such brilliant spy novels as A Coffin for Dimitrious *and* Dirty Story *and unquestionably one of the finest writers of espionage fiction in the English language, also wrote a series of "straight" detective short stories early in his career. These tales, which chronicle the cases of Dr. Jan Czissar, a refugee from Czechoslovakia who insinuates himself into Scotland Yard investigations, are quite different in tone and conception from Mr. Ambler's thrillers. "The Case of the Emerald Sky" is perhaps the best of them and amply demonstrates the more cerebral side of the author's talents.*

Assistant Commissioner Mercer of Scotland Yard stared, without speaking, at the card which Sergeant Flecker had placed before him.

There was no address, simply

DR. JAN CZISSAR
Late Prague Police

It was an inoffensive-looking card. An onlooker, who knew only that Dr. Czissar was a refugee Czech with a brilliant record of service in the criminal investigation department of the Prague police, would have been surprised at the expression of dislike that spread slowly over the assistant commissioner's healthy face.

Yet, had the same onlooker known the circumstances of Mercer's first encounter with Dr. Czissar, he would not have been surprised. Just one week had elapsed since Dr. Czissar had appeared out of the blue with a letter of introduction from the mighty Sir Herbert at the home office, and Mercer was still smarting as a result of the meeting.

Sergeant Flecker had seen and interpreted the expression. Now he spoke.

"Out, sir?"

Mercer looked up sharply. "No, sergeant. In, but too busy," he snapped.

Half an hour later Mercer's telephone rang.

"Sir Herbert to speak to you from the home office, sir," said the operator.

Sir Herbert said, "Hello, Mercer, is that you?" And then, without waiting for a reply: "What's this I hear about your refusing to see Dr. Czissar?"

Mercer jumped but managed to pull himself together. "I did not refuse to see him, Sir Herbert," he said with iron calm. "I sent down a message that I was too busy to see him."

Sir Herbert snorted. "Now look here, Mercer; I happen to know that it was Dr. Czissar who spotted those Seabourne murderers for you. Not blaming you, personally, of course, and I don't propose to mention the matter to the commissioner. You can't be right every time. We all know that as an organization there's nothing to touch Scotland Yard. My point is, Mercer, that you fellows ought not to be above learning a thing or two from a foreign expert. Clever fellows, these Czechs, you know. No question of poaching on your preserves. Dr. Czissar wants no publicity. He's grateful to this country and eager to help. Least we can do is to let him. We don't want any professional jealousy standing in the way."

If it were possible to speak coherently through clenched teeth, Mercer would have done so. "There's no question either of poaching on preserves or of professional jealousy, Sir Herbert. I was, as Dr. Czissar was informed, busy when he called. If he will write in for an appointment, I shall be pleased to see him."

"Good man," said Sir Herbert cheerfully. "But we don't want any of this red-tape business about writing in. He's in my office now. I'll send him over. He's particularly anxious to have a word with you about this Brock Park case. He won't keep you more than a few minutes. Good-bye."

Mercer replaced the telephone carefully. He knew that if he had replaced it as he felt like replacing it, the entire instrument would have been smashed. For a moment or two he sat quite still. Then, suddenly, he snatched the telephone up again.

"Inspector Cleat, please." He waited. "Is that you, Cleat? Is the commissioner in? . . . I see. Well, you might ask him as soon as he comes in if he could spare me a minute or two. It's urgent. Right."

He hung up again, feeling a little better. If Sir Herbert could have words with the commissioner, so could he. The old man wouldn't stand for his subordinates being humiliated and insulted by pettifogging politicians. Professional jealousy!

Meanwhile, however, this precious Dr. Czissar wanted to talk about the Brock Park case. Right! Let him! He wouldn't be able to pull that to pieces. It was absolutely watertight. He picked up the file on the case which lay on his desk.

Yes, absolutely watertight.

Three years previously, Thomas Medley, a widower of sixty with two adult children, had married Helena Merlin, a woman of forty-two. The four had since lived together in a large house in the London suburb of Brock Park. Medley, who had amassed a comfortable fortune, had retired from business shortly before his second marriage, and had devoted most of his time since to his hobby, gardening. Helena Merlin was an artist, a landscape painter, and in Brock Park it was whispered that her pictures sold for large sums. She dressed fashionably and smartly, and was disliked by her neighbors. Harold Medley, the son aged twenty-five, was a medical student at a London hospital. His sister, Janet, was three years younger, and as dowdy as her stepmother was smart.

In the early October of that year, and as a result of an extra heavy meal, Thomas Medley had retired to bed with a bilious attack. Such attacks had not been unusual. He had had an enlarged liver, and had been normally dyspeptic. His doctor had prescribed in the usual way. On his third day in bed the patient had been considerably better. On the fourth day, however, at about four in the afternoon, he had been seized with violent abdominal pains, persistent vomiting, and severe cramps in the muscles of his legs.

These symptoms had persisted for three days, on the last of which there had been convulsions. He had died that night. The doctor had certified the death as being due to gastroenteritis. The dead man's estate had amounted to, roughly, one hundred and ten thousand pounds. Half of it went to his wife. The remainder was divided equally between his two children.

A week after the funeral, the police had received an anonymous letter suggesting that Medley had been poisoned. Subsequently, they had received two further letters. Information had then reached them that several residents in Brock Park had received similar letters, and that the matter was the subject of gossip.

Medley's doctor was approached later. He had reasserted that the death had been due to gastroenteritis, but admitted that the possibility of the condition having been brought by the willful administration of poison had not occurred to him. The body had been exhumed by license of the home secretary, and an autopsy performed. No traces of poison had been found in the stomach; but in the liver, kidneys and spleen a total of 1.751 grains of arsenic had been found.

Inquiries had established that on the day on which the poisoning symptoms had appeared, the deceased had had a small luncheon consisting of breast of chicken, spinach (canned), and one potato. The cook had partaken of spinach from the same tin without suffering any ill effects. After his luncheon, Medley had taken a dose of the medicine prescribed for him by the doctor. It had been mixed with water for him by his son, Harold.

Evidence had been obtained from a servant that, a fortnight before the death, Harold had asked his father for one hundred pounds to settle a racing debt. He had been refused. Inquiries had revealed that Harold had lied. He had been secretly married for some time, and the money had been needed not to pay racing debts but for his wife, who was about to have a child.

The case against Harold had been conclusive. He had needed money desperately. He had quarreled with his father. He had known that he was the heir to a quarter of his father's estate. As a medical student in a hospital, he had been in a position to obtain arsenic. The poisoning that appeared had shown that the arsenic must have been administered at about the time the medicine had been taken. It had been the first occasion on which Harold had prepared his father's medicine.

The coroner's jury had boggled at indicting him in their verdict, but he had later been arrested and was now on remand. Further evidence from the hospital as to his access to supplies of arsenical drugs had been forthcoming. He would certainly be committed for trial.

Mercer sat back in his chair. A watertight case. Sentences began to form in his mind. "This Dr. Czissar, Sir Charles, is merely a time-wasting crank. He's a refugee and his sufferings have probably unhinged him a little. If you could put the matter to Sir Herbert, in that light . . ."

And then, for the second time that afternoon, Dr. Czissar was announced.

Mercer was angry, yet, as Dr. Czissar came into the room, he became conscious of a curious feeling of friendliness toward him. It was not entirely the friendliness that one feels toward an enemy one is about to destroy. In his mind's eye he had been picturing Dr. Czissar as an ogre. Now, Mercer saw that, with his mild eyes behind their thick spectacles, his round, pale face, his drab raincoat and his unfurled umbrella, Dr.

Czissar was, after all, merely pathetic. When, just inside the door, Dr. Czissar stopped, clapped his umbrella to his side as if it were a rifle, and said loudly: "Dr. Jan Czissar. Late Prague Police. At your service." Mercer very nearly smiled.

Instead he said: "Sit down, doctor. I am sorry I was too busy to see you earlier."

"It is so good of you . . ." began Dr. Czissar earnestly.

"Not at all, doctor. You want, I hear, to compliment us on our handling of the Brock Park case."

Dr. Czissar blinked. "Oh, no, Assistant Commissioner Mercer," he said anxiously. "I would like to compliment, but it is too early, I think. I do not wish to seem impolite, but . . ."

Mercer smiled complacently. "Oh, we shall convict our man, all right, doctor. I don't think you need to worry."

Dr. Czissar's anxiety became painful to behold. "Oh, but I do worry. You see—" he hesitated diffidently, "—he is not guilty."

Mercer hoped that the smile with which he greeted the statement did not reveal his secret exultation. He said blandly, "Are you aware, doctor, of all the evidence against him?"

"I attended the inquest," said Dr. Czissar mournfully. "But there will be more evidence from the hospital, no doubt. This young Mr. Harold could no doubt have stolen enough arsenic to poison a regiment without the loss being discovered."

The fact that the words had been taken out of his mouth disconcerted Mercer only slightly. He nodded. "Exactly."

A faint, thin smile stretched the doctor's full lips. He settled his glasses on his nose. Then he cleared his throat, swallowed hard and leaned forward. "Attention, please," he said sharply.

For some reason that he could not fathom, Mercer felt his self-confidence ooze suddenly away. He had seen that same series of actions, ending with the peremptory demand for attention, performed once before, and it had been the prelude to humiliation, to . . . He pulled himself up sharply. The Brock Park case was watertight. He was being absurd.

"I'm listening," he said.

"Good." Dr. Czissar wagged one solemn finger. "According to the medical evidence given at the inquest, arsenic was found in the liver, kidneys and spleen. No?"

Mercer nodded firmly. "One point seven five one grains. That shows that much more than a fatal dose had been administered. Much more."

Dr. Czissar's eyes gleamed. "Ah, yes. Much more. It is odd, is it not, that so much was found in the kidneys?"

"Nothing odd at all about it."

"Let us leave the point for the moment. Is it not true, Assistant Commissioner Mercer, that all postmortem tests for arsenic are for arsenic itself and not for any particular arsenic salt?"

Mercer frowned. "Yes, but it's unimportant. All arsenic salts are deadly poisons. Besides, when arsenic is absorbed by the human body, it turns to the sulphide. I don't see what you are driving at, doctor."

"My point is this, assistant commissioner, that usually it is impossible to tell from a delayed autopsy which form of arsenic was used to poison the body. You agree? It might be arsenious oxide, or one of the arsenates or arsenites, copper arsenite, for instance; or it might be a chloride, or it might be an organic compound of arsenic."

"Precisely."

"But," continued Dr. Czissar, "what sort of arsenic should we expect to find in a hospital, eh?"

Mercer pursed his lips. "I see no harm in telling you, doctor, that Harold Medley could easily have secured supplies of either salvarsan or neosalvarsan. They are both important drugs."

"Yes, indeed," said Dr. Czissar. "Very useful in one-tenth of a gram doses, but very dangerous in larger quantities." He stared at the ceiling. "Have you seen any of Helena Merlin's paintings, assistant commissioner?"

The sudden change of subject took Mercer unawares. He hesitated. Then: "Oh, you mean Mrs. Medley. No, I haven't seen any of her paintings."

"Such a chic, attractive woman," said Dr. Czissar. "After I had seen her at the inquest I could not help wishing to see some of her work. I found some in a gallery near Bond Street." He sighed. "I had expected something clever, but I was disappointed. She paints what she thinks instead of what is."

"Really? I'm afraid, doctor, that I must . . ."

"I felt," persisted Dr. Czissar, bringing his cowlike eyes once more to Mercer's, "that the thoughts of a woman who thinks of a field as blue and of a sky as emerald green must be a little strange."

"Modern stuff, eh?" said Mercer shortly. "I don't much care for it, either. And now, doctor, if you've finished, I'll ask you to excuse me. I . . ."

"Oh, but I have not finished yet," said Dr. Czissar kindly. "I think, assistant commissioner, that a woman who paints a landscape with a green sky is not only strange, but also interesting, don't you? I asked the gentlemen at the gallery about her. She produces only a few pictures—about six a year. He offered to sell me one of them for fifteen guineas. She earns one hundred pounds a year from her work. It is wonderful how expensively she dresses on that sum."

"She had a rich husband."

"Oh, yes. A curious household, don't you think? The daughter Janet is especially curious. I was so sorry that she was so much upset by the evidence at the inquest."

"A young woman probably would be upset at the idea of her brother being a murderer," said Mercer drily.

"But to accuse herself so violently of the murder. That was odd."

"Hysteria. You get a lot of it in murder cases." Mercer stood up and held out his hand. "Well, doctor, I'm sorry you haven't been able to upset our case this time. If you'll leave your address with the sergeant as you go, I'll see that you get a pass for the trial," he added with relish.

But Dr. Czissar did not move. "You are going to try this young man for murder, then?" he said slowly. "You have not understood what I have been hinting at?"

Mercer grinned. "We've got something better than hints, doctor—a first-class circumstantial case against young Medley. Motive, time and method of administration, source of the poison. Concrete evidence, doctor! Juries like it. If you can produce one scrap of evidence to show that we've got the wrong man, I'll be glad to hear it."

Dr. Czissar's back straightened, and his cowlike eyes flashed. He said, sharply, "I, too, am busy. I am engaged on a work on medical jurisprudence. I desire only to see justice done. I do not believe that on the evidence you have you can convict this young man under English law; but the fact of his being brought to trial could damage his career as a doctor. Furthermore, there is the real murderer to be considered. Therefore, in a spirit of friendliness, I have come to you instead of going to Harold Medley's legal advisers. I will now give you your evidence."

Mercer sat down again. He was very angry. "I am listening," he said grimly; "but if you . . ."

"Attention, please," said Dr. Czissar. He raised a finger. "Arsenic was found in the dead man's kidneys. It is determined that Harold Medley could have poisoned his father with either salvarsan or neosalvarsan. There is a contradiction there. Most inorganic salts of arsenic, white arsenic, for instance, are practically insoluble in water, and if a quantity of such a salt had been administered, we might expect to find traces of it in the kidneys. Salvarsan and neosalvarsan, however, are compounds of arsenic and are very soluble in water. If either of them had been administered through the mouth, we should *not* expect to find arsenic in the kidneys."

He paused; but Mercer was silent.

"In what form, therefore, was the arsenic administered?" he went on. "The tests do not tell us, for they detect only the presence of the element, arsenic. Let us then look among the inorganic salts. There is white arsenic, that is arsenious oxide. It is used for dipping sheep. We would not expect to find it in Brock Park. But Mr. Medley was a gardener. What about sodium arsenite, the weed-killer? But we heard at the inquest that the weed-killer in the garden was of the kind harmful only to weeds. We come to copper arsenite. Mr. Medley was, in my opinion, poisoned by a large dose of copper arsenite."

"And on what evidence," demanded Mercer, "do you base that opinion?"

"There is, or there has been, copper arsenite in the Medleys' house." Dr. Czissar looked at the ceiling. "On the day of the inquest, Mrs. Medley wore a fur coat. I have since found another fur coat like it. The price of the coat was four hundred guineas. Inquiries in Brock Park have told me that this lady's husband, besides being a rich man, was also a very mean and unpleasant man. At the inquest, his son told us that he had kept his marriage a secret because he was afraid that his father would stop his allowance or prevent his continuing his studies in medicine. Helena Medley had expensive tastes. She had married this man so that she could indulge them. He had failed her. That coat she wore, assistant commissioner, was unpaid for. You will find, I think, that she had other debts, and that a threat had been made by one of the creditors to approach her husband. She was tired of this man so much older than she was—this man who did not even justify his existence by spending his fortune on her. She poisoned her husband. There is no doubt of it."

"Nonsense!" said Mercer. "Of course we know that she was in debt. We are not fools. But lots of women are in debt. It doesn't make them murderers. Ridiculous!"

"All murderers are ridiculous," agreed Dr. Czissar solemnly; "especially the clever ones."

"But how on earth . . . ?" began Mercer.

Dr. Czissar smiled gently. "It was the spinach that the dead man had for luncheon before the symptoms of poisoning began that interested me," he said. "Why give spinach when it is out of season? Canned vegetables are not usually given to an invalid with gastric trouble. And then, when I saw Mrs. Medley's paintings, I understood. The emerald sky, assistant commissioner. It was a fine, rich emerald green, that sky—*the sort of emerald green that the artist gets when there is aceto-arsenite of copper in the paint!* The firm which supplies Mrs. Medley with her working materials will be able to tell you when she bought it. I suggest, too, that you take the picture—it is in the Summons Gallery—and remove a little of the sky for analysis. You will find that the spinach was prepared at her suggestion and taken to her husband's bedroom by her. Spinach is *green* and *slightly bitter* in taste. *So is copper arsenite.*" He sighed. "If there had not been anonymous letters . . ."

"Ah!" interrupted Mercer. "The anonymous letters! Perhaps you know . . ."

"Oh, yes," said Dr. Czissar simply. "The daughter Janet wrote them. Poor child! She disliked her smart stepmother and wrote them out of spite. Imagine her feelings when she found that she had—how do you say? —put a noose about her brother's throat. It would be natural for her to try to take the blame herself."

The telephone rang and Mercer picked up the receiver.

"The commissioner to speak to you, sir," said the operator.

"All right. Hello . . . Hello, Sir Charles. Yes, I did want to speak to you urgently. It was—" He hesitated. "—It was about the Brock Park case. I think that we will have to release young Medley. I've got hold of some new medical evidence that . . . Yes, yes, I realize that, Sir Charles, and I'm very sorry that . . . All right, Sir Charles, I'll come immediately."

He replaced the telephone.

Dr. Czissar looked at his watch. "But it is late and I must get to the museum reading room before it closes." He stood up, clapped his umbrella to his side, clicked his heels and said loudly: "Dr. Jan Czissar. Late Prague Police. At your service!"

The Other Hangman

JOHN DICKSON CARR

In his distinguished forty-year career, John Dickson Carr created two superior detectives, Dr. Gideon Fell and Sir Henry Merrivale, and some of the finest locked room and "impossible crime" novels and stories ever written. Almost all of his work is of the fair-play, classical crime-puzzle variety, and yet one story considered by many Carr aficionados to be among his top five short tales is a substantial departure in both style and content. Set in rural Pennsylvania, where Carr was born, "The Other Hangman" recounts the events surrounding a most unusual execution by hanging.

"Why do they electrocute 'em instead of hanging 'em in Pennsylvania? What" (said my old friend, Judge Murchison, dexterously hooking the spittoon closer with his foot) "do they teach you youngsters in these new-fangled law schools, anyway? That, son, *was* a murder case. It turned the Supreme Court's whiskers gray to find a final ruling, and for thirty years it's been argued about by lawyers in the back room of every saloon from here to the Pacific coast. It happened right here in this county— when they hanged Fred Joliffe for the murder of Randall Fraser.

"It was in '92 or '93; anyway, it was the year they put the first telephone in the court house, and you could talk as far as Pittsburgh except when the wires blew down. Considering it was the county seat, we were mighty proud of our town (population thirty-five hundred). The hustlers were always bragging about how thriving and growing our town was, and we had just got to the point of enthusiasm where every ten years we were certain the census taker must have forgotten half our population. Old Mark Sturgis, who owned the *Bugle Gazette* then, carried on something awful in an editorial when they printed in the almanac that we had a population of only 3265. We were all pretty riled about it, naturally.

"We were proud of plenty of other things, too. We had good reason to brag about the McClellan House, which was the finest hotel in the county; and I mind when you could get room and board, with apple pie for breakfast every morning, for two dollars a week. We were proud of our old county families, that came over the mountains when Braddock's army was scalped by the Indians in 1755, and settled down in log huts to dry their wounds. But most of all we were proud of our legal batteries.

"Son, it was a grand assembly! Mind, I won't say that all of 'em were long on knowledge of the statute books; but they knew their *Blackstone* and their *Greenleaf on Evidence,* and they were powerful speakers. *And* there were some—the top-notchers—full of graces and book knowledge and dignity, who were hell on the exact letter of the law. Scotch-Irish Presbyterians, all of us, who loved a good debate and a bottle o' whiskey. There was Charley Connell, a Harvard graduate and the district attorney, who had fine white hands, and wore a fine high collar, and made such pathetic addresses to the jury that people flocked for miles around to hear him; though he generally lost his cases. There was Judge Hunt, who prided himself on his resemblance to Abe Lincoln, and in consequence always wore a frock coat and an elegant plug hat. Why, there was your own grandfather, who had over two hundred books in his library, and people used to go up nights to borrow volumes of the encyclopedia.

"You know the big stone court house at the top of the street, with the flowers round it, and the jail adjoining? People went there as they'd go to a picture show nowadays; it was a lot better, too. Well, from there it was only two minutes' walk across the meadow to Jim Riley's saloon. All the cronies gathered there—in the back room, of course, where Jim had an elegant brass spittoon and a picture of George Washington on the wall to make it dignified. You could see the footpath worn across the grass until they built over that meadow. Besides the usual crowd, there was Bob Moran, the sheriff, a fine, strapping big fellow, but very nervous about doing his duty strictly. And there was poor old Nabors, a big, quiet, reddish-eyed fellow, who'd been a doctor before he took to drink. He was always broke, and he had two daughters—one of 'em consumptive—and Jim Riley pitied him so much that he gave him all he wanted to drink for nothing. Those were fine, happy days, with a power of eloquence and theorizing and solving the problems of the nation in that back room, until our wives came to fetch us home.

"Then Randall Fraser was murdered, and there was hell to pay.

"Now if it had been anybody else but Fred Joliffe who killed him, naturally we wouldn't have convicted. You can't do it, son, not in a little community. It's all very well to talk about the power and grandeur of justice, and sounds fine in a speech. But here's somebody you've seen walking the streets about his business every day for years; and you know when his kids were born, and saw him crying when one of 'em died; and you remember how he loaned you ten dollars when you needed it. . . .

Well, you can't take that person out in the cold light of day and string him up by the neck until he's dead. You'd always be seeing the look on his face afterwards. And you'd find excuses for him no matter what he did.

"But with Fred Joliffe it was different. Fred Joliffe was the worst and nastiest customer we ever had, with the possible exception of Randall Fraser himself. Ever seen a copperhead curled up on a flat stone? And a copperhead's worse than a rattlesnake—that won't strike unless you step on it, and gives warning before it does. Fred Joliffe had the same brownish color and sliding movements. You always remembered his pale little eye and his nasty grin. When he drove his cart through town—he had some sort of rag-and-bone business, you understand—you'd see him sitting up there, a skinny little man in a brown coat, peeping round the side of his nose to find something for gossip. And grinning.

"It wasn't merely the things he said about people behind their backs. Or to their faces, for that matter, because he relied on the fact that he was too small to be thrashed. He was a slick customer. It was believed that he wrote those anonymous letters that caused . . . but never mind that. Anyhow, I can tell you his little smirk *did* drive Will Farmer crazy one time, and Will *did* beat him within an inch of his life. Will's livery stable was burnt down one night a month later, with eleven horses inside, but nothing could ever be proved. He was too smart for us.

"That brings me to Fred Joliffe's only companion—I don't mean friend. Randall Fraser had a harness-and-saddle store in Market Street, a dusty place with a big dummy horse in the window. I reckon the only thing in the world Randall liked was that dummy horse, which was a dappled mare with vicious-looking glass eyes. He used to keep its mane combed. Randall was a big man with a fine mustache, a horseshoe pin in his tie, and sporty checked clothes. He was buttery polite, and mean as sin. He thought a dirty trick or a swindle was the funniest joke he ever heard. But the women liked him—a lot of them, it's no denying, sneaked in at the back door of that harness store. Randall itched to tell it at the barbershop, to show what fools they were and how virile he was; but he had to be careful. He and Fred Joliffe did a lot of drinking together.

"Then the news came. It was in October, I think, and I heard it in the morning, when I was putting on my hat to go down to the office. Old Withers was the town constable then. He got up early in the morning, although there was no need for it; and, when he was going down Market Street in the mist about five o'clock, he saw the gas still burning in the back room of Randall's store. The front door was wide open. Withers went in and found Randall lying on a pile of harness in his shirt sleeves, and his forehead and face bashed in with a wedging mallet. There wasn't much left of the face, but you could recognize him by his mustache and his horseshoe pin.

"I was in my office when somebody yelled up from the street that they had found Fred Joliffe drunk and asleep in the flour mill, with blood on his hands and an empty bottle of Randall Fraser's whiskey in his pocket. He was still in bad shape, and couldn't walk or understand what was going on, when the sheriff—that was Bob Moran I told you about—came to take him to the lockup. Bob had to drive him in his own rag-and-bone cart. I saw them drive up Market Street in the rain, Fred lying in the back of the cart all white with flour, and rolling and cursing. People were very quiet. They were pleased, but they couldn't show it.

"That is, all except Will Farmer, who had owned the livery stable that was burnt down.

" 'Now they'll hang him,' says Will. 'Now, by God they'll hang him.'

"It's a funny thing, son: I didn't realize the force of that until I heard Judge Hunt pronounce sentence after the trial. They appointed me to defend him, because I was a young man without any particular practice, and somebody had to do it. The evidence was all over town before I got a chance to speak with Fred. You could see he was done for. A scissors-grinder who lived across the street (I forget his name now) had seen Fred go into Randall's place about eleven o'clock. An old couple who lived up over the store had heard 'em drinking and yelling downstairs; at near on midnight they'd heard a noise like a fight and a fall; but they knew better than to interfere. Finally, a couple of farmers driving home from town at midnight had seen Fred stumble out of the front door, slapping his clothes and wiping his hands on his coat like a man with delirium tremens.

"I went to see Fred at the jail. He was sober, although he jerked a good deal. Those pale watery eyes of his were as poisonous as ever. I can still see him sitting on the bunk in his cell, sucking a brown-paper cigarette, wriggling his neck, and jeering at me. He wouldn't tell me anything, because he said I would go and tell the judge if he did.

" 'Hang *me?*' he says, and wrinkled his nose and jeered again. 'Hang *me?* Don't you worry about that, mister. Them so-and-so's will never hang me. They're too much afraid of me, them so-and-so's are. Eh, mister?'

"And the fool couldn't get it through his head right up until the sentence. He strutted away in court; making smart remarks, and threatening to tell what he knew about people, and calling the judge by his first name. He wore a dew dickey shirt front he bought to look spruce in.

"I was surprised how quietly everybody took it. The people who came to the trial didn't whisper or shove; they just sat still as death, and looked at him. All you could hear was a kind of breathing. It's funny about a courtroom, son: it has its own particular smell, which won't bother you unless you get to thinking about what it means, but you notice worn places and cracks in the walls more than you would anywhere else. You would hear Charley Connell's voice for the prosecution, a little thin sound in a big room, and Charley's footsteps creaking. You would hear a cough in the audience, or a woman's dress rustle, or the gas-jets whistling. It was dark in the rainy season, so they lit the gas-jets by two o'clock in the afternoon.

"The only defense I could make was that Fred had been too drunk to be responsible, and remembered nothing of that night (which he admitted was true). But, in addition to being no defense in law, it was a terrible frost besides. My own voice sounded wrong. I remember that six of the jury had whiskers, and six hadn't; and Judge Hunt, up on the bench with the flag draped on the wall behind his head, looked more like Abe Lincoln than ever. Even Fred Joliffe began to notice. He kept twitching round to look at people, a little uneasylike. Once he stuck out his neck at the jury and screeched: '*Say* something, can'tcha? Do something, can'tcha?'

"They did.

"When the foreman of the jury said: 'Guilty of murder in the first degree,' there was just a little noise from those people. Not a cheer, or anything like that. It hissed out all together, only once, like breath released, but it was terrible to hear. It didn't hit Fred until Judge Hunt was halfway through pronouncing sentence. Fred stood looking round with a wild, half-witted expression until he heard Judge Hunt say: '*And may God have mercy on your soul.*' Then he burst out, kind of pleading and kidding as though this was carrying the joke too far. He said: 'Listen, now, you don't *mean* that, do you? You can't fool me. You're only Jerry Hunt; I know who you are. You can't do that to me.' All of a sudden he began pounding the table and screaming: 'You ain't really agoing to hang me, are you?'

"But we were.

"The date of execution was fixed for the twelfth of November. The order was all signed. '. . . within the precincts of the said county jail, between the hours of 8 and 9 A.M., the said Frederick Joliffe shall be hanged by the neck until he is dead; an executioner to be commissioned by the sheriff for this purpose, and the sentence to be carried out in the presence of a qualified medical practitioner; the body to be interred . . .' And the rest of it. Everybody was nervous. There hadn't been a hanging since any of that crowd had been in office, and nobody knew how to go about it exactly. Old Doc Macdonald, the coroner, was to be there; and of course they got hold of Reverend Phelps the preacher; and Bob Moran's wife was going to cook pancakes and sausage for the last breakfast. Maybe you think that's fool talk. But think for a minute of taking somebody you've known all your life, and binding his arms one cold morning, and walking him out in your own backyard to crack his neck on a rope—all religious and legal, with not a soul to interfere. Then you begin to get scared of the powers of life and death, and the thin partition between.

"Bob Moran was scared white for fear things wouldn't go off properly. He had appointed big, slow-moving, tipsy Ed Nabors as hangman. This was partly because Ed Nabors needed the fifty dollars that was the fee, and partly because Bob had a vague idea that an ex-medical man would be better able to manage an execution. Ed had sworn to keep sober; Bob Moran said he wouldn't get a dime unless he *was* sober; but you couldn't always tell.

"Nabors seemed in earnest. He had studied up the matter of scientific hanging in an old book he borrowed from your grandfather, and he and the carpenter had knocked together a big, shaky-looking contraption in the jail yard. It worked all right in practice, with sacks of meal; the trap went down with a boom that brought your heart up in your throat. But once they allowed for too much spring in the rope, and it tore a sack apart. Then old Doc Macdonald chipped in about that fellow John Lee, in England—and it nearly finished Bob Moran.

"That was late on the night before the execution. We were sitting round the lamp in Bob's office, trying to play stud poker. There were tops and skipping ropes, all kinds of toys, all over the office. Bob let his kids play in there—which he shouldn't have done, because the door out of it led to a corridor of cells with Fred Joliffe in the last one. Of course the few other prisoners, disorderlies and chicken-thieves and the like, had been moved upstairs. Somebody had told Bob that the scent of an execution affects 'em like a cage of wild animals. Whoever it was, he was right. We could hear 'em shifting and stamping over our heads, and one old nigger singing hymns all night long.

"Well, it was raining hard on the tin roof; maybe that was what put

Doc Macdonald in mind of it. Doc was a cynical old devil. When he saw that Bob couldn't sit still, and would throw in his hand without even looking at the buried card, Doc says:

" 'Yes, I hope it'll go off all right. But you want to be careful about that rain. Did you read about that fellow they tried to hang in England?—and the rain had swelled the boards so's the trap wouldn't fall? They stuck him on it three times, but still it wouldn't work . . .'

"Ed Nabors slammed his hand down on the table. I reckon he felt bad enough as it was, because one of his daughters had run away and left him, and the other was dying of consumption. But he was twitchy and reddish about the eyes; he hadn't had a drink for two days, although there was a bottle on the table. He says:

" 'You shut up or I'll kill you. Damn you, Macdonald,' he says, and grabs the edge of the table. 'I tell you nothing *can* go wrong. I'll go out and test the thing again, if you'll let me put the rope around your neck.'

"And Bob Moran says: 'What do you want to talk like that for, anyway, Doc? Ain't it bad enough as it is?' he says. 'Now you've got me worrying about something else,' he says. 'I went down there a while ago to look at him, and he said the funniest thing I ever heard Fred Joliffe say. He's crazy. He giggled and said God wouldn't let them so-and-so's hang him. It was terrible, hearing Fred Joliffe talk like that. What time is it, somebody?'

"I was cold that night. I dozed off in a chair, hearing the rain, and that animal cage snuffling upstairs. The nigger was singing that part of the hymn about while the nearer waters roll, while the tempest still is high.

"They woke me about half past eight to say that Judge Hunt and all the witnesses were out in the jail yard, and they were ready to start the march. Then I realized that they were really going to hang him after all. I had to join behind the procession as I was sworn, but I didn't see Fred Joliffe's face and I didn't want to see it. They had given him a good wash, and a clean flannel shirt that they tucked under at the neck. He stumbled coming out of the cell, and started to go in the wrong direction; but Bob Moran and the constable each had him by one arm. It was a cold, dark, windy morning. His hands were tied behind.

"The preacher was saying something I couldn't catch; everything went off smoothly enough until they got halfway across the jail yard. It's a pretty big yard. I didn't look at the contraption in the middle, but at the witnesses standing over against the wall with their hats off; and I smelled the clean air after the rain, and looked up at the mountains where the sky was getting pink. But Fred Joliffe did look at it, and went down flat on his knees. They hauled him up again. I heard them keep on walking, and go up the steps, which were creaky.

"I didn't look at the contraption until I heard a thumping sound, and we all knew something was wrong.

"Fred Joliffe was not standing on the trap, nor was the bag pulled over his head, although his legs were strapped. He stood with his eyes closed and his face towards the pink sky. Ed Nabors was clinging with both hands to the rope, twirling round a little and stamping on the trap. It didn't budge. Just as I heard Ed crying something about the rain having swelled the boards, Judge Hunt ran past me to the foot of the contraption.

"Bob Moran started cursing pretty obscenely. 'Put him on and try it, anyway,' he says, and grabs Fred's arm. 'Stick that bag over his head and give the thing a chance.'

" 'In His Name,' says the preacher pretty steadily, 'you'll not do it if I can help it.'

"Bob ran over like a crazy man and jumped on the trap with both feet. It was stuck fast. Then Bob turned round and pulled an Ivor-Johnson .45 out of his hip pocket. Judge Hunt got in front of Fred, whose lips were moving a little.

" 'He'll have the law, and nothing but the law,' says Judge Hunt. 'Put that gun away, you lunatic, and take him back to the cell until you can make the thing work. Easy with him, now.'

"To this day I don't think Fred Joliffe had realized what happened. I believe he only had his belief confirmed that they never meant to hang him after all. When he found himself going down the steps again, he opened his eyes. His face looked shrunken and dazed like, but all of a sudden it came to him in a blaze.

" 'I knew them so-and-so's would never hang me,' says he. His throat was so dry he couldn't spit at Judge Hunt, as he tried to do; but he marched straight and giggling across the yard. 'I knew them so-and-so's would never hang me,' he says.

"We all had to sit down a minute, and we had to give Ed Nabors a drink. Bob made him hurry up, although we didn't say much, and he was leaving to fix the trap again when the court-house janitor came bustling into Bob's office.

" 'Call,' says he, 'on the new machine over there. Telephone.'

" 'Lemme out of here!' yells Bob. 'I can't listen to no telephone calls now. Come out and give us a hand.'

" 'But it's from Harrisburg,' says the janitor. 'It's from the governor's office. You got to go.'

" 'Stay here, Bob,' says Judge Hunt. He beckons to me. 'Stay here, and I'll answer it,' he says. We looked at each other in a queer way when we went across the Bridge of Sighs. The court-house clock was striking nine, and I could look down into the yard and see people hammering at the trap. After Judge Hunt had listened to that telephone call he had a hard time putting the receiver back on the hook.

" 'I always believed in Providence, in a way,' says he, 'but I never thought it was so personal like. Fred Joliffe is innocent. We're to call off this business,' says he, 'and wait for a messenger from the governor. He's got the evidence of a woman. . . . Anyway, we'll hear it later.'

"Now, I'm not much of a hand at describing mental states, so I can't tell you exactly what we felt then. Most of all was a fever and horror for fear they had already whisked Fred out and strung him up. But when we looked down into the yard from the Bridge of Sighs we saw Ed Nabors and the carpenter arguing over a crosscut saw on the trap itself; and the blessed morning light coming up in a glory to show us we could knock the ugly contraption to pieces and burn it.

"The corridor downstairs was deserted. Judge Hunt had got his wind back, and, being one of those stern elocutionists who like to make complimentary remarks about God, he was going on something powerful. He sobered up when he saw that the door to Fred Joliffe's cell was open.

" 'Even Joliffe,' says the judge, 'deserves to get this news first.'

"But Fred never did get that news, unless his ghost was listening. I told you he was very small and light. His heels were a good eighteen inches off the floor as he hung by the neck from an iron peg in the wall of the cell. He was hanging from a noose made in a child's skipping rope; black-faced, dead already, with the whites of his eyes showing in slits, and his heels swinging over a kicked-away stool.

"No, son, we didn't think it was suicide for long. For a little while we were stunned, half crazy, naturally. It was like thinking about your troubles at three o'clock in the morning.

"But, you see, Fred's hands were still tied behind him. There was a bump on the back of his head, from a hammer that lay beside the stool. Somebody had walked in there with the hammer concealed behind his back, had stunned Fred when he wasn't looking, had run a slip-knot in that skipping rope, and jerked him up aflapping to strangle there. It was the creepiest part of the business, when we'd got that through our heads, and we began loudly to tell each other where we'd been during the confusion. Nobody had noticed much. I was scared green.

"When we gathered round the table in Bob's office, Judge Hunt took hold of his nerve with both hands. He looked at Bob Moran, at Ed Nabors, at Doc Macdonald, and at me. One of us was the other hangman.

" 'This is a bad business, gentlemen,' says he, clearing his throat a couple of times like a nervous orator before he starts. 'What I want to know is, who under sanity would strangle a man when he thought we intended to do it, anyway, on a gallows?'

"Then Doc Macdonald turned nasty. 'Well,' says he, 'if it comes to that, you might inquire where that skipping rope came from, to begin with.'

" 'I don't get you,' says Bob Moran, bewildered like.

" 'Oh, don't you?' says Doc, and sticks out his whiskers. 'Well, then, who was so dead set on this execution going through as scheduled that he wanted to use a gun when the trap wouldn't drop?'

"Bob made a noise as though he'd been hit in the stomach. He stood looking at Doc for a minute, with his hands hanging down—and then he went for him. He had Doc back across the table, banging his head on the edge, when people began to crowd into the room at the yells. Funny, too; the first one in was the jail carpenter, who was pretty sore at not being told that the hanging had been called off.

" 'What do you want to start fighting for?' he says, fretful like. He was bigger than Bob, and had him off Doc with a couple of heaves. 'Why didn't you tell me what was going on? They say there ain't going to be any hanging. Is that right?'

"Judge Hunt nodded, and the carpenter—Barney Hicks, that's who it was; I remember now—Barney Hicks looked pretty peevish, and says:

" 'All right, all right, but you hadn't ought to fight all over the joint like that.' Then he looks at Ed Nabors. 'What I want is my hammer. Where's my hammer, Ed? I been looking all over the place for it. What did you do with it?'

"Ed Nabors sits up, pours himself four fingers of rye, and swallows it.

" 'Beg pardon, Barney,' says he in the coolest voice I ever heard. 'I must have left it in the cell,' he says, 'when I killed Fred Joliffe.'

"Talk about silences! It was like one of those silences when the magician at the Opera House fires a gun and six doves fly out of an empty box. I couldn't believe it. But I remember Ed Nabors sitting big in the corner by the barred window, in his shiny black coat and string tie. His hands were on his knees, and he was looking from one to the other of us, smiling a little. He looked as old as the prophets then; and he'd got enough liquor to keep the nerve from twitching beside his eye. So he just sat there, very quietly, shifting the plug of tobacco around in his cheek, and smiling.

" 'Judge,' he says in a reflective way, 'you got a call from the governor at Harrisburg, didn't you? Uh-huh. I knew what it would be. A woman had come forward, hadn't she, to confess Fred Joliffe was innocent and she had killed Randall Fraser? Uh-huh. The woman was my daughter. Jessie couldn't face telling it here, you see. That was why she ran away from me and went to the governor. She'd have kept quiet if you hadn't convicted Fred.'

" 'But why . . .' shouts the judge. *'Why . . .'*

" 'It was like this,' Ed goes on in that slow way of his. 'She'd been on pretty intimate terms with Randall Fraser, Jessie had. And both Randall and Fred were having a whooping lot of fun threatening to tell the whole town about it. She was pretty near crazy, I think. And, you see, on the night of the murder Fred Joliffe was too drunk to remember anything that happened. He thought he *had* killed Randall, I suppose, when he woke up and found Randall dead and blood on his hands.

" 'It's all got to come out now, I suppose,' says he, nodding. 'What did happen was that the three of 'em were in that back room, which Fred didn't remember. He and Randall had a fight while they were baiting Jessie; Fred whacked him hard enough with that mallet to lay him out, but all the blood he got was from a big splash over Randall's eye. Jessie . . . Well, Jessie finished the job when Fred ran away, that's all.'

" 'But, you damned fool,' cried Bob Moran, and begins to pound the table, 'why did you have to go and kill Fred when Jessie had confessed?'

" 'You fellows wouldn't have convicted Jessie, would you?' says Ed, blinking round at us. 'No. But, if Fred had lived after her confession, you'd have *had* to, boys. That was how I figured it out. Once Fred learned what did happen, that he wasn't guilty and she was, he'd never have let up until he'd carried that case to the Superior Court out of your hands. He'd have screamed all over the state until they either had to hang her or send her up for life. I couldn't stand that. As I say, that was how I figured it out, although my brain's not so clear these days. So,' says he, nodding and leaning over to take aim at the cuspidor, 'when I heard about that telephone call, I went into Fred's cell and finished *my* job.'

" 'But don't you understand,' says Judge Hunt, in the way you'd reason with a lunatic, 'that Bob Moran will have to arrest you for murder, and—'

"It was the peacefulness of Ed's expression that scared us then. He got up from his chair, and dusted his shiny black coat, and smiled at us.

" 'Oh, no,' says he very clearly. 'That's what you don't understand. You can't do a single damned thing to me. You can't even arrest me.'

" 'He's bughouse,' says Bob Moran.

" 'Am I?' says Ed affably. 'Listen to me. I've committed what you might call a perfect murder, because I've done it legally . . . Judge, what time did you talk to the governor's office, and get the order for the execution to be called off? Be careful now.'

"And I said, with the whole idea of the business suddenly hitting me:

" 'It was maybe five minutes past nine, wasn't it, judge? I remember the court-house clock striking when we were going over the Bridge of Sighs.'

" 'I remember it too,' says Ed Nabors. 'And Doc Macdonald will tell you that Fred Joliffe was dead before ever that clock struck nine. I have in my pocket,' says he, unbuttoning his coat, 'a court order which authorizes me to kill Fred Joliffe, by means of hanging by the neck—which I did—between the hours of eight and nine in the morning—which I also did. And I did it in full legal style before the order was countermanded. Well?'

"Judge Hunt took off his stovepipe hat and wiped his face with a bandana. We all looked at him.

" 'You can't get away with this,' says the judge, and grabs the sheriff's orders off the table. 'You can't trifle with the law in that way. And you can't execute sentence alone. Look here! "In the presence of a qualified medical practitioner." What do you say to that?'

" 'Well, I can produce my medical diploma,' says Ed, nodding again. 'I may be a booze-hister, and mighty unreliable, but they haven't struck me off the register yet. . . . You lawyers are hell on the wording of the law,' says he admiringly, 'and it's the wording that's done for you this time. Until you get the law altered with some fancy words, there's nothing in that document to say that the doctor and the hangman can't be the same person.'

"After a while Bob Moran turned round to the judge with a funny expression on his face. It might have been a grin.

" 'This ain't according to morals,' says he. 'A fine citizen like Fred shouldn't get murdered like that. It's awful. Something's got to be done about it. As you said yourself this morning, judge, he ought to have the law and nothing but the law. Is Ed right, judge?'

" 'Frankly, I don't know,' says Judge Hunt, wiping his face again. 'But, so far as I know, he is. What are you doing, Robert?'

" 'I'm writing him out a check for fifty dollars,' says Bob Moran, surprised like. 'We got to have it all nice and legal, haven't we?' "

The Couple Next Door

MARGARET MILLAR

Margaret Millar is married to the famous mystery writer Ross Macdonald, but hers is a distinctive voice in this field. Much of her work, in novels like Vanish in an Instant *(1952), the Edgar Award-winning* Beast in View *(1955),* A Stranger in my Grave *(1960), and* The Fiend *(1964), involves psychologically disturbed characters.*

Of course, as in "The Couple Next Door," it all depends on what you mean by "psychologically disturbed."

It was by accident that they lived next door to each other, but by design that they became neighbors—Mr. Sands, who had retired to California after a life of crime investigation, and the Rackhams, Charles and Alma. Rackham was a big, innocent-looking man in his fifties. Except for the accumulation of a great deal of money, nothing much had ever happened to Rackham, and he liked to listen to Sands talk, while Alma sat with her knitting, plump and contented, unimpressed by any tale that had no direct bearing on her own life. She was half Rackham's age, but the fullness of her figure, and her air of having withdrawn from life quietly and without fuss, gave her the stamp of middle age.

Two or three times a week Sands crossed the concrete driveway, skirted the eugenia hedge, and pressed the Rackhams' door chime. He stayed for tea or for dinner, to play gin or Scrabble, or just to talk. "That reminds me of a case I had in Toronto," Sands would say, and Rackham would produce martinis and an expression of intense interest, and Alma would smile tolerantly, as if she didn't really believe a single thing Sands, or anyone else, ever said.

They made good neighbors: the Rackhams, Charles younger than his years, and Alma older than hers, and Sands who could be any age at all. . .

It was the last evening of August and through the open window of Sands's study came the scent of jasmine and the sound of a woman's harsh, wild weeping.

He thought at first that the Rackhams had a guest, a woman on a crying jag, perhaps, after a quarrel with her husband.

He went out into the front yard to listen, and Rackman came around the hedge, dressed in a bathrobe.

He said, sounding very surprised, "Alma's crying."

"I heard."

"I asked her to stop. I begged her. She won't tell me what's the matter."

"Women have cried before."

"Not Alma." Rackham stood on the damp grass, shivering, his forehead streaked with sweat. "What do you think we should do about it?"

The *I* had become *we*, because they were good neighbors, and along with the games and the dinners and the scent of jasmine, they shared the sound of a woman's grief.

"Perhaps you could talk to her," Rackham said.

"I'll try."

"I don't think there is anything physically the matter with her. We both had a check-up at the Tracy clinic last week. George Tracy is a good friend of mine—he'd have told me if there was anything wrong."

"I'm sure he would."

"If anything ever happened to Alma I'd kill myself."

Alma was crouched in a corner of the davenport in the living room, weeping rhythmically, methodically, as if she had accumulated a hoard of tears and must now spend them all in one night. Her fair skin was blotched with patches of red, like strawberry birthmarks, and her eyelids were blistered from the heat of her tears. She looked like a stranger to Sands, who had never seen her display any emotion stronger than ladylike distress over a broken teacup.

Rackham went over and stroked her hair. "Alma, dear. What is the matter?"

"Nothing . . . nothing . . ."

"Mr. Sands is here, Alma. I thought he might be able—we might be able—"

But no one was able. With a long shuddering sob, Alma got up and lurched across the room, hiding her blotched face with her hands. They heard her stumble up the stairs.

Sands said, "I'd better be going."

"No, please don't. I—the fact is, I'm scared. I'm scared stiff. Alma's always been so quiet."

"I know that."

"You don't suppose—there's no chance she's losing her mind?"

If they had not been good neighbors Sands might have remarked that

Alma had little mind to lose. As it was, he said cautiously, "She might have had bad news, family trouble of some kind."

"She has no family except me."

"If you're worried, perhaps you'd better call your doctor."

"I think I will."

George Tracy arrived within half an hour, a slight, fair-haired man in his early thirties, with a smooth unhurried manner that imparted confidence. He talked slowly, moved slowly, as if there was all the time in the world to minister to desperate women.

Rackham chafed with impatience while Tracy removed his coat, placed it carefully across the back of the chair, and discussed the weather with Sands.

"It's a beautiful evening," Tracy said, and Alma's moans sliding down the stairs distorted his words, altered their meaning: *a terrible evening, an awful evening.* "There's a touch of fall in the air. You live in these parts, Mr. Sands?"

"Next door."

"For heaven's sake, George," Rackham said, "will you hurry up? For all you know, Alma might be dying."

"That I doubt. People don't die as easily as you might imagine. She's in her room?"

"Yes. Now will you *please*—"

"Take it easy, old man."

Tracy picked up his medical bag and went towards the stairs, leisurely, benign.

"He's always like that." Rackham turned to Sands, scowling. "Exasperating son-of-a-gun. You can bet that if he had a wife in Alma's condition he'd be taking those steps three at a time."

"Who knows?—perhaps he has."

"*I* know," Rackham said crisply. "He's not even married. Never had time for it, he told me. He doesn't look it but he's very ambitious."

"Most doctors are."

"Tracy is, anyway."

Rackham mixed a pitcher of martinis, and the two men sat in front of the unlit fire, waiting and listening. The noises from upstairs gradually ceased, and pretty soon the doctor came down again.

Rackham rushed across the room to meet him. "How is she?"

"Sleeping. I gave her a hypo."

"Did you talk to her? Did you ask her what was the matter?"

"She was in no condition to answer questions."

"Did you find anything wrong with her?"

"Not physically. She's a healthy young woman."

"Not *physically.* Does that mean—?"

"Take it easy, old man."

Rackham was too concerned with Alma to notice Tracy's choice of words, but Sands noticed, and wondered if it had been conscious or unconscious: Alma's a healthy young woman . . . Take it easy, old man.

"If she's still depressed in the morning," Tracy said, "bring her down to the clinic with you when you come in for your X-rays. We have a good neurologist on our staff." He reached for his coat and hat. "By the way, I hope you followed the instructions."

Rackham looked at him stupidly. "What instructions?"

"Before we can take specific X-rays, certain medication is necessary."

"I don't know what you're talking about."

"I made it very clear to Alma," Tracy said, sounding annoyed. "You were to take one ounce of sodium phosphate after dinner tonight, and report to the X-ray department at eight o'clock tomorrow morning without breakfast."

"She didn't tell me."

"Oh."

"It must have slipped her mind."

"Yes. Obviously. Well, it's too late now." He put on his coat, moving quickly for the first time, as if he were in a rush to get away. The change made Sands curious. He wondered why Tracy was suddenly so anxious to leave, and whether there was any connection between Alma's hysteria and her lapse of memory about Rackham's X-rays. He looked at Rackham and guessed, from his pallor and his worried eyes, that Rackham had already made a connection in his mind.

"I understood," Rackham said carefully, "that I was all through at the clinic. My heart, lungs, metabolism—everything fit as a fiddle."

"People," Tracy said, "are not fiddles. Their tone doesn't improve with age. I will make another appointment for you and send you specific instructions by mail. Is that all right with you?"

"I guess it will have to be."

"Well, good night, Mr. Sands, pleasant meeting you." And to Rackham, "Good night, old man."

When he had gone, Rackham leaned against the wall, breathing hard. Sweat crawled down the sides of his face like worms and hid in the collar of his bathrobe. "You'll have to forgive me, Sands. I feel—I'm not feeling very well."

"Is there anything I can do?"

"Yes," Rackham said. "Turn back the clock."

"Beyond my powers, I'm afraid."

"Yes . . . Yes, I'm afraid."

"Good night, Rackham." *Good night, old man.*

"Good night, Sands." *Good night old man to you, too.*

Sands shuffled across the concrete driveway, his head bent. It was a dark night, with no moon at all.

From his study Sands could see the lighted windows of Rackham's bedroom. Rackham's shadow moved back and forth behind the blinds as if seeking escape from the very light that gave it existence. Back and forth, in search of nirvana.

Sands read until far into the night. It was one of the solaces of growing old—if the hours were numbered, at least fewer of them need be wasted in sleep. When he went to bed, Rackham's bedroom light was still on.

They had become good neighbors by design; now, also by design, they became strangers. Whose design it was, Alma's or Rackham's, Sands didn't know.

There was no definite break, no unpleasantness. But the eugenia hedge seemed to have grown taller and thicker, and the concrete driveway a mile away. He saw the Rackhams occasionally; they waved or smiled or said, "Lovely weather," over the backyard fence. But Rackham's smile was thin and painful, Alma waved with a leaden arm, and neither of them cared about the weather. They stayed indoors most of the time, and when they did come out they were always together, arm in arm, walking slowly and in step. It was impossible to tell whose step led, and whose followed.

At the end of the first week in September, Sands met Alma by accident in a drugstore downtown. It was the first time since the night of the doctor's visit that he'd seen either of the Rackhams alone.

She was waiting at the prescription counter wearing a flowery print dress that emphasized the fullness of her figure and the bovine expression of her face. A drugstore length away, she looked like a rather dull, badly dressed young woman with a passion for starchy foods, and it was hard to understand what Rackham had seen in her. But then Rackham had never stood a drugstore length away from Alma; he saw her only in close-up, the surprising, intense blue of her eyes, and the color and texture of her skin, like whipped cream. Sands wondered whether it was her skin and eyes, or her quality of serenity which had appealed most to Rackham, who was quick and nervous and excitable.

She said, placidly, "Why, hello there."

"Hello, Alma."

"Lovely weather, isn't it?"

"Yes. . . . How is Charles?"

"You must come over for dinner one of these nights."

"I'd like to."

"Next week, perhaps. I'll give you a call—I must run now. Charles is waiting for me. See you next week."

But she did not run, she walked; and Charles was not waiting for her, he was waiting for Sands. He had let himself into Sands's house and was pacing the floor of the study, smoking a cigarette. His color was bad, and he had lost weight, but he seemed to have acquired an inner calm. Sands could not tell whether it was the calm of a man who had come to an important decision, or that of a man who had reached the end of his rope and had stopped struggling.

They shook hands, firmly, pressing the past week back into shape.

Rackham said, "Nice to see you again, old man."

"I've been here all along."

"Yes. Yes, I know. . . . I had things to do, a lot of thinking to do."

"Sit down. I'll make you a drink."

"No, thanks. Alma will be home shortly, I must be there."

Like a Siamese twin, Sands thought, *separated by a miracle, but returning voluntarily to the fusion—because the fusion was in a vital organ.*

"I understand," Sands said.

Rackham shook his head. "No one can understand, really, but you come very close sometimes, Sands. Very close." His cheeks flushed, like a boy's. "I'm not good at words or expressing my emotions, but I wanted to thank you before we leave, and tell you how much Alma and I have enjoyed your companionship."

"You're taking a trip?"

"Yes. Quite a long one."

"When are you leaving?"

"Today."

"You must let me see you off at the station."

"No, no," Rackham said quickly. "I couldn't think of it. I hate last-minute depot farewells. That's why I came over this afternoon to say good-bye."

"Tell me something of your plans."

"I would if I had any. Everything is rather indefinite. I'm not sure where we'll end up."

"I'd like to hear from you now and then."

"Oh, you'll hear from me, of course." Rackham turned away with an impatient twitch of his shoulders as if he was anxious to leave, anxious to start the trip right now before anything happened to prevent it.

"I'll miss you both," Sands said. "We've had a lot of laughs together."

Rackham scowled out of the window. "Please, no farewell speeches. They might shake my decision. My mind is already made up, I want no second thoughts."

"Very well."

"I must go now. Alma will be wondering—"

"I saw Alma earlier this afternoon," Sands said.

"Oh?"

"She invited me for dinner next week."

Outside the open window two hummingbirds fought and fussed, darting with crazy accuracy in and out of the bougainvillea vine.

"Alma," Rackham said carefully, "can be very forgetful sometimes."

"Not that forgetful. She doesn't know about this trip you've planned, does she? . . . Does she, Rackham?"

"I wanted it to be a surprise. She's always had a desire to see the world. She's still young enough to believe that one place is different from any other place. . . . You and I know better."

"Do we?"

"Good-bye, Sands."

At the front door they shook hands again, and Rackham again promised to write, and Sands promised to answer his letters. Then Rackham crossed the lawn and the concrete driveway, head bent, shoulders hunched. He didn't look back as he turned the corner of the eugenia hedge.

Sands went over to his desk, looked up a number in the telephone directory, and dialed.

A girl's voice answered, "Tracy clinic, X-ray department."

"This is Charles Rackham," Sands said.

"Yes, Mr. Rackham."

"I'm leaving town unexpectedly. If you'll tell me the amount of my bill I'll send you a check before I go."

"The bill hasn't gone through, but the standard price for a lower gastrointestinal is twenty-five dollars."

"Let's see, I had that done on the—"

"The fifth. Yesterday."

"But my original appointment was for the first, wasn't it?"

The girl gave a does-it-really-matter sigh. "Just a minute, sir, and I'll check." Half a minute later she was back on the line. "We have no record of an appointment for you on the first, sir."

"You're sure of that?"

"Even without the record book, I'd be sure. The first was a Monday. We do only gall bladders on Monday."

"Oh. Thank you."

Sands went out and got into his car. Before he pulled away from the curb he looked over at Rackham's house and saw Rackham pacing up and down the verandah, waiting for Alma.

The Tracy clinic was less impressive than Sands had expected, a converted two-story stucco house with a red tile roof. Some of the tiles were broken and the whole building needed paint, but the furnishings inside were smart and expensive.

At the reception desk a nurse wearing a crew cut and a professional smile told Sands that Dr. Tracy was booked solid for the entire afternoon. The only chance of seeing him was to sit in the second-floor waiting room and catch him between patients.

Sands went upstairs and took a chair in a little alcove at the end of the hall, near Tracy's door. He sat with his face half hidden behind an open magazine. After a while the door of Tracy's office opened and over the top of his magazine Sands saw a woman silhouetted in the door frame—a plump, fair-haired young woman in a flowery print dress.

Tracy followed her into the hall and the two of them stood looking at each other in silence. Then Alma turned and walked away, passing Sands without seeing him because her eyes were blind with tears.

Sands stood up. "Dr. Tracy?"

Tracy turned sharply, surprise and annoyance pinching the corners of his mouth. "Well? Oh, it's Mr. Sands."

"May I see you a moment?"

"I have quite a full schedule this afternoon."

"This is an emergency."

"Very well. Come in."

They sat facing each other across Tracy's desk.

"You look pretty fit," Tracy said with a wry smile, "for an emergency case."

"The emergency is not mine. It may be yours."

"If it's mine, I'll handle it alone, without the help of a poli—I'll handle it myself."

Sands leaned forward. "Alma has told you, then, that I used to be a policeman."

"She mentioned it in passing."

"I saw Alma leave a few minutes ago. . . . She'd be quite a nice-looking woman if she learned to dress properly."

"Clothes are not important in a woman," Tracy said, with a slight flush. "Besides, I don't care to discuss my patients."

"Alma is a patient of yours?"

"Yes."

"Since the night Rackham called you when she was having hysterics?"

"Before then."

Sands got up, went to the window, and looked down at the street.

People were passing, children were playing on the sidewalk, the sun shone, the palm trees rustled with wind—everything outside seemed normal and human and real. By contrast, the shape of the idea that was forming in the back of his mind was so grotesque and ugly that he wanted to run out of the office, to join the normal people passing on the street below. But he knew he could not escape by running. The idea would follow him, pursue him until he turned around and faced it.

It moved inside his brain like a vast wheel, and in the middle of the wheel, impassive, immobile, was Alma.

Tracy's harsh voice interrupted the turning of the wheel. "Did you come here to inspect my view, Mr. Sands?"

"Let's say, instead, your viewpoint."

"I'm a busy man. You're wasting my time."

"No. I'm giving you time."

"To do what?"

"Think things over."

"If you don't leave my office immediately, I'll have you thrown out." Tracy glanced at the telephone but he didn't reach for it, and there was no conviction in his voice.

"Perhaps you shouldn't have let me in. Why did you?"

"I thought you might make a fuss if I didn't."

"Fusses aren't in my line." Sands turned from the window. "Liars are, though."

"What are you implying?"

"I've thought a great deal about that night you came to the Rackhams' house. In retrospect, the whole thing appeared too pat; too contrived: Alma had hysterics and you were called to treat her. Natural enough, so far."

Tracy stirred but didn't speak.

"The interesting part came later. You mentioned casually to Rackham that he had an appointment for some X-rays to be taken the following day, September the first. It was assumed that Alma had forgotten to tell him. Only Alma *hadn't* forgotten. There was nothing to forget. I checked with your X-ray department half an hour ago. They have no record of any appointment for Rackham on September the first.

"Records get lost."

"This record wasn't lost. It never existed. You lied to Rackham. The lie itself wasn't important, it was the *kind* of lie. I could have understood a lie of vanity, or one to avoid punishment or to gain profit. But this seemed such a silly, senseless, little lie. It worried me. I began to wonder about Alma's part in the scene that night. Her crying was most unusual for a woman of Alma's inert nature. What if her crying was also a lie? And what was to be gained by it?"

"Nothing," Tracy said wearily. "Nothing was gained."

"But something was *intended*—and I think I know what it was. The scene was played to worry Rackham, to set him up for an even bigger scene. If that next scene has already been played, I am wasting my time here. Has it?"

"You have a vivid imagination."

"No. The plan was yours—I only figured it out."

"Very poor figuring, Mr. Sands." But Tracy's face was gray, as if mold had grown over his skin.

"I wish it were. I had become quite fond of the Rackhams."

He looked down at the street again, seeing nothing but the wheel turning inside his head. Alma was no longer in the middle of the wheel, passive and immobile; she was revolving with the others—Alma and Tracy and Rackham, turning as the wheel turned, clinging to its perimeter.

Alma, devoted wife, a little on the dull side. . . . What sudden passion of hate or love had made her capable of such consummate deceit? Sands imagined the scene the morning after Tracy's visit to the house. Rackham, worried and exhausted after a sleepless night: *"Are you feeling better now, Alma?"*

"Yes."

"What made you cry like that?"

"I was worried."

"About me?"

"Yes."

"Why didn't you tell me about my X-ray appointment?"

"I couldn't. I was frightened. I was afraid they would discover something serious the matter with you."

"Did Tracy give you any reason to think that?"

"He mentioned something about a blockage. Oh, Charles, I'm scared! If anything ever happened to you, I'd die. I couldn't live without you!"

For an emotional and sensitive man like Rackman, it was a perfect set-up: his devoted wife was frightened to the point of hysterics, his good friend and physician had given her reason to be frightened. Rackham was ready for the next step. . . .

"According to the records in your X-ray department," Sands said, "Rackham had a lower gastrointestinal X-ray yesterday morning. What was the result?"

"Medical ethics forbid me to—"

"You can't hide behind a wall of medical ethics that's already full of holes. What was the result?"

There was a long silence before Tracy spoke. "Nothing."

"You found nothing the matter with him?"

"That's right."

"Have you told Rackham that?"

"He came in earlier this afternoon, alone."

"Why alone?"

"I didn't want Alma to hear what I had to say."

"Very considerate of you."

"No, it was not considerate," Tracy said dully. "I had decided to back out of our—our agreement—and I didn't want her to know just yet."

"The agreement was to lie to Rackham, convince him that he had a fatal disease?"

"Yes."

"Did you?"

"No. I showed him the X-rays, I made it clear that there was nothing wrong with him. . . . I tried. I tried my best. It was no use."

"What do you mean?"

"He wouldn't believe me! He thought I was trying to keep the real truth from him." Tracy drew in his breath sharply. "It's funny, isn't it?—after days of indecision and torment I made up my mind to do the right thing. But it was too late. Alma had played her role too well. She's the only one Rackham will believe."

The telephone on Tracy's desk began to ring but he made no move to answer it, and pretty soon the ringing stopped and the room was quiet again.

Sands said, "Have you asked Alma to tell him the truth?"

"Yes, just before you came in."

"She refused?"

Tracy didn't answer.

"She wants him to think he is fatally ill?"

"I—yes."

"In the hope that he'll kill himself, perhaps?"

Once again Tracy was silent. But no reply was necessary.

"I think Alma miscalculated," Sands said quietly. "Instead of planning suicide, Rackham is planning a trip. But before he leaves, he's going to hear the truth—from you and from Alma." Sands went towards the door. "Come on, Tracy. You have a house call to make."

"No. I can't." Tracy grasped the desk with both hands, like a child resisting the physical force of removal by a parent. "I won't go."

"You have to."

"No! Rackham will ruin me if he finds out. That's how this whole thing started. We were afraid, Alma and I, afraid of what Rackham would do if she asked him for a divorce. He's crazy in love with her, he's obsessed!"

"And so are you?"

"Not the way he is. Alma and I both want the same things—a little peace, a little quiet together. We are alike in many ways."

"That I can believe," Sands said grimly. "You want the same things, a little peace, a little quiet—and a little of Rackham's money?"

"The money was secondary."

"A very close second. How did you plan on getting it?"

Tracy shook his head from side to side, like an animal in pain. "You keep referring to plans, ideas, schemes. We didn't start out with plans or schemes. We just fell in love. We've been in love for nearly a year, not daring to do anything about it because I knew how Rackham would react if we told him. I have worked hard to build up this clinic; Rackham could destroy it, and me, within a month."

"That's a chance you'll have to take. Come on, Tracy."

Sands opened the door and the two men walked down the hall, slowly and in step, as if they were handcuffed together.

A nurse in uniform met them at the top of the stairs. "Dr. Tracy, are you ready for your next—?"

"Cancel all my appointments, Miss Leroy."

"But that's imposs—"

"I have a very important house call to make."

"Will it take long?"

"I don't know."

The two men went down the stairs, past the reception desk, and out into the summer afternoon. Before he got into Sands's car, Tracy looked back at the clinic, as if he never expected to see it again.

Sands turned on the ignition and the car sprang forward.

After a time Tracy said, "Of all the people in the world who could have been at the Rackhams' that night, it had to be an ex-policeman."

"It's lucky for you that I was."

"Lucky." Tracy let out a harsh little laugh. "What's lucky about financial ruin?"

"It's better than some other kinds of ruin. If your plan had gone through, you could never have felt like a decent man again."

"You think I will anyway?"

"Perhaps, as the years go by."

"The years." Tracy turned, with a sigh. "What are you going to tell Rackham?"

"Nothing. You will tell him yourself."

"I can't. You don't understand, I'm quite fond of Rackham, and so is Alma. We—it's hard to explain."

"Even harder to understand." Sands thought back to all the times he had seen the Rackhams together and envied their companionship, their mutual devotion. Never, by the slightest glance or gesture of impatience or slip of the tongue, had Alma indicated that she was passionately in love with another man. He recalled the games of Scrabble, the dinners, the endless conversations with Rackham, while Alma sat with her knitting, her face reposeful, content. Rackham would ask, "Don't you want to play too, Alma?" And she would reply. "No, thank you, dear, I'm quite happy with my thoughts."

Alma, happy with her thoughts of violent delights and violent ends.

Sands said, "Alma is equally in love with you?"

"Yes." He sounded absolutely convinced. "No matter what Rackham says or does, we intend to have each other."

"I see."

The blinds of the Rackham house were closed against the sun. Sands led the way up the verandah steps and pressed the door chime, while Tracy stood, stony-faced and erect, like a bill collector or a process server.

Sands could hear the chimes pealing inside the house and feel their vibrations beating under his feet.

He said, "They may have gone already."

"Gone where?"

"Rackham wouldn't tell me. He just said he was planning the trip as a surprise for Alma."

"He can't take her away! He can't force her to leave if she doesn't want to go!"

Sands pressed the door chime again, and called out, "Rackham? Alma?" But there was no response.

He wiped the sudden moisture off his forehead with his coat sleeve. "I'm going in."

"I'm coming with you."

"No."

The door was unlocked. He stepped into the empty hall and shouted up the staircase, "Alma? Rackham? Are you there?"

The echo of his voice teased him from the dim corners.

Tracy had come into the hall. "They've left, then?"

"Perhaps not. They might have just gone out for a drive. It's a nice day for a drive."

"Is it?"

"Go around to the back and see if their car's in the garage."

When Tracy had gone, Sands closed the door behind him and shot the bolt. He stood for a moment listening to Tracy's nervous footsteps on the concrete driveway. Then he turned and walked slowly into the living room, knowing the car would be in the garage, no matter how nice a day it was for a drive.

The drapes were pulled tight across the windows and the room was cool and dark, but alive with images and noisy with the past:

"I wanted to thank you before we leave, Sands."

"You're taking a trip?"

"Yes, quite a long one."

"When are you leaving?"

"Today."

"You must let me see you off at the station. . . ."

But no station had been necessary for Rackham's trip. He lay in front of the fireplace in a pool of blood, and beside him was his companion on the journey, her left arm curving around his waist.

Rackham had kept his promise to write. The note was on the mantel, addressed not to Sands, but to Tracy.

Dear George:

You did your best to fool me but I got the truth from Alma. She could never hide anything from me, we are too close to each other. This is the easiest way out. I am sorry that I must take Alma along, but she has told me so often that she could not live without me. I cannot leave her behind to grieve.

Think of us now and then, and try not to judge me too harshly.

Charles Rackham

Sands put the note back on the mantel. He stood quietly, his heart pierced by the final splinter of irony: before Rackham had used the gun on himself, he had lain down on the floor beside Alma and placed her dead arm lovingly around his waist.

From outside came the sound of Tracy's footsteps and then the pounding of his fists on the front door.

"Sands, I'm locked out. Open the door. Let me in! Sands, do you hear me? Open this door!"

Sands went and opened the door.

Danger Out of the Past

ERLE STANLEY GARDNER

The creator of Perry Mason, Erle Stanley Gardner, was himself a trial lawyer who turned to fiction writing and became an amazing success. He produced hundreds of stories and novels in a wide variety of genres—see, for example, The Human Zero: The Science Fiction Stories of Erle Stanley Gardner *and* Whispering Sands: Stories of Gold Fever and the Western Desert *(both 1981), but it was as a mystery writer that he achieved his greatest fame. One of the great pulpsters, he created several dozen series characters, most of whom still await collection. Though without doubt a gifted writer, his considerable talents have been obscured by the sheer volume of his work, not all of which has been of the same calibre, a phenomenon that has also harmed the reputation of several other writers whose work appears in this book. At his best, though, as in "Danger Out of the Past," Gardner was as good as the best of them.*

The roadside restaurant oozed an atmosphere of peaceful prosperity. It was a green-painted building set in a white graveled circle in the triangle where the two main highways joined.

Five miles beyond, a pall of hazy smog marked the location of the city; but out here at the restaurant the air was pure and crystal clear.

George Ollie slid down from the stool behind the cash register and walked over to look out of the window. His face held an expression which indicated physical well-being and mental contentment.

In the seven short years since he had started working as a cook over the big range in the rear he had done pretty well for himself—exceptionally well for a two-time loser—although no one here knew that, of course. Nor did *anyone* know of that last job where a confederate had lost his head and pulled the trigger . . .

But all that was in the past. George Ollie, president of a luncheon club, member of the Chamber of Commerce, had no connection with that George Ollie who had been prisoner number 56289.

In a way, however, George owed something of his present prosperity to his criminal record. When he had started work in the restaurant, that bank job which had been "ranked" preyed on his mind. For three years he had been intent on keeping out of circulation. He had stayed in his room nights and had perforce saved all the money that he had made.

So, when the owner's heart had given out and it became necessary for him to sell almost on a moment's notice, George was able to make a down payment in cash. From then on, hard work, careful management, and the chance relocation of a main highway had spelled prosperity for the ex-con.

George turned away from the window, looked over the tables at the symmetrical figure of Stella, the head waitress, as she bent over the table taking the orders of the family that had just entered.

Just as the thrill of pride swept through George whenever he looked at the well-kept restaurant, the graveled parking place, and the constantly accelerating stream of traffic which furnished him with a constantly increasing number of customers—so did George thrill with a sense of possessive pride whenever he looked at Stella's smoothly curved figure.

There was no question but what Stella knew how to wear clothes. Somewhere, George thought, there must in Stella's past have been a period of prosperity, a period when she had worn the latest Parisian models with distinction. Now she wore the light-blue uniform, with the white starched cuffs above the elbow and the white collar, with that same air of distinction. She not only classed up the uniforms but she classed up the place.

When Stella walked, the lines of her figure rippled smoothly beneath the clothes. Customers looking at her invariably looked again. Yet Stella was always demure, never forward. She smiled at the right time and in the right manner. If the customer tried to get intimate, Stella always managed to create an atmosphere of urgency so that she gave the impression of an amiable, potentially willing young woman too busy for intimacies.

George could tell from the manner in which she put food down at a table and smilingly hurried back to the kitchen, as though on a matter of the greatest importance, just what was being said by the people at the table—whether it was an appreciative acknowledgment of skillful service, good-natured banter, or the attempt on the part of predatory males to make a date.

But George had never inquired into Stella's past. Because of his own history he had a horror of anything that even hinted of an attempt to inquire into one's past. The present was all that counted.

Stella herself avoided going to the city. She went on a shopping trip once or twice a month, attended an occasional movie, but for the rest stayed quietly at home in the little motel a couple of hundred yards down the roadway.

George was aroused from his reverie by a tapping sound. The man at the counter was tapping a coin on the mahogany. He had entered from the east door and George, contemplating the restaurant, hadn't noticed him.

During this period of slack time in the afternoon Stella was the only waitress on duty. Unexpectedly half a dozen tables had filled up and Stella was busy.

George departed from his customary post at the cash register to approach the man. He handed over a menu, filled a glass with water, arranged a napkin, spoon, knife, and fork, and stood waiting.

The man, his hat pulled well down on his forehead, tossed the menu to one side with a gesture almost of contempt.

"Curried shrimp."

"Sorry," George explained affably, "that's not on the menu today."

"Curried shrimp," the man repeated.

George raised his voice. Probably the other was hard of hearing. "We don't have them today, sir. We have . . ."

"You heard me," the man said. "Curried shrimp. Go get 'em."

There was something about the dominant voice, the set of the man's shoulders, the arrogance of manner, that tugged at George's memory. Now that he thought back on it, even the contemptuous gesture with which the man had tossed the menu to one side without reading it meant something.

George leaned a little closer.

"Larry!" he exclaimed in horror.

Larry Giffen looked up and grinned. "Georgie!" The way he said the name was contemptuously sarcastic.

"When . . . when did you . . . how did you get out?"

"It's okay, Georgie," Larry said. "*I* went out through the front door. Now go get me the curried shrimp."

"Look, Larry," George said, making a pretense of fighting the feeling of futility this man always inspired, "the cook is cranky. I'm having plenty of trouble with the help and . . ."

"You heard me," Larry interrupted. "Curried shrimp!"

George met Larry's eyes, hesitated, turned away toward the kitchen.

Stella paused beside the range as he was working over the special curry sauce.

"What's the idea?" she asked.

"A special."

Her eyes studied his face. "How special?"

"*Very* special."

She walked out.

Larry Giffen ate the curried shrimp. He looked around the place with an air of proprietorship.

"Think maybe I'll go in business with you, Georgie."

George Ollie knew from the dryness in his mouth, the feeling of his knees, that that was what he had been expecting.

Larry jerked his head toward Stella. "She goes with the joint."

Ollie, suddenly angry and belligerent, took a step forward. "She doesn't go with anything."

Giffen laughed, turned on his heel, started toward the door, swung back, said, "I'll see you after closing tonight," and walked out.

It wasn't until the period of dead slack that Stella moved close to George.

"Want to tell me?" she asked.

He tried to look surprised. "What?"

"Nothing."

"I'm sorry, Stella. I can't."

"Why not?"

"He's dangerous."

"To whom?"

"To you—to both of us."

She made a gesture with her shoulder. "You never gain anything by running."

He pleaded with her. "Don't get tangled in it, Stella. You remember last night the police were out here for coffee and doughnuts after running around like mad—those two big jobs, the one on the safe in the bank, the other on the theater safe?"

She nodded.

"I should have known then," he told her. "That's Larry's technique. He never leaves them anything to work on. Rubber gloves so there are no fingerprints. Burglar alarms disconnected. Everything like clockwork. No clues. No wonder the police were nuts. Larry Giffen never leaves them a clue."

She studied him. "What's he got on *you?*"

George turned away, then faced her, tried to speak, and couldn't.

"Okay," she said, "I withdraw the question."

Two customers came in, Stella escorted them to a table and went on with the regular routine. She seemed calmly competent, completely unworried. George Ollie, on the other hand, couldn't get his thoughts together. His world had collapsed. Rubber-glove Giffen must have found out about that bank job with the green accomplice, otherwise he wouldn't have dropped in.

News travels fast in the underworld. Despite carefully cultivated changes in his personal appearance, some smart ex-con while eating at the restaurant must have "made" George Ollie. He had said nothing to George, but had reserved the news as an exclusive for the ears of Larry Giffen. The prison underworld knew Big Larry might have use for George —as a farmer might have use for a horse.

And now Larry had "dropped in."

Other customers arrived. The restaurant filled up. The rush-hour waitresses came on. For two and a half hours there was so much business that George had no chance to think. Then business began to slacken. By eleven o'clock it was down to a trickle. At midnight George closed up.

"Coming over?" Stella asked.

"Not tonight," George said. "I want to do a little figuring on a purchase list."

She said nothing and went out.

George locked the doors, put on the heavy double bolts, and yet, even as he turned out the lights and put the bars in place, he knew that bolts wouldn't protect him from what was coming.

Larry Giffen kicked on the door at twelve-thirty.

George, in the shadows, pretended not to hear. He wondered what Larry would do if he found that George had ignored his threat, had gone away and left the place protected by locks and the law.

Larry Giffen knew better. He kicked violently on the door, then turned and banged it with his heel—banged it so hard that the glass rattled and threatened to break.

George hurried out of the shadows and opened the door.

"What's the idea of keeping me waiting, Georgie?" Larry asked with a solicitude that was overdone to the point of sarcasm. "Don't you want to be chummy with your old friend?"

George said, "Larry, I'm on the square. I'm on the legit. I'm staying that way."

Larry threw back his head and laughed. "You know what happens to rats, Georgie."

"I'm no rat, Larry. I'm going straight, that's all. I've paid my debts to the law and to you."

Larry showed big yellowed teeth as he grinned. "Ain't that nice, Georgie. *All* your debts paid! Now how about that National Bank job where Skinny got in a panic because the cashier didn't get 'em up fast enough?"

"I wasn't in on that, Larry."

Larry's grin was triumphant. "Says you! You were handling the getaway car. The cops got one fingerprint from the rearview mirror. The FBI couldn't classify that one print, but if anyone ever started 'em checking it with *your* file, Georgie, your fanny would be jerked off that cushioned stool by the cash register and transferred to the electric chair—the hot seat, Georgie . . . You never did like the hot seat, Georgie."

George Ollie licked dry lips. His forehead moistened with sweat. He wanted to say something but there was nothing he could say.

Larry went on talking. "I pulled a couple of jobs here. I'm going to pull just one more. Then I'm moving in with you, Georgie. I'm your new partner. You need a little protection. I'm giving it to you."

Larry swaggered over to the cash register, rang up No Sale, pulled the drawer open, raised the hood over the roll of paper to look at the day's receipts.

"Now, Georgie," he said, regarding the empty cash drawer, "you shouldn't have put away all that dough. Where is it?"

George Ollie gathered all the reserves of his self-respect. "Go to hell," he said. "I've been on the square and I'm going to stay on the square."

Larry strode across toward him. His open left hand slammed against the side of George's face with staggering impact.

"You're hot," Larry said, and his right hand swung up to the other side of George's face. "You're hot, Georgie," and his left hand came up from his hip.

George made a pretense at defending himself but Larry Giffen, quick as a cat, strong as a bear, came after him. "You're hot." . . . Wham . . . "You're hot." . . . Wham . . . "You're hot, Georgie."

At length Larry stepped back. "I'm taking a half interest. You'll run it for me when I'm not here, Georgie. You'll keep accurate books. You'll do all the work. Half of the profits are mine. I'll come in once in a while to look things over. Be damn certain that you don't try any cheating, Georgie.

"You wouldn't like the hot squat, Georgie. You're fat, Georgie. You're well fed. You've teamed up with that swivel-hipped babe, Georgie. I could see it in your eye. She's class, and she goes with the place, Georgie. Remember, I'm cutting myself in for a half interest. I'm leaving it to you to see there isn't any trouble."

George Ollie's head was in a whirl. His cheeks were stinging from the heavy-handed slaps of the big man. His soul felt crushed under a weight. Larry Giffen knew no law but the law of power, and Larry Giffen, his little malevolent eyes glittering with sadistic gloating, was on the move, coming toward him again, hoping for an opportunity to beat up on him.

George hadn't known when Stella had let herself in. Her key had opened the door smoothly.

"What's he got on you, George?" she asked.

Larry Giffen swung to the sound of her voice. "Well, well, little Miss Swivel-hips," he said. "Come here, Swivel-hips. I'm half owner in the place now. Meet your new boss."

She stood still, looking from him to George Ollie.

Larry turned to George.

"All right, Georgie, where's the safe? Give me the combination to the safe, Georgie. As your new partner I'll need to have it. I'll handle the day's take. Later on you can keep books, but right now, I need money. I have a heavy date tonight."

George Ollie hesitated a moment, then moved back toward the kitchen.

"I said give *me* the combination to the safe," Larry Giffen said, his voice cracking like a whip.

Stella was looking at him. George had to make it a showdown. "The dough's back here," he said. He moved toward the rack where the big butcher knives were hanging.

Larry Giffen read his mind. Larry had always been able to read him like a book.

Larry's hand moved swiftly. A snub-nosed gun nestled in Larry's big hand.

There was murder in the man's eye but his voice remained silky and taunting.

"Now, Georgie, you must be a good boy. Don't act rough. Remember, Georgie, I've done my last time. No one takes Big Larry alive. Give me the combination to the safe, Georgie. And I don't want any fooling!"

George Ollie reached a decision. It was better to die fighting than to be strapped into an electric chair. He ignored the gun, kept moving back toward the knife rack.

Big Larry Giffen was puzzled for a moment. George had always collapsed like a flat tire when Larry had given an order. This was a new

George Ollie. Larry couldn't afford to shoot. He didn't want noise and he didn't want to kill.

"Hold it, Georgie! You don't need to get rough." Larry put away his gun. "You're hot on that bank job, Georgie. Remember I can send you to the hot squat. That's all the argument I'm going to use, Georgie. You don't need to go for a shiv. Just tell me to walk out, Georgie, and I'll leave. Big Larry doesn't stay where he isn't welcome.

"But you'd better welcome me, Georgie boy. You'd better give me the combination to the safe. You'd better take me in as your new partner. Which is it going to be, Georgie?"

It was Stella who answered the question. Her voice was calm and clear. "Don't hurt him. You'll get the money."

Big Larry looked at her. His eyes changed expression. "Now that's the sort of a broad *I* like. Tell your new boss where the safe is. Start talking, babe, and remember you go with the place."

"There isn't any safe," George said hurriedly. "I banked the money."

Big Larry grinned. "You're a liar. You haven't left the place. I've been casing the joint. Go on, babe, tell me where the hell that safe is. Then Georgie here will give his new partner the combination."

"Concealed back of the sliding partition in the pie counter," Stella said.

"Well, well, well," Larry Giffen observed, "isn't *that* interesting?"

"Please don't hurt him," Stella pleaded. "The shelves lift out . . ."

"Stella!" George Ollie said sharply. "Shut up!"

"The damage has been done now, Georgie boy," Giffen said.

He slid back the glass doors of the pie compartment, lifted out the shelves, put them on the top of the counter, then slid back the partition disclosing the safe door.

"Clever, Georgie boy, clever! You called on your experience, didn't you? And now the combination, Georgie."

Ollie said, "You can't get away with it, Larry. I won't . . ."

"Now, Georgie boy, don't talk that way. I'm your partner. I'm in here fifty-fifty with you. You do the work and run the place and I'll take my half from time to time—But you've been holding out on me for a while, Georgie boy, so everything that's in the safe is part of my half. Come on with the combination—Of course, I could make a spindle job on it, but since I'm a half owner in the joint I hate to damage any of the property. Then you'd have to buy a new safe. The cost of that would have to come out of your half. You couldn't expect *me* to pay for a new safe."

Rubber-glove Giffen laughed at his little joke.

"I said to hell with you," George Ollie said.

Larry Giffen's fist clenched. "I guess you need a damn good working over, Georgie boy. You shouldn't be disrespectful . . ."

Stella's voice cut in. "Leave him alone. I said you'd get the money. George doesn't want any electric chair."

Larry turned back to her. "I like 'em sensible, sweetheart. Later on, I'll tell you about it. Right now it's all business. Business before pleasure. Let's go."

"Ninety-seven four times to the right," Stella said.

"Well, well, well," Giffen observed. "She knows the combination. We both know what that means, Georgie boy, don't we?"

George, his face red and swollen from the impact of the slaps, stood helpless.

"It means she really is part of the place," Giffen said. "I've got a half interest in you too, girlie. I'm looking forward to collecting on that too. Now what's the rest of the combination?"

Giffen bent over the safe; then, suddenly thinking better of it, he straightened, slipped the snub-nosed revolver into his left hand, and said, "Just so you don't get ideas, Georgie boy—but you wouldn't, you know. You don't like the idea of the hot squat."

Stella, white-faced and tense, called out the numbers. Larry Giffen spun the dials on the safe, swung the door open, opened the cash box.

"Well, well, well," he said, sweeping the bills and money into his pocket. "It *was* a good day, wasn't it?"

Stella said, "There's a hundred-dollar bill in the ledger."

Big Larry pulled out the ledger. "So there is, so there is," he said, surveying the hundred-dollar bill with the slightly torn corner. "Girlie, you're a big help. I'm glad you go with the place. I think we're going to get along swell."

Larry straightened, backed away from the safe, stood looking at George Ollie.

"Don't look like that Georgie boy. It isn't so bad. I'll leave you enough profit to keep you in business and keep you interested in the work. I'll just take off most of the cream. I'll drop in to see you from time to time, and, of course, Georgie boy, you won't tell anybody that you've seen me. Even if you did it wouldn't do any good because I came out the front door, Georgie boy. I'm smart. I'm not like you. I don't have something hanging over me where someone can jerk the rug out from under me at any time.

"Well, Georgie boy, I've got to be toddling along. I've got a little job at the supermarket up the street. They put altogether too much confidence in that safe they have. But I'll be back in a couple of hours, Georgie boy. I've collected on part of my investment and now I want to collect on the rest of it. You wait up for me, girlie. You can go get some shut-eye, Georgie."

Big Larry looked at Stella, walked to the door, stood for a moment searching the shadows, then melted away into the darkness.

"You," Ollie said to Stella, his voice showing his heartsickness at her betrayal.

"What?" she asked.

"Telling him about the safe—about that hundred dollars, giving him the combination . . ."

She said, "I couldn't stand to have him hurt you."

"You and the things you can't stand," Ollie said. "You don't know Rubber-glove Giffen. You don't know what you're in for now. You don't . . ."

"Shut up," she interrupted. "If you're going to insist on letting other people do your thinking for you, I'm taking on the job."

He looked at her in surprise.

She walked over to the closet, came out with a wrecking bar. Before he had the faintest idea of what she had in mind she walked over to the cash register, swung the bar over her head, and brought it down with crashing impact on the front of the register. Then she inserted the point of the bar, pried back the chrome steel, jerked the drawer open. She went to the back door, unlocked it, stood on the outside, inserted the end of the wrecking bar, pried at the door until she had crunched the wood of the door jamb.

George Ollie was watching her in motionless stupefaction. "What the devil are you doing?" he asked. "Don't you realize . . . ?"

"Shut up," she said. "What's this you once told me about a spindle job? Oh, yes, you knock off the knob and punch out the spindle—"

She walked over to the safe and swung the wrecking bar down on the knob of the combination, knocking it out of its socket, letting it roll crazily along the floor. Then she went to the kitchen, picked out a towel, polished the wrecking bar clean of fingerprints.

"Let's go," she said to George Ollie.

"Where?" he asked.

"To Yuma," she said. "We eloped an hour and a half ago—or hadn't you heard? We're getting married. There's no delay or red tape in Arizona. As soon as we cross the state line we're free to get spliced. You need someone to do your thinking for you. I'm taking the job.

"And," she went on, as George Ollie stood there, "in this state a husband can't testify against his wife, and a wife can't testify against her husband. In view of what I know now it might be just as well."

George stood looking at her, seeing something he had never seen before —a fierce, possessive something that frightened him at the same time it reassured him. She was like a panther protecting her young.

"But I don't get it," George said. "What's the idea of wrecking the place, Stella?"

"Wait until you see the papers," she told him.

"I still don't get it," he told her.

"You will," she said.

George stood for another moment. Then he walked toward her. Strangely enough he wasn't thinking of the trap but of the smooth contours under her pale blue uniform. He thought of Yuma, of marriage and of security, of a home.

It wasn't until two days later that the local newspapers were available in Yuma. There were headlines on an inside page:

RESTAURANT BURGLARIZED WHILE PROPRIETOR ON HONEYMOON
BIG LARRY GIFFEN KILLED IN GUN BATTLE WITH OFFICERS

The newspaper account went on to state that Mrs. George Ollie had telephoned the society editor from Yuma stating that George Ollie and she had left the night before and had been married in the Gretna Green across the state line. The society editor had asked her to hold the phone and had the call switched to the police.

Police asked to have George Ollie put on the line. They had a surprise for him. It seemed that when the merchant patrolman had made his regular nightly check of Ollie's restaurant at 1 A.M., he found it had been broken into. Police had found a perfect set of fingerprints on the cash register and on the safe. Fast work had served to identify the fingerprints as those of Big Larry Giffen, known in the underworld as Rubber-glove Giffen because of his skill in wearing rubber gloves and never leaving fingerprints. This was one job that Big Larry had messed up. Evidently he had forgotten his gloves.

Police had mug shots of Big Larry and in no time at all they had out a general alarm.

Only that afternoon George Ollie's head waitress and part-time cashier had gone to the head of the police burglary detail. "In case we should ever be robbed," she had said, "I'd like to have it so you could get a conviction when you get the man who did the job. I left a hundred-dollar bill in the safe. I've torn off a corner. Here's the torn corner. You keep it. That will enable you to get a conviction if you get the thief."

Police thought it was a fine idea. It was such a clever idea they were sorry they couldn't have used it to pin a conviction on Larry Giffen.

But Larry had elected to shoot it out with the arresting officers. Knowing his record, officers had been prepared for this. After the sawed-off shotguns had blasted the life out of Big Larry the police had found the bloodstained hundred-dollar bill in his pocket when his body was stripped at the morgue.

Police also found the loot from three other local jobs on him, cash amounting to some seven thousand dollars.

Police were still puzzled as to how it happened that Giffen, known to the underworld as the most artistic box man in the business, had done such an amateurish job at the restaurant. Giffen's reputation was that he had never left a fingerprint or a clue.

Upon being advised that his place had been broken into, George Ollie, popular restaurant owner, had responded in a way which was perfectly typical of honeymooners the world over.

"The hell with business," he had told the police. "I'm on my honeymoon."

A Matter of Public Notice

DOROTHY SALISBURY DAVIS

Frequently nominated for the Edgar Award of the Mystery Writers of America, Dorothy Salisbury Davis is an excellent practitioner of the arts of detection and suspense. Although her characters are often filled with self-doubt and have the odds stacked against them, they usually possess sufficient resiliency of spirit to overcome their opponents and emerge victorious. At her best, as in The Pale Betrayer *(1965),* Where the Dark Streets Go *(1969),* Shock Wave *(1972), and the present selection, she is close to the pinnacle of her field.*

. . . the victim, Mrs. Mary Philips, was the estranged wife of Clement Philips of this city who is now being sought by the police for questioning . . .

Nancy Fox reread the sentence. It was from the Rockland, Minnesota *Gazette,* reporting the latest of three murders to occur in the city within a month. "Estranged wife" was the phrase that gave her pause. Common newspaper parlance it might be, but for her it held a special meaning: for all its commonplaceness, it most often signals the tragic story of a woman suddenly alone—a story that she, Nancy Fox, could tell. Oh, how very well she could tell it!—being now an estranged wife herself.

How, she wondered, had Mary Philips taken her estrangement from a husband she probably once adored? Did he drink? Gamble? Was he unfaithful? Reason enough—any one of them—for some women. Or was it a cruelty surprised in him that had started the falling away of love, piece by piece, like the petals from a wasting flower?

Had the making of the final decision consumed Mary Philips's every thought for months and had the moment of telling it been too terrible to remember? And did it recur, fragmenting the peace it was supposed to have brought? Did the sudden aloneness leave her with the feeling that part of her was missing, that she might never again be a whole person?

Idle questions, surely, to ask now of Mrs. Philips. Mary Philips, age thirty-nine, occupation beauty operator, was dead—strangled at the rear of her shop with an electric cord at the hands of an unknown assailant. And Clement Philips was being sought by the police—in point of fact, by Captain Edward Allan Fox of the Rockland force, which was why Nancy Fox had read the story so interestedly in the first place.

Clement Philips was sought, found, and dismissed, having been two thousand miles from Rockland at the time of Mary Philips's murder. Several others, picked up after each of the three murders, were also dismissed. It was only natural that these suspects were getting testy, talking about their rights.

The chief of police was getting testy also. His was a long history of political survival in Rockland. Only in recent years had his work appeared worthy of public confidence, and that was due to the addition, since the war, of Captain Fox to the force. Fox knew it. No one knew his own worth better than "the Fox" did. And he knew how many years past retirement the old chief had stretched his tenure.

The chief paced back and forth before Captain Fox's desk, grinding one hand into the other behind his back. "I never thought the day would come when we'd turn up such a maniac in this town! He doesn't belong here, Fox!"

"Ah, but he does—by right of conquest," Fox said with the quiet sort of provocation he knew grated on the old man.

The chief whirled on him. "You never had such a good time in your life, did you?"

Fox sighed. He was accustomed to the bombast, the show of wrath that made his superior seem almost a caricature. He did not have to take it: the last of the chief's whipping boys was custodian now of the city morgue. "Once or twice before, sir," Fox said, his eyes unwavering before the chief's.

The old man gave ground. He knew who was running the force, and he was not discontented. He had correctly estimated Fox's ambition: what Fox had of power, he had only with the old man's sanction. "In this morning's brief for me and the mayor, you made quite a thing of the fact that all three victims were separated from their husbands. Now, I'm not very deep in this psychology business—and the missus and I haven't ever been separated more than the weekend it took to bury her sister—so you're going to have to explain what you meant. Does this separation from their husbands make 'em more—ah—attractive? Is that what you're getting at? More willing?"

Fox could feel a sudden pulsethrob at his temple. It was a lecher's picture the old man had conjured with his words and gestures, and his reference to Fox's own vulnerability—Nancy having left him—stirred him to a fury a weaker man would not have been able to control.

But he managed it, saying, "Only more available—and therefore more susceptible to the advances of their assailant."

The old man pulled at the loose skin of his throat. "It's interesting, Fox, how you go at it from the woman's point of view. The mayor says it makes damn good reading."

"Thank you, sir," Fox said for something that obviously was not intended as a compliment. "Do you remember Thomas Coyne?"

"Thomas Coyne," the chief repeated.

"The carpenter—the friend of Elsie Troy's husband," Fox prompted. Elsie Troy had been the first of the three victims. "We've picked him up again. No better alibi this time than last—this time, his landlady. I think he's too damned smug to have the conscience most men live with, so I've set a little trap for him. I thought maybe you'd like to be there."

"Think you can make a case against him?"

Fox rose and took the reports from where the old man had put them. "Chief," he said then, "there are perhaps a half dozen men in Rockland against whom a case could be made . . . including myself."

The old man's jaw sagged. A lot of other people were also unsure of Ed Fox—of the working mechanism they suspected ran him instead of a heart. "Let's see this Coyne fellow," the chief said. "I don't have much taste for humor at a time like this."

"I was only pointing up, sir, that our killer's mania is not apparent to either friends or victims—until it is too late."

The old man grunted and thrust his bent shoulders as far back as they would go—in subconscious imitation of the Fox's military bearing. On the way to the sun room—so called because of the brilliance of its lighting —where Thomas Coyne was waiting, the chief paused and asked, "Is it safe to say for sure now that Elsie Troy was the first victim? That we don't have a transient killer with Rockland just one stop on his itinerary?"

There had been several indications of such a possibility.

"I think we may assume that Elsie Troy was the beginning," Fox said. "I think now that her murder was a random business, unpremeditated. She was killed at night—in her bedroom, with the lights on and the window shades up. She was fully dressed, unmolested. It wasn't a set-up for murder. It was pure luck that someone didn't see it happening.

"But having walked out of Elsie Troy's house a free man, her assailant got a new sense of power—a thrill he'd never had in his life. And then there began in him what amounted to a craving for murder. How he chooses victims, I don't know. That's why I called attention to the . . . the state of suspension in the marriages of the victims." Fox shrugged. "At least, that's my reconstruction of the pattern."

"You make it sound like you were there," the old man said.

"Yes," Fox said, "I suppose I do." He watched the old man bull his neck and plow down the hall ahead of him, contemplating the bit of sadism in himself—in, he suspected, all policemen. It was their devil, as was avarice the plague of merchants, conceit the foe of actors, complacency the doctor's demon, pride the clergyman's. He believed firmly that man's worst enemy was within himself. His own, Fox thought grimly, had cost him a wife, and beyond that, God Almighty knew what else. There were times since Nancy's going when he felt the very structure of his being tremble. There was no joy without her, only the sometimes bitter pleasure of enduring pain.

Coyne sat in the bright light, as Fox had expected, with the serenity of a religious mendicant. His arms folded, he could wait out eternity by his manner. It was unnatural behavior for any man under police inquisition. Fox was himself very casual. "Well, Tom, it's about time for us to start all over again. You know the chief?"

Coyne made a gesture of recognition. The chief merely glared down at him, his face a wrinkled mask of distaste.

"April twenty-ninth," Fox led. "That was the night you decided finally that you had time to fix Mrs. Troy's back steps."

"Afternoon," Coyne corrected. "I was home at night."

"What do you call the dividing line between afternoon and night?"

"Dark—at night it gets dark . . . sir."

"And you want it understood that you were home *before* dark?"

"I was home before dark," Coyne said calmly.

There had never been reference in the newspaper to the hour of Elsie Troy's death, partly because the medical examiner could put it no closer than between seven and nine. The month being April, darkness fell by seven.

"Suppose you tell the chief just what happened while you were there."

"Nothing happened. I went there on my way home from work. I fixed the steps. Then I called in to her that the job was done. She came out and said, 'That's fine, Tom. I'll pay you next week.' I never did get paid, but I guess that don't matter now."

Told by melancholy rote, Fox thought, having heard even the philosophic ending before. But then, most people repeated themselves under normal circumstances, especially about grievances they never expected to be righted.

"What I can't understand, Tom, is why you decided to fix the steps that day, and not, say, the week before?"

Coyne shrugged. "I just had the time then, I guess."

"She hadn't called you?"

"No, sir," he said with emphasis.

"You say that as though she would not have called you under any circumstances."

Coyne merely shrugged again.

"As a matter of fact, it was the husband—when they were still together —who asked you to repair the steps, wasn't it, Tom?"

"I guess it was."

"And you happened to remember it on the day she was about to be murdered."

"I didn't plan it that way," Coyne said, the words insolent, but his manner still serene. He tilted his chair back.

"It's a funny thing, chief," Fox said. "Here's a man commissioned to do a job on a friend's house. He doesn't get around to it until the home has broken up. If it was me, I'd have forgotten all about the job under those circumstances—never done it at all."

"So would I," the chief said, "unless I was looking for an excuse to go there."

"Exactly," Fox said, still in a casual voice.

"It wouldn't be on account of you they broke up, would it, Coyne?" the chief suggested.

Coyne seemed to suppress a laugh. It was the first time his effort at control showed. "No, sir."

"Don't you like women?" the chief snapped.

"I'm living with one now," Coyne said.

"Mrs. Tuttle?" said Fox, naming Coyne's landlady.

"What's wrong with that? She's a widow."

Fox did not say what was wrong with it. But Mr. Thomas Coyne was not going to have it both ways: he had alibied himself with Mrs. Tuttle for the hours of all three murders. A paramour was not the most believable of witnesses. But then, from what Fox had seen of Mrs. Tuttle, he would not have called her the most believable of paramours, either.

With deliberate ease Fox then led Coyne through an account of his activities on the nights of the two subsequent murders. By the suspect's telling, they brought Coyne nowhere near the scenes.

Finally Fox exchanged glances with the old man. He had had more than enough of Coyne by now and very little confidence that the carpenter had been worth bringing in again. "You can go now, Tom," Fox said, "but don't leave town." He nodded at the policeman by the door. And then, after a pause, "By the way, Tom, when did you last go swimming?"

"Oh, two or three weeks ago."

"Where?"

"Baker's Beach," Coyne said, naming the public park.

Fox nodded, held the door for the chief, and then closed it behind them.

"That guy should go on the radio," the old man said. "He knows all the answers."

"Seems like it," Fox said.

The second victim, Jane Mullins, had been strangled on the beach. But if Tom Coyne, as he said, had gone swimming two or three weeks ago, that would account for the sand found in Coyne's room.

Sand and a stack of newspapers—the only clues to Thomas Coyne's interests . . . and a clue also to the personality of his landlady; Mrs. Tuttle was a very careless housekeeper to leave sand and old newspapers lying around for weeks. She might be as careless with time—even with the truth.

Three strangulations—all of women who lived alone—within a month. It was enough to set the whole of a city the size of Rockland—population one hundred and ten thousand—on edge. As the *Gazette* editorialized: "When murder can match statistics with traffic deaths, it is time to investigate the investigators."

Knowing Ed Fox so well, Nancy wondered if he had not planted that line with the *Gazette;* it had the Fox's bite. It would be like him, if he was not getting all the cooperation he wanted from his superiors.

She looked at the clock and poured herself another cup of coffee. She was due at the radio station at eleven. Her broadcast time was noon: "The Woman's Way."

How cynical she had become about him, and through him, about so many things. As much as anything, that cynicism had enabled her to make the break: the realization that she was turning into a bitter woman with a slant on the world that made her see first the propensity for evil in a man, and only incidentally his struggle against it. This philosophy might make Ed a good policeman, but it made her a poor educator. And she considered herself an educator despite his belittlement of her work. A radio commentator was responsible to her audience that they learn a little truth from her. Why just a little? Ed had always said to that.

She wondered if Ed thought about her at all these days, when she could scarcely think of anything except him. It was as though she bore his heelmark on her soul. A cruel image—oh, she had them. For a month she had lived apart from him, yet the morbid trauma of their life together still hung about her. If she could not banish the memories, she must find psychiatric help. That would greatly amuse Ed—one more useless occupation by his reckoning. Worse than useless, the enemy of justice: his hardest catch could escape the punishment that fitted his crime by a psychiatrist's testimony.

Nancy folded the morning paper and rinsed her coffee cup.

Strange, the occupations of the three victims: Mary Philips had operated a beauty parlor, Elsie Troy had run a nursery school. She could hear Ed lecture on that: why have children if you pushed them out of the house in rompers? And poor Jane Mullins had written advertising copy—to Ed, perhaps the most useless nonsense of all. Well, that would give Ed something in common with the murderer—contempt for his victims. Ed always liked to have a little sympathy for the murderer: it made him easier to find. And no man ever suffered such anguish of soul as did Ed Fox at the hour of his man's execution.

There, surely, was the worst moment in all her five years of marriage to him: the night Mort Simmons was executed. Simmons had shot a man and Ed had made the arrest and got the confession. Nancy had known her husband was suffering, and she had ventured to console him with some not very original remarks about his having only done his duty, and that doubts were perfectly natural at such an hour.

"Doubts!" he had screamed at her. "I have no more doubt about his guilt than the devil waiting for him at the gates of hell!"

She had thought a long time about that. Slowly, then, the realization had come to her that Ed Fox suffered when such a man died because, in the pursuit and capture of him, Ed identified himself with the criminal. And fast upon that realization the thought had taken hold of her that never in their marriage had she been that close to him.

Nancy opened her hand and saw the marks of her nails in the palm. She looked at the nails. They needed polish. A beauty operator, Mary Philips. If

Nancy had been in the habit of having her hair done by a professional, she might possibly have known Mrs. Philips. The shop was in the neighborhood where she and Ed had lived, where Ed still lived . . .

She caught up her purse and briefcase and forced her thoughts onto a recipe for which she had no appetite. Ed was not troubled that way in his work . . .

"Damn it, Fox, give them something! They're riding my back like a cartload of monkeys." This was the old man's complaint on the third day after Mary Philips's murder. Reporters were coming into Rockland from all over the country. The mayor had turned over the facilities of his own office to them.

So Captain Fox sat down and composed a description of a man who might have been the slayer. He did it aware of his cynicism.

The state police laboratory had been unable to bring out any really pertinent physical evidence in any of the cases. The murderer was a wily one—a maniac or a genius . . . except in the instance of Elsie Troy. Fox could not help but dwell on that random start to so successful a career.

The detective stood over the stenographer while she typed the description—twenty copies on the electric machine. He then dictated a few lines calculated to counteract the description, to placate the rising hysteria of all the lonely women in Rockland. So many lonely women, whether or not they lived alone . . . Did Nancy feel alarmed? he wondered. If she did, she had not called on him for reassurance. But then, she would not. There was that streak of stubborn pride in her that made her run like an animal from the hand most willing to help.

"Forty-eight complaints have already been investigated, twenty-one suspects questioned . . ." Give them statistics, Fox thought. Nowadays they mean more to people than words. Maybe figures didn't lie, but they made a convincing camouflage for the truth.

He handed out the release over the chief of police's name, and found himself free once more to do the proper work of a detective, something unrelated to public relations. Suspect number twenty-two had been waiting for over an hour in the sun room.

It gave Fox a degree of satisfaction to know that he was there— "Deacon" Alvin Rugg. Rugg with two g's. G as in God, he thought. The young man was a religious fanatic—either a fanatic or a charlatan, possibly both, in Fox's mind. And he was the Fox's own special catch, having been flushed out in the policeman's persistent search for something the three women might have had in common beside the shedding of their husbands. All three—Elsie Troy, Jane Mullins, and Mary Philips—were interested in a revivalist sect called Church of the Morning.

On his way to the sun room, Fox changed his mind about tackling the suspect there. Why not treat him as if he were only a witness?—the better to disarm him. He had no police record, young Mr. Rugg, except for a violation of the peace ordinance in a nearby town: the complaint had been filed against his father and himself—their zeal had simply begat too large a crowd.

Fox had the young man brought to the office, and there he offered him the most comfortable chair in the room. Rugg chose a straight one instead. Fox thought he might prove rugged, Rugg.

The lithe youth wore his hair crested around his head a little like a brushed-up halo, for it was almost the color of gold. His eyes were large, blue and vacuous, though no doubt some would call them deep.

"Church of the Morning," Fox started, trying without much success to keep the cynicism from his voice. "When did you join up?"

"I was called at birth," Alvin replied with a rotish piety.

He was older than he looked, Fox realized, and a sure phony. "How old are you, Rugg?"

"Twenty."

"Let's see your draft registration. This is no newspaper interview."

"Thirty-two," Rugg amended, wistful as a woman, and Fox did not press for the registration proof.

"What do you do for a living?"

"Odd jobs. I'm a handyman when I'm not doing the Lord's work."

"How do you get these . . . these odd jobs?"

"My father recommends me."

"That would be the Reverend Rugg?"

The young man nodded—there was scarcely the shadow of a beard on his face. Fox was trying to calculate how the women to whom his father recommended him would feel about Alvin of the halo. Fox himself would have had more feeling for a goldfish, but then he was not a lonely woman. He must look up some of them, those still among the living. Fox had gone to the revival tent the night before—he and one-tenth the population of Rockland, almost twelve thousand people. It did not seem so extraordinary, then, that all three victims had chanced to catch the fervor of the Church of the Morning.

"I suppose you talk religion with your employers?"

"That is why I am for hire, captain."

The arrogance of an angel on its way to hell, Fox thought. "Who was your mother?" he snapped, on the chance that this was the young man's point of vulnerability.

"A Magdalen," Rugg said. "I have never asked further. My father is a holy man."

Fox muttered a vulgarity beneath his breath. He was a believer in orthodoxy, himself. Revivalists were not for him, especially one like Reverend Rugg, whom he had heard last night speak of this boy, this golden lad, as sent to him like a pure spirit to reward the revivalist's belated penitence—this golden lad . . . of thirty-two.

"The reason I asked you to come in, Alvin," Fox said, forcing amiability upon himself, and quite as though he had not sent two officers to pick Rugg up, "I thought you might be able to help us on these murders. You've heard about them?"

"I . . . I had thought of coming in myself," Rugg said.

"When did that thought occur to you?"

"Well, two or three weeks ago at least—the first time, I mean. You see, I worked for that Mrs. Troy—cleaned her windows, things like that. Her husband was a bitter, vengeful man. He doesn't have the spiritual consolation his wife had."

A nice distinction of the present and past tense, Fox thought. But what Troy did have was an unbreakable alibi: five witnesses to his continuous presence at a poker table on the night Elsie Troy was slain.

"She told you that about him?" Fox prompted cheerfully.

"Well, not exactly. She wanted to make a donation to the church but she couldn't. He had their bank account tied up . . . she said."

The hesitation before the last two words was marked by Fox. Either the Ruggs had investigated Elsie Troy's finances, he thought, or Alvin was covering up an intimacy he feared the detective suspected or had evidence of.

"But Mrs. Troy ran a nursery school," Fox said blandly. "I don't suppose she took the little ones in out of charity, do you?"

"Her husband had put up the money for the school. He insisted his investment should be paid back to him first."

"I wouldn't call that unreasonable, would you, Alvin? A trifle unchivalrous, perhaps, but not unreasonable?"

A vivid dislike came into the boy's, the man's, eyes. He had suddenly made an enemy of him, Fox thought with grim satisfaction. He would soon provoke the unguarded word. "Didn't you and Mrs. Troy talk about anything besides money?"

"We talked about faith," Rugg said, and then clamped his lips.

"Did you also do chores for Mrs. Mullins?"

"No. But she offered once to get me a messenger's job at the advertising company where she worked. Said I could do a lot of good there."

"I'll bet," Fox said. "And how about Mary Philips? What was she going to do for you?" He resisted the temptation to refer to the beauty shop.

"Nothing. She was a very nice woman."

That, Fox thought, was a revelatory answer. It had peace of soul in it. The captain then proceeded to turn the heat on "Deacon" Rugg, and before half an hour was over, he got from the golden boy the admission that both Elsie Troy and Jane Mullins had made amatory advances. Seeking more than religion, the self-widowed starvelings! They kicked out husbands and then welcomed any quack in trousers. Lady breadwinners! Fox could feel the explosion of his own anger; it spiced his powers of inquisition.

Alvin Rugg was then given such mental punishment as might have made a less vulnerable sinner threaten suit against the city. But while the "deacon" lacked airtight alibis for the nights of the twenty-ninth of April, the sixteenth of May, and June second, he had been seen about his father's tent by many people, and he maintained his innocence through sweat and tears, finally sobbing his protestations on his knees.

The extent of the Fox's mercy was to leave Rugg alone to compose himself and find his own way to the street.

"Until tomorrow then, this is Nancy Fox going 'The Woman's Way.' "

Nancy gathered her papers so as not to make a sound the microphone could pick up. The newscaster took over. The next instant Nancy was listening with all the concentration of her being.

". . . a man about forty, quick of movement, near six feet tall, a hundred and sixty pounds, extremely agile; he probably dresses conservatively and speaks softly. One of his victims is thought to have been describing him when she told a friend, 'You never know when he is going to smile or when he isn't—he changes moods so quickly . . .' "

Nancy pressed her lips together and leaned far away from the table. Her breathing was loud enough to carry into the mike. That was her own husband the newscaster was describing—Ed Fox himself, right down to the unpredictable smile! Actually, it could be any of a dozen men, she tried to tell herself. Of course. Any of a hundred! What nonsense to put such a description over the air!

She had regained her composure by the time the reporter had finished his newscast. Then she had coffee with him, as she often did. But what a fantastic experience! Fantasy—that was the only word for it. The description had been part of a release from the office of the chief of police, which meant it had Ed's own approval.

"But now I'm going to tell you what it sounded like to me," the newsman said. "Like somebody—maybe on the inside—deliberately muddying up the tracks. I tell you somebody down there knows more than we're getting in these handouts."

"What a strange idea!" Nancy cried, and gave a deprecating laugh as hollow as the clink of her dime on the counter.

She spent the next couple of hours in the municipal library, trying to learn something about water rights. A bill on the water supply was before the city council. Two years of research would have been more adequate to the subject, she discovered. Once more she had dived into something only to crack her head in the shallows of her own ignorance. Then she drove out to the county fairgrounds to judge the cake contest of the Grange women. She fled the conversational suggestion that the murderer might be scouting there. Some women squealed with a sort of ecstatic terror.

A feeling of deepening urgency pursued her from one chore to the next: there was something she ought to do, something she must return to and attend to. And yet the specific identity of this duty did not reveal itself. Sometimes she seemed on the brink of comprehension . . . but she escaped. Oh, yes, that much of herself she knew: she was fleeing it, not it fleeing her.

With that admission she cornered herself beyond flight. There was a question hanging in the dark reaches of her mind, unasked now even as it was five years ago. Since the night Mort Simmons died in the electric chair, it clung like monstrous fungi at the end of every cavern through which she fled. And by leaving her husband's home she had not escaped it.

Ask it now, she demanded—ask it now!

She drove off the pavement and braked the car to a shrieking halt. "All right," she cried aloud. "I ask it before God—is Ed Fox capable of . . ." But she could not finish the sentence. She bent her head over the wheel and sobbed, "Eddie, oh, Eddie dear, forgive me . . ."

Without food, without rest, she drove herself until the day was spent, and with it most of her energy. Only her nerves remained taut. She returned just before dark to the apartment she had subleased from a friend. It was in no way her home: she had changed nothing in it, not even the leaf on the calendar. And so the place gave her no message when she entered—neither warning nor welcome.

She left the hall door ajar while she groped her way to the table where the lamp stood, and at the moment of switching on the light she sensed that someone had followed her into the apartment. Before she could fully see him, he caught her into his arms.

"Don't, please, don't!" she cried. Her struggling but made him tighten his grip.

"For God's sake, Nancy, it's me!"

"I know," she said, and leaped away as Ed gave up his grasp of her. She could taste the retch of fear. She whirled and looked at him as if she were measuring the distance between them.

"You knew?" he said incredulously. "You knew that it was me and yet you acted like that?"

She could only stare at him and nod in giddy acknowledgment of the truth.

His hands fell limp to his sides.

"My God," he murmured.

A world of revelation opened to her in that mute gesture, in the simple dropping of his hands.

Neither of them moved. She felt the ache that comes with unshed tears gathering in her throat as the bitter taste of fear now ran out. It was a long moment until the tears were loosed and welled into her eyes, a moment in which they measured each other in the other's understanding —or in the other's misunderstanding.

"I thought I might surprise an old love—if I surprised you," he said flatly. "And then when I realized you were afraid, it seemed so crazy— so inconsiderate a thing to do, with a maniac abroad." He stood, self-pilloried and miserable—immobile, lest one move of his start up the fear in her again.

At last she managed the words: "Eddie, I do love you."

Fox raised his arms and held them out to her and she ran to them with utter abandon.

Presently he asked, "How long have you been afraid of me?"

"I think since the night Mort Simmons was executed," she said, and then clinging to him again, "Oh, my dear, my beloved husband."

He nodded and lifted her fingers to his lips. "How did you conceal it? Fear kills love. They say like that." He snapped his fingers.

"I never called it fear," she said, lifting her chin—and that, she thought, that inward courage was what he mistook for pride—"not until . . ." She bit her lip against the confession of the final truth.

"Until the murder of one, two, three women," Fox said evenly, "with whose lives you knew I'd have no sympathy."

"I didn't know that exactly," she said. "I only knew your prejudices."

"Pride and prejudice," he mused. He pushed her gently an arm's distance from him. "Take another look at my prejudices, Nancy, and see who suffers most by them."

"May I come home now, Eddie?"

"Soon, darling, very soon." He picked up his hat from where it had fallen in their struggle. "But you must let me tell you when."

Fox drove to within a block of Thomas Coyne's boarding house. He parked the car and walked up the street to where the tail he had put on Coyne was sitting, a newspaper before him, in a nondescript Ford. Fox slipped in beside him.

"Coyne's in there," the other detective said. "Been there since he came home from work. Ten minutes ago he went down to the corner for a newspaper. Came right back."

Fox decided to talk first with Mrs. Tuttle. He approached her by way of the kitchen door, identified himself, and got a cup of warmed-over coffee at the table. A voluble, lusty, good-natured woman, she responded easily to his question—whether she was interested in the Church of the Morning. She shook her head. Fox described "Deacon" Alvin Rugg and his relationship to the murdered women.

Mrs. Tuttle clucked disapproval and admitted she had heard of him, but where she could not remember. To the captain's direct question as to whether she had ever seen the golden boy, she shook her head again. "I tell you, Mr. Fox, I like my men and my whiskey one-hundred proof, and my religion in a church with a stone foundation."

Fox laughed. "Anybody in the house here interested in the Revival?"

"What you want to know," she said, looking at him sideways, "is if it was Tom Coyne who told me about him. Isn't that it?"

Fox admitted to the bush he had been beating around. "I'd like to know if Coyne has shown any interest in the sect."

"I don't know for sure. He takes sudden fancies, that one does."

"I understand he has a very deep fancy for you," Fox said bluntly.

Mrs. Tuttle frowned, the good nature fleeing her face. She took his cup and saucer to the sink and clattered it into the dish basin.

"I'm sorry to be clumsy about a delicate matter," Fox said, getting up from the table and following to where he could see her face. Shame or wrath? he wondered. Perhaps both. "It was very necessary to Coyne that he confide that information to the police," he elaborated, in subtle quest of further information.

"Was it?" she said. "Then maybe it was necessary for him to come to me in the first place. Can you tell me that, mister?"

"If you tell me when it was he first came to you—in that sense, I mean," Fox said.

"A couple of nights ago," she said. "Till then it was just . . . well, we were pals, that's all."

Fox examined his own fingernails. "He didn't take very long to tell about it, did he?"

"Now answer my question to you," she said. "Did he come just so he could tell you him and me were—like that?"

Fox ventured to lay his hand on her arm. She pulled away from his touch as though it were fire. Her shame was deep, her affair shallow, he thought. "Just stay in the kitchen," he said. She would have her answer soon enough.

He moved through the hall and alerted the detective on watch at the front. Then he went upstairs. Thomas Coyne was sitting in his room, the newspaper open on the table before him, a pencil in his hand. He had been caught in the obviously pleasurable act of marking an item in the paper, and he gathered himself up on seeing Fox—like a bather surprised in the nude.

It gave an ironic sequence to the pretense on which Fox had come. "I wanted to see your swim trunks," Captain Fox said.

Coyne was still gaping. Slowly he uncoiled himself, and then pointed to the dresser drawer.

"You get them," Fox said, "I don't like to invade your privacy." He turned partially away, in fact, to suggest that he was unaware of the newspaper over which he had surprised the man. He waited until Coyne reached the dresser, and then moved toward the table, but even there Fox pointed to the picture on the wall beyond it, and remarked that he remembered its like from his schooldays. A similar print, he said, had hung in the study hall. On and on he talked, and if Coyne was aware of the detective's quick scrutiny of his marked newspaper, it was less fearful for the man to pretend he had not seen it.

My wife, Ellen, having left my bed and board, I am no longer responsible . . .

Fox had seen it. So, likely, had the husbands of Mary Philips and Jane Mullins and Elsie Troy given public notice some time or other. The decision he needed to reach instantly was whether he had sufficient evidence to indict Tom Coyne: it was so tempting to let him now pursue the pattern once more—up to its dire culmination.

The detective stood, his arms folded, while Coyne brought the swim trunks. "Here you are, captain," he said, having recovered his voice.

"Haven't worn them much," Fox said, not touching them.

"It's early," Coyne said.

"So it is," Fox said, "the fifth of June. Baker's Beach just opened Memorial Day, didn't it?"

There was no serenity in Coyne now. He realized the trap into which he had betrayed himself while under questioning by Fox and the chief of police. So many things he had made seem right—even an affair with Mrs. Tuttle; and now that one little thing, by Fox's prompting, was wrong. He would not have been allowed in the waters of Baker's Beach before the thirtieth of May. In order to account for the sand in his room following the murder of Jane Mullins, he had said he had gone swimming at Baker's Beach two or three weeks before.

"Like a god needs sacrifice," Fox said.

The chief had pride in his eyes, commending Captain Fox for so fine a job. They went upstairs together to see the mayor, and there the chief took major credit as his due. He announced, however, that this would be his last case before retirement, and he put his arm about Captain Fox as the reporters were invited in. Fox asked to be excused.

"Damn it, man, you've got to do the talking," the chief protested.

"Yes, sir, if you say," Fox said with unbecoming docility. "But first I want to call my wife."

"By all means," the chief said. "Here, use the mayor's phone."

Nancy answered at the first ring.

"Will you pick me up tonight, my dear, on your way home?" Fox said.

The Cat's-Paw

STANLEY ELLIN

Stanley Ellin is the author of ten novels in the crime field, including the brilliant The Key to Nicholas Street *(1953), but it is his short stories on which his fame justly rests. He writes them very slowly and the care he takes shows: he has received two Edgars from the Mystery Writers of America for such work as "The Blessington Method." "The Cat's-Paw" is one of his very best, and that is high praise indeed.*

There was little to choose among any of the rooms in the boarding house in their dingy, linoleum-floored, brass-bedsteaded uniformity, but the day he answered the advertisement on the *Help Wanted* page, Mr. Crabtree realized that one small advantage accrued to his room: the public telephone in the hallway was opposite his door, and simply by keeping an ear cocked he could be at the instrument a moment after the first shrill warning ring had sounded.

In view of this he closed his application for employment not only with his signature but with the number of the telephone as well. His hand shook a little as he did so; he felt party to a gross deception in implying that the telephone was his personal property, but the prestige to be gained this way, so he thought, might somehow weight the balance in his favor. To that end he tremorously sacrificed the unblemished principles of a lifetime.

The advertisement itself had been nothing less than a miracle. *Man wanted,* it said, *for hard work at moderate pay. Sober, honest, industrious former clerk, age forty-five–fifty preferred. Write all details. Box 111;* and Mr. Crabtree, peering incredulously through his spectacles, had read it with a shuddering dismay at the thought of all his fellows, age forty-five–fifty, who might be seeking hard work at moderate pay, and who might have read the same notice minutes, or perhaps, hours, before.

His answer could have served as a model Letter of Application for Employment. His age was forty-eight, his health excellent. He was unmarried. He had served one single firm for thirty years; had served it faithfully and well; had an admirable record for attendance and punctuality. Unfortunately, the firm had merged with another and larger; regrettably, many

239

capable employees had to be released. Hours? Unimportant. His only interest was in doing a good job no matter the time involved. Salary? A matter entirely in the hands of his prospective employer. His previous salary had been fifty dollars per week, but naturally that had come after years of proved worth. Available for an interview at any time. References from the following. The signature. And then, the telephone number.

All this had been written and rewritten a dozen times until Mr. Crabtree had been satisfied that every necessary word was there, each word in its proper place. Then, in the copperplate hand that had made his ledgers a thing of beauty, the final draft had been transferred to fine bond paper purchased toward this very contingency, and posted.

After that, alone with his speculations on whether a reply would come by mail, by telephone, or not at all, Mr. Crabtree spent two endless and heart-fluttering weeks until the moment when he answered a call and heard his name come over the wire like the crack of doom.

"Yes," he said shrilly, "I'm Crabtree! I sent a letter!"

"Calmly, Mr. Crabtree, calmly," said the voice. It was a clear, thin voice, which seemed to pick up and savor each syllable before delivering it, and it had an instant and chilling effect on Mr. Crabtree who was clutching the telephone as if pity could be squeezed from it.

"I have been considering your application," the voice went on with the same painful deliberation, "and I am most gratified by it. Most gratified. But before calling the matter settled, I should like to make clear the terms of employment I am offering. You would not object to my discussing it now?"

The word "employment" rang dizzily through Mr. Crabtree's head. "No," he said, "please do."

"Very well. First of all, do you feel capable of operating your own establishment?"

"My own establishment?"

"Oh, have no fears about the size of the establishment or the responsibilities involved. It is a matter of some confidential reports which must be drawn up regularly. You would have your own office, your name on the door, and, of course, no supervision directly over you. That should explain the need for an exceptionally reliable man."

"Yes," said Mr. Crabtree, "but those confidential reports . . ."

"Your office will be supplied with a list of several important corporations. It will also receive subscriptions to a number of financial journals which frequently make mention of those same corporations. You will note all such references as they appear, and, at the end of each day, consolidate them into a report which will be mailed to me. I must add that none of this calls for any theoretical work or literary treatment. Accuracy, brevity, clarity: those are the three measures to go by. You understand that, of course?"

"Yes, indeed," said Mr. Crabtree fervently.

"Excellent," said the voice. "Now your hours will be from nine to five, six days a week, with an hour off at noon for lunch. I must stress this: I am insistent on punctuality and attendance, and I expect you to be as conscientious about these things as if you were under my personal supervision every moment of the day. I hope I do not offend you when I emphasize this?"

"Oh, no, sir!" said Mr. Crabtree. "I . . ."

"Let me continue," the voice said. "Here is the address where you will appear one week from today, and the number of your room"—Mr. Crabtree without pencil or paper at hand pressed the numbers frantically into his memory—"and the office will be completely prepared for you. The door will be open, and you will find two keys in a drawer of the desk: one for the door and one for the cabinet in the office. In the desk you will also find the list I mentioned, as well as the materials needed in making out your reports. In the cabinet you will find a stock of periodicals to start work on."

"I beg your pardon," said Mr. Crabtree, "but those reports . . ."

"They should contain every single item of interest about the corporations on your list, from business transactions to changes in personnel. And they must be mailed to me immediately upon your leaving the office each day. Is that clear?"

"Only one thing," said Mr. Crabtree. "To whom—where do I mail them?"

"A pointless question," said the voice sharply, much to Mr. Crabtree's alarm. "To the box number with which you are already familiar, of course."

"Of course," said Mr. Crabtree.

"Now," said the voice with a gratifying return to its original deliberate tones, "the question of salary. I have given it a good deal of thought, since as you must realize, there are a number of factors involved. In the end, I let myself be guided by the ancient maxim: a good workman is worthy of his hire—you recall those words?"

"Yes," said Mr. Crabtree.

"And," the voice said, "a poor workman can be easily dispensed with. On that basis, I am prepared to offer you fifty-two dollars a week. Is that satisfactory?"

Mr. Crabtree stared at the telephone dumbly and then recovered his voice. "Very," he gasped. "Oh, very much so. I must confess I never..."

The voice brought him up sharply. "But that is conditional, you understand. You will be—to use a rather clumsy term—on probation until you have proved yourself. Either the job is handled to perfection, or there is no job."

Mr. Crabtree felt his knees turn to water at the grim suggestion. "I'll do my best," he said. "I most certainly will do my absolute best."

"And," the voice went on relentlessly, "I attach great significance to the way you observe the confidential nature of your work. It is not to be discussed with anyone, and since the maintenance of your office and supplies lies entirely in my hands there can be no excuse for a defection. I have also removed temptation in the form of a telephone which you will *not* find on your desk. I hope I do not seem unjust in my abhorrence of the common practice where employees waste their time in idle conversation during working hours."

Since the death of an only sister twenty years before, there was not a soul in the world who would have dreamed of calling Mr. Crabtree to make any sort of conversation whatsoever; but he only said, "No, sir. Absolutely not."

"Then you are in agreement with all the terms we have discussed?"

"Yes, sir," said Mr. Crabtree.

"Any further questions?"

"One thing," said Mr. Crabtree. "My salary. How . . ."

"It will reach you at the end of each week," said the voice, "in cash. Anything else?"

Mr. Crabtree's mind was now a veritable log-jam of questions, but he found it impossible to fix on any particular one. Before he could do so, the voice said crisply, "Good luck, then," and there was the click which told him his caller had hung up. It was only when he attempted to do the same that he discovered his hand had been clenched so tightly around the receiver that it cost him momentary anguish to disengage it.

It must be admitted that the first time Mr. Crabtree approached the address given him, it would not have surprised him greatly to find no building there at all. But the building was there, reassuring in its immensity, teeming with occupants who packed the banks of elevators solidly, and, in the hallways, looked through him and scurried around him with efficient disinterest.

The office was there too, hidden away at the end of a devious corridor of its own on the very top floor, a fact called to Mr. Crabtree's attention by a stairway across the corridor, which led up to an open door through which the flat gray of the sky could be seen.

The most impressive thing about the office was the CRABTREE'S AF-FILIATED REPORTS boldly stenciled on the door. Opening the door, one entered an incredibly small and narrow room made even smaller by the massive dimensions of the furniture that crowded it. To the right, immediately inside the door, was a gigantic filing cabinet. Thrust tightly against it, but still so large that it utilized the remainder of the wall space on that side, was a huge, old-fashioned desk with a swivel chair before it.

The window set in the opposite wall was in keeping with the furniture. It was an immense window, broad and high, and its sill came barely above Mr. Crabtree's knees. He felt a momentary qualm when he first glanced through it and saw the sheer dizzying drop below, the terrifying quality of which was heightened by the blind, windowless walls of the building directly across from him.

One look was enough; henceforth, Mr. Crabtree kept the bottom section of the window securely fastened and adjusted only the top section to his convenience.

The keys were in a desk drawer; pen, ink, a box of nibs, a deck of blotters, and a half dozen other accessories more impressive than useful were in another drawer; a supply of stamps was at hand; and, most pleasant, there was a plentiful supply of stationery, each piece bearing the letterhead, CRABTREE'S AFFILIATED REPORTS, the number of the office, and the address of the building. In his delight at this discovery Mr. Crabtree dashed off a few practice lines with some bold flourishes of the pen, and then, a bit alarmed at his own prodigality, carefully tore the sheet to minute shreds and dropped it into the wastebasket at his feet.

After that, his efforts were devoted wholly to the business at hand. The filing cabinet disgorged a dismayingly large file of publications which had to be pored over, line by line, and Mr. Crabtree never finished studying a page without the harrowing sensation that he had somehow bypassed the mention of a name which corresponded to one on the typed list he had found, as promised, in the desk. Then he would retrace the entire page with an awful sense of dallying at his work, and groan when he came to the end of it without finding what he had not wanted to find in the first place.

It seemed to him at times that he could never possibly deplete the monstrous pile of periodicals before him. Whenever he sighed with pleasure at having made some headway, he would be struck with the gloomy foreknowledge that the next morning would find a fresh delivery of mail at his door and, consequently, more material to add to the pile.

There were, however, breaks in this depressing routine. One was the preparation of the daily report, a task which, somewhat to Mr. Crabtree's surprise, he found himself learning to enjoy; the other was the prompt arrival each week of the sturdy envelope containing his salary down to the last dollar bill, although this was never quite the occasion for unalloyed pleasure it might have been.

Mr. Crabtree would carefully slit open one end of the envelope, remove the money, count it, and place it neatly in his ancient wallet. Then he would poke trembling exploratory fingers into the envelope, driven by the fearful recollection of his past experience to look for the notice that would tell him his services were no longer required. That was always a bad moment, and it had the unfailing effect of leaving him ill and shaken until he could bury himself in his work again.

The work was soon part of him. He had ceased bothering with the typed list; every name on it was firmly imprinted in his mind, and there were restless nights when he could send himself off to sleep merely by repeating the list a few times. One name in particular had come to intrigue him, merited special attention. Efficiency Instruments, Ltd. was unquestionably facing stormy weather. There had been drastic changes in personnel, talks of a merger, sharp fluctuations on the market.

It rather pleased Mr. Crabtree to discover that with the passage of weeks into months each of the names on his list had taken on a vivid personality for him. Amalgamated was steady as a rock, stolid in its comfortablesuccess; Universal was high-pitched, fidgety in its exploration of new techniques; and so on down the line. But Efficiency Instruments, Ltd. was Mr. Crabtree's pet project, and he had, more than once, nervously caught himself giving it perhaps a shade more attention than it warranted. He brought himself up sharply at such times; impartiality must be maintained, otherwise. . . .

It came without any warning at all. He returned from lunch, punctual as ever, opened the door of the office, and knew he was standing face to face with his employer.

"Come in, Mr. Crabtree," said the clear, thin voice, "and shut the door."

Mr. Crabtree closed the door and stood speechless.

"I must be a prepossessing figure," said the visitor with a certain relish, "to have such a potent effect on you. You know who I am, of course?"

To Mr. Crabtree's numbed mind, the large, bulbous eyes fixed unwinkingly on him, the wide, flexible mouth, the body, short and round as a barrel, bore a horrifying resemblance to a frog sitting comfortably at the edge of a pond, with himself in the unhappy role of a fly hovering close by.

"I believe," said Mr. Crabtree shakily, "that you are my employer, Mr. . . . Mr. . . ."

A stout forefinger nudged Mr. Crabtree's ribs playfully. "As long as the bills are paid, the name is unimportant, eh, Mr. Crabtree? However, for the sake of expedience, let me be known to you as—say—George Spelvin. Have you ever encountered the ubiquitous Mr. Spelvin in your journeyings, Mr. Crabtree?"

"I'm afraid not," said Mr. Crabtree miserably.

"Then you are not a playgoer, and that is all to the good. And if I may hazard a guess, you are not one to indulge yourself in literature or the cinema either?"

"I do try to keep up with the daily newspaper," said Mr. Crabtree stoutly. "There's a good deal to read in it, you know, Mr. Spelvin, and it's not always easy, considering my work here, to find time for other diversions. That is, if a man wants to keep up with the newspapers."

The corners of the wide mouth lifted in what Mr. Crabtree hoped was a smile. "That is precisely what I hoped to hear you say. Facts, Mr. Crabtree, facts! I wanted a man with a single-minded interest in facts, and your words now as well as your application to your work tell me I have found him in you. I am very gratified, Mr. Crabtree."

Mr. Crabtree found that the blood was thumping pleasantly through his veins. "Thank you. Thank you again, Mr. Spelvin. I know I've been trying very hard, but I didn't know whether . . . Won't you sit down?" Mr. Crabtree tried to get his arm around the barrel before him in order to swing the chair into position, and failed. "The office is a bit small. But very comfortable," he stammered hastily.

"I am sure it is suitable," said Mr. Spelvin. He stepped back until he was almost fixed against the window and indicated the chair. "Now I should like you to be seated, Mr. Crabtree, while I discuss the matter I came on."

Under the spell of that commanding hand Mr. Crabtree sank into the chair and pivoted it until he faced the window and the squat figure outlined against it. "If there is any question about today's report," he said, "I am afraid it isn't complete yet. There were some notes on Efficiency Instruments . . ."

Mr. Spelvin waved the matter aside indifferently. "I am not here to discuss that," he said slowly. "I am here to find the answer to a problem which confronts me. And I rely on you, Mr. Crabtree, to help me find that answer."

"A problem?" Mr. Crabtree found himself warm with a sense of well-being. "I'll do everything I can to help, Mr. Spelvin. Everything I possibly can."

The bulging eyes probed his worriedly. "Then tell me this, Mr. Crabtree: how would you go about killing a man?"

"I?" said Mr. Crabtree. "How would I go . . . I'm afraid I don't understand, Mr. Spelvin."

"I said," Mr. Spelvin repeated, carefully stressing each word, "how would you go about killing a man?"

Mr. Crabtree's jaw dropped. "But I couldn't. I wouldn't. That," he said, "that would be murder!"

"Exactly," said Mr. Spelvin.

"But you're joking," said Mr. Crabtree, and tried to laugh, without managing to get more than a thin, breathless wheeze through his constricted throat. Even that pitiful effort was cut short by the sight of the stony face before him. "I'm terribly sorry, Mr. Spelvin, terribly sorry. You can see it's not the customary . . . it's not the kind of thing . . ."

"Mr. Crabtree. In the financial journals you study so assiduously you will find my name—my own name—repeated endlessly. I have a finger in many pies, Mr. Crabtree, and it always prods the plum. To use the more blatant adjectives, I am wealthy and powerful far beyond your wildest dreams—granting that you are capable of wild dreams—and a man does not attain that position by idling his time away on pointless jokes, or in passing the time of day with hirelings. My time is limited, Mr. Crabtree. If you cannot answer my question, say so, and let it go at that!"

"I don't believe I can," said Mr. Crabtree piteously.

"You should have said that at once," Mr. Spelvin replied, "and spared me my moment of choler. Frankly, I did not believe you could answer my question, and if you had, it would have been a most disillusioning experience. You see, Mr. Crabtree, I envy, I deeply envy, your serenity of existence where such questions never even enter. Unfortunately, I am not in that position. At one point in my career, I made a mistake, the only mistake that has ever marked my rise to fortune. This, in time, came to the attention of a man who combines ruthlessness and cleverness to a dangerous degree, and I have been in the power of that man since. He is, in fact, a blackmailer, a common blackmailer who has come to set too high a price on his wares, and so, must now pay for them himself."

"You intend," said Mr. Crabtree hoarsely, "to kill him?"

Mr. Spelvin threw out a plump hand in protest. "If a fly rested in the palm of that hand," he said sharply, "I could not find the power to close my fingers and crush the life from it. To be blunt, Mr. Crabtree, I am totally incapable of committing an act of violence, and while that may be an admirable quality in many ways, it is merely an embarrassment now, since the man must certainly be killed." Mr. Spelvin paused. "Nor is this a task for a paid assassin. If I resorted to one, I would most assuredly be exchanging one blackmailer for another, and that is altogether impractical." Mr. Spelvin paused again. "So, Mr. Crabtree, you can see there is only one conclusion to be drawn: the responsibility for destroying my tormentor rests entirely on you."

"Me!" cried Mr. Crabtree. "Why, I could never—no, never!"

"Oh, come," said Mr. Spelvin brusquely. "You are working yourself into a dangerous state. Before you carry it any further, Mr. Crabtree, I should like to make clear that your failure to carry out my request means that when you leave this office today, you leave it permanently. I cannot tolerate an employee who does not understand his position."

"Not tolerate!" said Mr. Crabtree. "But that is not right, that is not right at all, Mr. Spelvin. I've been working hard." His spectacles blurred. He fumbled with them, cleaned them carefully, replaced them on his nose. "And to leave me with such a secret. I don't see it; I don't see it at all. Why," he said in alarm, "it's a matter for the police!"

To his horror Mr. Spelvin's face turned alarmingly red, and the huge body started to shake in a convulsion of mirth that rang deafeningly through the room.

"Forgive me," he managed to gasp at last. "Forgive me, my dear fellow. I was merely visualizing the scene in which you go to the authorities and tell them of the incredible demands put upon you by your employer."

"You must understand," said Mr. Crabtree, "I am not threatening you, Mr. Spelvin. It is only . . ."

"Threatening me? Mr. Crabtree, tell me, what connection do you think there is between us in the eyes of the world?"

"Connection? I work for you, Mr. Spelvin. I'm an employee here. I . . ."

Mr. Spelvin smiled blandly. "What a curious delusion," he said, "when one can see that you are merely a shabby little man engaged in some pitiful little enterprise that could not possibly be of interest to me."

"But you employed me yourself, Mr. Spelvin! I worte a letter of application!"

"You did," said Mr. Spelvin, "but unfortunately the position was already filled, as I informed you in my very polite letter of explanation. You look incredulous, Mr. Crabtree, so let me inform you that your letter and a copy of my reply rest securely in my files should the matter ever be called to question."

"But this office! These furnishings! My subscriptions!"

"Mr. Crabtree, Mr. Crabtree," said Mr. Spelvin shaking his head heavily, "did *you* ever question the source of your weekly income? The manager of this building, the dealers in supplies, the publishers who deliver their journals to you were no more interested in my identity than you were. It is, I grant, a bit irregular for me to deal exclusively in currency sent through the mails in your name, but have no fears for me, Mr. Crabtree. Prompt payments are the opiate of the businessman."

"But my reports!" said Mr. Crabtree who was seriously starting to doubt his own existence.

"To be sure, the reports. I daresay that the ingenious Mr. Crabtree, after receiving my unfavorable reply to his application, decided to go into business for himself. He thereupon instituted a service of financial reports and even attempted to make *me* one of his clients! I rebuffed him sharply, I can tell you (I have his first report *and* a copy of my reply to it), but he foolishly persists in his efforts. Foolishly, I say, because his reports are absolutely useless to me; I have no interest in any of the corporations he discusses, and why he should imagine I would have is beyond my reckoning. Frankly, I suspect the man is an eccentric of the worst type, but since I have had dealings with many of that type I merely disregard him, and destroy his daily reports on their arrival."

"Destroy them?" said Mr. Crabtree stupefied.

"You have no cause for complaint, I hope," said Mr. Spelvin with some annoyance. "To find a man of your character, Mr. Crabtree, it was necessary for me to specify *hard work* in my advertisement. I am only living up to my part of the bargain in providing it, and I fail to see where the final disposition of it is any of your concern."

"A man of my character," echoed Mr. Crabtree helplessly, "to commit murder?"

"And why not?" The wide mouth tightened ominously. "Let me enlighten you, Mr. Crabtree. I have spent a pleasant and profitable share of my life in observing the human species, as a scientist might study insects under glass. And I have come to one conclusion, Mr. Crabtree, one above all others which has contributed to the making of my own success. I have come to the conclusion that to the majority of our species it is the function that is important, not the motives, nor the consequences.

"My advertisement, Mr. Crabtree, was calculated to enlist the services of one like that; a perfect representative of the type, in fact. From the moment you answered that advertisement to the present, you have been living up to all my expectations: you have been functioning flawlessly with no thought of either motive or consequence.

"Now murder has been made part of your function. I have honored you with an explanation of its motives; the consequences are clearly defined. Either you continue to function as you always have, or, to put it in a nutshell, you are out of a job."

"A job!" said Mr. Crabtree wildly. "What does a job matter to a man in prison! Or to a man being hanged!"

"Oh, come," remarked Mr. Spelvin placidly. "Do you think I'd lead you into a trap which might snare me as well? I am afraid you are being obtuse, my dear man. If you are not, you must realize clearly that my own security is tied in the same package as yours. And nothing less than your permanent presence in this office and your steadfast application to your work is the guarantee of that security."

"That may be easy to say when you're hiding under an assumed name," said Mr. Crabtree hollowly.

"I assure you, Mr. Crabtree, my position in the world is such that my identity can be unearthed with small effort. But I must also remind you that should you carry out my request you will then be a criminal and, consequently, very discreet.

"On the other hand, if you do not carry out my request—and you have complete freedom of choice in that—any charges you may bring against me will be dangerous only to you. The world, Mr. Crabtree, knows nothing about our relationship, and nothing about my affair with the gentleman who has been victimizing me and must now become my victim. Neither his demise nor your charges could ever touch me, Mr. Crabtree.

"Discovering my identity, as I said, would not be difficult. But using that information, Mr. Crabtree, can only lead you to a prison or an institution for the deranged."

Mr. Crabtree felt the last dregs of his strength seeping from him. "You have thought of everything," he said.

"Everything, Mr. Crabtree. When you entered my scheme of things, it was only to put my plan into operation; but long before that I was hard at work weighing, measuring, evaluating every step of that plan. For example, this room, this very room, has been chosen only after a long and weary search as perfect for my purpose. Its furnishings have been selected and arranged to further that purpose. How? Let me explain that.

"When you are seated at your desk, a visitor is confined to the space I now occupy at the window. The visitor is, of course, the gentleman in question. He will enter and stand here with the window *entirely open* behind him. He will ask you for an envelope a friend has left. This envelope," said Mr. Spelvin tossing one to the desk. "You will have the envelope in your desk, will find it, and hand it to him. Then, since he is a very methodical man (I have learned that well), he will place the envelope in the inside pocket of his jacket—and at that moment one good thrust will send him out the window. The entire operation should take less than a minute. Immediately after that," Mr. Spelvin said calmly, "you will close the window to the bottom and return to your work."

"Someone," whispered Mr. Crabtree, "the police . . ."

"Will find," said Mr. Spelvin, "the body of some poor unfortunate who climbed the stairs across the hallway and hurled himself from the roof above. And they will know this because inside that envelope secured in his pocket is not what the gentleman in question expects to find there, but a neatly typewritten note explaining the sad affair and its motives, an apology for any inconvenience caused (suicides are great ones for apologies, Mr. Crabtree) and a most pathetic plea for a quick and peaceful burial. And," said Mr. Spelvin, gently touching his fingertips together, "I do not doubt he will get it."

"What," Mr. Crabtree said, "what if something went wrong? If the man opened the letter when it was given to him. Or . . . if something like that happened?"

Mr. Spelvin shrugged. "In that case the gentleman in question would merely make his way off quietly and approach me directly about the matter. Realize, Mr. Crabtree, that anyone in my friend's line of work expects occasional little attempts like this, and, while he may not be inclined to think them amusing, he would hardly venture into some precipitous action that might kill the goose who lays the golden eggs. No, Mr. Crabtree, if such a possibility as you suggest comes to pass, it means only that I must reset my trap, and even more ingeniously."

Mr. Spelvin drew a heavy watch from his pocket, studied it, then replaced it carefully. "My time is growing short, Mr. Crabtree. It is not that I find your company wearing, but my man will be making his appearance shortly, and matters must be entirely in your hands at that time. All I require of you is this: when he arrives, the window will be open." Mr. Spelvin thrust it up hard and stood for a moment looking appreciatively at the drop below. "The envelope will be in your desk." He opened the drawer and dropped it in, then closed the drawer firmly. "And at the moment of decision, you are free to act one way or the other."

"Free?" said Mr. Crabtree. "You said he would ask for the envelope!"

"He will. He will, indeed. But if you indicate that you know nothing about it, he will quietly make his departure, and later communicate with me. And that will be, in effect, a notice of your resignation from my employ."

Mr. Spelvin went to the door and rested one hand on the knob. "However," he said, "if I do *not* hear from him, that will assure me that you have successfully completed your term of probation and are to be henceforth regarded as a capable and faithful employee."

"But the reports!" said Mr. Crabtree. "You destroy them . . ."

"Of course," said Mr. Spelvin, a little surprised. "But you will continue with your work and send the reports to me as you have always done. I assure you, it does not matter to me that they are meaningless, Mr. Crabtree. They are part of a pattern, and your adherence to that pattern, as I have already told you, is the best assurance of my own security."

The door opened, closed quietly, and Mr. Crabtree found himself alone in the room.

The shadow of the building opposite lay heavily on his desk. Mr. Crabtree looked at his watch, found himself unable to read it in the growing dimness of the room, and stood up to pull the cord of the light over his head. At that moment a peremptory knock sounded on the door.

"Come in," said Mr. Crabtree.

The door opened on two figures. One was a small, dapper man, the other a bulky police officer who loomed imposingly over his companion. The small man stepped into the office and, wilth the gesture of a magician pulling a rabbit from a hat, withdrew a large wallet from his pocket, snapped it open to show the gleam of a badge, closed it, and slid it back into his pocket.

"Police," said the man succinctly. "Name's Sharpe."

Mr. Crabtree nodded politely. "Yes?" he said.

"Hope you don't mind," said Sharpe briskly. "Just a few questions."

As if this were a cue, the large policeman came up with an efficient-looking notebook and the stub of a pencil, and stood there poised for action. Mr. Crabtree peered over his spectacles at the notebook, and through them at the diminutive Sharpe. "No," said Mr. Crabtree, "not at all."

"You're Crabtree?" said Sharpe, and Mr. Crabtree started, then remembered the name on the door.

"Yes," he said.

Sharpe's cold eyes flickered over him and then took in the room with a contemptuous glance. "This your office?"

"Yes," said Mr. Crabtree.

"You in it all afternoon?"

"Since one o'clock," said Mr. Crabtree. "I go to lunch at twelve and return at one promptly."

"I'll bet," said Sharpe, then nodded over his shoulder. "That door open any time this afternoon?"

"It's always closed while I am working," said Mr. Crabtree.

"Then you wouldn't be able to see anybody going up that stairs across the hall there."

"No," replied Mr. Crabtree, "I wouldn't."

Sharpe looked at the desk, then ran a reflective thumb along his jaw. "I guess you wouldn't be in a position to see anything happening outside the window either."

"No, indeed," said Mr. Crabtree. "Not while I'm at work."

"Now," said Sharpe, "did you *hear* something outside of that window this afternoon? Something out of the ordinary, I mean."

"Out of the ordinary?" repeated Mr. Crabtree vaguely.

"A yell. Somebody yelling. Anything like that?"

Mr. Crabtree puckered his brow. "Why, yes," he said, "yes, I did. And not long ago either. It sounded as if someone had been startled—or frightened. Quite loud, too. It's always so quiet here I couldn't help hearing it."

Sharpe looked over his shoulder and nodded at the policeman who closed his notebook slowly. "That ties it up," said Sharpe. "The guy made the jump, and the second he did it he changed his mind, so he came down hollering all the way. Well," he said, turning to Mr. Crabtree in a burst of confidence, "I guess you've got a right to know what's going on here. About an hour ago some character jumped off that roof right over your head. Clear case of suicide, note in his pocket and everything, but we like to get all the facts we can."

"Do you know," said Mr. Crabtree, "who he was?"

Sharpe shrugged. "Another guy with too many troubles. Young, good-looking, pretty snappy dresser. Only thing beats me is why a guy who could afford to dress like that would figure he has more troubles than he can handle."

The policeman in uniform spoke for the first time. "That letter he left," he said deferentially, "sounds like he was a little crazy."

"You have to be a little crazy to take that way out," said Sharpe.

"You're a long time dead," said the policeman heavily.

Sharpe held the doorknob momentarily. "Sorry to bother you," he said to Mr. Crabtree, "but you know how it is. Anyhow, you're lucky in a way. Couple of girls downstairs saw him go by and passed right out." He winked as he closed the door behind him.

Mr. Crabtree stood looking at the closed door until the sound of heavy footsteps passed out of hearing. Then he seated himself in the chair and pulled himself closer to the desk. Some magazines and sheets of stationery lay there in mild disarray, and he arranged the magazines in a neat pile, stacking them so that all corners met precisely. Mr. Crabtree picked up his pen, dipped it into the inkbottle, and steadied the paper before him with his other hand.

Efficiency Instruments, Ltd., he wrote carefully, *shows increased activity . . .*

The Road to Damascus

MICHAEL GILBERT

Michael Gilbert is a lawyer in London who, since the late 1940s, has produced some twenty novels of detection and suspense, many of them featuring Inspector Hazelrigg. He is also a prolific short-story writer, having completed four collections as of this writing. His collection of spy tales, Game Without Rules, *is justly regarded as one of the great books of its kind. His novels and stories are quite naturally rich in legal lore, which serves to enhance his many interesting plots and characters.*

Everyone in Lamperdown knew that Mr. Behrens, who lived with his aunt at the Old Rectory and kept bees, and Mr. Calder, who lived in a cottage on the hilltop outside the village and was the owner of a deerhound called Rasselas, were the closest of close friends. They knew, too, that there was something out of the ordinary about both of them.

Both had a habit of disappearing. When Mr. Calder went he left the great dog in charge of the cottage; and Mr. Behrens would plod up the hill once a day to talk to the dog and see to his requirements. If both men happened to be away at the same time, Rasselas would be brought down to the Old Rectory where, according to Flossie, who did for the Behrenses, he would sit for hour after hour in one red plush armchair, staring silently at Mr. Behrens's aunt in the other.

There were other things. There was known to be a buried telephone line connecting the Old Rectory and the cottage; both houses had an elaborate system of burglar alarms; and Mr. Calder's cottage, according to Ken who had helped to build it, had steel plates inside the window shutters.

The villagers knew all this and, being countrymen, talked very little about it, except occasionally among themselves toward closing time. To strangers, of course, they said nothing.

That fine autumn morning Rasselas was lying, chin on ground, watching Mr. Calder creosote the sharp end of a wooden spile. He sat up suddenly and rumbled out a warning.

"It's only Arthur," said Mr. Calder. "We know him."

The dog subsided with a windy sigh.

Arthur was Mr. Calder's nearest neighbor. He lived in a converted railway carriage in the company of a cat and two owls, and worked in the woods which cap the North Downs from Wrotham Hill to the Medway —Brimstone Wood, Molehill Wood, Long Gorse Shaw, Whitehorse Wood, Tom Lofts Wood and Leg of Mutton Wood. It was a very old part of the country and, like all old things, it was full of ghosts. Mr. Calder could not see them, but he knew they were there. Sometimes when he was walking with Rasselas in the woods, the dog would stop, cock his head on one side and rumble deep in his throat, his yellow eyes speculative as he followed some shape flitting down the ride ahead of them.

"Good morning, Arthur," said Mr. Calder.

"Working, I see," said Arthur. He was a small, thick man, of great strength, said to have an irresistible attraction for women.

"The old fence is on its last legs. I'm putting this in until I can get it done properly."

Arthur examined the spile with an expert eye and said, "Chestnut. That should hold her for a season. Oak'd be better. You working too hard to come and look at something I found?"

"Never too busy for that," said Mr. Calder.

"Let's go in your car, it'll be quicker," said Arthur. "Bring a torch, too."

Half a mile along a rutted track they left the car, climbed a gate and walked down a broad ride, forking off it onto a smaller one. After a few minutes the trees thinned, and Mr. Calder saw that they were coming to a clearing where wooding had been going on. The trunks had been dragged away and the slope was a litter of scattered cordwood.

"These big contractors," said Arthur. "They've got no idea. They come and cut down the trees, and lug 'em off, and think they've finished the job. Then I have to clear it up. Stack the cordwood. Pull out the stumps where they're an obstruction to traffic."

What traffic had passed, or would ever pass again through the heart of this secret place, Mr. Calder could hardly imagine. But he saw that the workmen had cleared a rough path which followed the contour of the hill and disappeared down the other side, presumably joining the track they had come by somewhere down in the valley. At that moment the ground was a mess of tractor marks and turned earth. In a year the raw places would be skimmed over with grass and nettles and bluebells and kingcups and wild garlic. In five years there would be no trace of the intruders.

"In the old days," said Arthur, "we done it with horses. Now we do it with machinery. I'm not saying it isn't quicker and handier, but it don't seem altogether right." He nodded at his bulldozer, askew on the side of a hummock. Rasselas went over and sneered at it, disapproving of the oily smell.

"I was shifting this stump," said Arthur, "when the old cow slipped and came down sideways. She hit t'other tree a proper dunt. I thought I bitched up the works, but all I done was shift the tree a piece. See?"

Mr. Calder walked across to look. The tree which Arthur had hit was no more than a hollow ring of elm, very old and less than three feet high. His first thought was that it was curious that a heavy bulldozer crashing down onto it from above should not have shattered its frail shell altogether.

"Ah! You have a look inside," said Arthur.

The interior of the stump was solid concrete.

"Why on earth," said Mr. Calder, "would anyone bother—?"

"Just have a look at this."

The stump was at a curious angle, half uprooted so that one side lay much higher than the other.

"When I hit it," said Arthur, "I felt something give. Truth to tell, I thought I'd cracked her shaft. Then I took another look. See?"

Mr. Calder looked. And he saw.

The whole block—wooden ring, cement center and all—had been pierced by an iron bar. The end of it was visible, thick with rust, sticking out of the broken earth. He scraped away the soil with his fingers and presently found the U-shaped socket he was looking for. He sat back on his heels and stared at Arthur, who stared back, solemn as one of his own owls.

"Someone," said Mr. Calder slowly, "—God knows why—took the trouble to cut out this tree stump and stick a damned great iron bar right through the middle of it, fixed to open on a pivot."

"It would have been Dan Owtram who fixed the bar for 'em, I don't doubt," said Arthur. "He's been dead ten years now."

"Who'd Dan fix it for?"

"Why, for the military."

"I see," said Mr. Calder. It was beginning to make a little more sense.

"You'll see when you get inside."

"Is there something inside?"

"Surely," said Arthur. "I wouldn't bring you out all this way just to look at an old tree stump, now would I? Come around here."

Mr. Calder moved round to the far side and saw, for the first time, that when the stump had shifted it had left a gap on the underside. It was not much bigger than a badger's hole.

"Are you suggesting I go down *that?*"

"It's not so bad, once you're in," said Arthur.

The entrance sloped down at about forty-five degrees and was only really narrow at the start, where the earth had caved in. After a short slide Mr. Calder's feet touched the top of a ladder. It was a long ladder. He counted twenty rungs before his feet were on firm ground. He got out his torch and switched it on.

He was in a fair-sized chamber, cut out of the chalk. He saw two recesses, each containing a spring bed on a wooden frame; two or three empty packing cases, upended as table and seats; a wooden cupboard, several racks, and a heap of disintegrating blankets. The place smelled of lime and dampness and, very faintly, of something else.

A scrabbling noise announced the arrival of Arthur.

"Like something outer one of them last war films," he said.

"*Journey's End!*" said Mr. Calder. "All it needs is a candle in an empty beer bottle and a couple of gas masks hanging up on the wall."

"It was journey's end for him all right." Arthur jerked his head toward the far corner, and Mr. Calder swung his torch round.

The first thing he saw was a pair of boots, then the mildewy remains of a pair of flannel trousers, through gaps in which the leg bones showed white. The man was lying on his back. He could hardly have fallen like that; it was not a natural position. Someone had taken the trouble to straighten the legs and fold the arms over the chest after death.

The light from Mr. Calder's torch moved upward to the head, where it stayed for a long minute. Then he straightened up. "I don't think you'd better say much about this. Not for the moment."

"That hole in his forehead," said Arthur. "Its a bullet hole, ennit?"

"Yes. The bullet went through the middle of his forehead and out at the back. There's a second hole there."

"I guessed it was more up your street than mine," said Arthur. "What'll we do? Tell the police?"

"We'll have to tell them sometime. Just for the moment, do you think you could cover the hole up? Put some sticks and turf across?"

"I could do that all right. 'Twont really be necessary, though. Now the wooding's finished you won't get anyone else through here. It's all preserved. The people who do the shooting, they stay on the outside of the covers."

"One of them didn't," said Mr. Calder, looking down at the floor and showing his teeth in a grin.

Mr. Behrens edged his way through the crowd in the drawing room of Colonel Mark Bessendine's Chatham quarters. He wanted to look at one of the photographs on the mantelpiece.

"Thats the *Otrango*," said a girl near his left elbow. "It was grandfather's ship. He proposed to granny in the Red Sea. On the deck-tennis court, actually. Romantic, don't you think?"

Mr. Behrens removed his gaze from the photograph to study his informant. She had brown hair and a friendly face and was just leaving the puppy-fat stage. Fifteen or sixteen he guessed. "You must be Julia Bessendine," he said.

"And you're Mr. Behrens. Daddy says you're doing something very clever in our workshops. Of course, he wouldn't say what."

"That was his natural discretion," said Mr. Behrens. "As a matter of fact, it isn't hush-hush at all. I'm writing a paper for the Molecular Society on underwater torque reactions and the Navy offered to lend me its big test tank."

"Gracious!" said Julia.

Colonel Bessendine surged across.

"Julia, you're in dereliction of your duties. I can see that Mr. Behrens's glass is empty."

"Excellent sherry," said Mr. Behrens.

"Tradition," said Colonel Bessendine, "associates the Navy with rum. In fact, the two drinks that it really understands are gin and sherry. I hope our technical people are looking after you?"

"The Navy have been helpfulness personified. It's been particularly convenient for me, being allowed to do this work at Chatham. Only twenty minutes' run from Lamperdown, you see."

Colonel Bessendine said, "My last station was Devonport. A ghastly place. When I was posted back here I felt I was coming home. The whole of my youth is tied up with this part of the country. I was born and bred not far from Tilbury and I went to school at Rochester."

His face, thought Mr. Behrens, was like a waxwork. A clever waxwork, but one which you could never quite mistake for human flesh. Only the eyes were truly alive.

"I sometimes spent a holiday down here when I was a boy," said Mr. Behrens. "My aunt and uncle—he's dead now—bought the Old Rectory at Lamperdown after the First World War. Thank you, my dear, that was very nicely managed." This was to Julia, who had fought her way back to him with most of the sherry still in the glass. "In those days your school," he said to the girl, "was a private house. One of the great houses of the county."

"It must have been totally impracticable," said Julia Bessendine severely. "Fancy trying to *live* in it. What sort of staff did it need to keep it up?"

"They scraped along with twenty or thirty indoor servants, a few dozen gardeners and gamekeepers, and a cricket pro."

"Daddy told me that when he was a boy he used to walk out from school, on half holidays, and watch cricket on their private cricket ground. That's right, isn't it, daddy?"

"That's right, my dear. I think, Julia—"

"He used to crawl up alongside the hedge from the railway and squeeze through a gap in the iron railings at the top and lie in the bushes. And once the old lord walked across and found him, and instead of booting him out, he gave him money to buy sweets with."

"Major Furlong looks as if he could do with another drink," said Colonel Bessendine.

"Colonel Bessendine's father," said Mr. Behrens to Mr. Calder later that evening, "came from New Zealand. He ran away to sea at the age of thirteen, and got himself a job with the Anzac Shipping Line. He rose to be head purser on their biggest ship, the *Otrango*. Then he married. An Irish colleen, I believe. Her father was a landowner from Cork. That part of the story's a bit obscure, because her family promptly disowned her. They didn't approve of the marriage at all. They were poor but proud. Old Bessendine had the drawback of being twice as rich as they were."

"Rich? A purser?"

"He was a shrewd old boy. He bought up land in Tilbury and Grays and leased it to builders. When he died, his estate was declared for probate at eighty-five thousand pounds. I expect it was really worth a lot more. His three sons were all well educated and well behaved. It was the sort of home where the boys called their father 'sir,' and got up when he came into the room."

"We could do with more homes like that," said Mr. Calder. "Gone much too far the other way. What happened to the other two sons?"

"Both dead. The eldest went into the Army: he was killed at Dunkirk. The second boy was a flight lieutenant. He was shot down over Germany, picked up and put into a prison camp. He was involved in some sort of trouble there. Shot, trying to escape."

"Bad luck," said Mr. Calder. He was working something out with paper and pencil. "Go away." This was to Rasselas, who had his paws on the table and was trying to help him. "What happened to young Mark?"

"Mark was in the Marines. He was blown sky high in the autumn of 1940—the first heavy raid on Gravesend and Tilbury."

"But I gather he came down in one piece."

"Just about. He was in hospital for six months. The plastic surgeons did a wonderful job on his face. The only thing they couldn't put back was the animation."

"Since you've dug up such a lot of his family history, do I gather that he's in some sort of a spot?"

"He's in a spot all right," said Mr. Behrens. "He's been spying for the Russians for a long time and we've just tumbled to it."

"You're sure?"

"I'm afraid there's no doubt about it at all. Fortescue has had him under observation for the last three months."

"Why hasn't he been put away?"

"The stuff he's passing out is important, but it's not vital. Bessendine isn't a scientist. He's held security and administrative jobs in different naval stations, so he's been able to give details of the progress and success of various jobs—where a project has run smoothly, or where it got behind time, or flopped. There's nothing the other side likes more than a flop."

"How does he get the information out?"

"That's exactly what I'm trying to find out. It's some sort of post-office system, no doubt. When we've sorted that out, we'll pull him in."

"Has he got any family?"

"A standard pattern Army-type wife. And a rather nice daughter."

"It's the family who suffer in these cases," said Mr. Calder. He scratched Rasselas's tufted head, and the big dog yawned. "By the way, *we* had rather an interesting day, too. We found a body."

He told Mr. Behrens about this, and Mr. Behrens said, "What are you going to do about it?"

"I've telephoned Fortescue. He was quite interested. He's put me on to a Colonel Cawston, who was in charge of Irregular Forces in this area in 1940. He thinks he might be able to help us."

Colonel Cawston's room was littered with catalogues, feeding charts, invoices, paid bills and unpaid bills, seed samples, gift calendars, local newspapers, boxes of cartridges, and buff forms from the Ministry of Agriculture, Fisheries and Food.

Mr. Calder said, "It's really very good of you to spare the time to talk to me, colonel. You're a pretty busy man, I can see that."

"We shall get on famously," said the old man, "if you'll remember two things. The first is that I'm deaf in my left ear. The second, that I'm no longer a colonel. I stopped being that in 1945."

"Both points shall be borne in mind," said Mr. Calder, easing himself round onto his host's right-hand side.

"Fortescue told me you were coming. If that old bandit's involved, I suppose it's Security stuff?"

"I'm not at all sure," said Mr. Calder. "I'd better tell you about it. . . ."

"Interesting," said the old man, when he had done so. "Fascinating, in fact."

He went across to a big corner cupboard, dug into its cluttered interior and surfaced with two faded khaki-colored canvas folders, which he laid on the table. From one of them he turned out a thick wad of papers, from the other a set of quarter- and one-inch military maps.

"I kept all this stuff," he said. "At one time, I was thinking of writing a history of Special Operations during the first two years of the war. I never got round to it, though. Too much like hard work." He unfolded the maps, and smoothed out the papers with his bent and arthritic fingers.

"Fortescue told me," said Mr. Calder, "that you were in charge of what he called 'Stay-put Parties.'"

"It was really a very sound idea," said the old man. His frosty blue eyes sparkled for a moment, with the light of unfought battles. "They did the same thing in Burma. When you knew that you might have to retreat, you dug-in small resistance groups, with arms and food and wireless sets. They'd let themselves be overrun, you see, and operate behind the enemy lines. We had a couple of dozen posts like that in Kent and Sussex. The one you found would have been—Whitehorse Wood you said?—here it is, Post Six. That was a very good one. They converted an existing dene-hole—you know what a dene-hole is?"

"As far as I can gather," said Mr. Calder, "the original inhabitants of this part of the country dug them to hide in when *they* were overrun by the Angles and Saxons and such. A sort of pre-Aryan Stay-put Party."

"Never thought of it that way." The old man chuckled. "You're quite right, of course. That's exactly what it was. Now then. Post Six. We had three men in each—an officer and two NCOs." He ran his gnarled finger up the paper in front of him. "Sergeant Brewer. A fine chap that. Killed in North Africa. Corporal Stubbs. He's dead, too. Killed in a motor crash, a week after VE-Day. So your unknown corpse couldn't be either of *them.*"

There was a splendid inevitability about it all, thought Mr. Calder. It was like the unfolding of a Greek tragedy; or the final chord of a well-built symphony. You waited for it. You knew it was coming. But you were still surprised when it did.

"Bessendine," said the old man. "Lieutenant Mark Bessendine. Perhaps the most tragic of the lot, really. He was a natural choice for our work. Spoke Spanish, French and German. Young and fit. Front-line experience with the Reds in Spain."

"What exactly happened to him?"

"It was the first week in November 1940. Our masters in Whitehall had concluded that the invasion wasn't on. I was told to seal up all my posts and send the men back to their units. I remember sending Mark out that afternoon to Post Six—it hadn't been occupied for some weeks —told him to bring back any loose stores. That was the last time I saw him—in the flesh, as you might say. You heard what happened?"

"He got caught in the German blitz on Tilbury and Gravesend."

"That's right. Must have been actually on his way back to our HQ. The explosion picked him up and pushed him through a plate-glass window. He was damned lucky to be alive at all. Next time I saw him he was swaddled up like a mummy. Couldn't talk or move."

"Did you see him again?"

"I was posted abroad in the spring. Spent the rest of the war in Africa and Italy. . . . Now you happen to mention it, though, I thought I did bump into him once—at the big reception center at Calais. I went through there on my way home in 1945."

"Did he recognize you?"

"It was a long time ago. I can't really remember." The old man looked up sharply. "Is it important?"

"It might be," said Mr. Calder.

"If you're selling anything," said the old lady to Mr. Behrens, "you're out of luck."

"I am neither selling nor buying," said Mr. Behrens.

"And if you're the new curate, I'd better warn you that I'm a Baptist."

"I'm a practicing agnostic."

The old lady looked at him curiously, and then said, "Whatever it is you want to talk about, we shall be more comfortable inside, shan't we?"

She led the way across the hall, narrow and bare as a coffin, into a surprisingly bright and cheerful sitting room.

"You don't look to me," she said, "like the sort of man who knocks old ladies on the head and grabs their life's savings. I keep mine in the bank, such as they are."

"I must confess to you," said Mr. Behrens, "that I'm probably wasting your time. I'm in Tilbury on a sentimental errand. I spent a year of the war in an Air Force prison camp in Germany. One of my greatest friends there was Jeremy Bessendine. He was a lot younger than I was, of course, but we had a common interest in bees."

"I don't know what you were doing up in an airplane, at your time of life. I expect you dyed your hair. People used to do that in the 1914 war. I'm sorry, I interrupted you. Mr.—?"

"Behrens."

"My name's Galloway. You said Jeremy Bessendine."

"Yes. Did you know him?"

"I knew *all* the Bessendines. Father and mother, and all three sons. The mother was the sweetest thing, from the bogs of Ireland. The father, well, let's be charitable and say he was old-fashioned. Their house was on the other side of the road to mine. There's nothing left of it now. Can you see? Not a stick nor a stone."

Mr. Behrens looked out of the window. The opposite side of the road was an open space containing one row of prefabricated huts.

"Terrible things," said Mrs. Galloway. "They put them up after the war as a temporary measure. Temporary!"

"So that's where the Bessendines' house was," said Mr. Behrens, sadly. "Jeremy often described it to me. He was so looking forward to living in it again when the war was over."

"Jeremy was my favorite," said Mrs. Galloway. "I'll admit I cried when I heard he'd been killed. Trying to escape, they said."

She looked back twenty-five years, and sighed at what she saw. "If we're going to be sentimental," she said, "we shall do it better over a cup of tea. The kettle's on the boil." She went out into the kitchen but left the door open, so that she could continue to talk.

"John, the eldest, I never knew well. He went straight into the Army. He was killed early on. The youngest was Mark. He was a wild character, if you like."

"Wild? In what way?" said Mr. Behrens.

Mrs. Galloway arranged the teapot, cups, and milk jug on a tray and collected her thoughts. Then she said, "He was a rebel. Strong or weak?"

"Just as it comes," said Mr. Behrens.

"His two brothers, they accepted the discipline at home. Mark didn't. Jeremy told me that when Mark ran away from school—the second time —and his father tried to send him back, they had a real set-to, the father shouting, the boy screaming. That was when he went off to Spain to fight for the Reds. Milk and sugar?"

"Both," said Mr. Behrens. He thought of Mark Bessendine as he had seen him two days before. An ultracorrect, poker-backed, poker-faced regular soldier. How deep had the rebel been buried?

"He's quite a different sort of person now," he said.

"Of course, he would be," said Mrs. Galloway. "You can't be blown to bits and put together again and still be the same person, can you?"

"Why, no," said Mr. Behrens. "I suppose you can't."

"I felt very strange myself for a week or so, after it happened. And I was only blown across the kitchen and cracked my head on the stove."

"You remember that raid, then?"

"I most certainly do. It must have been about five o'clock. Just getting dark, and a bit misty. They came in low, and the next moment—*crump, bump*—we were right in the middle of it. It was the first raid we'd had —and the worst. You could hear the bombs coming closer and closer. I thought, I wish I'd stayed in Saffron Walden—where I'd been evacuated, you see—I'm for it now, I thought. And it's all my own fault for coming back like the posters told me not to. And the next moment I was lying on the floor, with my head against the stove, and a lot of warm red stuff running over my face. It was tomato soup."

"And that was the bomb that destroyed the Bessendines' house—and killed old Mr. and Mrs. Bessendine?"

"That's right. And it was the same raid that nearly killed Mark. My goodness!"

The last exclamation was nothing to do with what had gone before. Mrs. Galloway was staring at Mr. Behrens. Her face had gone pale. She said, "Jeremy! I've just remembered! When it happened they sent him home, on compassionate leave. He *knew* his house had been blown up. Why would he tell you he was looking forward to living in it after the war —when he must have known it wasn't there?"

Mr. Behrens could think of nothing to say.

"You've been lying, haven't you? Who are you? What's it all about?"

Mr. Behrens put down his teacup, and said, gently, "I'm sorry I had to tell you a lot of lies, Mrs. Galloway. Please don't worry about it too much. I promise you that nothing you told me is going to hurt anyone."

The old lady gulped down her own tea. The color came back slowly to her cheeks. She said, "Whatever it is, I don't want to know about it." She stared out of the window at the place where a big house had once stood, inhabited by a bullying father and a sweet Irish mother, and three boys. She said, "It's all dead and done with, anyway."

As Mr. Behrens drove home in the dusk, his tires on the road hummed the words back at him. *Dead and done with. Dead and done with.*

Mr. Fortescue, who was the manager of the Westminster branch of the London and Home Counties Bank, and a number of other things besides, glared across his broad mahogany desk at Mr. Calder and Mr. Behrens and said, "I have never encountered such an irritating and frustrating case."

He made it sound as if they, and not the facts, were the cause of his irritation.

Mr. Behrens said, "I don't think people quite realize how heavily the scales are weighted in favor of a spy who's learned his job and keeps his head. All the stuff that Colonel Bessendine is passing out is stuff he's officially entitled to know. Progress of existing work, projects for new work, personnel to be employed, Security arrangements. It all comes into his field. Suppose he *does* keep notes of it. Suppose we searched his house, found those notes in his safe. Would it prove anything?"

"Of course it wouldn't," said Mr. Fortescue, sourly. "That's why you've got to catch him actually handing it over. I've had three men—apart from you—watching him for months. He behaves normally—goes up to town once or twice a week, goes to the cinema with his family, goes to local drink parties, has his friends in to dinner. All absolutely above suspicion."

"Quite so," said Mr. Behrens. "He goes up to London in the morning rush hour. He gets into a crowded underground train. Your man can't get too close to him. Bessendine's wedged up against another man who happens to be carrying a briefcase identical with his own. . . ."

"Do you think that's how it's done?"

"I've no idea," said Mr. Behrens. "But I wager I could invent half a dozen other methods just as simple and just as impossible to detect."

Mr. Calder said, "When exactly did Mark Bessendine start betraying his country's secrets to the Russians?"

"We can't be absolutely certain. But it's been going on for a very long time. Back to the Cold War which nearly turned into a hot war—1947, perhaps."

"Not before that?"

"Perhaps you had forgotten," said Mr. Fortescue, "that until 1945 the Russians were on our side."

"I wondered," said Mr. Calder, "if before that he might have been spying for the Germans. Have you looked at the 'Hessel' file lately?"

Both Mr. Fortescue and Mr. Behrens stared at Mr. Calder, who looked blandly back at them.

Mr. Behrens said, "We never found out who Hessel was, did we? He was just a code name to us."

"But the Russians found out," said Mr. Calder. "The first thing they did when they got to Berlin was to grab all Admiral Canaris's records. If they found the Hessel dossier there—if they found out that he had been posing successfully for more than four years as an officer in the Royal Marines—"

"Posing?" said Mr. Fortescue, shaprly.

"It occurred to me as a possibility."

"If Hessel is posing as Bessendine, where's Bessendine?" said Mr. Fortescue.

"At the bottom of a pre-Aryan chalk pit in Whitehorse Wood, above Lamperdown," said Mr. Calder, "with a bullet through his head."

Mr. Fortescue looked at Mr. Behrens, who said, "Yes, it's possible. I had thought of that."

"Lieutenant Mark Bessendine," said Mr. Calder, slowly, as if he was seeing it all as he spoke, "set off alone on November afternoon, with orders to close down and seal up Post Six. He'd have been in battle dress and carrying his Army pay book and identity papers with him, because in 1940 everyone did that. As he was climbing out of the post, he heard, or saw, a strange figure. A civilian, lurking in the woods, where no civilian should have been. He challenged him. And the answer was a bullet, from Hessel's gun. Hessel had landed that day, or the day before, on the south coast, from a submarine. Most of the spies who were landed that autumn lasted less than a week. Right?"

"They were a poor bunch," said Mr. Fortescue. "Badly equipped, and with the feeblest cover stories. I sometimes wondered if they were people Canaris wanted to get rid of."

"Exactly," said Mr. Calder. "But Hessel was a tougher proposition. He spoke excellent English—his mother was English, and he'd been to an English public school. And here was a God-sent chance to improve his equipment and cover. Bessendine was the same size and build. All he had to do was to change clothes and instead of being a phony civilian, liable to be questioned by the first constable he met, he was a properly dressed, fully documented Army officer. Provided he kept on the move, he could go anywhere in England. No one would question him. It wasn't the sort of cover that would last forever. But that didn't matter. His pick-up was probably fixed for four weeks ahead—in the next no-moon period. So he put on Bessendine's uniform, and started out for Gravesend. Not, I need hardly say, with any intention of going back to headquarters. All he wanted to do was to catch a train to London."

"But the Luftwaffe caught him."

"They did indeed," said Mr. Calder. "They caught him—and they set him free. Free of all possible suspicion. When he came out of that hospital six months later, he had a new face. More. He was a new man. If anyone asked him anything about his past, all he had to say was—'Oh, that was before I got blown up. I don't remember very much about that.'"

"But surely," said Mr. Fortescue, "it wasn't quite as easy as that. Bessendine's family—" He stopped.

"You've seen it too, haven't you?" said Mr. Calder. "He had no family. No one at all. One brother was dead, the other was in a prison camp in Germany. I wonder if it was a pure coincidence that he should later have been shot when trying to escape. Or did Himmler send a secret instruction to the camp authorities? Maybe it was just another bit of luck. Like Mark's parents being killed in the same raid. His mother's family lived in Ireland —and had disowned her. His father's family—if it existed—was in New Zealand. Mark Bessendine was completely and absolutely alone."

"The first Hessel messages went out to Germany at the end of 1941," said Mr. Fortescue. "How did he manage to send them?"

"No difficulty there," said Mr. Calder. "The German shortwave transmitters were very efficient. You only had to renew the batteries. He'd have buried his in the wood. He only had to dig it up again. He had all the call signals and codes."

Mr. Behrens had listened to this in silence, with a half smile on his face.

Now he cleared his throat and said, "If this—um—ingenious theory is true, it does—um—suggest a way of drawing out the gentleman concerned, does it not . . . ?"

"I was very interested when you told me about this dene-hole," said Colonel Bessendine to Mr. Behrens. "I had heard about them as a boy, of course, but I've never actually seen one."

"I hope we shan't be too late," said Mr. Behrens. "It'll be dark in an hour. You'd better park your car here. We'll have to do the rest of the trip on foot."

"I'm sorry I was late," said Colonel Bessendine. "I had a job I had to finish before I go off tomorrow."

"Off?"

"A short holiday. I'm taking my wife and daughter to France."

"I envy you," said Mr. Behrens. "Over the stile here and stright up the hill. I hope I can find it from this side. When I came here before I approached it from the other side. Fork right here, I think."

They moved up through the silent woods, each occupied with his own, very different, thoughts.

Mr. Behrens said, "I'm sure this was the clearing. Look. You can see the marks of the workmen's tractors. And this—I think—was the stump."

He stopped, and kicked at the foot of the elm bole. The loose covering pieces of turf on sticks, laid there by Arthur, collapsed, showing the dark entrance.

"Good Lord!" said Colonel Bessendine. He was standing, hands in raincoat pockets, shoulders hunched. "Don't tell me that people used to live in a place like that?"

"It's quite snug inside."

"Inside? You mean you've actually been inside it?" He shifted his weight so that it rested on his left foot and his right hand came out of his pocket and hung loose.

"Oh, certainly," said Mr. Behrens. "I found the body, too."

There was a long silence. That's the advantage of having a false face, thought Mr. Behrens. It's unfair. You can do your thinking behind it, and no one can watch you actually doing it.

The lips cracked into a smile.

"You're an odd card," said Colonel Bessendine. "Did you bring me all the way here to tell me that?"

"I brought you here," said Mr. Behrens, "so that you could explain one or two things that have been puzzling me." He had seated himself on the thick side of the stump. "For instance, you must have known about this hideout, since you and Sergeant Brewer and Corporal Stubbs built it in 1940. Why didn't you tell me that when I started describing it to you?"

"I wasn't quite sure then," said Colonel Bessendine. "I wanted to make sure."

As he spoke his right hand moved with a smooth unhurried gesture into the open front of his coat and out again. It was now holding a flat blue-black weapon which Mr. Behrens, who was a connoisseur in such matters, recognized as a *Zyanidpistole* or cyanide gun.

"Where did they teach you that draw?" he said. "In the *Marineamt?*"

For the first time he thought that the colonel was genuinely surprised. His face still revealed nothing, but there was a note of curiosity in his voice.

"I learned in Spain to carry a gun under my arm and draw it quickly," he said. "There were quite a few occasions on which you had to shoot people before they shot you. Your own side, sometimes. It was rather a confused war in some ways."

"I imagine so," said Mr. Behrens. He was sitting like a Buddha in the third attitude of repose, his feet crossed, the palms of his hands pressed flat, one on each knee. "I only mentioned it because some of my colleagues had a theory that you were a German agent called Hessel."

In the colonel's eyes a glint of genuine amusement appeared for a moment, like a face at a window, and ducked out of sight again.

"I gather that you were not convinced by this theory?"

"As a matter of fact, I wasn't."

"Oh. Why?"

"I remembered what your daughter told me. That you used to crawl up alongside a hedge running from the railway line to the private cricket ground at the big house. I went along and had a look. You couldn't crawl up along the hedge now. It's too overgrown. But there *is* a place at the top—it's hidden by the hedge, and I scratched myself damnably getting into it—where two bars are bent apart. A boy could have got through them easily."

"You're very thorough," said the colonel. "Is there anything you *haven't* found out about me?"

"I would be interested to know exactly when you started betraying your country. And why. Did you mean to do it all along and falling in with

Hessel and killing him gave you an opportunity—the wireless and the codes and the call signs—?"

"I can clearly see," said the colonel, "that you have never been blown up. Really blown to pieces, I mean. If you had been, you'd know that it's quite impossible to predict what sort of man will come down again. You can be turned inside out, or upside down. You can be born again. Things you didn't know were inside you can be shaken to the top."

"Saul becoming Paul, on the road to Damascus."

"You *are* an intelligent man," said the colonel. "It's a pleasure to talk to you. The analogy had not occurred to me, but it is perfectly apt. My father was a great man for disciplining youth, for regimentation, and the New Order. Because he was my father, I rebelled against it. That's natural enough. Because I rebelled against it, I fought for the Russians against the Germans in Spain. I saw how those young Nazis behaved. It was simply a rehearsal for them, you know. A rehearsal for the struggle they had dedicated their lives to. A knightly vigil, if you like. I saw them fight, and I saw them die. Any that were captured were usually tortured. I tortured them myself. If you torture a man and fail to break him, it becomes like a love affair. Did you know that?"

"I, too, have read the work of the Marquis de Sade," said Mr. Behrens. "Go on."

"When I lay in hospital in the darkness with my eyes bandaged, my hands strapped to my sides, coming slowly back to life, I had the strangest feeling. I *was* Hessel, I *was* the man I had left lying in the darkness at the bottom of the pit. I had closed his eyes and folded his hands, and now I was him. His work was my work. Where he had left it off, I would take it up. My father had been right and Hitler had been right and I had been wrong. And now I had been shown a way to repair the mistakes and follies of my former life. Does that sound mad to you?"

"Quite mad," said Mr. Behrens. "But I find it easier to believe than the rival theory—that the accident of having a new face enabled you to fool everyone for twenty-five years. You may have had no family, but there were school friends and Army friends and neighbors. But I interrupt you. When you got out of hospital and decided to carry on Hessel's work, I suppose you used his wireless set and his codes?"

"Until the end of the war, yes. Then I destroyed them. When I was forced to work for the Russians I began to use other methods. I'm afraid I can't discuss them, even with you. They involve too many other people."

In spite of the peril of his position, Mr. Behrens could not suppress a feeling of deep satisfaction. Not many of his plans had worked out so exactly. Colonel Bessendine was not a man given to confidences. A mixture of carefully devised forces was now driving him to talk. The time and the place; the fact that Mr. Behrens had established a certain intellectual supremacy over him; the fact that he must have been unable, for so many years, to speak freely to anyone; the fact that silence was no longer important, since he had made up his mind to liquidate his audience. On this last point Mr. Behrens was under no illusions. Colonel Bessendine was on his way out. France was only the first station on a line which led to eastern Germany and Moscow.

"One thing puzzles me," said the colonel, breaking into his thoughts. "During all the time we have been talking here—and I cannot tell you how much I have enjoyed our conversation—I couldn't help noticing that you have hardly moved. Your hands, for instance, have been lying cupped, one on each knee. When a fly annoyed you just now, instead of raising your hand to brush it off you shook your head violently."

Mr. Behrens said, raising his voice a little, "If I were to lift my right hand a very well-trained dog, who has been approaching you quietly from the rear while we were talking, would have jumped for your throat."

The colonel smiled. "Your imagination does you credit. What happens if you lift your left hand? Does a genie appear from a bottle and carry me off?"

"If I raise my left hand," said Mr. Behrens, "you will be shot dead." And so saying, he raised it.

The two men and the big dog stared down at the crumpled body. Rasselas sniffed at it, once, and turned away. It was carrion and no longer interesting.

"I'd have liked to try to pull him down alive," said Mr. Behrens. "But with that foul weapon in his hand I dared not chance it."

"It will solve a lot of Mr. Fortescue's problems," said Mr. Calder. He was unscrewing the telescopic sight from the rifle he was carrying.

"We'll put him down beside Hessel. I've brought two crowbars along with me. We ought to be able to shift the stump back into its original position. With any luck, they'll lie there, undisturbed, for a very long time."

Side by side in the dark earth, thought Mr. Behrens. Until the Day of Judgment, when all hearts are opened and all thoughts known.

"We'd better hurry, too," said Mr. Calder. "It's getting dark, and I want to get back in time for tea."

Midnight Blue

ROSS MACDONALD

Ross Macdonald (Kenneth Millar), as every mystery reader knows, ranks with Dashiell Hammett and Raymond Chandler as one of the finest writers of the "hardboiled" private-eye story. These three men, the "Big Three" as they have been called, defined and shaped the fictional private eye and in the process created both a literary tradition and a transcendent form of literature. The chronicles of Lew Archer are lyrical studies of violence and human aberration, with strong sociological and metaphysical overtones. "Midnight Blue," perhaps the best of Archer's short cases, is vintage Macdonald—a "mini-novel" of considerable power and skill.

It had rained in the canyon during the night. The world had the colored freshness of a butterfly just emerged from the chrysalis stage and trembling in the sun. Actual butterflies danced in flight across free spaces of air or played a game of tag without any rules among the tree branches. At this height there were giant pines among the eucalyptus trees.

I parked my car where I usually parked it, in the shadow of the stone building just inside the gates of the old estate. Just inside the posts, that is—the gates had long since fallen from their rusted hinges. The owner of the country house had died in Europe, and the place had stood empty since the war. It was one reason I came here on the occasional Sunday when I wanted to get away from the Hollywood rat race. Nobody lived within two miles.

Until now, anyway. The window of the gatehouse overlooking the drive had been broken the last time that I'd noticed it. Now it was patched up with a piece of cardboard. Through a hole punched in the middle of the cardboard, bright emptiness watched me—human eye's bright emptiness.

"Hello," I said.

A grudging voice answered: "Hello."

The gatehouse door creaked open, and a white-haired man came out. A smile sat strangely on his ravaged face. He walked mechanically, shuffling in the leaves, as if his body was not at home in the world. He wore faded denims through which his clumsy muscles bulged like animals in a sack. His feet were bare.

I saw when he came up to me that he was a huge old man, a head taller than I was and a foot wider. His smile was not a greeting or any kind of a smile that I could respond to. It was the stretched, blind grimace of a man who lived in a world of his own, a world that didn't include me.

"Get out of here. I don't want trouble. I don't want nobody messing around."

"No trouble," I said. "I came up to do a little target shooting. I probably have as much right here as you have."

His eyes widened. They were as blue and empty as holes in his head through which I could see the sky.

"Nobody has the rights here that I have. I lifted up mine eyes unto the hills and the voice spoke and I found sanctuary. Nobody's going to force me out of my sanctuary."

I could feel the short hairs bristling on the back of my neck. Though my instincts didn't say so, he was probably a harmless nut. I tried to keep my instincts out of my voice.

"I won't bother you. You don't bother me. That should be fair enough."

"You bother me just *being* here. I can't stand people. I can't stand cars. And this is twice in two days you come up harrying me and harassing me."

"I haven't been here for a month."

"You're an Ananias liar." His voice whined like a rising wind. He clenched his knobbed fists and shuddered on the verge of violence.

"Calm down, old man," I said. "There's room in the world for both of us."

He looked around at the high green world as if my words had snapped him out of a dream.

"You're right," he said in a different voice. "I have been blessed, and I must remember to be joyful. Joyful. Creation belongs to all of us poor creatures." His smiling teeth were as long and yellow as an old horse's. His roving glance fell on my car. "And it wasn't you who come up here last night. It was a different automobile. I remember."

He turned away, muttering something about washing his socks, and dragged his horny feet back into the gatehouse. I got my targets, pistol, and ammunition out of the trunk, and locked the car up tight. The old man watched me through his peephole, but he didn't come out again.

Below the road, in the wild canyon, there was an open meadow backed by a sheer bank which was topped by the crumbling wall of the estate. It was my shooting gallery. I slid down the wet grass of the bank and tacked a target to an oak tree, using the butt of my heavy-framed .22 as a hammer.

While I was loading it, something caught my eye—something that glinted red, like a ruby among the leaves. I stooped to pick it up and found that it was attached. It was a red-enameled fingernail at the tip of a white hand. The hand was cold and stiff.

I let out a sound that must have been loud in the stillness. A jay bird erupted from a manzanita, sailed up to a high limb of the oak, and yelled down curses at me. A dozen chickadees flew out of the oak and settled in another at the far end of the meadow.

Panting like a dog, I scraped away the dirt and wet leaves that had been loosely piled over the body. It was the body of a girl wearing a midnight-blue sweater and skirt. She was a blond, about seventeen. The blood that congested her face made her look old and dark. The white rope with which she had been garrotted was sunk almost out of sight in the flesh of her neck. The rope was tied at the nape in what is called a granny's knot, the kind of knot that any child can tie.

I left her where she lay and climbed back up to the road on trembling knees. The grass showed traces of the track her body had made where someone had dragged it down the bank. I looked for tire marks on the shoulder and in the rutted, impacted gravel of the road. If there had been any, the rain had washed them out.

I trudged up the road to the gatehouse and knocked on the door. It creaked inward under my hand. Inside there was nothing alive but the spiders that had webbed the low black beams. A dustless rectangle in front of the stone fireplace showed where a bedroll had lain. Several blackened tin cans had evidently been used as cooking utensils. Gray embers lay on the cavernous hearth. Suspended above it from a spike in the mantel was a pair of white cotton work socks. The socks were wet. Their owner had left in a hurry.

It wasn't my job to hunt him. I drove down the canyon to the highway and along it for a few miles to the outskirts of the nearest town. There a drab green box of a building with a flag in front of it housed the Highway Patrol. Across the highway was a lumberyard, deserted on Sunday.

"Too bad about Ginnie," the dispatcher said when she had radioed the local sheriff. She was a thirtyish brunette with fine black eyes and dirty fingernails. She had on a plain white blouse, which was full of her.

"Did you know Ginnie?"

"My young sister knows her. They go—they went to high school to-gether. It's an awful thing when it happens to a young person like that. I knew she was missing—I got the report when I came on at eight—but I kept hoping that she was just off on a lost weekend, like. Now there's nothing to hope for, is there?" Her eyes were liquid with feeling. "Poor Ginnie. And poor Mr. Green."

"Her father?"

"That's right. He was in here with her high school counselor not more than an hour ago. I hope he doesn't come back right away. I don't want to be the one that has to tell him."

"How long has the girl been missing?"

"Just since last night. We got the report here about 3 A.M., I think. Apparently she wandered away from a party at Cavern Beach. Down the pike a ways." She pointed south toward the mouth of the canyon.

"What kind of a party was it?"

"Some of the kids from the Union High School—they took some wienies down and had a fire. The party was part of graduation week. I happen to know about it because my young sister Alice went. I didn't want her to go, even if it was supervised. That can be a dangerous beach at night. All sorts of bums and scroungers hang out in the caves. Why, one night when I was a kid I saw a naked man down there in the moonlight. He didn't have a woman with him either."

She caught the drift of her words, did a slow blush, and checked her loquacity. I leaned on the plywood counter between us.

"What sort of girl was Ginnie Green?"

"I wouldn't know. I never really knew her."

"Your sister does."

"I don't let my sister run around with girls like Ginnie Green. Does that answer your question?"

"Not in any detail."

"It seems to me you ask a lot of questions."

"I'm naturally interested, since I found her. Also, I happen to be a private detective."

"Looking for a job?"

"I can always use a job."

"So can I, and I've got one and I don't intend to lose it." She softened the words with a smile. "Excuse me; I have work to do."

She turned to her shortwave and sent out a message to the patrol cars that Virginia Green had been found. Virginia Green's father heard it as he came in the door. He was a puffy gray-faced man with red-rimmed eyes. Striped pajama bottoms showed below the cuffs of his trousers. His shoes were muddy, and he walked as if he had been walking all night.

He supported himself on the edge of the counter, opening and shutting his mouth like a beached fish. Words came out, half strangled by shock.

"I heard you say she was dead, Anita."

The woman raised her eyes to his. "Yes. I'm awfully sorry, Mr. Green."

He put his face down on the counter and stayed there like a penitent, perfectly still. I could hear a clock somewhere, snipping off seconds, and in the back of the room the L.A. police signals like muttering voices coming in from another planet. Another planet very much like this one, where violence measured out the hours.

"It's my fault," Green said to the bare wood under his face. "I didn't bring her up properly. I haven't been a good father."

The woman watched him with dark and glistening eyes ready to spill. She stretched out an unconscious hand to touch him, pulled her hand back in embarrassment when a second man came into the station. He was a young man with crew-cut brown hair, tanned and fit-looking in a Hawaiian shirt. Fit-looking except for the glare of sleeplessness in his eyes and the anxious lines around them.

"What is it, Miss Brocco? What's the word?"

"The word is bad." She sounded angry. "Somebody murdered Ginnie Green. This man here is a detective and he just found her body up in Trumbull Canyon."

The young man ran his fingers through his short hair and failed to get a grip on it, or on himself. "My God! That's terrible!"

"Yes," the woman said. "You were supposed to be looking after her, weren't you?"

They glared at each other across the counter. The tips of her breasts pointed at him through her blouse like accusing fingers. The young man lost the glaring match. He turned to me with a wilted look.

"My name is Connor, Franklin Connor, and I'm afraid I'm very much to blame in this. I'm a counselor at the high school, and I was supposed to be looking after the party, as Miss Brocco said."

"Why didn't you?"

"I didn't realize. I mean, I thought they were all perfectly happy and safe. The boys and girls had pretty well paired off around the fire. Frankly, I felt rather out of place. They aren't children, you know. They were all seniors, they had cars. So I said good night and walked home along the beach. As a matter of fact, I was hoping for a phone call from my wife."

"What time did you leave the party?"

"It must have been nearly eleven. The ones who hadn't paired off had already gone home."

"Who did Ginnie pair off with?"

"I don't know. I'm afraid I wasn't paying too much attention to the kids. It's graduation week, and I've had a lot of problems—"

The father, Green, had been listening with a changing face. In a sudden yammering rage his implosive grief and guilt exploded outward.

"It's your business to know! By God, I'll have your job for this. I'll make it *my* business to run you out of town."

Connor hung his head and looked at the stained tile floor. There was a thin spot in his short brown hair, and his scalp gleamed through it like bare white bone. It was turning into a bad day for everybody, and I felt the dull old nagging pull of other people's trouble, like a toothache you can't leave alone.

The sheriff arrived, flanked by several deputies and an HP sergeant. He wore a Western hat and a rawhide tie and a blue gabardine business suit which together produced a kind of gun-smog effect. His name was Pearsall.

I rode back up the canyon in the right front seat of Pearsall's black Buick, filling him in on the way. The deputies' Ford and an HP car followed us, and Green's new Oldsmobile convertible brought up the rear.

The sheriff said: "The old guy sounds like a looney to me."

"He's a loner, anyway."

"You never can tell about them hoboes. That's why I give my boys instructions to roust 'em. Well, it looks like an open-and-shut case."

"Maybe. Let's keep our minds open anyway, sheriff."

"Sure. Sure. But the old guy went on the run. That shows consciousness of guilt. Don't worry, we'll hunt him down. I got men that know these hills like you know your wife's geography."

"I'm not married."

"Your girl friend, then." He gave me a sideways leer that was no gift. "And if we can't find him on foot, we'll use the air squadron."

"You have an air squadron?"

"Volunteer, mostly local ranchers. We'll get him." His tires squealed on a curve. "Was the girl raped?"

"I didn't try to find out. I'm not a doctor. I left her as she was."

The sheriff grunted. "You did the right thing at that."

Nothing had changed in the high meadow. The girl lay waiting to have her picture taken. It was taken many times, from several angles. All the birds flew away. Her father leaned on a tree and watched them go. Later he was sitting on the ground.

I volunteered to drive him home. It wasn't pure altruism. I'm incapable of it. I said when I had turned his Oldsmobile:

"Why did you say it was your fault, Mr. Green?"

He wasn't listening. Below the road four uniformed men were wrestling a heavy covered aluminum stretcher up the steep bank. Green watched them as he had watched the departing birds, until they were out of sight around a curve.

"She was so young," he said to the back seat.

I waited, and tried again. "Why did you blame yourself for her death?"

He roused himself from his daze. "Did I say that?"

"In the Highway Patrol office you said something of the sort."

He touched my arm. "I didn't mean I killed her."

"I didn't think you meant that. I'm interested in finding out who did."

"Are you a cop—a policeman?"

"I have been."

"You're not with the locals."

"No. I happen to be a private detective from Los Angeles. The name is Archer."

He sat and pondered this information. Below and ahead the summer sea brimmed up in the mouth of the canyon.

"You don't think the old tramp did her in?" Green said.

"It's hard to figure out how he could have. He's a strong-looking old buzzard, but he couldn't have carried her all the way up from the beach. And she wouldn't have come along with him of her own accord."

It was a question, in a way.

"I don't know," her father said. "Ginnie was a little wild. She'd do a thing *because* it was wrong, *because* it was dangerous. She hated to turn down a dare, especially from a man."

"There were men in her life?"

"She was attractive to men. You saw her, even as she is." He gulped. "Don't get me wrong. Ginnie was never a *bad* girl. She was a little headstrong, and I made mistakes. That's why I blame myself."

"What sort of mistakes, Mr. Green?"

"All the usual ones, and some I made up on my own." His voice was bitter. "Ginnie didn't have a mother, you see. Her mother left me years ago, and it was as much my fault as hers. I tried to bring her up myself. I didn't give her proper supervision. I run a restaurant in town, and I don't get home nights till after midnight. Ginnie was pretty much on her own since she was in grade school. We got along fine when I was there, but I usually wasn't there.

"The worst mistake I made was letting her work in the restaurant over the weekends. That started about a year ago. She wanted the money for clothes, and I thought the discipline would be good for her. I thought I could keep an eye on her, you know. But it didn't work out. She grew up too fast, and the night work played hell with her studies. I finally got the word from the school authorities. I fired her a couple of months ago, but I guess it was too late. We haven't been getting along too well since then. Mr. Connor said she resented my indecision, that I gave her too much responsibility and then took it away again."

"You've talked her over with Connor?"

"More than once, including last night. He was her academic counselor, and he was concerned about her grades. We both were. Ginnie finally pulled through, after all, thanks to him. She was going to graduate. Not that it matters now, of course."

Green was silent for a time. The sea expanded below us like a second blue dawn. I could hear the roar of the highway. Green touched my elbow again, as if he needed human contact.

"I oughtn't to've blown my top at Connor. He's a decent boy, he means well. He gave my daughter hours of free tuition this last month. And he's got troubles of his own, like he said."

"What troubles?"

"I happen to know his wife left him, same as mine. I shouldn't have borne down so hard on him. I have a lousy temper, always have had." He hesitated, then blurted out as if he had found a confessor: "I said a terrible thing to Ginnie at supper last night. She always has supper with me at the restaurant. I said if she wasn't home when I got home last night that I'd wring her neck."

"And she wasn't home," I said. And somebody wrung her neck, I didn't say.

The light at the highway was red. I glanced at Green. Tear tracks glistened like snail tracks on his face.

"Tell me what happened last night."

"There isn't anything much to tell," he said. "I got to the house about twelve-thirty, and, like you said, she wasn't home. So I called Al Brocco's house. He's my night cook, and I knew his youngest daughter Alice was at the moonlight party on the beach. Alice was home all right."

"Did you talk to Alice?"

"She was in bed asleep. Al woke her up, but I didn't talk to her. She told him she didn't know where Ginnie was. I went to bed, but I couldn't sleep. Finally I got up and called Mr. Connor. That was about one-thirty. I thought I should get in touch with the authorities, but he said no, Ginnie had enough black marks against her already. He came over to the house and we waited for a while and then we went down to Cavern Beach. There was no trace of her. I said it was time to call in the authorities, and he agreed. We went to his beach house, because it was nearer, and called the sheriff's office from there. We went back to the beach with a couple of flashlights and went through the caves. He stayed with me all night. I give him that."

"Where are these caves?"

"We'll pass them in a minute. I'll show you if you want. But there's nothing in any of the three of them."

Nothing but shadows and empty beer cans, discarded contraceptives, the odor of rotting kelp. I got sand in my shoes and sweat under my collar. The sun dazzled my eyes when I half walked, half crawled, from the last of the caves.

Green was waiting beside a heap of ashes.

"This is where they had the wienie roast," he said.

I kicked the ashes. A half-burned sausage rolled along the sand. Sand fleas hopped in the sun like fat on a griddle. Green and I faced each other over the dead fire. He looked out to sea. A seal's face floated like a small black nose cone beyond the breakers. Farther out a water skier slid between unfolding wings of spray.

Away up the beach two people were walking toward us. They were small and lonely and distinct as Chirico figures in the long white distance.

Green squinted against the sun. Red-rimmed or not, his eyes were good. "I believe that's Mr. Connor. I wonder who the woman is with him."

They were walking as close as lovers, just above the white margin of the surf. They pulled apart when they noticed us, but they were still holding hands as they approached.

"It's Mrs. Connor," Green said in a low voice.

"I thought you said she left him."

"That's what he told me last night. She took off on him a couple of weeks ago, couldn't stand a high school teacher's hours. She must have changed her mind."

She looked as though she had a mind to change. She was a hard-faced blond who walked like a man. A certain amount of style took the curse off her stiff angularity. She had on a madras shirt, mannishly cut, and a pair of black Capri pants that hugged her long, slim legs. She had good legs.

Connor looked at us in complex embarrassment. "I thought it was you from a distance, Mr. Green. I don't believe you know my wife."

"I've seen her in my place of business." He explained to the woman: "I run the Highway Restaurant in town."

"How do you do," she said aloofly, then added in an entirely different voice: "You're Virginia's father, aren't you? I'm so sorry."

The words sounded queer. Perhaps it was the surroundings; the ashes on the beach, the entrances to the caves, the sea, and the empty sky which dwarfed us all. Green answered her solemnly.

"Thank you, ma'am. Mr. Connor was a strong right arm to me last night. I can tell you." He was apologizing. And Connor responded:

"Why don't you come to our place for a drink? It's just down the beach. You look as if you could use one, Mr. Green. You, too," he said to me. "I don't believe I know your name."

"Archer. Lew Archer."

He gave me a hard hand. His wife interposed. "I'm sure Mr. Green and his friend won't want to be bothered with us on a day like this. Besides, it isn't even noon yet, Frank."

She was the one who didn't want to be bothered. We stood around for a minute, exchanging grim, nonsensical comments on the beauty of the day. Then she led Connor back in the direction they had come from. Private property, her attitude seemed to say: trespassers will be fresh-frozen.

I drove Green to the Highway Patrol station. He said that he was feeling better, and could make it home from there by himself. He thanked me profusely for being a friend in need to him, as he put it. He followed me to the door of the station, thanking me.

The dispatcher was cleaning her fingernails with an ivory-handled file. She glanced up eagerly.

"Did they catch him yet?"

"I was going to ask you the same question, Miss Brocco."

"No such luck. But they'll get him," she said with female vindictive-
ness. "The sheriff called out his air squadron, and he sent to Ventura for
bloodhounds."

"Big deal."

She bridled. "What do you mean by that?"

"I don't think the old man of the mountain killed her. If he had, he
wouldn't have waited till this morning to go on the lam. He'd have taken
off right away."

"Then why did he go on the lam at all?" The word sounded strange
in her prim mouth.

"I think he saw me discover the body, and realized he'd be blamed."

She considered this, bending the long nail file between her fingers. "If
the old tramp didn't do it, who did?"

"You may be able to help me answer that question."

"Me help you? How?"

"You know Frank Connor, for one thing."

"I know him. I've seen him about my sister's grades a few times."

"You don't seem to like him much."

"I don't like him, I don't dislike him. He's just blah to me."

"Why? What's the matter with him?"

Her tight mouth quivered, and let out words: "*I* don't know what's the
matter with him. He can't keep his hands off of young girls."

"How do you know that?"

"I heard it."

"From your sister Alice?"

"Yes. The rumor was going around the school, she said."

"Did the rumor involve Ginnie Green?"

She nodded. Her eyes were as black as fingerprint ink.

"Is that why Connor's wife left him?"

"I wouldn't know about that. I never even laid eyes on Mrs. Connor."

"You haven't been missing much."

There was a yell outside, a kind of choked ululation. It sounded as much
like an animal as a man. It was Green. When I reached the door, he
was climbing out of his convertible with a heavy blue revolver in his
hand.

"I saw the killer," he cried out exultantly.

"Where?"

He waved the revolver toward the lumberyard across the road. "He
poked his head up behind that pile of white pine. When he saw me, he

ran like a deer. I'm going to get him."

"No. Give me the gun."

"Why? I got a license to carry it. And use it."

He started across the four-lane highway, dodging through the moving patterns of the Sunday traffic as if he were playing Parcheesi on the kitchen table at home. The sounds of brakes and curses split the air. He had scrambled over the locked gate of the yard before I got to it. I went over after him.

Green disappeared behind a pile of lumber. I turned the corner and saw him running halfway down a long aisle walled with stacked wood and floored with beaten earth. The old man of the mountain was running ahead of him. His white hair blew in the wind of his own movement. A burlap sack bounced on his shoulders like a load of sorrow and shame.

"Stop or I'll shoot!" Green cried.

The old man ran on as if the devil himself were after him. He came to a cyclone fence, discarded his sack, and tried to climb it. He almost got over. Three strands of barbed wire along the top of the fence caught and held him struggling.

I heard a tearing sound, and then the sound of a shot. The huge old body espaliered on the fence twitched and went limp, fell heavily to the earth. Green stood over him breathing through his teeth.

I pushed him out of the way. The old man was alive, though there was blood in his mouth. He spat it onto his chin when I lifted his head.

"You shouldn't ought to of done it. I come to turn myself in. Then I got ascairt."

"Why were you scared?"

"I watched you uncover the little girl in the leaves. I knew I'd be blamed. I'm one of the chosen. They always blame the chosen. I been in trouble before."

"Trouble with girls?" At my shoulder Green was grinning terribly.

"Trouble with cops."

"For killing people?" Green said.

"For preaching on the street without a license. The voice told me to preach to the tribes of the wicked. And the voice told me this morning to come in and give my testimony."

"What voice?"

"The great voice." His voice was little and weak. He coughed red.

"He's as crazy as a bedbug," Green said.

"Shut up." I turned back to the dying man. "What testimony do you have to give?"

"About the car I seen. It woke me up in the middle of the night, stopped in the road below my sanctuary."

"What kind of car?"

"I don't know cars. I think it was one of them foreign cars. It made a noise to wake the dead."

"Did you see who was driving it?"

"No. I didn't go near. I was ascairt."

"What time was this car in the road?"

"I don't keep track of time. The moon was down behind the trees."

Those were his final words. He looked up at the sky with his skycolored eyes, straight into the sun. His eyes changed color.

Green said: "Don't tell them. If you do, I'll make a liar out of you. I'm a respected citizen in this town. I got a business to lose. And they'll believe me ahead of you, mister."

"Shut up."

He couldn't. "The old fellow was lying, anyway. You know that. You heard him say yourself that he heard voices. That proves he's a psycho. He's a psycho killer. I shot him down like you would a mad dog, and I did right."

He waved the revolver.

"You did wrong, Green, and you know it. Give me that gun before it kills somebody else."

He thrust it into my hand suddenly. I unloaded it, breaking my fingernails in the process, and handed it back to him empty. He nudged up against me.

"Listen, maybe I did do wrong. I had provocation. It doesn't have to get out. I got a business to lose."

He fumbled in his hip pocket and brought out a thick sharkskin wallet. "Here. I can pay you good money. You say that you're a private eye; you know how to keep your lip buttoned."

I walked away and left him blabbering beside the body of the man he had killed. They were both victims, in a sense, but only one of them had blood on his hands.

Miss Brocco was in the HP parking lot. Her bosom was jumping with excitement.

"I heard a shot."

"Green shot the old man. Dead. You better send in for the meat wagon and call off your bloody dogs."

The words hit her like slaps. She raised her hand to her face, defensively. "Are you mad at me? Why are you mad at me?"

"I'm mad at everybody."

"You still don't think he did it."

"I know damned well he didn't. I want to talk to your sister."

"Alice? What for?"

"Information. She was on the beach with Ginnie Green last night. She may be able to tell me something."

"You leave Alice alone."

"I'll treat her gently. Where do you live?"

"I don't want my little sister dragged into this filthy mess."

"All I want to know is who Ginnie paired off with."

"I'll ask Alice. I'll tell you."

"Come on, Miss Brocco, we're wasting time. I don't need your permission to talk to your sister, after all. I can get the address out of the phone book if I have to."

She flared up and then flared down.

"You win. We live on Orlando Street, 224. That's on the other side of town. You will be nice to Alice, won't you? She's bothered enough as it is about Ginnie's death."

"She really was a friend of Ginnie's, then?"

"Yes. I tried to break it up. But you know how kids are—two motherless girls, they stick together. I tried to be like a mother to Alice."

"What happened to your own mother?"

"Father—I mean, she died." A greenish pallor invaded her face and turned it to old bronze. "Please. I don't want to talk about it. I was only a kid when she died."

She went back to her muttering radios. She was quite a woman, I thought as I drove away. Nubile but unmarried, probably full of untapped Mediterranean passions. If she worked an eight-hour shift and started at eight, she'd be getting off about four.

It wasn't a large town, and it wasn't far across it. The highway doubled as its main street. I passed the Union High School. On the green playing field beside it a lot of kids in mortarboards and gowns were rehearsing their graduation exercises. A kind of pall seemed to hang over the field. Perhaps it was in my mind.

Father along the street I passed Green's Highway Restaurant. A dozen cars stood in its parking space. A couple of white-uniformed waitresses were scooting around behind the plate-glass windows.

Orlando Street was a lower-middle-class residential street bisected by the highway. Jacaranda trees bloomed like low small purple clouds among its stucco and frame cottages. Fallen purple petals carpeted the narrow lawn in front of the Brocco house.

A thin, dark man, wiry under his T-shirt, was washing a small red Fiat in the driveway beside the front porch. He must have been over fifty, but his long hair was as black as an Indian's. His Sicilian nose was humped in the middle by an old break.

"Mr. Brocco?"

"That's me."

"Is your daughter Alice home?"

"She's home."

"I'd like to speak to her."

He turned off his hose, pointing its dripping nozzle at me like a gun. "You're a little old for her, ain't you?"

"I'm a detective investigating the death of Ginnie Green."

"Alice don't know nothing about that."

"I've just been talking to your older daughter at the Highway Patrol office. She thinks Alice may know something."

He shifted on his feet. "Well, if Anita says it's all right."

"It's okay, dad," a girl said from the front door. "Anita just called me on the telephone. Come in, Mr.—Archer, isn't it?"

"Archer."

She opened the screen door for me. It opened directly into a small square living room containing worn green frieze furniture and a television set which the girl switched off. She was a handsome, serious-looking girl, a younger version of her sister with ten years and ten pounds subtracted and a pony tail added. She sat down gravely on the edge of a chair, waving her hand at the chesterfield. Her movements were languid. There were blue depressions under her eyes. Her face was sallow.

"What kind of questions do you want to ask me? My sister didn't say."

"Who was Ginnie with last night?"

"Nobody. I mean, she was with me. She didn't make out with any of the boys." She glanced from me to the blind television set, as if she felt caught between. "It said on the television that she was with a man, that there was medical evidence to prove it. But I didn't see her with no man. Any man."

"Did Ginnie go with men?"

She shook her head. Her pony tail switched and hung limp. She was close to tears.

"You told Anita she did."

"I did not!"

"Your sister wouldn't lie. You passed on a rumor to her—a high school rumor that Ginnie had had something to do with one man in particular."

The girl was watching my face in fascination. Her eyes were like a bird's, bright and shallow and fearful.

"Was the rumor true?"

She shrugged her thin shoulders: "How would I know?"

"You were good friends with Ginnie."

"Yes. I was." Her voice broke on the past tense. "She was a real nice kid, even if she was kind of boy crazy."

"She was boy crazy, but she didn't make out with any of the boys last night."

"Not while I was there."

"Did she make out with Mr. Connor?"

"No. He wasn't there. He went away. He said he was going home. He lives up the beach."

"What did Ginnie do?"

"I don't know. I didn't notice."

"You said she was with you. Was she with you all evening?"

"Yes." Her face was agonized. "I mean no."

"Did Ginnie go away, too?"

She nodded.

"In the same direction Mr. Connor took? The direction of his house?"

Her head moved almost imperceptibly downward.

"What time was that, Alice?"

"About eleven o'clock, I guess."

"And Ginnie never came back from Mr. Connor's house?"

"I don't know. I don't know for certain that she went there."

"But Ginnie and Mr. Connor were good friends?"

"I guess so."

"How good? Like a boy friend and a girl friend?"

She sat mute, her birdlike stare unblinking.

"Tell me, Alice."

"I'm afraid."

"Afraid of Mr. Connor?"

"No. Not him."

"Has someone threatened you—told you not to talk?"

Her head moved in another barely perceptible nod.

"Who threatened you, Alice? You'd better tell me for your own protection. Whoever did threaten you is probably a murderer."

She burst into frantic tears. Brocco came to the door.

"What goes on in here?"

"Your daughter is upset, I'm sorry."

"Yeah, and I know who upset her. You better get out of here or you'll be sorrier."

He opened the screen door and held it open, his head poised like a dark and broken ax. I went out past him. He spat after me. The Broccos were a very emotional family.

I started back toward Connor's beach house on the south side of town but ran into a diversion on the way. Green's car was parked in the lot beside his restaurant. I went in.

The place smelled of grease. It was almost full of late Sunday lunchers seated in booths and at the U-shaped breakfast bar in the middle. Green himself was sitting on a stool behind the cash register counting money. He was counting it as if his life and his hope of heaven depended on the colored paper in his hands.

He looked up, smiling loosely and vaguely. "Yes, sir?" Then he recognized me. His face went through a quick series of transformations and settled for a kind of boozy shame. "I know I shouldn't be here working on a day like this. But it keeps my mind off my troubles. Besides, they steal you blind if you don't watch 'em. And I'll be needing the money."

"What for, Mr. Green?"

"The trial." He spoke the word as if it gave him a bitter satisfaction.

"Whose trial?"

"Mine. I told the sheriff what the old guy said. And what I did. I know what I did. I shot him down like a dog, and I had no right to. I was crazy with my sorrow, you might say."

He was less crazy now. The shame in his eyes was clearing. But the sorrow was still there in their depths, like stone at the bottom of a well.

"I'm glad you told the truth, Mr. Green."

"So am I. It doesn't help him, and it doesn't bring Ginnie back. But at least I can live with myself."

"Speaking of Ginnie," I said. "Was she seeing quite a lot of Frank Connor?"

"Yeah. I guess you could say so. He came over to help her with her studies quite a few times. At the house, and at the library. He didn't charge me any tuition, either."

"That was nice of him. Was Ginnie fond of Connor?"

"Sure she was. She thought very highly of Mr. Connor."

"Was she in love with him?"

"In love? Hell, I never thought of anything like that. Why?"

"Did she have dates with Connor?"

"Not to my knowledge," he said. "If she did, she must have done it behind my back." His eyes narrowed to two red swollen slits. "You think Frank Connor had something to do with her death?"

"It's a possibility. Don't go into a sweat now. You know where that gets you."

"Don't worry. But what about this Connor? Did you get something on him? I thought he was acting queer last night."

"Queer in what way?"

"Well, he was pretty tight when he came to the house. I gave him a stiff snort, and that straightened him out for a while. But later on, down on the beach, he got almost hysterical. He was running around like a rooster with his head chopped off."

"Is he a heavy drinker?"

"I wouldn't know. I never saw him drink before last night at my house." Green narrowed his eyes. "But he tossed down a triple bourbon like it was water. And remember this morning, he offered us a drink on the beach. A drink in the morning, that isn't the usual thing, especially for a high school teacher."

"I noticed that."

"What else have you been noticing?"

"We won't go into it now," I said. "I don't want to ruin a man unless and until I'm sure he's got it coming."

He sat on his stool with his head down. Thought moved murkily under his knitted brows. His glance fell on the money in his hands. He was counting tens.

"Listen, Mr. Archer. You're working on this case on your own, aren't you? For free?"

"So far."

"So go to work for me. Nail Connor for me, and I'll pay you whatever you ask."

"Not so fast," I said. "We don't know that Connor is guilty. There are other possibilities."

"Such as?"

"If I tell you, can I trust you not to go on a shooting spree?"

"Don't worry," he repeated. "I've had that."

"Where's your revolver?"

"I turned it in to Sheriff Pearsall. He asked for it."

We were interrupted by a family group getting up from one of the booths. They gave Green their money and their sympathy. When they were out of hearing, I said:

"You mentioned that your daughter worked here in the restaurant for a while. Was Al Brocco working here at the same time?"

"Yeah. He's been my night cook for six-seven years. Al is a darned good cook. He trained as a chef on the Italian line." His slow mind, punchy with grief, did a double-take. "You wouldn't be saying that he messed around with Ginnie?"

"I'm asking you."

"Shucks, Al is old enough to be her father. He's all wrapped up in his own girls, Anita in particular. He worships the ground she walks on. She's the mainspring of that family."

"How did he get on with Ginnie?"

"Very well. They kidded back and forth. She was the only one who could ever make him smile. Al is a sad man, you know. He had a tragedy in his life."

"His wife's death?"

"It was worse than that," Green said. "Al Brocco killed his wife with his own hand. He caught her with another man and put a knife in her."

"And he's walking around loose?"

"The other man was a Mex," Green said in an explanatory way. "A wetback. He couldn't even talk the English language. The town hardly blamed Al, the jury gave him manslaughter. But when he got out of the pen, the people at the Pink Flamingo wouldn't give him his old job back —he used to be chef there. So I took him on. I felt sorry for his girls, I guess, and Al's been a good worker. A man doesn't do a thing like that twice, you know."

He did another slow mental double-take. His mouth hung open. I could see the gold in its corners.

"Let's hope not."

"Listen here," he said. "You go to work for me, eh? You nail the guy, whoever he is. I'll pay you. I'll pay you now. How much do you want?"

I took a hundred dollars of his money and left him trying to comfort himself with the rest of it. The smell of grease stayed in my nostrils.

Connor's house clung to the edge of a low bluff about halfway between the HP station and the mouth of the canyon where the thing had begun:

a semicantilevered redwood cottage with a closed double garage fronting the highway. From the grapestake-fenced patio in the angle between the garage and the front door a flight of wooden steps climbed to the flat roof which was railed as a sun deck. A second set of steps descended the fifteen or twenty feet to the beach.

I tripped on a pair of garden shears crossing the patio to the garage window. I peered into the interior twilight. Two things inside interested me: a dismasted flattie sitting on a trailer, and a car. The sailboat interested me because its cordage resembled the white rope that had strangled Ginnie. The car interested me because it was an imported model, a low-slung Triumph two-seater.

I was planning to have a closer look at it when a woman's voice screeked overhead like a gull's:

"What do you think you're doing?"

Mrs. Connor was leaning over the railing on the roof. Her hair was in curlers. She looked like a blond Gorgon. I smiled up at her, the way that Greek whose name I don't remember must have smiled.

"Your husband invited me for a drink, remember? I don't know whether he gave me a rain check or not."

"He did not! Go away! My husband is sleeping!"

"Ssh. You'll wake him up. You'll wake up the people in Forest Lawn."

She put her hand to her mouth. From the expression on her face she seemed to be biting her hand. She disappeared for a moment, and then came down the steps with a multicolored silk scarf over her curlers. The rest of her was sheathed in a white satin bathing suit. Against it her flesh looked like brown wood.

"You get out of here," she said. "Or I shall call the police."

"Fine. Call them. I've got nothing to hide."

"Are you implying that we have?"

"We'll see. Why did you leave your husband?"

"That's none of your business."

"I'm making it my business, Mrs. Connor. I'm a detective investigating the murder of Ginnie Green. Did you leave Frank on account of Ginnie Green?"

"No. No! I wasn't even aware—" Her hand went to her mouth again. She chewed on it some more.

"You weren't aware that Frank was having an affair with Ginnie Green?"

"He wasn't."

"So you say. Others say different."

"What others? Anita Brocco? You can't believe anything *that* woman says. Why, her own father is a murderer, everybody in town knows that."

"Your own husband may be another, Mrs. Connor. You might as well come clean with me."

"But I have nothing to tell you."

"You can tell me why you left him."

"That is a private matter, between Frank and me. It has nothing to do with anybody but us." She was calming down, setting her moral forces in a stubborn, defensive posture.

"There's usually only the one reason."

"I had my reasons. I said they were none of your business. I chose for reasons of my own to spend a month with my parents in Long Beach."

"When did you come back?"

"This morning."

"Why this morning?"

"Frank called me. He said he needed me." She touched her thin breast absently, pathetically, as if perhaps she hadn't been much needed in the past.

"Needed you for what?"

"As his wife," she said. "He said there might be tr—" Her hand went to her mouth again. She said around it: "Trouble."

"Did he name the kind of trouble?"

"No."

"What time did he call you?"

"Very early, around seven o'clock."

"That was more than an hour before I found Ginnie's body."

"He knew she was missing. He spent the whole night looking for her."

"Why would he do that, Mrs. Connor?"

"She was his student. He was fond of her. Besides, he was more or less responsible for her."

"Responsible for her death?"

"How dare you say a thing like that!"

"If he dared to do it, I can dare to say it."

"He didn't!" she cried. "Frank is a good man. He may have his faults, but he wouldn't kill anyone. I know him."

"What are his faults?"

"We won't discuss them."

"Then may I have a look in your garage?"

"What for? What are you looking for?"

"I'll know when I find it." I turned toward the garage door.

"You mustn't go in there," she said intensely. "Not without Frank's permission."

"Wake him up and we'll get his permission."

"I will not. He got no sleep last night."

"Then I'll just have a look without his permission."

"I'll kill you if you go in there."

She picked up the garden shears and brandished them at me—a sick-looking lioness defending her overgrown cub. The cub himself opened the front door of the cottage. He slouched in the doorway groggily, naked except for white shorts.

"What goes on, Stella?"

"This man has been making the most horrible accusations."

His blurred glance wavered between us and focused on her. "What did he say?"

"I won't repeat it."

"I will, Mr. Conor. I think you were Ginnie Green's lover, if that's the word. I think she followed you to this house last night, around midnight. I think she left it with a rope around her neck."

Connor's head jerked. He started to make a move in my direction. Something inhibited it, like an invisible leash. His body slanted toward me, static, all the muscles taut. It resembled an anatomy specimen with the skin off. Even his face seemed mostly bone and teeth.

I hoped he'd swing on me and let me hit him. He didn't. Stella Connor dropped the garden shears. They made a noise like the dull clank of doom.

"Aren't you going to deny it, Frank?"

"I didn't kill her. I swear I didn't. I admit that we—that we were together last night, Ginnie and I."

"Ginnie and I?" the woman repeated incredulously.

His head hung down. "I'm sorry, Stella. I didn't want to hurt you more than I have already. But it has to come out. I took up with the girl after you left. I was lonely and feeling sorry for myself. Ginnie kept hanging around. One night I drank too much and let it happen. It happened more than once. I was so flattered that a pretty young girl—"

"You fool!" she said in a deep, harsh voice.

"Yes, I'm a moral fool. That's no surprise to you, is it?"

"I thought you respected your pupils, at least. You mean to say you brought her into our own house, into our own bed?"

"You'd left. It wasn't ours any more. Besides, she came of her own accord. She wanted to come. She loved me."

She said with grinding contempt: "You poor, groveling ninny. And to think you had the gall to ask me to come back here, to make you look respectable."

I cut in between them. "Was she here last night, Connor?"

"She was here. I didn't invite her. I wanted her to come, but I dreaded it, too. I knew that I was taking an awful chance. I drank quite a bit to numb my conscience—"

"What conscience?" Stella Connor said.

"I have a conscience," he said without looking at her. "You don't know the hell I've been going through. After she came, after it happened last night, I drank myself unconscious."

"Do you mean after you killed her?" I said.

"I didn't kill her. When I passed out, she was perfectly all right. She was sitting up drinking a cup of instant coffee. The next thing I knew, hours later, her father was on the telephone and she was gone."

"Are you trying to pull the old blackout alibi? You'll have to do better than that."

"I can't. It's the truth."

"Let me into your garage."

He seemed almost glad to be given an order, a chance for some activity. The garage wasn't locked. He raised the overhead door and let the daylight into the interior. It smelled of paint. There were empty cans of marine paint on a bench beside the sailboat. Its hull gleamed virgin white.

"I painted my flattie last week," he said inconsequentially.

"You do a lot of sailing?"

"I used to. Not much lately."

"No," his wife said from the doorway. "Frank changed his hobby to women. Wine and women."

"Lay off, eh?" His voice was pleading.

She looked at him from a great and stony silence.

I walked around the boat, examining the cordage. The starboard jib line had been sheared off short. Comparing it with the port line, I found that the missing piece was approximately a yard long. That was the length of the piece of white rope that I was interested in.

"Hey!" Connor grabbed the end of the cut line. He fingered it as if it was a wound in his own flesh. "Who's been messing with my lines? Did you cut it, Stella?"

"I never go near your blessed boat," she said.

"I can tell you where the rest of that line is, Connor. A line of similar length and color and thickness was wrapped around Ginnie Green's neck when I found her."

"Surely you don't believe I put it there?"

I tried to, but I couldn't. Small-boat sailers don't cut their jib lines, even when they're contemplating murder. And while Connor was clearly no genius, he was smart enough to have known that the line could easily be traced to him. Perhaps someone else had been equally smart.

I turned to Mrs. Connor. She was standing in the doorway with her legs apart. Her body was almost black against the daylight. Her eyes were hooded by the scarf on her head.

"What time did you get home, Mrs. Connor?"

"About ten o'clock this morning. I took a bus as soon as my husband called. But I'm in no position to give him an alibi."

"An alibi wasn't what I had in mind. I suggest another possibility, that you came home twice. You came home unexpectedly last night, saw the girl in the house with your husband, waited in the dark till the girl came out, waited with a piece of rope in your hands—a piece of rope you'd cut from your husband's boat in the hope of getting him punished for what he'd done to you. But the picture doesn't fit the frame, Mrs. Connor. A sailor like your husband wouldn't cut a piece of line from his own boat. And even in the heat of murder he wouldn't tie a granny's knot. His fingers would automatically tie a reef knot. That isn't true of a woman's fingers."

She held herself upright with one long, rigid arm against the door frame.

"I wouldn't do anything like that. I wouldn't do that to Frank."

"Maybe you wouldn't in daylight, Mrs. Connor. Things have different shapes at midnight."

"And hell hath no fury like a woman scorned? Is that what you're thinking? You're wrong. I wasn't here last night. I was in bed in my father's house in Long Beach. I didn't even know about that girl and Frank."

"Then why did you leave him?"

"He was in love with another woman. He wanted to divorce me and marry her. But he was afraid—afraid that it would affect his position in town. He told me on the phone this morning that it was all over with the other woman. So I agreed to come back to him." Her arm dropped to her side.

"He said that it was all over with Ginnie?"

Possibilities were racing through my mind. There was the possibility that Connor had been playing reverse English, deliberately and clumsily framing himself in order to be cleared. But that was out of far left field.

"Not Ginnie," his wife said. "The other woman was Anita Brocco. He met her last spring in the course of work and fell in love—what *he* calls love. My husband is a foolish, fickle man."

"Please, Stella. I said it was all over between me and Anita, and it is."

She turned on him in quiet savagery. "What does it matter now? If it isn't one girl it's another. Any kind of female flesh will do to poultice your sick little ego."

Her cruelty struck inward and hurt her. She stretched out her hand toward him. Suddenly her eyes were blind with tears.

"Any flesh but mine, Frank," she said brokenly.

Connor paid no attention to his wife.

He said to me in a hushed voice:

"My God, I never thought. I noticed her car last night when I was walking home along the beach."

"Whose car?"

"Anita's red Fiat. It was parked at the viewpoint a few hundred yards from here." He gestured vaguely toward town. "Later, when Ginnie was with me, I thought I heard someone in the garage. But I was too drunk to make a search." His eyes burned into mine. "You say a woman tied that knot?"

"All we can do is ask her."

We started toward my car together. His wife called after him:

"Don't go, Frank. Let him handle it."

He hesitated, a weak man caught between opposing forces.

"I need you," she said. "We need each other."

I pushed him in her direction.

It was nearly four when I got to the HP station. The patrol cars had gathered like homing pigeons for the change in shift. Their uniformed drivers were talking and laughing inside.

Anita Brocco wasn't among them. A male dispatcher, a fat-faced man with pimples, had taken her place behind the counter.

"Where's Miss Brocco?" I asked.

"In the ladies' room. Her father is coming to pick her up any minute."

She came out wearing lipstick and a light beige coat. Her face turned beige when she saw my face. She came toward me in slow motion, leaned with both hands flat on the counter. Her lipstick looked like fresh blood on a corpse.

"You're a handsome woman, Anita. Too bad about you."

"Too bad." It was half a statement and half a question. She looked down at her hands.

"Your fingernails are clean now. They were dirty this morning. You were digging in the dirt last night, weren't you?"

"No."

"You were, though. You saw them together and you couldn't stand it. You waited in ambush with a rope, and put it around her neck. Around your own neck, too."

She touched her neck. The talk and laughter had subsided around us. I could hear the tick of the clock again, and the muttering signals coming in from inner space.

"What did you use to cut the rope with, Anita? The garden shears?"

Her red mouth groped for words and found them. "I was crazy about him. She took him away. It was all over before it started. I didn't know what to do with myself. I wanted him to suffer."

"He's suffering. He's going to suffer more."

"He deserves to. He was the only man—" She shrugged in a twisted way and looked down at her breast. "I didn't want to kill her, but when I saw them together—I saw them through the window. I saw her take off her clothes and put them on. Then I thought of the night my father—when he—when there was all the blood in mother's bed. I had to wash it out of the sheets."

The men around me were murmuring. One of them, a sergeant, raised his voice.

"Did you kill Ginnie Green?"

"Yes."

"Are you ready to make a statement?" I said.

"Yes. I'll talk to Sheriff Pearsall. I don't want to talk here, in front of my friends." She looked around doubtfully.

"I'll take you downtown."

"Wait a minute." She glanced once more at her empty hands. "I left my purse in the—in the back room. I'll go and get it."

She crossed the office like a zombie, opened a plain door, closed it behind her. She didn't come out. After a while we broke the lock and went in after her.

Her body was cramped on the narrow floor. The ivory-handled nail file lay by her right hand. There were bloody holes in her white blouse and in the white breast under it. One of them had gone as deep as her heart.

Later Al Brocco drove up in her red Fiat and came into the station.

"I'm a little late," he said to the room in general. "Anita wanted me to give her car a good cleaning. Where is she, anyway?"

The sergeant cleared his throat to answer Brocco.

All us poor creatures, as the old man of the mountain had said that morning.

I'll Die Tomorrow

MICKEY SPILLANE

A former comic-book writer (he worked on such famous characters as Captain America and Captain Marvel), Frank Morrison Spillane eventually went on to become one of the best-selling mystery writers in history. Although heavily criticized for works that were then considered too sexy and violent, he captured the imagination of millions through the exploits of Mike Hammer, one of the great figures of the "hardboiled" school of fiction. His first seven novels, beginning with I, the Jury *in 1947 made his reputation, but throughout his career his talent has been consistently underestimated by those who objected to the racy life-styles of his characters.*

Despite his popularity, few readers are familar with his often excellent short stories, and we are happy to bring "I'll Die Tomorrow" to your attention.

The friendly looking gentleman in the neat charcoal gray suit was a killer. But like any good predator, his disguise was excellent. To all appearances, he was a moderately successful businessman with offices, perhaps, high in a Manhattan building, where the street fumes and noises didn't reach.

Offhand, you would guess his age in the late forties, and if asked to describe him, could do little more than say he was, well, average. No, there was nothing suspicious in his walk or talk or behavior and if you had any reason to trust anyone it would be this gentleman. Why, he even looked happy.

And with all of that, his disguise *was* perfect, simply because it was not an artificial disguise at all. It was real. He did have an office, although not in Manhattan, and he *was* happy. Rudolph Less was a man well satisfied with life, especially when he was working, and now he was on a job again.

Upstairs was a man he was going to kill and the going price on his demise was to be ten thousand lovely dollars that would go toward supporting his single secret pastime in his converted summer house on the island. He smiled at the thought, feeling a tiny, vicarious thrill touch his parts. Women, he thought, could be taught . . . or even forced . . . to do such wonderful things.

Yes, life was fine. Only the select few knew of his true nature and of his niche in life. Through these few, others could come by his services—and many had.

How many now? Was it forty-six times? Or forty-eight? Sometimes it was difficult to recall. Once he had kept track, but as in all other businesses, tabulating inventory became boring. Now it was better simply to look ahead.

It was a good business and of all those engaged in it, he was the best. No doubt of it. (He smiled at the doorman who smiled back, but the smile was only a gesture.) He was thinking of the many times he had read the accounts in the papers of his work. Always, the police were puzzled, or another was taken in custody. He chuckled when he thought of the three who had already died in the chair mistakenly. Wouldn't *that* shake up the administration if it ever came out! But they were only punks and the error of their death was really a boon to society, doing earlier what would have happened later anyway.

Things like that only added to his business reputation, though. It had paid off, really it had. He thought again of Theresa of the dark flesh and darker hair who had loved those things he had done to her. She really had. She had done things to him that in his frenzy of wild emotion he couldn't even recall. He could only remember the terrible pleasure of the experience. Well, he could get Theresa again now.

That's what being the best meant. They hired him because he never failed. For a brief second his face clouded as if he were angry with himself, then he shook his head dismissing the thought because it couldn't be.

It was too bad, he thought, that he hadn't checked further, but experience wasn't on his side then. He had cleared out too soon. He wasn't absolutely certain. He smiled again, tentatively. But they had paid him, so everything must have gone all right.

He couldn't help but think about it and try to recall the details merely to satisfy his desire for perfection. It had been his first contract, and a simple one. A kid called Buddy . . . he couldn't remember his last name, but he had a dime-size hole through his right ear that was supposed to be from a stray .45 bullet during the war. Buddy had hijacked seventeen grand from the paymaster to the Jersey City group and rather than remain a laughing stock to their pseudo dignity, Buddy had to go, but with no apparent connection to the group, of course.

It hadn't been difficult. Buddy was a talkative guy so he simply engaged him in conversation, walked him close to the water, enjoyed the final moment of conversation by telling Buddy who he was and what he was about to do and while Buddy stood dumfounded, with his mouth open and a light from the opposite shore visible through the hole in his ear, he chest-shot him and watched the body smash back into the water.

If only they had found the remains he could be satisfied. However, the river was running fast, it *had* been blowing up a storm, and the ocean was close by. Buddy (what *was* his last name?) never showed up, not even to reclaim the bundle of money he had left behind in his room. At the thought Rudolph Less breathed deeply and smiled, satisfied that his record was perfect. Yes, a good record. Big Tim Sheely of Detroit and the western senator and Marco Leppert who was a Mafia courier were on that list. He chuckled again. How the Mafia had searched for him! They killed four men thinking they had the right one each time and he was never even suspected. After their last failure it was the Mafia itself who gave him the job of axman to rid the organization of their own killers who blundered.

That job got him Joan, he remembered. Such a woman, such a hungry, hungry woman. She was so big all over. So big, so big. Everything so big. Yes, he would have Joan again too. Perhaps even Theresa and Joan together. Who knew what he could do then. It might be bad for his constitution, but he was in good health yet, he thought wryly. There were still some things to be experienced that he could stand.

He had no need to look at the wall directory before going into the elevator. He was part of the crowd now, seen, yet unnoticed. He coughed gently from the smoke of the cigar in the mouth of the man next to him but said nothing. Instead, he thought suddenly, *I'd like to kill him!*

Like Lew Smith who stood right in front of him in the back of the darkened theater and never felt the ice pick slide into his heart. He simply collapsed and they carried him out thinking that he had fainted, and no one saw Rudolph leave at all. Lew smelled of cigar smoke too. And Lew had bought him Francie who would make him sit back and watch while she did the damndest dance he ever did see until his eyes were bugging out and he could hardly breathe and when by the time she let him get his hands on her he had lost almost all his senses and had to be slapped back to normal. But Francie had smiled then and loved what he had done to her although she pouted a while over his bite marks.

He was breathing too heavily, and down the neck of the woman in front of him. She almost turned around, when he caught himself and forced his breath to come easier.

It was because he was getting close to his business arrangement again. It was like that lately. He tasted the fruits of success before the actual planting. But the conclusion was foregone anyway. Success was not problematical any longer. It was a certainty. That was why he could ask for so much to do so little.

Sometimes he wondered about those who lingered a few moments. What did they think? Who was he? What had they done to him that he should snuff out their lives? Oh, there were those who knew. He remembered that two even seemed relieved. For years they had lived in fear of this day and now it had come. There was no more fear for them. Actuality had arrived as a medium-sized man with a friendly smile and it was over very quickly without much pain at all because he was an expert at his work. He was quite sure that one man even whispered a quiet "Thank you" before he died.

Well, that was one thing about his method. There was no flight involved, no loud histrionics. They didn't know him, there was nothing fearful about his appearance and if anything registered at all, generally it was surprise.

Someday, maybe, he thought he might like to change his method. If he could get his assignment in the proper place he would like to try a few experiments. Like extensions of the things he had done with Lulu who had some savage blood and liked to be beaten in certain ways. Pain peculiarly inflicted with her fullest cooperation was her delight and she had taught him things his mind had begun to dwell on lately. He shrugged off the thought impatiently and looked up at the indicator over the operator's head. The car had stopped and the doors opened.

Sixteen.

He remembered *his* number sixteen.

She was a showgirl named Cindy Valentine who knew too much about the operations of another group through an already dead boy friend. The district attorney had her secretly marked for investigation, but money, being able to buy anything, bought the tip and now Cindy was being cancelled out.

Cindy Valentine, number sixteen, had been somewhat of a pleasure. In fact, it had been Cindy who had showed him the ultimate use to which he could put the many dollars he had accumulated. So far he merely rented an office from which he sold, and profitably, trinkets and novelties via pages of certain magazines. One employee really did all the work but it gave him a sense of well-being, a place in society. Daily, he commuted from his house. It wasn't much, but it was secluded. There was nothing he couldn't do there at his pleasure and he was so situated that there were no prying eyes at all. To the world outside, he lived a simple and secluded life. Sort of a friendly recluse, he thought.

Yes, Cindy had brought new meaning into his life. He had called ahead and said he was a jeweler who was instructed to let Miss Valentine have a single pick from his collection. She had been overjoyed at the thought and although she tried to cajole the name of his sponsor from him, he said he was sworn not to tell. Hers was a secret admirer. No doubt she had had many. She believed everything he told her. She squealed with delight when she admitted him to her apartment, seeing the flat sample case under her arm.

At first she didn't notice the flush in his face. She was too excited, then, in the living room, she saw his consternation and smiled. The filmy nylon negligee was all Cindy had on. Her smile grew impish and she had said, "Since you're going to give me something, I'm going to give you something." Then she let the negligee fall to the floor and when she was done he was a shaken but strangely elated man. She said, "Now you give me something," and looked at the case on the table. Well, he gave her something, all right. Very quickly and there was hardly any blood and he picked up his case and went out. They all called it a passion kill and in a way it had been.

Cindy certainly had introduced something new to his life. Now, rather than merely having the satisfaction of a job well done, he had an end result that was far greater than anything he had ever dreamed of. The satisfaction he would get tonight would be far greater than the satisfaction of job perfection he used to consider enough. Perfection was quite a word. It gnawed at him like a little mouse. If only he could have been sure of that first one, Buddy, the one with the hole in his ear.

Well, the one upstairs would merely add to his list of accomplishments. This was a curious one. Different insofar as he never had time to study the man. He would be alone in his office counting the weekly take, a secret office he used solely for bookkeeping and accounting purposes. He rented it under an assumed name and made a deliberate point to go there disguised. His operation was illegal and deftly concealed. Only after long and arduous investigation did Rudolph Less's client discover his whereabouts. Since his connection with the dead man would be obvious, it was necessary for his client to have an airtight alibi at the time of the kill, making Rudolph's talents necessary.

Ordinarily he wouldn't have gone for the second part of the arrangement, but lately he was beginning to enjoy new facets of an old thrill. The client said he could keep whatever money he found there in addition to his regular pay. Thousands extra! Enough to buy . . . well, if that man was right about that one down in Cuba he could bring her here at once. Complete muscular control, he had said. Think of it! He swallowed hard and dimmed the mental picture. Not yet. Later he could sit in his room savoring the anticipation when the job was done, but first the job.

He got out at twenty with two others but before the doors shut a giddy young girl ran up and grabbed his sleeve and said too loudly, "Mr. Bascomb? Are you Mr. Bascomb . . . they just called from downstairs and said . . ."

"I'm not Mr. Bascomb," he smiled. Inwardly he swore, something he hadn't done in years. He saw the elevator boy grinning at the girl's stammer of embarrassment before the doors closed. An incident like that could cause that boy to remember his face. But nevertheless, he'd never be back again, never see the boy again, and if he described anyone at all, or did the girl, it would be the average man of the street.

The girl walked off, her buttocks in violent motion. Ordinarily he would feel a warm glow at such a sight, but the momentary pleasure of another sort ahead that could be completely consummated overrode such a simple delight of watching a girl from behind.

Yet the sight introduced a new thought, something that had been on his mind for months now, something that touched him whenever he saw a young and pretty girl on the street. So far he had bought his pleasures. Oh, they had been expensive, but worth every bit of it. But the thrills and sensations they provided finally reached a limit. Repetition turned original wonders into almost commonplace boredom and it was getting more difficult all the time to find something *really* different.

There *was* one thing. Supposing, and it shouldn't be too difficult, that he could lure some unsuspecting girl . . . on the promise of a job, perhaps . . . or really, if one was honest about it, by actual force . . . that would take a car, maybe drugs; there would be untold risks but that would only add to the delicacy . . . yes, it was something to think about. Maybe after the one from Cuba. He would like to experience one with complete muscular control first.

Annoyed at himself he stopped and adjusted his coat, although there was no one in the corridor to see him. He held the leather folio more securely under his arm, feeling in it the flat contours of the Browning and the extended length of the silencer he had gotten from that odd man in Germany. Silencers were fine. Why didn't they fight wars with silencers? It shouldn't be expensive and think of how quietly and efficiently the war could be fought. Ah, the advantage of the bow and arrow. Too bad it was such a clumsy weapon.

He stopped at the door marked STAR DISTRIBUTING, smiled to himself and fitted the key he had been given into the lock. It opened easily and he stepped inside. As the diagram showed, he was in a small anteroom, and facing him was the lighted square of a frosted glass door. That had no lock. Rudolph Less smiled again.

He heard someone cough and nodded to himself. Feet shuffled and a chair scraped back. He heard a phone picked up and dialed and held his position. He could not enter while the phone was on. There was no need for someone else giving an alarm. The way it was, if done right, the body wouldn't be found until it started to stink and that would be several days. No, he could wait a minute.

Inside, his assignment said, "You got everything ready for tonight . . . yeah . . . yeah . . . okay, I'll call you. I'm going to make up the payroll now. Sure . . . sure . . . so long." The phone clicked and the man coughed again.

Rudolph said softly, "Now," and opened the door.

He smiled at his assignment.

His assignment looked startled, then frowned uncomprehendingly at the Browning with the silencer pointing at his chest. He was a big man, thick through the chest and neck, his hair gray at the sides. He was well dressed and from first glance Rudolph wouldn't have taken him for someone in the rackets. But appearances were deceiving, weren't they? Who would take *him* for an *eliminator?* Now that was a good word.

The man said, "What do you want?"

Rudolph's eyes took him in quickly. He was big, all right. Most likely it would take more than one shot. Two quick body hits to stop him if he tried to move, then a head shot to complete the job. One thing about a silencer, you could hear the bullets hit too. Not so much in the stomach, of course, but if they went through a rib or in the skull . . .

"What I want is your money," Rudolph said. It sounded peculiar to him. Shoddy, somehow. "Where is it?"

"In the safe, that's where, and if you expect . . ."

"If I don't get it I'll kill you anyway," Rudolph told him.

There was no mistaking the tone of his voice. The big guy nodded, was about to say something and stopped. He walked across the room to the safe and dragged out a small, obviously heavy, steel box. Rudolph saw the combination lock on it and waved the gun to the desk. He surely couldn't carry the box out of here. "Open it," he said.

The guy sat down and began spinning the dial. Outside there was a burst of laughter and a key rattled the lock. The door opened and two girls laughed again. A male voice joined theirs.

Rudolph's heart jumped, but then quieted. He had been in situations like this before. He put the gun into the folio, keeping his hand on it and casually sat down. The door to the office opened and a girl said, "Mr. Riley, your friend Mr. Brisson is here. Do you want . . ." she glanced around the door and saw Rudolph. "Oh," she giggled, "I'm sorry. I didn't know you had company. I thought this man was Mr. Brisson before."

"That's all right," Mr. Riley told her. "I'll be out shortly."

The girl giggled again and closed the door. Outside several more people came in and typewriters began to rattle. Two men were discussing a sales meeting.

Rudolph could feel the dryness of his skin, but still he could smell sweat. Sweat? Or was it fear. Someplace something had gone wrong. This was supposed to be an empty office. Just one man. Damn! Why didn't he do the job the way he had done all the others. That's what happens when you leave the details up to somebody else. Damn it all to hell! But you wouldn't know that was what Rudolph Less was thinking because he was smiling in a very friendly fashion.

The big man said softly, "You're in trouble, friend," and as he said it opened the lid of the box. The money was there as it was supposed to be. Packets of hundreds and Riley was dumping it out on the desk. He looked across the room at his smiling visitor. "You can't get out very well and pretty soon somebody will be coming in here. If you do get out you won't be a hard one to identify. Those girls out there are all artists and could sketch you to perfection. Show it to the papers and you'd be turned in in no time."

"That is problematical," Rudolph said.

"You picked a lousy time for a stickup, mister."

Rudolph smiled again. "Yes, I did." The smile didn't last long because Riley was smiling too.

He said, "Buddy, if I could get the jump on you, you'd be in a mess."

"Oh?" His teeth flashed and he lifted the Browning out of the folio.

"You had a key to this place, you came on a day when the payroll was

being made up and you came armed. A planned stickup. I kill you . . ."
he shrugged . . . "one day in court is all. Self-defense."

"That could hardly happen," Rudolph said. For some reason he felt
edgy. Events weren't at all like they should be. His assignment, a better
word than victim, was being too aggressive. What had to be done had to
be done quickly and his mind raced over the possibilities. Several were
available to him. He would take the money, of course. He would tell them
outside that Mr. Riley would be busy all day and not to disturb him. He'd
hate to leave his house, especially his paraphernalia he had so carefully
assembled, but he lived there under a fictitious name and he could do it
over again, perhaps this time with certain innovations he desired. Suntan,
hair dye, whiskers in any number of combinations could alter his appearance sufficiently. No, it wouldn't be an insurmountable problem at all.

He was so engrossed in this thoughts, that although his eyes were on
Riley, the big man's voice came to him as a steady drone.

". . . it took so long to find you. You're mighty clever, I guess you know.
Proof for a court of law would be impossible to obtain. And me, I don't
want to stick my neck out. I'm not going to kill somebody who needs
killing bad then pay for it myself. I'm a little on the smart side too.

"But contacts I made. Finally the right guy put me through. In returning a big favor I did him he put me in touch with you. We made the
arrangements together, you and I. Clever, eh?"

The big guy smiled and sucked in his breath. He was too big, Rudolph
thought. Maybe even two chest hits wouldn't do it. He carried five in the
Browning so what he'd have to do was give him four in the chest quickly
and then hold the last one for the coup. Nobody could take four. The
smashing impact in the lungs even prevents a yell and the only sound
would be the body falling. However, the noise outside would cover that
up.

Somehow the droning voice made sense. His mind, charged now to
frenzied activity, raced back over the words, picked them up and went
over them again. There was something here now that shouldn't be at all.
Something terrible if he heard right. The smile seemed frozen on his face
now and for the first time his eyes made a little rat's movement around
the room.

"I hired you to kill me," Riley said. "I never knew who you were or
where you were and I finally figured out the only way to have you in front
of me so you could die where I can see it happen without any heat coming
my way at all."

Rudolph's voice was strained. "You can't!"

"I have, pal, I have. But first let me tell you thanks. I have a nice straight business going for me and there won't be any heat. In fact, I'll be a hero. How about that."

He felt cold. He had never felt so cold as now. There was no spit in his mouth and his insides were rolling. Had he eaten earlier he was sure he would have vomited at the moment. For some reason he could hear the voices of Cindy and Lulu and Francie and Joan and all those others and far away mocking him with a Cuban accent the untasted one he hungered after, and somewhere from a deep invisible fog came the scared bleatings of the ones he would have had by cajolery or by force if necessary.

Would have had! Not at all! Not at all, Mr. Riley. "You forgot something, Mr. Riley," Rudolph said, bringing the Browning into line with his chest. "I have the gun."

"And I have one in this box under my hand, friend. A big fat .45 automatic for which I have a license."

Rudolph nodded sagely. "The moment you move your hand toward it I'll shoot you," he said softly.

"Fair enough," Riley said.

Rudolph was on his feet. What was the matter with this man? Was he mad! Then his hand moved and Rudolph pulled the trigger. The Browning jumped once . . . twice . . . three times . . . four . . . he could see the shots hitting his chest right in the heart area. Go down, damn you, go down! He had to go down. The big guy had the .45 out of the box when Rudolph Less pulled the trigger on the last shot and saw it rip into his arm, but it was the wrong arm. The other one had the .45.

And he was grinning, damn him!

He looked at the blood pumping from his arm. "This makes it all the better," he said, then laughed again and ripped open his shirt.

With mouth agape, Rudolph saw the overlapping plates of the bulletproof vest. Riley brought the gun up and pointed it at his head.

Rudolph was old looking now, sallow, his cheeks sunken in fear. His invincibility shattered for no reason, no reason at all. All those wonderful pleasures gone, gone, because this big fool in front of him had tricked him. Where had he made his mistake? It had to be somewhere. Where then?

He said, "Why?" His voice was weak, faltering.

Riley lifted a hand to his ear and felt for the piece of cosmetic wax that fitted so cleverly. Then he squeezed the trigger of the .45.

In the awlful blast of the gun that Rudolph could still hear while his skull was shattering into tiny bits his last remembrance was that the round hole in the nose of his final lover, the terrible .45, was exactly the same size as the one in the big guy's ear and that Riley's first name had to be Buddy.

For All the Rude People

JACK RITCHIE

Jack Ritchie is read devotedly by hundreds of thousands of readers in spite of the fact that he has only one published book, A New Leaf and Other Stories *(1971). His large following is composed of those who regularly read* Ellery Queen's Mystery Magazine *and* Alfred Hitchcock's Mystery Magazine, *publications which have featured scores of his well-crafted and intriguing stories. Further evidence of his excellence is the frequent appearance of his stories in mystery/crime anthologies, including a dozen and a half selections over almost a twenty-year period in the* Best Detective Stories of the Year. *He is also the creator of the only (as far as we know) private eye of the vampire persuasion.*

"How old are you?" I asked.

His eyes were on the revolver I was holding. "Look, mister, there's not much in the cash register, but take it all. I won't make no trouble."

"I am not interested in your filthy money. How old are you?"

He was puzzled. "Forty-two."

I clicked my tongue. "What a pity. From your point of view, at least. You might have lived another twenty or thirty years if you had just taken the very slight pains to be polite."

He didn't understand.

"I am going to kill you," I said, "because of the six-cent stamp and because of the cherry candy."

He did not know what I meant by the cherry candy, but he did know about the stamp.

Panic raced into his face. "You must be crazy. You can't kill me just because of that."

"But I can."

And I did.

When Dr. Briller told me that I had but four months to live, I was, of course, perturbed. "Are you positive you haven't mixed up the X-rays? I've heard of such things."

"I'm afraid not, Mr. Turner."

I gave it more earnest thought. "The laboratory reports. Perhaps my name was accidently attached to the wrong . . ."

He shook his head slowly. "I double-checked. I always do in cases like these. Sound medical practice, you know."

It was late afternoon and the time when the sun is tired. I rather hoped that, when my time came actually to die, it might be in the morning. Certainly more cheerful.

"In cases like this," Dr. Briller said, "a doctor is faced with a dilemma. Shall he or shall he not tell his patient? I always tell mine. That enables them to settle their affairs and to have a fling, so to speak." He pulled a pad of paper toward him. "Also, I'm writing a book. What do you intend doing with your remaining time?"

"I really don't know. I've just been thinking about it for a minute or two, you know."

"Of course," Briller said. "No immediate rush. But when you do decide, you will let me know, won't you? My book concerns the things that people do with their remaining time when they know just when they're going to die."

He pushed aside the pad. "See me every two or three weeks. That way we'll be able to measure the progress of your decline."

Briller saw me to the door. "I've already written up twenty-two cases like yours." He seemed to gaze into the future. "Could be a best seller, you know."

I have always lived a bland life. Not an unintelligent one, but bland.

I have contributed nothing to the world—and in that I have much in common with almost every soul on earth—but, on the other hand, I have not taken away anything, either. I have, in short, asked merely to be left alone. Life is difficult enough without undue association with people.

What can one do with the remaining four months of a bland life?

I have no idea how long I walked and thought on that subject, but eventually I found myself on the long curving bridge that sweeps down to join the lake drive. The sounds of mechanical music intruded themselves upon my mind and I looked down.

A circus, or very large carnival, lay below.

It was the world of shabby magic, where the gold is gilt, where the top-hatted ringmaster is as much a gentleman as the medals on his chest are authentic, and where the pink ladies on horseback are hard-faced and narrow-eyed. It was the domain of the harsh-voiced vendors and the short-change.

I have always felt that the demise of the big circus may be counted as one of the cultural advances of the twentieth century, yet I found myself descending the footbridge and in a few moments I was on the midway between the rows of stands where human mutations are exploited and exhibited for the entertainment of all children.

Eventually I reached the big top and idly watched the bored ticket-taker in his elevated box at one side of the main entrance.

A pleasant-faced man leading two little girls approached him and presented several cardboard rectangles which appeared to be passes.

The ticket-taker ran his finger down a printed list at his side. His eyes hardened and he scowled down at the man and the children for a moment. Then slowly and deliberately he tore the passes to bits and let the fragments drift to the ground. "These are no damn good," he said.

The man below him flushed. "I don't understand."

"You didn't leave the posters up," the ticket-taker snapped. "Beat it, crumb!"

The children looked up at their father, their faces puzzled. Would he do something about this?

He stood there and the white of anger appeared on his face. He seemed about to say something, but then he looked down at the children. He closed his eyes for a moment as though to control his anger, and then he said, "Come on, kids. Let's go home."

He led them away, down the midway, and the children looked back, bewildered, but saying nothing.

I approached the ticket-taker. "Why did you do that?"

He glanced down. "What's it to you?"

"Perhaps a great deal."

He studied me irritably. "Because he didn't leave up the posters."

"I heard that before. Now explain it."

He exhaled as though it cost him money. "Our advance man goes through a town two weeks before we get there. He leaves posters advertising the show any place he can—grocery stores, shoe shops, meat markets—any place that will paste them in the window and keep them there until the show comes to town. He hands out two or three passes for that. But what some of these jokers don't know is that we check up. If the posters aren't still up when we hit town, the passes are no good."

"I see," I said dryly. "And so you tear up the passes in their faces and in front of their children. Evidently that man removed the posters from the window of his little shop too soon. Or perhaps he had those passes *given* to him by a man who removed the posters from his window."

"What's the difference? The passes are no good."

"Perhaps there is no difference in that respect. But do you realize what you have done?"

His eyes were narrow, trying to estimate me and any power I might have.

"You have committed one of the most cruel of human acts," I said stiffly. "You have humiliated a man before his children. You have inflicted a scar that will remain with him and them as long as they live. He will take those children home and it will be a long, long way. And what can he say to them?"

"Are you a cop?"

"I am not a cop. Children of that age regard their father as the finest man in the world. The kindest, the bravest. And now they will remember that a man has been bad to their father—and he had been unable to do anything about it."

"So I tore up his passes. Why didn't he buy tickets? Are you a city inspector?"

"I am not a city inspector. Did you expect him to *buy* tickets after that humiliation? You left the man with no recourse whatsoever. He could not *buy* tickets and he could not create a well-justified scene, because the children were with him. He could do nothing. Nothing at all, but retreat with two children who wanted to see your miserable circus and now they cannot."

I looked down at the foot of his stand. There were the fragments of many more dreams—the debris of other men who had committed the capital crime of not leaving their posters up long enough. "You could at least have said, 'I'm sorry, sir. But your passes are not valid.' And then you could have explained politely and quietly why."

"I'm not paid to be polite." He showed yellow teeth. "And, mister, I *like* tearing up passes. It gives me a kick."

And there it was. He was a little man who had been given a little power and he used it like a Caesar.

He half rose. "Now get the hell out of here, *mister*, before I come down there and chase you all over the lot."

Yes. He was a man of cruelty, a two-dimensional animal born without feeling and sensitivity and fated to do harm as long as he existed. He was a creature who should be eliminated from the face of the earth.

If only I had the power to . . .

I stared up at the twisted face for a moment more and then turned on my heel and left. At the top of the bridge I got a bus and rode to the sports shop at Thirty-seventh.

I purchased a .32-caliber revolver and a box of cartridges.

Why do we *not* murder? Is it because we do not feel the moral justification for such a final act? Or is it more because we fear the consequences if we are caught—the cost to us, to our families, to our children?

And so we suffer wrongs with meekness, we endure them because to eliminate them might cause us even more pain than we already have.

But I had no family, no close friends. And four months to live.

The sun had set and the carnival lights were bright when I got off the bus at the bridge. I looked down at the midway and he was still in his box.

How should I do it? I wondered. Just march up to him and shoot him as he sat on his little throne?

The problem was solved for me. I saw him replaced by another man —apparently his relief. He lit a cigarette and strolled off the midway toward the dark lake front.

I caught up with him around a bend concealed by bushes. It was a lonely place, but close enough to the carnival so that its sounds could still reach me.

He heard my footsteps and turned. A tight smile came to his lips and he rubbed the knuckles of one hand. "You're asking for it, mister."

His eyes widened when he saw my revolver.

"How old are you?" I asked.

"Look, mister," he said swiftly. "I only got a couple of tens in my pocket."

"How old are you?" I repeated.

His eyes flicked nervously. "Thirty-two."

I shook my head sadly. "You could have lived into your seventies. Perhaps forty more years of life, if only you had taken the simple trouble to act like a human being."

His face whitened. "Are you off your rocker or something?"

"A possibility."

I pulled the trigger.

The sound of the shot was not so loud as I had expected, or perhaps it was lost against the background of the carnival noises.

He staggered and dropped to the edge of the path and he was quite dead.

I sat down on a nearby park bench and waited.

Five minutes. Ten. Had no one heard the shot?

I became suddenly conscious of hunger. I hadn't eaten since noon. The thought of being taken to a police station and being questioned for any length of time seemed unbearable. And I had a headache, too.

I tore a page from my pocket notebook and began writing.

A careless word may be forgiven. But a lifetime of cruel rudeness cannot. This man deserved to die.

I was about to sign my name, but then I decided that my initials would be sufficient for the time being. I did not want to be apprehended before I had a good meal and some aspirins.

I folded the page and put it into the dead ticket-taker's breast pocket.

I met no one as I returned up the path and ascended the footbridge. I walked to Weschler's, probably the finest restaurant in the city. The prices are, under normal circumstances, beyond me, but I thought that this time I could indulge myself.

After dinner, I decided an evening bus ride might be in order. I rather enjoyed that form of city excursion and, after all, my freedom of movement would soon become restricted.

The driver of the bus was an impatient man and clearly his passengers were his enemies. However, it was a beautiful night and the bus was not crowded.

At Sixty-eighth Street, a fragile, white-haired woman with cameo features waited at the curb. The driver grudgingly brought his vehicle to a stop and opened the door.

She smiled and nodded to the passengers as she put her foot on the first step, and one could see that her life was one of gentle happiness and very few bus rides.

"Well!" the driver snapped. "Is it going to take you all day to get in?"

She flushed and stammered. "I'm sorry." She presented him with a five-dollar bill.

He glared. "Don't you have any change?"

The flush deepened. "I don't think so. But I'll look."

The driver was evidently ahead on his schedule and he waited.

And one other thing was clear. He was enjoying this.

She found a quarter and held it up timorously.

"In the box!" he snapped.

She dropped it into the box.

The driver moved his vehicle forward jerkily and she almost fell. Just in time, she managed to catch hold of a strap.

Her eyes went to the passengers, as though to apologize for herself—for not having moved faster, for not having immediate change, for almost falling. The smile trembled and she sat down.

At Eighty-second, she pulled the buzzer cord, rose and made her way forward.

The driver scowled over his shoulder as he came to a stop. "Use the rear door. Don't you people ever learn to use the rear door?"

I am all in favor of using the rear door. Especially when a bus is crowded. But there were only a half a dozen passengers on this bus and they read their newspapers with frightened neutrality.

She turned, her face pale, and left by the rear door.

The evening she had had, or the evening she was going to have, had now been ruined. Perhaps many more evenings with the thought of it.

I rode the bus to the end of the line.

I was the only passenger when the driver turned it around and parked.

It was a deserted, dimly lit corner, and there were no waiting passengers at the small shelter at the curb. The driver glanced at his watch, lit a cigarette, and then noticed me. "If you're taking the ride back, mister, put another quarter in the box. No free riders here."

I rose from my seat and walked slowly to the front of the bus. "How old are you?"

His eyes narrowed. "That's none of your business."

"About thirty-five, I'd imagine," I said. "You'd have had another thirty years or more ahead of you." I produced the revolver.

He dropped the cigarette. "Take the money."

"I'm not interested in money. I'm thinking about a gentle lady and perhaps the hundreds of other gentle ladies and the kind, harmless men and the smiling children. You are a criminal. There is no justification for what you do to them. There is no justification for your existence."

And I killed him.

I sat down and waited.

After ten minutes, I was still alone with the corpse.

I realized that I was sleepy. Incredibly sleepy. It might be better if I turned myself in to the police after a good night's sleep.

I wrote my justification for the driver's demise on a sheet of note paper, added my initials and put the page in his pocket.

I walked four blocks before I found a taxi and took it to my apartment building.

I slept soundly and perhaps I dreamed. But if I did, my dreams were pleasant and innocuous, and it was almost nine before I woke.

After a shower and a leisurely breakfast, I selected my best suit. I remembered that I had not yet paid that month's telephone bill. I made out a check and addressed an envelope. I discovered that I was out of stamps. But no matter, I would get one on the way to the police station.

I was almost there when I remembered the stamp. I stopped in at a corner drugstore. It was a place I had never entered before.

The proprietor, in a semimedical jacket, sat behind the soda fountain reading a newspaper and a salesman was making notations in a large order book.

The proprietor did not bother to look up when I entered and he spoke to the salesman. "They've got his fingerprints on the notes, they've got his handwriting and they've got his initials. What's wrong with the police?"

The salesman shrugged. "What good are fingerprints if the murderer doesn't have his in the police files? The same goes for the handwriting if you got nothing to compare it with. And how many thousand people in the city got the initials L.T.?" He closed his book. "I'll be back next week."

When he was gone, the druggist continued reading the newspaper.

I cleared my throat.

He finished reading a long paragraph and then looked up. "Well?"

"I'd like a six-cent stamp, please."

It appeared almost as though I had struck him. He stared at me for fifteen seconds and then he left his stool and slowly made his way to the rear of the store toward a small barred window.

I was about to follow him, but a display of pipes at my elbow caught my attention.

After a while I felt eyes upon me and looked up.

The druggist stood at the far end of the store, one hand on his hip and the other disdainfully holding the single stamp. "Do you expect me to bring it to you?"

And now I remembered a small boy of six who had had five pennies. Not just one this time, but five, and this was in the days of penny candies.

He had been entranced at the display in the showcase—the fifty varieties of sweet things, and his mind had revolved in a pleasant indecision. The red whips? The licorice? The grab bags? But not the candy cherries. He didn't like those at all.

And then he had become conscious of the druggist standing beside the display case—tapping one foot. The druggist's eyes had smouldered with irritation—no, more than that—with anger. "Are you going to take all day for your lousy nickel?"

He had been a sensitive boy and he had felt as though he had received a blow. His precious five pennies were now nothing. This man despised them. And this man despised him.

He pointed numbly and blindly. "Five cents of that."

When he left the store, he had found that he had the candy cherries.

But that didn't really matter. Whatever it had been, he couldn't have eaten it.

Now I stared at the druggist and the six-cent stamp and the narrow hatred for anyone who did not contribute directly to his profits. I had no doubt that he would fawn if I purchased one of his pipes.

But I thought of the six-cent stamp and the bag of cherry candy I had thrown away so many years ago.

I moved toward the rear of the store and took the revolver out of my pocket. "How old are you?"

When he was dead, I did not wait longer than necessary to write a note. I had killed for myself this time and I felt the need of a drink.

I went several doors down the street and entered a small bar. I ordered a brandy and water.

After ten minutes, I heard the siren of a squad car.

The bartender went to the window. "It's just down the street." He took off his jacket. "Got to see what this is all about. If anybody comes in, tell them I'll be right back." He put the bottle of brandy on the bar. "Help yourself, but tell me how many."

I sipped the brandy slowly and watched the additional squad cars and finally the ambulance appear.

The bartender returned after ten minutes and a customer followed at his heels. "A short beer, Joe."

"This is my second brandy," I said.

Joe collected my change. "The druggist down the street got himself murdered. Looks like it was by the man who kills people because they're not polite."

The customer watched him draw a beer. "How do you figure that? Could have been just a holdup."

Joe shook his head. "No. Fred Masters—he's got the TV shop across the street—found the body and he read the note."

The customer put a dime on the bar. "I'm not going to cry about it. I always took my business someplace else. He acted like he was doing you a favor every time he waited on you."

Joe nodded. "I don't think anybody in the neighborhood's going to miss him. He always made a lot of trouble."

I had been about to leave and return to the drugstore to give myself up, but now I ordered another brandy and took out my notebook. I began making a list of names.

It was surprising how one followed another. They were bitter memories, some large, some small, some I had experienced and many more that I had witnessed—and perhaps felt more than the victims.

Names. And that warehouseman. I didn't know his name, but I must include him.

I remembered the day and Miss Newman. We were her sixth graders and she had taken us on another one of her excursions—this time to the warehouses along the river, where she was going to show us "how industry works."

She always planned her tours and she always asked permission of the places we visited, but this time she strayed or became lost and we arrived at the warehouse—she and the thirty children who adored her.

And the warehouseman had ordered her out. He had used language which we did not understand, but we sensed its intent, and he had directed it against us and Miss Newman.

She was small and she had been frightened and we retreated. And Miss Newman did not report to school the next day or any day after that and we learned that she had asked for a transfer.

And I who loved her, too, knew why. She could not face us after that.

Was he still alive? He had been in his twenties then, I imagined.

When I left the bar a half an hour later, I realized I had a great deal of work to do.

The succeeding days were busy ones and, among others, I found the warehouseman. I told him why he was dying because he did not even remember.

And when that was done, I dropped into a restaurant not far away.

The waitress eventually broke off her conversation with the cashier and strode to my table. "What do you want?"

I ordered a steak and tomatoes.

The steak proved to be just about what one could expect in such a neighborhood. As I reached for my coffee spoon, I accidentally dropped it to the floor. I picked it up. "Waitress, would you mind bringing me another spoon, please?"

She stalked angrily to my table and snatched the spoon from my fingers. "You got the shakes or something?"

She returned in a few moments and was about to deposit a spoon, with considerable emphasis, upon my table.

But then a sudden thought altered the harsh expression on her face. The descent of the arm diminuendoed, and when the spoon touched the tablecloth, it touched gently. Very gently.

She laughed nervously. "I'm sorry if I was sharp, mister."

It was an apology, and so I said, "That's quite all right."

"I mean that you can drop a spoon any time you want to. I'll be glad to get you another."

"Thank you." I turned to my coffee.

"You're not offended, are you, mister?" she asked eagerly.

"No. Not at all."

She snatched a newspaper from an empty neighboring table. "Here, sir, you can read this while you eat. I mean, it's on the house. Free."

When she left me, the wide-eyed cashier stared at her. "What's with all that, Mabel?"

Mabel glanced back at me with a trace of uneasiness. "You can never tell who he might be. You better be polite these days."

As I ate I read, and an item caught my eye. A grown man had heated pennies in a frying pan and tossed them out to some children who were making trick-or-treat rounds before Halloween. He had been fined a miserable twenty dollars.

I made a note of his name and address.

Dr. Briller finished his examination. "You can get dressed now, Mr. Turner."

I picked up my shirt. "I don't suppose that some new miracle drug has been developed since I was here last?"

He laughed lightly. "No, I'm afraid not." He watched me button the shirt. "By the way, have you decided what you're going to do with your remaining time?"

I had, but I thought I'd say, "Not yet."

He was faintly perturbed. "You really should, you know. Only about three months left. And be sure to let me know when you do."

While I finished dressing, he sat down at his desk and glanced at the newspaper lying there. "The killer seems to be rather busy, doesn't he?"

He turned a page. "But really the most surprising thing about the crimes seems to be the public's reaction. Have you read the 'Letters from the People' column recently?"

"No."

"These murders appear to be meeting with almost universal approval. Some of the letter writers even hint that they might be able to supply the murderer with a few choice names themselves."

I would have to get a paper.

"Not only that," Dr. Briller said, "but a wave of politeness has struck the city."

I put on my coat. "Shall I come back in two weeks?"

He put aside the paper. "Yes. And try to look at this whole thing as cheerfully as possible. We all have to go some day."

But his day was indeterminate and presumably in the distant future.

My appointment with Dr. Briller had been in the evening, and it was nearly ten by the time I left my bus and began the short walk to my apartment building.

As I approached the last corner, I heard a shot. I turned into Milding Lane and found a little man with a revolver standing over a newly dead body on the quiet and deserted sidewalk.

I looked down at the corpse. "Goodness. A policeman."

The little man nodded. "Yes, what I've done does seem a little extreme, but you see, he was using a variety of language that was entirely unnecessary."

"Ah," I said.

The little man nodded again. "I'd parked my car in front of this fire hydrant. Entirely inadvertently, I assure you. And this policeman was waiting when I returned to my car. And also he discovered that I'd forgotten my driver's license. I would not have acted as I did if he had simply written out a ticket—for I was guilty, sir, and I readily admit it —but he was not content with that. He made embarrassing observations concerning my intelligence, my eyesight, the possibility that I'd stolen the car, and finally on the legitimacy of my birth." He blinked at a fond memory. "And my mother was an angel, sir. An angel."

I remembered a time when I'd been apprehended while absentmind-edly jaywalking. I would contritely have accepted the customary warning, or even a ticket, but the officer had insisted upon a profane lecture before a grinning assemblage of interested pedestrians. Most humiliating.

The little man looked at the gun in his hand. "I bought this just today and actually I'd intended to use it on the superintendent of my apartment building. A bully."

I agreed. "Surly fellows."

He sighed. "But now I suppose I'll have to turn myself over to the police?"

I gave it thought. He watched me.

He cleared his throat. "Or perhaps I should just leave a note? You see, I've been reading in the newspapers about . . ."

I lent him my notebook.

He wrote a few lines, signed his initials and deposited the slip of paper between two buttons of the dead officer's jacket.

He returned the notebook. "I must remember to get one of these."

He opened the door of his car. "Can I drop you off anywhere?"

"No, thank you," I said. "It's a nice evening. I'd rather walk."

Pleasant fellow, I reflected, as I left him.

Too bad there weren't more like him.

Hangover

JOHN D. MACDONALD

He blew in like a fresh breeze at the end of the pulp era in the late 1940s, and immediately made his mark in every genre he touched—sports fiction, science fiction, mystery, horror, suspense. He paid his dues and success was his reward. John D. MacDonald, the creator of Travis McGee, now has sixty million books in print and new hardcover best sellers each year. And he deserves all of it—he is the master storyteller of this field, and he has enriched us all.

He dreamed that he had dropped something, lost something of value in the furnace, and he lay on his side trying to look down at an angle through a little hole, look beyond the flame down into the dark guts of the furnace for what he had lost. But the flame kept pulsing through the hole with a brightness that hurt his eyes, with a heat that parched his face, pulsing with an intermittent husky rasping sound.

With his awakening, the dream became painfully explicable—the pulsing roar was his own harsh breathing, the parched feeling was a consuming thirst, the brightness was transmuted into pain intensely localized behind his eyes. When he opened his eyes, a long slant of early morning sun dazzled him, and he shut his eyes quickly again.

This was a morning time of awareness of discomfort so acute that he had no thought for anything beyond the appraisal of the body and its functions. Though he was dimly aware of psychic discomforts that might later exceed the anguish of the flesh, the immediacy of bodily pain localized his attentions. Even without the horizontal brightness of the sun, he would have known it was early. Long sleep would have muffled the beat of the taxed heart to a softened, sedate, and comfortable rhythm. But it was early and the heart knocked sharply with a violence and in a cadence almost hysterical, so that no matter how he turned his head, he could feel it, a tack hammer chipping away at his mortality.

His thirst was monstrous, undiminished by the random nausea that teased at the back of his throat. His hands and feet were cool, yet where his thighs touched he was sweaty. His body felt clotted, and he knew that he had perspired heavily during the evening, an oily perspiration that left

323

an unpleasant residue when it dried. The pain behind his eyes was a slow bulging and shrinking, in contrapuntal rhythm to the clatter of his heart.

He sat on the edge of the bed, head bowed, eyes squeezed shut, cool trembling fingers resting on his bare knees. He felt weak, nauseated, and acutely depressed.

This was the great joke. This was a hangover. Thing of sly wink, of rueful guffaw. This was death in the morning.

He stood on shaky legs and walked into the bathroom. He turned the cold water on as far as it would go. He drank a full glass greedily. He was refilling the glass when the first spasm came. He turned to the toilet, half falling, cracking one knee painfully on the tile floor, and knelt there and clutched the edge of the bowl in both hands, hunched, miserable, naked. The water ran in the sink for a long time while he remained there, retching, until nothing more came but flakes of greenish bile. When he stood up, he felt weaker but slightly better. He mopped his face with a damp towel, then drank more water, drank it slowly and carefully, and in great quantity, losing track of the number of glasses. He drank the cold water until his belly was swollen and he could hold no more, but he felt as thirsty as before.

Putting the glass back on the rack, he looked at himself in the mirror. He took a quick, overly casual look, the way one glances at a stranger, the eye returning for a longer look after it is seen that the first glance aroused no undue curiosity. Though his face was grayish, eyes slightly puffy, jaws soiled by beard stubble, the long face with its even undistinguished features looked curiously unmarked in relation to the torment of the body.

The visual reflection was a first step in the reaffirmation of identity. You are Hadley Purvis. You are thirty-nine. Your hair is turning gray with astonishing and disheartening speed.

He turned his back on the bland image, on the face that refused to comprehend his pain. He leaned his buttocks against the chill edge of the sink, and a sudden unbidden image came into his mind, as clear and supernaturally perfect as a colored advertisement in a magazine. It was a shot glass full to the very brim with dark brown bourbon.

By a slow effort of will he caused the image to fade away. Not yet, he thought, and immediately wondered about his instinctive choice of mental phrase. Nonsense. This was a part of the usual morbidity of hangover —to imagine oneself slowly turning into an alcoholic. The rum sour on Sunday mornings had become a ritual with him, condoned by Sarah. And that certainly did not speak of alcoholism. Today was, unhappily, a working day, and it would be twelve-thirty before the first martini at Mario's. If anyone had any worries about alcoholism, it was Sarah, and her worries resulted from her lack of knowledge of his job and its requirements. After a man has been drinking for twenty-one years, he does not suddenly become a legitimate cause for the sort of annoying concern Sarah had been showing lately.

In the evening when they were alone before dinner, they would drink, and that certainly did not distress her. She liked her few knocks as well as anyone. Then she had learned somehow that whenever he went to the kitchen to refill their glasses from the martini jug in the deep freeze, he would have an extra one for himself, opening his throat for it, pouring it down in one smooth, long, silvery gush. By mildness of tone she had trapped him into an admission, then had told him that the very secrecy of it was "significant." He had tried to explain that his tolerance for alcohol was greater than hers, and that it was easier to do it that way than to listen to her tiresome hints about how many he was having.

Standing there in the bathroom, he could hear the early morning sounds of the city. His hearing seemed unnaturally keen. He realized that it was absurd to stand there and conduct mental arguments with Sarah and become annoyed at her. He reached into the shower stall and turned the faucets and waited until the water was the right temperature before stepping in, just barely warm. He made no attempt at first to bathe. He stood under the roar and thrust of the high nozzle, eyes shut, face tilted up.

As he stood there he began, cautiously, to think of the previous evening. He had much experience in this sort of reconstruction. He reached out with memory timorously, anticipating remorse and self-disgust.

The first part of the evening was, as always, easy to remember. It had been an important evening. He had dressed carefully yesterday morning, knowing that there would not be time to come home and change before going directly from the office to the hotel for the meeting, with its cocktails, dinner, speeches, movie, and unveiling of the new model. Because of the importance of the evening, he had taken it very easy at Mario's at lunchtime, limiting himself to two martinis before lunch, conscious of virtue—only to have it spoiled by Bill Hunter's coming into his office at three in the afternoon, staring at him with both relief and approval and saying, "Glad you didn't have one of those three-hour lunches, Had. The old man was a little dubious about your joining the group tonight."

Hadley Purvis had felt suddenly and enormously annoyed. Usually he liked Bill Hunter, despite his aura of opportunism, despite the cautious ambition that had enabled Hunter to become quite close to the head of the agency in a very short time.

"And so you said to him, 'Mr. Driscoll, if Had Purvis can't go to the party, I won't go either.' And then he broke down."

He watched Bill Hunter flush. "Not like that, Had. But I'll tell you what happened. He asked me if I thought you would behave yourself tonight. I said I was certain you realized the importance of the occasion, and I reminded him that the Detroit people know you and like the work you did on the spring campaign. So if you get out of line, it isn't going to do me any good either."

"And that's your primary consideration, naturally."

Hunter looked at him angrily, helplessly. "Damn it, Had . . ."

"Keep your little heart from fluttering. I'll step lightly."

Bill Hunter left his office. After he was gone, Hadley tried very hard to believe that it had been an amusing little interlude. But he could not. Resentment stayed with him. Resentment at being treated like a child. And he suspected that Hunter had brought it up with Driscoll, saying very casually, "Hope Purvis doesn't put on a floor show tonight."

It wasn't like the old man to have brought it up. He felt that the old man genuinely liked him. They'd had some laughs together. Grown-up laughs, a little beyond the capacity of a boy scout like Hunter.

He had washed up at five, then gone down and shared a cab with Davey Tidmarsh, the only one of the new kids who had been asked to come along. Davey was all hopped up about it. He was a nice kid. Hadley liked him. Davey demanded to know what it would be like, and in the cab Hadley told him.

"We'll be seriously outnumbered. There'll be a battalion from Detroit, also the bank people. It will be done with enormous seriousness and a lot of expense. This is a pre-preview. Maybe they'll have a mockup there. The idea is that they get us all steamed up about the new model. Then, all enthused, we whip up two big promotions. The first promotion is a carnival deal they will use to sell the new models to the dealers and get them all steamed up. That'll be about four months from now. The second promotion will be the campaign to sell the cars to the public. They'll make a big fetish of secrecy, Davey. There'll be uniformed company guards. Armed."

It was as he had anticipated, only a bit bigger and gaudier than last year.

Everything seemed to get bigger and gaudier every year. It was on the top floor of the hotel, in one of the middle-sized convention rooms. They were carefully checked at the door, and each was given a numbered badge to wear. On the left side of the room was sixty feet of bar. Along the right wall was the table where the buffet would be. There was a busy rumble of male conversation, a blue haze of smoke. Hadley nodded and smiled at the people he knew as they worked their way toward the bar. With drink in hand, he went into the next room—after being checked again at the door—to look at the mockup.

Hadley had to admit that it had been done very neatly. The mockup was one-third actual size. It revolved slowly on a chest-high pedestal, a red-and-white convertible with the door open, with the model of a girl in a swimming suit standing beside it, both model girl and model car bathed in an excellent imitation of sunlight. He looked at the girl first, marveling at how cleverly the sheen of suntanned girl had been duplicated. He looked at the mannekin's figure and thought at once of Sarah and felt a warm wave of tenderness for her, a feeling that she was his luck and, with her, nothing could ever go wrong.

He looked at the lines of the revolving car and, with the glibness of long practice, he made up phrases that would be suitable for advertising it. He stood aside for a time and watched the manufactured delight on the faces of those who were seeing the model for the first time. He finished his drink and went out to the bar. With the first drink, the last traces of irritation at Bill Hunter disappeared. As soon as he had a fresh drink, he looked Bill up and said, "I'm the man who snarled this afternoon."

"No harm done," Hunter said promptly and a bit distantly. "Excuse me, Had. There's somebody over there I have to say hello to."

Hadley placed himself at the bar. He was not alone long. Within ten minutes he was the center of a group of six or seven. He relished these times when he was sought out for his entertainment value. The drinks brought him quickly to the point where he was, without effort, amusing. The sharp phrases came quickly, almost without thought. They laughed with him and appreciated him. He felt warm and loved.

He remembered there had been small warnings in the back of his mind, but he had ignored them. He would know when to stop. He told the story about Jimmy and Jackie and the punch card over at Shor's, and knew he told it well, and knew he was having a fine time, and knew that everything was beautifully under control.

But, beyond that point, memory was faulty. It lost continuity. It became episodic, each scene bright enough, yet separated from other scenes by a grayness he could not penetrate.

He was still at the bar. The audience had dwindled to one, a small man he didn't know, a man who swayed and clung to the edge of the bar. He was trying to make the small man understand something. He kept shaking his head. Hunter came over to him and took his arm and said, "Had, you've got to get something to eat. They're going to take the buffet away soon."

"Smile, pardner, when you use that word 'got.' "

"Sit down and I'll get you a plate."

"Never let it be said that Hadley Purvis couldn't cut his own way through a solid wall of buffet." As Hunter tugged at his arm, Hadley finished his drink, put the glass on the bar with great care, and walked over toward the buffet, shrugging his arm free of Hunter's grasp. He took a plate and looked at all the food. He had not the slightest desire for food. He looked back. Hunter was watching him. He shrugged and went down the long table.

Then, another memory. Standing there with plate in hand. Looking over and seeing Bill Hunter's frantic signals. Ignoring him and walking steadily over to where Driscoll sat with some of the top brass from Detroit. He was amused at the apprehensive expression on Driscoll's face. But he sat down and Driscoll had to introduce him.

Then, later. Dropping something from his fork. Recapturing it and glancing up to trap a look of distaste on the face of the most important man from Detroit, a bald, powerful-looking man with a ruddy face and small bright blue eyes.

He remembered that he started brooding about that look of distaste. The others talked, and he ate doggedly. They think I'm a clown. I'm good enough to keep them laughing, but that's all. They don't think I'm capable of deep thought.

He remembered Driscoll's frown when he broke into the conversation, addressing himself to the bald one from Detroit and taking care to pronounce each word distinctly, without slur.

"That's a nice-looking mockup. And it is going to make a lot of vehicles look old before their time. The way I see it, we're in a period of artificially accelerated obsolescence. The honesty has gone out of the American product. The great God is turnover. So all you manufacturers are straining a gut to make a product that wears out, or breaks, or doesn't last or, like your car, goes out of style. It's the old game of rooking the consumer. You have your hand in his pocket, and we have our hand in yours."

He remembered his little speech vividly, and it shocked him. Maybe it was true. But that had not been the time or place to state it, not at this festive meeting, where everybody congratulated each other on what a fine new sparkling product they would be selling. He felt his cheeks grow hot as he remembered his own words. What a thing to say in front of Driscoll! The most abject apologies were going to be in order.

He could not remember the reaction of the man from Detroit, or Driscoll's immediate reaction. He had no further memories of being at the table. The next episode was back at the bar, a glass in his hand, Hunter beside him speaking so earnestly you could almost see the tears in his eyes. "Good Lord, Had! What did you say? What did you do? I've never seen him so upset."

"Tell him to go do something unspeakable. I just gave them a few clear words of ultimate truth. And now I intend to put some sparkle in that little combo."

"Leave the music alone. Go home, please. Just go home, Had."

There was another gap, and then he was arguing with the drummer. The man was curiously disinclined to give up the drums. A waiter gripped his arm.

"What's your trouble?" Hadley asked him angrily. "I just want to teach this clown how to stay on top of the beat."

"A gentleman wants to see you, sir. He is by the cloakroom. He asked me to bring you out."

Then he was by the cloakroom. Driscoll was there. He stood close to Hadley. "Don't open your mouth, Purvis. Just listen carefully to me while I try to get something through your drunken skull. Can you understand what I'm saying?"

"Certainly I can—"

"Shut up! You may have lost the whole shooting match for us. That speech of yours. He told me he wasn't aware of the fact that I hired Commies. He said that criticisms of the American way of life make him physically ill. Know what I'm going back in and tell him?"

"No."

"That I got you out here and fired you and sent you home. Get this straight. It's an attempt to save the contract. Even if it weren't, I'd still fire you, and I'd do it in person. I thought I would dread it. I've known you a long time. I find out, Purvis, that I'm actually enjoying it. It's such a damn relief to get rid of you. Don't open your mouth. I wouldn't take you back if you worked for free. Don't come back. Don't come in tomorrow. I'll have a girl pack your personal stuff. I'll have it sent to you by messenger along with your check. You'll get both tomorrow before noon. You're a clever man, Purvis, but the town is full of clever men who can hold liquor. Good-bye."

Driscoll turned on his heel and went back into the big room. Hadley remembered that the shock had penetrated the haze of liquor. He remembered that he had stood there, and he had been able to see two men setting up a projector, and all he could think about was how he would tell Sarah and what she would probably say.

And, without transition, he was in the Times Square area on his way home. The sidewalk would tilt unexpectedly, and each time he would take a lurching step to regain his balance. The glare of the lights hurt his eyes. His heart pounded. He felt short of breath.

He stopped and looked in the window of a men's shop that was still open. The sign on the door said OPEN UNTIL MIDNIGHT. He looked at his watch. It was a little after eleven. He had imagined it to be much later. Suddenly it became imperative to him to prove both to himself and to a stranger that he was not at all drunk. If he could prove that, then he would know that Driscoll had fired him not for drinking, but for his opinions. And would anyone want to keep a job where he was not permitted to have opinions?

He gathered all his forces and looked intently into the shop window. He looked at a necktie. It was a gray wool tie with a tiny figure embroidered in dark red. The little embroidered things were shaped like commas. He decided that he liked it very much. The ties in that corner of the window were priced at three-fifty. He measured his stability, cleared his throat, and went into the shop.

"Good evening, sir."

"Good evening. I'd like that tie in the window, the gray one on the left with the dark-red pattern."

"Would you please show me which one, sir?"

"Of course." Hadley pointed it out. The man took a duplicate off a rack.

"Would you like this in a box, or shall I put it in a bag?"

"A bag is all right."

"It's a very handsome tie."

He gave the man a five-dollar bill. The man brought him his change. "Thank you, sir. Good night."

"Good night." He walked out steadily, carrying the bag. No one could have done it better. A very orderly purchase. If he ever needed proof of his condition, the clerk would remember him. "Yes, I remember the gentleman. He came in shortly before closing time. He bought a gray tie. Sober? Perhaps he'd had a drink or two. But he was as sober as a judge."

And somewhere between the shop and home all memory ceased. There was a vague something about a quarrel with Sarah, but it was not at all clear. Perhaps because the homecoming scene had become too frequent for them.

He dried himself vigorously on a harsh towel and went into the bedroom. When he thought of the lost job, he felt quick panic. Another one wouldn't be easy to find. One just as good might be impossible. It was a profession that fed on gossip.

Maybe it was a good thing. It would force a change on them. Maybe a new city, a new way of life. Maybe they could regain something that they had lost in the last year or so. But he knew he whistled in the dark. He was afraid. This was the worst of all mornings-after.

Yet even that realization was diffused by the peculiar aroma of unreality that clung to all his hangover mornings. Dreams were always vivid, so vivid that they became confused with reality. With care, he studied the texture of the memory of Driscoll's face and found therein a lessening of his hope that it could have been dreamed.

He went into his bedroom and took fresh underwear from the drawer. He found himself thinking about the purchase of the necktie again. It seemed strange that the purchase should have such retroactive importance. The clothing he had worn was where he had dropped it beside his bed. He picked it up. He emptied the pockets of the suit. There was a skein of dried vomit on the lapel of the suit. He could not remember having been ill. There was a triangular tear in the left knee of the trousers, and he noticed for the first time an abrasion on his bare knee. He could not remember having fallen. The necktie was not in the suit pocket. He began to wonder whether he had dreamed about the necktie. In the back of his mind was a ghost image of some other dream about a necktie.

He decided that he would go to the office. He did not see what else he could do. If his memory of what Driscoll had said was accurate, maybe by now Driscoll would have relented. When he went to select a necktie after he had shaved carefully, he looked for the new one on the rack. It was not there. As he was tying the one he had selected he noticed a wadded piece of paper on the floor beside his wastebasket. He picked it up, spread it open, read the name of the shop on it, and knew that the purchase of the tie had been real.

By the time he was completely dressed, it still was not eight o'clock. He felt unwell, though the sharpness of the headache was dulled. His hands were shaky. His legs felt empty and weak.

It was time to face Sarah. He knew that he had seen her the previous evening. Probably she had been in bed, had heard him come in, had gotten up as was her custom and, no doubt, there had been a scene. He hoped he had not told her of losing the job. Yet, if it had been a dream, he could not have told her. If he had told her, it would be proof that it had not been a dream. He went through the bathroom into her bedroom, moving quietly. Her bed had been slept in, turned back where she had gotten out.

He went down the short hall to the small kitchen. Sarah was not there. He began to wonder about her. Surely the quarrel could not have been so bad that she had dressed and left. He measured coffee into the top of the percolator and put it over a low gas flame. He mixed frozen juice and drank a large glass. The apartment seemed uncannily quiet. He poured another glass, drank half of it, and walked up the hallway to the living room.

Stopping in the doorway, he saw the necktie, recognized the small pattern. He stood there, glass in hand, and looked at the tie. It was tightly knotted. And above the knot, resting on the arm of the chair, was the still, unspeakable face of Sarah, a face the shiny hue of fresh eggplant.

The Santa Claus Club

JULIAN SYMONS

Julian Symons is a courageous man. His is one of the finest critical voices commenting on the mystery and suspense field, yet he has not hesitated to stick his neck out by publishing fiction within it, and his work is of consistently high quality. His book reviews for the Sunday Times *of London have set the standard for all the others. As a fiction writer he is best known for his stories of Inspector Bland (whose name certainly does not describe these books). A talented poet and essayist, he is a worthy successor to the late Anthony Boucher as crime fiction's man of letters.*
"The Santa Claus Club" is evidence of his considerable talents.

It is not often, in real life, that letters are written recording implacable hatred nursed over the years, or that private detectives are invited by peers to select dining clubs, or that murders occur at such dining clubs, or that they are solved on the spot by logical deduction.

The case of The Santa Claus Club provided an example of all these rarities.

The case began one day a week before Christmas, when Francis Quarles went to see Lord Acrise. He was a rich man, Lord Acrise, and an important one—the chairman of this big building concern and the director of that big insurance company and the consultant to the government on many matters.

He had been a harsh, intolerant man in his prime, and was still hard enough in his early seventies, Quarles guessed, as he looked at the beaky nose, jutting chin, and stony blue eyes under thick brows. They sat in the study of Acrise's house just off the Brompton Road.

"Just tell me what you think of these."

These were three letters, badly typed on a machine with a worn ribbon. They were all signed with the name James Gliddon. The first two contained vague references to some wrong done to Gliddon by Acrise in the past. They were written in language that was wild, but unmistakably threatening.

"You have been a white sepulcher for too long, but now your time has come . . . You don't know what I'm going to do, now I've come back,

333

but you won't be able to help wondering and worrying . . . The mills of God grind slowly, but they're going to grind you into little bits for what you've done to me."

The third letter was more specific. "So the thief is going to play Santa Claus. That will be your last evening alive. *I shall be there,* Joe Acrise, and I shall watch with pleasure as you squirm in agony."

Quarles looked at the envelopes. They were plain and cheap. The address was typed, and the word "personal" was on top of the envelope. "Who is James Gliddon?"

The stony eyes glared at him. "I'm told you're to be trusted. Gliddon was a school friend of mine. We grew up together in the slums of Nottingham. We started a building company together. It did well for a time, then went bust. There was a lot of money missing. Gliddon kept the books. He got five years for fraud."

"Have you heard from him since then? I see all these letters are recent."

"He's written half a dozen letters, I suppose, over the years. The last one came—oh, seven years ago, I should think. From the Argentine." Acrise stopped, then said abruptly, "Snowin tried to find him for me but he'd disappeared."

"Snowin?"

"My secretary. Been with me twelve years."

He pressed a bell. An obsequious, fattish man, whose appearance somehow put Quarles in mind of an enormous mouse, scurried in.

"Snowin? Did we keep any of those old letters from Gliddon?"

"No, sir. You told me to destroy them."

"The last one came from the Argentine, right?"

"From Buenos Aires to be exact, sir."

Acrise nodded, and Snowin scurried out. Quarles said, "Who else knows this story about Gliddon?"

"Just my wife." Acrise bared yellow teeth in a grin. "Unless somebody's been digging into my past."

"And what does this mean, about you playing Santa Claus?"

"I'm this year's chairman of The Santa Claus Club. We hold our raffle and dinner next Monday."

Then Quarles remembered. The Santa Claus Club had been formed by ten rich men. Each year they met, every one of them dressed up as Santa Claus, and held a raffle. The members took turns to provide the prize that was raffled—it might be a case of Napoleon brandy, a modest cottage with some exclusive salmon fishing rights attached to it, a Constable painting.

Each Santa Claus bought one ticket for the raffle, at a cost of one thousand guineas. The total of ten thousand guineas was given to a Christmas charity. After the raffle the assembled Santa Clauses, each accompanied by one guest, ate a traditional Christmas dinner.

The whole thing was a combination of various English characteristics: enjoyment of dressing up, a wish to help charities, and the desire also that the help given should not go unrecorded. The dinners of The Santa Claus Club got a good deal of publicity, and there were those who said that it would have been perfectly easy for the members to give their money to charities in a less conspicuous manner.

"I want you to find Gliddon," Lord Acrise said. "Don't mistake me, Mr. Quarles. I don't want to take action against him, I want to help him. I wasn't to blame—don't think I admit that—but it was hard that Jimmy Gliddon should go to jail. I'm a hard man, have been all my life, but I don't think my worst enemies would call me mean. Those who've helped me know that when I die they'll find they're not forgotten. Jimmy Gliddon must be an old man now. I'd like to set him up for the rest of his life."

"To find him by next Monday is a tall order," Quarles said. "But I'll try."

He was at the door when Acrise said casually, "By the way, I'd like you to be my guest at The Santa Clause Club dinner on Monday night."

Did that mean, Quarles wondered, that he was to act as official poison taster if he did not find James Gliddon?

There were two ways of trying to find Gliddon—by investigation of his career after leaving prison, and through the typewritten letters. Quarles took the job of tracing the past, leaving the letters to his secretary, Molly Player.

From Scotland Yard, Quarles found out that Gliddon had spent nearly four years in prison, from 1913 to late in 1916. He had joined a Nottinghamshire Regiment when he came out, and the records of this regiment showed that he had been demobilized in August 1919, with the rank of sergeant. In 1923 he had been given a sentence of three years for an attempt to smuggle diamonds. Thereafter, all trace of him in Britain vanished.

Quarles made some expensive telephone calls to Buenos Aires, where a letter had come from seven years earlier. He learned that Gliddon had lived in the city from a time just after the war until 1955. He ran an import-export business, and was thought to have been living in other South American republics during the war. His business was said to have been a cloak for smuggling, both of drugs and of suspected Nazis, whom he got out of Europe into the Argentine.

In 1955 a newspaper had accused Gliddon of arranging the entry into the Argentine of a Nazi war criminal named Hermann Breit. Gliddon threatened to sue the paper, and then disappeared. A couple of weeks later a battered body was washed up just outside the city.

"It was identified as Gliddon," the liquid voice said over the telephone. "But you know, Señor Quarles, in such matters the police are sometimes happy to close their files."

"There was still some doubt?"

"Yes. Not very much, perhaps, but in these cases there is often a doubt."

Molly Player found out nothing useful about the paper and envelopes. They were of the sort that could be bought in a thousand stores and shops in London and elsewhere. She had more luck with the typewriter. Its key characteristics identified the machine as a Malward portable of a model which the company had ceased producing ten years ago. The typeface had proved unsatisfactory, and only some three hundred machines of this sort had been made.

The Malward Company was able to provide her with a list of the purchasers of these machines, and Molly started to check and trace them, but had to give it up as a bad job.

"If we had three weeks I might get somewhere. In three days it's impossible," she said to Quarles.

Lord Acrise made no comment on Quarles's recital of failure. "See you on Monday evening, seven-thirty, black tie," he said, and barked with laughter. "Your host will be Santa Claus."

"I'd like to be there earlier."

"Good idea. Any time you like. You know where it is—Robert the Devil Restaurant."

The Robert the Devil Restaurant is situated inconspicuously in Mayfair. It is not a restaurant in the ordinary sense of the word, for there is no public dining room, but simply several private rooms, which can accommodate any number of guests from two to thirty. Perhaps the food is not quite the best in London, but it is certainly the most expensive.

It was here that Quarles arrived at half-past six, a big suave man, rather too conspicuously elegant perhaps in a midnight-blue dinner jacket. He talked to Albert, the maitre d'hotel, whom he had known for some years, took unobtrusive looks at the waiters, went into and admired the kitchens.

Albert observed his activities with tolerant amusement. "You are here on some sort of business, Mr. Quarles?"

"I am a guest, Albert. I am also a kind of bodyguard. Tell me, how many of your waiters have joined you in the past twelve months?"

"Perhaps half a dozen. They come, they go."

"Is there anybody at all on your staff—waiters, kitchen staff, anybody —who has joined you this year and is over sixty years old?"

Albert thought, then shook his head decisively. "No. There is no such one."

The first of the guests came just after seven. He was the brain surgeon, Sir James Erdington, with a guest whom Quarles recognized as the Arctic explorer, Norman Endell.

After that they came at intervals of a minute or two—a minister in the government, one of the three most important men in the motor industry, a general promoted to the peerage to celebrate his retirement, a theatrical producer named Roddy Davis who had successfully combined commerce and culture. As they arrived, the hosts went into a special dressing room to put on their Santa Claus clothes, while the guests drank sherry.

At seven-twenty-five Snowin scurried in, gasped, "Excuse me, place names, got to put them out," and went into the dining room. Through the open door Quarles glimpsed a large oval table, gleaming with silver and bright with roses.

After Snowin came Lord Acrise, jutting-nosed and fearsome-eyed. "Sorry to have kept you waiting," he barked, and asked conspiratorially, "Well?"

"No sign."

"False alarm. Lot of nonsense. Got to dress up now."

He went into the dressing room with his box—each of the hosts had a similar box, labeled SANTA CLAUS—and came out again bewigged, bearded, and robed. "Better get the business over, and then we can enjoy ourselves. You can tell 'em to come in," he said to Albert.

This referred to the photographers who had been clustering outside and who now came into the room specially provided for holding the raffle. In the center of the room was a table and on this table stood this year's prize —two exquisite T'ang horses. On the other side of the table were ten chairs arranged in a semicircle, and on these sat the Santa Clauses. The guests stood inconspicuously at the side.

The raffle was conducted with the utmost seriousness. Each Santa Claus had a numbered slip. These slips were dropped into a bowl, mixed up, and then Acrise put in his hand and drew out one of them. Flashbulbs exploded.

"The number drawn is eight," Acrise announced, and Roddy Davis waved the counterfoil in his hand. "Isn't that *wonderful?* It's my ticket." He went over to the horses and picked up one. More flashes. "I'm bound to say that they couldn't have gone to *anybody* who'd have appreciated them more."

Quarles, standing near the general, whose face was as red as his robe, heard him mutter something uncomplimentary. Charity, he reflected, was not universal, even in a gathering of Santas. More flashes, the photographers disappeared, and Quarles's views about the nature of charity were reinforced when, as they were about to go into the dining room, Erdington said, "Forgotten something, haven't you, Acrise?"

With what seemed dangerous quietness Acrise answered, "Have I? I don't think so."

"It's customary for the club and guests to sing "Noel" before we go in to dinner."

"You didn't come to last year's dinner. It was agreed then that we should give it up. Carols after dinner, much better."

"I must say I thought that was *just* for last year, because we were late," Roddy Davis fluted. "I'm sure that's what was agreed. I think myself it's rather pleasant to sing "Noel" before we go in and start eating too much."

"Suggest we put it to the vote," Erdington said sharply.

Half a dozen of the Santas now stood looking at each other with subdued hostility. It was a situation that would have been totally ludicrous, if it had not been also embarrassing for the guests.

Then suddenly the Arctic explorer, Endell, began to sing "Noel, Noel" in a rich bass. There was the faintest flicker of hesitation, and then guests and Santas joined in. The situation was saved.

At dinner Quarles found himself with Acrise on one side of him and Roddy Davis on the other. Endell sat at Acrise's other side, and beyond him was Erdington.

Turtle soup was followed by grilled sole, and then three great turkeys were brought in. The helpings of turkey were enormous. With the soup they drank a light, dry sherry, with the sole Chassagne Montrachet, with the turkey an Alexe Corton, heavy and powerful.

"And who are *you?*" Roddy Davis peered at Quarles's card and said, with what seemed manifest untruth, "Of course I know your name."

"I am a criminologist." This sounded better, he thought, than private detective.

"I remember your monograph on criminal calligraphy. Quite fascinating."

So Davis did know who he was—it would be easy, Quarles thought, to underrate the intelligence of the round-faced man who beamed so innocently to him.

"These beards really do get in the way rather," Davis said. "But there, one must suffer for tradition. Have you known Acrise long?"

"Not very. I'm greatly privileged to be here." Quarles had been watching, as closely as he could, the pouring of the wine and the serving of the food. He had seen nothing suspicious. Now, to get away from Davis's questions, he turned to his host.

"Damned awkward business before dinner," Acrise said. "Might have been, at least. Can't let well alone, Erdington." He picked up his turkey leg, attacked it with Elizabethan gusto, then wiped his mouth and fingers with a napkin. "Like this wine?"

"It's excellent."

"Chose it myself. They've got some good burgundies here." Acrise's speech was slightly slurred, and it seemed to Quarles that he was rapidly getting drunk.

"Do you have any speeches?"

"What's that?"

"Are any speeches made after dinner?"

"No speeches. Just sing carols. But I've got a little surprise for 'em."

"What sort of surprise?"

"Very much in the spirit of Christmas, and a good joke too. But if I told you it wouldn't be a surprise now, would it?"

Acrise had almost said "shurprise." Quarles looked at him and then returned to the turkey.

There was a general cry of pleasure as Albert himself brought in the great plum pudding, topped with holly and blazing with brandy.

"That's the most wonderful pudding I've ever seen in my life," Endell said. "Are we really going to eat it?"

"Of course we're going to eat it," Acrise said irritably. He stood up, swaying a little, and picked up the knife beside the pudding.

"I don't like to be critical, but our chairman is really *not* cutting the pudding very well," Roddy Davis whispered to Quarles.

And indeed, it was more of a stab than a cut that Acrise made at the pudding. Albert took over, and cut it quickly and efficiently. Bowls of brandy butter were circulated.

Quarles leaned toward Acrise. "Are you all right?"

"Of course I'm all right." The slurring was very noticeable now. Acrise ate no pudding, but he drank some more wine, and dabbed at his lips. When the pudding was finished he got slowly to his feet again, and toasted the queen.

Cigars were lighted. Acrise was not smoking. He whispered something to the waiter, who nodded and left the room. Acrise got up again, leaning heavily on the table.

"A little surprise," he said. "In the spirit of Christmas."

Quarles had thought that he was beyond being surprised by the activities of The Santa Claus Club, but still he was astonished by sight of the three figures who entered the room. They were led by Snowin, somehow more mouselike than ever, wearing a long white smock and a red nightcap with a tassel.

He was followed by an older man dressed in a kind of gray sackcloth, with a face so white that it might have been covered in plaster of Paris. This man carried chains which he shook.

At the rear came a middle-aged lady, who sparkled so brightly that she seemed to be completely hung with tinsel.

"I am Scrooge," said Snowin.

"I am Marley," wailed gray sackcloth, clanking his chains.

"And I," said the middle-aged lady with abominable sprightliness, "am the ghost of Christmas past."

There was a murmur round the table, and slowly the murmur grew to a ripple of laughter.

"We have come," said Snowin in a thin mouse voice, "to perform for you our own interpretation of A Christmas Carol—oh, sir, what's the matter?"

Lord Acrise stood up in his robes, tore off his wig, pulled at his beard, tried to say something. Then he clutched at the side of his chair and fell sideways, so that he leaned heavily against Endell and slipped slowly to the floor.

There ensued a minute of confused activity. Endell made some sort of exclamation and rose from his chair, slightly obstructing Quarles. Erdington was first beside the body, holding the wrist in his hand, listening for the heart. Then they were all crowding round, the red-robed Santas, the guests, the actors in their ludicrous clothes. Snowin, at Quarles's left shoulder, was babbling something, and at his right were Roddy Davis and Endell.

"Stand back," Erdington snapped. He stayed on his knees for another few moments, looking curiously at Acrise's puffed, distorted face, bluish around the mouth. Then he stood up. "He's dead."

There was a murmur of surprise and horror, and now they all drew back, as men do instinctively from the presence of death.

"Heart attack?" somebody said. Erdington made a noncommittal noise. Quarles moved to his side.

"I'm a private detective, Sir James. Lord Acrise feared an attempt on his life and asked me to come along here."

"You seem to have done well so far," Erdington said dryly.

"May I look at the body?"

"If you wish."

As soon as Quarles bent down he caught the smell of bitter almonds. When he straightened up Erdington raised his eyebrows.

"He's been poisoned. There's a smell like purssic acid, but the way he died precludes cyanide, I think. He seemed to become very drunk during dinner, and his speech was blurred. Does that suggest anything to you?"

"I'm a brain surgeon, not a physician." Erdington stared at the floor, then said, "Nitrobenzene?"

"That's what I thought. We shall have to notify the police." Quarles went to the door and spoke to a disturbed Albert. Then he returned to the room and clapped his hands.

"Gentlemen. My name is Francis Quarles, and I am a private detective. Lord Acrise asked me to come here tonight because he had received a threat that this would be his last evening alive. The threat said: 'I shall be there, and I shall watch with pleasure as you squirm in agony.' Lord Acrise has been poisoned. It seems certain that the man who made the threat is in this room."

"Gliddon," a voice said. Snowin had divested himself of the white smock and red nightcap, and now appeared as his customary respectable self.

"Yes. This letter, and others he had received, were signed with the name of James Gliddon, a man who bore a grudge against Lord Acrise which went back nearly half a century. Gliddon became a professional smuggler and crook. He would now be in his late sixties."

"But damn it, man, this Gliddon's not here." That was the general, who took off his wig and beard. "Lot of tomfoolery."

In a shamefaced way the other members of The Santa Claus Club removed their facial trappings. Marley took off his chains and the middle-aged lady discarded her cloak of tinsel.

"Isn't he here? But Lord Acrise is dead."

Snowin coughed. "Excuse me, sir, but would it be possible for my colleagues from our local dramatic society to retire? Of course, I can stay myself if you wish. It was Lord Acrise's idea that we should perform our skit on *A Christmas Carol* as a seasonable novelty, but—"

"Everybody must stay in this room until the police arrive. The problem, as you will all realize, is how the poison was administered. All of us ate the same food and drank the same wine. I sat next to Lord Acrise, and I watched as closely as possible to make sure of this. I watched the wine being poured, the turkey being carved and brought to the table, the pudding being cut and passed round. After dinner some of you smoked cigars or cigarettes, but not Acrise."

"Just a moment." It was Roddy Davis who spoke. "This sounds fantastic, but wasn't it Sherlock Holmes who said that when you'd eliminated all other possibilities, even a fantastic one might be right? Supposing that some poison in powder form had been put on to Acrise's food—through the saltcellars, say—"

Erdington was shaking his head, but Quarles unscrewed both the salt and pepper shakers and tasted their contents. "Salt and pepper. And in any case other people used these. Hello, what's this?"

Acrise's napkin lay crumpled on his chair, and Quarles had picked it up and was staring at it.

"It's Acrise's napkin," Endell said. "What's remarkable about that?"

"It's a napkin, but not the one Acrise used. He wiped his mouth half a dozen times on his napkin, and wiped his greasy fingers on it too, when he'd gnawed a turkey bone. He must certainly have left grease marks on it. But look at this napkin."

He held it up, and they saw that it was spotless. Quarles said softly, "The murderer's mistake."

"I'm quite baffled," Roddy Davis said. "What does it mean?"

Quarles turned to Erdington. "Sir James and I agreed that the poison used was probably nitrobenzene. This is deadly as a liquid, but it is also poisonous as a vapor, isn't that so?"

Erdington nodded. "You'll remember the case of the unfortunate young man who used shoe polish containing nitrobenzene on damp shoes, put them on and wore them, and was killed by the fumes."

"Yes. Somebody made sure that Lord Acrise had a napkin that had been soaked in nitrobenzene but was dry enough to use. The same person substituted the proper napkin, the one belonging to the restaurant, after Acrise was dead."

"Nobody's left the room," said Roddy Davis.

"No."

"That means the murder napkin must still be here."

"It does."

"Then what are we waiting for? I vote that we submit to a search."

There was a small hubbub of protest and approval. "That won't be necessary," Quarles said. "Only one person here fulfills all the qualifications of the murderer."

"James Gliddon?"

"No. Gliddon is almost certainly dead. But the murderer is somebody who knew about Acrise's relationship with Gliddon, and tried to be clever by writing the letters to lead us along a wrong track. Then the murderer is somebody who had the opportunity of coming in here before dinner and who knew exactly where Acrise would be sitting. There is only one person who fulfills all of these qualifications.

"He removed any possible suspicion from himself, as he thought, by being absent from the dinner table, but he arranged to come in afterwards to exchange the napkins. He probably put the poisoned napkin into the clothes he discarded. As for motive, long-standing hatred might be enough, but he is also somebody who knew that he would benefit handsomely when Acrise died—stop him, will you?"

But the general, with a tackle reminiscent of the days when he had been the best wing three-quarter in the country, had already brought to the floor Lord Acrise's mouselike secretary, Snowin.

The Wager

ROBERT L. FISH

Robert L. Fish (1912–1981) is probably best known as the author of
Mute Witness, *the novel on which the film* Bullitt *was based. But he was
also the author of many novels of distinction and a number of elegant short
stories of which "The Wager," in its intricacy and its almost poisonously
ebullient sense of pace, may be the most elegant of all.*

I suppose if I were watching television coverage of the return of a lunar
mission and Kek Huuygens climbed out of the command module after
splashdown, I shouldn't be greatly surprised. I'd be even less surprised to
see Kek hustled aboard the aircraft carrier and given a thorough search
by a suspicious customs official. Kek, you see, is one of those men who turn
up at very odd times in unexpected places. Also, he is rated by the customs
services of nearly every nation in the world as the most talented smuggler
alive. Polish by birth, Dutch by adopted name, the holder of a valid U.S.
passport, multilingual, a born sleight-of-hand artist, Kek is an elusive
target for the stolid bureaucrat who thinks in terms of hollow shoe heels
and suitcases with false bottoms. Now and then over the years, Kek has
allowed me to publish a little of his lore in my column. When I came
across him last, however, he was doing something very ordinary in a
commonplace setting. Under the critical eye of a waiter, he was nursing
a beer at a table in that little sunken-garden affair in Rockefeller Center.

Before I got to his table, I tried to read the clues. Kek had a good tan
and he looked healthy. But his suit had a shine that came from wear rather
than from silk thread. A neat scissors trim didn't quite conceal the fact
that his cuffs were frayed. He was not wearing his usual boutonniere.

"I owe you three cognacs from last time—Vaduz, wasn't it?—and I'm
buying," I said as I sat down.

"You are a man of honor," he said and called to the waiter, naming
a most expensive cognac. Then he gave me his wide friendly smile. "Yes,
you have read the signs and they are true—but not for any reasons you
might imagine. Sitting before you, you can observe the impoverishment
that comes from total success. Failure can be managed, but success can
be a most difficult thing to control. . . ."

344

Hidden inside every Kek Huuygens aphorism there is a story some-where. But if you want it produced, you must pretend complete indiffer-ence. "Ah, yes," I said, "failure is something you know in your heart. Success is something that lies in the eye of the beholder. I think—"

"Do you want to hear the story or don't you?" Kek said. "You can't use it in your column, though, I warn you."

"Perhaps in time?"

"Perhaps in time, all barbarous customs regulations will be repealed," he said. "Perhaps the angels will come down to rule the earth. Until then, you and I alone will share this story." That was Kek's way of saying "Wait until things have cooled off."

It all began in Las Vegas (Huuygens said) and was primarily caused by two unfortunate factors: one, that I spoke the word "banco" aloud and, two, that it was heard. I am still not convinced that the player against me wasn't the world's best card manipulator, but at any rate, I found myself looking at a jack and a nine, while the best I could manage for myself was a six. So I watched my money disappear, got up politely to allow the next standee to take my place and started for the exit. I had enough money in the hotel safe to pay my bill and buy me a ticket back to New York —a simple precaution I recommend to all who never learn to keep quiet in a baccarat game—and a few dollars in my pocket, but my financial position was not one any sensible banker would have lent money against. I was sure something would turn up, as it usually did, and in this case it turned up even faster than usual, because I hadn't even reached the door before I was stopped.

The man who put his hand on my arm did so in a completely friendly manner, and I recalled him as being one of the group standing around the table during the play. There was something faintly familiar about him, but even quite famous faces are disregarded at a baccarat table; one is not there to collect autographs. The man holding my arm was short, heavy, swarthy and of a type to cause instant distaste on the part of any discern-ing observer. What caught and held my attention was that he addressed me by name—and in French. "M'sieu Huuygens?" he said. To my abso-lute amazement, he pronounced it correctly. I acknowledged that I was, indeed, M'sieu Kek Huuygens. "I should like to talk with you a moment and to buy you a drink," he said.

"I could use one," I admitted, and I allowed him to lead me into the bar. As we went, I noticed two men who had been standing to one side studying their fingernails; they now moved with us and took up new positions to each side, still studying their nails. One would think that fingernails were a subject that could quickly bore, but apparently not to those two. As I sat down beside my chubby host, I looked at him once more, and suddenly recognition came.

He saw the light come on in the little circle over my head and smiled, showing a dazzling collection of white teeth, a tribute to the art of the dental laboratory.

"Yes," he said, "I am Antoine Duvivier," and waved over a waiter. We ordered and I returned my attention to him. Duvivier, as you must know —even newspapermen listen to the radio, I assume—was the president of the island of St. Michel in the Caribbean, or had been until his loyal subjects decided that presidents should be elected, after which he departed in the middle of the night, taking with him most of his country's treasury. He could see the wheels turning in my head as I tried to see how I could use this information to my advantage, and I must say he waited politely enough while I was forced to give up on the problem. Then he said, "I have watched you play at baccarat."

We received our drinks and I sipped, waiting for him to go on.

"You are quite a gambler, M'sieu Huuygens," he said, "but, of course, you would have to be, in your line of work." He saw my eyebrows go up and added quite coolly, "Yes, M'sieu Huuygens, I have had you investigated, and thoroughly. But please permit me to explain that it was not done from idle curiosity. I am interested in making you a proposition."

I find, in situations like this, the less said the better, so I said nothing.

"Yes," he went on, "I should like to offer you—" He paused, as if reconsidering his words, actually looking embarrassed, as if he were guilty of a *gaffe*. "Let me rephrase that," he said and searched for a better approach. At last he found it. "What I meant was, I should like to make a *wager* with you, a wager I am sure should be most interesting to a gambler such as yourself."

This time, of course, I had to answer, so I said, "Oh?"

"Yes," he said, pleased at my instant understanding. "I should like to wager twenty thousand dollars of my money, against two dollars of yours, that you will *not* bring a certain object from the Caribbean through United States Customs and deliver it to me in New York City."

I must admit I admire bluntness, even though the approach was not particularly unique. "The odds are reasonable," I admitted. "One might even say generous. What type of object are we speaking of?"

He lowered his voice. "It is a carving," he said "A Tien Tse Huwai, dating back to eight centuries before Christ. It is of ivory and is not particularly large; I imagine it could fit into your coat pocket, although, admittedly, it would be bulky. It depicts a village scene—but you, I understand, are an art connoisseur; you may have heard of it. In translation, its name is *The Village Dance.*" Normally, I can control my features, but my surprise must have shown, for Duvivier went on in the same soft voice. "Yes, I have it. The carving behind that glass case in the St. Michel National Gallery is a copy—a plastic casting, excellently done, but a copy. The original is at the home of a friend in Barbados. I could get it that far, but I was afraid to attempt bringing it the rest of the way; to have lost it would have been tragic. Since then, I have been looking for a man clever enough to get it into the States without being stopped by customs." He suddenly grinned, those white blocks of teeth almost blinding me. "I am offering ten thousand-to-one odds that that clever man is *not* you."

It was a cute ploy, but that was not what interested me at the moment.

"M'sieu," I said simply, "permit me a question: I am familiar with the Tien *Village Dance.* I have never seen it, but it received quite a bit of publicity when your National Gallery purchased it, since it was felt—if you will pardon me—that the money could have been used better elsewhere. However, my surprise a moment ago was not that you have the carving; it was at your offer. The Tien, many years in the future, may, indeed, command a large price, but the figure your museum paid when you bought it was, as I recall, not much more than the twenty thousand dollars you are willing to—ah—wager to get it into this country. And that value could only be realized at a legitimate sale, which would be difficult, it seems to me, under the circumstances."

Duvivier's smile had been slowly disappearing as I spoke. Now he was looking at me in disappointment.

"You do not understand, m'sieu," he said, and there was a genuine touch of sadness in his voice at my incogitancy. "To you, especially after your losses tonight, I am sure the sum of twenty thousand dollars seems a fortune, but, in all honesty, to me it is not. I am not interested in the monetary value of the carving; I have no intention of selling it. I simply wish to own it." He looked at me with an expression I have seen many times before—the look of a fanatic, a zealot. A Collector, with a capital C. "You cannot possibly comprehend," he repeated, shaking his head. "It is such an incredibly lovely thing. . . ."

Well, of course, he was quite wrong about my understanding, or lack of it; I understood perfectly. For a moment, I almost found myself liking the man; but only for a moment. And a wager is a wager, and I had to admit I had never been offered such attractive odds before in my life. As for the means of getting the carving into the United States, especially from Barbados, I had a thought on that, too. I was examining my idea in greater detail when his voice broke in on me.

"Well?" he asked, a bit impatiently.

"You have just made yourself a bet," I said. "But it will require a little time."

"How much time?" Now that I was committed, the false friendliness was gone from both voice and visage; for all practical purposes, I was now merely an employee.

I thought a moment. "It's hard to say. It depends," I said at last. "Less than two months but probably more than one."

He frowned. "Why so long?" I merely shrugged and reached for my glass. "All right," he said grudgingly. "And how do you plan on getting it through customs?" My response to this was to smile at him gently, so he gave up. "I shall give you a card to my friend in Barbados, which will release the carving into your care. After that"—he smiled again, but this time it was a bit wolfish for my liking—"our wager will be in effect. We will meet at my apartment in New York."

He gave me his address, together with his telephone number, and then handed me a second card with a scrawl on it to a name in Barbados, and that was that. We drank up, shook hands and I left the bar, pleased to be working again and equally pleased to be quitted of Duvivier, if only for a while.

Huuygens paused and looked at me with his satanic eyebrows tilted sharply. I recognized the expression and made a circular gesture over our glasses, which was instantly interpreted by our waiter. Kek waited until we were served, thanked me gravely and drank. I settled back to listen, sipping. When next Huuygens spoke, however, I thought at first he was changing the subject, but I soon learned this was not the case.

Anyone who says the day of travel by ship has passed (Huuygens went on) has never made an examination of the brochures for Caribbean cruises that fill and overflow the racks of travel agencies. It appears that between sailings from New York and sailings from Port Everglades—not to mention Miami, Baltimore, Norfolk and others—almost everything afloat must be pressed into service to transport those Americans with credit cards and a little free time to the balmy breezes and shimmering sands of the islands. They have trips for all seasons, as well as for every taste and pocketbook. There are bridge cruises to St. Lucia, canasta cruises to Trinidad, gold cruises to St. Croix. There are seven-day cruises to the Bahamas, eight-day cruises to Jamaica, thirteen-day cruises to Martinique; there are even—I was not surprised to see—three-day cruises to nowhere. And it struck me that even though it was approaching summer, a cruise would be an ideal way to travel; it had been one of my principal reasons for requiring so much time to consummate the deal.

So I went to the travel agency in the hotel lobby and was instantly inundated with schedules and pamphlets. I managed to get the reams of propaganda to my room without a bellboy, sat down on the bed and carefully made my selection. When I had my trip laid out to my satisfaction, I descended once again to the hotel lobby and presented my program to the travel agent there. He must have thought I was insane, but I explained I suffered from Widget Syndrome and required a lot of salt air, after which he shrugged and picked up the phone to confirm my reservations through New York. They readily accepted my credit card for the bill —which I sincerely hoped to be able to honor by the time it was presented —and two days later, I found myself in Miami, boarding the *M.V. Andropolis* for a joyous sixteen-day cruise. It was longer than I might have chosen, but it was the only one that fit my schedule and I felt that I had —or would, shortly—earn the rest.

I might as well tell you right now that it was a delightful trip. I should have preferred to have taken along my own feminine companionship, but my finances would not permit it; there are, after all, such hard-cash outlays as bar bills and tips. However, there was no lack of unattached women aboard, some even presentable, and the days—as they say—fairly flew. We had the required rum punch in Ocho Rios, fought off the beggars in Port-au-Prince, visited Bluebeard's Castle in Charlotte Amalie and eventually made it to Barbados.

Barbados is a lovely island, with narrow winding roads that skirt the ocean and cross between the Caribbean and Atlantic shores through high stands of sugarcane that quite efficiently hide any view of approaching traffic; but my rented car and I managed to get to the address I had been given without brushing death more than three or four times. The man to whom I presented the ex-president's card was not in the least perturbed to be giving up the carving; if anything, he seemed relieved to be rid of its responsibility. It was neatly packaged in straw, wrapped in brown paper and tied with twine, and I left it exactly that way as I drove back to the dock through the friendly islanders, all of whom demonstrated their happy, carefree insouciance by walking in the middle of the road.

There was no problem about carrying the package aboard. Other passengers from the *M. V. Andropolis* were forming a constant line, like ants, to and from the ship, leaving empty-handed to return burdened with Wedgewood, Hummel figures, camera lenses and weirdly woven straw hats that did not fit. I gave up my boarding pass at the gangplank, climbed to my proper deck and locked myself in my stateroom, interested in seeing this carving upon which M'sieu Antoine Duvivier was willing to wager the princely sum of twenty-thousand United States dollars.

The paper came away easily enough. I eased the delicate carving from its bed of straw and took it to the light of my desk lamp. At first I was so interested in studying the piece for its authenticity that the true beauty of the carving didn't strike me; but when I finally came to concede that I was, indeed, holding a genuine Tien Tse Huwai in my hands and got down to looking at the piece itself, I had to admit that M'sieu Duvivier, whatever his other failings, was a man of excellent taste. I relished the delicate nuances with which Tien had managed his intricate subject, the warmth he had been able to impart to his cold medium, the humor he had been genius enough to instill in the ivory scene. Each figure in the relaxed yet ritualistic village dance had his own posture, and although there were easily forty or fifty men and women involved, carved with infinite detail on a plaque no larger than six by eight inches and possibly three inches in thickness, there was no sense of crowding. One could allow himself to be drawn into the carving, to almost imagine movement or hear the flutes. I enjoyed the study of the masterpiece for another few minutes and then carefully rewrapped it and tucked it into the air-conditioning duct of my stateroom, pleased that the first portion of my assignment had been completed with such ease. I replaced the grillwork and went upstairs to the bar, prepared to enjoy the remaining three or four days of balmy breezes—if not shimmering sands, since Barbados had been our final port.

The trip back to Miami was enjoyable but uneventful. I lost in the shuffleboard tournament, largely due to a near-sighted partner, but in compensation I picked up a record number of spoons from the bottom of the swimming pool and received in reward, at the captain's party, a crystal ashtray engraved with a design of Triton either coming up or going down for the third time. What I am trying to say is that, all in all, I enjoyed myself completely and the trip was almost compensation for the thorough—and humiliating—search I had to suffer when I finally went through customs in Miami. As usual, they did everything but disintegrate my luggage, and they handled my person in a manner I normally accept only from young ladies. But at last I was free of customs—to their obvious chagrin—and I found myself in the street in one piece. So I took myself and my luggage to a hotel for the night.

And the next morning I reboarded the *M. V. Andropolis* for its next trip—in the same cabin—a restful three-day cruise to nowhere. . . .

Huuygens smiled at me gently. My expression must have caused the waiter concern—he probably thought I had left my wallet at home—for he hurried over. To save myself embarrassment, I ordered another round and then went back to staring at Huuygens.

I see (Kek went on, his eyes twinkling) that intelligence has finally forced its presence upon you. I should have thought it was rather obvious. These Caribbean cruise ships vary their schedules, mixing trips to the islands with these short cruises to nowhere, where they merely wander aimlessly upon the sea and eventually find their way back—some say with considerable luck—to their home port. Since they touch no foreign shore, and since even the ships' shops are closed during these cruises, one is not faced with the delay or embarrassment of facing a customs agent upon one's return. Therefore, if one were to take a cruise *preceding* a cruise to nowhere and were to be so careless as to inadvertently leave a small object —in the air-conditioning duct of his stateroom, for example—during the turnaround, he could easily retrieve it on the second cruise and walk off the ship with it in his pocket, with no fear of discovery.

Which, of course, is what I did. . . .

The flight to New York was slightly anticlimactic, and I called M'sieu Duvivier as soon as I landed at Kennedy. He was most pleasantly surprised, since less than a month had actually elapsed, and said he would expect me as fast as I could get there by cab.

The ex-president of St. Michel lived in a lovely apartment on Central Park South, and as I rode up in the elevator, I thought of how pleasant it must be to have endless amounts of money at one's disposal; but before I had a chance to dwell on that thought too much, we had arrived and I found myself pushing what I still think was a lapis lazuli doorbell set in a solid-gold frame. It made one want to weep. At any rate, Duvivier himself answered the door, as anxious as any man I have ever seen. He didn't even wait to ask me in or inquire as to my taste in aperitifs.

"You have it?" he asked, staring at my coat pocket.

"Before we go any further," I said, "I should like you to repeat the exact terms of our wager. The *exact* terms, if you please."

He looked at me in irritation, as if I were being needlessly obstructive.

"All right," he said shortly. "I wagered you twenty thousand dollars of my money against two dollars of yours that you would *not* bring me a small carving from Barbados through United States Customs and deliver it to me in New York. Is that correct?"

I sighed. "Perfectly correct," I said and reached into my pocket. "You are a lucky man. You won." And I handed him his two dollars. . . .

I stared across the table at Huuygens. I'm afraid my jaw had gone slack. He shook his head at me, a bit sad at my lack of comprehension.

"You can't possibly understand," he said, almost petulantly. "It is so incredibly lovely. . . .

A Fool About Money

NGAIO MARSH

Unlike authors of science fiction and Westerns, crime writers do receive honors from their governments, although it helps to live in the British Commonwealth of Nations. Ngaio Marsh is Dame Commander, Order of the British Empire, and has a theater at Canterbury University named after her. She is also (arguably) the best-known citizen of New Zealand in the world at large.

Her wonderful mystery and suspense stories need no introduction, and "A Fool About Money" will receive none here.

"Where money is concerned," Harold Hancock told his audience at the enormous cocktail party, "my poor Hersey—and she won't mind my saying so, will you, darling?—is the original dumbbell. Did I ever tell you about her trip to Dunedin?"

Did he ever tell them? Hersey thought. Wherever two or three were gathered did he ever fail to tell them? The predictable laugh, the lovingly coddled pause, and the punchline led into and delivered like an act of God —did he, for pity's sake, ever tell them!

Away he went, mock-serious, empurpled, expansive, and Hersey put on the comic baby face he expected of her. Poor Hersey, they would say, such a goose about money. It's a shame to laugh.

"It was like this—" Harold began. . . .

It had happened twelve years ago when they were first in New Zealand. Harold was occupied with a conference in Christchurch and Hersey was to stay with a friend in Dunedin. He had arranged that she would draw on his firm's Dunedin branch for money and take in her handbag no more than what she needed for the journey. "You know how you are," Harold said.

He arranged for her taxi, made her check that she had her ticket and reservation for the train, and reminded her that if on the journey she wanted cups of tea or synthetic coffee or a cooked lunch, she would have to take to her heels at the appropriate stations and vie with the competitive male. At this point her taxi was announced and Harold was summoned to a long-distance call from London.

"You push off," he said. "Don't forget that fiver on the dressing table. You won't need it but you'd better have it. Keep your wits about you. Bye, dear."

He was still shouting into the telephone when she left.

She had enjoyed the adventurous feeling of being on her own. Although Harold had said you didn't in New Zealand, she tipped the taxi driver and he carried her suitcase to the train and found her seat, a single one just inside the door of a Pullman car.

A lady was occupying the seat facing hers and next to the window.

She was well dressed, middle-aged and of a sandy complexion with noticeably light eyes. She had put a snakeskin dressing case on the empty seat beside her.

"It doesn't seem to be taken," she said, smiling at Hersey.

They socialized—tentatively at first and, as the journey progressed, more freely. The lady (in his version Harold always called her Mrs. X) confided that she was going all the way to Dunedin to visit her daughter. Hersey offered reciprocative information. In the world outside, plains and mountains performed a grandiose kind of measure and telegraph wires leaped and looped with frantic precision.

An hour passed. The lady extracted a novel from her dressing case and Hersey, impressed by the handsome appointments and immaculate order, had a good look inside the case.

The conductor came through the car intoning, "Ten minutes for refreshments at Ashburton."

"Shall you join in the onslaught?" asked the lady. "It's a free-for-all."

"Shall you?"

"Well—I might. When I travel with my daughter we take turns. I get the morning coffee and she gets the afternoon. I'm a bit slow on my pins, actually."

She made very free use of the word "actually."

Hersey instantly offered to get their coffee at Ashburton and her companion, after a proper show of diffidence, gaily agreed. They explored their handbags for the correct amount. The train uttered a warning scream and everybody crowded into the corridor as it drew up to the platform.

Hersey left her handbag with the lady (an indiscretion heavily emphasized by Harold) and sprinted to the refreshment counter where she was blocked off by a phalanx of men. Train fever was running high by the time she was served and her return trip with brimming cups was hazardous indeed.

The lady was holding both their handbags as if she hadn't stirred an inch.

Between Ashburton and Oamaru, a long stretch, they developed their acquaintanceship further, discovered many tastes in common, and exchanged confidences and names. The lady was called Mrs. Fortescue. Sometimes they dozed. Together, at Oamaru, they joined in an assault on the dining room and together they returned to the carriage where Hersey scuffled in her stuffed handbag for a powder compact. As usual it was in a muddle.

Suddenly a thought struck her like a blow in the wind and a lump of ice ran down her gullet into her stomach. She made an exhaustive search but there was no doubt about it.

Harold's fiver was gone.

Hersey let the handbag fall in her lap, raised her head, and found that her companion was staring at her with a very curious expression on her face. Hersey had been about to confide her awful intelligence but the lump of ice was exchanged for a coal of fire. She was racked by a terrible suspicion.

"Anything wrong?" asked Mrs. Fortescue in an artificial voice.

Hersey heard herself say, "No. Why?"

"Oh, nothing," she said rather hurriedly. "I thought—perhaps—like me, actually, you have bag trouble."

"I do, rather," Hersey said.

They laughed uncomfortably.

The next hour passed in mounting tension. Both ladies affected to read their novels. Occasionally one of them would look up to find the other one staring at her. Hersey's suspicions increased rampantly.

"Ten minutes for refreshments at Palmerston South," said the conductor, lurching through the car.

Hersey had made up her mind. "Your turn!" she cried brightly.

"Is it? Oh. Yes."

"I think I'll have tea. The coffee was awful."

"So's the tea actually. Always. Do we," Mrs. Fortescue swallowed, "do we really want anything?"

"I do," said Hersey very firmly and opened her handbag. She fished out her purse and took out the correct amount. "And a bun," she said. There was no gainsaying her. "I've got a headache," she lied. "I'll be glad of a cuppa."

When they arrived at Palmerston South, Hersey said, "Shall I?" and reached for Mrs. Fortescue's handbag. But Mrs. Fortescue muttered something about requiring it for change and almost literally bolted. "All that for nothing!" thought Hersey in despair. And then, seeing the elegant drersing case still on the square seat, she suddenly reached out and opened it.

On top of the neatly arranged contents lay a crumpled five-pound note.

At the beginning of the journey when Mrs. Fortescue had opened the case, there had, positively, been no fiver stuffed in it. Hersey snatched the banknote, stuffed it into her handbag, shut the dressing case, and leaned back, breathing short with her eyes shut.

When Mrs. Fortescue returned she was scarlet in the face and trembling. She looked continuously at her dressing case and seemed to be in two minds whether or not to open it. Hersey died a thousand deaths.

The remainder of the journey was a nightmare. Both ladies pretended to read and to sleep. If ever Hersey had read guilt in a human countenance it was in Mrs. Fortescue's.

"I ought to challenge her," Hersey thought. "But I won't. I'm a moral coward and I've got back my fiver."

The train was already drawing into Dunedin station and Hersey had gathered herself and her belongings when Mrs. Fortescue suddenly opened her dressing case. For a second or two she stared into it. Then she stared at Hersey. She opened and shut her mouth three times. The train jerked to a halt and Hersey fled.

Her friend greeted her warmly. When they were in the car she said, "Oh, before I forget! There's a telegram for you."

It was from Harold.

It said: "You forgot your fiver, you dumbbell. Love Harold."

Harold had delivered the punchline. His listeners had broken into predictable guffaws. He had added the customary coda: "And she didn't know Mrs. X's address, so she couldn't do a thing about it. So of course to this day Mrs. X thinks Hersey pinched her fiver."

Hersey, inwardly seething, had reacted in the sheepish manner Harold expected of her when from somewhere at the back of the group a wailing broke out.

A lady erupted as if from a football scrimmage. She looked wildly about her, spotted Hersey, and made for her.

"At last, at last!" cried the lady. "After all these years!"

It was Mrs. Fortescue.

"It *was* your fiver!" she gabbled. "It happened at Ashburton when I minded your bag. It was, it was!"

She turned on Harold. "It's all your fault," she amazingly announced. "And mine of course." She returned to Hersey. "I'm dreadfully inquisitive. It's a compulsion. I—I—couldn't resist. I looked at your passport. I looked at everything. And my own handbag was open on my lap. And the train gave one of those recoupling jerks and both our handbags were upset. And I could see you," she chattered breathlessly to Hersey, "coming back with that ghastly coffee.

"So I shoveled things back and there was the fiver on the floor. Well, I had one and I thought it was mine and there wasn't time to put it in my bag, so I slapped it into my dressing case. And then, when I paid my luncheon bill at Oamaru, I found my own fiver in a pocket of my bag."

"Oh, my God!" said Hersey.

"Yes. And I couldn't bring myself to confess. I thought you might leave your bag with me if you went to the loo and I could put it back. But you didn't. And then, at Dunedin, I looked in my dressing case and the fiver was gone. So I thought you knew I knew." She turned on Harold.

"You must have left *two* fivers on the dressing table," she accused.

"Yes!" Hersey shouted. "You did, you did! There were two. You put a second one out to get change."

"Why the hell didn't you say so!" Harold roared.

"I'd forgotten. You know yourself," Hersey said with the glint of victory in her eye, "It's like you always say, darling, I'm such a fool about money."

And Three to Get Ready . . .

H.L. GOLD

One of the most famous editors in the history of science fiction and a man whose stewardship of Galaxy *magazine changed the face of that genre, Horace L. Gold was also a fine craftsman for the pulp magazines, working in a variety of fields. His finest science-fiction stories can be found in* The Old Die Rich and Other Stories *(1955).*

The stories he bought as an editor frequently featured protagonists with special powers, operating in worlds of their own that may or may not have been real. "And Three to Get Ready . . ." is one of the finest stories of this kind, proving that an editor can set high standards for his writers.

Usually, people get committed to the psycho ward by their families or courts, but this guy came alone and said he wanted to be put away because he was deadly dangerous. Miss Nelson, the dragon at the reception desk, put in a call for Dr. Schatz and he took me along just in case. I'm a psycho-ward orderly, which means I'm big and know gentle judo to put these poor characters into pretzel shapes that don't hurt them, but keep them from hurting themselves or somebody else.

He was sitting there, hunched together as if he was afraid that he'd make a move that might kill anyone nearby, and about as dangerous looking as a wilted carnation. Not much bigger than one, either. Maybe five four, one hundred and twenty-five pounds, slender shoulders, slender hands, little feet, the kind of delicate face no guy would ever pick for himself, but a complexion you'd switch with if you've got a beard of Brillo like mine that needs shaving every damned day.

"Do you have this gentleman's history, Miss Nelson?" asked Dr. Schatz, before talking to the patient.

Her prim lips got even tighter. "I'm afraid not, doctor. He . . . says it would be like committing suicide to give it to me."

The little fellow nodded miserably.

"But we must have at least your name—" Dr. Schatz began.

He skittered clear over to the end of the bench and huddled there, shaking. "But that's exactly what I can't give you! Not only mine— *anybody's!*"

One thing you've got to say for these psychiatrists: they may feel surprised, but they never show it. Tell them you can't eat soup with anything except an egg-beater and they'll even manage to look as if they do that, too. I guess it's something you learn. I'm getting pretty good at it myself, but not when I come up against something as new as this twitch's line. I couldn't keep my eyebrows down.

Dr. Schatz, though, nodded and gave him a little smile and suggested going up to the mental hygiene office, where there wouldn't be so many people around. The little guy got up and came right along. They went into Schatz's office and I went to the room adjoining, with just a thin door I could hear through and open in a hurry if anything happened. You'd be surprised how seldom anything does happen, but it doesn't pay to take chances.

"Now, suppose you tell me what's bothering you," I heard Dr. Schatz say quietly. "Or isn't that possible, either?"

"Oh, I can tell you *that,*" the little guy said. "I just can't tell you my —my name. Or yours, if I knew it. Or anyone else's."

"Why?"

The little guy was silent for a minute. I could hear him breathing hard and I knew he was pushing the words up to his mouth, trying to make them come out.

"When I say somebody's name three times," he whispered, "the person dies."

"I see." You can't throw Dr. Schatz that easy. "Only persons?"

"Well . . ." The little guy hitched his chair closer; I heard it shriek and grate on the cement floor. "Look, I'm here because it's driving me nuts, doc. You think I am already, so I've got to convince you I'm not. I have to give you proof that I'm right."

The doctor waited. They always do at times like that; it kind of forces the patients to say things they maybe didn't want to.

"The first one was Willard Greenwood," said the little guy in a slow, tense voice. "You remember him—the undersecretary down in Washington. A healthy man, right? Good career ahead of him. I see his name in the papers. Willard Greenwood. It has a . . . a *round* sound to it. I find myself saying it. I say it three times. Right out loud while I'm looking at his picture. So what happens?"

"Greenwood committed suicide last week," Dr. Schatz said. "He'd evidently had psychological difficulty for some time."

"Yes. I didn't think much about it. A coincidence, like. But then I see a newsreel of this submarine launching a few days ago. *The Barnacle.* I say the name out loud three times, same as anybody else might. You've done that yourself sometimes, haven't you? Haven't you?"

"Of course. Names occasionally have a fascination."

"Sure. So *The Barnacle* runs into something and sinks. I began to suspect what was going on so, like an experiment you might say, I picked another name out of the papers. I figured it ought to be somebody who isn't psycho, like Greenwood turned out to be, or old and sick, or a submarine which might be expected to run into danger. It had to be somebody young and healthy. I picked the name out of the school news. A girl named Clara Newland. Graduating from Emanuel High. Seventeen."

"She died?"

The little guy gave a kind of sob. "Automobile crash. She was the only one who was killed. The others all only got hurt. Last Sunday."

"Those could be coincidences, you know," Dr. Schatz said very gently. "Perhaps you said other names aloud and nothing happened, but you remember those because something did."

The guy kicked his chair back; I could hear it slide. He probably got up and leaned over the desk; they do that when they're all excited. I put my hand on the knob and got ready.

"As soon as I knew what was going on," he said, "I stopped saying names three times. I didn't dare say them even *once*, because that might make me say them again and then again—and you know what the payoff would be. But then last night . . ."

"Yes?" Dr. Schatz said, prompting him when he halted.

"A bar got held up. It was when the customers had left and the bartender was getting ready to lock the place. Two guys. There was a scuffle and the bartender was killed. The cops came. One of the crooks was shot; the other got away. The crook who was shot was—"

I opened the door a slit and looked in. He was showing a clipping to Schatz, with his finger pointing shakily at one place.

"Paul Michaels," said the doctor.

"Don't say it!" the little guy yelled. I was ready to race in, but Dr. Schatz made a warning motion that the guy wouldn't notice that told me I wasn't needed. "I don't want to say it! If I do, it'll be three times and he'll die!"

"I think I understand," Schatz said. "You're afraid to mention names three times because of the result, and—well, what do you want us to do?"

"Keep me here. Stop me from saying names three times. Save God knows how many people from me. Because I'm deadly!"

Schatz said we'd do our best, and he got the guy committed for observation. It wasn't easy, because he still wouldn't give his name, and Dr. Merriman, the head of the psychiatric department, almost had another heart attack fighting about it.

We got together, Dr. Schatz and I, after the little guy had his pajamas and stuff issued and a bed assigned to him.

"That's a hell of a thing to carry around," I said, "thinking people die when you say their names three times. It would drive anybody batty."

"A vestige of childhood," he told me, and explained how kids unconsciously believe their wishes can do anything. I could remember some of that from my own childhood—my old man was a holy terror with his strap and many's the time I wished he was dead—and then got scared that maybe he would die and it would all be my fault. But I outgrew it, which Schatz said most people do. Only there are some who don't, like our little nameless friend, and they often get themselves twisted up like this.

"But that Paul Michaels," I said. "The crook who got shot. He's in the critical ward right here in this hospital."

"It's a city hospital," he answered, lighting a butt and looking tired. "Everything the private hospitals won't touch, we get. That's why we have this patient, too."

"Any special instructions?" I asked.

"I don't think so. This kind of case is seldom either suicidal or homicidal, unless the guilt feelings get out of hand. Keep him calm, that's all. Sedation if he needs it."

I had plenty to do around the mental hygiene ward without the little guy to worry about, but he wasn't much trouble. Until about an hour or two after supper, that is. I had some beds to move around and a tough customer to get into the hydrotherapy room, so I didn't pay much attention to the little guy and his restless eyes.

He came up to *me*, twitchy as hell, and grabbed my arm with both his hands.

"I keep thinking about that—that name," he babbled. "I keep wanting to say it. *Do* something! Don't let me say it!"

"Who?" I asked, blank for a minute, and then I remembered. "You mean this crook Paul Michaels—"

He got white and jumped up and tried to stop my mouth, but I'd already said it. I tried to calm him down and finally had the nurse give him some phenobarb, all the time explaining that the name had slipped out and I was sorry. You know, soothing him.

He said, trembling, "Now I know I'm going to say it. I just know I will." And he shuffled over to the window and sat there holding his head, looking sick.

I got to bed about midnight, still wondering about the poor little guy who thought he could kill people that easy. I had the next morning off, but I didn't take it. There were cops all over the place and Dr. Schatz looked real worried.

"I don't know how our new patient is going to take this," he said, shaking his head. "That Paul Michaels we had here—"

"*Had?*" I repeated. "What do you mean, had? He transferred to a prison hospital or something?"

"He's dead," Schatz said.

I closed my mouth after a few seconds. "Aw, nuts," I grumbled, disgusted with myself. "I was almost believing the little guy did it. Michaels was shot up bad. Hell, he was on the critical list."

"That's right. There'd be nothing remarkable if he died . . . from the bullet wound. But his throat was slit."

"And the little guy?"

"We have him full of Nembutal. He was shouting that he had said Michaels's name three times and that Michaels would have to die and he would be responsible."

"You haven't told him yet," I said.

"Naturally not. It would really put him into a spin."

It was a solid mess from top floor to basement, so I had to give up my morning off. The patients, except the little guy who was in isolation, all found out about Michaels somehow—you can't stop things like that from spreading—and I had a time handling them. In between, though, I learned how the case was developing.

There was this old cop Slattery we generally have for cases like Michaels sitting outside the critical ward, watching who went in and out. There had been somebody with Michaels on the stickup, see, who made it while Michaels was plugged, and the cops don't take chances that maybe the accomplice or someone from the underworld might want to get at the patient when he's helpless. They always put a guard on.

Well, Slattery is all right, but he maybe isn't so alert any more, and somebody slipped past him late at night, cut Michaels's neck with probably a razor blade, and then got out again without Slattery noticing. The other patients were all doped up or asleep, so they were no help. Slattery, though, swore nobody except nurses on duty in the ward or on the floor went past him. He claimed he didn't fall asleep once during the night, and the funny thing is the nurses said the same. Or maybe it's not so funny; they like the old man and might do a little lying to help him off a rough spot.

Well, that put the girls on an even worse spot. If they were telling the truth, that Slattery had been awake the whole night, then one of them must have done it. Because Slattery had said that only the nurses went in and out of the ward. Captain Warren, the homicide man, jumped on that fast and got the girls to line up in front of Slattery.

"Well, Slattery?" Warren said. "One of these nurses must have been the killer. Do you recognize one who went in there with no business to? Or did one of them act suspicious, and which was it?"

Slattery looked unhappy as he went down the line and stared at the girls' faces. He shook his head figuring, I guess, that he was in for some real trouble now.

"It was pretty dim in the ward," he mumbled. "All they keep on is a little night light—just enough so the girls can find their way around without tripping, but not bright enough to keep the patients awake. I can't even be sure which nurses went in and out."

"Nothing suspicious?" Slattery demanded.

"Search me. They were nurses and my job is to keep anybody else out. As long as they were nurses and it was so dim there, one of them could have had an Army rifle under her uniform and I wouldn't know."

Captain Warren questioned the girls, got nowhere, and had them all checked to see if one didn't know Michaels well enough to want to knock him off.

I got all that from Sally Norton, one of the homely babes in the mental hygiene ward, when she came back from the grilling to go on duty. She went to her locker to change and then ran back, yipping, and grabbed Dr. Schatz. She had her uniform held up in front of her, like a shield, kind of, and she was shaking it angrily.

"Just take a look at this, doctor!" she said. "Came back clean from the laundry yesterday and I haven't even worn it yet, and look at it now!"

"If there's anything wrong with the laundry, take it up with them," he said, annoyed. "I'm having enough trouble keeping my patients quiet with all this racket going on over Michaels."

"But that's just it. I wouldn't be surprised if it has something to do with Michaels." And she showed him the sleeve, where there were red spots down near the wrist.

Schatz called in Captain Warren and Dr. Merriman, the head of the mental hygiene department. Merriman looked sicker than usual; he kept his hand inside his jacket, over his heart. All this excitement wasn't doing him any more good than it was doing the patients.

Warren was interested, all right. Being there in the hospital, it was easy to run a test and prove the spots were blood, human, type B—which happened to be Michaels's blood type. He wasn't the only one in the hospital with that type, of course, but it isn't so common that Captain Warren could disregard it.

Warren started to give Sally a bad time, but Dr. Merriman cut in and told him about the little guy and the story about saying names three times.

"What in hell kind of nonsense is this?" Warren asked. "I'm looking for evidence, not a screwball fairy tale some nut thought up."

"Exactly," Dr. Schatz said fast; he'd been trying to head off Dr. Merriman, but hadn't dared to interrupt. "It's a fairly typical delusion with no more basis in fact than witches or goblins. I can't sanction questioning a disturbed patient because of it."

"You don't have to bother," said Warren. "I've got more important things—"

"The point," Dr. Merriman went on, "is that this man claimed he was afraid to mention—specifically, mind you—the name of Paul Michaels. That was why he wanted to be committed, in fact."

Warren looked baffled. "You mean you think he said Michaels's name three times and Michaels died because of that?"

"Certainly not," Merriman said stiffly. "It's a remarkable coincidence that deserves investigation, that's all. Or perhaps my idea of police work differs from yours."

I don't know how Schatz managed it, but he let Captain Warren know that Dr. Merriman was getting on in years and ought to be humored. So I went along with them to the little guy's bed, where he was just coming out of the sedative. He was still groggy, but he saw us coming and ducked his left hand under the blanket.

Well, that's all you have to do to get a cop suspicious, make a sudden move like running out of a bank at high noon or duck one hand under a blanket. Warren hauled it out, with the little guy resisting and trying to hide his pinky in his palm. The cop straightened out the pinky. It was colored red under the fingernail.

"Blood?" I asked, confused, and then got busy because the little guy was trying to pull away while Captain Warren took some scrapings.

It wasn't blood. It was lipstick, according to the lab test.

"There," said Dr. Schatz, satisfied, "you see? You've upset my patient, and for what?"

"Plenty," Warren said between his teeth, "and I'm going to upset him some more."

He had me hold the little guy down—I didn't want to until Dr. Merriman overrode Schatz's objections and ordered me to—while two cops put the little guy into Sally Norton's stained uniform and painted his mouth with lipstick.

You know, with that slender build of his and the cap on, he didn't look bad. Better than Sally, if you want to know, but who doesn't?

"All right," Schatz said, "he could have gotten past Slattery in that dim light. Admitted. But what makes you think he did? And why should he have done so?"

"The lipstick on the pinky," said Warren. "If you want to do a decent job, you don't just slap it on—you shape it with your little finger. Why? That depends. If the guy's psycho, he could have done Michaels in just because. But suppose he's the guy who was with Michaels on the job— Michaels was the only one who could have identified him. But Michaels was in a coma. So this character had to get into the hospital somehow and slit Michaels's throat to keep him from talking. Either way, it figures."

Dr. Merriman nodded. "That was my own opinion, captain."

"You're lying! You're lying!" the little guy screamed. "I said his name three times and he died! They always die! It's the curse I have to bear!"

"We'll see," said Dr. Merriman. "Say *my* name three times."

The little guy cowered away. "I—I can't. I have enough deaths on my conscience now."

"You heard me!" Dr. Merriman shouted, turning a dangerous red in the face. "Say my name three times!"

The little guy looked appealingly at Dr. Schatz, who said soothingly, "Go ahead. I know you're convinced it works, but it's completely contrary to logic. Wishes *can't* kill. This may prove it to you."

The little guy said Dr. Merriman's name three times, pale and shaking and looking about ready to throw up with fear.

Warren put Slattery—*and* another guard—on the psycho ward, and started a check on the little guy's fingerprints.

When I got to work the next day, the ward was a tomb. It might as well have been. Sally Norton was crying and Dr. Schatz was all pinch-faced and the little guy was practically running around the room yelling that he shouldn't have been forced to do it.

"Do what?" I wanted to know.

"Dr. Merriman died last night," Schatz said.

I looked at the little guy in horror. "Him?"

"No, no, of course not," said Schatz, but it was in a flat voice, not the impatient way he would have told me a day ago. "Dr. Merriman had a cardiac lesion. He could have gone at any time. There may even have been a deep unconscious wish to escape the pain and fear, and this patient's delusion could have given Dr. Merriman a psychological escape. It's the principle behind voodooism. The victim wills himself to death; the hexer merely supplied the suggestion."

It was pretty bad for a while, until Captain Warren showed up with a big grin on his face. It soured when he heard that Dr. Merriman had died, but he threw out the idea that the little guy had done it.

Matter of fact, he had the cops put the arm on him and said, "Arnold Roach, I arrest you for complicity in the murder—" And so forth and so on.

The little guy, whose name turned out to be what Warren said, had been unlucky enough to leave some fingerprints around. They had him, sure enough, except that he stuck to this whammy story and hired a good psychiatrist, who got him an insanity plea. So we have him back in the ward here. And if you think he's given up and started mentioning people's names even once, let alone three times, you're battier than he is. He screams whenever somebody mentions *any* name. It's a hell of a job remembering not to call the patients by name when he's around. "Look, what do you think?" I asked Dr. Schatz. "Is the guy psychotic or did he cop a lucky plea?"

Dr. Schatz ran his hand across his mouth and talked through his fingers. "I think he's psychotic. There's never any proof of that, of course, but his behavior bears me out. It's definitely psychotic."

"And what about this story of his about saying names three times? All right, maybe he made up those items before he showed up here—after all, they were dead already and nobody could say he had or hadn't said their names three times before they died. And Michaels—the little guy helped him shuffle out with a razor across the throat. But what about Dr. Merriman?"

"I've already told you," Schatz said tiredly. "Cardiac lesion and hypothetical death wish triggered by suggestion."

I put the mop back in the bucket and began wringing it after a fast swab at the floor. I didn't feel happy and I showed it.

"That's a guess," I answered. "What if the little guy is right and people *do* die when he says their names three times?"

"Why don't you try it and see?" he asked.

I almost upset the pail. "Me? You're the psychiatrist. Why don't you?"

"Because I know it's purely a childish delusion. I don't need any proof."

"That," I said, leaning on the mop, "is not a scientific attitude, doctor."

"The devil with it," he grunted in annoyance. "If it's bothering you that much, I'll do it."

But he always seems to have something else to do whenever I remind him.

"J"

ED McBAIN

The 87th Precinct series by Ed McBain, the alter ego of novelist Evan Hunter, is beyond question the finest group of police procedurals by an American writer (arguably, the finest by any writer in any language). Among its many virtues are meticulous attention to procedural detail, superb characterization, insightful social commentary, and an unsurpassed sense of realism. To date there have been thirty-four novels and one collection in the saga of Steve Carella, Meyer Meyer, Cotton Hawes, and the other members of the 87th Squad. "J," one of a handful of shorter works in the series, is a poignant and memorable novella about the squad's search for the brutal slayer of a rabbi.

It was the first of April, the day for fools.

It was also Saturday, and the day before Easter.

Death should not have come at all, but it had. And, having come, perhaps it was justified in its confusion. Today was the fool's day, the day for practical jokes. Tomorrow was Easter, the day of the bonnet and egg, the day for the spring march of finery and frills. Oh, yes, it was rumored in some quarters of the city that Easter Sunday had something to do with a different sort of march at a place called Calvary, but it had been a long long time since death was vetoed and rendered null and void, and people have short memories, especially where holidays are concerned.

Today, Death was very much in evidence, and plainly confused. Striving as it was to reconcile the trappings of two holidays—or perhaps three —it succeeded in producing only a blended distortion.

The young man who lay on his back in the alley was wearing black, as if in mourning. But over the black, in contradiction, was a fine silken shawl, fringed at both ends. He seemed dressed for spring, but this was the fool's day, and Death could not resist the temptation.

The black was punctuated with red and blue and white. The cobbled floor of the alley followed the same decorative scheme, red and blue and white, splashed about in gay spring abandon. Two overturned buckets of paint, one white, one blue, seemed to have ricocheted off the wall of the building and come to disorderly rest on the alley floor. The man's shoes were spattered with paint. His black garment was covered with paint. His hands were drenched in paint. Blue and white, white and blue, his black garment, his silken shawl, the floor of the alley, the brick wall of the building before which he lay—all were splashed with blue and white.

The third color did not mix well with the others.

The third color was red, a little too primary, a little too bright.

The third color had not come from a paint can. The third color still spilled freely from two dozen open wounds on the man's chest and stomach and neck and face and hands, staining the black, staining the silken shawl, spreading in a bright red pool on the alley floor, suffusing the paint with sunset, mingling with the paint but not mixing well, spreading until it touched the foot of the ladder lying crookedly along the wall, encircling the paintbrush lying at the wall's base. The bristles of the brush were still wet with white paint. The man's blood touched the bristles, and then trickled to the cement line where brick wall touched cobbled alley, flowing in an inching stream downward toward the street.

Someone had signed the wall.

On the wall, someone had painted, in bright, white paint, the single letter *J*. Nothing more—only *J*.

The blood trickled down the alley to the city street.

Night was coming.

Detective Cotton Hawes was a tea drinker. He had picked up the habit from his minister father, the man who'd named him after Cotton Mather, the last of the red-hot Puritans. In the afternoons, the good Reverend Jeremiah Hawes had entertained members of his congregation, serving tea and cakes which his wife Matilda baked in the old, iron, kitchen oven. The boy, Cotton Hawes, had been allowed to join the tea-drinking congregation, thus developing a habit which had continued to this day.

At eight o'clock on the night of April first, while a young man lay in an alleyway with two dozen bleeding wounds shrieking in silence to the passersby on the street below, Hawes sat drinking tea. As a boy, he had downed the hot beverage in the book-lined study at the rear of the parish house, a mixture of Oolong and Pekoe which his mother brewed in the kitchen and served in English bone-china cups she had inherited from her grandmother. Tonight, he sat in the grubby, shopworn comfort of the 87th Precinct squadroom and drank, from a cardboard container, the tea Alf Miscolo had prepared in the clerical office. It was hot tea. That was about the most he could say for it.

The open, mesh-covered windows of the squadroom admitted a mild spring breeze from Grover Park across the way, a warm seductive breeze which made him wish he were outside on the street. It was criminal to be catching on a night like this. It was also boring. Aside from one wife-beating squeal, which Steve Carella was out checking this very minute, the telephone had been ominously quiet. In the silence of the squadroom, Hawes had managed to type up three overdue D.D. reports, two chits for gasoline and a bulletin-board notice to the men of the squad reminding them that this was the first of the month and time for them to cough up fifty cents each for the maintenance of Al Miscolo's improvised kitchen. He had also read a half dozen FBI flyers, and listed in his little black memo book the license plate numbers of two more stolen vehicles.

Now he sat drinking insipid tea and wondering why it was so quiet. He supposed the lull had something to do with Easter. Maybe there was going to be an egg-rolling ceremony down South Twelfth Street tomorrow. Maybe all the criminals and potential criminals in the 87th were home dyeing. Eggs, that is. He smiled and took another sip of the tea. From the clerical office beyond the slatted rail divider which separated the squadroom from the corridor, he could hear the rattling of Miscolo's typewriter. Above that, and beyond it, coming from the iron-runged steps which led upstairs, he could hear the ring of footsteps. He turned toward the corridor just as Steve Carella entered it from the opposite end.

Carella walked easily and nonchalantly toward the railing, a big man who moved with fine-honed athletic precision. He shoved open the gate in the railing, walked to his desk, took off his jacket, pulled down his tie and unbuttoned the top button of his shirt.

"What happened?" Hawes asked.

"The same thing that always happens," Carella said. He sighed heavily and rubbed his hand over his face. "Is there any more coffee?" he asked.

"I'm drinking tea."

"Hey, Miscolo!" Carella yelled. "Any coffee in there?"

"I'll put on some more water!" Miscolo yelled back.

"So what happened?" Hawes asked.

"Oh, the same old jazz," Carella said. "It's a waste of time to even go out on these wife-beating squeals. I've never answered one yet that netted anything."

"She wouldn't press charges," Hawes said knowingly.

"Charges, hell. There wasn't even any beating, according to her. She's got blood running out of her nose, and a shiner the size of a half dollar, and she's the one who screamed for the patrolman—but the minute I get there, everything's calm and peaceful." Carella shook his head. " 'A beating, officer?' " he mimicked in a high, shrill voice. " 'You must be mistaken, officer. Why, my husband is a good, kind, sweet man. We've been married for twenty years, and he never lifted a finger to me. You must be mistaken, sir.' "

"Then who yelled for the cop?" Hawes asked.

"That's just what I said to her."

"What'd she answer?"

"She said, 'Oh, we were just having a friendly little family argument.' The guy almost knocked three teeth out of her mouth, but that's just a friendly little family argument. So I asked her how she happened to have a bloody nose and a mouse under her eye and—catch this, Cotton—she said she got them ironing."

"What?"

"Ironing."

"Now, how the hell—"

"She said the ironing board collapsed and the iron jumped up and hit her in the eye, and one of the ironing-board legs clipped her in the nose. By the time I left, she and her husband were ready to go on a second honeymoon. She was hugging him all over the place, and he was sneaking his hand under her dress, so I figured I'd come back here where it isn't so sexy."

"Good idea," Hawes said.

"Hey, Miscolo!" Carella shouted, "Where's that coffee?"

"A watched pot never boils!" Miscolo shouted back cleverly.

"We've got George Bernard Shaw in the clerical office," Carella said. "Anything happen since I left?"

"Nothing. Not a peep."

"The streets are quiet, too," Carella said, suddenly thoughtful.

"Before the storm," Hawes said.

"Mmmm."

The squadroom was silent again. Beyond the meshed window, they could hear the myriad sounds of the city, the auto horns, the muffled cries, the belching of buses, a little girl singing as she walked past the station house.

"Well, I suppose I ought to type up some overdue reports," Carella said.

He wheeled over a typing cart, took three Detective Division reports from his desk, inserted carbon between two of the sheets and began typing.

Hawes stared at the distant lights of Isola's buildings and sucked in a draught of mesh-filtered spring air.

He wondered why it was so quiet.

He wondered just exactly what all those people were doing out there.

Some of those people were playing April Fool's Day pranks. Some of them were getting ready for tomorrow, which was Easter Sunday. And some of them were celebrating a third and ancient holiday known as Passover. Now that's a coincidence which could cause one to speculate upon the similarity of dissimilar religions and the existence of a single, all-powerful God, and all that sort of mystic stuff, if one were inclined toward speculation. Speculator or not, it doesn't take a big detective to check a calendar, and the coincidence was there, take it or leave it. Buddhist, atheist, or Seventh Day Adventist, you had to admit there was something very democratic and wholesome about Easter and Passover coinciding the way they did, something which gave a festive air to the entire city. Jew and Gentile alike, because of a chance mating of the Christian and the Hebrew calendars, were celebrating important holidays at almost the same time. Passover had officially begun at sunset on Friday, March thirty-first, another coincidence, since Passover did not always fall on the Jewish Sabbath; but this year, it did. And tonight was April first, and the traditional second *seder* service, the annual reenactment of the Jews' liberation from Egyptian bondage, was being observed in Jewish homes throughout the city.

Detective Meyer Meyer was a Jew.

Or at least, he thought he was a Jew. Sometimes he wasn't quite certain. Because if he was a Jew, he sometimes asked himself, how come he hadn't seen the inside of a synagogue in twenty years? And if he was a Jew, how come two of his favorite dishes were roast pork and broiled lobster, both of which were forbidden by the dietary laws of the religion? And if he was such a Jew, how come he allowed his son Alan—who was thirteen and who had been *bar mitzvahed* only last month—to play post office with Alice McCarthy, who was as Irish as a four-leaf clover?

Sometimes, Meyer got confused.

Sitting at the head of the traditional table on this night of the second *seder*, he didn't know quite how he felt. He looked at his family, Sarah and the three children, and then he looked at the *seder* table, festively set with a floral centerpiece and lighted candles and the large platter upon which were placed the traditional objects—three matzos, a roasted shankbone, a roasted egg, bitter herbs, charoses, watercress—and he still didn't know exactly how he felt. He took a deep breath and began the prayer.

"And it was evening," Meyer said, "and it was morning, the sixth day. Thus the heaven and the earth were finished, and all the host of them. And on the seventh day, God had finished His work which He had made: and He rested on the seventh day from His work which He had done. And God blessed the seventh day, and hallowed it, because that in it He rested from all His work, which God had created in order to make it."

There was a certain beauty to the words, and they lingered in his mind as he went through the ceremony, describing the various objects on the table and their symbolic meaning. When he elevated the dish containing the bone and the egg, everyone sitting around the table took hold of the dish, and Meyer said, "This is the bread of affliction which our ancestors ate in the land of Egypt; let all those who are hungry, enter and eat thereof, and all who are in distress, come and celebrate the Passover."

He spoke of his ancestors, but he wondered who he—their descendant —was.

"Wherefore is this night distinguished from all other nights?" he asked. "Any other night, we may eat either leavened or unleavened bread, but on this night only unleavened bread; all other nights, we may eat any species of herbs, but on this night only bitter herbs . . ."

The telephone rang. Meyer stopped speaking and looked at his wife. For a moment, both seemed reluctant to break the spell of the ceremony. And then Meyer gave a slight, barely discernible shrug. Perhaps, as he went to the telephone, he was recalling that he was a cop first, and a Jew only second.

"Hello?" he said.

"Meyer, this is Cotton Hawes."

"What is it, Cotton?"

"Look, I know this is your holiday—"

"What's the trouble?"

"We've got a killing," Hawes said.

Patiently, Meyer said, "We've always got a killing."

"This is different. A patrolman called in about five minutes ago. The guy was stabbed in the alley behind—"

"Cotton, I don't understand," Meyer said. "I switched the duty with Steve. Didn't he show up?"

"What is it, Meyer?" Sarah called from the dining room.

"It's all right, it's all right," Meyer answered. "Isn't Steve there?" he asked Hawes, annoyance in his voice.

"Sure, he's out on the squeal, but that's not the point."

"What *is* the point?" Meyer asked. "I was right in the middle of—"

"We need you on this one," Hawes said. "Look, I'm sorry as hell. But there are aspects to—Meyer, this guy they found in the alley—"

"Well, what about him?" Meyer asked.

"We think he's a rabbi," Hawes said.

2

The sexton of the Isola Jewish Center was named Yirmiyahu Cohen, and when he introduced himself, he used the Jewish word for sexton, *shamash.* He was a tall, thin man in his late fifties, wearing a somber black suit and donning a skullcap the moment he, Carella and Meyer reentered the synagogue.

The three had stood in the alley behind the synagogue not a moment before, staring down at the body of the dead rabbi and the trail of mayhem surrounding him. Yirmiyahu had wept openly, his eyes closed, unable to look at the dead man who had been the Jewish community's spiritual leader. Carella and Meyer, who had both been cops for a good long time, did not weep.

There is plenty to weep at if you happen to be looking down at the victim of a homicidal stabbing. The rabbi's black robe and fringed prayer shawl were drenched with blood, but happily, they hid from view the multiple stab wounds in his chest and abdomen, wounds which would later be examined at the morgue for external description, number, location, dimension, form of perforation and direction and depth of penetration. Since twenty-five percent of all fatal stab wounds are cases of cardiac penetration, and since there was a wild array of slashes and a sodden mass of coagulating blood near or around the rabbi's heart, the two detectives automatically assumed that a cardiac stab wound had been the cause of death, and were grateful for the fact that the rabbi was fully clothed. They had both visited the mortuary and seen naked bodies on naked slabs, no longer bleeding, all blood and all life drained away, but skin torn like the flimsiest cheesecloth, the soft interior of the body deprived of its protective flesh, turned outward, exposed, the ripe wounds gaping and open, had stared at evisceration and wanted to vomit.

The rabbi had owned flesh, too, and at least a part of it had been exposed to his attacker's fury. Looking down at the dead man, neither Carella nor Meyer wanted to weep, but their eyes tightened a little and their throats went peculiarly dry because death by stabbing is a damn frightening thing. Whoever had handled the knife had done so in apparent frenzy. The only exposed areas of the rabbi's body were his hands, his neck, and his face—and these, more than the apparently fatal, hidden incisions beneath the black robe and the prayer shawl, shrieked bloody murder to the night. The rabbi's throat showed two superficial cuts which almost resembled suicidal hesitation cuts. A deeper horizontal slash at the front of his neck had exposed the trachea, carotids and jugular vein, but these did not appear to be severed—at least, not to the layman eyes of Carella and Meyer. There were cuts around the rabbi's eyes and a cut across the bridge of his nose.

But the wounds which caused both Carella and Meyer to turn away from the body were the slashes on the insides of the rabbi's hands. These, they knew, were the defense cuts. These spoke louder than all the others, for they immediately reconstructed the image of a weaponless man struggling to protect himself against the swinging blade of an assassin, raising his hands in hopeless defense, the fingers cut and hanging, the palms slashed to ribbons. At the end of the alley, the patrolman who'd first arrived on the scene was identifying the body to the medical examiner as the one he'd found. Another patrolman was pushing curious bystanders behind the police barricade he'd set up. The laboratory boys and photographers had already begun their work.

Carella and Meyer were happy to be inside the synagogue again.

The room was silent and empty, a house of worship without any worshippers at the moment. They sat on folding chairs in the large, empty room. The eternal light burned over the ark in which the Torah, the five books of Moses, was kept. Forward of the ark, one on each side of it, were the lighted candelabra, the *menorah*, found by tradition in every Jewish house of worship.

Detective Steve Carella began the litany of another tradition. He took out his notebook, poised his pencil over a clean page, turned to Yirmiyahu, and began asking questions in a pattern that had become classic through repeated use.

"What was the rabbi's name?" he asked.

Yirmiyahu blew his nose and said, "Solomon. Rabbi Solomon."

"First name?"

"Yaakov."

"That's Jacob," Meyer said. "Jacob Solomon."

Carella nodded and wrote the name into his book.

"Are you Jewish?" Yirmiyahu asked Meyer.

Meyer paused for an instant, and then said, "Yes."

"Was he married or single?" Carella asked.

"Married," Yirmiyahu said.

"Do you know his wife's name?"

"I'm not sure. I think it's Havah."

"That's Eve," Meyer translated.

"And would you know where the rabbi lived?"

"Yes. The house on the corner."

"What's the address?"

"I don't know. It's the house with the yellow shutters."

"How do you happen to be here right now, Mr. Cohen?" Carella asked. "Did someone call to inform you of the rabbi's death?"

"No. No, I often come past the synagogue. To check the light, you see."

"What light is that, sir?" Carella asked.

"The eternal light. Over the ark. It's supposed to burn at all times. Many synagogues have a small electric bulb in the lamp. We're one of the few synagogues in the city who still use oil in it. And, as *shamash*, I felt it was my duty to make certain the light—"

"Is this an Orthodox congregation?" Meyer asked.

"No. It's Conservative," Yirmiyahu said.

"There are three types of congregation now," Meyer explained to Carella. "Orthodox, Conservative and Reform. It gets a little complicated."

"Yes," Yirmiyahu said emphatically.

"So you were coming to the synagogue to check on the lamp," Carella said. "Is that right?"

"That's correct."

"And what happened?"

"I saw a police car at the side of the synagogue. So I walked over and asked what the trouble was. And they told me."

"I see. When was the last time you saw the rabbi alive, Mr. Cohen?"

"At evening services."

"Services start at sundown, Steve. The Jewish day—"

"Yes, I know," Carella said. "What time did services end, Mr. Cohen?"

"At about seven-thirty."

"And the rabbi was here? Is that right?"

"Well, he stepped outside when services were over."

"And you stayed inside. Was there any special reason?"

"Yes. I was collecting the prayer shawls and the *yarmelkas*, and I was putting—"

"*Yarmelkas* are skullcaps," Meyer said. "Those little black—"

"Yes, I know," Carella said. "Go ahead, Mr. Cohen."

"I was putting the *rimonim* back onto the handles of the scroll."

"Putting the what, sir?" Carella asked.

"Listen to the big Talmudic scholar," Meyer said, grinning. "Doesn't even know what *rimonim* are. They're these decorative silver covers, Steve, shaped like pomegranates. Symbolizing fruitfulness, I guess."

Carella returned the grin. "Thank you," he said.

"A man has been killed," Yirmiyahu said softly.

The detectives were silent for a moment. The banter between them had been of the faintest sort, mild in comparison to some of the grisly humor that homicide detectives passed back and forth over a dead body. Carella and Meyer were accustomed to working together in an easy, friendly manner, and they were accustomed to dealing with the facts of sudden death, but they realized at once that they had offended the dead rabbi's sexton.

"I'm sorry, Mr. Cohen," he said. "We meant no offense, you understand."

The old man nodded stoically, a man who had inherited a legacy of years and years of persecution, a man who automatically concluded that all Gentiles looked upon a Jew's life as a cheap commodity. There was unutterable sadness on his long, thin face, as if he alone were bearing the oppressive weight of the centuries on his narrow shoulders.

The synagogue seemed suddenly smaller. Looking at the old man's face and the sadness there, Meyer wanted to touch it gently and say, "It's all right, *tsadik*, it's all right," the Hebrew word leaping into his mind—*tsadik*, a man possessed of saintly virtues, a person of noble character and simple living.

The silence persisted. Yirmiyahu Cohen began weeping again, and the detectives sat in embarrassment on the folding chairs and waited.

At last Carella said, "Were you still here when the rabbi came inside again?"

"I left while he was gone," Yirmiyahu said. "I wanted to return home.

This is the *Pesach*, the Passover. My family was waiting for me to conduct the *seder.*"

"I see." Carella paused. He glanced at Meyer.

"Did you hear any noise in the alley, Mr. Cohen?" Meyer asked. "When the rabbi was out there?"

"Nothing."

Meyer sighed and took a package of cigarettes from his jacket pocket. He was about to light one when Yirmiyahu said, "Didn't you say you were Jewish?"

"Huh?" Meyer said. He struck the match.

"You are going to *smoke* on the second day of *Pesach?*" Yirmiyahu asked.

"Oh. Oh, well . . ." The cigarette felt suddenly large in Meyer's hand, the fingers clumsy. He shook out the match. "You—uh—you have any other questions, Steve?" he asked.

"No," Carella said.

"Then I guess you can go, Mr. Cohen," Meyer said. "Thank you very much."

"*Shalom,*" Yirmiyahu said, and shuffled dejectedly out of the room.

"You're not supposed to smoke, you see," Meyer explained to Carella, "on the first two days of Passover, and the last two, a good Jew doesn't smoke, or ride, or work, or handle money or—"

"I thought this was a Conservative synagogue," Carella said. "That sounds like Orthodox practice to me."

"Well, he's an old man," Meyer said. "I guess the customs die hard."

"The way the rabbi did," Carella said grimly.

3

They stood outside in the alley where chalk marks outlined the position of the dead body. The rabbi had been carted away, but his blood still stained the cobblestones, and the rampant paint had been carefully side-stepped by the laboratory boys searching for footprints and fingerprints, searching for anything which would provide a lead to the killer.

J, the wall read.

"You know, Steve, I feel funny on this case," Meyer told Carella.

"I do, too."

Meyer raised his eyebrows, somewhat surprised. "How come?"

"I don't know. I guess because he was a man of God." Carella shrugged. "There's something unworldly and naive and—pure, I guess—about rabbis and priests and ministers and I guess I feel they shouldn't be touched by all the dirty things in life." He paused. "Somebody's got to stay untouched, Meyer."

"Maybe so," Meyer paused. "I feel funny because I'm a Jew, Steve." His voice was very soft. He seemed to be confessing something he would not have admitted to another living soul.

"I can understand that," Carella said gently.

"Are you policemen?"

The voice startled them. It came suddenly from the other end of the alley, and they both whirled instantly to face it.

Instinctively, Meyer's hand reached for the service revolver holstered in his right rear pocket.

"Are you policemen?" the voice asked again. It was a woman's voice, thick with a Yiddish accent. The street lamp was behind the owner of the voice. Meyer and Carella saw only a frail figure clothed in black, pale white hands clutched to the breast of the black coat, pinpoints of light burning where the woman's eyes should have been.

"We're policemen," Meyer answered. His hand hovered near the butt of his pistol. Beside him, he could feel Carella tensed for a draw.

"I know who killed the *rov*," the woman said.

"What?" Carella asked.

"She says she knows who killed the rabbi," Meyer whispered in soft astonishment.

His hand dropped to his side. They began walking toward the street end of the alley. The woman stood there motionless, the light behind her, her face in shadow, the pale hands still, her eyes burning.

"Who killed him?" Carella said.

"I know the *rotsayach*," the woman answered. "I know the murderer."

"Who?" Carella said again.

"Him!" the woman shouted, and she pointed to the painted white *J* on the synagogue wall. "The *sonei Yisroel!* Him!"

"The anti-Semite," Meyer translated. "She says the anti-Semite did it."

They had come abreast of the woman now. The three stood at the end of the alley with the street lamp casting long shadows on the cobbles. They could see her face. Black hair and brown eyes, the classic Jewish face of a woman in her fifties, the beauty stained by age and something else, a fine-drawn tension hidden in her eyes and on her mouth.

"What anti-Semite?" Carella asked. He realized he was whispering. There was something about the woman's face and the blackness of her coat and the paleness of her hands which made whispering a necessity.

"On the next block," she said. Her voice was a voice of judgment and doom. "The one they call Finch."

"You saw him kill the rabbi?" Carella asked. You saw him do it?"

"No." She paused. "But I know in my heart that he's the one . . ."

"What's your name, ma'am?" Meyer asked.

"Hannah Kaufman," she said. "I know it was him. He said he would do it, and now he has started."

"He said he would do what?" Meyer asked the old woman patiently.

"He said he would kill all the Jews."

"You heard him say this?"

"*Everyone* has heard him."

"His name is Finch?" Meyer asked her. "You're sure?"

"Finch," the woman said. "On the next block. Over the candy store."

"What do you think?" he asked Carella.

Carella nodded. "Let's try him."

4

If America is a melting pot, the 87th Precinct is a crucible. Start at the River Harb, the northernmost boundary of the precinct territory, and the first thing you hit is exclusive Smoke Rise, where the walled-in residents sit in white-Protestant respectability in houses set a hundred feet back from private roads, admiring the greatest view the city has to offer. Come out of Smoke Rise and hit fancy Silvermine Road where the aristocracy of apartment buildings have begun to submit to the assault of time and the encroachment of the surrounding slums. Forty-thousand-dollar-a-year executives still live in these apartment buildings, but people write on the walls here, too: limericks, prurient slogans, which industrious doormen try valiantly to erase.

There is nothing so eternal as Anglo-Saxon etched in graphite.

Silvermine Park is south of the road, and no one ventures there at night. During the day, the park is thronged with governesses idly chatting about the last time they saw Sweden, gently rocking shellacked blue baby buggies. But after sunset, not even lovers will enter the park. The Stem, further south, explodes the moment the sun leaves the sky. Gaudy and incandescent, it mixes Chinese restaurants with Jewish delicatessens, pizza joints with Greek cabarets offering belly dancers. Threadbare as a beggar's sleeve, Ainsley Avenue crosses the center of the precinct, trying to maintain a dignity long gone, crowding the sidewalks with austere but dirty apartment buildings, furnished rooms, garages and a sprinkling of sawdust saloons. Culver Avenue turns completely Irish with the speed of a leprechaun. The faces, the bars, even the buildings seem displaced, seem to have been stolen and transported from the center of Dublin; but no lace curtains hang in the windows. Poverty turns a naked face to the streets here, setting the pattern for the rest of the precinct territory. Poverty rakes the backs of the Culver Avenue Irish, claws its way onto the white and tan and brown and black faces of the Puerto Ricans lining Mason Avenue, flops onto the beds of the whores on *La Vía de Putas,* and then pushes its way into the real crucible, the city side streets where different minority groups live cheek by jowl, as close as lovers, hating each other. It is here that Puerto Rican and Jew, Italian and Negro, Irishman and Cuban are forced by dire economic need to live in a ghetto which, by its very composition, loses definition and becomes a meaningless tangle of unrelated bloodlines.

Rabbi Solomon's synagogue was on the same street as a Catholic church. A Baptist storefront mission was on the avenue leading to the next block. The candy store over which the man named Finch lived was owned by a Puerto Rican whose son had been a cop—a man named Hernandez.

Carella and Meyer paused in the lobby of the building and studied the nameplates in the mailboxes. There were eight boxes in the row. Two had nameplates. Three had broken locks. The man named Finch lived in apartment 33 on the third floor.

The lock on the vestibule door was broken. From behind the stairwell, where the garbage cans were stacked before being put out for collection in the morning, the stink of that evening's dinner remains assailed the nostrils and left the detectives mute until they had gained the first-floor landing.

On the way up to the third floor, Carella said, "This seems too easy, Meyer. It's over before it begins."

On the third-floor landing, both men drew their service revolvers. They found apartment 33 and bracketed the door.

"Mr. Finch?" Meyer called.

"Who is it?" a voice answered.

"Police. Open up."

The apartment and the hallway went still.

"Finch?" Meyer said.

There was no answer. Carella backed off against the opposite wall. Meyer nodded. Bracing himself against the wall, Carella raised his right foot, the leg bent at the knee, then released it like a triggered spring. The flat of his sole collided with the door just below the lock. The door burst inward, and Meyer followed it into the apartment, his gun in his fist.

Finch was a man in his late twenties, with a square crew-cut head and bright green eyes. He was closing the closet door as Meyer burst into the room. He was wearing only trousers and an undershirt, his feet bare. He needed a shave, and the bristles on his chin and face emphasized a white scar that ran from just under his right cheek to the curve of his jaw. He turned from the closet with the air of a man who has satisfactorily completed a mysterious mission.

"Hold it right there," Meyer said.

There's a joke they tell about an old woman on a train who repeatedly asks the man sitting beside her if he's Jewish. The man, trying to read his newspaper, keeps answering, "No, I'm not Jewish." The old lady keeps pestering him, tugging at his sleeve, asking the same question over and over again. Finally the man puts down his newspaper and says, "All right, all right, damn it! I'm Jewish."

And the old lady smiles at him sweetly and says, "You know something? You don't look it."

The joke, of course, relies on a prejudice which assumes that you can tell a man's religion by looking at his face. There was nothing about Meyer Meyer's looks or speech which would indicate that he was Jewish. His face was round and clean-shaven, he was thirty-seven years old and completely bald, and he possessed the bluest eyes this side of Denmark. He was almost six feet tall and perhaps a trifle overweight, and the only conversation he'd had with Finch were the few words he'd spoken through the closed door, and the four words he'd spoken since he entered the apartment, all of which were delivered in big-city English without any noticeable trace of accent.

But when Meyer Meyer said, "Hold it right there," a smile came onto Finch's face, and he answered, "I wasn't going any place, Jewboy."

Well, maybe the sight of the rabbi lying in his own blood had been too much for Meyer. Maybe the words *"sonei Yisroel"* had recalled the days of his childhood when, one of the few Orthodox Jews in a Gentile neighborhood, and beearing the double-barreled name his father had foisted upon him, he was forced to defend himself against every hoodlum who crossed his path, invariably against overwhelming odds. He was normally a very patient man. He had borne his father's practical joke with amazing good will, even though he sometimes grinned mirthlessly through bleeding lips. But tonight, this second night of Passover, after having looked down at the bleeding rabbi, after having heard the tortured sobs of the sexton, after having seen the patiently suffering face of the woman in black, the words hurled at him from the other end of the apartment had a startling effect.

Meyer said nothing. He simply walked to where Finch was standing near the closet, and lifted the .38 high above his head. He flipped the gun up as his arm descended, so that the heavy butt was in striking position as it whipped toward Finch's jaw.

Finch brought up his hands, but not to shield his face in defense. His hands were huge, with big knuckles, the imprimatur of the habitual street fighter. He opened the fingers and caught Meyer's descending arm at the wrist, stopping the gun three inches from his face.

He wasn't dealing with a kid; he was dealing with a cop. He obviously intended to shake that gun out of Meyer's fist and then beat him senseless on the floor of the apartment. But Meyer brought up his right knee and smashed it into Finch's groin, and then, his wrist still pinioned, he bunched his left fist and drove it hard and straight into Finch's gut. That did it. The fingers loosened and Finch backed away a step just as Meyer brought the pistol back across his own body and then unleashed it in a backhand swipe. The butt cracked against Finch's jaw and sent him sprawling against the closet wall.

Miraculously, the jaw did not break. Finch collided with the closet, grabbed the door behind him with both hands opened wide and flat against the wood, and then shook his head. He blinked his eyes and shook his head again. By what seemed to be sheer will power, he managed to stand erect without falling on his face.

Meyer stood watching him, saying nothing, breathing hard. Carella, who had come into the room, stood at the far end, ready to shoot Finch if he so much as raised a pinky.

"Your name Finch?" Meyer asked.

"I don't talk to Jews," Finch answered.

"Then try *me*," Carella said. "What's your name?"

"Go to hell, you and your Jewboy friend both."

Meyer did not raise his voice. He simply took a step closer to Finch, and very softly said, "Mister, in two minutes, you're gonna be a cripple because you resisted arrest."

He didn't have to say anything else, because his eyes told the full story, and Finch was a fast reader.

"Okay," Finch said, nodding. "That's my name."

"What's in the closet, Finch?" Carella asked.

"My clothes."

"Get away from the door."

"What for?"

Neither of the cops answered. Finch studied them for ten seconds, and quickly moved away from the door. Meyer opened it. The closet was stacked high with piles of tied and bundled pamphlets. The cord on one bundle was untied, the pamphlets spilling onto the closet floor. Apparently, this bundle was the one Finch had thrown into the closet when he'd heard the knock on the door. Meyer stooped and picked up one of the pamphlets. It was badly and cheaply printed, but the intent was unmistakable. The title of the pamphlet was "The Bloodsucker Jew."

"Where'd you get this?" Meyer asked.

"I belong to a book club," Finch answered.

"There are a few laws against this sort of thing," Carella said.

"Yeah?" Finch answered. "Name me one."

"Happy to. Section 1340 of the Penal Law—libel defined."

"Maybe you ought to read Section 1342," Finch said. " *'The publication is justified when the matter charged as libelous is true, and was published with good motives and for justifiable ends.'* "

"Then let's try Section 514," Carella said. " *'A person who denies or aids or incites another to deny any person because of race, creed, color or national origin . . .'* "

"I'm not trying to incite anyone," Finch said, grinning.

"Nor am I a lawyer," Carella said. "But we can also try Section 700, which defines discrimination, and Section 1430, which makes it a felony to perform an act of malicious injury to a place of religious worship."

"Huh?" Finch said.

"Yeah," Carella answered.

"What the hell are you talking about?"

"I'm talking about the little paint job you did on the synagogue wall."

"What paint job? What synagogue?"

"Where were you at eight o'clock tonight, Finch?"

"Out."

"Where?"

"I don't remember."

"You better *start* remembering."

"Why? Is there a section of the Penal Law against loss of memory?"

"No," Carella said. "But there's one against homicide."

5

The team stood around him in the squad room.

The team consisted of Detectives Steve Carella, Meyer Meyer, Cotton Hawes, and Bert Kling. Two detectives from Homicide South had put in a brief appearance to legitimize the action, and then went home to sleep, knowing full well that the investigation of a homicide is always left to the precinct discovering the stiff. The team stood around Finch in a loose semicircle. This wasn't a movie sound stage, so there wasn't a bright light shining in Finch's eyes, nor did any of the cops lay a finger on him. These days, there were too many smart-assed lawyers around who were ready and able to leap upon irregular interrogation methods when and if a case finally came to trial. The detectives simply stood around Finch in a loose, relaxed semicircle, and their only weapons were a thorough familiarity with the interrogation process and with each other, and the mathematical superiority of four minds pitted against one.

"What time did you leave the apartment?" Hawes asked.

"Around seven."

"And what time did you return?" Kling asked.

"Nine, nine-thirty. Something like that."

"Where'd you go?" Carella asked.

"I had to see somebody."

"A rabbi?" Meyer asked.

"No."

"Who?"

"I don't want to get anybody in trouble."

"You're in plenty of trouble yourself," Hawes said. "Where'd you go?"

"No place."

"Okay, suit yourself," Carella said. "You've been shooting your mouth off about killing Jews, haven't you?"

"I never said anything like that."

"Where'd you get these pamphlets?"

"I found them."

"You agree with what they say?"

"Yes."

"You know where the synagogue in this neighborhood is?"

"Yes."

"Were you anywhere near it tonight between seven and nine?"

"No."

"Then where were you?"

"No place."

"Anybody see you there?" Kling asked.

"See me where?"

"The no place you went to."

"Nobody saw me."

"You went no place," Hawes said, "and nobody saw you. Is that right?"

"That's right."

"The invisible man," Kling said.

"That's right."

"When you get around to killing all these Jews," Carella said, "how do you plan to do it?"

"I don't plan to kill anybody," he said defensively.

"Who you gonna start with?"

"Nobody."

"Ben-Gurion?"

"Nobody."

"Or maybe you've already started."

"I didn't kill anybody, and I'm not gonna kill anybody. I want to call a lawyer."

"A Jewish lawyer?"

"I wouldn't have—"

"What wouldn't you have?"

"Nothing."

"You like Jews?"

"No."

"You hate them?"

"No."

"Then you like them."

"No. I didn't say—"

"You either like them or you hate them. Which?"

"That's none of your goddamn business!"

"But you agree with the crap in those hate pamphlets, don't you?"

"They're not hate pamphlets."

"What do you call them?"

"Expressions of opinion."

"Whose opinion?"

"Everybody's opinion!"

"Yours included?"

"Yes, mine included!"

"Do you know Rabbi Solomon?"

"No."

"What do you think of rabbis in general?"

"I never think of rabbis."

"But you think of Jews a lot, don't you?"

"There's no crime against think—"

"If you think of Jews you must think of rabbis. Isn't that right?"

"Why should I waste my time—"

"The rabbi is the spiritual leader of the Jewish people, isn't he?"

"I don't know anything about rabbis."

"But you must know that."

"What if I do?"

"Well, if you said you were going to kill the Jews—"

"I never said—"

"—then a good place to start would be with—"

"I never said anything like that!"

"We've got a witness who heard you! A good place to start would be with a rabbi, isn't that so?"

"Go shove your rabbi—"

"Where were you between seven and nine tonight?"

"No place."

"You were behind that synagogue, weren't you?"

"No."

"You were painting a *J* on the wall, weren't you?"

"No! No, I wasn't!"

"You were stabbing a rabbi!"

"You were killing a Jew!"

"I wasn't any place near that—"

"Book him, Cotton. Suspicion of murder."

"Suspicion of—I'm telling you I wasn't—"

"Either shut up or start talking, you bastard." Carella said.
Finch shut up.

6

The girl came to see Meyer Meyer on Easter Sunday.

She had reddish-brown hair and brown eyes, and she wore a dress of bright persimmon with a sprig of flowers pinned to the left breast. She stood at the railing and none of the detectives in the squadroom even noticed the flowers; they were too busy speculating on the depth and texture of the girl's rich curves.

The girl didn't say a word. She didn't have to. The effect was almost comic, akin to the cocktail-paarty scene where the voluptuous blond takes out a cigarette and four hundred men are stampeded in the rush to light it. The first man to reach the slatted rail divider was Cotton Hawes, since he was single and unattached. The second man was Hal Willis, who was also single and a good red-blooded American boy. Meyer Meyer, an old married poop, contented himself with ogling the girl from behind his desk. The word *"shtik"* crossed Meyer's mind, but he rapidly pushed the thought aside.

"Can I help you, miss?" Hawes and Willis asked simultaneously.

"I'd like to see Detective Meyer," the girl said.

"Meyer?" Hawes asked, as if his manhood had been maligned.

"Meyer?" Willis repeated.

"Is he the man handling the murder of the rabbi?"

"Well we're *all* sort of working on it," Hawes said modestly.

"I'm Artie Finch's girl friend," the girl said. "I want to talk to Detective Meyer."

Meyer rose from his desk with the air of a man who has been singled out from the stag line by the belle of the ball. Using his best radio announcer's voice, and his best company manners, he said, "Yes, miss, I'm Detective Meyer."

He held open the gate in the railing, all but executed a bow, and led the girl to his desk. Hawes and Kling watched as the girl sat and crossed her legs. Meyer moved a pad into place with all the aplomb of a General Motors executive.

"I'm sorry miss," he said. "What was your name?"

"Eleanor," she said. "Eleanor Fay."

"F-A-Y-E?" Meyer asked, writing.

"F-A-Y."

"And you're Arthur Finch's fiancée? Is that right?"

"I'm his girl friend," Eleanor corrected.

"You're not engaged?"

"Not officially, no." She smiled demurely, modestly and sweetly. Across the room, Cotton Hawes rolled his eyes toward the ceiling.

"What did you want to see me about, Miss Fay?" Meyer asked.

"I wanted to see you about Arthur. He's innocent. He didn't kill that man."

"I see. What do you know about it, Miss Fay?"

"Well, I read in the paper that the rabbi was killed sometime between seven-thirty and nine. I think that's right, isn't it?"

"Approximately, yes."

"Well, Arthur couldn't have done it. I know where he was during that time."

"And where was he?" Meyer asked.

He figured he knew just what the girl would say. He had heard the same words from an assortment of molls, mistresses, fiancées, girl friends and just plain acquaintances of men accused of everything from disorderly conduct to first-degree murder. The girl would protest that Finch was with her during that time. After a bit of tooth-pulling, she would admit that—well—they were alone together. After a little more coaxing, the girl would reluctantly state, the reluctance adding credulity to her story, that —well—they were alone in intimate circumstances together. The alibi having been firmly established, she would then wait patiently for her man's deliverance.

"And where was he?" Meyer asked, and waited patiently.

"From seven to eight," Eleanor said, "he was with a man named Bret Loomis in a restaurant called The Gate, on Culver and South Third."

"What?" Meyer said surprised.

"Yes. From there, Arthur went to see his sister in Riverhead. I can give you the address if you like. He got there at about eight-thirty and stayed a half hour or so. Then he went straight home."

"What time did he get home?"

"Ten o'clock."

"He told us nine, nine-thirty."

"He was mistaken. I know he got home at ten because he called me the minute he was in the house. It was ten o'clock."

"I see. And he told you he'd just got home?"

"Yes." Eleanor Fay nodded and uncrossed her legs. Willis, at the water cooler, did not miss the sudden revealing glimpse of nylon and thigh.

"Did he also tell you he'd spent all that time with Loomis first and then with his sister?"

"Yes, he did."

"Then why didn't he tell *us?*" Meyer asked.

"I don't know why. Arthur is a person who respects family and friends. I suppose he didn't want to involve them with the police."

"That's very considerate of him," Meyer said dryly, "especially since he's being held on suspicion of murder. What's his sister's name?"

"Irene Granavan. Mrs. Carl Granavan."

"And her address?"

"Nineteen-eleven Morris Road. In Riverhead."

"Know where I can find this Bret Loomis?"

"He lives in a rooming house on Culver Avenue. The address is 3918. It's near Fourth."

"You came pretty well prepared, didn't you, Miss Fay?" Meyer asked.

"If you don't come prepared," Eleanor answered, "why come at all?"

7

Bret Loomis was thirty-one years old, five feet six inches tall, bearded. When he admitted the detectives to the apartment, he was wearing a bulky black sweater and tight-fitting dungarees. Standing next to Cotton Hawes, he looked like a little boy who had tried on a false beard in an attempt to get a laugh out of his father.

"Sorry to bother you, Mr. Loomis," Meyer said. "We know this is Easter, and—"

"Oh, yeah?" Loomis said. He seemed surprised. "Hey, that's right, ain't it? It's Easter. I'll be damned. Maybe I oughta go out and buy myself a pot of flowers."

"You didn't know it was Easter?" Hawes asked.

"Like, man, who ever reads the newspapers? Gloom, gloom! I'm fed up to here with it. Let's have a beer, celebrate Easter. Okay?"

"Well, thanks," Meyer said, "but—"

"Come on, so it ain't allowed. Who's gonna know besides you, me and the bedpost? Three beers coming up."

Meyer looked at Hawes and shrugged. Hawes shrugged back. Together, they watched Loomis as he went to the refrigerator in one corner of the room and took out three bottles of beer.

"Sit down," he said. "You'll have to drink from the bottle because I'm a little short of glasses. Sit down, sit down."

The detectives glanced around the room, puzzled.

"Oh," Loomis said, "you'd better sit on the floor. I'm a little short of chairs."

The three men squatted around a low table which had obviously been made from a tree stump. Loomis put the bottles on the table top, lifted his own bottle, said "Cheers," and took a long drag at it.

"What do you do for a living, Mr. Loomis?" Meyer asked.

"I live," Loomis said.

"What?"

"I *live* for a living. That's what I do."

"I meant, how do you support yourself?"

"I get payments from my ex-wife."

"*You* get payments?" Hawes asked.

"Yeah. She was so delighted to get rid of me that she made a settlement. A hundred bucks a week. That's pretty good, isn't it?"

"That's very good," Meyer said.

"You think so?" Loomis seemed thoughtful. "I think I coulda boosted it to *two* hundred if I held out a little longer. The bitch was running around with another guy, you see, and was all hot to marry him. He's got plenty of loot. I bet I coulda boosted it to two hundred."

"How long do these payments continue?" Hawes asked, fascinated.

"Until I get married again—which I will never ever do as long as I live. Drink your beer. It's good beer." He took a drag at his bottle and said, "What'd you want to see me about?"

"Do you know a man named Arthur Finch?"

"Sure. He in trouble?"

"Yes."

"What'd he do?"

"Well, let's skip that for the moment, Mr. Loomis," Hawes said. "We'd like you to tell us—"

"Where'd you get that white streak in your hair?" Loomis asked suddenly.

"Huh?" Hawes touched his left temple unconsciously. "Oh, I got knifed once. It grew back this way."

"All you need is a blue streak on the other temple. Then you'll look like the American flag," Loomis said, and laughed.

"Yeah," Hawes said. "Mr. Loomis, can you tell us where you were last night between seven and eight o'clock?"

"Oh, boy," Loomis said, "this is like 'Dragnet,' ain't it? 'Where were you on the night of December twenty-first? All we want are the facts.' "

"Just like 'Dragnet,' " Meyer said dryly. "Where were you, Mr. Loomis?"

"Last night? Seven o'clock?" He thought for a moment. "Oh, sure."

"Where?"

"Olga's pad."

"Who?"

"Olga Trenovich. She's like a sculptress. She does these crazy little statues in wax. Like she drips the wax all over everything. You dig?"

"And you were with her last night?"

"Yeah. She had like a little session up at her pad. A couple of colored guys on sax and drums and two other kids on trumpet and piano."

"You got there at seven, Mr. Loomis?"

"No. I got there at six-thirty."

"And what time did you leave?"

"Gosssshhhhh, who remembers?" Loomis said. "It was the wee, small hours."

"After midnight, you mean?" Hawes asked.

"Oh, sure. Two, three in the morning," Loomis said.

"You got there at six-thirty and left at two or three in the morning? Is that right?"

"Yeah."

"Was Arthur Finch with you?"

"Hell, no."

"Did you see him at all last night?"

"Nope. Haven't seen him since—let me see—last month sometime."

"You were *not* with Arthur Finch in a restaurant called The Gate?"

"When? Last night, you mean?"

"Yes."

"Nope. I just told you. I haven't seen Artie in almost two weeks." A sudden spark flashed in Loomis's eyes and he looked at Hawes and Meyer guiltily.

"Oh-oh," he said. "What'd I just do? Did I screw up Artie's alibi?"

"You screwed it up fine, Mr. Loomis," Hawes said.

8

Irene Granavan, Finch's sister, was a twenty-one-year-old girl who had already borne three children and was working on her fourth, in her fifth month of pregnancy. She admitted the detectives to her apartment in a Riverhead housing development, and then immediately sat down.

"You have to forgive me," she said. "My back aches. The doctor thinks maybe it'll be twins. That's all I need is twins." She pressed the palms of her hands into the small of her back, sighed heavily, and said, "I'm always having a baby. I got married when I was seventeen, and I've been pregnant ever since. All my kids think I'm a fat woman. They've never seen me that I wasn't pregnant." She sighed again. "You got any children?" she asked Meyer.

"Three," he answered.

"I sometimes wish . . ." She stopped and pulled a curious face, a face which denied dreams.

"What do you wish, Mrs. Granavan?" Hawes asked.

"That I could go to Bermuda. Alone." She paused. "Have you ever been to Bermuda?"

"No."

"I hear it's very nice there," Irene Granavan said wistfully, and the apartment went still.

"Mrs. Granavan," Meyer said, "we'd like to ask you a few questions about your brother."

"What's he done now?"

"Has he done things before?" Hawes said.

"Well, you know . . ." She shrugged.

"What?" Meyer asked.

"Well, the fuss down at City Hall. And the picketing of that movie. You know."

"We don't know, Mrs. Granavan."

"Well, I hate to say this about my own brother, but I think he's a little nuts on the subject. You know."

"What subject?"

"Well, the movie, for example. It's about Israel, and him and his friends picketed it and all, and handed out pamphlets about Jews, and . . . You remember, don't you? The crowd threw stones at him and all. There were a lot of concentration-camp survivors in the crowd, you know." She paused. "I think he must be a little nuts to do something like that, don't you think?"

"You said something about City Hall, Mrs. Granavan. What did your brother—"

"Well, it was when the mayor invited this Jewish assemblyman—I forget his name—to make a speech with him on the steps of City Hall. My brother went down and—well, the same business. You know."

"You mentioned your brother's friends. What friends?"

"The nuts he hangs out with."

"Would you know their names?" Meyer wanted to know.

"I know only one of them. He was here once with my brother. He's got pimples all over his face. I remember him because I was pregnant with Sean at the time, and he asked if he could put his hands on my stomach to feel the baby kicking. I told him he certainly could not. That shut *him* up, all right."

"What was his name, Mrs. Granavan?"

"Fred. That's short for Frederick. Frederick Schultz."

"He's German?" Meyer asked.

"Yes."

Meyer nodded briefly.

"Mrs. Granavan," Hawes said, "was your brother here last night?"

"Why? Did he say he was?"

"Was he?"

"No."

"Not at all?"

"No. He wasn't here last night. I was home alone last night. My husband bowls on Saturdays." She paused. "I sit home and hug my fat belly, and he bowls. You know what I wish sometimes?"

"What?" Meyer asked.

And, as if she had not said it once before, Irene Granavan said, "I wish I could go to Bermuda sometime. Alone."

"The thing is," the house painter said to Carella, "I'd like my ladder back."

"I can understand that," Carella said.

"The brushes they can keep, although some of them are very expensive brushes. But the ladder I absolutely need. I'm losing a day's work already because of those guys down at your lab."

"Well, you see—"

"I go back to the synagogue this morning, and my ladder and my brushes and even my paints are all gone. And what a mess somebody made of that alley! So this old guy who's sexton of the place, he tells me the priest was killed Saturday night, and the cops took all the stuff away with them. I wanted to know what cops, and he said he didn't know. So I called headquarters this morning, and I got a runaround from six different cops who finally put me through to some guy named Grossman at the lab."

"Yes, Lieutenant Grossman," Carella said.

"That's right. And he tells me I can't have my goddamn ladder back until they finish their tests on it. Now what the hell do they expect to find on my ladder, would you mind telling me?"

"I don't know, Mr. Cabot. Fingerprints, perhaps."

"Yeah, *my* fingerprints! Am I gonna get involved in murder *besides* losing a day's work?"

"I don't think so." Carella said, smiling.

"I shouldn't have taken that job, anyway," Cabot said. "I shouldn't have even bothered with it."

"Who hired you for the job, Mr. Cabot?"

"The priest did."

"The rabbi, you mean?" Carella asked.

"Yeah, the priest, the rabbi, whatever the hell you call him." Cabot shrugged.

"And what were you supposed to do, Mr. Cabot?"

"I was supposed to paint. What do you think I was supposed to do?"

"Paint what?"

"The trim. Around the windows and the roof."

"White and blue?"

"White around the windows, and blue for the roof trim."

"The colors of Israel," Carella said.

"Yeah," the painter agreed. Then he said, "What?"

"Nothing. Why did you say you shouldn't have taken the job, Mr. Cabot?"

"Well, because of all the arguing first. He wanted it done for Peaceable, he said, and Peaceable fell on the first. But I couldn't—"

"Peaceable? You mean Passover?"

"Yeah, Peaceable, Passover, whatever the hell you call it." He shrugged again.

"You were about to say?"

"I was about to say we had a little argument about it. I was working on another job, and I couldn't get to his job until Friday, the thirty-first. I figured I'd work late into the night, you know, but the priest told me I couldn't work after sundown. So I said why can't I work after sundown, so he said the Sabbath began at sundown, not to mention the first day of Peace—Passover, and that work wasn't allowed on the first two days of Passover, nor on the Sabbath neither, for that matter. Because the Lord rested on the Sabbath, you see. The seventh day."

"Yes, I see."

"Sure. So I said, 'Father, I'm not of the Jewish faith,' is what I said, 'and I can work any day of the week I like.' Besides, I got a big job to start on Monday, and I figured I could knock off the church all day Friday and Friday night or, if worse came to worse, Saturday, for which I usually get time and a half. So we compromised."

"How did you compromise?"

"Well, this priest was of what you call the Conservative crowd, not the Reformers, which are very advanced, but still these Conservatives don't follow all the old rules of the religion is what I gather. So he said I could work during the day Friday, and then I could come back and work Saturday, provided I knocked off at sundown. Don't ask me what kind of crazy compromise it was. I think he had in mind that he holds mass at sundown and it would be a mortal sin if I was outside painting while everybody was inside praying, and on a very special high holy day, at that."

"I see. So you painted until sundown Friday?"

"Right."

"And then you came back Saturday morning?"

"Right. But what it was, the windows needed a lot of putty, and the sills needed scraping and sanding, so by sundown Saturday, I still wasn't finished with the job. I had a talk with the priest, who said he was about to go inside and pray, and could I come back after services to finish off the job? I told him I had a better idea. I would come back Monday morning and knock off the little bit that had to be done before I went on to this very big job I got in Majesta—it's painting a whole factory; that's a big job. So I left everything right where it was in back of the church. I figured, who'd steal anything from right behind a church. Am I right?"

"Right," Carella said.

"Yeah. Well, you know who'd steal them from right behind a church?"

"Who?"

"The cops!" Cabot shouted. "That's who! Now how the hell do I get my ladder back, would you please tell me? I got a call from the factory today. They said if I don't start work tomorrow, at the latest, I can forget all about the job. And me without a ladder!"

"Maybe we've got a ladder downstairs you can borrow," Carella said.

"Mister, I need a tall painter's ladder. This is a very high factory. Can you call this Captain Grossman and ask him to please let me have my ladder back? I got mouths to feed."

"I'll talk to him, Mr. Cabot," Carella said. "Leave me your number, will you?"

"I tried to borrow my brother-in-law's ladder—he's a paper hanger—but he's papering this movie star's apartment, downtown on Jefferson. So just try to get *his* ladder. Just try."

"Well, I'll call Grossman," Carella said.

"The other day, what she done, this movie actress, she marched into the living room wearing only this towel, you see? She wanted to know what—"

"I'll call Grossman," Carella said.

As it turned out, he didn't have to call Grossman, because a lab report arrived late that afternoon, together with Cabot's ladder and the rest of his working equipment, including his brushes, his putty knife, several cans of linseed oil and turpentine, a pair of paint-stained gloves and two dropcloths. At about the same time the report arrived, Grossman called from downtown, saving Carella a dime.

"Did you get my report?" Grossman asked.

"I was just reading it."

"What do you make of it?"

"I don't know," Carella said.

"Want my guess?"

"Sure. I'm always interested in what the layman thinks," Carella answered him.

"Layman, I'll give you a hit in the head!" Grossman answered, laughing. "You notice the rabbi's prints were on those paint-can lids, and also on the ladder?"

"Yes, I did."

"The ones on the lids were thumbprints, so I imagine the rabbi put those lids back onto the paint cans or, if they were already on the cans, pushed down on them to make sure they were secure."

"Why would he want to do that?"

"Maybe he was moving the stuff. There's a tool shed behind the synagogue. Had you noticed that?"

"No, I hadn't."

"Tch-tch, big detective. Yeah, there's one there, all right, about fifty yards behind the building. So I figure the painter rushed off, leaving his junk all over the backyard, and the rabbi was moving it to the tool shed when he was surprised by the killer."

"Well, the painter did leave his stuff there, that's true. He expected to come back Monday morning."

"Today, yeah," Grossman said. "But maybe the rabbi figured he didn't want his backyard looking like a pigsty, especially since this is Passover. So he took it into his head to move the stuff over to the tool shed. This is just speculation, you understand."

"No kidding?" Carella said. "I thought it was sound, scientific deduction."

"Go to hell. Those *are* thumbprints on the lids, so it's logical to conclude he pressed down on them. And the prints on the ladder seem to indicate he was carrying it."

"This report said you didn't find any prints but the rabbi's," Carella said. "Isn't that just a little unusual?"

"You didn't read it right," Grossman said. "We found a portion of a print on one of the paintbrushes. And we also—"

"Oh, yeah," Carella said, "here it is. This doesn't say much, Sam."

"What do you want me to do? It seems to be a tented-arch pattern, like the rabbi's, but there's too little to tell. The print could have been left on that brush by someone else."

"Like the painter?"

"No. We've pretty much decided the painter used gloves while he worked. Otherwise, we'd have found a flock of similar prints on all the tools."

"Then who left that print on the brush? The killer?"

"Maybe."

"But the portion isn't enough to get anything positive on?"

"Sorry, Steve."

"So your guess on what happened is that the rabbi went outside after services to clean up the mess. The killer surprised him, knifed him, made a mess of the alley, and then painted that *J* on the wall. Is that it?"

"I guess so, though—"

"What?"

"Well, there was a lot of blood leading right over to that wall, Steve. As if the rabbi had crawled there after he'd been stabbed."

"Probably trying to get to the back door of the synagogue."

"Maybe," Grossman said. "One thing I can tell you. Whoever killed him must have been pretty much of a mess when he got home. No doubt about that."

"Why do you say that?"

"That spattered paint all over the alley," Grossman said. "It's my guess the rabbi threw those paint cans at his attacker."

"You're a pretty good guesser, Sam," Carella told him, grinning.

"Thanks," Grossman said.

"Tell me something."

"Yeah?"

"You ever solve any murders?"

"Go to hell," Grossman said, and he hung up.

9

Alone with his wife that night in the living room of their apartment, Meyer tried to keep his attention *off* a television series about cops and *on* the various documents he had collected from Rabbi Solomon's study in the synagogue. The cops on television were shooting up a storm, blank bullets flying all over the place and killing hoodlums by the score. It almost made a working man like Meyer Meyer wish for an exciting life of romantic adventure.

The romantic adventure of *his* life, Sarah Lipkin Meyer, sat in an easy chair opposite the television screen, her legs crossed, absorbed in the fictional derring-do of the policemen.

"Ooooh, *get* him!" Sarah screamed at one point, and Meyer turned to look at her curiously, and then went back to the rabbi's books.

The rabbi kept a ledger of expenses, all of which had to do with the synagogue and his duties there. The ledger did not make interesting reading, and told Meyer nothing he wanted to know. The rabbi also kept a calendar of synagogue events and Meyer glanced through them reminiscently, remembering his own youth and the busy Jewish life centering around the synagogue in the neighborhood adjacent to his own. *March twelfth,* the calendar read, *regular Sunday breakfast of the Men's Club. Speaker, Harry Pine, director of Commission on International Affairs of*

American Jewish Congress. Topic: The Eichmann Case.

Meyer's eye ran down the list of events itemized in Rabbi Solomon's book:

March 12, 7:15 P.M.

Youth Group meeting.

March 18, 9:30 A.M.

Bar mitzvah services for Nathan Rothman. Kiddush after services. Open invitation to Center membership.

March 22, 8:45 P.M.

Clinton Samuels, Assistant Professor of Philosophy in Education, Brandeis University, will lead discussion in "The Matter of Identity for the Jews in Modern America."

March 26

Eternal Light Radio. "The Search" by Virginia Mazer, biographical script on Lillian Wald, founder of Henry Street Settlement in New York.

Meyer looked up from the calendar. "Sarah?" he said.

"Shhh, shhh, just a minute," Sarah answered. She was nibbling furiously at her thumb, her eyes glued to the silent television screen. An ear-shattering volley of shots suddenly erupted, all but smashing the picture tube. The theme music came up, and Sarah let out a deep sigh and turned to her husband.

Meyer looked at her curiously, as if seeing her for the first time, remembering the Sarah Lipkin of long, long ago and wondering if the Sarah Meyer of today was very much different from that initial exciting image. "Nobody's lips kin like Sarah's lips kin," the fraternity boys had chanted, and Meyer had memorized the chant, and investigated the possibilities, learning for the first time in his life that every cliché bears a kernel of folklore. He looked at her mouth now, pursed in puzzlement as she studied his face. Her eyes were blue, and her hair was brown, and she had a damn good figure and splendid legs, and he nodded in agreement with his youthful judgment.

"Sarah, do you feel any identity as a Jew in modern America?" he asked.

"What?" Sarah said.

"I said—"

"Oh, boy," Sarah said. "What brought *that* on?"

"The rabbi, I guess." Meyer scratched his bald pate. "I guess I haven't felt so much like a Jew since—since I was confirmed, I guess. It's a funny thing."

"Don't let it trouble you," Sarah said gently. "You *are* a Jew."

"Am I?" he asked, and he looked straight into her eyes.

She returned the gaze. "You have to answer that one for yourself," she said.

"I know I—well, I get mad as hell thinking about this guy Finch. Which isn't good, you know. After all, maybe he's innocent."

"Do you think so?"

"No. I think he did it. But is it *me* who thinks that, Meyer Meyer, detective second grade? Or is it Meyer Meyer who got beat up by the *goyim* when he was a kid, and Meyer Meyer who heard his grandfather tell stories about pogroms, or who listened to the radio and heard what Hitler was doing in Germany, or who nearly strangled a German colonel with his bare hands just outside—"

"You can't separate the two, darling," Sarah said.

"Maybe you can't. I'm only trying to say I never much felt like a Jew until this case came along. Now, all of a sudden . . ." He shrugged.

"Shall I get your prayer shawl?" Sarah said smiling.

"Wise guy," Meyer said. He closed the rabbi's calendar, and opened the next book on the desk. The book was a personal diary. He unlocked it, and began leafing through it.

Friday, January 6

Shabbat, Parshat Shemot. I lighted the candles at four-twenty-four. Evening services were at six-fifteen. It has been a hundred years since the Civil War. We discussed the Jewish Community of the South, then and now.

January 18

It seems odd to me that I should have to familiarize the membership about the proper blessings over the Sabbath candles. Have we come so far toward forgetfulness?

Baruch ata adonai elohenu melech haolam asher kidshanu b'mitzvotav vitzivanu l'hadlick ner shel shabbat.

Blessed are Thou O Lord our God, King of the universe who hast sanctified us by Thy laws and commanded us to kindle the Sabbath Light.

Perhaps he is right. Perhaps the Jews are doomed.

January 20

I had hoped that the Maccabean festival would make us realize the hardships borne by the Jews two thousand years ago in comparison to our good and easy lives today in a democracy. Today, we have the freedom to worship as we desire, but this should impose upon us the responsibility of enjoying that freedom. And yet, Hanukkah has come and gone, and it seems to me The Feast of Lights taught us nothing, gave us nothing more than a joyous holiday to celebrate.

The Jews will die, he says.

February 2

I believe I am beginning to fear him. He shouted threats at me today, said that I, of all the Jews, would lead the way to destruction. I was tempted to call the police, but I understand he has done this before. There are those in the membership who have suffered his harangues and who seem to feel he is harmless. But he rants with the fervor of a fanatic, and his eyes frighten me.

February 12

A member called today to ask me something about the dietary laws. I was forced to call the local butcher because I did not know the prescribed length of the *hallaf,* the slaughtering knife. Even the butcher, in jest, said to me that a real rabbi would know these things. I *am* a real rabbi. I believe in the Lord, my God, I teach His will and His law to His people. What need a rabbi know about *shehitah,* the art of slaughtering animals? Is it important to know that the slaughtering knife must be twice the width of the throat of the slaughtered animal, and no more than fourteen finger-breadths in length? The butcher told me that the knife must be sharp and smooth, with no perceptible notches. It is examined by passing finger and fingernail over both edges of the blade before and after slaughtering. If a notch is found, the animal is then unfit. Now I know. But is it necessary to know this? Is it not enough to love God, and to teach His ways?

His anger continues to frighten me.

February 14

I found a knife in the ark today, at the rear of the cabinet behind the Torah.

March 8

We had no further use of the Bibles we replaced, and since they were old and tattered, but nonetheless ritual articles containing the name of God, we buried them in the backyard, near the tool shed.

March 22

I must see about contacting a painter to do the outside of the synagogue. Someone suggested a Mr. Frank Cabot who lives in the neighborhood. I will call him tomorrow, perhaps. Passover will be coming soon, and I would like the temple to look nice.

The mystery is solved. It is kept for trimming the wick in the oil lamp over the ark.

The telephone rang. Meyer, absorbed in the diary, didn't even hear it. Sarah went to the phone and lifted it from the cradle.

"Hello?" she said. "Oh, hello, Steve. How are you?" She laughed and said, "No, I was watching television. That's right." She laughed again. "Yes, just a minute, I'll get him." She put the phone down and walked to where Meyer was working. "It's Steve," she said. "He wants to speak to you."

"Huh?"

"The phone. Steve."

"Oh," Meyer nodded. "Thanks." He walked over to the phone and lifted the receiver. "Hello, Steve," he said.

"Hi. Can you get down here right away?"

"Why? What's the matter?"

"Finch," Carella said. "He's broken jail."

10

Finch had been kept in the detention cells of the precinct house all day Sunday where, it being Easter, he had been served turkey for his midday meal. On Monday morning, he'd been transported by van to headquarters downtown on High Street where, as a felony offender, he participated in that quaint police custom known simply as "the line-up." He had been mugged and printed afterward in the basement of the building, and then led across the street to the Criminal Courts Building where he had been arraigned for first-degree murder and, over his lawyer's protest, ordered to be held without bail until trial. The police van had then transported him crosstown to the house of detention on Canopy Avenue where he'd remained all day Monday, until after the evening meal. At that time, those offenders who had committed, or who were alleged to have committed, the most serious crimes, were once more shackled and put into the van, which carried them uptown and south to the edge of the River Dix for transportation by ferry to the prison on Walker Island.

He'd made his break, Carella reported, while he was being moved from the van to the ferry. According to what the harbor police said, Finch was still handcuffed and wearing prison garb. The break had taken place at about 10 P.M. It was assumed that it had been witnessed by several dozen hospital attendants waiting for the ferry which would take them to Dix Sanitarium, a city-owned-and-operated hospital for drug addicts, situated in the middle of the river about a mile and a half from the prison. It was also assumed that the break had been witnessed by a dozen or more water rats who leaped among the dock pilings and who, because of their size, were sometimes mistaken for pussy cats by neighborhood kids who played near the river's edge. Considering the fact that Finch was dressed in drab gray uniform and handcuffs—a dazzling display of sartorial elegance, to be sure, but not likely to be seen on any other male walking the city streets —it was amazing that he hadn't yet been picked up. They had, of course, checked his apartment first, finding nothing there but the four walls and the furniture. One of the unmarried detectives on the squad, probably hoping for an invitation to go along, suggested that they look up Eleanor Fay, Finch's girl. Wasn't it likely he'd head for her pad? Carella and Meyer agreed that it was entirely likely, clipped their holsters on, neglected to offer the invitation to their colleague, and went out into the night.

It was a nice night, and Eleanor Fay lived in a nice neighborhood of old brownstones wedged in between new, all-glass apartment houses with garages below the sidewalk. April had danced across the city and left her subtle warmth in the air. The two men drove in one of the squad's sedans, the windows rolled down. They did not say much to each other, April had robbed them of speech. The police radio droned its calls endlessly; radio motor patrolmen all over the city acknowledged violence and mayhem.

"There it is," Meyer said. "Just up ahead."

"Now try to find a parking spot," Carella complained.

They circled the block twice before finding an opening in front of a drugstore on the avenue. They got out of the car, left it unlocked, and walked briskly in the balmy night. The brownstone was in the middle of the block. They climbed the twelve steps to the vestibule, and studied the nameplates alongside the buzzers. Eleanor Fay was in apartment 2B. Without hesitation, Carella pressed the buzzer for apartment 5A. Meyer took the doorknob in his hand and waited. When the answering click came, he twisted the knob, and silently they headed for the steps to the second floor.

Kicking in a door is an essentially rude practice. Neither Carella nor Meyer were particularly lacking in good manners, but they were looking for a man accused of murder, and a man who had successfully broken jail. It was not unnatural to assume this was a desperate man, and so they didn't even discuss whether or not they would kick in the door. They

aligned themselves in the corridor outside apartment 2B. The wall opposite the door was too far away to serve as a springboard. Meyer, the heavier
of the two men, backed away from the door, then hit it with his shoulder.
He hit it hard and close to the lock. He wasn't attempting to shatter the
door itself, an all but impossible feat. All he wanted to do was spring the
lock. All the weight of his body concentrated in the padded spot of arm
and shoulder which collided with the door just above the lock. The lock
itself remained locked, but the screws holding it to the jamb could not
resist the force of Meyer's fleshy battering ram. The wood around the
screws splintered, the threads lost their friction grip, the door shot inward
and Meyer followed it into the room. Carella, like a quarterback carrying
the ball behind powerful interference, followed Meyer.

It's rare that a cop encounters raw sex in his daily routine. The naked
bodies he sees are generally cold and covered with caked blood. Even
vice-squad cops find the act of love sordid rather than enticing. Eleanor
Fay was lying full length on the living-room couch with a man. The
television set in front of the couch was going, but nobody was watching
either the news or the weather.

When the two men with drawn guns piled into the room behind the
imploding door, Eleanor Fay sat bolt upright on the couch, her eyes wide
in surprise. She was naked to the waist. She was wearing tight-fitting black
tapered slacks and black high-heeled pumps. Her hair was disarranged and
her lipstick had been kissed from her mouth, and she tried to cover her
exposed breasts with her hands the moment the cops entered, realized the
task was impossible, and grabbed the nearest article of clothing, which
happened to be the man's suit jacket. She held it up in front of her like
the classic, surprised heroine in a pirate movie. The man beside her sat
up with equal suddenness, turned toward the cops, then turned back to
Eleanor, puzzled, as if seeking an explanation from her.

The man was not Arthur Finch.

He was a man in his late twenties. He had a lot of pimples on his face,
and a lot of lipstick stains. His white shirt was open to the waist. He wore
no undershirt.

"Hello, Miss Fay," Meyer said.

"I didn't hear you knock," Eleanor answered. She seemed to recover
instantly from her initial surprise and embarrassment. With total disdain
for the two detectives, she threw the jacket aside, rose and walked like a
burlesque queen to a hard-backed chair over which her missing clothing
was draped. She lifted a brassiere, shrugged into it, clasped it, all as if she

were alone in the room. Then she pulled a black, long-sleeved sweater over her head, shook out her hair, lighted a cigarette, and said. "Is breaking and entering only a crime for criminals?"

"We're sorry, miss," Carella said. "We're looking for your boy friend."

"Me?" the man on the couch asked. "What'd *I* do?"

A glance of puzzlement passed between Meyer and Carella. Something like understanding, faint and none too clear, touched Carella's face.

"Who are you?" he said.

"You don't have to tell them anything," Eleanor cautioned. "They're not allowed to break in like this. Private citizens have rights, too."

"That's right, Miss Fay," Meyer said. "Why'd you lie to us?"

"I didn't lie to anybody."

"You gave us false information about Finch's whereabouts on—"

"I wasn't aware I was under oath at the time."

"You weren't. But you were damn well maliciously impeding the progress of an investigation."

"The hell with you *and* your investigation. You horny bastards bust in here like—"

"We're sorry we spoiled your party," Carella said. "Why'd you lie about Finch?"

"I thought I was helping you," Eleanor said. "Now get the hell out of here."

"We're staying a while, Miss Fay," Meyer said, "so get off your high horse. How'd you figure you were helping us? By sending us on a wild-goose chase confirming alibis you knew were false?"

"I didn't know anything. I told you just what Arthur told me."

"That's a lie."

"Why don't you get out?" Eleanor said. "Or are you hoping I'll take off my sweater again?"

"What you've got, we've already seen, lady," Carella said. He turned to the man. "What's your name?"

"Don't tell him," Eleanor said.

"Here or uptown, take your choice," Carella said. "Arthur Finch has broken jail, and we're trying to find him. If you want to be accessories to—"

"Broken jail?" Eleanor went a trifle pale. She glanced at the man on the couch, and their eyes met.

"Wh—when did this happen?" the man asked.

"About ten o'clock tonight."

The man was silent for several moments. "That's not so good," he said at last.

"How about telling us who you are," Carella suggested.

"Frederick Schultz," the man said.

"That makes it all very cozy, doesn't it?" Meyer said.

"Get your mind out of the gutter," Eleanor said. "I'm not Finch's girl, and I never was."

"Then why'd you say you were?"

"I didn't want Freddie to get involved in this thing."

"How could he possibly get involved?"

Eleanor shrugged.

"What is it? Was Finch with Freddie on Saturday night?"

Eleanor nodded reluctantly.

"From what time to what time?"

"From seven to ten," Freddie said.

"Then he couldn't have killed the rabbi."

"Who said he did?" Freddie answered.

"Why didn't you tell us this?"

"Because . . ." Eleanor started, and then stopped dead.

"Because they had something to hide," Carella said. "Why'd he come to see you, Freddie?"

Freddie did not answer.

"Hold it," Meyer said. "This is the other Jew-hater, Steve. The one Finch's sister told me about. Isn't that right, Freddie?"

Freddie did not answer.

"Why'd he come to see you, Freddie? To pick up those pamphlets we found in his closet?"

"You the guy who prints that crap, Freddie?"

"What's the matter, Freddie? Weren't you sure how much of a crime was involved?"

"Did you figure he'd tell us where he got the stuff, Freddie?"

"You're a real good pal, aren't you, Freddie? You'd send your friend to the chair rather than—"

"I don't owe him anything!" Freddie said.

"Maybe you owe him a lot. He was facing a murder rap, but he never once mentioned your name. You went to all that trouble for nothing, Miss Fay."

"It was no trouble," Eleanor said thinly.

"No," Meyer said. "You marched into the precinct with a tight dress and a cockamamie bunch of alibis that you knew we'd check. You figured once we found those to be phony, we wouldn't believe anything else Finch said. Even if he told us where he *really* was, we wouldn't believe it. That's right, isn't it?"

"You finished?" Eleanor asked.

"No, but I think you are," Meyer answered.

"You had no right to bust in here. There's no law against making love."

"Sister," Carella said, "*you* were making hate."

11

Arthur Finch wasn't making anything when they found him.

They found him at ten minutes past two, on the morning of April fourth. They found him in his apartment because a patrolman had been sent there to pick up the pamphlets in his closet. They found him lying in front of the kitchen table. He was still handcuffed. A file and rasp were on the table top, and there were metal filings covering the enamel and a spot on the linoleum floor, but Finch had made only a small dent in the manacles. The filings on the floor were floating in a red, sticky substance.

Finch's throat was open from ear to ear.

The patrolman, expecting to make a routine pick-up, found the body and had the presence of mind to call his patrol-car partner before he panicked. His partner went down to the car and radioed the homicide to headquarters, who informed Homicide South and the detectives of the 87th Squad.

The patrolmen were busy that night. At 3 A.M., a citizen called in to report what he thought was a leak in a water main on South Fifth. The radio dispatcher at headquarters sent a car to investigate, and the patrolman found that nothing was wrong with the water main, but something was interfering with the city's fine sewage system.

The men were not members of the Department of Sanitation, but they nonetheless climbed down a manhole into the stink and garbage, and located a man's black suit caught on an orange crate and blocking a pipe, causing the water to back up into the street. The man's suit was spattered with white and blue paint. The patrolmen were ready to throw it into the nearest garbage can when one of them noticed it was also spattered with something that could have been dried blood. Being conscientious law-enforcement officers, they combed the garbage out of their hair and delivered the garment to their precinct house—which happened to be the 87th.

Meyer and Carella were delighted to receive the suit.

It didn't tell them a goddamned thing about who owned it, but it nonetheless indicated to them that whoever had killed the rabbi was now busily engaged in covering his tracks and this, in turn, indicated a high state of anxiety. Somebody had heard the news broadcast announcing Finch's escape. Somebody had been worried about Finch establishing an alibi for himself that would doubtlessly clear him.

With twisted reasoning somebody figured the best way to cover one homicide was to commit another. And somebody had hastily decided to get rid of the garments he'd worn while disposing of the rabbi.

The detectives weren't psychologists, but two mistakes had been committed in the same early morning, and they figured their prey was getting slightly desperate.

"It has to be another of Finch's crowd," Carella said. "Whoever killed Solomon painted a *J* on the wall. If he'd had time, he probably would have drawn a swastika as well."

"But why would he do that?" Meyer asked. "He'd automatically be telling us that an anti-Semite killed the rabbi."

"So? How many anti-Semites do you suppose there are in this city?"

"How many?" Meyer asked.

"I wouldn't want to count them," Carella said. "Whoever killed Yaakov Solomon was bold enough to—"

"Jacob," Meyer corrected.

"Yaakov, Jacob, what's the difference? The killer was bold enough to presume there were plenty of people who felt *exactly* the way he did. He painted that *J* on the wall and dared us to find *which* Jew-hater had done the job," Carella paused. "Does this bother you very much, Meyer?"

"Sure, it bothers me."

"I mean, my saying—"

"Don't be a boob, Steve."

"Okay. I think we ought to look up this woman again. What was her name? Hannah something. Maybe she knows—"

"I don't think that'll help us. Maybe we ought to talk to the rabbi's wife. There's indication in his diary that he knew the killer, that he'd had threats. Maybe she knows who was baiting him."

"It's four o'clock in the morning," Carella said. "I don't think it's a good idea right now."

"We'll go after breakfast."

"It won't hurt to talk to Yirmiyahu again, either. If the rabbi was threatened, maybe—"

"Jeremiah," Meyer corrected.

"What?"

"Jeremiah. Yirmiyahu is Hebrew for Jeremiah."

"Oh. Well, anyway, him. It's possible the rabbi took him into his confidence, mentioned this—"

"Jeremiah," Meyer said again.

"What?"

"No." Meyer shook his head. "That's impossible. He's a holy man. And if there's anything a really good Jew despises, it's—"

"What are you talking about?" Carella said.

"—it's killing. Judaism teaches that you don't murder, unless in self-defense." His brow suddenly furrowed into a frown. "Still, remember when I was about to light that cigarette? He asked me if I was Jewish—remember? He was shocked that I would smoke on the second day of Passover."

"Meyer, I'm a little sleepy. Who are you talking about?" Carella wanted to know.

"Yirmiyahu. Jeremiah. Steve, you don't think—"

"I'm just not following you, Meyer."

"You don't think . . . you don't think the rabbi painted that wall *himself,* do you?"

"Why would . . . what do you mean?"

"To tell us who'd stabbed him? To tell us who the killer was?"

"How would—"

"Jeremiah," Meyer said.

Carella looked at Meyer silently for a full thirty seconds. Then he nodded and said, *"J. "*

12

He was burying something in the backyard behind the synagogue when they found him. They had gone to his home first and awakened his wife. She was an old Jewish woman, her head shaved in keeping with the Orthodox tradition. She covered her head with a shawl, and she sat in the kitchen of her ground-floor apartment and tried to remember what had happened on the second night of Passover. Yes, her husband had gone to the synagogue for evening services. Yes, he had come home directly after services.

"Did you see him when he came in?" Meyer asked.

"I was in the kitchen," Mrs. Cohen answered. "I was preparing the *seder.* I heard the door open, and he went in the bedroom."

"Did you see what he was wearing?"

"No."

"What was he wearing during the *seder?*"

"I don't remember."

"Had he changed his clothes, Mrs. Cohen? Would you remember that?"

"I think so, yes. He had on a black suit when he went to temple. I think he wore a different suit after." The old woman looked bewildered. She didn't know why they were asking these questions. Nonetheless, she answered them.

"Did you smell anything strange in the house, Mrs. Cohen?"

"Smell?"

"Yes. Did you smell paint?"

"Paint? No. I smelled nothing strange."

They found him in the yard behind the synagogue.

He was an old man with sorrow in his eyes and in the stoop of his posture. He had a shovel in his hands, and he was patting the earth with the blade. He nodded, as if he knew why they were there. They faced each other across the small mound of freshly turned earth at Yirmiyahu's feet.

Carella did not say a solitary word during the questioning and arrest. He stood next to Meyer Meyer, and he felt only an odd sort of pain.

"What did you bury, Mr. Cohen?" Meyer asked. He spoke very softly. It was five o'clock in the morning, and night was fleeing the sky. There was a slight chill on the air. The wind seemed to penetrate to the sexton's marrow. He seemed on the verge of shivering. "What did you bury, Mr. Cohen? Tell me."

"A ritual object," the sexton answered.

"*What,* Mr. Cohen?"

"I have no further use for it. It is a ritual object. I am sure it had to be buried. I must ask the *rov.* I must ask him what the Talmud says." Yirmiyahu fell silent. He looked at the mound of earth at his feet. "The *rov* is dead, isn't he?" he said, almost to himself. "He is dead." He looked sadly into Meyer's eyes.

"Yes," Meyer answered.

"Baruch dayyan haemet," Yirmiyahu said. "You are Jewish?"

"Yes," Meyer answered.

"Blessed be God the true judge," Yirmiyahu translated, as if he had not heard Meyer.

"What did you bury, Mr. Cohen?"

"The knife," Yirmiyahu said. "The knife I used to trim the wick. It *is* a ritual object, don't you think? It should be buried, don't you think?" He paused. "You see . . ." His shoulders began to shake. He began weeping suddenly. "I killed," he said. The sobs started somewhere deep within the man, started wherever his roots were, started in the soul of the man, in the knowledge that he had committed the unspeakable crime—thou shalt not kill, thou shalt not kill. "I killed," he said again, but this time there were only tears, no sobs.

"Did you kill Arthur Finch?" Meyer asked.

The sexton nodded.

"Did you kill Rabbi Solomon?"

"He . . . you see . . . he was working. It was the second day of Passover, and he was working. I was inside when I heard the noise. I went to look and . . . he was carrying paints, paint cans in one hand, and . . . and a ladder in the other. He was *working.* I . . . took the knife from the ark, the knife I used to trim the wick. I had told him before this. I had told him he was not a *real* Jew, that his new . . . his new ways would be the end of the Jewish people. And this, *this!* To work on the second day of Passover!"

"What happened, Mr. Cohen?" Meyer asked gently.

"I—the knife was in my hand. I went at him with the knife. He—he tried to stop me. He threw paint at me. I—I—" The sexton's right hand came up as if clasped around a knife. The hand trembled as it unconsciously reenacted the events of that night. "I cut him. I cut him. . . . I killed him."

Yirmiyahu stood in the alley with the sun intimidating the peaks of the buildings now. He stood with his head bent, staring down at the mound of earth which covered the buried knife. His face was thin and gaunt, a face tormented by the centuries. The tears still spilled from his eyes and coursed down his cheeks. His shoulders shook with the sobs that came from somewhere deep in his guts. Carella turned away because it seemed to him in that moment that he was watching the disintegration of a man, and he did not want to see it.

Meyer put his arm around the sexton's shoulder.

"Come, *tsadik*," he said. "Come. You must come with me now."

The old man said nothing. His hands hung loosely at his sides.

They began walking slowly out of the alley. As they passed the painted
J on the synagogue wall, the sexton said, *"Olov ha-shalom."*

"What did he say?" Carella asked.

"He said, 'Peace be upon him.' "

"Amen," Carella said.

They walked silently out of the alley together.

Burial Monuments Three

EDWARD D. HOCH

Edward D. Hoch, one of the most prolific and popular of today's writers of criminous short stories, has probably invented more series detective characters than any writer, past or present. No less than a baker's dozen have appeared in three novels, four collections, and hundreds of short stories in Ellery Queen's Mystery Magazine *and other leading crime digests. "Burial Monuments Three," however, a nonseries story, is one of his finest tales yet—the strong, underplayed account of a vacationing newsman and a strange young woman whose lives intersect in a sleepy rural hamlet.*

The country was strange to him after he'd turned off the main road. He'd entered it suddenly, unexpectedly, and marveled that such a place could rest undiscovered just a mile or so off the turnpike. He slowed his little car, as much for the breathtaking view as for the sudden clanking that came from the motor.

The road had petered out into dust, and as soon as the car hit the unfamiliar surface it had begun its strange complaints. Hampton slowed almost to a stop, taking the rest of the dusty trail in low gear, heading downward into a sort of valley that seemed filled with lush fruit trees. Beyond the orchards he passed level pastures and gently grazing cows. Farther on, he came to an unmarked crossroad, and as he pondered the map he took from his glove compartment, a farmer's truck slowed to a stop beside him.

"Having trouble, mister?"

"The car's acting up. Is there a garage anywhere nearby?"

"Nearest garage would be in Random Corners. Go straight down this road for about three miles. You can't miss it."

"Thanks." Hampton waved an arm at the helpful farmer and continued down the dusty road.

He probably would have driven right past the little general store that marked all there was of Random Corners, except that he caught sight of the battered twin gas pumps standing at the side of the building. The garage, he determined, must be around back, and he pulled in by the pumps.

"Want gas?" someone called from inside the store. A tired-looking man with a lantern jaw appeared in the doorway.

"Something's wrong with the car. A farmer told me you had a garage here."

"Sure." The man came forward, down the steps to the little car. "Don't work much on these foreign jobs, though."

Hampton opened the hood for him and they puttered around together, working among the wires and spark plugs. After about a half hour the tired-looking man brought some new plugs and parts from the little garage around the rear of the store. "That should fix you up," he said. "Best I can do, anyway." He wiped the grease from his hands and went back into the general store.

Hampton followed him up the rotting wooden steps and through a rusty screen door advertising a popular brand of bread. "What do I owe you?" he asked.

The man wet the stub of his pencil in his mouth and wrote some figures on a scrap of paper. "Comes to eleven-ninety-five for parts, and I guess another five dollars for labor. That sound all right?"

"Sure." Hampton reached for his wallet.

"Got a special this week on charcoal. For picnics, you know."

"Get many picnickers around here?"

"Not many," the man answered sadly. "That's why we got the special."

"I see." He paid the man for the auto repair.

"Don't get much of anything around Random Corners. Except cows."

"It seems a pleasant enough place," Hampton said, making conversation.

"Nice in the summer. Turnpike keeps everybody away, though. They just pass us by. You visiting someone?"

"No. Just on vacation. Exploring some back roads."

The man peered more intently in Hampton's direction, adjusting his glasses for a better look. "Haven't I seen you before? What'd you say your name was?"

Hampton smiled a bit. It always happened, sooner or later. "I didn't, but it's Steve Hampton. You've probably seen me on television."

"You're that news guy!"

"That's right. But this month I'm just a vacation guy."

"Wait till I tell folks you stopped here to get your car fixed!"

The screen door banged and another customer entered. She was a young blond girl, with hair hanging loosely halfway down her back. She wore no makeup, and didn't need any. Hampton guessed her to be about nineteen or twenty, though she might have been younger. The man's shirt she wore was neat and tight, tucked into clean but well-worn jeans.

"Morning, Harry," she said, ignoring Hampton at first.

"Morning, Janie. How's things up in the woods?"

She flushed a bit as she noticed Hampton staring at her. "Same as down here, Harry. Got my order?"

"Just a minute." He checked over the list in front of him, penciled on a torn piece of gray cardboard. "Everything but the potatoes, Janie. Want to get them out of the storeroom yourself?"

"Sure." She vanished into the back with a jaunty swing of her hips.

"Cute girl," Hampton said. He still noticed cute girls, even at forty-one.

"Sure is," the man agreed. "Her name's Janie Mason. Lives up in the woods, all alone. Too bad about her."

"What's too bad?" Hampton asked, feeling the beginning of a chill on the back of his neck.

"Oh, she's had a hard life. It's left her a little bit . . . strange, you know. She lives in her own world, and nobody bothers much with her."

"You mean she's mentally retarded?"

"Retarded, mixed up. I don't know what you call it back in the city. There were four of them up there ten years ago, and now she's all alone. Her father, mother, and uncle all died."

"Died?" He was about to pursue it when the girl returned, carrying a sack of potatoes.

"That's everything I think." She took out some money and paid Harry.

"Can you manage it all right, Miss Janie?"

She nodded and lifted the two bags with difficulty.

"I'll help," Hampton said, for no good reason except that she was a cute girl.

She flashed him a grateful smile. "Thanks a lot."

"Where's your car?"

"I don't have a car. I walk."

He blinked and stared at her. "Well, I don't, I'm afraid I didn't realize . . ." But there was only one way out. "Well, I've got my car. I'll give you a ride home if you're not afraid of strangers."

"Thanks. I stopped being afraid of anything a long time ago." She followed him to the little car and waited while he piled the bags in the back seat. Then she said, "You're Steve Hampton, aren't you? I see you on television every night."

"The price of fame," he said with a smile. "I'm on vacation, really. I picked this little valley because I figured nobody would know me here."

"We have television sets," she said a bit indignantly. "Just like in the city."

"I know. I stand corrected." He gunned the engine and started off, pleased that it seemed to be running well again. "Now, which way is home?"

"Straight down this road. It isn't far."

"Do you live alone?"

"Yes. You really are a newsman, aren't you?" The breeze from the open windows had caught at her hair. "I heard you and Harry talking about me, back at the store."

It was his turn to blush, and he hoped she didn't notice. "I'm sorry about that. I don't usually talk about people behind their backs."

She turned toward him in the front seat. "Why not? Everyone else does."

He swerved the car a bit to avoid a cow at the side of the road. "How do you manage it, living alone out here?"

"I manage."

"Don't you want to get away, meet people your own age?"

"I promised I'd stay," she said quietly. "When all the others left."

There was a catch in her voice as she spoke the words, and he decided not to pursue the subject for the moment. After all, he was only giving her a ride home. "Are we nearly there?"

"Right up here on the left."

They passed a patch of woods that suddenly ended to reveal a small plot of farmland and a shabby house and barn, both in need of painting. The television antenna seemed the only modern touch in sight, and even this was cocked at a precarious angle.

"How do you manage to take care of it all by yourself?" he asked, pulling the car up in front.

"It's not easy. I've had to sell off all the cows and pigs. I guess maybe someday I'll have to get rid of everything." She'd grown serious, but suddenly her mood brightened. "Anyway, thanks for the ride. It's nearly a mile's walk, and these bags can get heavy."

"Could I carry them into the house for you, as long as I've come this far?"

"Thanks." Inside, she motioned him toward a table and said, "At least this calls for a cup of coffee."

He hesitated, but knew he would accept. There was something about his first step over the threshold that had decided him. The place had a not-quite-right feeling about it that roused his curiosity. It was something like entering another world, a world he'd never known. "All right," he told her. "A quick one."

She went busily to work with the coffeepot on the somewhat primitive stove. "It'll just be a minute."

"You really do live here alone," he said.

"I do now, for a while."

"But this house is so strange. You have the shades pulled on all the windows."

"The neighbors snoop," she answered simply. "You really are a newsman, aren't you? Curious about everything."

"Not a snooper, I hope. Not while I'm on vacation." He sipped the coffee. "This is very good."

"Let me snoop for a while. I know from the TV magazine that you're married, with children and all. Where are they?"

"I'm married, yes. With children and all. But right now I'm vacationing from that, too."

"You've left your wife?"

He took another swallow of coffee. "It's a long, dull story. Just like my marriage. Let's talk about something more pleasant, like you."

She smiled, enjoying the compliment, enjoying the perhaps unaccustomed role of being a woman. "What brought you to Random Corners, though? People don't come here much on vacation. Are you after a story?"

"Are there any here to find?"

Her expression was suddenly conspiratorial, as if the young woman of a moment ago had been replaced by a little girl. "I could show you something," she confided. "I could show you where they're buried."

"Who? Your family?"

"Yes."

"And where is that?"

"Near here, back in the woods."

He was beginning to think the man in the store might have been right about her. "Do you want to show me?"

"I could. If you promise not to use it on television."

"I promise."

"Then we'll go. So come on."

Go, he thought. *Down the rabbit hole with Alice, along the yellow brick road with Dorothy, into the woods with Janie Mason.*

Outside, the clouds of a possible storm were gathering on the western horizon, a blot on the perfect summer's day. "Is it far?" he asked the girl as they started back across the fields. He didn't want to be caught in the rain.

"Not far."

She led him through knee-high grass that looked as if it had gone untended for years, and suddenly he felt transported to the past, to some long-forgotten afternoon of his own youth. Was it only chance that had led him to Random Corners and this girl?

"What happened to your family, Janie?" he asked her as they reached the edge of the woods. "How did they die?" They were questions he had to ask, though he almost feared the answers.

She paused by a tree, running her fingers over the rough bark as if she'd never felt it before. "How did they die? I thought you knew. I thought Harry told you. They were murdered. All of them were murdered."

They went farther into the woods, and now Hampton could barely make out the sky with its thickening clouds. Occasionally the pace forced him to pause and catch his breath, but Janie Mason seemed as fresh as when they'd started.

Finally she stopped and held up a finger for silence, like someone entering a great cathedral. "We're here," she announced in a whisper.

Ahead, in a little clearing, he could make out the tops of three crude gravestones among the weeds. He walked a bit closer, with reverence to match her mood, until he could read the names scratched upon the stone:

HENRY MASON, DEVOTED FATHER

ANNA MASON, LOVING MOTHER

ROBERT MASON, LOYAL UNCLE

The year of their deaths was scratched on the stones too, and it was the same for each of them—three years earlier. Both father and mother had been in their early forties. The uncle had been a few years younger.

"Who killed them?" he asked her.

"Me," she answered simply, but then went on: "Or you. Or all of us. Did you ever think that a crime as personal as murder could be the product of so many hands?" The child Janie had gone, and she was an adult once more, a lovely young lady standing in a clearing in the woods.

"You sound like a philosopher," he said. "All I asked was who killed them."

"It was a member of the family." She turned her face away as she spoke.

"How old were you then, Janie?"

"Seventeen. I was seventeen that summer."

"And a member of the family killed them?"

"Yes."

"But there were only the four of you?"

"Yes. No others."

"Was it a double murder and a suicide?"

"In a way you could call it that, yes."

"Who buried them here?"

"I did."

"Yourself? Alone?"

"Yes."

"But wasn't there a funeral?"

She smiled slightly. "There was a funeral, but nobody came to it. I brought them back here in the wheelbarrow, one at a time, and said some prayers over them. Then I buried them."

"Yes," he said quietly; and then, "We'd better be getting back soon. It's going to rain."

She glanced up at the sky, seeing the filtered gray light through the curtain of leaves. "I know a place where we can go. Over here."

She led him to the opposite side of the clearing, to a low flat rock that protruded from a hillside. She scurried beneath the rock as the wind began to come up, and motioned for him to follow.

"It's a cave!" he said, surprised.

"Not really, just a little shelter. It only goes back about ten feet into the hill. I built it the first year, when I used to come here and sit by the graves. I scooped it out myself with a shovel. You're dry in here when it rains, and you can see the three graves."

"Why do you want to see them?" he asked, lying beside her on his stomach.

"Why? Because we should honor the dead, I guess. No matter what they were in life."

The darkening scene before them was lit suddenly by a blinding flash of lightning that seemed to play among the trees, and the thunder which followed immediately blended into the torrent of rain on the leaves. He turned to face this strange girl at his side, and saw a second flash of lightning whiten her skin with an eerie glow. In that instant she might have been a witch or a murderess, but in the next she was only a girl named Janie Mason. He slipped his arm gently around her taut body.

"Do you come here often with men?" he asked, not really caring. His wife was a lifetime away just then, in another world.

"Does it matter?"

"No."

"Does it matter if I killed them?"

Thunder crashed above the trees. He shifted position and drew her closer. "You didn't kill anybody."

"How do you know?"

"I know. I've met a few murderers in my time, and you're not one of them. How did it happen?"

She stared out at the rain, seeing perhaps something that was beyond his vision. "My father caught them together, and then he killed them."

He nodded. It was the oldest story in the world, brother against brother; as old as Cain and Abel. "Tell me about the day they died. Tell me why you buried them yourself, rather than call the police."

"Yes," she said vaguely. "The day they died." She fell silent then, and for a time there was only the sound of the rain. Nothing else moved, not the birds nor the animals. All waited in silence for the rain to stop. "The day they died," she began finally, breaking the silence. "The day they died the sun was shining, and it was in the spring. I remember I was out in the fields, working with my father, and my uncle was back in the house with mother."

"And what happened?" he urged.

"There was something—some sound that I didn't even hear. But father did. His ears perked up a bit, like a dog hearing one of those high-pitched whistles. He turned and stared at the house, and then without a word he put down the posthole digger he was using and walked back across the field. I didn't know what to do, so I just stayed there, working, until I heard mother scream."

"You knew then what it was."

"No, not really. I couldn't imagine it being anything more serious than a mouse."

"Farm wives don't scream at mice."

"No, I suppose not."

"How was it done? How did he kill them?"

She stared out at the rain. "With an ax, like the Bordens."

"Except that the Bordens were probably killed by Lizzie, their daughter."

Overhead, the lightning crackled again, then the thunder swept over them with a roar, coming like a giant wave on some distant beach, but the rain began to let up a bit as the storm moved somewhere beyond them. "I didn't kill anybody," she said.

"I know you didn't. I told you that. But what about the funeral? Wasn't there a police investigation?"

"There are no police in Random Corners. I would have had to call in the state troopers."

"Why didn't you?"

"There were reasons." She stared into his eyes. "A mystery may exist for strangers like yourself that is only a passing curiosity to local residents. No one here ever worried that the police weren't called, or that there was no formal funeral for them."

"How many people live here?"

"Only about a dozen, and they mind their own business. They don't like strangers, especially police."

"Would that include me?"

"Maybe."

The rain had almost stopped, and he pulled himself out of the little cave. She followed, and he stood for a moment facing her.

"Did it happen like you say?" he asked.

"Yes. My father found them like that and killed them."

"And you buried them."

"Yes."

"All three, right? Just like that."

"Yes."

"I don't believe you. I don't think any girl could bury her parents and uncle by herself like that, and simply go on living here. What's the truth Janie? One of those graves is empty, isn't it?"

"What do you mean?" Her face froze at his words.

"Your father didn't kill himself, did he? His grave is empty, isn't it?"

"I have a shovel if you want to dig," she told him. "I keep it back in the cave."

"Why? To dig them up, or to bury more?"

She didn't answer. She had disappeared back into the cave, and when she reappeared she had a rusty, long-handled shovel in one hand. "Here, dig if you want to!"

"I don't want to," he said. "I've got to be getting back." Somewhere overhead he caught the sound of a passing jet, and for a moment he was back in the world of reality. Then the sound gradually faded, leaving him facing this strange girl with the shovel she held outstretched to him.

"Dig," she said again.

He took the rusty shovel from her and plunged it into the wet earth of her father's grave. "If I lived here, I'd know. Wouldn't I, Janie?"

"Yes."

"I'd know what everyone in Random Corners knows—that your father killed them and then buried them back here, with an extra, empty grave for himself."

Her frightened eyes darted from his face, back toward the woods through which they'd come. He followed her gaze and saw a sudden shaft of sunlight catch the rain-drenched leaves; that, and something more— a man, walking toward them, with a woodsman's ax hanging loosely from his right hand.

"No," Janie whispered, the word catching in her throat.

"I'd know that your father was still right here in Random Corners, Janie. I'd know that, even though his name was Henry, everybody called him Harry when they shopped at his little store and gas station."

The tired man with the latern jaw stepped into the clearing and paused, facing them with his ax. "How much does he know, Janie?"

"Everything," she sobbed. "He knows your grave is empty, and he knows you never went away."

"Hello, Mr. Mason," Hampton said quietly, feeling the smooth wood of the shovel's handle against his sweating palms. "You warned me she was mixed up, but I wouldn't listen, would I?"

"My wife and brother were evil," he said quietly. "Removing them was God's justice, not mine. It was a kindness, really, and everyone in town knew it. That's why nobody ever told the police. I made an extra grave for myself, and moved down to the store, and nobody ever told." He shifted the ax and started to raise it. "Until now."

"Don't kill him, daddy!" the girl screamed. "He won't tell anyone!"

But the ax kept coming, until it was level with Henry Mason's head. "He'll tell the whole country on the TV. That's what he came here for in the first place!"

Hampton saw the ax coming at him, and he dodged to one side as the blade caught the padded shoulder of his jacket. Then, in a motion he'd practiced on the golf course a thousand times, he brought the long-handled shovel around in a wide arc before Henry Mason could swing his ax again. He was aiming at the weapon, or the man, or both—and the edge of the shovel caught Mason along the left temple with a dull, clanging sound.

It hardly seemed that the blow was enough to kill a man, but perhaps Henry Mason had lived too long already.

"We'll have to call the police," Hampton told the girl.

She looked up from the ground, where she held her father's head in her arms. "What good will that do? We'll bury him in his grave, and no one will ever know."

"We can't do that, Janie!"

"We can. We will. You were just a stranger passing through. Why should you suffer for this?"

Why, indeed? suddenly he was anxious to be back with his family, back to the relative normalcy of New York, where at least madness came in more familiar varieties. "I don't know," he said.

"Don't think about it. We'll do it."

He stood staring down at the body of the man he had killed. Then, after a time, he shifted his gaze to the waiting gravestone. He knew what he was doing was wrong, but he knew, too, that it was the only way out for him. No one had come to Mason's first funeral, and no one would miss him now. The people of Random Corners never asked questions.

He bent and picked up the shovel.

The Murder
and Fatal Woman

JOYCE CAROL OATES

These are two short and terrifying suspense stories by Joyce Carol Oates, probably the most prolific and honored short-story writer in the history of American literature, Guggenheim Fellow, winner of the National Book Award and member of the Institute of Arts and Letters. It is a little-known fact that William Faulkner sustained himself during his out-of-print decade partly by writing for Ellery Queen's Mystery Magazine *and similar markets; Joyce Carol Oates, in a similar pinch, could almost certainly do the same. In these stories the genre fractures underneath her protagonists, driving them and the reader to that pure and terrible place beneath purpose from which the best of Oates's fiction has always emerged.*

THE MURDER

A gunshot.

The crowd scrambles to its feet, turmoil at the front of the room, a man lies dying.

The smell of gunpowder is everywhere.

It has not happened. He stands there, alive, living. His shoulders loom up thick and square: the cut of his dark suit is jaunty. He is perfect. He shuffles a stack of papers and leans forward confidently against the podium. Those hands are big as lobster claws. He adjusts the microphone, bending it up to him. He is six and a half feet tall, my father, much taller than the man who has just introduced him, and this gesture—abrupt and a little comic—calls our attention to the fact.

Mr. Chairman, I want to point out no less than five irregularities in this morning's session.

That voice. It is in my head. I am leaning forward, anxious not to miss anything. What color is his suit exactly? I don't know. I am not in Washington with him; I am watching this on television. It is important that I know the color of his suit, of his necktie, across the distance. That voice! It is enough to paralyze me, safe here, safe here at home.

It is evident that the Sawyer report was not taken seriously by this committee . . . we wish to question the integrity of these proceedings. . . . A ripple of applause. His voice continues, gaining strength. Nothing has really begun yet—the men are jockeying for position, preparing themselves with stacks of papers, words, definitions. It has the air of a play in rehearsal, not yet ready to be viewed by the public, the dialogue only partly memorized, the actors fumbling to get hold of the story, the plot.

Look at him standing there. He speaks without hesitation, as if his role is written and he possesses it utterly. So sizable a man, my father!—the very soles of his shoes are enough to stamp out ordinary people. His voice is aristocratic. His voice is savage. Listen to that voice. *I request a definition of your curious phrase "creeping internationalism of American institutions"*—

Laughter. The camera shifts to show the audience in the gallery, a crowd of faces. I am one of those faces.

—most respectfully request a definition of "bleeding-heart humanists"—

Scattered laughter, the laughter of individuals. It is mocking, dangerous. The distinguished men of the committee sit gravely, unsmiling, and their counterparts in the audience are silent. Who are the people, like my father, who dare to laugh? They are dangerous men.

He was almost shot, some months ago. The man was apprehended at once. He had wanted to kill my father, to warn my father. But the shot had gone wild; the future was untouched.

His voice continues. The session continues. When the camera scans the audience I lean forward, here in Milwaukee. I need to see, to *see.* Is his murderer there in the audience?

My father is a man who will be murdered.

There are reasons for his murder. Look. Look at my mother: she is striding towards this room, her face flushed and grim. She is seeking me out. Her hair is in crazy tufts, uncombed, gray hair with streaks of red.

She jerks the door open. "What the hell?" she cries. "Are you still watching that?"

She stands in the doorway of my room and will not enter. It is one of her eccentricities—not to enter my room.

"Have you been watching that all day?" she says.

"It's—it's a very important hearing—"

"Turn it off! You need to go out and get some air."

I get to my feet.

My fingers on the knob—my head bowed—I stand above my father. He is a handsome man, but he cannot help me. He is a very handsome man. People stare after him. In the street, in a hotel lobby, anywhere people stare.

He was born to be stared at by women.

I am prepared to take my place in this story.

I am twenty-three and I have a life somewhere ahead of me, I believe. As I brush my long black hair I think about this life ahead of me, waiting. You see my fresh, unlined face, these two enormous strands of black hair, the white part in the center of my skull, the eyes. Dark eyes, like his. You see the pale, rather plain face, the ears pierced with tiny golden dots, almost invisible. You are dismayed as I walk across the room because my shoulders are slumped as if in weariness. I am round-shouldered, and I have grown to an unwomanly height. Deep inside me is a spirit that is also round-shouldered. Smaller women dart ahead of me, through doors or into waiting arms. I lumber along after them, a smile on my face, perspiring inside my dark, plain clothes. I am weighed down by something sinister that gathers in my face, a kind of glower, a knowledge perhaps.

I wake suddenly, as always. I sit up in bed. I remember the hearings and wonder if anything has happened to him overnight. There are no sessions scheduled for today. I dress slowly and brush my hair. I am preparing myself for anything, and it may be to review the clippings on my bureau—articles on him or by him, some with photographs.

He has moved away permanently.

Always, he has traveled. I remember him carrying a single suitcase, backing away, saying good-bye. His hearty, happy good-byes! I would follow him on the globe in his old study, so many times, pressing my forefinger against the shape of the country. There, there he was. Precisely there.

He is going to visit. I know this. He is nearby. This morning he is nearby.

My mother: nearly as tall as I, in slacks and an old sweater, in old bedroom slippers, a cigarette in her mouth. She smokes perpetually, squinting against the smoke irritably; right now she is arguing on the telephone, one of her sisters. They are both going on a trip around the world, leaving in August. She doesn't really want me to join her, but she keeps after me, nagging me, trying to make me give in. Her sturdy legs are too much for me, her thick thighs, her robust face, her pocketbooks and hats and shoes. She is on the telephone in the kitchen, hunched over, barking with sudden laughter, one side of her face squinting violently against the smoke.

The house: three floors, too large for my mother and me. You could drift through the downstairs and never find anything to sit on. A statue from Ceylon—a ram with sharp, cruel horns—canvases on the walls, like exclamations. A crystal chandelier hangs from the ceiling, large and dangerous. Over the parquet floor there is an immense Oriental rug, rich as a universe. On the mantel there are more statues, smaller ones, figures of human beings and sacred animals, and a large ornamental dagger in its fur sheath, everything filmed over lightly with dust. Everything is pushed together: there is hardly room to walk through it. We live in the back rooms. My mother strides out occasionally to add another table or lamp to the debris, her cigarette smartly in her mouth, the shrewd cold eye of a collector taking in everything, adding it up, dismissing it. We enter the house through the back door.

The street: a city street, town houses and apartment buildings and enormous old homes. On a weekday morning like today you expect to see a face high at one of the windows of these homes, an attic window maybe. You expect to hear a faint scream. We watch television along this street and read the newspapers, staring at the pictures of men in public life.

The water: Lake Michigan frosted and pointed at the shore, a look of polar calm, absolute cold, absolute zero. It is zero here. I can hear the waves beneath the ice. I can hear the waves at the back of my head, always. We who live on the edge of the lake never leave the lake: we carry it around with us in our heads. My father lived in this house for fifteen years, and so he must carry the sound of the waves in his head too.

I was conceived, of course, to the rhythm of Lake Michigan.

He is approaching this house, driving a large car. He eyes the house from a block away, respectful of the enemy. He brakes the car suddenly, because he sees a tall figure appear, coming around the side of the house, her shoulders hunched against the wind. She walks with the hard stride of a soldier getting from one point to another, wanting only to get from one point to another.

A car slows at the curb, and I stare at it, amazed. At such times I may be pretty. But the glower returns, the doubt.

"Audrey! Don't be alarmed, just get in . . . can you talk with me for a few minutes?"

We stare at each other. His face is melancholy for a moment, as if my flat stare has disappointed him. But then he smiles. He smiles and says, "Please get in! You must be freezing!"

"I didn't—I didn't know you were in town—"

"Yes, I am in town. I am here. Have you had breakfast yet?"

"No. Yes. I mean—"

"Get in. Or are you afraid your mother is watching?"

I cannot believe that he is here, that I am so close to him. "But what —what do you want?" I hear myself stammering. He gets out of the car, impatient with me, and seizes my hands. He kisses me, and I recoil from his fierce good humor.

"Forget about your unfortunate mother and come take a ride with me," he says. "Surely you can spare your father ten minutes?" And he gives me a shake, he grips my elbow in the palm of his big hand. There is nothing to do but give in. We drive off, two giant people in a giant automobile.

He says, "And now, my dear, tell me everything!—what you are doing with your life, what your expectations are, whether you can spare your father a month or so of your company—"

I begin to talk. My life: what is there to say about it? I have written him. I imagine him ripping open the envelopes with a big fatherly smile, scanning the first few lines, and then being distracted by a telephone, some person. In one hand he holds my letters. In the other hand he holds the letters from his women. He loses these letters. He crumples them and sticks them in his pockets or thrusts them into drawers, but he loses them in the end.

"And mother is planning—"

"No, never mind your mother. I am not interested in morbid personalities!" he cries.

His sideways grin, his face, his thick dark hair. I laugh at his words. They are not funny, and yet they win me to laughter.

"Audrey, I've moved into another dimension. You know that. You understand me, don't you?"

He squeezes my hand.

"I woke up missing you the other day," he says.

I stare at the dashboard of the car. My eyes are dazzled by the gauges, the dials. I can think of nothing to say. My body is large and heavy and cunning.

"Why are you looking away from me? You won't even look at me!" he says. "And that peculiar little smile—what is that?" He turns the rearview mirror above the windshield so that I can see myself.

"Do you hate me very much?" he says gently.

When I packed to leave that afternoon, my mother stood in the doorway and said in a level, unalarmed voice: "So you're going to live the high life with that bastard? So you're going to move out of here, eh? Please don't plan on coming back, then."

She was amused and cynical, smoking her cigarettes. I was opening and closing drawers.

"I don't mean . . . I don't want to hurt you . . ." I stammered.

"What?"

My suitcases are packed. I am making an end of one part of my life. In the background, beneath my mother's voice, there is the sound of water, waves.

"Women are such fools. I hate women," my mother says.

Some time ago a woman came to visit my mother. I was about fifteen then, and I had just come home from school; I remember that my feet were wet and my hair frizzy and bedraggled, an embarrassment as I opened the door. The woman stared at me. She had a long, powdered face, the lips drawn up sharply into a look of tired festivity. Something had gone on too long. She had been smiling too long. The eyes were bright and beautiful, the lashes black, the hair black but pulled sharply back from her face, almost hidden by a dark mink hat. Though it was winter, she looked warm. Her cheeks were reddened. The lips were coated with lipstick that had formed a kind of crust. She was glittering and lovely, and she reached out to take hold of my wrist.

"Audrey. You're Audrey . . ."

Her eyelids were pinkened, a dark dim pink. I smelled a strange fruity odor about her—not perfume, not powder—something sweet and overdone. Her bare fingers squeezed mine in a kind of spasm.

Then my mother hurried downstairs. The two women looked at each other gravely, as if recognizing each other, but for several seconds they said nothing. They moved forward, both with a slow, almost drugged air: they might have been hurrying to meet and only now, at the last moment, were they held back. "Am I too early?" the woman said.

"No. No. Of course not," my mother said.

The woman took off her coat and let it fall across a sofa—the bronze of her dress clashed with the things in the room. The woman was a surprise, a holiday, a treat.

"I can't seem to stop shivering," the woman laughed.

That evening my mother drank too much. She told me bitterly, "Women are such fools! I hate women."

We take a private car from the airport to the hotel. It is Washington, and yet my father doesn't telephone to say that he is back. "Tomorrow it all begins again," he says. "I want us to have a few hours alone." But he is energetic and eager for it to begin, and I am eager to be present, to watch him. I am scanning the crowds on the sidewalk, for he is in danger, someone could rush up to him at any moment.

He is in an excellent mood. He is bringing me into his life, checking me into the hotel, into a room next to his; he is my father, taking care of me, solicitous and exaggerated. The hotel reminds me of my mother's home—so much ornamentation, rugs thick and muffling, furniture with delicate curved legs.

"Well, this is my home. I live here most of the year," he declares.

We have drinks in the lounge. We chat. I ask him, "Has anyone ever tried to shoot you again?" He laughs—of course not! Who would want to shoot him? He smiles indulgently, as if I've said the wrong thing, and he turns to call the waitress over to him. Another martini, please. There is joy in the way he eats, the way he drinks.

It occurs to me that he is a man with many enemies.

"Why do you look so somber?" he asks me.

"I was worried—I was thinking—"

"Don't worry over me, please, I assure you I don't need it!" he laughs. He pats my hand with a hand that is just like it, though larger. "You sound like a—" and he pauses, his smile tightening as he tries to think of the right word. He is a man who knows words, he knows how to choose the right words, always, but he cannot think of the right word now. And so finally he says, strangely, "—like a woman."

Who is watching us?

Some distance away I see a woman . . . she is standing unnaturally still, alone, watching us. She stands soldily, her feet in low-heeled shoes, and she wears a dark coat buttoned up to the neck, very trim and spare. I find myself thinking in disappointment, *She isn't very pretty.* But really, I can't see her face across the crowded lobby. I feel dizzy with her presence. I would like to point her out to my father.

But he doesn't seem to notice her. He looks everywhere; it is a habit of his to scan everyone's face, to keep an eye on the entrance; but his gaze doesn't settle upon that woman.

We get into a taxi and ride off. It is a suspension of myself, this drifting along in the cab, between the hotel and the chamber where the hearings are taking place. From time to time my father asks me something, as if to keep me attached to him. Or he squeezes my hand.

Photographers move forward to take his picture. They maneuver to get my father and to exclude other people. My father, accustomed to attention, waves genially but does not slow down. He has somewhere to get to: he is a man who has somewhere to be, people waiting for him. I look around the sidewalk to see who is watching us here. I expect to see the woman again, but of course she could not have gotten here so quickly. Is his murderer in this crowd, the man who will leap forward someday and kill my father? Even my father's face, behind its bright mask, is a face of fear.

He too is looking for his murderer.

In the gallery one of his associates sits with me. *Your father is a wonderful man,* he tells me. The proceedings begin. People talk at great length. There is continual movement, spectators in and out, attorneys rising to consult with one another, committee members leaving and returning. I understand nothing will be decided. I understand that no one is here for a decision.

"Mr. Chairman," my father says, barely bothering to stand, "I wish to disagree . . ."

I look around the room, and there she is. She is standing at the very back. She is alone, listening to my father's words, standing very still. She is my secret, this woman! I watch her: her attention never moves from him.

She is staring at *him.* She doesn't notice anyone in the room except him. Her eyes are large, fawnish, very bright.

"Do you hate me very much?" he must ask them all.

Over the weekend we go to one party after another. My father is handsome and noisy with success. I sit and listen to him talking about the terrible, unfathomable future of the United States. I listen to his friends, their agreement. *Everything is accelerated, a totally new style evolves every four or five years now, it's seized upon, mastered, and discarded—a continual revolution,* he says. These conversations are important, they determine the conditions of the world.

"But do you think things are really so bad?" I ask my father when we are alone.

"Have you been listening to all that?" he teases.

I am dragged into taxis, out of taxis. The ceilings of the hotel corridors are very high. The menu for room service lists a bag of potato chips for one dollar. Always there is the sound of a machine whirring, a mechanism to clear the air. We meet in the coffee shop, and eventually we go out to the street, to get in a cab. Once I looked over the roof of the car and saw that woman again—I saw her clearly. She was staring at us. Her purse was large, and she carried it under her arm.

"There is someone—"

"What?" says my father.

"Someone is—"

But the taxi driver needs directions, and I really have nothing to say. I am silent.

Evening: we are shown into a crowded room, a penthouse apartment. The height is apparent; everyone seems elongated, dizzy, walking on the tips of their toes. I watch my father closely; he stands in a circle of people. In this room, awaiting him, there is a woman, and she will look at him in a certain way. They will approach each other, their eyes locking. His elbows move as he gestures; he bumps into someone and apologizes with a laugh.

I find a place to sit. The evening passes slowly. I am sitting alone, and people move around me. I sit quietly, waiting. From time to time my father checks on me, my hair plaited and smooth, my face chaste, innocent.

"Not bored, are you, sweetheart?" he says.

Women are placed strategically in this room: one here, one there, one in a corner, one advancing from the left, one already at his side, leaning against him, her hand on his wrist, the little lips, the dainty nostrils.

I will go to my father and take his arm and tell him quite gently, *You are going to die.*

My face is silent, fixed, my lips frozen into a kind of smile learned from watching other women.

No, I will say nothing. I will not tell him. I am silent. The shot will be precise and as near to silence as a gunshot can be. It will tear into his heart from the corner of a crowded room.

It is a way of making an end.

FATAL WOMAN

The first, the very first time, I became aware of my power over men, I was only twelve years old.

I remember distinctly. Because that was the year of the terrible fire downtown, the old Tate Hotel, where eleven people were burned to death and there was such a scandal. The hotel owner was charged with negligence and there was a trial and a lot of excitement. Anyway, I was walking downtown with one of my girl friends, Holly Turnbull, and there was a boardwalk or something by the hotel, which was just a ruin, what was left of it, and you could smell the smoke, such an ugly smell, and I was looking at the burnt building and I said to Holly: "My God do you smell *that?*" Thinking it was burnt flesh. I swear it was. But Holly pulled my arm and said, "Peggy, there's somebody watching us!"

Well, this man was maybe my father's age. He was just standing there a few yards away, watching me. He wore a dark suit, a white shirt, but no tie. His face was wrinkled on one side, he was squinting at me so hard his left eye was almost closed. You'd think he was going to smile or say something funny, grimacing like that. But no. He just stared. Stared and stared and stared. His lips moved but I couldn't hear what he said—it was just a mumble. It wasn't meant for me to hear.

My hair came to my waist. It was light brown, always shiny and well brushed. I had nice skin: no blemishes. Big brown eyes. A pretty mouth. Figure just starting to be what it is today. I didn't know it, but that man was the first, the very first, to look at me in that special way.

He scared me, though. He smelled like something black and scorched and ugly. Holly and I both ran away giggling, and didn't look back.

As I grew older my attractiveness to men increased and sometimes I almost wished I was an elderly woman!—free at last from the eyes and the winks and the whistles and the remarks and sometimes even the nudges. But that won't be for a while, so I suppose I must live with it. Sometimes I want to laugh, it seems so silly. It seems so crazy. I study myself in the mirror from all angles and I'm not being modest when I say that, in my opinion, I don't *seem* that much prettier than many women I know. Yet I've been in the presence of these women and it always happens if a man or a boy comes along he just skims over the others and when he notices me he stares. There must be something about me, an aura of some kind, that I don't know about.

Only a man would know.

I got so exasperated once, I asked: What is it? Why are you bothering *me?* But it came out more or less humorously.

Gerry Swanson was the first man who really dedicated himself to me —didn't just ogle me or whistle or make fresh remarks—but really fell in love and followed me around and ignored his friends' teasing. He walked by our house and stood across the street, waiting, just waiting for a glimpse of me, and he kept meeting me by accident downtown or outside the high school, no matter if I was with my girl friends and they all giggled like crazy at the sight of him. Poor Gerry Swanson, everybody laughed. I blushed so, I couldn't help it. It made me happy that he was in love with me, but it frightened me too, because he was out of school a few years and seemed a lot older than the boys I knew. (I had a number of boy friends in high school—I didn't want to limit myself to just one. I was very popular; it interfered with my schoolwork to some extent, but I didn't care. For instance, I was the lead in the spring play when I was only a sophomore, and I was on the cheerleading squad for three years, and I was First Maid-in-Waiting to the Senior Queen. I wasn't voted Senior Queen because, as my boy friends said, all the girls were jealous of me and deliberately voted against me, but *all* the boys voted for me. I didn't exactly believe them. I think some of the girls probably voted for me—I had lots of friends—and naturally some of the boys would have voted for other candidates. That's only realistic.) When Gerry came along, I was sixteen. He was working for his father's construction company and I was surprised he would like a girl still in high school, but he did; he telephoned all the time and took me out, on Sundays mainly, to the matinee downtown, because my father didn't trust him, and he tried to buy me things, and wrote letters, and made such a fool of himself everybody laughed at him, and I couldn't help laughing myself. I asked him once what it was: *Why* did he love me so much?

He just swallowed and stared at me and couldn't say a word.

As I've grown older this attractiveness has gradually increased, and in recent weeks it has become something of a nuisance. Maybe I dress provocatively—I don't know. Certainly I don't amble about with my bare midriff showing and my legs bare up to the buttocks, like many other girls, and I've recently had my hair cut quite short, for the warm weather. I have noticed, though, that my navy-blue dress seems to attract attention; possibly it fits my body too tightly. I don't know. I wish certain men would just ignore me. For instance, a black man on the street the other day— a black *police* man, who should know better—was staring at me from behind his sunglasses with the boldest look you could imagine. It was shocking. It was really rude. I gave him a cold look and kept right on walking, but I was trembling inside. Later, I wondered if maybe I should have pretended not to notice. I wondered if he might think I had snubbed him because of the color of his skin—but that had nothing to do with it, not a thing! I'm not prejudiced in any way and never have been.

At the hospital there are young attendants, college-age boys, at the very time of life when they are most susceptible to visual stimulation; they can't help noticing me, and staring and staring. When I took the elevator on Monday to the tenth floor, where Harold's room is, one of the attendants hurried to get on with me. The elevator was empty except for us two. The boy blushed so his face went beet red. I tried to make things casual by remarking on the weather and the pretty petunias out front by the sidewalk, but the boy was too nervous and he didn't say a word until the door opened on the tenth floor and I stepped out. "You're so beautiful!" —he said. But I just stepped out and pretended not to hear and walked down the corridor.

Eddie telephoned the other evening, Wednesday. He asked about Harold and I told him everything I knew, but then he didn't say good-bye, he just kept chattering and chattering—then he asked suddenly if he could come over to see me. That very night. His voice quavered and I was just so shocked!—but I should have seen it coming over the years. I should have seen it coming. I told him it was too late, I was going to bed, but could he please put my daughter on the phone for a minute? That seemed to subdue him.

In church I have noticed our minister watching me, sometimes out of the corner of his eye, as he gives his sermon. He is a few years younger than I am, and really should know better. But I've had this certain effect all my life—when I'm sitting in an audience and there are men addressing the group. I first noticed it, of course, in junior and senior high school, but it didn't seem to be so powerful then. Maybe I wasn't so attractive then. It's always the same: the man addressing us looks around the room, smiling, talking more or less to everyone, and then his eye happens to touch upon me and his expression changes abruptly and sometimes he even loses the thread of what he is saying, and stammers, and has to repeat himself. After that he keeps staring helplessly at me and addresses his words only to me, as if the rest of the audience didn't exist. It's the strangest thing. . . . If I take pity on him I can somehow "release" him, and allow him to look away and talk to the others; it's hard to explain how I do this—I give a nearly imperceptible nod and a little smile and I *will* him to be released, and it works, and the poor man is free.

I take pity on men, most of the time.

Sometimes I've been a little daring, I admit it. A little flirtatious. Once at Mirror Lake there were some young Italian men on the beach, and Harold saw them looking at me, and heard one of them whistle, and there was an unpleasant scene. . . . Harold said I encouraged them by the way I walked. I don't know: I just don't know. It seems a woman's body sometimes might be flirtatious by itself, without the woman herself exactly knowing.

The telephone rang tonight and when I picked up the receiver no one answered.

"Eddie," I said, "is this Eddie? I know it's you, dear, and you shouldn't do this—you know better—what if Barbara finds out, or one of the children? My daughter would be heartbroken to know her own husband is making telephone calls like this—You know better, dear!"

He didn't say a word, but he didn't hang up. I was the one to break the connection.

When I turned off the lights downstairs just now, and checked the windows, and checked the doors to make sure they were locked, I peeked out from behind the living-room shade and I could see someone standing across the street, on the sidewalk. It was that black policeman! But he wasn't in his uniform. I don't think he was in his uniform. He's out there right now, standing there, waiting, watching this house. Just like Gerry Swanson used to.

I'm starting to get frightened.

Everyone tells me to be strong, not to break down—about Harold, they mean; about the way the operation turned out. Isn't it a pity? they say. But he's had a full life, a rich life. You've been married how long—? Happily married. Of course. And your children, and the grandchildren. "A full, rich life." And they look at me with that stupid pity, never seeing me, not *me*, never understanding anything. What do I have to do with an old man, I want to scream at them. What do I have to do with an old dying man?

One of them stood on the sidewalk that day, staring at me. No, it was on a boardwalk. The air stank with something heavy and queer and dark. I giggled, I ran away and never looked back. Now one of them is outside the house at this very moment. He's waiting, watching for me. If I move the blind, he will see me. If I snap on the light and raise the blind even a few inches, he will see me. What has he to do with that old man in the hospital, what have I to do with that old man . . . ? But I can't help being frightened.

For the first time in my life I wonder—what is going to happen?

Agony Column

BARRY N. MALZBERG

If it didn't happen this way it should have. It might not have been easier to take but at least, like the London patrolman on the scene, we could have called it passion—desire is more bearable than design. Perhaps.

Gentlemen:

I enclose my short story, "Three for the Universe," and know you will find it right for your magazine, *Astounding Spirits.*

Yours very truly,
Martin Miller

Dear Contributor:

Thank you for your recent submission. Unfortunately, although we have read it with great interest, we are unable to use it in *Astounding Spirits.* Due to the great volume of submissions we receive, we cannot grant all contributors a personal letter, but you may be sure that the manuscript has been reviewed carefully and its rejection is no com ment upon its literary merit but may be dependent upon one of many factors.

Faithfully,
The Editors

Dear Editors:

The Vietnam disgrace must be brought to an end! We have lost on that stained soil not only our national honor but our very future. The troops must be brought home and we must remember that there is more honor in dissent than in unquestioningly silent agreement.

Sincerely,
Martin Miller

Dear Sir:

Thank you for your recent letter to the editors. Due to the great volume of worthy submissions we are unable to print every good letter we receive and therefore regretfully inform you that while we will not be publishing it, this is no comment upon the value of your opinion.

Very truly yours,
The Editors

Dear Congressman Forthwaite:

I wish to bring your attention to a serious situation which is developing on the West Side. A resident of this neighborhood for five years now, I have recently observed that a large number of streetwalkers, dope addicts and criminal types are loitering at the intersection of Columbus Avenue and Twenty-fourth Street at almost all hours of the day, offending passersby with their appearance and creating a severe blight on the area. In addition, passersby are often threateningly asked for "handouts" and even "solicited." I know that you share with me a concern for a Better West Side and look forward to your comments on this situation as well as some kind of concrete action.

Sincerely,
Martin Miller

Dear Mr. Millow:

Thank you for your letter. Your concern for our West Side is appreciated and it is only through the efforts and diligence of constituents such as yourself that a better New York can be conceived. I have forwarded your letter to the appropriate precinct office in Manhattan and you may expect to hear from them soon.

Gratefully yours,
Alwyn D. Forthwaite

Dear Gentlemen:

In May of this year I wrote Congressman Alwyn D. Forthwaite a letter of complaint, concerning conditions of the Columbus Avenue–West Twenty-fourth Street intersection in Manhattan and was informed by him that this letter was passed on to your precinct office. Since four months have now elapsed, and since I have neither heard from you nor observed any change in the conditions pointed out in my letter, I now write to ask whether or not that letter was forwarded to you and what you have to say about it.

Sincerely,
Martin Miller

Dear Mr. Milner:

Our files hold no record of your letter.

N.B. Karsh
Captain, #33462

Dear Sirs:

I have read Sheldon Novack's article in the current issue of *Cry* with great interest but feel that I must take issue with his basic point, which is that sex is the consuming biological drive from which all other activities stem and which said other activities become only metaphorical for. This strikes me as a bit more of a projection of Mr. Novack's own functioning than that reality which he so shrewdly contends he apperceives.

Sincerely,
Martin Miller

Dear Mr. Milton:

Due to the great number of responses to Sheldon A. Novack's "Sex and Sexuality: Are We Missing Anything?" in the August issue of *Cry*, we will be unable to publish your own contribution in our "Cry from the City" Column, but we do thank you for your interest.

Yours,
The Editors

Dear Mr. President:

I was shocked by the remarks apparently attributed to you in today's newspapers on the public assistance situation. Surely, you must be aware of the fact that social welfare legislation emerged from the compassionate attempt of 1930 politics to deal with human torment in a systematized fashion, and although many of the cruelties you note are inherent to the very system, they do not cast doubt upon its very legitimacy. Our whole national history has been one of coming to terms with collective consciousness as opposed to the law of the jungle, and I cannot understand how you could have such a position as yours.

Sincerely,
Martin Miller

Dear Mr. Meller:

Thank you very much for your letter of October eighteenth to the president. We appreciate your interest and assure you that without the concern of citizens like yourself the country would not be what it has become. Thank you very much and we do look forward to hearing from you in the future on matters of national interest.

Mary L. McGinnity
Presidential Assistant

Gentlemen:
I enclose herewith my article, "Welfare: Are We Missing Anything?" which I hope you may find suitable for publication in *Insight Magazine*.

Very truly yours,
Martin Miller

Dear Contributor:
The enclosed has been carefully reviewed and our reluctant decision is that it does not quite meet our needs at the present time. Thank you for your interest in *Insight*.

The Editors

Dear Senator Partch:
Your vote on the Armament Legislation was shameful.

Sincerely,
Martin Miller

Dear Dr. Mallow:
Thank you for your recent letter to Senator O. Stuart Partch and for your approval of the senator's vote.

L.T. Walters
Congressional Aide

Dear Susan Saltis:
I think your recent decision to pose nude in that "art-photography" series in *Men's Companion* was disgraceful, filled once again with those timeless, empty rationalizations of the licentious which have so little intrinsic capacity for damage except when they are subsumed, as they are in your case, with abstract and vague "connections" to platitudes so enormous as to risk the very demolition of the collective personality.

Yours very truly,
Martin Miller

Dear Sir:

With pleasure and in answer to your request, we are enclosing a photograph of Miss Susan Saltis as she appears in her new movie, *Chariots to the Holy Roman Empire.*

> Very truly yours,
> Henry T. Wyatt
> Publicity Director

Gentlemen:

I wonder if *Cry* would be interested in the enclosed article which is not so much an article as a true documentary of the results which have been obtained from my efforts over recent months to correspond with various public figures, entertainment stars, etc., etc. It is frightening to contemplate the obliteration of self which the very devices of the twentieth century compel, and perhaps your readers might share my (not so retrospective) horror.

> Sincerely,
> Martin Miller

Dear Sir:

As a potential contributor to *Cry*, I am happy to offer you our "Writer's Subscription Discount," meaning that for only five dollars and fifty cents you will receive not only a full year's subscription (twenty-eight percent below newsstand rates, fourteen percent below customary subscriptions) but in addition our year-end special issue, *Cry in the Void*, at no extra charge.

> Subscription Dept.

Dear Contributor:

Thank you very much for your article, "Agony Column." It has been considered here with great interest and it is the consensus of the Editorial Board that while it has unusual merit it is not quite right for us. We thank you for your interest in *Cry* and look forward to seeing more of your work in the future.

> Sincerely,
> The Editors

Dear Congressman Forthwaite:

Nothing has been done about the conditions I mentioned in my letter of about a year ago. Not one single thing!

Bitterly,
Martin Miller

Dear Mr. Mills:

Please accept our apologies for the delay in answering your good letter. Congressman Forthwaite has been involved, as you know, through the winter in the Food Panel and has of necessity allowed some of his important correspondence to await close attention.

Now that he has the time he thanks you for your kind words of support.

Yours truly,
Ann Ananauris

Dear Sir:

The Adams multiple murders are indeed interesting not only for their violence but because of the confession of the accused that he "did it so that someone would finally notice me." Any citizen can understand this —the desperate need to be recognized as an individual, to break past bureaucracy into some clear apprehension of one's self-worth, is one of the most basic of human drives, but it is becoming increasingly frustrated today by a technocracy which allows less and less latitude for the individual to articulate his own identity and vision and be heard. Murder is easy: it is easy in the sense that the murderer does not need to embark upon an arduous course of training in order to accomplish his feat; his excess can come from the simple extension of sheer human drives . . . aided by basic weaponry. The murderer does not have to cultivate "contacts" or "fame" but can simply, by being *there,* vault past nihilism and into some clear, cold connection with the self. More and more the capacity for murder lurks within us; we are narrow, and driven, we are almost obliterated from any sense of existence, we need to make that singing leap past accomplishment and into acknowledgment and *recognition.* Perhaps you would print this letter?

Hopefully,
Martin Miller

Dear Sir:

Thank you for your recent letter. We regret being unable to use it due to many letters of similar nature being received, but we look forward to your expression of interest.

Sincerely,
John Smith for the Editors

Dear Mr. President:

I intend to assassinate you. I swear that you will not live out the year. It will come by rifle or knife, horn or fire, dread or terror, but it will come, and there is no way that you can AVOID THAT JUDGMENT TO BE RENDERED UPON YOU.

Fuck You,
Martin Miller

Dear Reverend Mellbow:

As you know, the president is abroad at the time of this writing, but you may rest assured that upon his return your letter, along with thousands of other and similar expressions of hope, will be turned over to him and I am sure that he will appreciate your having written.

Very truly yours,
Mary L. McGinnity
Presidential Assistant

Last Rendezvous

JEAN L. BACKUS

Growing old and the loneliness and unhappiness that comes with advancing years is not a unique theme in the criminous short story, but seldom has it been done better than in novelist Jean L. Backus's "Last Rendezvous." This bittersweet and touching account of an elderly woman's confrontation with her past was deservedly nominated for a best short story Edgar by the Mystery Writers of America in 1978.

I resented the old woman's approach, not having driven one hundred and fifty miles along a rugged coast highway to be an unwilling dinner partner at Little River Inn. Particularly so early in my short stay. But I'd been told thirty or forty years ago that a lady was always kind to old people since she herself would be old one day, and perhaps unhappy and lonely as well. Now my time had come, and I had no need to be reminded of my age and circumstances. But as usual I hated to be in the position of rejecting anyone.

"No," I said, as she stood waiting by my table, "nobody's with me. I'm alone." Which was the solitary truth—family dead, friends dead or moved away, everyone I'd ever loved gone off without me.

"It's not good for a woman to eat by herself," she said, sitting in the opposite chair. "And that makes two of us. What are you drinking?"

"Gin and tonic, no fruit." Even then I should have told her I was in a poor mood for company, because her voice and gestures jangled my nerve ends. I looked at her more closely. Short gray hair, carelessly brushed, a blue pants suit, wrinkled and slightly soiled; she looked neglected. My own hair was white, but so far I had not neglected my appearance.

"Why, that's what I drink too," she said, beaming. "I'll have one tonight, I think. Where are you from?"

"The Bay Region."

"I used to live there," she said. "I live here now. This is as close to a home as I'll ever get, unless they put me in the booby hatch someday. What are you going to eat?"

"Petrale sole." I'd stayed at the inn and dined in this room at this table before. Tonight, the sole, tomorrow night the salmon. The next morning I'd be gone, leaving behind all that was precious and good in my life. Only memories now, but once a man had sat opposite me at this table, he down from the north, I up from the south.

For fourteen years we'd met every other month for a weekend together, walking on the beach at the mouth of the river, driving around the headland to watch the surf on the rocks at sunset, and retiring to the same cottage after a superb and leisurely dinner.

"And apricot cobbler." I spoke aloud, out of my thoughts.

"We have rhubarb cobbler tonight," the hostess said at my side. And to the woman across from me, "Miss Barnes, did you ask the lady if she minded your sitting with her?"

"Yes, I did." Miss Barnes flushed unbecomingly. "She didn't tell me I couldn't."

I said, "Perhaps you'll excuse me after all. I intend to eat very slowly tonight, and I have something serious to think about." Immediately I wished I'd kept still. Miss Barnes looked about to weep. But it was too late. The hostess, after a prolonged argument, led her away to another table, somewhere behind me.

The waitress brought me a bowl of clam chowder, and normally I'd have savored every spoonful. As it was, I could hardly swallow. By the time the salad arrived, however, my thoughts were back on Jim and how he'd always ordered oil and vinegar while I took the roquefort dressing.

Food had been one of the things we had in common, although he was married, a drygoods merchant in Eureka, while I was single, a librarian from Concord. I had hobbies and friends, I kept up with the news and theaters and concerts, I read a lot; I was fairly well content. When I met him, he had no interest beyond his work and his children, whom he adored and for whom he maintained the semblance of a marriage. Periodically he had to get away from his wife, and one time we turned up separately here at the inn. Our rooms happened to be next to each other, and on our way to dinner we collided as we locked our doors.

But we sat at separate tables to eat. I certainly hadn't thought of a possible friendship, much less an affair, on that first meeting. Yet, as we acknowledged later, both of us felt the impact of looking at a stranger and thinking how nice it would be if we could have been together.

Call it luck as I did, or fate as Jim did, we kept colliding all the next day—in the village, up Fern Canyon, and finally on the headland at sunset. "This is silly," Jim said as he left his car to come sit in mine.

"Tomorrow let's spend the day together."

It took another accidental weekend before I accepted what Jim said had been obvious and inevitable to him from the beginning. Probably it was his immediate honesty about his family situation that persuaded me to let my unexpectedly insistent fantasies become a reality, because I was never in any doubt as to the source of his interest in me, and if I were honest, the source of my interest in him. We represented adventure without danger, excitement without consequences, love without responsibility . . .

Behind me, Miss Barnes asked for a doggie bag because her little dog was starving, she said, and anyway, she couldn't eat all her sole. Suddenly I couldn't finish mine either.

The hostess came to refill my water glass. "Sorry about that," she said quietly. "Poor Miss Barnes has a habit of accosting the other guests, and tonight you were elected. It must be very annoying; I do apologize."

"It's all right," I told her. "Only I feel sorry for her because she seems so lonely, and—well, isn't she a bit out of touch?"

"Out of touch," the hostess said. "She's senile, poor thing. I'm afraid we're going to have to do something about her." I winced and covered it with a cough. Then she added, "Oh, you aren't eating. Isn't the fish all right?"

"It's perfect, thank you."

She nodded and moved away, while I took another bite of sole, remembering how Jim had always called it ambrosia and said we were the gods. Laying my fork down again, I got out a cigarette and my lighter.

"Could I have that little bit of fish you're not going to eat?" Miss Barnes asked, right at my elbow. "It's for my dog."

"What about bones? I never give my dog fish for fear of his choking on a bone."

"My dog eats anything I give her," Miss Barnes said, holding her doggie bag open. Then she leaned closer, her voice barely audible. "That's a lie. I want the fish for my lunch tomorrow. You see, retirement isn't all it's supposed to be these days."

Silently I transferred the remnant of my sole to the doggie bag and was relieved when the waitress came to lead Miss Barnes back to her own table.

Thought of my own retirement, not so far off now, was so unnerving that I left the dessert, finished my coffee, and went out through the bar onto the long front porch of the old inn, with the rose vines climbing up to the wooden scrollwork of the gabled windows and eaves. In front was the parking area where my car stood among others, and beyond the highway running below the property were the rocks with the sea pounding the shore under the dark old windblown cypresses.

I considered what I wanted to do and decided to get my Sheltie and feed him before we walked down the hill to the beach.

Miss Barnes was right behind me. "Is your doggie with you?"

"Locked in the car."

"Oh, dear, they say it's dangerous leaving children and animals in locked cars."

"I left the window partly open," I said. "Anyway, I'm going to feed him now and then go to bed."

Her smiled faded. "Oh, dear. I thought maybe you and I could go for a walk."

"Not tonight." And hastily I added, "Thanks."

"I'm sorry." Her eyes filled with weak tears. "I'm being tiresome, aren't I? It's a part of growing old not to know when you're being tiresome. That and being retired. What about you? Are you retired?"

"Not yet." But I would be. Any day now.

She shook her head. "You won't find it easy when you do. People die or drop away from you, and finally you're alone, with nothing but your regrets to sustain you." She looked far out to sea where a fishing vessel was beating the waves back to port. "I was young once, you know, and there was a man who found me attractive. But nothing came of it."

"Why not? Did you quarrel?"

"Oh, it was my fault." She faced me, lips quivering. "You see, I didn't trust him. He said he would leave his wife for me, but I thought he was just trying to—oh, you know. Then he died, and I discovered he'd gone ahead and started a divorce. If he'd lived, I think he would have come after me again. By the time I found out what I truly wanted, it was too late."

"I'm sorry," I said, and helpless to comfort her, I escaped to my car, put Star on his leash, and took him to my room for his meal. He gobbled it as usual, finding no strange smell from the phenobarb I'd put in the food I'd brought from home.

When I was sure Miss Barnes had disappeared, I took Star down the path through the red alders and young firs, past the Oregon grape and elderberry bushes, and across the highway to the beach at the mouth of the river. Here the water was calm, and I let Star run in and out of the waves, his barking already muted and uncertain. He got all wet and shook himself feebly when I whistled him back and restored the leash.

He was my second Sheltie, Jim having given me both dogs to remind me of him during our separations, he said. When the first Star sickened and died, I was inconsolable and felt it was a bad omen. But Jim simply went out and bought the second puppy for me. Now the second Star was twelve years old and I couldn't bear to see the way he was aging, because it was like a reflection of my own state.

We walked around to the point where I stood hypnotized by the surf pounding up and over the glistening black rocks and falling back, leaving ruffles of white foam . . .

"The seahorses are riding high tonight," Jim said in my ear.

I felt his arm around me, and leaned back wanting only to preserve and extend the love and security he gave me. Wanting it harder and oftener as the years rolled by, worrying that he was tired of me, resenting the sterile two months between our weekends, frequently mistrusting his ultimate intentions. In this I was unreasonable, for I'd known from the beginning ours would be love without responsibility, but the force of resentment swept me along anyway.

And sensing this in me, he tried to make it all right again by saying, "Oh, God, I'd give my life to go south with you tomorrow."

"Do it then."

"I can't. You know I can't, not unless—"

"Not unless she divorces you, which she won't, or the children become mature enough not to be damaged." I threw back the words he always used whenever I spoke of the future. Not that I often did, because I respected his love for his children, his desire to protect them, or their image of him. But that didn't prevent the slow rot of distrust from growing in my mind . . .

I sighed and turned to go, thinking of Miss Barnes. "I thought he was just trying to—oh, you know."

My poor old Star came dragging after me, already asleep on his feet from what I'd put in his food. Finally I had to pick him up and carry him like a baby in my arms. He died an hour after I got back to my room, and I sat weeping all night because I lacked the courage to finish what I'd started.

When daylight came, I wrapped the body in a blanket and carried it out to the car where I placed it on the passenger seat. Then I sat there beside him until it was time for the dining room to open.

I couldn't eat, but the coffee helped, and so did being seated at the table near the fireplace where Jim and I had always sat. Until the last morning when I'd come here alone while he still slept in the cottage we'd shared for the past two nights.

Presently I went out to the car again, and with Star's body beside me, drove off to visit our favorite headland and sit watching the water burst on the rocks for the rest of the day. I'd have given anything to bury Star there under a carpet of Indian paintbrush, lupines, and poppies, but it was public property.

I returned to the inn after sundown and had barely seated myself and ordered a drink in the dining room when Miss Barnes came to my table.

"Good evening," she said, face aglow. "How's your sweet little dog today? Not locked in the car again, I hope."

"My dog? Star?" I swallowed. "Oh, he died last night."

"Why, you poor thing! What happened?"

"Please. If you don't mind, I can't talk about it."

"Of course not. I'll sit down and keep you company—"

"Please don't, Miss Barnes. Please leave me alone."

The hostess heard me and led the old woman away.

I ordered the salmon and toyed with it. After refusing berry cobbler, I went straight to my room and sat down to wonder what I should do about Star's body, which was still in the car. I couldn't think where to take it, or whom to ask for help. All I could think about was poor old Miss Barnes, and how in a way I resembled her: not accosting strangers in the dining room, not yet; but inside, where it counted, and where I'd worked for eight long years to contain it. Now, if I could, I had to recall the last night Jim and I ever had together. Not as I would like to remember it, but as it really happened . . .

He had said that his wife was going to tell his children if he didn't give me up.

"Oh, Jim, no! She wouldn't."

"Well, she said she would. And it will devastate the kids. The youngest isn't quite fifteen, and I can't stand even the thought of their disillusion and hurt."

"What did you tell her then?"

"I said I'd think about it."

He didn't look at me as he spoke, and believing he'd already made his choice, I lost control. I said unspeakable things, made unreasonable accusations and threats. I was beside myself, and all the resentment and distrust in my festering mind came out until at last we faced each other, pale and shaking, utterly washed up, and we both knew it.

Jim was the first to break the silence. "Before I left home, I thought of another way, if you're willing. I'd rather die with you than live without you."

Shaken to my fibers, I finally agreed.

So we made our pact and went to bed for the last time, close and warm together as if nothing had changed. Only in the morning he didn't wake up—and I did.

After weeping for a time, I'd gone for breakfast which I didn't eat and driven straight home, a journey I don't remember. Nobody ever came after me, though I presumed his wife must have had difficulty convincing the authorities who she was because nobody would have recognized her as the woman who'd been registered as Jim's wife so often at the cottage.

Later when I went to Eureka and read his obituary in the local paper, I discovered she'd had enough influence to hush up the circumstances. Death from a heart attack, the notice read. But it should have said murder, because at the last minute and without saying so to Jim, I had panicked and failed to keep the suicide pact we'd made . . .

I stirred at last, calm and not unhappy as I got the bottle and swallowed the rest of the phenobarb tablets Jim had handed me eight years ago on the night, when in my madness, I believed he intended that only I should die . . .

The Real Shape of the Coast

JOHN LUTZ

When "The Real Shape of the Coast" first appeared in Ellery Queen's Mystery Magazine *in 1971, Ellery Queen wrote by way of introduction: "A most unusual background for crime and detection—the State Institution for the Criminal Incurably Insane; and a most unusual dramatis personae—mainly, the six patients in Cottage D. But it is not, as you might expect, the doctor in charge who is the detective; and it is not the attendant or any sane person. The detective is one of the patients. An incurably insane criminal the detective? Surely a 'first'—perhaps the most unusual 'first' in the one hundred and thirty years since Poe's preternaturally sane Dupin." A powerful and disturbing story . . .*

Where the slender peninsula crooks like a beckoning finger in the warm water, where the ocean waves crash in umbrellas of foam over the low-lying rocks to roll and ebb on the narrow white-sand beaches, there squats in a series of low rectangular buildings and patterns of high fences the State Institution for the Criminal Incurably Insane. There are twenty of the sharp-angled buildings, each rising bricked and hard out of sandy soil like an undeniable fact. Around each building is a ten-foot redwood fence topped by barbed wire, and these fences run to the sea's edge to continue as gossamer networks of barbed wire that stretch out to the rocks.

In each of the rectangular buildings live six men, and on days when the ocean is suitable for swimming it is part of their daily habit—indeed, part of their therapy—to go down to the beach and let the waves roll over them, or simply to lie in the purging sun and grow beautifully tan. Sometimes, just out of the grasping reach of the waves, the men might build things in the damp sand, but by evening those things would be gone. However, some very interesting things had been built in the sand.

The men in the rectangular buildings were not just marking time until their real death. In fact, the "Incurably Insane" in the institution's name was something of a misnomer; it was just that there was an absolute minimum of hope for these men. They lived in clusters of six not only for security's sake, but so that they might form a more or less permanent sensitivity group—day-in, day-out group therapy, with occasional informal gatherings supervised by young Dr. Montaign. Here under the subtle and skillful probings of Dr. Montaign the men bared their lost souls—at least, some of them did.

Cottage D was soon to be the subject of Dr. Montaign's acute interest. In fact, he was to study the occurrences there for the next year and write a series of articles to be published in influential scientific journals.

The first sign that there was something wrong at Cottage D was when one of the patients, a Mr. Rolt, was found dead on the beach one evening. He was lying on his back near the water's edge, wearing only a pair of khaki trousers. At first glance it would seem that he'd had a drowning accident, only his mouth and much of his throat turned out to be stuffed with sand and with a myriad of tiny colorful shells.

Roger Logan, who had lived in Cottage D since being found guilty of murdering his wife three years before, sat quietly watching Dr. Montaign pace the room.

"This simply won't do," the doctor was saying. "One of you has done away with Mr. Rolt, and that is exactly the sort of thing we are in here to stop."

"But it won't be investigated too thoroughly, will it?" Logan said softly. "Like when a convicted murderer is killed in a prison."

"May I remind you," a patient named Kneehoff said in his clipped voice, "that Mr. Rolt was not a murderer." Kneehoff had been a successful businessman before his confinement, and now he made excellent leather wallets and sold them by mail order. He sat now at a small table with some old letters spread before him, as if he were a chairman of the board presiding over a meeting. "I might add," he said haughtily, "that it's difficult to conduct business in an atmosphere such as this."

"I didn't say Rolt was a murderer," Logan said, "but he is—was— supposed to be in here for the rest of his life. That fact is bound to impede justice."

Kneehoff shrugged and shuffled through his letters. "He was a man of little consequence—that is, compared to the heads of giant corporations."

It was true that Mr. Rolt had been a butcher rather than a captain of industry, a butcher who had put things in the meat—some of them unmentionable. But then Kneehoff had merely run a chain of three dry-cleaning establishments.

"Perhaps you thought him inconsequential enough to murder," William Sloan, who was in for pushing his young daughter out of a fortieth-story window, said to Kneehoff. "You never did like Mr. Rolt."

Kneehoff began to splutter. "You're the killer here, Sloan! You and Logan!"

"I killed no one," Logan said quickly.

Kneehoff grinned. "You were proved guilty in a court of law—of killing your wife."

"They didn't prove it to me. I should know whether or not I'm guilty!"

"I know your case," Kneehoff said gazing dispassionately at his old letters. "You hit your wife over the head with a bottle of French Chablis wine, killing her immediately."

"I warn you," Logan said heatedly, "implying that I struck my wife with a wine bottle—and French Chablis at that—is inviting a libel suit!"

Noticeably shaken, Kneehoff became quiet and seemed to lose himself in studying the papers before him. Logan had learned long ago how to deal with him; he knew that Kneehoff's "company" could not stand a lawsuit.

"Justice must be done," Logan went on. "Mr. Rolt's murderer, a real murderer, must be caught and executed."

"Isn't that a job for the police?" Dr. Montaign asked gently.

"The police!" Logan laughed. "Look how they botched my case! No, this is a job for *us*. Living the rest of our lives with a murderer would be intolerable."

"But what about Mr. Sloan?" Dr. Montaign asked. "You're living with him."

"His is a different case," Logan snapped. "Because they found him guilty doesn't mean he is guilty. He says he doesn't remember anything about it, doesn't he?"

"What's your angle?" Brandon, the unsuccessful mystery bomber, asked. "You people have always got an angle, something in mind for yourselves. The only people you can really trust are the poor people."

"My angle is justice," Logan said firmly. "We must have justice!"

"Justice for all the people!" Brandon suddenly shouted, rising to his feet. He glanced about angrily and then sat down again.

"Justice," said old Mr. Heimer, who had been to other worlds and could listen to and hear metal, "will take care of itself. It always does, no matter where."

"They've been waiting a long time," Brandon said, his jaw jutting out beneath his dark mustache. "The poor people, I mean."

"Have the police any clues?" Logan asked Dr. Montaign.

"They know what you know," the doctor said calmly. "Mr. Rolt was killed on the beach between nine-fifteen and ten—when he shouldn't have been out of Cottage D."

Mr. Heimer raised a thin speckled hand to his lips and chuckled feebly. "Now, maybe that's justice."

"You know the penalty for leaving the building during unauthorized hours," Kneehoff said sternly to Mr. Heimer. "Not death, but confinement to your room for two days. We must have the punishment fit the crime and we must obey the rules. Any operation must have rules in order to be successful."

"That's exactly what I'm saying," Logan said. "The man who killed poor Mr. Rolt must be caught and put to death."

"The authorities are investigating," Dr. Montaign said soothingly.

"Like they investigated my case?" Logan said in a raised and angry voice. "They won't bring the criminal to justice! And I tell you we must not have a murderer here in Compound D!"

"Cottage D," Dr. Montaign corrected him.

"Perhaps Mr. Rolt was killed by something from the sea," William Sloan said thoughtfully.

"No," Brandon said, "I heard the police say there was only a single set of footprints near the body and it led from and to the cottage. It's obviously the work of an inside subversive."

"But what size footprints?" Logan asked.

"They weren't clear enough to determine the size," Dr. Montaign said. "They led to and from near the wooden stairs that come up to the rear yard, then the ground was too hard for footprints."

"Perhaps they were Mr. Rolt's own footprints," Sloan said.

Kneehoff grunted. "Stupid! Mr. Rolt went to the beach, but he did not come back."

"Well—" Dr. Montaign rose slowly and walked to the door. "I must be going to some of the other cottages now." He smiled at Logan. "It's interesting that you're so concerned with justice," he said. A gull screamed as the doctor went out.

The five remaining patients of Cottage D sat quietly after Dr. Montaign's exit. Logan watched Kneehoff gather up his letters and give their edges a neat sharp tap on the table top before slipping them into his shirt pocket. Brandon and Mr. Heimer seemed to be in deep thought, while Sloan was peering over Kneehoff's shoulder through the open window out to the rolling sea.

"It could be that none of us is safe," Logan said suddenly. "We must get to the bottom of this ourselves."

"But we are at the bottom," Mr. Heimer said pleasantly, "all of us."
Kneehoff snorted. "Speak for yourself, old man."

"It's the crime against the poor people that should be investigated," Brandon said. "If my bomb in the Statue of Liberty had gone off . . . And I used my whole week's vacation that year going to New York."

"We'll conduct our own investigation," Logan insisted, "and we might as well start now. Everyone tell me what he knows about Mr. Rolt's murder."

"Who put you in charge?" Kneehoff asked. "And why should we investigate Rolt's murder?"

"Mr. Rolt was our friend," Sloan said.

"Anyway," Logan said, "we must have an orderly investigation. Somebody has to be in charge."

"I suppose you're right," Kneehoff said. "Yes, an orderly investigation."

Information was exchanged, and it was determined that Mr. Rolt had said he was going to bed at nine-fifteen, saying good night to Ollie, the attendant, in the TV lounge. Sloan and Brandon, the two other men in the lounge, remembered the time because the halfway commercial for "Monsters of Main Street" was on, the one where the box of detergent soars through the air and snatches everyone's shirt. Then at ten o'clock, just when the news was coming on, Ollie had gone to check the beach and discovered Mr. Rolt's body.

"So," Logan said, "the approximate time of death has been established. And I was in my room with the door open. I doubt if Mr. Rolt could have passed in the hall to go outdoors without my noticing him, so we must hypothesize that he did go to his room at nine-fifteen, and sometime between nine-fifteen and ten he left through his window."

"He knew the rules," Kneehoff said. "He wouldn't have just walked outside for everyone to see him."

"True," Logan conceded, "but it's best not to take anything for granted."

"True, true," Mr. Heimer chuckled, "take nothing for granted."

"And where were *you* between nine and ten?" Logan asked.

"I was in Dr. Montaign's office," Mr. Heimer said with a grin, "talking to the doctor about something I'd heard in the steel utility pole. I almost made him understand that all things metal are receivers, tuned to different frequencies, different worlds and vibrations."

Kneehoff, who had once held two of his accountants prisoner for five days without food, laughed.

"And where were *you?*" Logan asked.

"In my office, going over my leather-goods vouchers," Kneehoff said. Kneehoff's "office" was his room, toward the opposite end of the hall from Logan's room.

"Now," Logan said, "we get to the matter of motive. Which of us had reason to kill Mr. Rolt?"

"I don't know," Sloan said distantly. "Who'd do such a thing—fill Mr. Rolt's mouth with sand?"

"You were his closest acquaintance," Brandon said to Logan. "You always played chess with him. Who knows what you and he were plotting?"

"What about you?" Kneehoff said to Brandon. "You tried to choke Mr. Rolt just last week."

Brandon stood up angrily, his mustache bristling. "That was the week *before* last!" He turned to Logan. "And Rolt always beat Logan at chess —that's why Logan hated him."

"He didn't *always* beat me at chess," Logan said. "And I didn't hate him. The only reason he beat me at chess sometimes was because he'd upset the board if he was losing."

"You don't like to get beat at anything," Brandon said, sitting down again. "That's why you killed your wife, because she beat you at things. How middle class, to kill someone because of that."

"I didn't kill my wife," Logan said patiently. "And she didn't beat me at things. Though she was a pretty good businesswoman," he added slowly, "and a good tennis player."

"What about Kneehoff?" Sloan asked. "He was always threatening to kill Mr. Rolt."

"Because he laughed at me!" Kneehoff spat out. "Rolt was a braggart and a fool, always laughing at me because I have ambition and he didn't. He thought he was better at everything than anybody else—and you, Sloan—Rolt used to ridicule you and Heimer. There isn't one of us who didn't have motive to eliminate a piece of scum like Rolt."

Logan was on his feet, almost screaming. "I won't have you talk about the dead like that!"

"All I was saying," Kneehoff said, smiling his superior smile at having upset Logan, "was that it won't be easy for you to discover Rolt's murderer. He was a clever man, that murderer, cleverer than you."

Logan refused to be baited. "We'll see about that when I check the alibis," he muttered, and he left the room to walk barefoot in the surf.

On the beach the next day Sloan asked the question they had all been wondering.

"What are we going to do with the murderer if we do catch him?" he asked, his eyes fixed on a distant ship that was just an irregularity on the horizon.

"We'll extract justice," Logan said. "We'll convict and execute him— eliminate him from our society!"

"Do you think we should?" Sloan asked.

"Of course we should!" Logan snapped. "The authorities don't care who killed Mr. Rolt. The authorities are probably glad he's dead."

"I don't agree that it's a sound move," Kneehoff said, "to execute the man. I move that we don't do that."

"I don't hear anyone seconding you," Logan said. "It has to be the way I say if we are to maintain order here."

Kneehoff thought a moment, then smiled. "I agree we must maintain order at all costs," he said. "I withdraw my motion."

"Motion, hell!" Brandon said. He spat into the sand. "We ought to just find out who the killer is and liquidate him. No time for a motion—time for action!"

"Mr. Rolt would approve of that," Sloan said, letting a handful of sand run through his fingers.

Ollie the attendant came down to the beach and stood there smiling, the sea breeze rippling his white uniform. The group on the beach broke up slowly and casually, each man idling away in a different direction.

Kicking the sun-warmed sand with his bare toes, Logan approached Ollie.

"Game of chess, Mr. Logan?" Ollie asked.

"Thanks, no," Logan said. "You found Mr. Rolt's body, didn't you, Ollie?"

"Right, Mr. Logan."

"Mr. Rolt was probably killed while you and Sloan and Brandon were watching TV."

"Probably," Ollie agreed, his big face impassive.

"How come you left at ten o'clock to go down to the beach?"

Ollie turned to stare blankly at Logan with his flat eyes. "You know I always check the beach at night, Mr. Logan. Sometimes the patients lose things."

"Mr. Rolt sure lost something," Logan said. "Did the police ask you if Brandon and Sloan were in the TV room with you the whole time before the murder?"

"They did and I told them yes." Ollie lit a cigarette with one of those transparent lighters that had a fishing fly in the fluid. "You studying to be a detective, Mr. Logan?"

"No, no," Logan laughed. "I'm just interested in how the police work, after the way they messed up my case. Once they thought I was guilty I didn't have a chance."

But Ollie was no longer listening. He had turned to look out at the ocean. "Don't go out too far, Mr. Kneehoff!" he called, but Kneehoff pretended not to hear and began moving in the water parallel with the beach.

Logan walked away to join Mr. Heimer who was standing in the surf with his pants rolled above his knees.

"Find out anything from Ollie?" Mr. Heimer asked, his body balancing slightly as the retreating sea pulled the sand and shells from beneath him.

"Some things," Logan said, crossing his arms and enjoying the play of the cool surf about his legs. The two men—rather than the ocean—seemed to be moving as the tide swept in and out and shifted the sand beneath the sensitive soles of their bare feet. "It's like the ocean," Logan said, "finding out who killed Mr. Rolt. The ocean works and works on the shore, washing in and out until only the sand and rock remain—the real shape of the coast. Wash the soil away and you have bare rock; wash the lies away and you have bare truth."

"Not many can endure the truth," Mr. Heimer said, stooping to let his hand drag in an incoming wave, "even in other worlds."

Logan raised his shoulders. "Not many ever learn the truth," he said, turning and walking through the wet sand toward the beach. Amid the onwash of the wide shallow wave he seemed to be moving backward, out to sea . . .

Two days later Logan talked to Dr. Montaign, catching him alone in the TV lounge when the doctor dropped by for one of his midday visits. The room was very quiet; even the ticking of the clock seemed slow, lazy, and out of rhythm.

"I was wondering, doctor," Logan said, "about the night of Mr. Rolt's murder. Did Mr. Heimer stay very late in your office?"

"The police asked me that," Dr. Montaign said with a smile. "Mr. Heimer was in my office until ten o'clock, then I saw him come into this room and join Brandon and Sloan to watch the news."

"Was Kneehoff with them?"

"Yes, Kneehoff was in his room."

"I was in my room," Logan said, "with my door open to the hall, and I didn't see Mr. Rolt pass to go outdoors. So he must have gone out through his window. Maybe the police would like to know that."

"I'll tell them for you," Dr. Montaign said, "but they know Mr. Rolt went out through his window because his only door was locked from the inside." The doctor cocked his head at Logan, as was his habit. "I wouldn't try to be a detective," he said gently. He placed a smoothly manicured hand on Logan's shoulder. "My advice is to forget about Mr. Rolt."

"Like the police?" Logan said.

The hand patted Logan's shoulder soothingly.

After the doctor had left, Logan sat on the cool vinyl sofa and thought. Brandon, Sloan and Heimer were accounted for, and Kneehoff couldn't have left the building without Logan seeing him pass in the hall. The two men, murderer and victim, might have left together through Mr. Rolt's window—only that wouldn't explain the single set of fresh footprints to and from the body. And the police had found Mr. Rolt's footprints where he'd gone down to the beach farther from the cottage and then apparently walked up the beach through the surf to where his path and the path of the murderer crossed.

And then Logan saw the only remaining possibility—the only possible answer.

Ollie, the man who had discovered the body—Ollie alone had had the opportunity to kill! And after doing away with Mr. Rolt he must have noticed his footprints leading to and from the body; so at the wooden stairs he simply turned and walked back to the sea in another direction, then walked up the beach to make his "discovery" and alert the doctor.

Motive? Logan smiled. Anyone could have had motive enough to kill the bragging and offensive Mr. Rolt. He had been an easy man to hate.

Logan left the TV room to join the other patients on the beach, careful not to glance at the distant white-uniformed figure of Ollie painting some deck chairs at the other end of the building.

"Tonight," Logan told them dramatically, "we'll meet in the conference room after Dr. Montaign leaves and I promise to tell you who the murderer is. Then we'll decide how best to remove him from our midst."

"Only if he's guilty," Kneehoff said. "You must present convincing, positive evidence."

"I have proof," Logan said.

"Power to the people!" Brandon cried, leaping to his feet.

Laughing and shouting, they all ran like schoolboys into the waves.

The patients sat through their evening session with Dr. Montaign, answering questions mechanically and chattering irrelevantly, and Dr. Montaign sensed a certain tenseness and expectancy in them. Why were they anxious? Was it fear? Had Logan been harping to them about the murder? Why was Kneehoff not looking at his letters, and Sloan not gazing out the window?

"I told the police," Dr. Montaign mentioned, "that I didn't expect to walk up on any more bodies on the beach."

"You?" Logan stiffened in his chair. "I thought it was Ollie who found Mr. Rolt."

"He did, really," Dr. Montaign said, cocking his head. "After Mr. Heimer left me I accompanied Ollie to check the beach so I could talk to him about some things. He was the one who saw the body first and ran ahead to find out what it was."

"And it was Mr. Rolt, his mouth stuffed with sand," Sloan murmured.

Logan's head seemed to be whirling. He had been so sure! Process of elimination. It had to be Ollie! Or were the two men, Ollie and Dr. Montaign, in it together? They had to be! But that was impossible! There had been only one set of footprints.

Kneehoff! It must have been Kneehoff all along! He must have made a secret appointment with Rolt on the beach and killed him. But Rolt had been walking alone until he met the killer, who was also alone! And *someone* had left the fresh footprints, the single set of footprints, to and from the body.

Kneehoff must have seen Rolt, slipped out through his window, intercepted him, and killed him. But Kneehoff's room didn't have a window! Only the two end rooms had windows, Rolt's room and Logan's room!

A single set of footprints—they could only be his own! *His own!*

Through a haze Logan saw Dr. Montaign glance at his watch, smile, say his good-byes, and leave. The night breeze wafted through the wide open windows of the conference room with the hushing of the surf, the surf wearing away the land to bare rock.

"Now," Kneehoff said to Logan, and the moon seemed to light his eyes, "who exactly is our man? Who killed Mr. Rolt? And what is your evidence?"

Ollie found Logan's body the next morning, face down on the beach, the gentle lapping surf trying to claim him. Logan's head was turned and half buried and his broken limbs were twisted at strange angles, and around him the damp sand was beaten with, in addition to his own, four different sets of footprints.

Hercule Poirot
in the Year 2010

JON L. BREEN

There have been any number of parody-pastiches in the mystery field, the greater percentage of them take-offs on Conan Doyle's Sherlock Holmes. Perhaps the best of the Holmes parodies was Robert L. Fish's delightful "Shlock Homes" series, but the premier parodist working today is certainly critic and writer Jon L. Breen, whose targets include such past and present giants as S.S. Van Dine's Philo Vance, Ellery Queen's EQ, Ed McBain's 87th Precinct, and John D. MacDonald's Travis McGee. "Hercule Poirot in the Year 2010" is not only a marvelous pastiche of Agatha Christie and her Belgian detective, but a fine detective story in its own right. Along with the best of Breen's other parodies, it will appear in a forthcoming collection provocatively titled Hair of the Sleuthhound.

"It's *Mrs.* Harbottle," the elderly lady insisted to the ticket-taker on the New York–London underground. "Missus, spelled M-I-S-S-U-S." She fumbled with her change and her ticket and walked away muttering to herself. I'm proud I was Justin Harbottle's wife, she thought, and proud to be his widow and none of this miz rubbish. Here in America, you'd think they'd never heard of miss and missus.

She sat in the window seat of the six-passenger compartment, fumbling with her parcels. She did like a window seat, though there was little reason to covet one on the New York–London underground. Little reason for a window at all really, since there was nothing to see. She hoped her seatmates would be nice. Forty-five minutes is a long time to spend with strangers, especially when one is getting on and every minute is precious.

The young gentleman who took the seat across from her nodded pleasantly. He was a nice-looking gentleman, but there was something about him that spelled foreigner to her. Not American foreigner, of course, but European foreigner. Which was silly really, as her children so often reminded her, since in the United States of Europe every European is every Briton's countryman; but it was hard for a girl—a lady—who had grown up in a time when they were all different countries to adjust to the changing times.

Let her children laugh—they were kind really, understanding even when she insisted on modestly wearing her bikini when they went to the beach at Brighton, though the French and Italian and even the California beaches were now so much more accessible.

More passengers. An American man and his wife. Even now you could always tell an American. They were so impatient, always glancing at their watches. The wife was nice looking, but the husband looked a brute, like a rock singer of her youth, though of course rock singers would be before his time no doubt. Or would they? It was so hard to keep track of the time going by.

Would they be going soon? No, there's one more passenger. Looks a big heavy-set man. Why, it was Gaylord Tenney, Mr. Harbottle's former business partner! Mrs. Harbottle was terribly embarrassed. Not that she held a grudge against Tenney for having cheated Justin Harbottle out of his half of the business and hastened his death, but surely Tenney would be equally embarrassed to find her sitting there. It would be a terribly awkward experience.

She almost got up and rushed off to await the next car, but after all, she wanted to get home to London and one couldn't let other people run one's life, especially someone like Gaylord Tenney who had done enough damage already.

But he didn't look the slightest bit embarrassed. He merely nodded all around and opened his newspaper calmly, as if none of his fellow passengers was anyone he recognized. But Mrs. Harbottle felt a general stiffening, as if the remaining passengers either knew him or sensed the sort of character he was behind his dignified mustache and tastefully tailor-made gray suit that would have passed muster even in the more sartorially exacting seventies of Mrs. Harbottle's youth. Imagine the cheek of the man, just sitting there like that!

Well, as Mrs. Harbottle had always told herself, one would just have to make the best of it.

Alice Lane nudged her husband almost imperceptibly and got no reaction. Nudging him more perceptibly, she heard a whispered "I know, I know." So he had recognized Gaylord Tenney as well. Right here in the same car with them, going to London.

The devil with him, Alice said to herself, fixing her chin determinedly.

So he was going to England—her ancestral home, Counterbridge House, the last stately home left in England, was hers and no one else's. Tenney didn't have a leg to stand on with his false claim, so there was no need to worry.

She cast a fond glance at her husband. He was so American! Could he be happy in an English country mansion with an acre and a half of vast inherited lands? True, she was of the American side of the family and had never been to England, but she'd seen so many of those historical TV programs imported from the BBC that she knew she would feel right at home.

No need to think any more about Gaylord Tenney. Counterbridge House would be hers, an acre and a half all hers to roam in this crowded world.

Alex Lane looked at his watch for the hundredth time. Why weren't they moving, blast it? Not that there was any great hurry now—with that damned Gaylord Tenney in the same car they would arrive in London simultaneously.

Alex ran a hand through his unfashionably long and sleek black hair. Was Tenney's claim to Counterbridge any good? Who could tell? But, if it was, the ten million dollars Alex was counting on from the sale of Counterbridge House to the television interests would fly out the window and Alex Lane would be ruined financially.

He fingered the letter in his pocket, the letter making the offer. Still there. He hadn't told Alice about it yet, but that would come in time.

Sven Petrocelli felt the slight rumble that meant the New York–London underground was getting under way. Good. Finally. Once it got going the ride would be so smooth you couldn't tell it from standing still. A quick transfer to the Peking line and he'd be in China by dinnertime. But it would have to be a quick transfer.

Could he make it before Gaylord Tenney had an opportunity to give him away to Scotland Yard? How they'd like to get him, but only Tenney knew who he was and only Tenney could denounce him.

If only some kind soul would eliminate Tenney.

Plunge the car into darkness first—that would be easy enough to do. Any experienced underground traveler would know it could be done by pulling the alarm switch next to each seat, an action that could easily be taken out of the view of the other passengers. The switches, obsolete now, had been quite necessary during the transport war of the 1990s. Then, of course, a quick thrust of some sharp implement into Tenney's heart, and back into the seat quickly before the lights went back on. Who would know which of them did it?

If only someone would do that.

Maybe someone is planning it and that's why *I* thought of it, Sven mused. He had had some mind-reading training before the trouble, but it was dangerous to delve any further in that area without really knowing what you were doing. Instead, Sven would concentrate on willing Tenney dead.

What a tense group they were, Mrs. Harbottle mused. She made a tentative attempt to start some conversation.

"Are you French?" she asked the young, foreign-looking gentleman.

He seemed to bristle. "I am European," he said, in an indeterminate accent. "And so I believe are you."

"Yes," she said, determined to ignore his rudeness. Well, he wasn't French then, or he'd have proudly proclaimed it. "Will you be staying long in London?"

A rueful smile played at the corners of his mouth. "Not any longer than I can help," he said. Seeing Mrs. Harbottle's face, he added hastily, "Not that I mean to reflect poorly on London, one of our greatest European cities."

A little mollified, she thought, He's not a European at all. No true European talks that silly patriotic way. True he doesn't look Chinese, but—

The young foreigner seemed to be a thousand miles away, and their brief conversation was definitely concluded. What was he thinking about so hard?

Alice Lane found the English lady so tiresome. She tried to engage her on the subject of British history, but all she could talk about was shopping, shopping.

"Yes, I often shop in America. Not New York, it's so expensive, just like London really."

Obviously not upper class. Oh, for some intelligent conversation to take her mind off Tenney. But conversation with whom? The young man looked to be meditating, Alex was tense and stiff as a board, and one could hardly start a conversation with Tenney himself.

How could he sit there so calmly, reading his newspaper, knowing there were at least two people in the car who could cheerfully murder him? How?

Alice paused in her thoughts to scream. The car was suddenly plunged into darkness. She sensed movement about her but could not tell who was moving where.

The lights were off perhaps thirty seconds, though it seemed a half hour. Toward the end, amid unindifferentiated gasps and groans, Mrs. Harbottle piped up cheerfully, "Well, I think we have a bit of a problem. No need to worry, though."

"No need to worry," Alex Lane echoed in a near-hysterical voice. "Who knows how deep we are in the Atlantic, in total darkness, with no—"

He broke off when the lights went back on. More gasps and shrieks were vented as the four surviving passengers viewed the body of Gaylord Tenney, bleeding all over his newspaper, a dagger in his heart. Quite dead.

Sven Petrocelli might have observed with a faint smile on his face: Someone actually did it.

Alice Lane stared horror-stricken. Alex, she wanted to cry out loud, Alex, what have you done?

Alex Lane darted nervous eyes at his wife. If she goes to prison, he wondered, do I still get the property?

Mrs. Harbottle looked calmly at the body. I don't know who did this, she thought, I only know I didn't.

Just how old is he? Colonel Hart-Winston asked himself as he gazed across the desk at his visitor. One couldn't just ask, of course, that would never do, but one surely wondered, knowing something of the Belgian's past history. Let's see, it was now 2010, and he reportedly retired from the police early in the last century. Surely one hundred and fifty was a conservative guess, but it hardly seemed possible. The egg-shaped head was smooth and unwrinkled, the mustaches as black as ever.

"Transplants, mon ami," said Hercule Poirot.

"Eh? What's that, Mr. Poirot?" Colonel Hart-Winston, jolted from his rather rude silence, turned even a shade redder than his norm. "Transplants, do you say?"

"But yes. My American doctor tells me I lead the league in transplants, though I don't know what league he refers to. And, more happily, artificial replacements. I was most pleased when I no longer had to depend on the unfortunate victims of accidents to keep me going. Very little of me, in any event, is the original part.

"Except, of course, the little gray cells. Those, I am pleased to say, are not amenable to transplant, and no method has been found to produce them artificially, though we all know what is being done with computers and androids and—but a thousand pardons, colonel. I am growing garrulous in my old age, which you were so diligently attempting to guess at a moment ago."

"Forgive me. Intolerably rude. But how the deuce did you know I was speculating on your age? You don't read minds, surely?"

"Does the prospect alarm you?"

"Frankly, yes. This case has gone beyond the mind reader, which is about the only sort of detective left around these days. You're one of the few great detectives left, in the old sense."

"And with all the mind readers available, why do you suddenly need the old warhorse Poirot, so effectively put out of business by the new breed?"

"You'll be back in business before you know. Have you heard about thought therapy, Mr. Poirot?"

"A branch of psychiatry that gained importance in the 1980s, I believe. Most successful in curing serious mental disturbances. Do I gather that thought therapy is aiding criminals in escaping law enforcement?"

"We've been hearing for some time that thought therapists can teach people to so manipulate their conscious minds as to be immune to our thought readers. But I never had a specific example of it until our present case. I have four suspects in the murder of Gaylord Tenney—four suspects only—and one of them *has* to be the murderer. Anything else is physically impossible, and yet the thought readings on all four indicate innocence of the crime!

"I have only two alternatives: a physically impossible murder or some form of jamming our thought readings. I feel the latter is more likely, but in any case our people—highly strung mental gymnasts, you know the type—can do no more. Simple mind reading has been adequate to all crime-solving purposes for so long they know nothing else to do. That is why I have come to you."

"I have come to *you.*"

"Yes, yes. Figuratively speaking, of course. Called you in. But, Mr. Poirot, I want your assurance you are not a mind reader. To employ an outside mind reader is against regulations, and really I hardly think you would do us much good if your old methods have been tainted with our new ones."

"Rest assured, sir, the little gray cells are still working."

"I'm relieved to hear it. I think the best starting point is for you to read the account of the murder that Ms. Oliver, our mind-wave recorder, has gleaned from the information of our mental investigators. I think you will find her account rather pleasantly old-fashioned in style. While you read, perhaps you will enjoy a glass of sherry?"

"A most interesting story," remarked Hercule Poirot. "How are you able to get all the thoughts of the persons on the train—and is it a train? —with such accuracy?"

"It's not generally known, Mr. Poirot, but when necessary we can recreate any thought on any underground car. As the term used to be, the cars are bugged. Of course, the thought records are only used in the case of a serious crime or other emergency such as this one. People must, after all, have some privacy, mustn't they? In any case, you see our problem. All think innocent, yet one must be guilty."

"A trifling problem for the little gray cells, mon ami."

"Trifling? Surely not."

"Quite trifling. Proof is another matter, however. If I could name the murderer, could you then use some extra mind-reading weapons to go a step deeper and dredge out the real evil thoughts underneath the innocent surface? For surely these thought therapists can only go so deep with their implantations."

"Yes, I feel sure we could. But we cannot subject them all to that, Mr. Poirot. After all, the three innocent ones would have reason to complain. We could only proceed that way on one person and then only when we are sure."

"Bien. I, Hercule Poirot, am sure. Your stenographer, Ms. Oliver, is she, I wonder, some relative of an old friend of mine, Ariadne Oliver, the detective novelist?"

"Granddaughter, I believe. That's where she gets the style."

"I thought so. Dear Mrs. Oliver, a lovely gracious lady, and always looking for some new twist on the least-likely-person solution. The narrator did it, or the policeman did it, or a supposed victim did it, or everybody did it, or nobody did it. But one thing that Mrs. Oliver could never do, and she probably wished she could, was to follow the thoughts of one of her characters, have that character overtly think in an innocent way, say through thoughts that I am not guilty, I did not do it, and then turn out to be the murderer.

"That, of course, would be against the rules of fair play; it would be cheating, and thus forbidden. But now, at last, that is possible, and yet, alas, there is no one who writes detective novels any more. Truly a pity."

"You were about to name the murderer, Mr. Poirot," the colonel nodded.

"But of course. The key is the phenomenon of compensation. The person under thought therapy must concentrate very hard on *thinking innocent.* The *actually innocent* person does not. Therefore the person undergoing thought therapy must be a little bit stronger, a little more emphatic.

"This person feels a need not just to have normal thoughts and normal reactions of surprise and horror and the imputation of guilt to others. This person needs to think *in an innocent way,* to say in his thoughts: *I did not do it. I am not guilty.*

"And you will note only one of the suspects did this, only one had this uncharacteristic thought. You remember from Ms. Oliver's account that only one person thought: I don't know who did this; I only know I didn't."

"Mrs. Harbottle!" the colonel exclaimed, reaching for the phone.

Hercule Poirot sighed. "If only Mrs. Oliver could be here to see this."

Merrill-Go-Round

MARCIA MULLER

Female private eyes have made several fictional appearances in recent years, usually with limited success because (a) they were written by males and (b) they tended to talk and act like male private eyes. Sharon McCone, the protagonist of Edwin of the Iron Shoes *(1977) and two forthcoming novels,* Ask the Cards a Question *and* The Cheshire Cat's Eye, *is the one notable exception because (a) her creator, Marcia Muller, is a woman, and (b) she is a sensitively drawn character who talks and acts in a believable feminine fashion. "Merrill-Go-Round" is McCone's first recorded short case—a private-eye story that is also a "woman's story," in the best sense of that term.*

I clung to the metal pole as the man in the red coat and straw hat pushed the lever forward. The blue pig with the bedraggled whisk-broom tail on which I sat moved upward to the strains of "Casey Waltzed on with the Strawberry Blond." As the carousel picked up speed, the pig rose and fell with a rocking motion and the faces of the bystanders slipped swiftly past.

I smiled, feeling more like a child than a thirty-year-old woman, enjoying the stir of the breeze on my long black hair. When the red-coated operator stepped onto the platform and began taking tickets, I got down from the pig—reluctantly. I followed him as he weaved his way through lions and horses, ostriches and giraffes, continuing our conversation.

"It was only yesterday," I shouted above the din of the music. "The little girl came in alone, at about three-thirty. Are you sure you don't remember her?"

The old man turned, clinging to a camel for support. His was the weathered face of one who has spent most of his life outdoors. "I'm sure, Miss McCone. Look at them." He flung out an arm. "This is Monday, and the place is packed with kids. On a Sunday we have ten times as many. How do you expect me to remember one, out of all the rest?"

"I have a picture." I rummaged in my shoulder bag. When I looked up, the man was several yards away, taking a ticket from the rider of a purple toad.

I hurried up and thrust the picture into the old man's hand. "This is the missing child. Surely she'd stand out, with all that curly red hair."

His eyes, in their web of wrinkles, narrowed. He stared at the color photo. Then he gave it back to me. "No," he said. "She's a beautiful kid. But no, I didn't see her yesterday. Sorry."

I looked around. "Is there any way out of here besides the regular exit?"

He continued on his way. "The other doors are locked. There's no way that kid could have left but through the exit. If her mother claims she got on the carousel and disappeared, she's crazy. Either the kid never came in or the mother missed her when she left, that's all." Done collecting tickets, he leaned against a stationary pony, his face serious. "The parents shouldn't let their kids ride alone."

"Merrill is ten, over the age when the park regulations say they can."

He shook his head. "Maybe so, but when you've seen as many kids get hurt as I have, it makes you think twice about those regulations. They get excited, they forget to hang on. That mother was a fool to let her little girl ride this thing alone."

Silently I agreed. The carousel was dangerous in more ways than one. Merrill Smith, according to her mother, Evelyn, had gotten on it the previous afternoon and had never gotten off.

Outside the round blue building that housed the carousel, I crossed to where my client sat on a bench next to the ticket booth. Although the sun was shining, Evelyn Smith had drawn her coat tightly around her thin frame. Her dull red hair fluffed in curls over her upturned collar, and her lashless blue eyes regarded me solemnly as I approached. I marveled, for the second time since Evelyn had given me Merrill's picture, that this homely woman could have produced such a beautiful child.

"Does the operator remember her?" Evelyn asked eagerly.

"There were so many kids here that he couldn't. I'll have to locate the woman who was in the ticket booth yesterday."

"But I bought Merrill's ticket for her."

"Just the same, she may remember something." I sat down on the cold stone bench and put my hand on Evelyn's arm. "Look, don't you think it would be better to go to the police? They have the resources for dealing with disappearances. I'm only one person and . . ."

"No!" Her normally pallid face whitened until it seemed translucent. "No, Sharon. I want you."

"But, Evelyn, I don't know where to go next. You've already contacted

Merrill's school and her friends. I can question the ticket-booth woman and personnel at the children's playground, but I'm afraid the answer will be the same. And, in the meantime, your little girl has been missing . . ."

"No. Please."

I was silent for a moment. When I looked up, Evelyn's pale eyes were on my face. There was something coldly analytical there, something that didn't fit with a distressed mother.

Evelyn glanced away. "You just look like someone who can help, Sharon. You're part Indian, aren't you?"

"One-eighth Shoshone. The rest is Scotch-Irish, but the Indian blood came out in me."

"It shows in your face."

"That doesn't mean I have any special Indianlike skills for tracking people down," I said lightly.

"Oh, I know that. I was just curious."

But it didn't fit with the upset mother either. Why would she be thinking of my heritage rather than her little girl? I made a quick decision. "All right, I'll give it a try. But you have to help me. Try to think of anywhere else Merrill might have gone."

Evelyn closed her eyes. "There's the place where we used to live. Merrill was happy there; the woman in the first-floor flat was nice to her. Merrill might have gone back there. She doesn't really like the new apartment."

I wrote down the address. "I'll try it, but if I haven't come up with anything by tonight, promise me you'll call the police."

She stood up, a small smile curving her lips. "Okay, but I know you'll find her. I just know it!"

She turned, her hands thrust deep in her pockets, and I watched her narrow back retreat through the brightly painted futuristic shapes of the new children's playground. I wished I had the same confidence in my abilities as my client did.

I remained on the bench for a few minutes. Traffic whizzed by on the other side of the eucalyptus grove that screened this corner of San Francisco's Golden Gate Park but, caught up in thoughts of Evelyn Smith, I barely noticed it.

My client was a brand-new member of All Souls Cooperative, the legal services outfit for which I was a private investigator. She'd come in this morning and told her story to my boss, Hank Zahn. After her insistent refusal of police help, he'd sent her to me.

It was Evelyn's unreasonable fear of the police that bothered me most about this case. Any normal middle-class mother would have been on the phone to them minutes after her child's disappearance. Instead, Evelyn had waited until the next day and then contacted a lawyer. Why? What was she afraid of?

Well, I decided, when a client comes to you with a story that seems less than candid, the best place to look is into that client's own life. Perhaps the neighbor at the old address could shed some light on her strange behavior. If I didn't turn up any leads from the park personnel, that was where I'd look next.

By three that afternoon, almost twelve hours after Merrill Smith's disappearance, I was still empty-handed. The park personnel knew nothing; the old neighbor wasn't home. Dejectedly I drove my battered red MG to the Bernal Heights district of the city and the big brown Victorian that housed All Souls.

I nodded at Ted, the secretary, and made my way down the long central hall to my office—a room that was little more than a converted closet. There I curled up in my overstuffed armchair and stared at the wall. My thoughts, such as they were, were interrupted by a knock on the door. My boss, Hank Zahn, came in and perched on the desk.

"You find that missing kid?" he asked.

I shook my head. "It's a strange case."

"That should please you. It's been pretty dull around here lately."

It was true. All Souls' clients—a placid lower-to-middle-income group —had been even more law abiding of late than usual. I'd had little excitement. Still, it was more satisfying than the security guard job I'd had before college and more above-board than the assignments they'd tried to hand me at the big detective agency I'd gone to work for after I'd gotten my degree. Hank, an old friend from UC Berkeley, had given me the job with All Souls after the big agency and I had agreed to differ on my role in a particularly messy divorce action.

"This case does provide a challenge," I said.

"No leads?"

"Only one left to check out." I glanced at my watch. "And I may as well do that now."

I left Hank contemplating my tiny office. Maybe one day he would decide I rated something better and move me into a room with a window.

Once again I drove to Evelyn Smith's former address, on Fell Street across from the Panhandle of the park. It was a decaying area that had never recovered from the hippie invasion of the sixties. The house itself was a three-flat Victorian with a fire escape snaking up its facade. I studied the mailboxes and rang the bell of the ground-floor flat.

A young woman in a pink bathrobe answered. Her eyes were sleep-swollen and her blond hair was tangled.

"I'm sorry I woke you," I said.

"That's okay. I was just catching a few winks while the baby naps. What can I do for you?"

"Evelyn Smith sent me," I said, showing her my license. "Her little girl has disappeared and she thought she might have come back here."

"Evvie? What do you know! I haven't heard from her since she moved."

"And you haven't seen Merrill?"

"No. Why on earth would Evvie think she'd come here?"

"She said Merrill had been happy here and that you'd been especially nice to her."

The woman frowned. "Yes, I was nice to Merrill, but that was four years ago. And I seriously doubt Merrill was happy at all. In fact, that was the reason I went out of my way with her."

"Oh? Why wasn't she happy?"

"The usual. Evvie and Bob fought all the time. Then he moved out and, a few months later, Evvie found a smaller place for her and the little girl."

So Evelyn was divorced. She'd told me she was a single mother. "What did they fight about?"

"Toward the end, everything, but mainly about the kid." She paused, thoughtful. "You know, that's an odd thing. I hadn't thought of it in ages."

"What is that?"

"Merrill. How two homely people could have such a beautiful kid. Evvie, so awkward and skinny. And Bob, with that dark-red hair and awful complexion. It was Merrill being so beautiful that caused their problems."

"How so?"

"Bob adored her. He doted on that child. And Evvie was jealous. At first she accused Bob of spoiling Merrill, and then she turned really vicious. She made cracks about unnatural relationships, if you know what I mean. *Then* she started to take it out on the kid. I tried to help, but there wasn't much I could do. Evvie Smith acted like she hated her own child."

Evelyn Smith's new apartment was in a pleasant modern building on the north side of the park. I followed a carpeted hallway to the rear of the building.

Evelyn was as pale as she had been that morning. She admitted me, her eyes anxiously searching my face.

"Did you find out anything?" she asked.

I hesitated. "A little. I'd like to see Merrill's room."

She nodded and took me there. The room was decorated in yellow, with big felt cut-outs of animals on the walls. The bed was neatly made up with ruffled quilts, and everything was in place, except for a second-grade reader that lay open on the desk. The room had the look of being lovingly cared for.

Evelyn was staring at a tiger on the wall beside her. "She's crazy about animals," she said softly. "That's why she enjoys the merry-go-round so much."

I glanced at Merrill's name, printed in childish letters on the flyleaf of the reader. Evelyn seemed a genuinely devoted mother; perhaps her jealousy had vanished once her husband was out of the picture. "Evelyn," I said, "I understand you're divorced."

She nodded. "Three years ago."

"Where does your ex-husband live?"

"Here in town, on a houseboat at Mission Creek."

"Do you still love him?"

She started, then colored. "What's that got to do with anything?"

"A lot. You're protecting him."

She fell silent, fingering the second-grade reader. "What makes you say that?"

"It's a common occurrence: the father snatches the child whom the mother has custody of. The mother doesn't want to bring in the police because she still loves the father and doesn't want to get him in trouble. So she hires a private investigator to get the child back. Why didn't you tell me what had happened? It would have saved so much time."

She looked up, her eyes filling with tears. "Because I don't know if he really has her. I tried to call him; there wasn't any answer. I thought you would find out . . ."

"How could I, when you didn't even tell me he existed?"

"I don't know. I don't want to get him in trouble. All I want is my little girl back. Please, Sharon!" The tears spilled over.

"Take it easy," I said, patting her arm. "You'll get her back."

My task had been simplified: ascertain that Bob Smith had the little girl; wait, watch unobtrusively; and, when the moment was right, a reverse snatch, back to mommy. Simple. But . . . there was one stop I wanted to make before the houseboat on Mission Creek.

The late-afternoon fog had crept through the redwood and eucalyptus groves of the park by the time I reached the carousel. It was shut for the night, and the old man I'd spoken with earlier had gone. In the ticket booth a gray-haired woman who had not been on duty earlier was counting cash into a bank-deposit bag.

"I don't know where he lives," she said when I asked about the carousel operator. "Is it important?"

"Yes. I want to ask him if he saw a certain man here yesterday."

The woman's eyes were keen with interest. "Maybe I could help you. I was on duty then."

"You're the Sunday cashier?"

"Sundays and afternoons."

I pulled out Merrill's picture. "Do you remember her?"

The woman smiled. "Of course. You don't forget such a beautiful child. She and her mother used to come here every Sunday afternoon and ride the carousel. Her mother still comes. She sits on that bench over there and watches the children and looks sad as can be. Did her little girl die?"

I stared. "When was the last time you saw the child?"

"Maybe three years ago but, like I said, you don't forget a child like that. Is she dead?"

I shook my head, thinking of the second-grade reader in the neat-as-a-pin room that supposedly belonged to a ten-year-old. "No, she's not dead. She's fine."

It was dark when I parked at Mission Creek. A hodgepodge of ramshackle boats lined the shore and falling-down piers. Their lights shone off the black water of the narrow channel. Waves slapped against the pilings as I hurried out on the main pier, my footsteps echoing on the rough planking. Bob Smith's boat was near the end, between two hulking fishing craft. A dim light on the porch highlighted peeling blue paint. I knocked on the door and waited.

The lines of the fishing craft creaked as it rose and fell with the tide. Behind me there was a rustling sound. Rats, I thought. I glanced over my shoulder, seized with the eerie sensation of being watched. No one— whom I could see. Footsteps sounded inside the houseboat.

The little girl who answered the door had curly red-gold hair. Her T-shirt was grimy and there was a rip in her jeans, but in spite of it she was beautiful.

"Hello, Merrill."

"Hi. Who are you?"

"A friend of your mom."

It was the wrong answer. She stiffened.

"And your dad," I added.

Merrill relaxed. "You want to see him?"

"Yes, I'd like to."

Bob Smith had shaggy dark-red hair and a complexion pitted with acne scars. His eyes regarded me through rimless glasses.

I introduced myself and showed him my license. "Mr. Smith, your ex-wife hired me this morning to find Merrill. She claims your daughter disappeared on the merry-go-round in Golden Gate Park yesterday afternoon."

He blinked. "That's preposterous. Yesterday afternoon we were out on our sailboat. All afternoon."

The little girl reappeared, an orange cat draped over her shoulder. She regarded me quizzically. "Are you really a friend of my mom?"

"Really."

She set the cat down on the gangplank and began to play with a rusty anchor that served as decoration.

I turned back to Bob Smith. "I know Evvie's story is preposterous. I see you have custody of Merrill."

"Yes, ever since the divorce three years ago."

"Did Evvie abuse Merrill?"

He glanced away. "You have to understand that Evvie isn't too stable. She has her problems, but she refuses to undergo therapy. There's no question that she loves Merrill, but . . . What's this about her claiming Merrill was missing?"

"I'll get to that. Has Evvie tried to regain custody recently?"

"Yes, but they put the question to Merrill and she chose to stay with me. I suppose this so-called disappearance is another manifestation of Evvie's sickness."

"Your ex-wife may be disturbed, but she's also very clever. Failing to get custody, she hired me to kidnap the child."

"And you'd do that?"

I smiled, thinking of my past employment problems. "No. Some investigators might, but not me. Evvie constructed an elaborate scenario and actually had me believing *you'd* taken the child—because I was convinced I'd discovered that myself. She probably figured a woman would be more sympathetic and willing to believe it."

The orange cat nudged against my ankles. Merrill said, "Daddy, I'm hungry."

Bob Smith opened his mouth in reply, but his features suddenly took on a look of shock.

I felt a rush of air behind me and started to turn. Merrill cried out.

I pivoted, almost losing my balance, and came face to face with Evelyn. She was clutching Merrill around the shoulders, her left arm under the child's neck.

"Daddy!"

Bob Smith started forward. "Evvie, what the hell . . ."

Evelyn's face was pale, like a soapstone sculpture. "Don't come near me!"

Bob rushed forward, past me.

Evelyn drew back, and her right hand came up, bearing a knife.

I recoiled, at the same time thinking, Just like the knife I make salads with! And then, Salads—at a time like this!

Evelyn began backing toward the end of the pier, dragging Merrill with her. The little girl's feet scraped on the rough planking. Her small face was blank with shock.

Bob Smith groaned and turned to me. He spread his hands. "It's all starting again. All over again."

I pushed past him. Evelyn and Merrill were almost to the end of the pier. The black water of the channel glistened behind them.

"Evvie," I called, "please come back."

"No! I knew you'd find out and then wouldn't bring Merrill to me. You're too smart. I should have hired someone stupid."

"Evvie, you've no place to go."

"I don't care. I don't have anyplace to go anyway."

"Come on. Sure you do." I held out my hand, unsure that she could see it in the blackness.

"No. No way. I want to stay out here. Just Merrill and me and the water . . ." Her voice died out. In the flickering lights off the water, I could see the gleam of the knife.

Bob Smith came up behind me. "I'll call the police."

I nodded and pushed him back.

"Evvie," I called, "what about the animals?"

"The what?" She sounded further and further away.

"The animals. The ones Merrill's so crazy about."

"What animals?"

"On the merry-go-round. The giraffes and the camels and the . . ."

"And the zebras, mommy." A small voice, scared, but somehow understanding. "And what about the ostrich? What about the purple toad?"

There was a long silence. Then Evvie's voice, weak: "You want to see the animals?"

"I want to go to the merry-go-round, mommy. With you. Like we used to do."

I began edging closer. "The other day I rode on the greatest blue pig."

Merrill: "Was that the one with the tail falling off?"

"Yes. The most awful tail I've ever seen in a pig." Closer.

"I'd love to ride that pig. Please, mommy."

Evelyn's head turned, toward the water, toward oblivion for her and her little girl.

"Evvie," I said, "come on back here. We have to go ride the merry-go-round."

Her head turned toward me.

"Please, mommy!"

"Just the three of us?" she asked. "Not Bob too?"

"Not Bob."

She sighed, and the blade of the knife flashed—downward, where it clattered on the planks of the pier. Wearily she released her hold on Merrill.

I stepped forward and kicked the knife into the water.

Merrill stumbled toward me. Behind, Bob Smith gasped in relief. Merrill stopped, looking back at her mother. Then she reached up and clasped Evvie's hand.

I took Evelyn's arm. "Are you all right, Merrill?" I asked.

Merrill looked up at me. "I'm all right. Will mommy be okay?"

"Yes. Yes, she will—now."

A Craving for Originality

BILL PRONZINI

There are crime stories and then there are crime stories. "A Craving for Originality" is that type known as the reductio ad absurdum—*in this case, a wildly satirical look at the hack writer, the entire spectrum of contemporary fiction, and the dull, flat, dreary, uninspired lives of most people. The crime which is perpetrated in these pages is one of the most bizarre in the annals of mysterydom, as you'll discover when Charlie Hackman finally succeeds in his search for originality.*

Charlie Hackman was a professional writer. He wrote popular fiction, any kind from sexless Westerns to sexy Gothics to oversexed historical romances, whatever the current trends happened to be. He could be counted on to deliver an acceptable manuscript to order in two weeks. He had published nine million words in a fifteen-year career, under a variety of different names (Allison St. Cyr being the most prominent), and he couldn't tell you the plot of any book he'd written more than six months ago. He was what is euphemistically known in the trade as "a dependable wordsmith," or "a versatile pro," or "a steady producer of commercial commodities."

In other words, he was well named: Hackman was a hack.

The reason he was a hack was not because he was fast and prolific, or because he contrived popular fiction on demand, or because he wrote for money. It was because he was and did all these things with no ambition and no sense of commitment. It was because he wrote without originality of any kind.

Of course, Hackman had not started out to be a hack; no writer does. But he had discovered early on, after his first two novels were rejected with printed slips by thirty-seven publishers each, that (a) he was not very good, and (b) what talent he did possess was in the form of imitations. When he tried to do imaginative, ironic, meaningful work of his own he failed miserably; but when he imitated the ideas and visions of others, the blurred carbon copies he produced were just literate enough to be publishable.

Truth to tell, this didn't bother him very much. The one thing he had

482

always wanted to be was a professional writer; he had dreamed of nothing else since his discovery of the Hardy Boys and Tarzan books in his preteens. So from the time of his first sale he accepted what he was, shrugged, and told himself not to worry about it. What was wrong with being a hack, anyway? The writing business was full of them—and hacks, no less than nonhacks, offered a desirable form of escapist entertainment to the masses; the only difference was, his readership had nondiscriminating tastes. Was his product, after all, any less honorable than what television offered? Was he hurting anybody, corrupting anybody? No. Absolutely not. So what was wrong with being a hack?

For one and a half decades, operating under this cheerful set of rationalizations, Hackman was a complacent man. He wrote from ten to fifteen novels per year, all for minor and exploitative paperback houses, and earned an average annual sum of twenty-five thousand dollars. He married an ungraceful woman named Grace and moved into a suburban house on Long Island. He went bowling once a week, played poker once a week, argued conjugal matters with his wife once a week, and took the train into Manhattan to see his agent and editors once a week. Every June he and Grace spent fourteen pleasant days at Lake George in the Adirondacks. Every Christmas Grace's mother came from Pennsylvania and spent fourteen miserable days with them.

He drank a little too much sometimes and worried about lung cancer because he smoked three packs of cigarettes a day. He cheated moderately on his income tax. He coveted one of his neighbors' wives. He read all the current paperback best sellers, dissected them in his mind, and then reassembled them into similar plots for his own novels. When new acquaintances asked him what he did for a living he said, "I'm a writer," and seldom failed to feel a small glow of pride.

That was the way it was for fifteen years—right up until the morning of his fortieth birthday.

Hackman woke up on that morning, looked at Grace lying beside him, and realized she had put on at least forty pounds since their marriage. He listened to himself wheeze as he lighted his first cigarette of the day. He got dressed and walked downstairs to his office, where he read the half page of manuscript still in his typewriter (an occult pirate novel, the latest craze). He went outside and stood on the lawn and looked at his house. Then he sat down on the porch steps and looked at himself.

I'm not just a writer of hack stories, he thought sadly, I'm a liver of a hack life.

Fifteen years of cohabiting with trite fictional characters in hackneyed fictional situations. Fifteen years of cohabiting with an unimaginative wife in a trite suburb in a hackneyed life-style in a conventional world. Hackman the hack, doing the same things over and over again; Hackman the hack, grinding out books and days one by one. No uniqueness in any of it, from the typewriter to the bedroom to the Adirondacks.

No originality.

He sat there for a long while, thinking about this. No originality. Funny. It was like waking up to the fact that, after forty years, you've never tasted pineapple, that pineapple was missing from your life. All of a sudden you craved pineapple; you wanted it more than you'd ever wanted anything before. Pineapple or originality—it was the same principle.

Grace came out eventually and asked him what he was doing. "Thinking that I crave originality," he said, and she said, "Will you settle for eggs and bacon?" Trite dialogue, Hackman thought. Hackneyed humor. He told her he didn't want any breakfast and went into his office.

Originality. Well, even a hack ought to be able to create something fresh and imaginative if he applied himself; even a hack learned a few tricks in fifteen years. How about a short story? Good. He had never written a short story; he would be working in new territory already. Now how about a plot?

He sat at his typewriter. He paced the office. He lay down on the couch. He sat at the typewriter again. Finally the germ of an idea came to him and he nurtured it until it began to develop. Then he began to type.

It took him all day to write the story, which was about five thousand words long. That was about his average wordage per day on a novel, but on a novel he never revised so much as a comma. After supper he went back into the office and made pen-and-ink corrections until eleven o'clock. Then he went to bed, declined Grace's reluctant offer of "a birthday present," and dreamed about the story until 6 A.M. At which time he got up, retyped the pages, made some more revisions in ink, and retyped the story a third time before he was satisfied. He mailed it that night to his agent.

Three days later the agent called about a new book contract. Hackman asked him, "Did you have a chance to read the short story I sent you?"

"I read it, all right. And sent it straight back to you."

"Sent it back? What's wrong with it?"

"It's old hat," the agent said. "The idea's been done to death."

Hackman went out into the backyard and lay down in the hammock. All right, so maybe he was doomed to hackdom as a writer; maybe he just wasn't capable of *writing* anything original. But that didn't mean he couldn't *do* something original, did it? He had a quick mind, a good grasp of what was going on in the world. He ought to be able to come up with at least one original idea, maybe even an idea that would not only satisfy his craving for originality but change his life, get him out of the stale rut he was in.

He closed his eyes.

He concentrated.

He thought about jogging backward from Long Island to Miami Beach and then applying for an entry in the Guinness Book of World Records.

Imitative.

He thought about marching naked through Times Square at high noon, waving a standard paperback contract and using a bullhorn to protest man's literary inhumanity to man.

Trite.

He thought about adopting a red-white-and-blue disguise and robbing a bank in each one of the original thirteen states.

Derivative.

He thought about changing his name to Holmes, finding a partner named Watson, and opening a private inquiry agency that specialized in solving the unsolved and insoluble.

Parrotry.

He thought about doing other things legal and illegal, clever and foolish, dangerous and harmless.

Unoriginal. Unoriginal. Unoriginal.

That day passed and several more just like it. Hackman became obsessed with originality—so much so that he found himself unable to write, the first serious block he had had as a professional. It was maddening, but every time he thought of a sentence and started to type it out, something would click in his mind and make him analyze it as original or banal. The verdict was always banal.

He thought about buying a small printing press, manufacturing bogus German Deutsche marks in his basement, and then flying to Munich and passing them at the Oktoberfest.

Counterfeit.

Hackman took to drinking a good deal more than his usual allotment of alcohol in the evenings. His consumption of cigarettes rose to four packs a day and climbing. His originality quotient remained at zero.

He thought about having a treasure map tattooed on his chest, claiming to be the sole survivor of a gang of armored car thieves, and conning all sorts of greedy people out of their life savings.

Trite.

The passing days turned into passing weeks. Hackman still wasn't able to write; he wasn't able to do much of anything except vainly overwork his brain cells. He knew he couldn't function again as a writer or a human being until he did something, *anything* original.

He thought about building a distillery in his garage and becoming Long Island's largest manufacturer and distributor of bootleg whiskey.

Hackneyed.

Grace had begun a daily and voluble series of complaints. Why was he moping around, drinking and smoking so much? Why didn't he go into his office and write his latest piece of trash? What were they going to do for money if he didn't fulfill his contracts? How would they pay the mortgage and the rest of their bills? What was the *matter* with him, anyway? Was he going through some kind of midlife crisis or what?

Hackman thought about strangling her, burying her body under the acacia tree in the backyard—committing the perfect crime.

Stale. Bewhiskered.

Another week disappeared. Hackman was six weeks overdue now on an occult pirate novel and two weeks overdue on a male-action novel; his publishers were upset, his agent was upset; where the hell were the manuscripts? Hackman said he was just polishing up the first one. "Sure you are," the agent said over the phone. "Well, you'd better have it with you when you come in on Friday. I mean that, Charlie. You'd better deliver."

Hackman thought about kidnapping the star of Broadway's top musical extravaganza and holding her for a ransom of one million dollars plus a role in her next production.

Old stuff.

He decided that things couldn't go on this way. Unless he came up with an original idea pretty soon, he might just as well shuffle off this mortal coil.

He thought about buying some rat poison and mixing himself an arsenic cocktail.

More old stuff.

Or climbing a utility pole and grabbing hold of a high-tension wire.

Prosaic. Corny.

Or hiring a private plane to fly him over the New Jersey swamps and then jumping out at two thousand feet.

Ho-hum.

Damn! He couldn't seem to go on, he couldn't seem *not* to go on. So what was he going to do?

He thought about driving over to Pennsylvania, planting certain carefully faked documents inside Grace's mother's house, and turning the old bat in to the FBI as a foreign spy.

Commonplace.

On Friday morning he took his cigarettes (the second of the five packs a day he was now consuming) and his latest hangover down to the train station. There he boarded the express for Manhattan and took a seat in the club car.

He thought about hijacking the train and extorting twenty million dollars from the state of New York.

Imitative.

When the train arrived at Penn Station he trudged the six blocks to his agent's office. In the elevator on the way up an attractive young blond gave him a friendly smile and said it was a nice day, wasn't it?

Hackman thought about making her his mistress, having a torrid affair, and then running off to Acapulco with her and living in sin in a villa high above the harbor and weaving Mexican *serapes* by day and drinking tequila by night.

Hackneyed.

The first thing his agent said to him was, "Where's the manuscript, Charlie?" Hackman said it wasn't ready yet, he was having a few personal problems. The agent said, "You think you got problems? What about *my* problems? You think I can afford to have hack writers missing deadlines and making editors unhappy? That kind of stuff reflects back on me, ruins my reputation. I'm not in this business for my health, so maybe you'd better just find yourself another agent."

Hackman thought about bashing him over the head with a paperweight, disposing of the body, and assuming his identity after first gaining sixty pounds and going through extensive plastic surgery.

Motheaten. Threadbare.

Out on the street again, he decided he needed a drink and turned into the first bar he came to. He ordered a triple vodka and sat brooding over it. I've come to the end of my rope, he thought. If there's one original idea in this world, I can't even imagine what it is. For that matter, I can't even imagine a partly original idea, which I'd settle for right now because maybe there *isn't* anything completely original any more.

"What am I going to do?" he asked the bartender.

"Who cares?" the bartender said. "Stay, go, drink, don't drink—it's all the same to me."

Hackman sighed and got off his stool and swayed out onto East Fifty-second Street. He turned west and began to walk back toward Grand Central, jostling his way through the midafternoon crowds. Overhead, the sun glared down at him between the buildings like a malevolent eye.

He was nearing Madison Avenue, muttering clichés to himself, when the idea struck him.

It came out of nowhere, full-born in an instant, the way most great ideas (or so he had heard) always do. He came to an abrupt standstill. Then he began to smile. Then he began to laugh. Passersby gave him odd looks and detoured around him, but Hackman didn't care. The idea was all that mattered.

It was inspired.

It was imaginative.

It was meaningful.

It was original.

Oh, not one-hundred-percent original—but that was all right. He had already decided that finding total originality was an impossible goal. This idea was close, though. It was close and it was wonderful and he was going to do it. Of course he was going to do it; after all these weeks of search and frustration, how could he *not* do it?

Hackman set out walking again. His stride was almost jaunty and he was whistling to himself. Two blocks south he entered a sporting goods store and found what he wanted. The salesman who waited on him asked if he was going camping. "Nope," Hackman said, and winked. "Something *much* more original than that."

He left the store and hurried down to Madison to a bookshop that specialized in mass-market paperbacks. Inside were several long rows of shelving, each shelf containing different categories of fiction and nonfiction, alphabetically arranged. Hackman stepped into the fiction section, stopped in front of the shelf marked HISTORICAL ROMANCES, and squinted at the titles until he located one of his own pseudonymous works. Then he unwrapped his parcel.

And took out the woodsman's hatchet.

And got a comfortable grip on its handle.

And raised it high over his head.

And—

Whack! Eleven copies of *Love's Tender Fury* by Allison St. Cyr were drawn and quartered.

A male customer yelped; a female customer shrieked. Hackman took no notice. He moved on to the shelf marked OCCULT PIRATE ADVENTURE, raised the hatchet again, and—

Whack! Nine copies of *The Devil Daughter of Jean Lafitte* by Adam Caine were exorcised and scuttled.

On to ADULT WESTERNS. And—

Whack! Four copies of *Ryder Rides the Outlaw Trail* by Galen McGee bit the dust.

Behind the front counter a chubby little man was jumping up and down, waving his arms. "What are you doing?" he kept shouting at Hackman. "What are you doing?"

"Hackwork!" Hackman shouted back. "I'm a hack writer doing hackwork!"

He stepped smartly to GOTHIC SUSPENSE. And—

Whack! Five copies of *Mansion of Dread* by Melissa Ann Farnsworth were reduced to rubble.

On to MALE ACTION SERIES, and—

Whack! Ten copies of Max Ruffe's *The Grenade Launcher #23: Blowup at City Hall* exploded into fragments.

Hackman paused to survey the carnage. Then he nodded in satisfaction and turned toward the front door. The bookshop was empty now, but the chubby little man was visible on the sidewalk outside, jumping up and down and semaphoring his arms amid a gathering crowd. Hackman crossed to the door in purposeful strides and threw it open.

People scattered every which way when they saw him come out with the hatchet aloft. But they needn't have feared; he had no interest in people, except as bit players in this little drama. After all, what hack worth the name ever cared a hoot about his audience?

He began to run up Forty-eighth Street toward Fifth Avenue, brandishing the hatchet. Nobody tried to stop him, not even when he lopped off the umbrella shading a frankfurter vendor's cart.

"I'm a hack!" he shouted.

And shattered the display window of an exclusive boutique.

"I'm Hackman the hack!" he yelled.

And halved the product and profits of a pretzel vendor.

"I'm Hackman the hack and I'm hacking my way to glory!" he bellowed.

And sliced the antenna off an illegally parked Cadillac limousine.

He was almost to Fifth Avenue by this time. Ahead of him he could see a red signal light holding up crosstown traffic; this block of Forty-eighth Street was momentarily empty. Behind him he could hear angry shouts and what sounded like a police whistle. He looked back over his shoulder. Several people were giving pursuit, including the chubby little man from the bookshop; the leader of the pack, a blue uniform with a red face atop it, was less than fifty yards distant.

But the game was not up yet, Hackman thought. There were more bookstores along Fifth; with any luck he could hack his way through two or three before they got him. He decided south was the direction he wanted to go, pulled his head around, and started to sprint across the empty expanse of Forty-eighth.

Only the street wasn't empty any longer; the signal on Fifth had changed to green for the eastbound traffic.

He ran right out in front of an oncoming car.

He saw it too late to jump clear, and the driver saw him too late to brake or swerve. But before he and the machine joined forces, Hackman had just enough time to realize the full scope of what was happening—and to feel a sudden elation. In fact, he wished with his last wish that he'd thought of this himself. It was the crowning touch, the final fillip, the *coup de grâce;* it lent the death of Hackman, unlike the life of Hackman, a genuine originality.

Because the car which did him in was not just a car; it was a New York City taxicab.

Otherwise known as a hack.

Tranquillity Base

ASA BABER

Asa Baber's short stories and articles have appeared in Playboy *and similar markets for well over a decade; he is the author of one novel,* Land of a Million Elephants. *"Tranquility Base" may be the finest—it is absolutely the most terrifying—short story to emerge from the late-sixties, shoot-at-the-moon, one-small-step, bang-'em-all-up ambience. It is probably for that very reason that it took Mr. Baber ten years to sell the story, and when he did it appeared in a small, university-affiliated publication. Here it is, hopefully rescued and restored for that fraction of eternity Tranquillity Base has left us.*

Union Station, Chicago, after five in the afternoon. What a day, what a day, with the heat in the streets. But Avery is happy after work and he hums to himself as he walks down the steep incline towards the concourse. He has his light tan suit coat thrown recklessly over his shoulder: his forefinger tugs the minor weight and that gesture flexes his bicep. He has his sleeves rolled a bit too high, but all the better to show his new vacation tan.

Once into the cavernous station with its cathedral light, with its steady stream of visitors and its strangely muffled echoes at this hour—only the shuffling sound of thousands of shoes crossing the floor—Avery buys his paper at the candy counter and moves into the flow that leads to the Burlington line. If there is an eternal special moment to his days, it is this time when he senses the sleek silver tube waiting for him in double-deckered air-conditioned comfort. Oh how he longs for the silence and focus of that ride to Highlands. No one bothers him, yet he recognizes many of the faces, conductors and commuters, all brothers and sisters in this journey westward that leads out of the city and its grit.

Avery is getting himself ready, sorting out the signals, smelling as he passes through steam from the airbrakes that faint tinge of uric acid that lies in the railroad bed. His ears hear the hiss and groan from the undercarriage. Somewhere far off two flatcars jolt together.

He calibrates the distance to the middle of his train. He will walk two cars past that. It is his guessing game with the engineer, for when the train stops at Highlands there is only one exit that crosses the tracks. If Avery winds up ahead of that magic point he will have to tramp through milkweed and cinders to get back to the spot. If he is too cautious he will have to wait in line while others more lucky pass across. But there are times when Avery is winner, when he is *there*. That makes his day, and he trots down the cement stairs in first place, and his children cheer him from the station wagon, and Ellen beams at his little triumph.

Today he feels no special ease, not even knowing that things have gone well for him (for the world, really—for the universe). Yes, he hums, and as much as he can, he struts. He is conscious of that secret roll of fat that suit coats usually hide. He hums to blot out his habit (especially when he is tired) of talking to himself. Only last week Collins—who rides the same train, but never with Avery—had confronted him at the office and asked Avery if he was all right; it seems he had seen Avery mumbling to himself as he boarded the train. Avery laughed it off very heartily, but he knew he would have to watch his public image.

Looking at him walking towards you on the platform, you would find him easy to like or ignore. Of average height and average weight for a man of thirty-five; hair a little thinning with silver streaks in the brown crew cut; jowls a bit flabby, and two worry lines that crease his forehead vertically and come to rest under the sinuses; a face eager to please, tired, wary, probably proud.

The headlines all say the same thing. The world is going home tonight for a special extravaganza and the newspapers cater to it. There are transcripts, feature articles, biographies, pictures, quotations from leaders and confidants, best wishes even in advertisements. There is the feeling that one has been included, that each and every one is part of the venture.

As he passes the middle of the train, Avery hears a sharp whistle. It pierces his ears and makes him wince. He looks around, but no one else seems to have heard it. Avery walks again—whistle again. He turns; nothing. He shakes his head and nods to a conductor who has been watching him. He continues on his way.

Then it comes, a fierce slap on the back, and a greeting shouted in his ear, "Brooks, you son-of-a-bitch!"

Avery checks his happy reaction of surprise that someone knows him, for he turns and looks up into a fat face that he does not recognize. But he keeps his grin on and his hand out; he doesn't want to muff it. "Whatdeyuh say!"

"Brooks, you bastard!" Affection again from this unplaceable.

Avery searches his memory hard. He runs through old school yearbooks and company rosters. He still has to fake it. "Yep. It's me, all right."

"Brooks Avery on the five-twenty! You live out this way?"

"Sure do. We moved here last year." Avery searches wildly: no special insignias on the lapel of the seersucker; a raincoat thrown over the arm that carries the briefcase—there's a clue, a big D in Gothic print on the light clear skin of the case, a skin so lucid at this angle that it appears almost phosphorescent. In his fast associations Avery assumes that the material was stripped from some exotic animal in Argentina or Peru. Smart shoes of the same mysterious hide (more nearly boots than shoes), a straw hat with a paisley band.

"Goddamn, Brooksy, it's been fifteen great years, hasn't it?"

Avery smiles and nods. There is a hint, and he works on it; fifteen years ago means college; still nothing.

The Anonymous reaches out and pats Avery's waistline. "Looks like you've put on a little too, baby! A pound a year, I always say." He laughs and Avery laughs with him. As usual when standing beside someone taller, Avery pulls in his backbone and shifts his weight to his toes. "Come on, let's hit the bar car and I'll buy you a drink."

Avery feels like a dude and apologizes. "Look, I'm sorry, but we don't have bar cars."

"The hell you say! No bar car for me and my buddy?" He flips a big arm around Avery's shoulders and they begin to walk again towards the head of the train. "You ought to see the bar car on the Orient Express —until it hits Yugoslavia, of course, and then they take it off."

"Really?" Avery says; he is damned if he is going to make countryboy comments such as "You sure have been around."

"Yes, really, by Christ! I've never seen anything like it. There you are whizzing along the Adriatic, coming into Trieste eating grapes and drinking wine, and zip boom bah they switch a few railroad cars and you're in Starvationville. I mean it. STARVATIONVILLE! Nothing to eat until you hit the Turkish border. And then it's goat's cheese and bread. My God I thought I was going to die."

Avery stops, uncertain, and holds out his hand. "This is where I get on."

But the arm does not leave the shoulders and the hand is ignored. They simply climb through the double doors together. "Let's hit the smoking car. Okay?" the man says. "I've still got to have my coffin nails."

"Yeah, me too," snickers Avery. They file into the aisle. "You want to sit upstairs? Only single seats—" he gets rather desperate "—but we could read the paper."

"Sure, sure." The guy is all amenable. "Got to read up for the Big Happening."

"Yep," says Avery as he slides into the narrow seat. "It's really incredible, isn't it?"

"I'll say it is. Makes you wonder, doesn't it?" says his amigo as he sits in the seat behind him.

"Sure does. I wish them luck."

"Sure as hell do. They'll need more than that, a lot more."

"Skill," nods Avery. He holds the front-page section over his shoulder. "Here you go."

"Naww, that's okay. Give me the Sports."

"No, go ahead, take it."

They settle back in silence. Avery lights a cigarette and takes that first delicious puff. The air conditioning and nicotine work on him, comfort him, and for a moment he does not care who the man is. Avery has had a long day.

He can see himself in the window. He brushes his palms across his temples. He checks his wristwatch and precisely to the minute he feels the sudden small jolt as the train pulls out. He catches a hard tap on the shoulder and he turns. The face is almost touching his and it blows smoke at him as it says: "Liftoff!" Then the face laughs loudly at its own joke.

Avery plays the game. "Roger. The clock is started."

They seem to have exhausted that lingo so they settle back again and read. Now out of the station, the sunlight pours on his forearm and Avery lowers the shade only to find it raised again by his copilot. That might be a pugnacious gesture and Avery checks behind him to see what this is all about. He gets a friendly wink: "Got to see the city too. May buy a house out this way and I want to see what I'll be riding through."

"You don't live out here?" Avery asks.

"Yes I do," says the face with a confirming nod.

Avery cannot cope with that paradox so he ignores it. He looks out over the dreary familiar scene: rickety back porch stairs that climb three and four stories, crawling up the grimy apartment walls as if they are separate stilts leaning for rest on the dark bricks; old refrigerators tied closed with ropes; cinders and innertubes; the sparkle of glass from a thousand facets of backyard earth, glittering as if this was a moon's surface; rotting wooden fences and, enclosing the properties of factories and stores, rusted mesh fences with barbed wire crowning their fringes; junked cars and twisted rails; steel structures on the skyline; children swinging on clotheslines or running through alleys or staring out of windows; all the old and clearly known elements of this part of town.

"How's Ellen?" comes the voice after long silence.

Tone and content frighten Avery. Just how much did this interrogator know? "She's fine, just fine."

"Fourteen years is a long time."

That remark floats for a moment, and Avery is about to turn and say "Look, who are you?" but the voice leans into his ear and whispers, "Don't tell old Dave that fourteen years isn't a long time." And he nudges Avery's shoulder. "Huh? Isn't it true? Fourteen-year itch twice what the seven-year itch is, huh?"

Avery has to laugh. It comes out modest but knowing. "There's an itch sometimes, all right." And there is relief in his laugh too, for now he has a name to work with. He uses it immediately. "Yes sir, Dave, there is an itch. I guess you know, huh?"

"Don't look at me, Brooksy, I never did the deed. I spend my time wandering, baby." Great guffaws. "I figured . . . I figured if a man gets married, he's stuck in earth orbit, you know?" He laughs with tears in his eyes now. "No apogee, no perigee!" His large hands make crude circles in the air.

Avery has to laugh with him. "I guess you broke out of that."

"Out with the pulsars, Brooks, out of sight!"

Their laughter dies down slowly and they return to their reading, shaking their heads at their good time and understanding, flipping the newspapers occasionally with their wrists.

Once past the tight homes of Cicero, the scene outside the windows begins to change towards greenery. The yellow heavy sky slowly lifts and by the time they hit Cissna Park there is a sense of clean air and trees.

Avery makes his preparations for descent. He tightens his tie and rolls down his sleeves. The air conditioning has made him feel spruce again and he wants to greet his family in full dress. He stubs out his last cigarette and puts on a false friendly air. "Well, Dave, it's been great."

"Ohhoho" comes a deep rumbling laugh from the huge frame. "How about a drink on me, Brooksy? You aren't going to run out on me, are you?"

Avery shrugs uneasily. "Next stop is my stop, Dave. Got to meet the wife and kids."

"All the better. Buy them all a drink!"

"Well, the kids don't drink, Dave. I don't want to put you to any trouble."

"No trouble! No trouble, kid!" He chucks Avery not too gently under the chin. They are moving down the stairs before Avery knows it. "I mean, how often do we get together? Every fifteen years? You think I don't have time to drink with a buddy I haven't seen for fifteen years?"

Avery pulls the sliding doors open and stands in the vestibule of the car. Out here it is hotter. He nods at the conductor. "You see, Dave, Ellen and the kids . . . you know . . . this is their worst hour . . . it's chaos at home, really."

"No trouble! Chance to meet your kids. How are they? Nice bunch?"

"Oh, they're great, Dave, really great. Beautiful."

The train crosses the tollway bridge. The arm comes back over Avery's shoulder and a sigh leads into a statement: "One thing I regret, Brooks, about not getting married. No kids of my own. I love the little bastards." The arm gestures and chokes Avery slightly. "What do we build roads like that for if it's not for our children? Huh?"

"That's a great road, Dave. Goes up to Milwaukee."

"Kids—the only reason to get married as I see it."

"It's one of the main ones, that's for sure."

"You bet your sweet ass it is. Something to lead your life for." He points at the headlines of the folded paper. "Something to run risks for, by God."

Avery tries to think through the moments ahead. His wife will be waiting in the parking lot. How will she handle this one? She is good at picking up his signals and if he plays it right she will not ask too many questions or make it embarrassing for him. But it is going to take some diplomacy on his part. He hates days like this when the obligations never end and rest never comes.

Off the train at almost the right point, across the tracks, Avery pounds rapidly down the steps hoping to have time to warn his wife. But there is no shaking the big lug at his side. Avery watches Ellen's face through the tinted windshield. He sees the children asking questions of her. He comes up to the driver's side and she opens the window.

"Honey, you remember Dave?"

Only the slightest pause on her part, only the hitch of an eyebrow and lip before she comes through, that beauty: "Dave! How are you? Nice to see you."

Avery is brushed aside and he hears a kiss as Dave leans in the window.

"Ellen, I'll be damned if you've changed a bit."

Very cautious this time: "Same to you, Dave," and a frantic look at Avery, who shrugs his shoulders and gives her a reassuring wink.

Avery opens the door and Ellen starts to get out of the front seat, but she is pushed back by the large hand that flips the bucket and paws its way into the back with the children. Avery clears his throat and makes the introductions rapidly. "Kids, this is an old friend of mine. His name is Dave, kids. Dave, this is Tony and Mark."

"Dave who?" asks Tony.

Oh you wise-ass punk, thinks Avery, but his embarrassment is covered by guffaws from Dave. "Dave who? Dave whoever, that's who!" says the voice in the back seat.

"That's a weird name," says Mark. "Dave Whoever."

Avery turns the air conditioner to maximum. He wants to cover the drive home with chatter. "Tony's eleven and Mark's six."

Ellen picks up his frantic mood and fills in too. "They're both very excited about tonight, Brooks, and I promised them they could stay up if they were good boys. They can watch until one of them misbehaves. When one goes to bed, the other goes."

Avery wants to ramble on; he has a speech already outlined, but the voice interrupts. "These are great kids, just great. I should have known, though. Good breeding! Good stock!"

Ellen blushes. "Dave, really, I—"

"Don't be silly! Good stock, by God. Plump and healthy. Prime! Prime!" He cups Tony's head as if he is palming a basketball. "I just love kids, I tell you." The children move away from him.

"What are you doing with yourself these days, Dave?" Ellen asks. She is still uneasy and her voice cracks.

"Oh, stuff and things, here and there." A silence. "Finance, mostly, international finance. Sales. A little lobbying on the side."

"Dave really gets around, honey," says Avery. "He was telling me about Turkey."

"How interesting!" Ellen turns so that she can watch the children. "How long were you there?"

"Oh, I'm there almost every year. I make a run out to the Mideast every six months or so. Good pickings out there."

Avery laughs. "I'll bet you do a hell of a business anywhere you go."

"That's about right," Dave answers seriously.

Avery turns off County Line Road and heads for Oak Street. "You know, it's nice to see some of my classmates really make it big," he says.

Dave shrugs and ruffles Tony's hair, pinches Mark's cheeks. "You hear that, boys? Your old man is trying to make himself modest. He lives out here in a damn fine spread, good wife, luscious children, and he tries to build me up. What do you think of that, guys?" The children simply stare at him.

"Come on, Dave, you've probably stashed away your first million by now."

Dave laughs and rubs his stomach. "Well, I knew I was fat, but not that fat! No sir, I didn't know it showed."

Avery pounds the steering wheel in his discovery and chuckles. "There, you see, Ellen? A real go-getter!"

Ellen shifts in her seat. "Well I think Dave is right, Brooks. You shouldn't run yourself down in front of the boys." She turns again towards the back seat. "Brooks is doing very well."

"Aww, cut it, Ellen."

"Of course I shouldn't tell you this, Dave, but Brooks is going to be managing the Central Bank Card."

"Ellen, this is still confidential." He looks at his guest in the mirror. "Don't listen to her, Dave, she's biased."

Ellen slaps his forearm. "I'm proud of you but not biased. Sometimes you think I'm—"

"—my own severest critic . . . I know, honey. Let's just cut the shop-talk."

Dave pulls Mark onto his knees and leans forward. "Come on, Ellen, tell me what Brooks is doing."

"I just did. The Central Bank Card? For the whole Midwest? You know?"

"Do I know?" And then to Mark. "Do we know?" Mark giggles. "You bet your skin we know! The charge card to end all charge cards!"

Avery shakes his head. "End a few careers too. You ought to see the people who apply. You would not believe it. In debt, prison records, divorced and paying too much alimony, people right out of the ghettos. . . . They have no money sense, none at all."

Dave punches Mark's stomach with his forefinger. "Your dad will sort them out, huh boy?" Mark giggles again.

Avery wheels into the driveway. In the full summer, wet and rich, the oaks and elms seem to drip sap and the lilac bush still holds its bloom and roses droop. The garage door opens with a signal from somewhere inside the car. They pull in next to the Volkswagen. The garage door shuts and lights come on. As he exits into the living room, Avery smells the odor of thick grass freshly cut mingling with traces of gasoline. "Tony! How many times have I told you to wash the lawn mower after you're done!"

But Avery does not have it in him to be a stern father tonight. For one thing, he has a policy of not scolding the children in front of guests. For another, he wants to watch television. He picks up the automatic tuner and presses the button.

The rest of the crew have followed him in. They all stand while the set warms up and flashes into color. They see an animated film describing what will be happening. "They're landing!" screams Tony.

Dave pulls the boy against him and rubs his shoulders. "Not yet, champ. This is just a cartoon, sort of."

Tony does not pull away immediately and Mark sidles up to get attention too. Dave notices this and holds the shorter boy's head against his hip. "You guys are okay in my book."

Both Avery and Ellen beam. Avery rubs his hands together as if he is washing them. "How about a little drink, Dave?"

"Whatever you've got, old buddy."

"Bourbon? Scotch?"

Dave walks to the kitchen with him. "I'll tell you what I really like— maybe you've got it, maybe you haven't."

"Name your poison."

"Well, the last time I was in Bangkok I had a banana liqueur. . . ."

Avery stumbles on his words. "I'm afraid we don't—"

"It was sweet as mother's milk."

"Dave, we haven't got—"

"That's okay. Just give me a tequila sour . . . and if you haven't got that, a little bourbon is okay by me."

Avery sighs fast. "A black label Daniels coming right up!"

Dave leaves for the living room again. Ellen enters fast to corner Avery. "Who *is* he?"

"Ellen, why isn't the ice maker working?"

"There's ice in the bucket, Brooks. Who is he?"

"He's who he says he is. He's Dave. He's a classmate."

"Was he in your fraternity?"

"Don't think so, Ellen. Hand me the jigger."

She stamps her foot. "I'm trying to talk to you, Brooks Avery! I don't have anything to feed that man. I don't like him just barging in here."

"Shhh! Now settle yourself down and feed him whatever you were going to feed us and act like the nice girl you usually are. Let's watch the tube and enjoy life, okay?"

"What made you bring him home? Why didn't you call?"

"Ellen, this is not the first time I've brought someone home with me. He is an old friend and he is a wealthy friend. All right? In my business you do not kick people of substance out your door. Now let's go."

The issue is closed. They come smiling back into the living room. They find Dave leading the boys in a poem he has taught them. They are trying to recite it while he pinches and tickles them:

> Oh I'm being eaten by a boa constrictor
> a boa constrictor a boa constrictor
> Oh I'm being eaten by a boa constrictor
> and I think that I shall die—
>
> Oh no, it's eating my toe
>
> Oh sin, it's up to my shin!
> Oh me, it's up to my knee!

"Drink, Dave?" Avery tries to hand the glass over in the wiggling crowd.

"Not yet, thanks. Set it over there. We're busy here." The face is red and happy.

> Oh my, it's up to my thigh!
> Oh fiddle, it's up to my middle!

There are great howls of laughter here, for Dave is prodding both their stomachs.

> Oh mess, it's up to my chest!
> Oh heck, it's up to my neck!
> Oh dear, it's up to my ear!

And then the three clowns collapse with muted sounds of suffocation:

> Glub, glub, glub!

Avery gets the children calmed down and seated in front of the TV. "Now you guys watch, because this is *history*. Man's first landing on the moon." But in fact there is not much to see except long shots of the control room. The boys wander in and out while Avery tries to play host. He raises his glass. "A little sentiment, Dave. Luck to those guys tonight."

"I'll drink to that. And to the machine that brought them there and has to get them back."

"Yes sir, to that too."

"You think there isn't money riding on this shot?" Dave asks this almost meanly.

"No sir! I know there is. I know that."

"Listen, some of the people I represent have got their hearts in their throats right now."

"The banks aren't *un*involved, you know," says Avery with some pride.

"People have got to dream, Brooks. We need this thing. It's going to open our eyes."

"Right, Dave; dream the impossible dream." Now with the good smoky scotch in his gullet Avery feels expansive and aware. Ellen comes and sits beside him. They drink and small-talk.

Dinner comes and goes, a meal unnoticed in the excitement of the time: food eaten without being seen, TV tables nearly toppled as hands search vaguely across the surfaces for crackers, herring, ham, cheese, wine, all the time the eyes and ears strain to be sociable and yet not miss the moments of black-and-white wonder. The boys are frozen without motion.

"Good picture—great picture—fantastic! Jesus, all those miles!" Dave roars his approval. His face is swelling as he drinks.

Ellen brings in strawberry shortcake and a canister of whipped cream. There is coffee too but the men go back to whiskey. After the two-hour show the screen fills with color and commentators again. Ellen pushes the children out of the room, but not before Avery gets his hugs from them and Dave gets the same.

The room is gently spinning for Avery in that familiar soft first-edge of a high. Things have gone so well! He cannot keep all compliments back. "Dave, you are great with kids. Just great."

Dave spreads his hands in a gesture of humility. "Like I said, Brooksy, they're my life."

"You should get married, Dave. I mean it. Have kids of your own."

"Oh. I do okay."

Avery takes this as studsmanship and he leers. "Lots of war stories, huh? I'll bet you do okay." But that buddy-buddy locker-room approach does not spur reaction. Avery is slightly embarrassed at his own crudity and he regroups with a serious topic. "How about some words of wisdom, Mr. Financier? A little shoptalk before we get too blotto."

Spread hands again. "You name it."

"Dave. Dave." Avery mutters affectionately, "I'm small potatoes. I'm not in your league. Just pick up your briefcase there and tell me what will make my million for me." The briefcase goes to the lap and again Avery is fascinated by the object. It seems to pick up the colors from the TV and melt them into a magic palette of patterns and moving structures. "Dave, that is the goddamndest hunk of leather I ever saw. What the hell is it?"

A private laugh. "If I told you, you wouldn't believe it."

"I would, I would. Cross my heart."

But he is leafing through papers and does not answer. Avery does not pursue the subject because there might be a hot tip coming up. Finally, Dave throws his hands up in despair. "Christ, Brooks, I don't know where to begin. We're spread out all over the place, you know? I could talk about teak from Cambodia or oil from South Africa or munitions from here. We are so damned diversified!"

"Boy," says Avery into the echo chamber of his glass, "I'll bet you really get around."

The conversation goes on in counterpart with the TV. Avery cannot remember all that is being said. His eyes cross lightly once or twice. He notices Ellen come into the room and turn down the volume on the set. And he sees two towheads peeking around the corner from the stairs. "Get back in bed!" he yells once.

Then a silly mood hits him. The TV picture with all its flip-flopping challenges Avery. He stands and sprays whipped cream on the TV screen. It is a delightful feeling, a sort of freedom that surges over him in a flash. Ellen grabs futilely for the can and catches an eyeful of the stuff and runs crying from the room. Avery paints a cream mustache on the tempered glass, two fat dots for eyes, a jiggly hairline, a sloppy mouth.

And of course the regrets come on as fast as the urge did. Something snaps inside his head and he realizes his absurdity. He stands there with the can dripping. Avery tries a laugh. Nothing. He walks carefully across the carpet. "It wasn't just the liquor," he says. "I'm not that drunk." He turns and sees his wife cleaning the TV with a paper towel. She is crying. "Ellen, honey, it was just a joke."

"How do you expect the boys to get to sleep? As if they haven't had enough excitement! Listen to them up there bouncing on their beds."

"So they'll make good astronauts," Avery ad-libs. "So they'll go to Mars and Venus and Saturn."

"Not Saturn," says Dave with a smile and a nudge in Avery's side.

Avery smiles back and plays straight man. "Why not Saturn?"

Dave starts to laugh, and it rolls from somewhere in his gut and infects the room, and tears come into his eyes as he tries to push the answer out. Even Ellen laughs.

"Why not Saturn?" Avery asks again, prompting.

"Because—" handkerchief goes to eyes "—because she eats her children!" And if the line is not that funny, so what, because the sight of that huge man doubled up and gasping for breath is riotous, and Ellen and Avery join him in a release of nerves. It is a special happy thing like a roller-coaster ride, and they hit the highs and lows at different times so that when one stops laughing another begins again, and the children know from the sounds that something is going on, and they run down the stairs again into the middle of the helpless hystericals, and they are hugged.

"What's so funny?" asks Mark uneasily after a time; this triggers another wave of amusement, but not for too long.

"It is your bedtime for the last time!" says Ellen severely.

Dave crosses and takes each boy by the hand. He is serious and dignified. "Let me do the honors, Ellen."

She gasps and pretends embarrassment. "Why I'll do no such thing! You're a guest in this house—"

Avery holds up his hands. "Ellen! Ellen. Here is a man who loves children, and he doesn't get this kind of chance very often. Just stop being the careful mother."

But it is really out of both their hands. Dave is leading the kids up the stairs in a cute hippety-hop dance that synchronizes with the poem they are chanting again.

The door shuts at the top of the stairs and Avery hugs his wife warmly. "Your bedtime too, sweet."

"But I've got to clean up, Brooks."

"Can't you ever accept a favor? I'll scrape the dishes and load the washer. Dave will put the kids to sleep. Now take advantage of our hospitality before it melts."

She yawns widely, grins sweetly. "Dave will have to sleep—"

"—in the hide-a-bed in the playroom. I know."

She climbs the stairs slowly, already unzipping her dress. "The sheets are in—"

"Ellen, I *know.*"

"Kiss the boys for me," is her last reminder as she rounds the corner.

Avery pours himself another scotch, light this time with water. There is still a wrap-up of the day and night beaming out of the TV. Avery laughs at his own idiocy with the whipped cream. He can still see white streaks of the stuff in the corners of the picture tube. He sits and stares dully, hardly listening to the low voices coming from the set.

How much time passes he cannot guess. He awakens to the sound of footsteps coming down the stairs. He turns to the TV and hears the anthem, sees the flag, and then the picture cuts to garbled haze.

Dave walks slowly into the room, straightening his tie. Avery hops up with the sleep still in his eyes. He punches the set off. "How about a nightcap, buddy?"

"No thanks," says Dave in a quiet voice. "I'm full."

Avery scratches the back of his neck and yawns. "No offense, Dave, no offense. It's just been a long day. You won't mind sleeping in the basement, will you? We've got it all fixed up; it's dry and there's a couch down there and—" Avery watches as Dave picks up his briefcase, puts on his raincoat and hat. He is nonplussed only for a moment. "Great idea, Dave. Walk will do us good." He starts to get his windbreaker but is stopped by Dave's outstretched hand.

"Been nice seeing you, Brooks."

Avery won't take the shake. He doesn't understand. "Hey, wait a minute, guy, you can't leave now. It's after one in the morning! This isn't New York, you know. We don't have cabs cruising right down the middle of Oak Street at this hour. Come on, Dave, this is crazy."

"Sorry, Brooksy, I've got to move along. Don't worry about me."

"Well I by Christ am going to worry about you." Avery is getting a little angry. "There's no reason for you to go storming off."

The big hand grasps his shoulder and Avery has to admit that it transmits comfort and power to him. "Brooks, who's storming? I've got to be in Atlanta by noon today." Avery sulks. "Brooks, I am not afraid of the dark."

Avery sees he has lost. "At least let me drive you to the cabstand in LaGrange."

"Wouldn't hear of it, Brooksy. Wouldn't want to waste your time."

"Dave, this is crazy!"

The big face laughs and pats him again. "Maybe I'll see you in another fifteen years, huh?"

"Maybe," says Avery halfheartedly.

"Tell Ellen good-bye for me. And thank her for the food." He rubs his stomach. "It was great."

"Nothing to it, Dave." They shake hands firmly. "And listen, listen . . ." Avery slows because he is choked up about this. "I just want to say that you were great with the kids."

Dave punches him on the bicep. "Take it from me, Brooks, those are delectable children. Some of the best."

"Anytime you're in this part of the world, Dave . . ."

"You bet, Brooks." He is already out the door and down the flagstones. "Good night!"

Avery watches the large white back disappear into the shadows. He closes the door softly and stands there a minute nodding affectionately. Then he sweeps his eyes around the room and flips the switches.

The moon lights his way up the stairs. He is a little dizzy at the top and he goes straight to the bathroom, takes two bicarbonate tablets, brushes his teeth, makes himself drink a glass of water.

He opens his bedroom door and hears the spasmodic snore of his wife over the rumble of the air conditioner. He laughs to himself and thinks that sometime he will tape her nightsounds.

He goes down the hallway and carefully twists the boys' doorknob. He imagines himself sly as a snake or burglar as he opens the door without a squeak.

His first thought is: What a great trick! But that does not last more than a millisecond, for there is something final and real and infinite about the two skeletons on the beds, something the moonlight cannot hide. These are the bones of his children, disjointed but arranged properly, like rifles field-stripped for inspection. There is no pose to them. They lie stiff as exhibits, picked clean to the slivers.

In the midst of his nausea and disbelief Avery starts to scream for his wife. But he controls that impulse and tries to think, fights to keep from fainting. He shuts the door and stumbles down the stairs, slams open the front door and runs into the yard. All his instincts cannot keep him from trembling wildly. He falls shaking on the sidewalk and his heart races. He screams for help and screams again, waits for his echoes to simmer, waits for lights to turn on in the houses across the way. No response, so he screams again and again in a high cracking falsetto that astounds him. His voice meets nothing but the trimmed tropic beauty of the summer suburb and the full moon.

The Cabin in the Hollow

JOYCE HARRINGTON

Joyce Harrington's first published short story, "The Purple Shroud," won the Edgar Award, but many familiar with her work feel that this one, published two years later, is even better. It is a story of unspeakable horror made bearable only by the writer's use of the inferential. If the story was not structured in this particular way it might be impossible to take, but that may make the effect of this all the more painful since Miss Harrington enables us to apprehend this situation every step of the way. Joyce Harrington, the author of two mystery novels, resides in New York and is still at the outset of a remarkable career.

The dream came again last night. It seems like it came almost before I was asleep and lasted all night, even a few seconds after I woke up. Although I know that can't be true. I read in a magazine once about the scientists who measure dreams, and make lines on charts, and they all say that dreams only last a few seconds. They hook people up to machines while they're sleeping, and the machines can tell when they're dreaming and when not. I'd surely like to find out if my dream really lasts all night. But I wouldn't like to be hooked up to any machine. No sirree.

It's always summer in the dream. That's how I knew it was a dream the first time it came. It was full summer and the air was all hazy and lazy with the smell of hot dirt and piney woods. It seemed so real that when I woke up I almost thought I'd left the real world behind and was waking into a nightmare of coming to the city and living through the winter in three cold rooms high up in a rat-trap building without even a dirt yard and no real job after five months of walking the hard pavements.

In the dream I was standing in a dirt road that went uphill and around a bend. I knew I'd been climbing that road for a spell because I felt sweaty and just a mite tired, but a good kind of tired. On one side of the road was a big patch of horse nettles. Just beyond them and going on up the hillside was a clump of spindly pitch pines. On the other side of the road were some more horse nettles and then a grassy place with some boulders and a scramble of jack oaks going on down the hill.

I dreamed I just went over and set down in the grassy place with my

back against a boulder and looked out over the hills and hollows and let
the sun beat down on me. I set there for a long time. Maybe it was just
a few seconds like the dream scientists say, but I watched the sun cross
over the sky and listened to the click beetles and the bees buzzing around
where there was a pipe vine crawling all over a dead tree trunk.

That's all there was that first time, except for some red squirrels carrying on in amongst the jack oaks, and my hand itching for my shotgun.

The dream came several times after that, maybe five or six. And it's
always the same—the road and the horse nettles and the trees with the
squirrels frisking in amongst them. But each time I have the dream
something else is added on at the end. The second time of the dream I
was setting there in the grassy place watching the squirrels and wishing
for my shotgun, and I started to feel hungry like it was getting to be
dinnertime. I got up from the grassy place and commenced walking on
up the road. By and by I came to a big huckleberry bush hanging right
out over the road. I stopped and ate some. Ate a lot, but there were plenty,
and then I took off my hat and filled it to take some home to Glenna.
That was the end that time.

Each time the dream came it would be the same, and each time at the
end I would be a little further along that road and the sun would be a little
further down the sky. Until finally, the way it was last night, I came to
a bend in the road and I stood there with my hat full of huckleberries,
knowing, just knowing, that when I got around that bend there would be
a cabin with wood smoke coming from the chimney, and Glenna would
be there with dinner on the table and the kids playing around in the
dooryard. That was when I woke up, right there at the bend in the road
with home just a few steps away.

I got up then. Gray winter light was coming in the window, and there
was dirty gray snow on the window ledge. It was cold under the quilt even
though I had my long johns on. I jumped out of bed. Well, call it a bed,
but it's just a mattress on the floor. Got dressed in a hurry because I
wanted to get down to the unemployment office early so I wouldn't have
to wait so long in line.

Glenna had a pot of coffee going and she had the gas oven on full blast
with the door open so it was warmer in the kitchen. She was crumbling
dry biscuits into bowls for the kids. She doused the crumbs with hot coffee
and carefully measured a spoonful of condensed milk into each of the four
bowls. Her hand shook a little over Calvin's bowl so he got a little extra.

"I'll just have some coffee," I said, before she could start crumbling up some biscuit for me. I wanted her to save some for herself. She was wearing the dress she always wore when she was in her last months and couldn't get into anything else. Not that she had much else to get into, but she loved that faded old calico dress with its lace-trimmed collar and its tiny buttons at the throat and the careful smocking across the front. Her mother had made it for her while she was waiting on Calvin to be born, and she'd worn it for each and every child after him.

The kids ate quietly and fast. Too quiet. It wasn't natural for kids to be that quiet. Glenna's raised them up to be polite and respectful to their elders, but this quiet was something else. Something lost and not right.

For maybe the hundredth time I thought about mornings back home with everyone hustling around doing their chores and the old cow yelling her head off for somebody to come and milk her. Calvin had taken on that chore when he was ten. Denzil fed the chickens and slopped the hogs, and Vergil hauled in wood for the stove. Even LaDonna did her part, setting out plates on the table just so, like a little five-year-old mother, while Glenna fried sausage and cut thick slices of homemade bread.

It would be warm and smoky inside the house. The dogs would come in and lie beside the stove; and everybody would be brighteyed and laughing and telling what they'd seen outside that morning. Could be a possum sleeping in the woodpile or a fog rolling in over the hill or a deer come down to drink from the pond. It was all good news, better than what we heard on the portable radio when it was working. Then the school bus would come beeping around the bend and the boys would moan and groan and trudge off with their books and lunch buckets, unless it was planting or harvest or just time to go after squirrel.

Whenever I got to thinking like that I'd have to stop and remember it wasn't always that good.

I made myself think about the times when there was too much rain or not enough rain and the corn didn't do so good. The time the cow sickened and had to be put down, and Glenna cried so to see her old friend go like that. Or the time that lightning struck the big old mockernut tree and it fell on the barn and caved in the roof.

But worst of all was the time the man came in a big Chrysler car with a paper in his pocket and said he owned everything that was underneath of our land. Not he himself, but the company he worked for and that amounted to the same thing. He showed me the paper and there was my daddy's signature at the bottom plain as if I saw him put it there myself.

My daddy learned to sign his name after he was a grown man and many's the night I'd seen him practicing to get it just right, so I'd recognize it anywhere. It was daddy who'd insisted that I learn how to read and figure and study about the world outside our hills so when the time came I could make up my own mind whether to stay or go. But he'd never told me anything about this paper.

The company man puffed himself up inside his sharp plaid city suit and made ready to read the paper out loud. Well, "Excuse me," I said, "I'd like to read that paper myself." I was polite and all, but I did want him to know that hillbilly though I might be, I was not ignorant.

A lot of good my pride did me, because that paper said exactly what he said it did, in amongst the whereases and the aforesaids. It said that my daddy had sold the mineral rights under our land to the company for two hundred dollars, and the company could come in any time they liked and take out whatever they could find there. Only they couldn't touch the cabin or the outbuildings.

"Do you understand what the paper says?" he asked, reaching for it with a soft white hand.

"Means you're planning to do a little digging," I answered. We were standing on the porch all this time, and Glenna was standing just inside the door with LaDonna hiding behind her skirt.

The company man laughed a fat jolly ha-ha-ha and said, "That's exactly right. We've got to do a little digging and get that coal out. I'm glad you understand, sir. Saves time that way. And trouble. Now, we'll give you a chance to get your crops in before we start." He pulled another piece of paper from his pocket. "Now, let's see. We've got the shovels and the crew scheduled to start in about three weeks. Okay? See you then."

He stepped down off the porch, moving smartly for a short fat man.

"Corn won't be ready in three weeks," I called after him.

I guess he didn't hear me. He just went straight to his big black car and got in. The car was a bit dusty on top of its polish and I wondered how many country roads he'd traveled and how many pieces of paper he'd brought into the hills and hollows. He nosed the car on up the road, and I guessed that Avery Spencer, over the hill and down the next hollow, would be in line to get some good news too. I turned to Glenna and saw the fear in her brown eyes and in her white pinched lips.

I don't know how long I was lost in remembering, but my back was starting to feel blistered. I'd been standing in front of the open oven door to soak up some heat. It's funny how that oven heat doesn't warm your bones. It just makes your skin hot. Nothing like the sun heat in the dream that seemed to warm from the inside out. Only that heat didn't last past waking up. Wish I could carry that dream sun inside me all through the day, walking through the gray snow and the icy puddles with the wind coming around the corners of buildings sudden like and blasting right through my old hunting jacket.

I had a swallow of coffee left in my cup. It was pretty light in color and tasted weak. Glenna must be trying to make the coffee go farther than it's supposed to. She was clearing off the table now and the kids were putting on their jackets to go to school. At least they got the free hot lunch along with their letters. Calvin, being in junior high school, minded a lot having to line up for the free lunch tickets in full sight of all the other kids. I think if it was only for himself he wouldn't do it. Would rather go hungry. But he always managed to carry something home in his pocket, some bread or an apple, or sometimes a piece of meat wrapped up in a sheet of notebook paper.

The kids left quietly, only Calvin stopping to say, "Good-bye, dad. Bye, ma." I'd have to be leaving soon myself if I was going to pick up on any jobs that might be offered today. Glenna was washing up the breakfast bowls in cold water. She looked tired and her belly made it awkward for her at the sink. Her soft brown hair that used to be curly and bouncy hung limp on her shoulders. She said it was because she lacked rainwater to wash it with.

"I best be going now," I said.

"Yes."

"I'll surely get something today."

"Yes."

"We can always get the welfare."

"Yes." Her dull eyes flashed for just a moment. "No. No, we can't do that."

But the sparkle had flared and was gone, and I knew it would be gone forever if we once took the welfare. It hurt my heart something fierce to see my pretty Glenna, who used to laugh and sing, who knew all the old songs and could play the zither till it brought tears of pleasure to your eyes, to see my lady-wife brought so low and downhearted. Maybe she'd perk up after the baby came.

"How are you feeling?" I asked her.

"All right. A little tired."

"Will it be soon?"

"Next week, maybe. Maybe sooner. Or later. I wish . . ."

Her voice trailed off, but I knew she was wishing she didn't have to have this baby in the city hospital where the doctors raced around from one to the next and the nurses didn't have time to hold her hand and say a few words of comfort. I knew she was wishing for her own bedstead with the carved posts that she'd clung to when the pains came fast, for the granny-woman who'd caught each and every one of the other babies, for her mother and her own kind of womenfolk clustering around holding her hand and giving her encouraging words and sips of honey-sweetened ginger tea to ease her time.

"Got to go now," I said. There was no way to say anything else.

All the way down to the unemployment office I kept trying to get back inside the dream, to be walking that dirt road instead of these chilly, slopped-over, crowded city sidewalks, feeling the sun on my back instead of the eyes of the hundreds of people walking behind me or riding in cars or buses if they were lucky. Oh, I know they weren't looking at me. Like as not, they didn't even see me or know I was there. It was just that there was no peace in feeling that hurrying multitude all around me, not like the peace of country roads where a man could be alone and feel right with himself.

But the more I tried to remember the dream, the more my remembering turned to the old home and how it was when the bulldozers came. They started in on the trees first. Cut the trees down and blasted out the stumps. They had trucks going up and down the road hauling those logs away. It was like seeing dear friends cut down in their prime and carted away in a never-ending funeral procession.

Glenna wouldn't step foot outside the cabin once they started their chopping and blasting. She tried to keep the kids inside too. But the boys just wouldn't be kept. To Denzil and Vergil it was better than a revival meeting, but I could see Calvin turning thoughtful and silent as he watched them gouging away at the hillside.

I was no better. I'd gotten in what corn was ready for picking, but there was a lot left still in the ear that I'd never see the benefit of. But once the 'dozers and the power shovels started tearing chunks out of the land it seemed like I got paralyzed. Could do nothing but listen to the hungry grinding and wait and watch while the face of the hillside changed like the face of a beautiful woman turned haggard and old before her time by a great sorrow. The animals couldn't take it any better than we could. Both dogs disappeared one night and we never saw them again. The sow littered early and ate her farrow. The chickens ran around pecking at each other and the hens almost stopped laying entirely.

I'd seen strip-mined land once before. It was in the southern part of the state where we'd gone once to visit with some of Glenna's kin. There was a place where there'd once been a hill, covered with trees older than the oldest person around those parts. When we saw it, the shovels had finished their work and gone away. There was no sign of any hill, just blackened holes and trenches and scattered rocks like bones sticking out of a half-rotted corpse. Round and about there were heaps of earth just shoved aside with the life gone out of it. As far as we could see there was no growing thing.

The people there said that in dry weather when the wind blew, the gritty dust rose in great clouds and covered everything for miles around, and when it rained the black mud crept into the hollows smothering everything in its path. In one place there'd been a mud avalanche that covered a whole cabin, and a baby was crushed to death when the walls caved in. Those people hadn't been able to stop the shovels from coming, and now that it was all over and the land was dead, they didn't know what to do. They just hung on.

Before the shovels started in on our hillside I went to see the preacher, hoping he could give me some advice on how to stop them and maybe help me get together with some of the others whose land was threatened. I told him about the paper with my daddy's signature on it, and what I'd seen of land that had been worked over by those shovels. He said I should hold fast and pray to God. He said I should render unto Caesar, and I should have faith in God and in our president to see the right thing done. He said it was possible that the government would make the company put everything back the way it was before. I said I didn't see how they could do that since it took a while to grow a tree.

Later on I heard that the company had given the preacher a donation for his Bible study school, but I don't know if that was true.

We hung on. We watched the shovels take huge bites out of the hill, chew them up and spit them out at the edge of the cornfield. We watched the trucks come up the road empty and go down full, and we ate their dust. The day the bulldozer flattened Glenna's kitchen garden I spoke what was on my mind.

"Glenna," I said after supper that night, "it's time to go."

"I guess so," she answered. "Where can we go?"

"I've thought about that some." I was trying to sound very calm and sensible, but truth of the matter was that I was scared by what I was going to say. "I don't see how we can start up another place, even if I knew of another place to start. We haven't got the money to buy land. Anyway, I'd just be setting on it waiting for the shovels to come over the hill and start in again."

"Then what can we do?"

I think Glenna knew what I had in mind. There wasn't much that we kept secret from each other, and although she never said much it seemed she could almost read my thoughts sometimes. I was just filling in words to keep from getting to the point.

"I'm still a young man, Glenna, and I've got my health and my strength. I can read and write and figure. But most of all I'm willing to work. And I do believe that any man, he's willing to work, can find a job to do."

"You mean we're going to the city."

"Well, yes." We were sitting at the plank table, and Glenna got up to stack the supper dishes and heat the water in the big tin dishpan.

"Oh, I fear it. I don't like it and I fear it," she whispered.

"It'll be all right, Glenna," I told her. "There are lots and lots of people who do okay in cities. Maybe there are some bad ones there, but so are there anywhere. And along of the bad ones I'll bet there are ten times as many good folk, helping and kind. Only we don't ever get to hear of them. And the kids'll get to go to good schools and make something of themselves and not be poor dirty farmers like their daddy." I was telling all this to Glenna, but I was telling it to myself as well, bolstering up my plan every way I could.

"I recollect the time Acey Doolittle went to Indianapolis and had his car stolen and all his money and had to hitchhike back home."

"Aw, Glenna, he was drunk at the time and you know it."

I'd done an awful lot of talking for one time and I was afraid that any more and I'd start losing faith in my decision.

"Guess I'll go to bed now," I said. "We'll be pretty busy from tomorrow, selling off the hogs and chickens and deciding what we can carry along with us in the car."

I reached the unemployment office in record time—twenty minutes of fast walking. Running more like. Running in front of the memory of the little house in the hollow with its shutters closed up so it couldn't look out at the creeping deadness all around it, and us driving away in the old Chevy with every mortal thing we could carry packed inside and tied on top. Now the old Chevy sat out in the street with its wheels gone and its seats and engine gone and all the glass smashed out. Nobody even wanted to haul its carcass away for junk.

I gave in my name to the lady at the front desk. She ought to know it by heart by this time since she heard it darn near every morning. But somehow she never seemed to remember. I knew her name all right. She had it on a little metal plate on her desk. Miss I. Fonseca. She had stiff bright yellow hair and blue on her eyelids and a lot of red lipstick on her mouth. Her voice was hard and loud, but more than that it was disconnected some way, as if the things she had to say had nothing to do with Miss I. Fonseca.

I went and found a plastic chair to sit on and wait and the back section of a newspaper to read while I was waiting. I was about halfway through the Help Wanted ads, wondering how on earth I was ever going to get the experience that everybody seemed to want even for a job of janitoring, when Miss I. Fonseca called my name.

"Mr. Powell will see you now," she said in that loud and distant way of hers.

I'd seen Mr. Powell before and he'd given me a few jobs of casual labor over the months. I never thought to see the day when I would be beholden to a colored man for a job of work. But Mr. Powell was kind and polite and seemed to understand the hardships of a country person in the city. He told me once that his own people had come up from the South years ago when he was a kid, so I guess he remembered the way of it.

I walked over to his cubicle lined around with green metal walls halfway up and frosted glass the rest of the way.

"Morning, Mr. Mayhew," he said. "Have a seat. How's it going?"

"Morning, sir. Okay, I guess." I set down and waited.

He shuffled through a stack of cards on his desk and pulled one out.

"It says here on your card that you can read and write and do arithmetic."

"Yes, sir."

"Well, I just had a call from Mossbacker's Warehouse. Seems a forklift tipped over and landed on their checker. They need a replacement right away. Think you can handle it?"

"Yes, sir." I had no notion of what a checker was supposed to do, but

I wasn't about to tell that to Mr. Powell, decent as he was.

"It's easy work," he said. "All you have to do is mark off on a checklist whatever goes in or comes out of the warehouse and add it up at the end. And if you work out all right, the job might last until the regular man gets out of the hospital. If you get over there right away you'll be able to get in a good seven hours. Here's the address." He scribbled on a slip of paper. "And the directions how to get there."

I stood up. "Thank you, Mr. Powell. I'll sure do my best." He held out his hand and I took it. I'd never shaken the hand of a colored man before, but this was a man who was helping me to stand tall and not looking down on me for a dumb redneck. Sometimes the old ways of thinking and doing need to be shook up a little. I turned to leave.

"Ah . . . Mr. Mayhew . . ."

I turned back in the doorway.

"The warehouse is about three miles from here. Have you got bus fare?"

I hesitated, then started to say yes although all I had was enough to buy a cup of coffee for my lunch, and that wasn't enough for bus fare. But before I could say anything, Mr. Powell was around his desk and pressing some coins into my hand.

"It's just a loan. You can pay me back." He clapped me on the shoulder. "Good luck. I'll call and tell them you're on the way."

I ran out of the unemployment office and all the way to the bus stop, no room in my head or my heart now for memories. I was a man with a job of work to do and impatient to get at it and prove myself. The bus came within a few minutes and I took that as a good omen. I was on my way. We'd be all right now.

I scarcely noticed the dreary city landscape as the bus rolled along. I kept thinking of all the things we needed and how we could get some of them in just a few hours. We could all go down to the store after I got home from work and have a good time deciding what we needed most. Maybe I could keep enough back for a little present for Glenna, a growing plant or a shiny hair clip, something to cheer her up. Before I finished thinking about all the ham hocks and beans we'd be able to buy, the bus reached my stop and I jumped off happy as a kid diving off a barn rafter into a pile of hay.

The job was easy, just like Mr. Powell said. But it was cold. I stood out on the loading dock all morning checking in a shipment of automobile parts. The crates were all marked with what was inside them, and all I had to do was find the right place on the checklist and make a mark against it. Then the forklift went on inside the warehouse.

I worked slowly at first, to be sure I got everything right, but I soon got the hang of it and speeded up. My hands got numb but I tried not to let that slow me down. I would have worked right through lunchtime, but everybody else knocked off so there was nothing for me to check. A canteen wagon came around and I borrowed fifty cents against my day's pay and bought some hot soup and coffee.

We all sat around an oil stove just inside the warehouse and warmed ourselves against the afternoon's work. There were about eight other men working there. I didn't say very much, just made myself known, and listened while they discussed the accident that had brought me such good luck. The regular checker had suffered two broken ribs and a dislocated shoulder. No one knew when he'd be able to come back to work. I was sorry for his pain, but grateful for my chance to work a few days and get some of that experience I didn't seem to have.

We finished unloading the automobile parts during the afternoon and started working on an outgoing shipment of machine tools. Five o'clock came and I was ready to go on working all night if need be, but I went to the office and collected my day's pay, less the fifty cents lunch money. The boss asked me if I could come back next day and I said that wild horses couldn't keep me away if he wanted me there. He laughed and said I was a good worker all right, and he'd see me in the morning.

With thirteen dollars and fifty cents in my pocket I felt like a millionaire. Even so, I decided to walk home because the bus fare would just buy a quart of milk for the kids. I walked back along the bus route, looking in the shop windows along the way. I came to a dime store and went into its bright lights and warm thick popcorn-and-candy smell. They had some plants way in the back of the store, but they looked so sad and droopy it would only make Glenna more down-hearted to set eyes on one of them. I could have got her a goldfish in a bowl for ninety-nine cents, but I was afraid it would freeze to death before I got it home. So I settled for a bright green plastic hair barrette with yellow daisies on it for forty-nine cents plus tax.

I practically ran the rest of the way and was on our block before it really got dark. I passed the old Chevy where it sat ringed round with street filth and gray slush. Some kids were jumping on top of it. The rear license plate was gone and I thought that was a good thing so nobody could find out it was mine and give me parking tickets. The front plate, the one that said

WEST VIRGINIA—ALMOST HEAVEN, was still in place. I guess nobody wanted that, or believed it was true.

The hallway was dark, as always. The super hardly ever bothered to put new light bulbs in. They always got stolen after a few days. But I knew my way by feel and by smell. There were always the same number of steps going up and coming down, and I ran up those four flights and around those dark landings like I was running up to Salvation Johnny's camp meeting to be saved. I couldn't wait to lay my day's earnings before Glenna and tell her that I might be working steady for a while.

The door of the apartment was locked and I was glad of that. Glenna often forgot to keep the door locked. We'd never had a lock on the door back home. In the city it was best to keep your door locked. I banged on the door and yelled for her to open up. There was no sound from inside. I thought maybe she and the kids had gone out or maybe her time had come and they'd all gone to the hospital. I got out my key and unlocked the door.

It was dark in the apartment, but what came out at me and almost bowled me over was the smell. The gas smell came billowing out of there into my face like a suffocating demon. I must have yelled because I got a lungful of it that made me dizzy. I know that I reached inside the door and flicked on the overhead light. I know that I ran into the kitchen and threw a chair at the window.

After that things are a little mixed up, but I know what I saw. I saw my old shotgun lying on the kitchen table with a piece of paper propped up against it. I saw Glenna setting on a kitchen chair with her head lying on the open oven door. LaDonna was lying at her feet. I think I turned the gas off then.

I went into the next room where the kids slept and I saw Denzil and Vergil clutching at each other on the floor in a corner, and the dried blood on their faces. I saw where Calvin had tried to crawl out of the room in spite of the terrible wound in his chest and hadn't been able to make it. I went back to the kitchen.

Cold air was coming in the broken window. The gas smell was less, but I was still dizzy and there was a distant clanging sound in my head. I felt like I was moving through thick layers of clutching invisible fog. I raised Glenna up. Her face was so flushed she looked like she had a terrible consuming fever. But when I put my lips on her forehead she was cold. I laid her head back down.

I remembered the piece of paper on the table. I went over and picked it up. It was a piece of Calvin's notebook paper. I felt it in my hands, the dry rustle of it, and I smelled the schoolroom smell of it, but it was a long time before I could bring myself to read it. It was written in pencil, in Glenna's careful schoolgirl handwriting, all the letters formed as though the teacher were standing over her with a paddle ready to swat if she did it wrong.

It said, "I can't bear to birth my baby in this place. I'm going Home, and I'm taking the children with me. Sweet Jesus forgive me." That was all.

I put the paper back on the table and I went over and closed the apartment door. And locked it. I went and picked Glenna up off the chair and carried her into the bedroom. She was heavy, but I made it all right. I laid her on the mattress, straight and neat. Then I put each of the children in their own beds and covered them up. I cleaned the shotgun as best I could and put it away. And then I went to bed.

I lay down beside Glenna and pulled the quilt over both of us. I closed my eyes, and the dream came right away. I was standing in the dirt road, but this time I had my shotgun in my hand. I sat in the grassy place, and when the squirrels started carrying on I was ready for them, and I got five. I tied them together and hung them over my gun barrel. When I got to the huckleberry bush I laid the gun and the squirrels in the road, and picked my hat full of berries.

I went on up the road and at the bend I could already smell wood smoke and hear the kids shouting and laughing. I rounded the bend and it was all just as I knew it would be. I left the squirrels on the porch and took the berries inside to Glenna. She was setting in her old rocker nursing a tiny new girl baby. Calvin helped me skin the squirrels, and Denzil and Vergil each begged for a tail to hang on their belts. Everything was the way it was supposed to be.

But sometimes, after I go to bed in that cabin in the hollow, after the kids are all quietened down, and maybe Glenna's sitting up late doing some mending, sometimes when I go to sleep I'll have a dream of people trying to talk to me, of being in ice-cold water up to my neck, of being struck by lightning and the shock of it passing through my whole body. But it's never very real. It's not a real place and nothing you could even call a nightmare. And it doesn't happen very often, just once in a while.

Life just goes on in that cabin in the woods. The seasons come and go. The trees stand tall. Glenna grows her runner beans and her squash and tomatoes. The boys and I go hunting, and the girls will learn to make butter and bake bread. And somehow I know that no power shovel is ever going to come over this hill.

Peckerman

ROBERT S. PHILLIPS

Rimbaud, as the protagonist of this story would grimly concede, barely had half of it. Robert Phillips, a highly regarded poet, essayist and anthologist, has appeared in The Arbor House Treasury of Horror and the Supernatural, *his short stories were collected in* The Land of Lost Content *(Vanguard Press, 1970), and new stories are appearing in* The Hudson Review, New Letters, *and* New England Review. *He has recently completed his first novel.*

> *Je est un autre.*
> —Rimbaud

For Peckerman, the whole business began one hot August morning when his wife, reading the morning paper at the breakfast table while he hunched over a second mug of coffee, said: "How odd, dear. There's a new rock-and-roll singer with your name!"

At the time Peckerman only grunted. It did seem funny that someone else should be named Barry Peckerman. Even funnier that he had not changed it. Barry Peckerman (*this* Barry Peckerman, not the rising rock star) was resigned to his name. At the university library, where he was head of the reference department, people spoke of and to "Mr. Peckerman" in hushed tones—which, he realized, may have been due more to their speaking within a library than for any other reason.

Nevertheless, they did not laugh to his face, as they did first, when he was a boy (at summer camp the Gentiles had jeered him in the showers, and later in the Army much was made of the first two syllables of his last name and their appropriateness to shortarm inspection.) Somehow through the years it came to seem not so much that he failed to live up to his name—he was of merely average endowment—but that his name had failed to live up to *him.* He was, after all, a successful reference librarian, the owner of a fine personal library as well. He drove a Buick.

Generally Peckerman did not think about his name any more. It never appeared in the newspapers, except the day he was born, forty-five years ago, and the day he was married. Still, it was *his* name, and when his wife took note of the rock (*not* rock-and-roll—even *he* had kept up sufficiently to know the latter was passé among the young) star, he reached for the paper and read rather guardedly.

The other Barry Peckerman lived on the West coast and had just cut his first album. The newspaper photograph revealed a youth who looked like every other that Peckerman saw shamble in and out of the library: hair too long, aviator glasses, mustache, shirt open to reveal a hairless chest, lots of chains around his neck. "I hope he can sing better than he looks," was Peckerman's comment to his wife. He gathered his papers and sandwich, stuffed them in his briefcase, and left.

While maneuvering the Buick through traffic he gave the other Barry Peckerman one second thought, but only one: was it a coincidence this young man had the same name? Or was he, perhaps, a former student at the university who, for whatever reason, had appropriated Peckerman's name for his own? Peckerman knew it had been the rage, a few years back, for the truly outrageous rock singers to take names equally outrageous. Wasn't there a Sid Vicious? (Which his wife once pronounced Sid *Viscous.*) Wasn't there a Johnny Rotten and a Jello Biafra? There was, he recalled with a wince, a punk rock group who called themselves The Dead Kennedys. Now that was going too far! Compared to those turbulent souls, this young Barry Peckerman looked mild indeed. Doubtless he would go the way of most would-be rock stars.

That was the last Peckerman thought of it. Until well into the autumn, when two students stopped before his desk in the information alcove and the boy demanded, "Hey—are you his father? *She* wants to know." The girl on his arm snickered. They both wore silver jackets that looked like astronaut gear.

"Am I *whose* father?" Peckerman replied, his voice considerably lower than the boy's. This was, after all, the library. His mind began framing a response, since indeed Peckerman was no one's father. Their's had been a childless marriage, at first by choice (he had to get through graduate school, and his teaching assistantship stipend was small), then later by circumstance. Try as they might, they could not have a baby. Another reason, perhaps, why he was self-conscious about his name?

"Barry Peckerman's dad, of course. Are you? We saw your nameplate and wondered."

Peckerman's eyes fell to the copper desk plate bearing his first and last names. It had been a gift, sometime back, commemorating fifteen years of library service.

"I'm afraid not," Peckerman said with a superior smile. "No relation." He wanted to add, "Thank God," but restrained himself.

"I told her you weren't, but she wanted to check it out anyway."

"Too bad," the girl said, speaking finally. "He could take real good care of you in your old age. If he wanted to. He's making real good bread."

"I'm afraid I don't get the point," Peckerman said, flashing again his superior smile.

"Don't you keep up with the charts, man?" the boy asked. "Barry Peckerman's got the number-one single in the country."

"He does?" The only charts Peckerman consulted, from time to time, were the *New York Times Book Review* lists of fiction and nonfiction best sellers. He did so out of a sense of duty, of "keeping up." Most of the books listed were rubbish.

"Where've you been, another planet?" the girl asked. "Jesus, you can't even turn on the radio without hearing it."

"I doubt that. Besides, I tend to listen to FM. Stations that carry opera, that sort of thing."

"Flip over to AM sometime," the youth said. "You'll hear a lot of Barry Peckerman for sure." He paused, then added, "Way out—that you both should have the same name. I mean, a name like *that.*"

"Like *what?*" Peckerman asked, taking umbrage.

"Like *Pecker*man! I mean, it's not exactly Smith or Jones, is it?"

"No, it isn't," Peckerman said with dignity. He dismissed the couple by beginning to shuffle some papers.

Late that afternoon, driving home, Peckerman snapped on the car radio, something he rarely did because the stations were all disco or rock. The first thing he heard was an announcer who shouted, "and now, the one you've been waiting for, the big one, the one that's climbed to number-one position on the charts in just six short weeks—the one everyone's talking about—Barry Peckerman and 'Kiss the Jelly off My Belly'!"

Peckerman pursed his lips and drove while Barry Peckerman thumped and shouted the song. The whole performance took just three minutes. But to Peckerman it seemed much longer. It was crude, unbearable. He switched to another station—only to hear the same song. He switched again. Same song. Desperately Peckerman turned the dial from station to station, but they all seemed to be playing the same thing. Finally he flipped off the radio in disgust.

Once home he felt exhausted. It was a nice house, described by the realtor who sold it to them, years ago, as "a dreamy Dutch Colonial with a pillared verandah." It was big on antique charm with nooks and crannies and generations of love. He had bought it in the days of the five percent mortgage, and five thousand down. This night he discovered his wife in the kitchen, making one of his favorite recipes, veal birds from the *Fannie Farmer Cookbook.* "What's that funny look on your face?" she asked.

He decanted some white wine for an aperitif. "Funny look?"

"You're smiling rather oddly. Like Peter Lorre."

"Oh . . . I just heard that young Barry Peckerman. You know, the one you saw in the paper? Heard him about five times, in fact."

"So what about him?"

"Can't sing. He'll be a real fly-by-night. One record, then poof! Gone with the wind."

"A pity," his wife said, taking the glass of wine he offered. It was Waterford crystal, part of a set they began when they got engaged. "If someone's going to have your name, he should at least be good at what he does."

"That's what *I* say."

The next day, bending toward the water fountain in the library basement, Peckerman was passed by the custodian who said, "Hey, Mr. Peckerman! I bought your record. Never knew you could sing so purty! Ha!" Peckerman waved the man away. It was impertinent in the least, especially since he was the janitor, and a black at that.

A few days later a student thrust a record under Peckerman's nose and demanded that he autograph the label. "If I can't get the real Barry Peckerman's, I can get yours. Nobody'll know the difference anyhow."

"Take that thing out of my face!" he snapped. "I *am* the real Barry Peckerman."

"Oh yeah? You sing, man?"

"No, and in my opinion, neither does that other. What I meant to say is, I had the name long before what's-his-name."

"What's-his-name? That's funny. Sorry if I made you mad. It was a joke. You older guys don't know how to take a joke." The student backed away.

Ever precise, Peckerman fired to his back: "You didn't make me mad; you made me *angry.*"

Within weeks, Peckerman's mail began to include all manner of letters from screwballs or practical jokesters. At home his telephone began to ring at all hours.

"Hey, like, wow!" one girl said into the receiver at 3 A.M. one Sunday morning. "I was just sort of looking through the phone book, and I couldn't believe it. Barry Peckerman, right here in town! Out of sight!"

Peckerman soon had his phone number changed. His wife could not understand why he was inconveniencing all her friends, who now must learn a new number, and one of whom had failed to reach her in time for a bridge luncheon she had looked forward to for a month.

"Something had to be done, my dear," he said vaguely, without elaboration. She was unaware of the torment which had become his, especially at work, where she never ventured. She knew remarkably little about his professional life. His job was to work with the young, and they were the very ones aware of this other Peckerman. He even took his prized copper nameplate off the desk and hid it in a drawer. Still the students came, often not for reference assistance at all, but to make his life sheer hell. And it was not only the students. In a staff meeting, Dr. Lynch, director of the university libraries, had made amusing reference to the very famous celebrity who still found time, between engagements at Vegas and so forth, to man the reference desk. Everyone tittered, especially Lee Ackart, who smoked like a stack, had yellow teeth, and whom Peckerman detested even though she was a horse for work.

That same week, when their best friends came for Saturday night supper, they arrived bearing a recording of "Kiss the Jelly off My Belly" instead of the usual and expected bottle of wine. "We thought you'd find this screamingly funny," the wife gushed. "Have you heard it yet?" the husband inquired.

"As much as I care to, thank you," Peckerman said, brushing the record aside. To compound his rage, he had not bought a table wine because this couple invariably brought one. Now there would be none with dinner, unless he drove downtown to make a quick purchase. Should he excuse himself and do so? He weighed the disappointment of the former against the inconvenience of the latter. In the end, he decided to make the couple suffer with him and served none. It was not a successful evening. The friends left immediately after dessert. Peckerman told his wife he didn't care if he ever saw either of them again.

All of which was but a prelude to the nightmare which was Peckerman's when the other Peckerman released an album, including of course "Kiss the Jelly off My Belly" (what *was* that supposed to mean?) and nine other songs, all sounding to Peckerman's ears the same. The album, like the single before it, quickly climbed the charts. Within weeks it, too, was number one. Peckerman now could not even flip the dials of the television in search of a news program or a good old English movie without hearing his own name taken in vain.

It was Barry Peckerman's image to be a slightly naughty Peck's bad boy. He had a very sexy image, apparently, like Tom Jones before him. *Tom Jones* indeed, Peckerman fumed; and what would Fielding think of that? At least Fielding was dead, did not suffer the ignominy. Once the reference librarian sat stupefied in his own living room and heard Johnny Carson ask the young singer how he got his unusual name.

"Ya mean, Barry?" the youth asked insolently.

Roar of audience laughter.

"No, no. *Pecker*man," Johnny Carson volleyed with a wink.

More laughter.

"Well, uh, it's a made-up name. My girl friend gave it to me, if you really want to know."

"Oh?" said Carson, looking puckish. "And how did she come up with that particular name?"

"I'd show you, but this is a family program," came the reply.

Extreme roar of laughter.

So far as Peckerman could tell, this became a much-repeated anecdote, revealing what often passes for wit in our illiterate age. Wasn't it Dr. Johnson, he recalled, who said: "The size of a man's understanding might always be justly measured by his mirth"? If so, young Peckerman possessed no understanding at all; instead, he was more concerned with measuring the size of something else.

One morning, entering the library, Peckerman found a crudely printed sign taped to the back of his chair: I'D SHOW YOU, BUT THIS IS A FAMILY LIBRARY. As luck would have it, Peckerman was late, the reference room was already populated. No telling how many had seen the hateful sign. As he removed it and threw it into the trash basket, a guffaw arose from the students and faculty bent over books in feigned concentration.

"Did you hear the singer Barry Peckerman had a vasectomy last week?" the dean asked him in the parking lot.

"No," Peckerman said weakly.

"The operation took place last Monday, Tuesday, Wednesday and Thursday!" the dean roared. He seemed to find the joke so funny, he had to pound the fender of his Jeep with the palm of his hand for emphasis.

Peckerman needed a rest. He still had a week's vacation left, and just before Christmas he booked a room in a rural Vermont inn he had heard about from his colleagues. When he and Mrs. Peckerman entered the lobby, after an eight-hour drive through whirling and drifting snow, there seemed to be a great many people assembled for such a tiny inn. Then he saw it. There was a banner over the front desk: SILVER FOX INN WELCOMES BARRY PECKERMAN!

There were flowers everywhere, and all the sofas and chairs were filled with nubile teenage girls, all of whom turned smiles in his direction, and then turned back again. More girls were stationed at the windows. He noticed the call letters of a local radio station on a smaller banner. Peckerman felt ill. He approached the desk clerk, who was cleaning his fingernails with the tines of a fork.

"Yes, sir, may I help you? If it's about a room, I'm afraid we're booked solid."

Peckerman implored. "Please keep your voice down. This is between you and me, okay?"

"Certainly, sir. In my position, I have to keep many confidences. Why, I could tell you stories . . ."

"I'm sure you could. Look, my name is Barry Peckerman, and there's been some—"

The desk clerk's face cracked like an eggshell. "You? *You're* Barry Peckerman? Ha, ha, ha. And I'm Robert Redford. Hey, gang, get this! This guy says *he's* Barry Peckerman!"

The room rippled with hysterical laughter.

A whipped man, Peckerman attempted to maintain composure. "You don't understand. I happen to have the same name as the singer. Rather, he has the same name as I. But it *is* my name, see?" Peckerman produced his driver's license and passed it across the desk like some adolescent attempting to buy beer. "Now, I do have a reservation in this inn, which I expect you to honor. We've had a long drive. So if you can just have someone show us up to our room—"

During this ramble the clerk's expression changed from mirth to disbelief to indignation. "Your name *is* Peckerman?"

"Yes, yes. Barry Y. Peckerman."

"Well, why didn't you say so when you made your reservation?"

"I did."

"I mean, why didn't you say you weren't *the* Barry Peckerman? The radio station's here, the high school band is coming any minute, the whole town has turned out. We've even given you the fucking bridal suite!" He threw the fork down with disgust.

"I'm sorry. A regular room will do."

"There *aren't* any regular rooms left. We're overbooked now. Because Barry Peckerman was supposed to come. We even had the piano tuned!"

"Who the hell is this old creep?" a genuinely creepy-looking woman asked, rising from a wicker chair by the fire, gathering her moss-colored coat about her, and leaving. She was followed by a bevy of the others. Soon the lobby was virtually empty. In the corner the radio station interviewer packed his equipment between curses.

"We thought we were going to *see* somebody," the bellhop said, throwing the Peckermans' two suitcases upon the bed. "What a rip-off."

When they finally were alone, Peckerman removed the heavy Samsonite suitcases from the king-size bed (he would have none of the new soft luggage) and collapsed on it. He remained there most of the week, reading *Middlemarch*, which he had brought in the 1909, Houghton Mifflin three-volume edition. When he tired of that, he read year-old issues of *Yankee* and *Vermont Life* which his wife found in the lobby.

"You're really acting very silly," his wife kept saying.

"There's no earthly reason why I have to face those people again," he replied from the enormous white-and-pink bed which dominated the white-and-pink bridal suite. There had been a magnum of champagne, compliments of the management, in the room when they arrived. It was, of course, for the other Peckerman and he expected it to be withdrawn in indignation. After a day, when it was not, he had more ice sent up and drank the entire thing himself one snowy afternoon. He became quite drunk. His wife sat by his side all evening, patting his hand and asking again and again why he was so unhappy.

When Peckerman returned to the library the first week in January, he found a note to report to the director's office. The director sat behind his enormous desk, the principal adornment of which was a glass jar full of dull brown candy. "Have a horehound drop," the director always said. Peckerman imagined this was an affectation acquired after a recent president of the United States kept jelly beans on his desk. At least jelly beans were palatable. After declining the horehounds, Peckerman sat studying the director, who said, "I wanted to explain, Barry, about a decision we made in staff meeting while you were gone."

"Yes?"

"For some time, we've contemplated giving an annual award to the most proficient library trainee. A plaque on the wall, to which we add a name each year."

"Wonderful idea. A real incentive-builder."

"Yes. Well, there was considerable sentiment here to call it the Barry Peckerman Award. You can't imagine how the junior staff looks up to your standard of professionalism."

"That's nice to hear." Peckerman was embarrassed. While he never had articulated it, he realized now he had longed for some kind of continuity, of immortality, which he could never acquire through offspring. Having his name literally attached to this great library would effect just that.

"Unfortunately," the director continued, "there were those who thought the name Barry Peckerman on such a plaque would appear . . . well, frankly, ridiculous. Become an object of ridicule. Cheapen the whole idea, diminish the effect of the award, as it were. The singer, you know."

"Yes, I know," Peckerman sighed. A great prize had just been handed him, then rudely yanked away.

"So we're calling it the Library Award for Outstanding Service. It has a certain ring to it, don't you think?"

"Indeed."

"And it's hard to argue with a name like that."

"Quite so."

"An unassailable name."

"Definitely."

"I'm so glad you agree it was for the best. Funny thing, that whippersnapper having the same name."

"Hilarious."

Not long after that, Peckerman came home to find his wife supine on the living-room sofa, eyes closed. On the stereo, loudly, the second new album by Barry Peckerman was playing. The album cover lay on the Persian carpet announcing its title, *Ballocks Up!* A four-color poster of Peckerman had come with the recording. His wife had unfolded it and taped it to the mirror over the mantelpiece.

"Isn't he wonderful?" she sighed.

"Is he?" Peckerman genuinely asked, heavy of heart.

"Oh my yes. I didn't use to listen to this kind of music, as you well know. But he's something else."

"He is that. He's a common thief! He stole my name."

"Well, it's a cute name, when you think about it. At least, for him it is. They say he has to have his trousers especially made just to accommodate him . . ."

Peckerman swallowed his rage. "What's for dinner?"

"There are some cold cuts in the refrigerator. Help yourself. I just want to meditate here a while longer."

Meditate, she calls it, he thought. I just may regurgitate.

After that, she seemed lost to him. Not that she listened to young Peckerman's records all day. And she removed the poster from the mirror without his having to ask. But how could he feel affection towards some-one who had become a fan of the bane of his existence? Her affections were vicariously alienated. Peckerman took to sleeping in the guest room. His wife never questioned the move. Was she relieved? It was after two weeks of sleeping in the guest room, alone, that Peckerman decided to take revenge.

Originally he halfheartedly thought he would board an airplane, fly to Hollywood or Vegas or wherever, and stalk the rock star and murder him. But what would that solve? The singer in all probability would become in death more famous than in life, like Jean Harlow or Marilyn Monroe, James Dean or Elvis Presley. Night after night Peckerman sat in his darkened living room, lined with the great books of the nineteenth cen-tury, plotting the best course of action. He was so involved in his plot, it became necessary to take a leave of absence from the library. He had not been performing well. He was rude to students. The director at-tributed his behavior to gross disappointment over the naming of the award. Perhaps he and the staff had made a mistake?

Peckerman forgot to shave, didn't eat. His wife advised him to see that marvelous young Dr. Smelly, who, in addition to being a fine psychiatrist, had (she pointed out) managed to adjust to his own name perfectly well.

Peckerman began to traffic in drugs. In a college town, the supply and the demand are always there. One need merely lift the rock and peer underneath. Peckerman crawled under that rock and became a pusher. Soon his clients included students from five universities within a two-hundred-mile radius. He dealt only with the young. Peckerman refused to do business with faculty, though it would have given him enormous satisfaction to give Lee Ackart a bad trip. Lee had laughed at him in staff meeting.

In time Peckerman widened his activities to include the selling of sex. White slavery, involving young women and even younger boys, became part of his repertoire. He quit the library altogether, of course—he had no time for that. The dean and the director, unaware of his feverish activities in crime, felt the poor man had fallen into depression and idleness. They imagined him sitting at home, unshaven, in a darkened living room, perhaps slowly sipping Chablis.

Peckerman's wife couldn't account for all the comings and goings of her husband, or his late hours, or all the telephone calls made to and from the separate bedroom where he had established himself, as on a beach-head, some months before. But she did know that Peckerman seemed happier than he had in years. There was an elastic spring to his walk that she had never noticed before. At breakfast he was absolutely radiant. Every day he left the house whistling, going about his job of debauching and debasing the young.

That, of course, was merely the short-term motive. The other, the greatly desired, motive took longer. Peckerman finally managed to get himself arrested. When the story broke, it broke big. He was convicted of trafficking in drugs and sex, of pimping teenaged male prostitutes, and was even proven to have become a Communist. His picture appeared in all the bigger newspapers. Some carried two photographs—one of Peckerman as he had appeared just a few years before (a mild-mannered man with a librarian's haircut), and the new Peckerman (an aging man with shoulder-length silver hair and a wild glint in his eye). He looked like a cross between Charles Manson and Howard Hughes.

His deeds had been so dastardly, his character change so extreme, that his name gave coinage to a new phrase in the language. To "pull a Peckerman" came to mean to do anything really gross. He was notorious.

And the fame of *this* Barry Peckerman did not die. The public, after all, has more rock singers to worship than truly outrageous criminals. The former librarian was sentenced to prison. His hair was cut short and he served fifteen years of his sentence, given early release for good behavior. While incarcerated the perpetrator revamped the entire prison library cataloguing system for the state of Illinois. They had been, unbelievably, still using the old Dewey system. As he worked in the various state prison libraries, Peckerman sought news stories about the other Barry Peckerman. But after the first year or so, there were none. Peckerman had managed to bring about Peckerman's ruin.

It is years later.

Peckerman is sitting in a bar attached to a bowling alley in Venice, California. The walls are knotty pine, a stuffed marlin hangs over the bar. His wife has, of course, long divorced him. Since prison he has been drifting, town to town, state to state, doing handyman work. It surprised him to discover he can, after all, work with his hands. In the bar a younger man, though by no means young, is brooding over his drink. Peckerman prods him into conversation. The younger man's eyes look burnt out. He has a huge paunch which falls over his beaded belt. His polyester shirt is not clean.

"I used to be a singer once," the younger man slurs.

"I thought so," Peckerman replies. He has recognized the face within the face. How many times had he studied those posters and album covers!

"What's your name?"

"Barry," the other says. He burps, then continues, "Peckerman."

"Barry Peckerman!" the older man wants to say. "Not *the* Barry Peckerman! The monster from back East—the Communist and whoremonger and everything!" But he draws the line. He has had his satisfaction. Instead he quietly asks, "What happened?"

"I'm not even sure, man. Everything turned to shit. You know the story about the king that could turn everything he touched into gold? Well, I had the opposite touch. Everything I touched turned to shit."

"Do you still sing?"

"Are you kidding me? I even changed my professional name, to Barry Peck. Like Gregory Peck, get it? Got a gig in Elizabeth, New Jersey, and still they hated me. Some folks recognized me, shouted up to the stage, "Hey, Peckerman, are you related to *him?*"

"Upsetting."

"I'll say. The funny thing is, it was all over by then. I only had one big hit anyhow, 'Kiss the Jelly off My Belly.' Everything else was garbage. I probably wouldn't have been on the scene much longer, you know?"

"Fascinating," Peckerman replies dryly. "So what do you call yourself these days?"

"Johnson. My real name's Ray Johnson. And you?"

"Green. Bob Green. Glad to meet you." Peckerman shakes Ray Johnson's hand. "My wife was a great admirer of yours."

"She was?"

"Unquestionably."

The two men quickly became friends, without really knowing one another at all. Currently they share a one-bedroom house in Sausalito.

A Simple, Willing Attempt

ELIZABETH MORTON

Elizabeth Morton is the pseudonym of a cellist and medical books production editor who presently lives in Rockland County, New York; her short-short story, "Namesake," appeared in The Arbor House Treasury of Horror and the Supernatural, *and she has also been published in the science-fiction market. This story was written in celebration of Ms. Morton's move from the relatively genteel Amish country to the more baroque interstices of New York; it is, like the works of Albert Payson Terhune and others, a dog story only by indirection. It is foremost a Manhattan story.*

So at the end I thought of the Doberman. The Doberman that would have saved me trouble if I had truly understood the conditions.

My Doberman is named Titus. I bought him for protection a year ago. "Protection" is an important service in this city; faith has gone the way of the trolley. The question might be who will protect us against ourselves, of course, but that is sheerly metaphysical. In any case the answer is that *we* will protect ourselves and I do what I must.

I have Titus.

Consider the Doberman. When I opened the door at six, Titus did not come to greet me. Instead he stood in the small bedroom toward the rear, whining. Breezes from an open window scattered some things from my dresser at his feet but he didn't seem to notice. He whined again. "What is it?" I said. I was alert from the outset. I want to make that clear. I was not naive. One fine-tunes apprehension in this city, becomes suspicious of circumstance. "Tell me, Titus," I said.

He did not move. His legs trembled. "What's wrong, boy?" I said. Why do we never call our pets *man?* He whimpered, his jaws locked. "Let's open your mouth, boy," I said, getting down on my knees to face him.

He would have none of it so I ran a finger over his muzzle. (Such a stupid act but I was concerned and what did I know?) Titus had always been quite firm about anyone stroking his head. But he only whined again and dropped to his knees. He started to drool.

Rabies? Lockjaw? Animals can give tetanus, I thought, but do they get it? I've always been slightly in awe of this animal and I regard Titus as

531

a motile, biscuit-chomping weapon—but I am a woman with some feeling. I did not want him to suffer; even a defective weapon should be fixed. "I'll take you to the veterinarian," I said, "if you don't stop this at once."

Titus groaned yet again, that shaking sigh. I should have pointed out earlier in this hasty memoir (but it is coming out, as you may have noticed, under enormous pressure) that there is a veterinarian on the ground floor of this large apartment building: a fool's parade of pets and anxious owners stalks through the lobby during daylight hours. I have used Dr. Stone's services a couple of times because he was so convenient, otherwise I would hardly have noticed him. Outside of his routine duties, which he seemed to perform efficiently, he was a lazy and shiftless sort. Used to be. But Stone's imminence made me press Titus once more. "Come on, boy," I said, hoping he would follow reasonably. "We'll find out what your mouth problem is."

To my relief, Titus followed me quietly out of the apartment and into the gray hallway where we waited patiently for the elevator and boarded it, joining a fat man and two blunt-faced adolescents who stared at us all the way down. Titus sniveled, but held his ground. "That dog is *frozen*," one of the adolescents said. "Frozen *solid*," said the other. Everyone laughed except for Titus, myself and the fat man. On the ground floor I watched the adolescents skim across the lobby and out the door with an intruder's panache, exchanged a look of disgust with the fat man, then turned left and went up the four stairs to Stone's office. The door was open, even though it was after posted hours. Stone, no less than the rest of us, is greedy: he will not let a concerned (paying) owner go unheeded. Androcles was the last member of the profession who took the long view.

The waiting room was empty, but not for long; Titus and I stared at copies of *The Pet Dealer* on a long table until Stone emerged in a flurry of yelps from the rear. I do not have the time to characterize him except to say that he does not suffer from age, humility or compassion. "He can't seem to open his mouth," I said. "Can dogs get lockjaw?

"You mean that one, right?" Stone said. "So, I'll take a look." He pulled on Titus's collar and they trotted toward the door. "Read a magazine," Stone said. "I'll be back in a minute."

"I'm in the building," I said. I gave him my name. "Remember? You can call me. My number is in your file. You *have* a file?"

"I'll call you then," Stone said, "if you don't have the patience to wait."

"I don't want to wait," I said. "I'm upstairs; let me know when the examination is done. That way I can have a drink—I work hard too, you know." I got up, started for the door. "Just find out what's wrong with the dog."

"I'll call you," Stone said. "Argue responsibility with yourself." He led Titus through the door, into another swirl of yelping.

I left the reception room. The adolescents were not on the elevator but the fat man was. "They didn't come from any floor in *this* building," he said bitterly. "There's no security. Anything can happen in this place. Don't you think anything can happen?" I did not answer. I did not want to take our relationship one step beyond where it was. If strangers do not want to hurt you, they want an involvement. *"Frozen,"* I heard him mutter as I got out. It did not disturb me.

In my apartment, I made myself a scotch and water, thinking of life in a city where protection is a major service; where dogs are weapons and weapons are a way of greeting. The phone rang just as I had decided, yet again, that the conditions of my life were tolerable after all, I had a job that I loved and the scotch, which I endured, and the fear neutralized by Titus. "This is Dr. Stone," the voice said, "what are you doing? This is Dr. Stone, do you hear me?"

"I hear you," I said. I took another swallow of scotch: it broadened me somewhat. "What do you mean, what am I doing? I'm sitting here by the phone, thinking about lockjaw which for all I know is contagious. I'm thinking of the city and my life. I'm thinking—"

"Get out of the apartment now."

"What's that?" I took another swallow. "I don't think it's worth the rent and I keep *looking* but I'm not ready—"

"It's not funny," Stone said. His voice had the tone of the boy saying *that dog is frozen.* "Get out now. Come downstairs to my office."

I put down the glass. Through the haze of scotch and fatigue I felt a small stab of implication. "What is this?"

"I'll tell you downstairs. I'll meet you in the lobby."

"You tell me now."

"Shut up and get out of there."

"Good-bye," I said.

"You fool," he said rapidly, "I got your dog's mouth open."

"That's what you were supposed to do, *doctor.*"

"Wait. Listen to me," Stone said urgently, "Get out of that apartment *now.*"

I stared into the mouthpiece. "What?—"

"There were two fingers in that dog's mouth."

I put down the phone then, my hand reflexively numb, and heard the sounds inside the bedroom closet.

The door seemed to move slightly and it was only then, looking down, that I saw the thin strip of blood spreading from the closet . . .

I heard the knob within the closet turn.

What had the fat man said?

But I knew nothing of the fat man; I had refused to become involved. I dealt only with myself and my biscuit-tracking weapon. And so, even before I saw the face, even before I saw the dull revolver that was held in the hand that had not been ruined, even before all that, in fine and pure constancy, unmoving like Titus, I thought of the Doberman and his simple, willing attempt.

The phone began to ring again.

Oh God oh Stone oh Titus, I am *frozen*.

Crime Wave in Pinhole

JULIE SMITH

The small-town Southern sheriff isn't frequently a heroic figure—indeed, his image, which is usually that of a beer-bellied racist, is often the opposite. And while they occasionally have some redeeming features (as in the Virgil Tibbs stories of John Ball, such as In the Heat of the Night*), they do not often seem to use the brains they were born with.*

Not so in Julie Smith's "Crime Wave in Pinhole," a wonderful story about a very competent Southerner, and one of the very best stories in the mystery field written in dialect.

Doggonedest thing come in the mail yesterday—a letter of commendation from the Miami Police Department, thankin' me for solvin' a murder case. Me, Harry January, Pinhole, Mississippi's chief of police and sole officer of the law! I figured my brethren on the Bay of Biscayne had taken leave of their senses.

But I got to studyin' on the thing a while and I looked up the date I was supposed to've perpetrated this triumph and the whole thing come back to me. Blamed if I *didn't* solve a murder for them peckerwoods— it just wasn't no big thing at the time.

It happened the day Mrs. Flossie Chestnut come in, cryin' and takin' on cause her boy Johnny'd been kidnapped. Least that was her suspicion, but I knew that young'un pretty well and in my opinion there wasn't no kidnapper in Mississippi brave enough for such a undertakin'. Bein' as it was my duty, however, I took down a report of the incident, since he *could've* got hit by a car or fell down somebody's well or somethin'.

Mrs. Flossie said she hadn't seen a sign of him since three o'clock the day before when she caught him ridin' his pony standin' up. Naturally she told him he oughtn't to do it 'cause he could break his neck and it probably wasn't too easy on the pony neither. Then she emphasized her point by the administration of a sound hidin' and left him repentin' in the barn.

She wasn't hardly worried when he didn't show up for supper, on account of that was one of his favorite tricks when he was sulkin'. Seems his practice was to sneak in after ever'body else'd gone to sleep, raid the

535

icebox, and go to bed without takin' a bath. Then he'd come down to breakfast just like nothin' ever happened. Only he didn't that mornin' and Mrs. Flossie had ascertained his bed hadn't been slept in.

I told Mrs. Flossie he would likely be home in time for lunch and sent her on back to her ranch-style home with heated swimmin' pool and green-house full of orchids. Come to think about it, her and her old man were 'bout the only folks in town had enough cash to warrant holdin' their offspring for ransom, but I still couldn't believe it. Some say Pinhole got its name cause it ain't no bigger'n one, and the fact is we just don't have much crime here in the country. I spend most of my mornin's playin' gin rummy with Joshua Clow, who is retired from the drygoods business, and Mrs. Flossie had already played merry heck with my schedule.

But there wasn't no sense grumblin' about it. I broadcast a missin' juvenile report on the police radio and commenced to contemplatin' what to do next. Seemed like the best thing was to wait till after lunch, see if the little varmint turned up, and, if he didn't, get up a search party. It was goin' to ruin my day pretty thorough, but I didn't see no help for it.

'Long about that time, the blessed phone rang. It was young Judy Scarborough, down at the motel, claimin' she had gone and caught a live criminal without my assistance and feelin' mighty pleased with herself. Seems she had noticed that a Mr. Leroy Livingston, who had just checked in at her establishment, had a different handwritin' when he registered than was on the credit card he used to pay in advance. Young Judy called the credit company soon as her guest went off to his room and learned the Mr. Livingston who owned the card was in his sixties, whereas her Mr. Livingston wasn't a day over twenty-five.

It sounded like she had a genuine thief on her hands, so I went on over and took him into custody. Sure enough, his driver's license and other papers plainly indicated he was James Williamson of Little Rock, Arkansas. Among his possessions he had a employee identification card for Mr. Leroy Livingston of the same town from a department store where Mr. Livingston apparently carried out janitorial chores.

So I locked up Mr. Williamson and got on the telephone to tell Mr. Livingston we had found his missin' credit card. His boss said he was on vacation and give me the number of his sister, with whom he made his home. I called Miss Livingston to give her the glad tidin's, and she said her lovin' brother was in Surfside, Florida. Said he was visitin' with a friend of his youth, a Catholic priest whose name she couldn't quite recollect, 'cept she knew he was of Italian descent.

By this time I was runnin' up quite a little phone bill for the taxpayers of Pinhole, but I can't never stand not to finish what I start. So I called my brother police in Surfside, Florida, meanwhile motionin' for Mrs. Annie Johnson to please set down, as she was just come into the station. Surfside's finest tells me there is a Father Fugazi at Holy Name Church, and I jot down the number for future reference.

"What can I do for you, Annie?" I says then, and Mrs. Annie gets so agitated I thought I was goin' to have to round up some smellin' salts. Well, sir, soon's I got her calmed down, it was like a instant replay of that mornin's colloquy with Mrs. Flossie Chestnut. Seems her boy Jimmy has disappeared under much the same circumstances as young Johnny Chestnut. She punished him the day before for somethin' he was doin' and hadn't laid eyes on him since. Just to make conversation and get her mind off what might'a happened I says, casual like, "Mind if I ax you what kind'a misbehavior you caught him at?" And she turns every color in a Mississippi sunset.

But she sees it's her duty to cooperate with the law and she does. "I caught him makin' up his face," she says.

"Beg pardon?"

"He was experimentin' with my cosmetics," she says this time, very tight-lipped and dignified, and I begin to see why she is upset. But I figure it's my duty to be reassurin'.

"Well, now," says I, "I reckon it was just a childish prank—not that it didn't bear a lickin' for wastin' perfectly good face paint—but I don't 'spect it's nothin' to be embarrassed about. Now you run along home and see if he don't come home to lunch."

Sweat has begun to pour off me by this time as I realize I got two honest-to-Pete missin' juveniles and a live credit-card thief on my hands. Spite of myself, my mind starts wanderin' to the kind of trouble these young'uns could've got theirselves into, and it ain't pretty.

I broadcast another missin' juvenile report and start thinkin' again. Bein' as it was a Saturday I knew it wouldn't do no good callin' up the school to see if they was in attendance. But what I could do, I could call up Liza Smith, who's been principal for two generations and knows ever'thing about every kid in Pinhole.

She tells me Jimmy and Johnny is best friends and gives me two examples of where they like to play. Lord knows how she knew 'em. One is a old abandoned culvert 'bout two miles out of town and the other is a giant oak tree on ol' man Fisher's land, big enough to climb in but no good for buildin' a treehouse, on account of the boys have to trespass just to play there. Which is enough in itself to make Fisher get out his shotgun.

It was time to go home for lunch and my wife Helen is the best cook in Mississippi. But I didn't have no appetite. I called her and told her so. Then I took me a ride out to the culvert and afterwards to ol' man Fisher's place. No Jimmy and no Johnny in neither location.

So's I wouldn't have to think too much about the problem I got, I called up Father Fugazi in Surfside. He says, yes indeed, he had lunch with his ol' friend Leroy Livingston three days ago and made a date with him to go on a auto trip to DeLand the very next day. But Livingston never showed up. Father Fugazi never suspected nothin', he just got his feelin's hurt. But in the frame of mind I was in, I commenced to suspect foul play.

Now I got somethin' else to worry about, and I don't need Frannie Mendenhall, the town busybody and resident old maid, bustlin' her ample frame through my door, which she does about then. Doggone if Frannie ain't been hearin' noises again in the vacant house next door. Since this happens reg'lar every six months, I'm inclined to pay it no mind, but Frannie says the noises was different this time—kinda like voices, only more shrill. I tell Frannie I'll investigate later, but nothin' will do but what I have to do it right then.

Me and Frannie go over to that vacant house and I climb in the window I always do, but this time it's different from before. Because right away I find somethin' hadn't oughta be there—a blue windbreaker 'bout the right size for a eight-year-old, which is what Jimmy and Johnny both are. I ask Frannie if those noises coulda been kids' voices and she says didn't sound like it but it could be. I ask her if she heard any grown-ups' voices as well. She says she ain't sure. So I deduce that either Jimmy or Johnny or both has spent the night in the vacant house, either in the company of a kidnapper or not.

I go back to the station and call the Chestnuts and the Johnsons. Ain't neither Jimmy nor Johnny been home to lunch, but ain't no ransom notes arrived either. Oh, yeah, and Johnny's favorite jacket's a blue windbreaker. And sure enough, it ain't in his closet.

No sooner have I hung up the phone than my office is a reg'lar beehive of activity again. Three ladies from the Baptist church have arrived, in as big a huff as I have noticed anybody in all month. Turns out half the goods they was about to offer at a church bake sale that very afternoon have mysteriously disappeared and they are demandin' instant justice. There ain't no question crime has come to the country. I say I will launch an immediate investigation and I hustle those pillars of the community out of my office.

Course I had my suspicions 'bout who the thieves were—and I bet you can guess which young rascals I had in mind—but that still didn't get me no forrader with findin' 'em.

I made up my mind to take a walk around the block in search of inspiration, but first I called the Dade County, Florida, sheriff's office— which is in charge of Surfside, which is a suburb of Miami. I asked if they had any unidentified bodies turn up in the last few days and they acted like they thought I was touched, but said they'd check.

I walked the half block up to the square, said hello to the reg'lars sittin' on the benches there, and passed a telephone pole with some sorta advertisement illegally posted on it. I was halfway around the square without a idea in my head when all of a sudden it come to me—the meanin' of that poster on the telephone pole. It said the circus was comin' to town.

I doubled back and gave it a closer squint. It said there was gone to be a big time under the big top on October 19, which was that very Saturday. But the date had been pasted over, like on menus when they hike up the prices and paste the new ones over the old ones. I peeled the pasted-over date off and saw that the original one was October 18, which was the day before. Course I don't know when that date's been changed, but it gives me a idea. I figure long as them circus folks ain't changed their minds again, they oughta be pitchin' tents on the fairgrounds right about then.

It ain't but five minutes before I'm out there makin' inquiries, which prove fruitful in the extreme. Come to find out, two young gentlemen 'bout eight years of age have come 'round seekin' careers amid the sawdust and the greasepaint not half an hour before. They have been politely turned down and sent to pat the ponies, which is what I find 'em doin'.

In case you're wonderin', as were the Chestnuts and the Johnsons, it wasn't nothin' at all to study out once I seen that poster. I thought back to one young'un ridin' his pony standin' up and another one tryin' on his mama's pancake and I couldn't help concludin' that Johnny and Jimmy had aspirations to gainful employment, as a trick rider and a clown respectively.

Then I see that the date of the engagement has been changed and I figure the boys didn't catch onto that development till they had done run away from home and found nothin' at the fairgrounds 'cept a sign advisin' 'em accordingly. Course they could hardly go home, bein' as their pride had been sorely injured by the lickin's they had recently undergone, so they just hid out overnight in the vacant house, stole baked goods from the Baptist ladies to keep theirselves alive, and hared off to join the circus soon's it showed up.

That's all there was to it.

All's well that ends well, I says to the Chestnuts and the Johnsons, 'cept for one little detail—them kids, says I, is going to have to make restitution for them cakes and cookies they helped theirselves to. And I'm proud to say that come the next bake sale them two eight-year-olds got out in the kitchen and rattled them pots and pans till they had produced some merchandise them Baptist ladies was mighty tickled to offer for purchase.

Meanwhile, I went back to the station and found the phone ringin' dang near off the hook. It was none other than the Miami Police Department sayin' they had gotten a mighty interestin' call from the sheriff's office. Seems the body of a man in his sixties had floated up on the eighteenth hole of a golf course on the shore of Biscayne Bay three days previous and they was handlin' the case. So far's they knew, they said, it was a John Doe with a crushed skull, and could I shed any further light?

I told 'em I reckoned Father Fugazi in Surfside most likely could tell 'em their John Doe was Leroy Livingston of Little Rock, Arkansas, and that I had a pretty good idea who robbed and murdered him.

Then I hung up and had me a heart-to-heart with Mr. James Williamson, credit-card thief and guest of the people of Pinhole. He crumbled like cold bacon in no time a-tall, and waxed pure eloquent on the subject of his own cold-blooded attack on a helpless senior citizen.

I called them Miami police back and said to send for him quick, 'cause Pinhole didn't have no use in the world for him. So I guess there ain't no doubt I solved a murder in Miami. I just didn't hardly notice it.

Watching Marcia

MICHAEL D. RESNICK

Michael D. Resnick, the author of Birthright *and* The Soul Eater *(New American Library, 1981), will most likely be recognized within the decade as a major figure in science fiction. He has never worked in the mystery and suspense field and only marginally with the short-story form, a dual reluctance which the following story indicates is a major loss to aficionados of either or both forms. "Watching Marcia" is a chilling and nearly flawless paradigm which, by reason of subject and handling, could not be published in the taboo-laden contemporary genre mystery magazines, an unfortunate circumstance which the editors of this anthology now remedy in this more permanent form. The voice of the watcher, the terror of the watched, the fine and rending line which bind them . . .*

Tuesday, June 7

Marcia walks from the living room to the bathroom and I panic for a minute as I lose sight of her, but then she comes back in view and I peer intently through my telescope (a Celestron C90, two hundred and thirty-nine dollars retail and worth every penny of it).

She lets her robe drop to the floor and a little moan escapes my lips. Then she is in the shower and the bathroom fills with steam, and it seems that even through the steam I can see her rubbing soap over her naked breasts, sliding her hands down her body, stroking that delicious area between her legs with just the hint of a smile on her face.

After an eternity she emerges, clean and pink and glowing with health, her skin still slick with water, and for a moment I can imagine myself in the bathroom with her, patting her dry, rubbing the water away from secret areas that only she and I share, licking her dry and then licking her moist again.

The thought fascinates me, and I find, to my surprise, that I have been rubbing my own body in the very same way, and producing, not surprisingly, the very same results.

I think I'm in love.

Wednesday, June 8

My lunch break is almost over and I wait by a tobacco stand in Marcia's office building. The smell of the cigars, even though they're all wrapped in cellophane and stacked in boxes, irritates my nostrils, and I find myself wondering why Royal Jamaicans cost twice as much as Royal Caribbeans when they both look so much alike. Finally she emerges from the elevator, her tight little ass fighting against her tight little skirt, her heels click-click-clicking in an almost sexual rhythm on the dirty tile floor.

She walks right by me without noticing, which is not unexpected—after all, I am the watcher and she is the watched—and I fall into step behind her, mesmerized by the twin globes of her buttocks as they race ahead of me like some sexual incarnation of Affirmed and Alydar locked in an eternal neck-and-neck struggle. I think of a horrible pun about no quarter being asked and emit a falsetto cackle which draws a few strange stares, but Marcia, everything moving in sync, shaking, bobbing, twitching, does not turn around.

She walks into the bookstore (I know her habits and could have been waiting for her there, but then I wouldn't have been able to watch her walk) and goes right to the romance section while I punch in and walk to my station at the cash register. She bends over to look at a title at the bottom of one of the racks, and her skirt climbs up her thighs and it is all I can do not to scream as inch after inch of that smooth white flesh which I know so well is revealed to me. I wonder if she is wearing panties (I woke up late this morning and didn't get a chance to check) and hope that she is; that soft, slippery little mound of ecstasy is for my eyes only. I start thinking of all the things I want to do to it with my lips, my tongue, my teeth, my fingers—and suddenly I realize that I have been staring blankly at the place where Marcia had been but that now she is standing in front of me with a pile of paperbacks and I am so nervous that I have to count her change three times before I get it right.

She smiles at me, an amused kind of smile, and I mumble and apologize and have to dig my fingers into my palms to keep from ripping her blouse open and covering her tits with love-bites right there in front of everyone. She takes her books and her change and walks out, Alydar and Affirmed jostling each other furiously for position. I wipe the sweat from my face and feel very stupid.

Which, by the way, is all wrong. Would a stupid person have had enough sense to demand that Marcia write down her phone number the first time she paid for her books with a Visa card? Without her name and number I'd never have been able to confirm her address in the directory, and without her address I wouldn't have been able to rent the apartment across the street, or set up my Celestron C90 three-and-one-half-inch refractive scope with its off-axis guiding system, or learned about the tiny mole on the inside of her left thigh. So there.

In point of fact, I am possessed of enormous animal cunning (which is a very nice word and reminds me of all kinds of things I'd like to do with Marcia). When I started writing notes and slipping them under her door, I knew better than to do it in my own handwriting or even on my own typewriter. Do you know how much work it was to cut out the letters from newspaper headlines to spell I WANT TO EAT YOU? (I did it all in 48-point Tempo Bold, but I couldn't find a capital *Y* for YOU. I hope she doesn't think she's dealing with an illiterate.)

And I drove all the way to Greenwich, Connecticut, to mail her the vibrator and the K-Y Jelly. I mean, not just to the Bronx or even Scarsdale, but to *Connecticut* for God's sake!

So I guess that shows you who's stupid and who's not.

Thursday, June 9

Marcia and I wake up together, or maybe I should say that we wake up at the same time. I place my eye to the Celestron and zero in and can almost see her clit pulsating. Then I look at her breasts and utter a howl of anguish because her nipples are not erect and she should know—damn it, she *must* know!—that she looks like only half a woman when they're like that. I want to suck and bite them erect, but I just stare and stare and get madder and madder at her.

She yawns, and hangs up her robe, and starts to get dressed. She puts her bra on first and then her panties, and I am beside myself with rage. *Everyone* knows that you're supposed to do it the other way around. It's just out-and-out *wrong*, and if I were there I'd take that goddamned vibrator and shove it so far up her ass that it would break her teeth.

I'm so upset that I don't even follow her to work like I always do. Ordinarily I like to watch her raise her hand and jiggle her breasts when she signals the bus, and try to get a peek up her skirt as she takes an aisle seat, but she has ruined everything today.

If she doesn't start showing a little consideration, I'll do something bad to her.

Yes I will.

Friday, June 10

I'm so mad I could almost kill her!

She didn't wear a bra today, and just walked to the bus stop, bouncing and flopping for everyone to see. I mean, you could see *everything!* The bus was a couple of minutes late, and some tall, gray-haired guy carrying a briefcase stopped to talk to her while we were waiting, and her nipples almost stuck right through her sweater. They didn't have any goddamned trouble standing up for *him!*

And the bus driver, who never notices anything, not even dogs crossing the street in front of him, gave her a great big smile when she shook her boobs in his face. If she'd have paused in front of him one more second I'd have cut his cock off and fed it to those dogs that he's always trying to hit.

Those tits and that cunt and that ass are *mine* to look at—nobody else's! No woman I love can flaunt herself like some five-buck-a-shot hooker, that's all I've got to say.

It had just better never happen again.

Or else.

Saturday, June 11

She goes to the beach today, and I sit a few hundred yards away on a park bench, binoculars in hand, and watch her.

She finds a nice secluded spot and removes her wraparound, and she is wearing a skimpy little royal-blue bikini, and it seems like the second she takes a deep breath her tits will pop right out of it. I tremble a little as I study her through the binoculars (Power Optics 30 x 80, one hundred and sixty-nine dollars without the tripod, lens caps free), and I decide that I don't want anyone else to see her like this. Bikinis may be all very well for unattached girls, but Marcia is mine, and you can even see that goddamned mole right next to her pussy, for Christ's sake! I make a mental note to tell her to dress more modestly in the future, wipe away a little stream of spittle that has somehow rolled down to my chin, and go back to looking at her.

A young blond man, all tanned and hairy and with his cock almost bursting out of his tight swimming trunks, stops by to talk to her. To *my* Marcia!

I reach into my purse and fondle the .22-caliber Beretta, letting my fingers slide over it and seek out all its crevices, much as they would like to do with Marcia, and decide to count to twenty. But on fourteen he shrugs and walks away, and Marcia turns onto her belly, golden buttocks reflecting the sun, begging, *begging* to be violated, and never knows that she saved his life by only six seconds.

Sunday, June 12

I get up at seven-thirty, turn off my alarm (a General Electric clock-radio, AM/FM, twenty-two-ninety-five at the local discount house, but it doesn't have a Snooze-Alarm, which was a terrible mistake but one with which I must live), and train my Celestron on her, but Marcia is becoming slovenly and she just lays there, eyes shut, the succulent mounds of her breasts rising and falling regularly, sound asleep.

Nine comes, then ten, and she's still asleep, and I don't dare take my eyes off her for fear that while I'm not looking she'll wake up and I'll miss the daily unveiling of her treasures, and suddenly I am overcome by a sense of having been misused. Has she no consideration for me? Doesn't she know how long I have been sitting motionless, my eye glued to the telescope? It's unfair, no two ways about it, and I make up my mind to alleviate the situation, so without taking my eyes from her body I reach blindly behind me and finally manage to locate the telephone.

I call her, and a moment later she sits up in the bed, the covers falling to her thigh, and I see that her nipples are erect, but it doesn't please me because I know she has been dreaming of *him,* of shoving her tits into his blond face and sticking him in her mouth and having his corrupt blond hands exploring every inch of her, and when she picks up the phone a moment later I am so mad that I don't trust myself to speak and all I can do is breathe heavily into the receiver.

I wait until my head stops throbbing and the screeching noise in my ears goes away, and then I dial her number again.

"Hello?" she says.

I stare at her and forget the receiver is in my hand, and she hangs up again. But now she is up for the day, and after I watch her go into the shower and come out and dry herself off and powder her body, I call a third time. This time I am in perfect control of myself. This time I will lay down the law to her.

"Hello?" she says again.

"Hello, Marcia," I say softly.

"Who is this?" she says.

"Marcia, I don't like the way things have been going between us," I say. "You've got to stop."

"Is this some kind of joke?" she asks, but I am looking at her through the scope and I know she doesn't think it's funny.

"If we're going to remain lovers," I say, "if you're going to open your ripe juicy body to me, then we've got to come to an understanding."

"Marlene, is this you?" she snaps. "I don't think much of your sense of humor, Marlene!"

"Who's Marlene?" I demand. "Are you seeing someone named Marlene?"

"Who *is* this?" she yells.

"You keep away from Marlene," I warn her. "I don't want to hear about her again." Then I realize that I am getting away from the point and that I am yelling too, so I take a deep breath and lower my voice and say, very casually and conversationally, "If you say one word to the blond guy, just one word, I'll kill him."

She hangs up the phone and starts pacing around her apartment.

She looks worried.

I smile. I have made my point. Things will improve between us now.

Monday, June 13

Marcia wears a bra today, and very unrevealing pants. She scrutinizes everyone at the bus stop, scanning each face ever so carefully, but I am too smart for her and I stay in my room, watching her from the window. I don't wait for her at the cigar stand either. When she walks into the bookstore I nod to her and smile pleasantly and she looks right through me. She browses for a few minutes but doesn't buy anything, and I can tell she is still thinking about our little chat.

Good. Even though it was our very first conversation and we haven't even been properly introduced, I am glad to see that she is a serious girl and considers what I have said very carefully.

I think this is the beginning of a very long and beautiful and trusting relationship.

Tuesday, June 14

I leave work early and race home to watch Marcia's face when she opens the package. I wait an hour for her, but finally she arrives, and puts the package down next to her mail on the kitchen table and looks at it like it might be a bomb. Finally she opens it and pulls out the black bra with the little holes cut out so that her nipples can peek through, and the black lace panties with the crotch removed, and then she sees the message: I

ACHE FOR YOUR HOT LITTLE BODY. (I have given up Tempo Bold and switched to 96-point Erber, which is much more impressive and really gets my message across.)

She begins to cry and a warm glow suffuses me as I realize that I have brought tears of happiness to the woman I love.

Wednesday, June 15

Today begins like all other days, with the unveiling, and proceeds like all the others, but somewhere along the way something goes wrong, because when I get on the bus to go home Marcia is not on it. Panic-stricken, I get off at the next block and begin back-tracking. I bump into people without noticing, and twist my ankle painfully on a curb, but I continue and finally I find her.

She is sitting at a bar, and as I look in the window I see that she has a drink in her hand, but because of my inexperience in such matters I cannot tell from the shape of the glass what kind of drink it is. The place is not doing much business at this hour. There is a couple seated at a table, and three businessmen are positioned at various spots along the bar, but that is enough.

I go into a drugstore across the street and look up the bar's number in the directory and dial it and ask for Marcia. The bartender sounds surprised, but he calls her name and then I see him bring the phone over to her.

"Marcia," I say harshly, "this can't go on."

"Who is this?" she says, her voice shaking.

"You can't keep exhibiting yourself like this," I continue, "flaunting your ass in front of those three men like some kind of trollop. I won't stand for it."

"Why can't you leave me alone?" she shrieks.

"Get out of there at once or I'm going to be very cross with you," I warn her and hang up the phone.

I watch her scream something into the receiver before she realizes the line is dead. Everyone turns and stares at her and suddenly she throws a handful of money on the bar and walks out and summons a cab.

I must remember to tell her not to overtip bartenders in the future.

Thursday, June 16

Marcia doesn't get out of bed to take her shower this morning. I know she's not having her period and I start to worry that she might be feeling under the weather, but then she jumps like she's had an electric shock and stares at the phone, and I can tell by her attitude that it must be ringing and she is probably afraid that I am still mad at her.

Once she gets to know me better she'll discover that I'm really a very warm and caring person who almost never carries a grudge. I decide to call and tell her that she is forgiven, but when the phone rings she buries her head under a pillow and since there is nothing more to watch except for a few trembling lumps under the blanket I decide to go to work without her.

All day long I wonder who would have been calling her at eight in the morning, and it puts me in a very foul mood by the time I return home. I watch Marcia for a few hours before going to bed and I feel better.

Friday, June 17

The unveiling is glorious today, as always, and I become so engrossed that I almost miss the bus. Still, there is a certain sameness to it, it lacks a certain spark, and I find myself wishing that she would do something a little different, so I call her at her office just after lunchtime.

"Hello?" she says in a brisk, businesslike voice. "May I help you?"

"You certainly may," I answer. "I sent you a present three days ago and you haven't even tried it on yet." I think I hear something at the other end of the line, perhaps a gasp or a sob, but she doesn't say anything, so I continue: "I think you should wear it to bed tonight, Marcia. After all, I spent a lot of time selecting it, and it seems very ungracious of you not to wear it at least once."

She hangs up the phone, or perhaps we are cut off. I spend the rest of the afternoon putting new mystery and science-fiction titles in the racks and setting aside the old ones for the distributor to take away. Someone comes in right at closing and I miss my regular bus, but somehow it doesn't bother me at all because I have already seen Marcia in the dress she is wearing today and I am looking forward with almost frenzied eagerness to seeing her wear my present tonight.

I walk up the stairs to my apartment and unlock the door. I haven't eaten all day and suddenly I realize that I am ravenously hungry, but I decide to take a quick look at Marcia first. I race to the Celestron, hoping against hope that she has decided against waiting until bedtime to put on the bra and panties. I press my eye to the sight, and I stare, and suddenly I emit a howl of rage.

She has pulled all her shades down!

Horrified, I turn the scope from her bedroom to the other rooms. In each of them the flimsy little curtains have been pulled together and the shades have been drawn. I dial her on the phone to demand an explanation, and the operator tells me she has just changed to an unlisted number.

This is intolerable! All ties are broken, all vows unmade, and I race down the stairs and across the street. I know that the ungrateful, spiteful, back-stabbing bitch will never answer the doorbell, so I climb up the creaky wooden stairs to her back door. It is locked, but I break the window and reach my hand through and let myself in.

She is running from the bedroom when I get there but I grab her by the arm (it doesn't feel anywhere near as soft as I had thought it would) and hurl her onto the bed.

"Who are you?" she blubbers, tears streaming down her face and mingling with her mascara. "I know you from somewhere! What do you want with me?"

"You can't treat me like this!" I scream. "Not after all we've meant to each other!"

"My God!" she says, her eyes suddenly going wide with horror. "You're that strange woman from the bookstore!"

I pull the knife from my purse.

"Slut!" I scream, and plunge it into her belly.

She howls in pain and spits blood.

"Cunt!" I rage, and stab her in the throat.

She tries to scream again, but it comes out as a wet gurgle.

"I loved you!" I say, burying the knife in her again and again. "We could have been so happy! Why did you have to spoil it? Why do all of you always have to spoil it?"

She doesn't say anything, of course. She is past saying anything ever again, and before I can mourn my lost love in private there is the body to be disposed of. I leave her apartment, return to my own, pick up a pair of plastic leaf bags and some masking tape, and pull my Volkswagen (a Beetle, twenty-three hundred dollars new, and *still* a great car) into the alley behind her building.

Then I go upstairs, slip one of the bags over her head and torso and the other over her legs, tape them together, hoist her over my shoulder, hobble back down to the alley, and place her in the trunk.

I drive to the local supermarket and pull around to the back, where they keep their huge metal dumpster, and I deposit her with all the other refuse and rubbish that will be picked up tomorrow morning.

(I was worried the first time I did it, but human hands never touch the dumpster. The truck reaches out with its long mechanical arms and lifts the dumpster high in the air and turns it upside down, and since they never found Phyllis or Joan or Martha I know that they won't find Marcia either. The selfish, unfeeling slut will be crushed into a tiny compact cube along with the tin cans and broken crates and will be deposited in some foul-smelling hole in the ground and that will be that and no one will ever know what happened to her. (Though if she ever treated other lovers in the same high-handed, uncaring fashion, there will be some at least who can hazard a guess, who might even congratulate me if they knew.)

And if the police come by (though of course they never do) I will just look shocked and say yes, I had seen her on occasion. She seemed like kind of a cold fish, if you ask me.

Lovers?

I'll smile and shake my head and say no, not her, she just wasn't the type.

Besides, what would a gray-haired little old neighbor lady know about that?

Wednesday, July 6

I think I'm in love.

Her name is Sharon, and she's much more sensitive than Marcia. No trashy romance novels for her, oh no; she comes in at two on the dot every afternoon and goes right to the poetry section. She's polite and refined, and she has the longest, most beautiful legs I ever saw. (And I'll bet she doesn't have a gross ugly mole like Marcia did.)

Her breasts are high and firm and I just know that her nipples stand out proudly. I dreamed about her the last four nights in a row, and I thought I would go crazy when July 4 came on a weekday and we had to close the store. I spent most of the day standing across the street, hoping Sharon would pass by to look at our new window display. We can't be kept apart like this any longer. It just isn't fair.

I wonder if she has a Visa card?

Somebody Cares

TALMAGE POWELL

Like Ed McBain's 87th Precinct novella, "Somebody Cares" is a police procedural with emphasis not so much on detection as on characterization. The two stories are completely different in tone and handling, however; Talmage Powell's tale is a sensitive study of a hard-bitten cop and a female homicide victim, the latter a "nobody," a Jane Doe (or Mary Smith) who led an empty, lonely life with no friends, no one seeming to care if she lived or died. Yet as Powell quietly demonstrates, "There are no total strangers in this world. Somebody cares."

Being teamed with Odus Martin wasn't an inviting prospect, but I didn't intend to let it blight the pleasure of my promotion to plainclothes.

His own reaction was buried deep in his personal privacy. I, the greenie fresh out of uniform, was accepted as just another chore. Martin volunteered no helpful advice; neither did he pass judgment on me. I suspected that he would be slow to praise and reluctant to criticize.

If my partner's almost inhuman taciturnity made him a poor companion, I had compensations. A ripple of pleasure raced through me each time I entered the squadroom. To me it was not a barren bleak place of scarred desks, hard chairs, dingy walls, and stale tobacco.

My first days as Martin's partner were busy ones. We rounded up suspects in a knifing case. Martin questioned them methodically and dispassionately. He decided a man named Greene was lying. He had Greene brought back and after seven hours and fifteen minutes of additional questioning by Martin, Greene signed a statement attesting his guilt.

Martin's attitude irritated me. A man's life had been cut short with a knife. Another man would spend his best years behind bars. Wives, mothers, children, brothers, sisters were affected. Their lives would never again be quite the same, no matter how strong they were or how much they managed to forget.

But to Odus Martin it was all a chore, nothing more. A small chore at that, one of many in an endless chain.

When I mentioned the families, Martin looked at me as if I were a truant and not-too-bright schoolboy. "Everybody in this world has some-one," he said. "Accept that—and quit worrying about it."

"I'm not necessarily worrying," I said, an edge creeping into my voice.

He shrugged and bent over some paper work on his desk. His manner was a dismissal—a reduction of me to a neuter, meaningless zero.

"Since you put it that way," I said argumentatively, "how about the nameless tramp the county has to bury?"

He looked up at me slowly. "Somewhere, Jenks, somebody misses that tramp. You take my word for it. There are no total strangers in this world. Somebody cares—somebody always cares."

I hadn't expected this bit of philosophy from him. It caused me to give him a second glance. But he still reminded me of a slab of silvery-gray casting in iron.

As the weeks passed, I learned to get along with Martin. I adopted a cool manner toward him, but only as a protective device. I told myself I'd never let a quarter of a century of violence and criminals turn me into an unsmiling robot, as had happened to Odus Martin.

I paid him the respect due a first-rate detective. His movements, mental as well as physical, were slow, thorough, and objective. He made colorless —hence, uninteresting—newspaper copy. This, coupled with his close-mouthed habits, caused most reporters to dislike him. Martin didn't mind in the least.

But when it came to criminals he had the instincts of a stalking leopard. As I became better acquainted with him, I realized these were not natural endowments—they were the cumulative conditioning and results of twenty-five years. He seemed never to have forgotten the smallest trick that experience had taught him.

The day Greene was arraigned, I put a question to Martin that had been bothering me. "You decided Greene was lying when he told us his alibi. Why? How could you be sure?"

"He looked me straight and forthrightly in the eye with every word he spoke," Martin explained.

This drew a complete blank with me.

Martin glanced at me and said patiently, "Greene *normally* was a very shifty-eyed character."

Well, I knew I could learn a lot from this guy, if I were sufficiently perceptive and alert myself. He didn't regard it as his place to teach. He was a cop.

As usual, I was fifteen minutes early to work the morning after the murder of Mary Smith. Martin was coming from the squadroom when I arrived. He was moving with the slow-motion, elephantine gait that covered distance like a mild sprint. It was clear he'd just got in and had intended to leave without waiting for me.

I fell in step beside him. "What's up?"

"Girl been killed."

"Where?"

"In Hibernia Park."

She lay as if sleeping under some bushes where she'd been dragged and hurriedly and ineffectually hidden. It was a golden day, filled with the freshness of morning, the grass and trees of the park dewy and vividly green.

Squad cars and uniformed men had already cordoned off the area. Men from the lab reached the scene about the same time as Martin and I. Efficiently, they started the routine of photography and footprint moulage.

I had not, as yet, the objectivity of the rest of them. The girl drew and held my attention. She was small, fine of bone, and sparsely fleshed. Her face had a piquant quality. She might have been almost pretty, if she'd known how to fix herself up.

As it was, she lay drab and colorless in her cheap, faded cotton dress, dull brown hair framing her face.

Her attitude of sleep, face toward the sky, became a horror when my eyes followed the lines her dragging heels had made. The lines ended beyond a flat stone. The stone was crusted with dark, dried blood. It was obvious that she'd been knocked down there, as she came along the walkway. The back of her head had struck the stone. Perhaps she'd died instantly. Her assailant had dragged her quickly to the bushes, concealing the body long enough for him to get far away from the park.

Looking again at her, I shivered slightly. What in your nineteen or twenty years, I asked silently of her, brought you to this?

The murder scene yielded little. Her purse, if she'd had one, was gone. She wore no jewelry, although she might have had a cheap watch or ID bracelet. The golden catch from such an item was found near the flat stone by one of the lab men.

Later in the squadroom, Martin and I sat and looked at the golden clasp.

"Mugged, robbed, murdered," Martin decided. "I wonder how much she was carrying in her purse. Five dollars? Ten?"

He held the catch so that it caught the light. "We'll check the pawn-shops. A hoodlum this cheap will try to pawn the watch. Nothing from Missing Persons?"

I'd just finished the routine in that department. I shook my head.

"Nothing from the lab, either," Martin said. "Her clothes came from any bargain basement. No laundry marks. Washed them herself. No scars or identifying marks. No bridgework in the mouth. We'll run the finger-prints, but I'm not hopeful. The P.M. will establish the cause of death as resulting from compound fracture of the skull, probably late last night."

"None of it will tell us who she is," I said.

"That's what I'm saying. But somebody will turn up, asking for her. Somebody will claim her. Girl that young—she can't die violently and disappear without it affecting someone. Meantime, all we got is this clasp."

We took it to all the pawnshops in the city. No watch with such a clasp missing had been pawned.

Martin next picked up every punk who had a mugging or mugging attempt on his record. We questioned each one of them. The task ate up two days, and when it was over we had placed nobody near Hibernia Park at the right time.

The girl's body remained in the morgue. No one inquired about her. She wasn't reported missing. She continued to be an unclaimed Jane Doe.

"It means," Martin said, "that she has no family here. She must have come here to work, maybe from a farm upstate. Lucky for us that we live in a reasonably small city. We'll check all the rooming houses—places where such a girl might have lived."

We did it building by building, block by teeming block, from landlord to landlady to building super.

Martin would take one side of the street, I the other. Our equipment was a picture of the girl, and the question was always the same. So were all the answers.

We spent two fatiguing, monotonous days of this. Then about midaf-ternoon the third day, I came disconsolately from a cheaper apartment building and saw Martin waving to me from a long porch across the street.

I waited for a break in traffic and crossed over. The rooming house was an old gables-and-gingerbread monstrosity, three stories, a mansion in its day, but long since chopped into small apartments and sleeping rooms.

A small, gray, near-sighted woman hovered in the hallway behind Odus Martin.

"This is Mrs. Carraway," Martin said.

The landlady and I nodded our new acquaintance.

"May we see Mary Smith's room?" Martin asked.

Mary Smith, I thought. I'd begun to think you'd remain Jane Doe forever, Mary Smith.

"Since you're police officers I guess it's all right," Mrs. Carraway said.

"You've seen my credentials," Martin said. "We'll take full responsibility."

We followed Mrs. Carraway to a small clean room at the end of the hallway. She stood in the open doorway while we examined the room.

The furnishings were typical—mismatched bed, bureau, chest of drawers, and worn carpet, faded curtains.

A neat person, Mary Smith. The few items of clothing she'd owned were pressed and properly placed in the closet and chest of drawers.

The room reflected a lonely life. There were no photos, no letters. Nothing of a personal nature except the clothing and a few magazines on a bedside table.

"How long she lived with you?" Martin asked.

"A little over two months," Mrs. Carraway said in her cautious, impersonal voice.

"When did you see her last?"

"A week ago Thursday when she paid a month's rent."

"She have any callers?"

"Callers?"

"Boy friend, perhaps."

"Not that I know of." Mrs. Carraway pursed her lips. "I'm not a nosy landlady. She seemed like a quiet, nice girl. So long as they pay their rent and don't raise a disturbance—that's all I'm concerned with."

"Know where she came from?"

"No. She came and looked at the room and said she'd take it. She said she was employed. I checked, to make sure."

"Where was that?"

"At the Cloverleaf Restaurant. She's a waitress."

Martin thanked her, and we started from the room.

Mrs. Carraway said, "Is she in serious trouble?"

"Pretty much," Martin said. "I'm sure she won't be coming back."

"What'll I do with her things?"

"We'll let you know."

Mrs. Carraway followed us to the front door. "I've told you everything

I know. I'm not an unkind person. But whatever she's done is none of my business. You'd just be wasting my time to be calling me in as a witness."

"We'll trouble you no more than we have to," Martin said.

We returned to the unmarked police car parked in the middle of the block. Martin got behind the wheel and drove in silence.

"Any doubt of her identity?" I asked.

"I don't think so. We'll check fingerprints in the room against the Jane Doe to be sure. But the landlady showed no hesitation when she saw the picture. She was Mary Smith, right enough."

Hello, Mary Smith, I thought. Hello, stranger. Who were you?

A man named Blakeslee was the owner of the Cloverleaf, a large drive-in on the south side of town. He was a slender, dark, harried-looking fellow, about forty.

He was checking the cash register when we arrived. We showed him our credentials, and with a gesture of annoyance he led us to a small office off the kitchen.

"Well," he said, closing the door, "what's this all about?"

"Got a Mary Smith on your payroll?" Martin asked.

"I did have. She quit without notice. A lot of them do. You've no idea what it is to keep help nowadays."

"What were the circumstances?"

"Circumstances?" He shrugged. "She didn't show up for a couple of days, so I put another girl on. There weren't any circumstances, as you put it."

"Did you wonder if maybe she was sick?"

"I figured she'd have called in. She's not the first to quit like that. I haven't time to be running around checking on them. What's your interest in her?"

"She's dead."

"What's that?" After his initial start, Blakeslee raised his hand and stroked his chin. "Why, that's too bad," he said in a tone without real meaning.

"The papers carried a story," Martin said. "Unidentified girl murdered."

"I don't recall seeing it. Probably wouldn't have connected it with Mary Smith anyway. How did it happen?"

"She was apparently on her way home. We think she was knocked down for whatever of value she was carrying."

"It couldn't have been much."

"Can you tell us anything about her?"

"Only that she came to work here. She seemed nice enough, always on time. Too quiet to make many friends."

"Where did she work formerly?"

"She came here from Crossmore." Blakeslee spread his hands. "I wish I could help. But after all, what was she to me?"

Martin and I took the expressway out of town. The drive to Crossmore, a small town in the next county, required only forty minutes.

I wondered how many restaurants there were in Crossmore. Very few, I guessed. We had at least that much in our favor.

However, Martin drove right on through the village.

"I'm playing a hunch," he said.

Just beyond Crossmore, overlooking the busy highway, were the rolling hills and meadows and buildings of the county-supported orphanage.

Martin turned into a winding driveway which was shaded by tall pines. He stopped before an old colonial-type home that had been converted into an administration building. More recent structures of frame and brick housed dorms and classrooms. Beyond there were barns and workshops.

A few minutes later we were in the office of Dr. Spreckles, the superintendent. A wiry, sandy man, Spreckles struck me as being a pleasant individual who nevertheless knew how to run things.

He looked at the picture of Mary Smith that the lab boys had made.

"Yes," he said. "She was one of our girls." His lips tightened slightly. "We hope she has done nothing to reflect on the training she received here."

"She hasn't," Martin assured him. "Who were her people?"

Spreckles went behind his desk and sat down. "She had none. She was born out of wedlock in the county hospital to a woman who gave her name only as Mary Smith. As soon as she was able to get about, the mother abandoned the child."

"The girl grew up here?"

"Yes."

"Never adopted?"

"No," Spreckles said slowly, resting his elbows on his desk and steepling his fingers. "As a child, she was quite awkward, too quiet, too shy. She lived here until she was eighteen."

"Who were her friends?"

"Strangely enough," Spreckles frowned, "I can't say. I don't think she had any really close ones. She was a face in a crowd, you might say. Never precocious. Not at the bottom of her classes, you understand, but not at the top. I do wish you'd tell me what difficulty she's in."

"She's dead," Martin said. "A mugger killed her during a robbery attempt."

"How terrible!" Spreckles made an honest attempt to muster genuine grief, but he simply didn't have it. He was shocked and upset by the passing forever of an impersonal image, but that was all . . .

As we drove back through Crossmore, Martin broke his silence—with a single utterance. It was softly spoken but the most vicious oath I'd ever heard. It was so unlike Martin that I stared at him out of the corner of my eyes.

But I let the silence return and stay that way. Right then, he had the look about him of a heavy-chested, steel-gray tomcat whose wounds have been rubbed with turpentine and salt.

We returned to grinding routine. The pawnshops. Still no watch. The vicinity of Hibernia Park—questioning all the people, one by one, who lived in the area. No one had glimpsed a man coming from the park about the time she was killed.

At night I was too tired to sleep. I wondered what this was getting us, if we'd ever catch the man. Yet there wasn't the slightest letdown in Martin's determination. I only wished I shared it . . .

Martin and I returned to the squadroom late Wednesday afternoon. A few minutes afterward, a uniformed policeman walked in and handed Martin an inexpensive woman's watch.

My scalp pulled tight. I crossed to Martin's desk as he opened a drawer. He shook the golden clasp from a small manila envelope. The clasp matched the broken band of the watch perfectly.

Martin stood up. His nostrils were flaring. "Where'd this come from?"

"The personal effects of a guy named Biddix," the man in uniform said. "He was in a poker game we just broke up in an old loft. The desk sergeant said you'd want to see the watch."

Martin's big hand closed over the tiny timepiece. I followed him out of the office.

Biddix was a dried-up, seedy little fellow in his late sixties. He'd been separated from the other poker players and put in a solitary cell.

When the cell door opened, Biddix took one look at Martin's face and backed against the wall.

Martin held out his hand and opened it. "Where'd you get this?"

"Look . . ." Biddix swallowed. "If it's stolen, I swear I had nothing to do with it."

"It was torn from a murdered girl's wrist," Martin said.

The dead-gray of Biddix's beard stubble suddenly blended exactly with the color of his skin.

"A guy put the watch in the game," Biddix said. "And that's the truth, so help me!"

"Which one?"

"He left before he was raided."

"What's his name?"

"Edgar Collins."

"Know where he lives?"

"Sure. In a flop on East Maple Street, number 311."

We went out. The cell door clanged behind us. Biddix came over and stood holding the bars. "I didn't know anything about the watch."

"Sure," Martin said.

"You'll put me in with the others now, won't you?"

"No," Martin said. "Not yet."

We got the location of Edgar Collins's room from the building super, went up one flight, and eased to the door.

The house was hot and the hallway smelled of age and many people. We listened. After a little, we heard a bedspring creak.

We put our shoulders to the door, and it flew open. A stringy, big-boned, bald-headed man sprang off the bed and dropped the tabloid he'd been reading. He was tall and stooped. He wore dirty khaki pants and a dirty undershirt.

"What's the big idear?" he demanded.

"Your name Edgar Collins?" Martin asked.

"So what if it is?"

"We're police officers. We want to talk to you."

"Yeah? What about?"

"A girl who was killed in Hibernia Park. If you're innocent, you got nothing to worry about. If not . . . We've got a shoe-track moulage to start. We'll find plenty of other things with the help of the lab boys, once we know where to start looking."

Collins stared at us. An explosion took place behind his pale eyes. He lunged toward the open window.

Martin got between me and Collins and grabbed the man first. He dragged Collins back in the room. Collins threw punches at Martin in blind panic.

Martin hit him three times in the face. Collins fell on the floor, wrapped his arms about his head, and began rolling back and forth.

"I didn't mean it," he said, babbling. "She fell on the stone. She was a stranger, nothing to me. It was an accident . . . please . . . give me a break! I didn't mean it, I tell you."

For a moment I thought Odus Martin was going to start hitting the man again.

A volunteer minister performed graveside rites the next morning. Martin and I stood with our hats in our hands.

I looked at the casket and thought: Good-bye, Mary Smith—that name will do as well as any. No father, no mother, no one. Killed by a man who never saw you before.

The sun was shining, but the day felt bleak and dismal.

Then, as we returned to headquarters, it came to me that Odus Martin had been right. There are no absolute strangers in this world, no zeros.

The death of Mary Smith had affected Odus Martin. Because I was his partner, it had affected me. Through us, it seemed to me, the human race had recognized the importance of her and expressed its unwillingness to let her die as an animal dies.

Mary Smith had lived and died in loneliness, but she had not been alone.

I didn't say anything of this to Odus Martin. He was a hard man to talk to. Anyhow, I felt that he understood it already, probably much more deeply than I ever could.

Jode's Last Hunt

BRIAN GARFIELD

Brian Garfield is special. Very few crime writers have worked so effectively in the Western genre as this exceptional talent has, although much of his work in the latter field has appeared under several pen names. He has served as both president of the Western Writers of America and director of the Mystery Writers of America. He won an Edgar Award for Hopscotch, *perhaps his best-known work.*

"Jode's Last Hunt" artfully combines his love of the West with his talent for the story of suspense.

The night watchman thought he saw a flicker in the woods. He stepped off the platform and looked away and then looked again, but there was nothing.

Could be a squirrel. Sunday dawn was always jumpy. Any other morning the mill would be working—shifts moving in and out—but Sunday was silent because that was the Keenmeier management: pious about the Sabbath. On Sunday the only face he'd see would be the day watchman's at eight o'clock and that was still three hours away.

Red shafts of light slanted through the lodgepoles. He looked at his watch. Another half hour he'd do another round of inspection.

He walked to his car and got in. The coffee was still hot, but there was only half a cup left. He thought about saving it, but it would only get cool. He drank it down.

His eyes drifted along the length of the paper mill out of habit. It looked new and raw—they hadn't bothered with much paint. Smoke had discolored the buildings in patches. The big metal chutes were coated with ugly splashes. Along the parking lot the pines had been stained by the mill's outpourings.

He could hear the river. It birled over rocks just below the mill. Those rocks were colored by the guck that poured out of the mill's spouts through the spillway. Once in a while he walked over there and just looked at the colors on the rocks. Weird and very pretty—metallic colors, hard and brilliant.

Something flickered again in the corner of his vision and he looked that way into the woods.

He was reaching for the door handle to get out of the car when the mill blew up.

Sheriff Ben Jode in his Grant County sheriff car made the turn off a paved road into the graded ranch drive. It lifted him to a rise where he put the brakes on and stopped at the crest to reconnoiter the situation.

Over across the valley was a mountain with a top shaped just like a biscuit, even to the corrugated cliffs that ran around its sides. That mesa dominated the valley. It was the highest point in the range; the other mountains swept gracefully away from it to either side, tier by tier. There were still white spots on the peaks—the remains of winter snow.

The valley was undulant, high-country terrain—yellow grass slopes dotted with piñon and juniper and scrub oak. He counted more than forty horses on the near pasture.

The road slumped into the valley. The main house was set up on a hilltop with a commanding view of its surroundings; below it the outbuildings and work headquarters were some distance away—corrals, two windmills, tack sheds, crew quarters, barn, silo. The house was isolated on its hilltop.

Several police cars of various persuasions stood parked askew a hundred yards or so below the house. Jode started driving down toward them. He made out a local cop car from Aravaipa town, two Highway Patrol cruisers, a white Rincon County sheriff car, and even a station wagon with a dome light on top of it—Fort Defiance Indian Reservation Apache Police. This was twenty miles outside the reservation. It made Jode grin.

He went down the drive slowly and parked a distance behind the other cars. Cops in various uniforms were hunkered behind the cars. They were clutching rifles and riot guns and a variety of such artillery. The Rincon sheriff, as tall as Jode and sixty pounds heavier, had a bullhorn in his hand.

Someone inside the house was shooting deliberately, without hurry, with a rifle. The reports were thin in the high air; the house was downwind and the shots almost seemed distant rumors, but Jode could see the pinpoint flashes from the windows.

Jode crouched low and made his way over to the Rincon sheriff.

"Out of your bailiwick, but I'm glad to have you, Ben."

Jode said, "I picked up the radio call. Looks like everybody did. Who's the guy in mufti?"

"FBI. Name of Vickers."

"FBI?"

"He's out of his bailiwick too."

The rifle kept popping at intervals. Not shooting at the cops, Jode noticed. Shooting at tires. The bullets were flattening nearly every tire on the various police cars. Jode looked back over his shoulder. He'd left his car far enough back; that rifle would have to be uncannily accurate to reach it from the house. At the moment the rifle wasn't even trying for it—there were plenty of easy targets right here up front.

"You're going to have quite a bill for tires."

The Rincon sheriff grunted.

Jode said, "Who've you got forted up in the house?"

"Maria Skelton."

Jode felt the shock. It grenaded into him. "You're putting me on."

"No, sir."

"All alone?"

"All alone except she's got that rifle, and she knows just exactly how to use it."

Jode laughed out loud.

"Yeah, well, it's very humorous," the Rincon sheriff said. "You notice she's got all the shutters closed. We can't get tear gas in there. I been yelling at her for an hour on the bullhorn. Didn't do no good, except about five minutes ago she took a notion to start target practice on our radial tires. Seems to have plenty ammunition up there." He looked down the row of cars at the fellow in the gray business suit. "Vickers wants to burn her out."

"Does he now?"

"I'll tell you, Ben, twenty cops against one woman and we had to resort to burning down a sixty-thousand-dollar house to get her out? How you figure that's going to look in the newspapers tomorrow morning?"

"Not too good, Roy."

"Yeah. Well, there you are then. I figure the only thing to do is wait her out. Sooner or later she'll get tired or she'll get bored."

"That could take quite a while."

"You got any other ideas? I'd appreciate a suggestion if you got one, Ben."

"My county line's seven miles way. It's your jurisdiction, not mine."

"I don't mind deferring to you," the Rincon sheriff said. "You been at this longer than I have. And besides—"

The Rincon sheriff didn't finish it, but the meaning was clear enough. Jode might be a little past his prime, but he was a leader. They all knew him in this corner of the Southwest. The combat medals from Korea. The reform ticket on which he'd come into the sheriff's office. The fact that Grant County used to be the most corrupt county in Arizona until Jode took the job; now it was one of the cleanest counties. The fact that the mob types who'd tried to establish a real estate foothold had been run out ignominiously. And the spectacular solution Jode had provided to the string of psycho murders of teenage girls back in '68. When he'd brought the Breucher kid in that afternoon, there'd been TV news cameras all over the court-house lawn. The news films had been picked up by the networks and Jode had been in the limelight, a national celebrity for two days.

Jode had 16 mm prints of those news films at home.

But since that episode it had been downhill for years. Things were quiet. Nobody messed around in Jode's jurisdiction. It was a big deal if his deputies had to arrest a routine gas station holdup team. Most of the time it was a matter of keeping drunks quiet in the roadside taverns and taking care of traffic duty.

Jode was still revered by people like the Rincon sheriff and rural folk who thought of him as a cross between John Wayne and Buford Pusser. He knew it and he enjoyed it. But it was glory in the past and now they treated him as if he'd already retired. At times he felt things slipping away from him.

He kept remembering the Hollywood producers who'd talked to him back in 1968 when he was hot news. They'd wanted to make a movie about him, but finally they backed away. It would take something new and fresh—a new triumph to rekindle the legend of Ben Jode, get his name back in the headlines, and bring the TV vans pouring back into Grant County.

The woman forted up in the shuttered house—now there was a head-line maker!

Jode knew quite a bit about her. Everybody did. He'd never met her, but he knew the stories.

Maria Skelton had been a champion rodeo rider. She wasn't Indian, but she'd grown up on the Fort Defiance Reservation. Her parents were missionaries. She knew horses and she knew the wild country—it was said she used to hang out with an Indian family that ran white lightning out of a still back up in the Biscuit peaks, and Maria ran pack trains of the stuff along the back trails, or at least that was the rumor. She had a wild reputation as a kid. Then she took to winning horse-show ribbons and rodeos.

And along about 1961 she'd appeared in some Western movies. She didn't last too long as a movie star, but she'd invested her movie money and rodeo winnings; she bought this ranch in 1963. She'd settled down to develop the place into an important horse-breeding outfit and to enjoy life with her bridegroom who was a fun-loving stunt man she'd met when she was working in Hollywood. Between them they worked on the Appaloosa breeding strain that they hoped would make the ranch world famous.

Maria had a reputation for being in and out of trouble constantly. They said she had a hearty tendency to get drunk and lay about her with chairs and handbags. For a slim small woman she managed to create quite a ruckus. She'd busted up some of the classier bars in California and Arizona. On one occasion it took four Hollywood cops to subdue her.

Then apparently as she'd got into her thirties she'd begun to grow up —laying off the firewater, staying closer to home, taking the horse-ranching job seriously.

Her bridegroom began to get bored. Or that was the story.

Then the Keenmeier lumber outfit alongside the ranch had decided to go into the paper business. It had built the enormous paper mill right on the bank of the river that separated the two properties.

The smoke and stink from the mill had begun to foul the air on the whole plateau. The effluents from the paper mill did unspeakable things to the river.

It had been common knowledge all through the high country: Maria was upset. She'd been yelling at the state's environmental protection people. But the board numbered some people who were not to be believed. She'd got nowhere with them. She'd had to quit using the river to water her stock; she'd had to drill wells.

About that time her stunt-man husband evidently had got tired of the bucolic sameness of life on the isolated ranch with a wife who'd suddenly turned soberside. So he'd taken off for Los Angeles where rumor had it he was living with a TV starlet and doing movie stunt work and refusing to answer his wife's phone calls.

They said there were community property legal problems involved in the settlement that had made Maria even more miserable.

About ten days ago somebody had tried to set fire to the baled paper on the mill's loading platform. But heavily compressed paper does not burn readily. The matches had done minimal damage. It was common knowledge Maria was the culprit, but there was no proof.

"She went and did it this time," the Rincon sheriff told him. "Dynamite."

"The paper mill?"

"Sure enough. Good thing she's not an explosives expert. She didn't use enough dynamite. Didn't set the charges in the right places. All she did was knock off a corner of the building."

"Anybody hurt?"

"No. I guess that's why she picked Sunday morning—nobody around to get hurt. The night watchman spotted her running away this morning right after the blast. Called my office. We headed out here and you can see the rest of the story for yourself."

"What's she trying to prove, Roy?"

"God knows what goes on inside the head of a crazy woman." The Rincon sheriff looked up at the house with jaundiced resignation.

A cop made a run from one car to another. Maria's rifle spoke. Kicked up some dust, sending the cop leaping to cover. The Rincon sheriff said, "She's just having herself some sport. If she'd wanted to hit him she'd have hit him."

"I'll tell you," Jode said, "I've got an idea."

In the night he took three of the deputies and moved in on the house; circling wide while the Rincon sheriff tried to divert Maria by firing at the front of the house, Jode eased up on the back.

Jode pried a shutter open with a tire iron. He stood aside then. Two deputies threw tear-gas canisters inside.

They gave the gas a little time to spread. Then they fitted on their gas masks and climbed into the dark house.

They spread through the house. Open a door, throw a gas canister through it, wait. Then go in. You'd know if she was in there—you'd hear the coughing.

They split up, going into various rooms, peering through their gas masks, hunting for Maria.

They didn't find her.

Jode searched every room, but there was no sign of Maria. He went outside and waved the Rincon sheriff up the hill. The posse approached hesitantly, wary of Maria's rifle. Two deputies came out of the house behind Jode, stripping off their gas masks; they stood there coughing, clearing their lungs.

As the Rincon sheriff approached the house one deputy walked away from the house past Jode. The deputy was still wearing his gas mask and that puzzled Jode a bit. Some suspicion stirred in him, but then the Rincon sheriff met him and they both turned to go inside—to conduct a more thorough search this time.

Jode went inside in his gas mask, throwing windows open to clear the place out. Peering into crannies. He glanced into the utility closet where the furnace and water heater were. He was about to turn away when something caught his eye—a boot. He went around behind the furnace and found that the boot was attached to a body.

Not a dead body. A live deputy, neatly tied up and gagged, wearing only his drawers and shirt sleeves. Shorty, the smallest of the deputies.

"Oh, no," Jode said.

By the time he reached the front door he heard the mesh of the car's starter. The car drove away fast.

"My car," he said to the Rincon sheriff. "She's got my damn car."

"That deputy in the gas mask leaving the house—"

"That was her."

The Rincon sheriff threw his hat violently to the floor. Jode went outside and watched the dust diminish in the moonlit distance, silver on the hills.

The two men looked at each other. The Rincon sheriff's mouth began to twitch. Then they both started to laugh.

Jode was half asleep in the swivel chair behind his desk. It was getting dark and the deputies went around the room turning on the lamps. After all these weeks they were still gossiping about Maria Skelton. A legend had started up.

"Maybe she's dead. Out there in the hills someplace."

"Me, I heard she's down in Mexico getting up an army of mercenaries to come back and wipe out the Keenmeier mill."

"Naw. I heard she went back to Hollywood. Getting her face fixed up by one of them plastic surgeons so nobody'll ever recognize her. Wants to get a job in the movies."

Jode said, "All of you shut up. I've heard all I care to hear about the woman."

And then Maria walked into his office.

She didn't come in voluntarily. She was handcuffed to Vickers, the FBI agent. Vickers was yawning with great apparent fatigue. "I want her locked up for the night so I can get some sleep before I have to drive her the rest of the way down to Phoenix."

They put her in a cell. Jode said, "What about the handcuffs?"

"She keeps the handcuffs on. Damn slippery eel!" The FBI man glared at Maria and returned with Jode to the front office. Jode noticed the fingernail scratches on Vickers's face.

Vickers said, "I spotted her out in bare-eye daylight over in Albuquerque of all places. She was coming out of a bar drunk as a coot. She crossed state lines getting to Albuquerque, and they found your car down in Socorro, so that makes it a federal case. My case." Vickers challenged Jode to dispute it. Jode didn't say anything.

Without asking permission, Vickers used the phone to call his district office in Phoenix. Listening to him talk, Jode knew what the FBI man was thinking: it was only a three-hour drive to Phoenix on the Interstate and Vickers couldn't be *that* tired, but he obviously wanted to trundle into Phoenix in the morning instead of the middle of the night because he wanted plenty of sunlight for the cameras. He wanted the news media to have plenty of time to set up for the triumphant arrival.

Jode had no love for the FBI man.

"You can sack out in the side room there. The night-duty cot."

Vickers didn't thank him, just went into the side room and shut the door, yawning ostentatiously.

Jode went back into the cells and shooed the wide-eyed deputies out. Maria was glaring at them like a caged cougar. When they left she glared at Jode the same way.

He said, "You may as well get some sleep."

"I don't need any sleep." She was still half drunk, he saw.

"That was pretty dumb, blowing up the paper mill."

"No. What was dumb was two things. I didn't blow up enough of it. And I got spotted by the watchman. Those things were dumb. Blowing up the mill wasn't dumb. That stinking paper mill. Listen, if I get another chance at it I'll finish the job."

Jode said, "What's it like being a movie star?"

"That puking paper mill," she said. "Ruining the earth. Poisoning the planet."

"Is it kind of fun out there in Hollywood? Wild parties like they say?"

"You let me get another load of dynamite out there and we'll see about that paper mill."

The office was a hubbub, all the deputies excitedly talking. Jode said, "I'm fed up. That FBI man's trying to sleep. Now you can all get in your cars and go home or go out and patrol the county highways. Doesn't make any nevermind to me, but just get yourselves out of here."

When he was alone in the office he looked in on Vickers. The FBI man was pretending to be asleep on the cot. After a few moments he began to snore. Jode made a face and shut the door, closing out the offending sound. He went back to the desk but didn't sit down. A thought had exploded into his mind. He went back into the cells.

She glared at him. He stood at the door and spoke. "Funny about Hollywood. I mean the way celebrities sometimes get to be movies stars. Athletes, they do it all the time—Jim Brown, Joe Namath. You got in the movies because you were a rodeo star, right? All it takes is some kind of famousness, don't matter what kind. You can get into the movies, right? A cop like Eddie Egan, for example—he's in that TV series now."

"It helps if you can act."

"What?"

"That was my problem, the reason I didn't last in pictures. I had the looks and I could ride a horse. Period."

All this time Jode was thinking very fast. Abruptly he left the cellblock.

He set things up swiftly. He took a rifle and a box of cartridges outdoors and put them in his jeep. He detached the glass face of the fuel gauge, which read nearly empty because he'd been meaning to fill it on his way home for supper but had forgotten. He broke off a piece of a paper match and used it to wedge the fuel needle over against the "full" mark. Then he replaced the glass. He drove the jeep around to the front and parked it in the No Parking zone and went back into the office, leaving the keys dangling in the ignition.

Vickers was genuinely asleep by now. Carefully Jode relieved him of the keys to the handcuffs.

In the cells he motioned Maria to come to the barred door. She hung back.

"I just want to take those things off your hands."

"What for?"

"You don't need them inside a cell, for Pete's sake."

"What about Vickers?"

"The hell with Vickers."

"You can say that again."

He unlocked the handcuffs and took them off her wrists. She watched him dubiously.

Then he unlocked the cell door. He didn't open it, but she knew it was unlocked. He went away, back to the office.

He crept into the side room, then silently and carefully placed the handcuffs, the handcuff keys, and the cell-door keys on the blanket beside the sleeping Vickers.

When he withdrew from the room he closed the door on Vickers and went back to his desk and sat.

After a while Maria came suspiciously into the room.

"Just one thing," Jode said. "Anybody asks, that FBI guy went soft on you, turned you loose."

She didn't answer.

"It doesn't matter what you say, lady, they'll take my word over yours. I'm just telling you what to say to make it easier on yourself."

"Why?"

"Maybe I just don't like the FBI."

"Nuts."

Jode smiled. "Don't try the main roads. I'll have to set up roadblocks. You head back in the hill country. You got a few hours while I make noise around here."

"Jode, you're crazy or what?"

"You're pretty good back in the hills. Raised on the reservation, right? But I'm just a little better. I'm going to catch you."

Now she smiled. She didn't speak. Her smile was as much as *That'll be the day, Jode. Old man.*

Fifty-one? Old?

She tossed her head and strode out.

In a moment Jode heard the sound of the jeep rolling away. He smiled.

He gave her twenty minutes to get clear of town, then he got on the radio and had the roadblocks set up. A couple of deputies came in for instructions. Vickers was waking up; Jode opened the door and the deputies looked in at Vickers as he sat up, looking in bafflement at the keys and handcuffs on the bed.

Jode said, "I step out for fifteen minutes and look what happens. She must've seduced him or something."

The deputies restrained Vickers when he tried to get to Jode.

When the undersheriff arrived, rubbing sleep from his eyes, Jode told him to hold the fort. "I got an idea where she might be. You keep tabs on my roadblocks. I'll be in touch—may take a day or two. Keep hunting, right?"

Jode got in his sheriff car and drove toward the mountains. He went up some back roads, found nothing, tried other back roads. She hadn't had much gas.

Probably she'd head for the reservation, he reasoned. And finally he found the jeep up in the foothills near the reservation fence where Maria had run out of gas. He looked inside and saw the fuel gauge still jammed over on the "full" mark. He lifted the faceplate off and removed the piece of match. The needle fell over to "empty."

Jode took the rotor out of his own car, disabling it so that Maria couldn't double back and steal it. You couldn't count on her not knowing how to hot-wire a car; she was a pretty astute lady. Then he looked up at the towering mountains ahead. There was a whole range of them between here and the Biscuit.

He went back to the car, got out a backpack, strapped it on, and slung the rifle over his shoulder.

And started tracking. On foot.

Her spoor took him high, back into the mountain passes. Once he found a place where she had stopped and thought about setting up an ambush. He looked back down the slopes from this point—he could see for miles, all the way out onto the plain to the town. So she'd seen him coming after her. She knew he was back there. But she'd decided against waiting for him.

She had something else on her mind.

The paper mill, he reckoned.

He kept climbing. He was going to have to catch her fast because he'd given her this chance, and she'd meant it when she'd said she'd take care of that paper mill. It put an urgency in him, because he knew if he didn't nail her fast there wouldn't be much in the way of headlines for him.

So he put on an added burst of speed.

And walked right into her trap.

It was just on sundown. She disarmed him efficiently. At gunpoint she forced him to build a fire; then she told him to take off his belt and make a loop, and when she had him the way she wanted him she sat down on his rear and pulled the belt up tight, fastening his hands together behind his back. She used a rifle sling on his feet and when he was trussed up properly she retreated to the fire.

She said, "I didn't see the point in the both of us freezing to death in the dark. This way I can keep an eye on you and at the same time we can have a nice cozy fire. Besides, you didn't put any food in the jeep."

"Sorry. I forgot."

She raided his pack for food. Jode said, "How about me?"

"Suffer. I'm not untying your hands. And I'm damned if I'll spoon-feed you."

So he went hungry.

After a while he said, "You could just kill me, I suppose."

"What for?"

"I'm going to make trouble for you otherwise."

"Well, I don't kill people. What do you think I am?"

"You don't mind blowing up buildings."

"This is Friday night, Jode. Sunday's my day for blowing up buildings. With nobody in them to get hurt."

"You got the dynamite right handy, have you?"

"Right where I left it. Not two hundred yards upstream from the mill. Cached it in a beaver hole by the riverbank."

"Well, then you've got the whole thing figured out, haven't you?"

"Sure have."

"Except one thing."

She said, "What thing?"

"Me. I don't aim to let you do it."

"You don't have a whole lot of choice, Jode."

He considered that. "Well, look, you may blow up the building all right, but sooner or later I'm going to catch you."

"Somebody will. I doubt it'll be you. You're not fast enough."

She washed the last of her meal down with coffee, glanced at him, made a face, and brought the coffee over to him. He tipped his head back and she gave him all he wanted to drink. Close up to him that way she seemed small and fragile; he marveled at her physical stamina. She was a good-looking woman, he couldn't deny it. How old did she have to be? Well, somewhere short of forty, he reckoned. But not far short of it. She could have passed for a lot less, though.

"If you know you're going to get nailed anyway, why do it?"

"Because it's got to be done. The damn paper mills of the world are destroying everything anybody ever had that was worth living for. I'll tell you, that paper mill is everything that's wrong with the world. They run it with a big computer that just doesn't listen. The computers run the industrialists and the polluters—they just think they're human beings.

The computers run the government too. Government just sits by while the paper mill ruins my marriage and my ranch and the whole damn world."

"You going to rail against everything that's happened since the year eighteen and twelve?"

"I'm talking about paper mills and everything they stand for. Among other things, of course, they stand for paper. The world is strangling to death, Jode, in a big old bureaucratic snarl of paper. How many forms and reports you got to fill out every time you go and arrest somebody for denting his neighbor's car or letting his dog loose on private property?"

"Well, you do have a point there."

"Somebody has got to stand up and make a very loud statement right here and now about the damn paper mills in the world, Jode. Because if we just let them go on and on the way they're going now, the whole world is going to drown in a sea of paper and get poisoned to death by the junk that comes out of those flumes in the river and those smokestacks on the top. And I'm just the person to make a very loud statement about all that. I've had plenty of practice being loud and obstreperous and obnoxious. I've been a pain in the neck to everybody ever knew me. It's my chance to do my penance, and I'm taking it. Man I wish I had a drink. You haven't got any puma sweat in that pack, by any chance?"

"No. I had a couple beers, but I drank them on the way up."

"Inconsiderate of you."

"Yeah, well if I'd known we were going to have a picnic together I'd have saved them."

"That paper mill's ruining the whole valley under the Biscuit."

"You already said that."

"Maybe this time you're listening."

"Lady, what if I agree with you? It still doesn't matter. I still got the laws to enforce."

"Why? That law is wrong, Jode, and you know it. Any law that lets a computer poison the earth for the people is wrong."

"The Keenmeier brothers aren't computers. They're real. I've met them."

"The Keenmeier brothers are pencil-pushing accountants. All they know is numbers. You call that a human being?"

"Well—"

"You think I'm some kind of ecology freak?"

"I don't know, Maria. All I know is I'm the sheriff and you're the bad guy and I've got to arrest you and take you in."

"Well, you didn't do a very good job of that, did you?"

"We're still a long way from the finish line," he said. And then he realized what was happening. How distracting she was being. Trying to get his guard down, trying to make sure he was too occupied seeing her side of it and sympathizing about her plight to worry about escaping.

He thought about all those TV cameras again. Hollywood. It brought him back to reality. He started burning his brain to figure out a way to get loose and get the drop on Maria. There had to be a way.

But he was still trussed up at dawn when Maria said, "So long," and walked away into the mountains, heading down-slope toward the pass by the Biscuit and the valley below—toward the ranch, the river, and the Keenmeier paper mill.

Feverishly Jode tried to get loose. He started shredding the flesh off his wrists, but the belts were tight.

It took him nearly two hours of rubbing the belt against the blade of a quartz outcrop before the leather parted. He unstrapped his feet and stood up, a bit wobbly and cramped. He stamped around to quicken the circulation.

Then he started down the mountain.

He kept imagining the headlines. His future when Hollywood filmed *The Ben Jode Story* with Jode himself playing the title role. He ran pell-mell down the canyons.

"Now quit this," he told himself, "don't be so stupid. You twist your ankle you'll never catch up." So he forced himself to slow down and move with reasonable care through the rocks.

He still had the rifle sling. He'd left the near-empty pack up on the mountain because it would only have slowed him down; he'd eaten and drunk what he could and now he was traveling light. He had a use for the rifle sling; everything else had been superfluous.

It took him the rest of the day to get down onto the slope of the Biscuit with the cliffs looming high above him. The valley was still ten miles away, but he kept going in the night—it was a quarter moon, enough to see by, and he knew damn well *she* wouldn't stop. She had that Sunday morning appointment at the paper mill. And anyhow there was no need for light to follow her tracks. He didn't need to follow tracks. He knew where she was going.

It must have been three in the morning when he finally came down off the foothills and into the valley. So footsore he could hardly keep moving, but he did.

From a hillside he surveyed the night. Dark spots on yonder hills might be scrubs and might be grazing horses; he kept looking until one of the scrubs moved and he knew it was a horse. Maybe half a mile down. He went that way.

This hour of the night a horse was bound to be skittish and he worked his way carefully, staying downwind, making a loop in the rifle sling. An ambush wasn't going to work; he came around a piñon slowly into the horse's eyeline and started speaking with soft persuasion.

"Ho boy, take it easy now, ho."

He kept talking while the Appaloosa eyed him suspiciously. It snorted a couple of times and pawed the earth. A gelding, about fourteen hands. Handsome spotted coat. Bright-eyed, a young one. He kept talking amiably.

"Gentle down now, ho boy, ho."

The gelding whickered and then he had the loop around its muzzle. He patted the horse's neck and talked to it for a while before he swung up bareback, clinging to the end of the rifle sling that he kept wrapped around his knuckles.

The horse pitched him off, but he made it a point to keep his grip on the end of the sling. He climbed on again and got bucked off again, but after the third try the horse was resigned to the idea and only did a few token scampers before settling down.

Jode eased his bruised hip to one side and rode awkwardly, sitting on one buttock mostly, walking the horse for the first half mile or so. Then he knew that wasn't going to do. He wasn't the only one out here with a reason to snag a horse—and these were Maria's horses. She'd have snagged one a lot faster than Jode did. So she still had a good jump on him and he had to move as fast as the horse could take him.

He came over the last hill and got off the horse, turned it loose, and threw the rifle sling around his waist, cinching it up in case there'd be a later use for it. He ran down into the trees, guided by the sound of the river somewhere in the pines.

He came in through the woods and found Maria skulking near the mill —moving crouched over, backing up—paying out wire.

Jode searched the trees swiftly and found the plunger about forty yards behind her. She was still backing toward it, uncoiling the wire. It meant she'd already set the charges under the mill and she was ready to hook up the wires and blow the detonators. He was just in time.

He crept up behind the plunger and waited behind a tree until she backed right up to him and then he grabbed her.

She struggled so much that she put him in mind of a wolverine he'd cornered once. But he got the rifle sling around her and pinioned her arms with it. Neither of them cried out; it was a silent struggle, and he had the advantage of weight. He used her belt to bind her wrists and then he sat her down to tie her ankles. She glared her rage at him.

Jode grinned. "Guess I knew one more shortcut than you did. Did I tell you my daddy used to take me hunting up along the Biscuit all the time?"

"Well, I guess you got your movie deal."

"Bet your bottom."

She sat there staring through her frustrated tears at the paper mill over there through the trees. The night watchman sat in his car drinking coffee. Water frothed over the rocks and Jode saw the fantastic colors.

"Beautiful, aren't they?" she said.

"What?"

"Another five years every tree on that bank will be dead. That stuff gets into the roots."

The water swirled over the fancy colors in the rocks. Jode looked at the ugly stains on the pines, at the smoke stains on the stacks of the mill. He smelled the pervasive stink.

He heard the car before he saw it. He looked that way, saw it flickering through the pines, recognized it, and therefore wasn't surprised when it pulled in beside the watchman's car and Jode saw the man in the gray business suit at the wheel.

Vickers glared around with hard, angry eyes.

So the FBI man wasn't as dumb as he seemed. He'd figured this out for himself.

"Well, hell," Jode said. He fixed the wires onto the plunger.

"What the hell you doing, Jode?" She was excited.

Jode pushed the plunger and the blast threw him back flat on the earth.

Pieces of paper mill hurtled through the forest. A wave of sudden heat swept over him, curling the pine needles around them.

He kept his arms over his face until the debris settled. When he sat up he saw the two cars half buried under debris. A door opened, shoving stuff aside. Vickers came out and stood on top of the junkpile. The watchman came struggling out.

Jode pushed her down—slowly because it was movement, not presences, that Vickers would see if he looked. On the ground he worked the leather bindings loose and freed her. Then they crept, belly-flat and worm-slow, until they were far back in the shadowed woods.

When he looked back he could see the two men climbing through the rubble. Nothing left of the mill above its foundation. A tall, heavy pine had toppled across the site. He said, "You used enough dynamite this time for sure."

"Jode, what on earth did you do that for?"

He considered the wreckage; he took her hand and walked her away through the pines, and after a little while he began unaccountably to laugh. "Beats hell out of me, honey."

Many Mansions

ROBERT SILVERBERG

Perhaps the ultimate crime story, this, murder in several dimensions and with a plethora of motives. Robert Silverberg, author of Lord Valentine's Castle *and* Majipoor Chronicles, *the latter due to be published at about the same time as this anthology, is the author of several hundred novels and short stories. Although his reputation rests (at least for the moment) on his science fiction, he is clearly one of the five or ten most powerful and accomplished voices in all of postwar American fiction.*

It's been a rough day. Everything gone wrong. A tremendous tieup on the freeway going to work, two accounts canceled before lunch, now some inconceivable botch by the weather programmers. It's snowing outside. Actually snowing. He'll have to go out and clear the driveway in the morning. He can't remember when it last snowed. And of course a fight with Alice again. She never lets him alone. She's at her most deadly when she sees him come home exhausted from the office. Ted why don't you this, Ted get me that. Now, waiting for dinner, working on his third drink in forty minutes, he feels one of his headaches coming on. Those miserable killer headaches that can destroy a whole evening. What a life! He toys with murderous fantasies. Take her out by the reservoir for a friendly little stroll, give her a quick hard shove with his shoulder. She can't swim. Down, down, down. Glub. Good-bye, Alice. Free at last.

In the kitchen she furiously taps the keys of the console, programming dinner just the way he likes it. Cold vichyssoise, baked potato with sour cream and chives, sirloin steak blood-rare inside and charcoal-charred outside. Don't think it isn't work to get the meal just right, even with the autochef. All for him. The bastard. Tell me, why do I sweat so hard to please him? Has he made me happy? What's he ever done for me except waste the best years of my life? And he thinks I don't know about his other women. Those lunchtime quickies. Oh, I wouldn't mind at all if he dropped dead tomorrow. I'd be a great widow—so dignified at the funeral, so strong, hardly crying at all. And everybody thinks we're such a close couple. Married eleven years and they're still in love. I heard someone say that only last week. If they only knew the truth about us. If they only knew.

Martin peers out the window of his third-floor apartment in Sunset Village. Snow. I'll be damned. He can't remember the last time he saw snow. Thirty, forty years back, maybe, when Ted was a baby. He absolutely can't remember. White stuff on the ground—when? The mind gets wobbly when you're past eighty. He still can't believe he's an old man. It rocks him to realize that his grandson Ted, Martha's boy, is almost forty. I bounced that kid on my knee and he threw up all over my suit. Four years old then. Nixon was president. Nobody talks much about Tricky Dick these days. Ancient history. McKinley, Coolidge, Nixon. Time flies. Martin thinks of Ted's wife Alice. What a nice tight little ass she has. What a cute pair of jugs. I'd like to get my hands on them. I really would. You know something, Martin? You're not such an old ruin yet. Not if you can get it up for your grandson's wife.

His dreams of drowning her fade as quickly as they came. He is not a violent man by nature. He knows he could never do it. He can't even bring himself to step on a spider; how then could he kill his wife? If she'd die some other way, of course, without the need of his taking direct action, that would solve everything. She's driving to the hairdresser on one of those manual-access roads she likes to use and her car swerves on an icy spot, and she goes into a tree at eighty kilometers an hour. Good. She's shopping on Union Boulevard and the bank is blown up by an activist; she's nailed by flying debris. Good. The dentist gives her a new anesthetic and it turns out she's fatally allergic to it. Puffs up like a blowfish and dies in five minutes. Good. The police come, long faces, snuffly noses. Terribly sorry, Mr. Porter. There's been an awful accident. Don't tell me it's my wife, he cries. They nod lugubriously. He bears up bravely under the loss, though.

"You can come in for dinner now," she says. He's sitting slouched on the sofa with another drink in his hand. He drinks more than any man she knows, not that she knows all that many. Maybe he'll get cirrhosis and die. Do people still die of cirrhosis, she wonders, or do they give them liver transplants now? The funny thing is that he still turns her on, after eleven years. His eyes, his face, his hands. She despises him but he still turns her on.

The snow reminds him of his young manhood, of his days long ago in the East. He was quite the ladies' man then. And it wasn't so easy to get some action back in those days, either. The girls were always worried about what people would say if anyone found out. *What people would say!* As if doing it with a boy you liked was something shameful. Or they'd worry about getting knocked up. They made you wear a rubber. How awful that was: like wearing a sock. The pill was just starting to come in, the original pill, the old one-a-day kind. Imagine a world without the pill! ("Did they have dinosaurs when you were a boy, grandpa?") Still, Martin had made out all right. Big muscular frame, strong earnest features, warm inquisitive eyes. You'd never know it to look at me now. I wonder if Alice realizes what kind of stud I used to be. If I had the money I'd rent one of those time machines they've got now and send her back to visit myself around 1950 or so. A little gift to my younger self. He'd really rip into her. It gives Martin a quick riffle of excitement to think of his younger self ripping into Alice. But of course he can't afford any such thing.

As he forks down his steak he imagines being single again. Would I get married again? Not on your life. Not until I'm good and ready, anyway, maybe when I'm fifty-five or sixty. Me for bachelorhood for the time being, just screwing around like a kid. To hell with responsibilities. I'll wait two, three weeks after the funeral, a decent interval, and then I'll go off for some fun. Hawaii, Tahiti, Fiji, someplace out there. With Nolie. Or Maria. Or Ellie. Yes, with Ellie. He thinks of Ellie's pink thighs, her soft heavy breasts, her long radiant auburn hair. Two weeks in Fiji with Ellie. Two weeks in Ellie with Fiji. Yes. Yes. Yes. "Is the steak rare enough for you, Ted?" Alice asks. "It's fine," he says.

She goes upstairs to check the children's bedroom. They're both asleep, finally. Or else faking it so well that it makes no difference. She stands by their beds a moment, thinking, I love you, Bobby, I love you, Tink. Tink and Bobby, Bobby and Tink. I love you even though you drive me crazy sometimes. She tiptoes out. Now for a quiet evening of television. And then to bed. The same old routine. Christ. I don't know why I go on like this. There are times when I'm ready to explode. I stay with him for the children's sake, I guess. Is that enough of a reason?

He envisions himself running hand in hand along the beach with Ellie. Both of them naked, their skins bronzed and gleaming in the tropical sunlight. Palm trees everywhere. Grains of pink sand under foot. Soft transparent wavelets lapping the shore. A quiet cove. "No one can see us here," Ellie murmurs. He sinks down on her firm sleek body and enters her.

A blazing band of pain tightens like a strip of hot metal across Martin's chest. He staggers away from the window, dropping into a low crouch as he stumbles toward a chair. The heart. Oh, the heart! That's what you get for drooling over Alice. Dirty old man. "Help," he calls feebly. "Come on, you filthy machine, help me!" The medic, activated by the key phrase, rolls silently toward him. Its sensors are already at work scanning him, searching for the cause of the discomfort. A telescoping steel-jacketed arm slides out of the medic's chest and, hovering above Martin, extrudes an ultrasonic injection snout. "Yes," Martin murmurs, "that's right, damn you, hurry up and give me the drug!" Calm. I must try to remain calm. The snout makes a gentle whirring noise as it forces the relaxant into Martin's vein. He slumps in relief. The pain slowly ebbs. Oh, that's much better. Saved again. Oh. Oh. Oh. Dirty old man. Ought to be ashamed of yourself.

Ted knows he won't get to Fiji with Ellie or anybody else. Any realistic assessment of the situation brings him inevitably to the same conclusion. Alice isn't going to die in an accident, any more than he's likely to murder her. She'll live forever. Unwanted wives always do. He could ask for a divorce, of course. He'd probably lose everything he owned, but he'd win his freedom. Or he could simply do away with himself. That was always a temptation for him. The easy way out, no lawyers, no hassles. So it's that time of the evening again. It's the same every night. Pretending to watch television, he secretly indulges in suicidal fantasies.

Bare-bodied dancers in gaudy luminous paint gyrate lasciviously on the screen, nearly large as life. Alice scowls. The things they show on TV nowadays! It used to be that you got this stuff only on the X-rated channels, but now it's everywhere. And look at him, just lapping it up! Actually she knows she wouldn't be so stuffy about the sex shows except that Ted's fascination with them is a measure of his lack of interest in her. Let them show screwing and all the rest on TV, if that's what people want. I just wish Ted had as much enthusiasm for me as he does for the television stuff. So far as sexual permissiveness in general goes, she's no prude. She used to wear nothing but trunks at the beach, until Tink was born and she started to feel a little less proud of her figure. But she still dresses as revealingly as anyone in their crowd. And gets stared at by everyone but her own husband. *He* watches the TV cuties. His other women must use him up. Maybe I ought to step out a bit myself, Alice thinks. She's had her little affairs along the way. Not many, nothing very serious, but she's had some. Three lovers in eleven years, that's not a great many, but it's a sign that she's no puritan. She wonders if she ought to get involved with somebody now. It might move her life off dead center while she still has the chance, before boredom destroys her entirely. "I'm going up to wash my hair," she announces. "Will you be staying down here till bedtime?"

There are so many ways he could do it. Slit his wrists. Drive his car off the bridge. Swallow Alice's whole box of sleeping tabs. Of course those are all old-fashioned ways of killing yourself. Something more modern would be appropriate. Go into one of the black taverns and start making loud racial insults? No, nothing modern about that. It's very 1975. But something genuinely contemporary does occur to him. Those time machines they've got now: suppose he rented one and went back, say, sixty years, to a time when one of his parents hadn't yet been born. And killed his grandfather. Find old Martin as a young man and slip a knife into him. If I do that, Ted figures, I should instantly and painlessly cease to exist. I would never have existed, because my mother wouldn't ever have existed. Poof. Out like a light. Then he realizes he's fantasizing a murder again. Stupid: if he could ever murder anyone, he'd murder Alice and be done with it. So the whole fantasy is foolish. Back to the starting point is where he is.

She is sitting under the hair-dryer when he comes upstairs. He has a peculiarly smug expression on his face and as soon as she turns the dryer off she asks him what he's thinking about. "I may have just invented a perfect murder method," he tells her. "Oh?" she says. He says, "You rent a time machine. Then you go back a couple of generations and murder one of the ancestors of your intended victim. That way you're murdering the victim too, because he won't ever have been born if you kill off one of his immediate progenitors. Then you return to your own time. Nobody can trace you because you don't have any fingerprints on file in an era before your own birth. What do you think of it?" Alice shrugs. "It's an old one," she says. "It's been done on television a dozen times. Anyway, I don't like it. Why should an innocent person have to die just because he's the grandparent of somebody you want to kill?"

They're probably in bed together right now, Martin thinks gloomily. Stark naked side by side. The lights are out. The house is quiet. Maybe they're smoking a little grass. Do they still call it grass, he wonders, or is there some new nickname now? Anyway the two of them turn on. Yes. And then he reaches for her. His hands slide over her cool, smooth skin. He cups her breasts. Plays with the hard little nipples. Sucks on them. The other hand wandering down to her parted thighs. And then she. And then he. And then they. And then they. Oh, Alice, he murmurs. Oh, Ted, *Ted,* she cries. And then they. Go to it. Up and down, in and out. Oh. Oh. Oh. She claws his back. She pumps her hips. Ted! Ted! Ted! The big moment is arriving now. For her, for him. Jackpot! Afterward they lie close for a few minutes, basking in the afterglow. And then they roll apart. Good night, Ted. Good night, Alice. Oh, Jesus. They do it every night, I bet. They're so young and full of juice. And I'm all dried up. Christ, I hate being old. When I think of the man I once was. When I think of the women I once had. Jesus. Jesus. God, let me have the strength to do it just once more before I die. And leave me alone for two hours with Alice.

She has trouble falling asleep. A strange scene keeps playing itself out obsessively in her mind. She sees herself stepping out of an upright coffin-sized box of dark gray metal, festooned with dials and levers. The time machine. It delivers her into a dark, dirty alleyway, and when she walks forward to the street she sees scores of little antique automobiles buzzing around. Only they aren't antiques: they're the current models. This is the year 1947. New York City. Will she be conspicuous in her futuristic clothes? She has her breasts covered, at any rate. That's essential back here. She hurries to the proper address, resisting the temptation to browse in shop windows along the way. How quaint and ancient everything looks. And how dirty the streets are. She comes to a tall building of red brick. This is the place. No scanners study her as she enters. They don't have annunciators yet or any other automatic home-protection equipment. She goes upstairs in an elevator so creaky and unstable that she fears for her life. Fifth floor. Apartment 5J. She rings the doorbell. *He* answers. He's terribly young, only twenty-four, but she can pick out signs of the Martin of the future in his face, the strong cheekbones, the searching blue eyes. "Are you Martin Jamieson?" she asks. "That's right," he says. She smiles. "May I come in?" "Of course," he says. He bows her into the apartment. As he momentarily turns his back on her to open the coat closet she takes the heavy steel pipe from her purse and lifts it high and brings it down on the back of his head. *Thwock.* She takes the heavy steel pipe from her purse and lifts it high and brings it down on the back of his head. *Thwock.* She takes the heavy steel pipe from her purse and lifts it high and brings it down on the back of his head. *Thwock.*

Ted and Alice visit him at Sunset Village two or three times a month. He can't complain about that; it's as much as he can expect. He's an old old man and no doubt a boring one, but they come dutifully, sometimes with the kids, sometimes without. He's never gotten used to the idea that he's a great-grandfather. Alice always gives him a kiss when she arrives and another when she leaves. He plays a private little game with her, copping a feel at each kiss. His hand quickly stroking her butt. Or sometimes when he's really rambunctious it travels lightly over her breasts. Does she notice? Probably. She never lets on, though. Pretends it's an accidental touch. Most likely she thinks it's charming that a man of his age would still have at least a vestige of sexual desire left. Unless she thinks it's disgusting, that is.

The time-machine gimmick, Ted tells himself, can be used in ways that don't quite amount to murder. For instance. "What's that box?" Alice asks. He smiles cunningly. "It's called a panchronicon," he says. "It gives you a kind of televised reconstruction of ancient times. The salesman loaned me a demonstration sample." She says, "How does it work?" "Just step inside," he tells her. "It's all ready for you." She starts to enter the machine, but then, suddenly suspicious, she hesitates on the threshold. He pushes her in and slams the door shut behind her. *Wham!* The controls are set. Off goes Alice on a one-way journey to the Pleistocene. The machine is primed to return as soon as it drops her off. That isn't murder, is it? She's still alive, wherever she may be, unless the saber-tooth tigers have caught up with her. So long, Alice.

In the morning she drives Bobby and Tink to school. Then she stops at the bank and the post office. From ten to eleven she has her regular session at the identity-reinforcement parlor. Ordinarily she would go right home after that, but this morning she strolls across the shopping-center plaza to the office that the time-machine people have just opened. TEM-PONAUTICS, LTD., the sign over the door says. The place is empty except for two machines, no doubt demonstration models, and a bland-faced, smiling salesman. "Hello," Alice says nervously. "I just wanted to pick up some information about the rental costs of one of your machines."

Martin likes to imagine Alice coming to visit him by herself some rainy Saturday afternoon. "Ted isn't able to make it today," she explains. "Something came up at the office. But I knew you were expecting us, and I didn't want you to be disappointed. Poor Martin, you must lead such a lonely life." She comes close to him. She is trembling. So is he. Her face is flushed and her eyes are bright with the unmistakable glossiness of desire. He feels a sense of sexual excitement too, for the first time in ten or twenty years, that tension in the loins, that throbbing of the pulse. Electricity. Chemistry. His eyes lock on hers. Her nostrils flare, her mouth goes taut. "Martin," she whispers huskily. "Do you feel what I feel?" "You know I do," he tells her. She says, "If only I could have known you when you were in your prime!" He chuckles. "I'm not altogether senile yet," he cries exultantly. Then she is in his arms and his lips are seeking her fragrant breasts.

"Yes, it came as a terrible shock to me," Ted tells Ellie. "Having her disappear like that. She simply vanished from the face of the earth, as far as anyone can determine. They've tried every possible way of tracing her and there hasn't been a clue." Ellie's flawless forehead furrows in a fitful frown. "Was she unhappy?" she asks. "Do you think she may have done away with herself?" Ted shakes his head. "I don't know. You live with a person for eleven years and you think you know her pretty well, and then one day something absolutely incomprehensible occurs and you realize how impossible it is ever to know another human being at all. Don't you agree?" Ellie nods gravely. "Yes, oh, yes, certainly!" she says. He smiles down at her and takes her hands in his. Softly he says, "Let's not talk about Alice any more, shall we? She's gone and that's all I'll ever know." He hears a pulsing symphonic crescendo of shimmering angelic choirs as he embraces her and murmurs, "I love you, Ellie. I love you."

She takes the heavy steel pipe from her purse and lifts it high and brings it down on the back of his head. *Thwock.* Young Martin drops instantly, twitches once, lies still. Dark blood begins to seep through the dense blond curls of his hair. How strange to see Martin with golden hair, she thinks, as she kneels beside his body. She puts her hand to the bloody place, probes timidly, feels the deep indentation. Is he dead? She isn't sure how to tell. He isn't moving. He doesn't seem to be breathing. She wonders if she ought to hit him again, just to make certain. Then she remembers something she's seen on television, and takes her mirror from her purse. Holds it in front of his face. No cloud forms. That's pretty conclusive: you're dead, Martin. R.I.P. Martin Jamieson, 1923–1947. Which means that Martha Jamieson Porter (1948–   ) will never now be conceived, and that automatically obliterates the existence of her son Theodore Porter (1968–   ). Not bad going, Alice, getting rid of unloved husband and miserable shrewish mother-in-law all in one shot. Sorry, Martin. Bye-bye, Ted. (R.I.P. Theodore Porter, 1968–1947. Eh?) She rises, goes into the bathroom with the steel pipe, and carefully rinses it off. Then she puts it back into her purse. Now to go back to the machine and return to 2006, she thinks. To start my new life. But as she leaves the apartment, a tall, lean man steps out of the hallway shadows and clamps his hand powerfully around her wrist. "Time Patrol," he says crisply, flashing an identification badge. "You're under arrest for temponautic murder, Mrs. Porter."

Today has been a better day than yesterday, low on crises and depressions, but he still feels a headache coming on as he lets himself into the house. He is braced for whatever bitchiness Alice may have in store for him this evening. But, oddly, she seems relaxed and amiable. "Can I get you a drink, Ted?" she asks. "How did your day go?" He smiles and says, "Well, I think we may have salvaged the Hammond account after all. Otherwise nothing special happened. And you? What did you do today, love?" She shrugs. "Oh, the usual stuff," she says. "The bank, the post office, my identity-reinforcement session."

If you had the money, Martin asks himself, how far back would you send her? 1947, that would be the year, I guess. My last year as a single man. No sense complicating things. Off you go, Alice baby, to 1947. Let's make it March. By June I was engaged and by September Martha was on the way, though I didn't find that out until later. Yes: March 1947. So. Young Martin answers the doorbell and sees an attractive girl in the hall, a woman, really, older than he is, maybe thirty or thirty-two. Slender, dark-haired, nicely constructed. Odd clothing: a clinging gray tunic, very short, made of some strange fabric that flows over her body like a stream. How it achieves that liquid effect around the pleats is beyond him. "Are you Martin Jamieson?" she asks. And quickly answers herself. "Yes, of course, you must be. I recognize you. How handsome you were!" He is baffled. He knows nothing, naturally, about this gift from his aged future self. "Who are you?" he asks. "May I come in first?" she says. He is embarrassed by his lack of courtesy and waves her inside. Her eyes glitter with mischief. "You aren't going to believe this," she tells him, "but I'm your grandson's wife."

"Would you like to try out one of our demonstration models?" the salesman asks pleasantly. "There's absolutely no cost or obligation." Ted looks at Alice. Alice looks at Ted. Her frown mirrors his inner uncertainty. She also must be wishing that they had never come to the Temponautics showroom. The salesman, pattering smoothly onward, says, "In these demonstrations we usually send our potential customers fifteen or twenty minutes into the past. I'm sure you'll find it fascinating. While remaining in the machine, you'll be able to look through a viewer and observe your own selves actually entering this very showroom a short while ago. Well? Will you give it a try? You go first, Mrs. Porter. I assure you it's going to be the most unique experience you've ever had." Alice, uneasy, tries to back off, but the salesman prods her in a way that is at once gentle and unyielding, and she steps reluctantly into the time machine. He closes the door. A great business of adjusting fine controls ensues. Then the salesman throws a master switch. A green glow envelops the machine and it disappears, although something transparent and vague—a retinal after-image? the ghost of the machine?—remains dimly visible. The salesman says, "She's now gone a short distance into her own past. I've programmed the machine to take her back eighteen minutes and keep her there for a total elapsed interval of six minutes, so she can see the entire opening moments of your visit here. But when I return her to Now Level, there's no need to match the amount of elapsed time in the past, so that from our point of view she'll have been absent only some thirty seconds. Isn't that remarkable, Mr. Porter? It's one of the many extraordinary paradoxes we encounter in the strange new realm of time travel." He throws another switch. The time machine once more assumes solid form. *"Voila!"* cries the salesman. "Here is Mrs. Porter, returned safe and sound from her voyage into the past." He flings open the door of the time machine. The passenger compartment is empty. The salesman's face crumbles. "Mrs. Porter?" he shrieks in consternation. "Mrs. Porter? I don't understand! How could there have been a malfunction? This is impossible! Mrs. Porter? *Mrs. Porter?*"

She hurries down the dirty street toward the tall brick building. This is the place. Upstairs. Fifth floor, apartment 5J. As she starts to ring the doorbell, a tall, lean man steps out of the shadows and clamps his hand powerfully around her wrist. "Time Patrol," he says crisply, flashing an identification badge. "You're under arrest for contemplated temponautic murder, Mrs. Porter."

"But I haven't any grandson," he sputters. "I'm not even mar—" She laughs. "Don't worry about it!" she tells him. "You're going to have a daughter named Martha and she'll have a son named Ted and I'm going to marry Ted and we'll have two children named Bobby and Tink. And you're going to live to be an old, old man. And that's all you need to know. Now let's have a little fun." She touches a catch at the side of her tunic and the garment falls away in a single fluid cascade. Beneath it she is naked. Her nipples stare up at him like blind pink eyes. She beckons to him. "Come on!" she says hoarsely. "Get undressed, Martin! You're wasting time!"

Alice giggles nervously. "Well, as a matter of fact," she says to the salesman, "I think I'm willing to let my husband be the guinea pig. How about it, Ted?" She turns toward him. So does the salesman. "Certainly, Mr. Porter. I know you're eager to give our machine a test run, yes?" No, Ted thinks, but he feels the pressure of events propelling him willy-nilly. He gets into the machine. As the door closes on him he fears that claustrophobic panic will overwhelm him; he is reassured by the sight of a handle on the door's inner face. He pushes on it and the door opens, and he steps out of the machine just in time to see his earlier self coming into the Temponautics showroom with Alice. The salesman is going forward to greet them. Ted is now eighteen minutes into his own past. Alice and the other Ted stare at him, aghast. The salesman whirls and exclaims, "Wait a second, you aren't supposed to get out of—" How stupid they all look! How bewildered! Ted laughs in their faces. Then he rushes past them, nearly knocking his other self down, and erupts into the shopping-center plaza. He springs in a wild frenzy of exhilaration toward the parking area. Free, he thinks. I'm free at last. And I didn't have to kill anybody.

Suppose I rent a machine, Alice thinks, and go back to 1947 and kill Martin. Suppose I really do it. What if there's some way of tracing the crime to me? After all, a crime committed by a person from 2006 who goes back to 1947 will have consequences in our present day. It might change all sorts of things. So they'd want to catch the criminal and punish him, or better yet prevent the crime from being committed in the first place. And the time-machine company is bound to know what year I asked them to send me to. So maybe it isn't such an easy way of committing a perfect crime. I don't know. God, I can't understand any of this. But perhaps I can get away with it. Anyway, I'm going to give it a try. I'll show Ted he can't go on treating me like dirt.

They lie peacefully side by side, sweaty, drowsy, exhausted in the good exhaustion that comes after a first-rate screw. Martin tenderly strokes her belly and thighs. How smooth her skin is, how pale, how transparent! The little blue veins so clearly visible. "Hey," he says suddenly. "I just thought of something. I wasn't wearing a rubber or anything. What if I made you pregnant? And if you're really who you say you are. Then you'll go back to the year 2006 and you'll have a kid and he'll be his own grandfather, won't he?" She laughs. "Don't worry much about it," she says.

A wave of timidity comes over her as she enters the Temponautics office. This is crazy, she tells herself. I'm getting out of here. But before she can turn around, the salesman she spoke to the day before materializes from a side room and gives her a big hello. Mr. Friesling. He's practically rubbing his hands together in anticipation of landing a contract. "So nice to see you again, Mrs. Porter." She nods and glances worriedly at the demonstration models. "How much would it cost," she asks, "to spend a few hours in the spring of 1947?"

Sunday is the big family day. Four generations sitting down to dinner together: Martin, Martha, Ted and Alice, Bobby and Tink. Ted rather enjoys these reunions, but he knows Alice loathes them, mainly because of Martha. Alice hates her mother-in-law. Martha has never cared much for Alice, either. He watches them glaring at each other across the table. Meanwhile old Martin stares lecherously at the gulf between Alice's breasts. You have to hand it to the old man, Ted thinks. He's never lost the old urge. Even though there's not a hell of a lot he can do about gratifying it, not at his age. Martha says sweetly, "You'd look ever so much better, Alice dear, if you'd let your hair grow out to its natural color." A sugary smile from Martha. A sour scowl from Alice. She glowers at the older woman. "This *is* its natural color," she snaps.

Mr. Friesling hands her the standard contract form. Eight pages of densely packed type. "Don't be frightened by it, Mrs. Porter. It looks formidable but actually it's just a lot of empty legal rhetoric. You can show it to your lawyer, if you like. I can tell you, though, that most of our customers find no need for that." She leafs through it. So far as she can tell, the contract is mainly a disclaimer of responsibility. Temponautics, Ltd., agrees to bear the brunt of any malfunction caused by its own demonstrable negligence, but wants no truck with acts of God or with accidents brought about by clients who won't obey the safety regulations. On the fourth page Alice finds a clause warning the prospective renter that the company cannot be held liable for any consequences of actions by the renter which wantonly or wilfully interfere with the already-determined course of history. She translates that for herself: *If you kill your husband's grandfather, don't blame us if you get in trouble.* She skims the remaining pages. "It looks harmless enough," she says. "Where do I sign?"

As Martin comes out of the bathroom he finds Martha blocking his way. "Excuse me," he says mildly, but she remains in his path. She is a big fleshy woman. At fifty-eight she affects the fashions of the very young, with grotesque results; he hates that aspect of her. He can see why Alice dislikes her so much. "Just a moment," Martha says. "I want to talk to you, father." "About what?" he asks. "About those looks you give Alice. Don't you think that's a little too much? How tasteless can you get?" "Tasteless? Are you anybody to talk about taste, with your face painted green like a fifteen-year-old?" She looks angry: he's scored a direct hit. She replies, "I just think that at the age of eighty-two you ought to have a greater regard for decency than to go staring down your own grandson's wife's front." Martin sighs. "Let me have the staring, Martha. It's all I've got left."

He is at the office, deep in complicated negotiations, when his autosecretary bleeps him and announces that a call has come in from a

Mr. Friesling, of the Union Boulevard Plaza office of Temponautics, Ltd. Ted is puzzled by that: what do the time-machine people want with him? Trying to line him up as a customer? "Tell him I'm not interested in time-trips," Ted says. But the autosecretary bleeps again a few moments later. Mr. Friesling, it declares, is calling in reference to Mr. Porter's credit standing. More baffled than before, Ted orders the call switched over to him. Mr. Friesling appears on the desk screen. He is small-featured and bright-eyed, rather like a chipmunk. "I apologize for troubling you, Mr. Porter," he begins. "This is strictly a routine credit check, but it's altogether necessary. As you surely know, your wife has requested rental of our equipment for a fifty-nine-year time-jaunt, and inasmuch as the service fee for such a trip exceeds the level at which we extend automatic credit, our policy requires us to ask you if you'll confirm the payment schedule that she has requested us to—" Ted coughs violently. "Hold on," he says. "My wife's going on a time-jaunt? What the hell, this is the first time I've heard of that!"

She is surprised by the extensiveness of the preparations. No wonder they charge so much. Getting her ready for the jaunt takes hours. They inoculate her to protect her against certain extinct diseases. They provide her with clothing in the style of the mid-twentieth century, ill-fitting and uncomfortable. They give her contemporary currency, but warn her that she would do well not to spend any except in an emergency, since she will be billed for it at its present-day numismatic value, which is high. They make her study a pamphlet describing the customs and historical background of the era and quiz her in detail. She learns that she is not under any circumstances to expose her breasts or genitals in public while she is in 1947. She must not attempt to obtain any mind-stimulating drugs other than alcohol. She should not say anything that might be construed as praise of the Soviet Union or of Marxist philosophy. She must bear in mind that she is entering the past solely as an observer, and should engage in minimal social interaction with the citizens of the era she is visiting. And so forth. At last they decide it's safe to let her go. "Please come this way, Mrs. Porter," Friesling says.

After staring at the telephone a long while, Martin punches out Alice's number. Before the second ring he loses his nerve and disconnects. Immediately he calls her again. His heart pounds so furiously that the medic, registering alarm on its delicate sensing apparatus, starts toward him. He waves the robot away and clings to the phone. Two rings. Three. Ah.

"Hello?" Alice says. Her voice is warm and rich and feminine. He has his screen switched off. "Hello? Who's there?" Martin breathes heavily into the mouthpiece. Ah. Ah. Ah. Ah. "Hello? Hello? Hello? Listen, you pervert, if you phone me once more—" *Ah. Ah. Ah.* A smile of bliss appears on Martin's withered features. Alice hangs up. Trembling, Martin sags in his chair. Oh, that was good! He signals fiercely to the medic. "Let's have the injection now, you metal monster!" He laughs. Dirty old man.

Ted realizes that it isn't necessary to kill a person's grandfather in order to get rid of that person. Just interfere with some crucial event in that person's past, is all. Go back and break up the marriage of Alice's grandparents, for example. (How? Seduce the grandmother when she's eighteen? "I'm terribly sorry to inform you that your intended bride is no virgin, and here's the documentary evidence." They were very grim about virginity back then, weren't they?) Nobody would have to die. But Alice wouldn't ever be born.

Martin still can't believe any of this, even after she's slept with him. It's some crazy practical joke, most likely. Although he wishes all practical jokes were as sexy as this one. "Are you really from the year 2006?" he asks her. She laughs prettily. "How can I prove it to you?" Then she leaps from the bed. He tracks her with his eyes as she crosses the room, breasts jiggling gaily. What a sweet little body. How thoughtful of my older self to ship her back here to me. If that's what really happened. She fumbles in her purse and extracts a handful of coins. "Look here," she says. "Money from the future. Here's a dime from 1993. And this is a two-dollar piece from 2001. And here's an old one, a 1979 Kennedy half dollar." He studies the unfamiliar coins. They have a greasy look, not silvery at all. Counterfeits? They won't necessarily be striking coins out of silver forever. And the engraving job is very professional. A two-dollar piece, eh? Well, you never can tell. And this. The half dollar. A handsome young man in profile. "Kennedy?" he says. "Who's Kennedy?"

So this is it at last. Two technicians in gray smocks watch her, soberfaced, as she clambers into the machine. It's very much like a coffin, just as she imagined it would be. She can't sit down in it: it's too narrow. Gives her the creeps, shut up in here. Of course, they've told her the trip won't take any apparent subjective time, only a couple of seconds. *Woosh!* and she'll be there. All right. They close the door. She hears the lock clicking shut. Mr. Friesling's voice comes to her over a loudspeaker. "We wish you a happy voyage, Mrs. Porter. Keep calm and you won't get into any difficulties." Suddenly the red light over the door is glowing. That means the jaunt has begun: she's traveling backward in time. No sense of acceleration, no sense of motion. One, two, three. The light goes off. That's it. I'm in 1947, she tells herself. Before she opens the door, she closes her eyes and runs through her history lessons. World War II has just ended. Europe is in ruins. There are forty-eight states. Nobody has been to the moon yet or even thinks much about going there. Harry Truman is president. Stalin runs Russia and Churchill—is Churchill still prime minister of England? She isn't sure. Well, no matter. I didn't come here to talk about prime ministers. She touches the latch and the door of the time machine swings outward.

He steps from the machine into the year 2006. Nothing has changed in the showroom. Friesling, the two poker-faced technicians, the sleek desks, the thick carpeting, all the same as before. He moves bouncily. His mind is still back there with Alice's grandmother. The taste of her lips, the soft urgent cries of her fulfillment. Who ever said all women were frigid in the old days? They ought to go back and find out. Friesling smiles at him. "I hope you had a very enjoyable journey, Mr.—ah—" Ted nods. "Enjoyable and useful," he says. He goes out. Never to see Alice again —how beautiful! The car isn't where he remembers leaving it in the parking area. You have to expect certain small peripheral changes, I guess. He hails a cab, gives the driver his address. His key does not fit the front door. Troubled, he thumbs the annunciator. A woman's voice, not Alice's, asks him what he wants. "Is this the Ted Porter residence?" he asks. "No, it isn't," the woman says, suspicious and irritated. The name on the doorplate, he notices now, is McKenzie. So the changes are not all so small. Where do I go now? If I don't live here, then where? "Wait!" he yells to the taxi, just pulling away. It takes him to a downtown cafe, where he phones Ellie. Her face, peering out of the tiny screen, wears an odd frowning expression. "Listen, something very strange has happened," he begins, "and I need to see you as soon as—" "I don't think I know you," she says. "I'm Ted," he tells her. "Ted who?" she asks.

How peculiar this is, Alice thinks. Like walking into a museum diorama and having it come to life. The noisy little automobiles. The ugly clothing. The squat, dilapidated twentieth-century buildings. The chaos. The oily, smoky smell of the polluted air. Wisps of dirty snow in the streets. Cans of garbage just sitting around as if nobody's ever heard of the plague. Well, I won't stay here long. In her purse she carries her kitchen carver, a tiny nickel-jacketed laser-powered implement. Steel pipes are all right for dream-fantasies, but this is the real thing, and she wants the killing to be quick and efficient. Criss, cross, with the laser beam, and Martin goes. At the street corner she pauses to check the address. There's no central info number to ring for all sorts of useful data, not in these primitive times; she must use a printed telephone directory, a thick tattered book with small smeary type. Here he is: Martin Jamieson, 504 West Forty-fifth. That's not far. In ten minutes she's there. A dark brick structure, five or six stories high, with spidery metal fire escapes running down its face. Even for its day it appears unusually run down. She goes inside. A list of tenants is posted just within the front door. Jamieson, 3A. There's no elevator and of course no liftshaft. Up the stairs. A musty hallway lit by a single dim incandescent bulb. This is apartment 3A. Jamieson. She rings the bell.

Ten minutes later Friesling calls back, sounding abashed and looking dismayed: "I'm sorry to have to tell you that there's been some sort of error, Mr. Porter. The technicians were apparently unaware that a credit check was in process and they sent Mrs. Porter off on her trip while we were still talking." Ted is shaken. He clutches the edge of the desk. Controlling himself with an effort, he says, "How far back was it that she wanted to go?" Friesling says, "It was fifty-nine years. To 1947." Ted nods grimly. A horrible idea has occurred to him. 1947 was the year that his mother's parents met and got married. What is Alice up to?

The doorbell rings. Martin, freshly showered, is sprawled out naked on his bed, leafing through the new issue of *Esquire* and thinking vaguely of going out for dinner. He isn't expecting any company. Slipping into his bathrobe, he goes toward the door. "Who's there?" he calls. A youthful, pleasant female voice replies, "I'm looking for Martin Jamieson." Well, okay. He opens the door. She's perhaps twenty-seven, twenty-eight years old, *very* sexy, on the slender side but well built. Dark hair, worn in a strangely boyish short cut. He's never seen her before. "Hi," he says tentatively. She grins warmly at him. "You don't know me," she tells him, "but I'm a friend of an old friend of yours. Mary Chambers? Mary and I grew up together in—ah—Ohio. I'm visiting New York for the first time, and Mary once told me that if I ever come to New York I should

be sure to look up Martin Jamieson, and so—may I come in?" "You bet,"
he says. He doesn't remember any Mary Chambers from Ohio. But what
the hell, sometimes you forget a few. What the hell.

He's much more attractive than she expected him to be. She has always
known Martin only as an old man, made unattractive as much by his
coarse lechery as by what age has done to him. Hollow-chested, stoop-
shouldered, pleated jowly face, sparse strands of white hair, beady eyes of
faded blue—a wreck of a man. But this Martin in the doorway is sturdy,
handsome, untouched by time, brimming with life and vigor and virility.
She thinks of the carver in her purse and feels a genuine pang of regret
at having to cut this robust boy off in his prime. But there isn't such a
great hurry, is there? First we can enjoy each other, Martin. And then the
laser.

"When is she due back?" Ted demands. Friesling explains that all
concepts of time are relative and flexible; so far as elapsed time at Now
Level goes, she's already returned. "What?" Ted yells. "Where is she?"
Friesling does not know. She stepped out of the machine, bade the
Temponautics staff a pleasant good-bye, and left the showroom. Ted puts
his hand to his throat. What if she's already killed Martin? Will I just
wink out of existence? Or is there some sort of lag, so that I'll fade
gradually into unreality over the next few days? "Listen," he says raggedly,
"I'm leaving my office right now and I'll be down at your place in less than
an hour. I want you to have your machinery set up so that you can
transport me to the exact point in space and time where you just sent my
wife." "But that won't be possible," Friesling protests. "It takes hours to
prepare a client properly for—" Ted cuts him off. "Get everything set up,
and to hell with preparing me properly," he snaps. "Unless you feel like
getting slammed with the biggest negligence suit since this time-machine
thing got started, you better have everything ready when I get there."

He opens the door. The girl in the hallway is young and good-looking,
with close-cropped dark hair and full lips. Thank you, Mary Chambers,
whoever you may be. "Pardon the bathrobe," he says, "but I wasn't
expecting company." She steps into his apartment. Suddenly he notices
how strained and tense her face is. Country girl from Ohio, suddenly
having second thoughts about visiting a strange man in a strange city? He
tries to put her at her ease. "Can I get you a drink?" he asks. "Not much of a

selection, I'm afraid, but I have scotch, gin, some blackberry cordial—"
She reaches into her purse and takes something out. He frowns. Not a gun,
exactly, but it does seem like a weapon of some sort, a little glittering metal
device that fits neatly in her hand. "Hey," he says, "what's—" "I'm so
terribly sorry, Martin," she whispers, and a bolt of terrible fire slams into his
chest.

She sips the drink. It relaxes her. The glass isn't very clean, but she isn't
worried about picking up a disease, not after all the injections Friesling
gave her. Martin looks as if he can stand some relaxing too. "Aren't you
drinking?" she asks. "I suppose I will," he says. He pours himself some
gin. She comes up behind him and slips her hand into the front of his
bathrobe. His body is cool, smooth, hard. "Oh, Martin," she murmurs.
"Oh! Martin!"

Ted takes a room in one of the commercial hotels downtown. The first
thing he does is try to put a call through to Alice's mother in Chillicothe.
He still isn't really convinced that his little time-jaunt flirtation has re-
troactively eliminated Alice from existence. But the call convinces him,
all right. The middle-aged woman who answers is definitely not Alice's
mother. Right phone number, right address—he badgers her for the
information—but wrong woman. "You don't have a daughter named
Alice Porter?" he asks three or four times. "You don't know anyone in
the neighborhood who does? It's important." All right. Cancel the old
lady, ergo cancel Alice. But now he has a different problem. How much
of the universe has he altered by removing Alice and her mother? Does
he live in some other city, now, and hold some other job? What has
happened to Bobby and Tink? Frantically he begins phoning people.
Friends, fellow workers, the man at the bank. The same response from
all of them: blank stares, shakings of the head. We don't know you, fellow.
He looks at himself in the mirror. Okay, he asks himself. Who am I?

Martin moves swiftly and purposefully, the way they taught him to do
in the army when it's necessary to disarm a dangerous opponent. He
lunges forward and catches the girl's arm, pushing it upward before she
can fire the shiny whatzis she's aiming at him. She turns out to be stronger
than he anticipated, and they struggle fiercely for the weapon. Suddenly
it fires. Something like a lightning-bolt explodes between them and knocks

him to the floor, stunned. When he picks himself up he sees her lying near the door with a charred hole in her throat.

The telephone's jangling clatter brings Martin up out of a dream in which he is ravishing Alice's luscious young body. Dry-throated, gummy-eyed, he reaches a palsied hand toward the receiver. "Yes?" he says. Ted's face blossoms on the screen. "Grandfather!" he blurts. "Are you all right?" "Of course I'm all right," Martin says testily. "Can't you tell? What's the matter with you, boy?" Ted shakes his head. "I don't know," he mutters. "Maybe it was only a bad dream. I imagined that Alice rented one of those time machines and went back to 1947. And tried to kill you so that I wouldn't ever have existed." Martin snorts. "What idiotic nonsense! How can she have killed me in 1947 when I'm here alive in 2006?"

Naked, Alice sinks into Martin's arms. His strong hands sweep eagerly over her breasts and shoulders and his mouth descends to hers. She shivers with desire. "Yes," she murmurs tenderly, pressing herself against him. "Oh, yes, yes, yes!" They'll do it and it'll be fantastic. And afterward she'll kill him with the kitchen carver while he's lying there savoring the event. But a troublesome thought occurs. If Martin dies in 1947, Ted doesn't get to be born in 1968. Okay. But what about Tink and Bobby? They won't get born either, not if I don't marry Ted. I'll be married to someone else when I get back to 2006, and I suppose I'll have different children. Bobby? Tink? What am I doing to you? Sudden fear congeals her, and she pulls back from the vigorous young man nuzzling her throat. "Wait," she says. "Listen, I'm sorry. It's all a big mistake. I'm sorry, but I've got to get out of here right away!"

So this is the year 1947. Well, well, well. Everything looks so cluttered and grimy and ancient. He hurries through the chilly streets toward his grandfather's place. If his luck is good and if Friesling's technicians have calculated things accurately, he'll be able to head Alice off. That might even be her now, that slender woman walking briskly half a block ahead of him. He steps up his pace. Yes, it's Alice, on her way to Martin's. Well done, Friesling! Ted approaches her warily, suspecting that she's armed. If she's capable of coming back to 1947 to kill Martin, she'd kill him just as readily. Especially back here where neither one of them has any legal existence. When he's close to her he says in a low, hard, intense voice, "Don't turn around, Alice. Just keep walking as if everything's perfectly normal." She stiffens. "Ted?" she cries, astonished. "Is that you, Ted?" "Damned right it is." He laughs harshly. "Come on. Walk to the corner and turn to your left around the block. You're going back to your machine and you're going to get the hell out of the twentieth century without harming anybody. I know what you were trying to do, Alice. But I caught you in time, didn't I?"

Martin is just getting down to real business when the door of his apartment bursts open and a man rushes in. He's middle-aged, stocky, with weird clothes—the ultimate in zoot suits, a maze of vividly contrasting colors and conflicting patterns, shoulders padded to resemble shelves —and a wild look in his eyes. Alice leaps up from the bed. "Ted!" she screams. "My God, what are you doing here?" "You murderous bitch," the intruder yells. Martin, naked and feeling vulnerable, his nervous system stunned by the interruption, looks on in amazement as the stranger grabs her and begins throttling her. "Bitch! Bitch! Bitch!" he roars, shaking her in a mad frenzy. The girl's face is turning black. Her eyes are bugging. After a long moment Martin breaks finally from his freeze. He stumbles forward, seizes the man's fingers, peels them away from the girl's throat. Too late. She falls limply and lies motionless. "Alice!" the intruder moans. "Alice, Alice, what have I done?" He drops to his knees beside her body, sobbing. Martin blinks. "You killed her," he says, not believing that any of this can really be happening. "You actually killed her!"

Alice's face appears on the telephone screen. Christ, how beautiful she is, Martin thinks, and his decrepit body quivers with lust. "There you are," he says. "I've been trying to reach you for hours. I had such a strange dream—that something awful had happened to Ted—and then your phone didn't answer, and I began to think maybe the dream was a premonition of some kind, an omen, you know—" Alice looks puzzled. "I'm afraid you have the wrong number, sir," she says sweetly, and hangs up.

She draws the laser and the naked man cowers back against the wall in bewilderment. "What the hell is this?" he asks, trembling. "Put that thing down, lady. You've got the wrong guy." "No," she says. "You're the one I'm after. I hate to do this to you, Martin, but I've got no choice. You have to die." "Why?" he demands. "*Why?*" "You wouldn't understand it even if I told you," she says. She moves her finger toward the discharge stud. Abruptly there is a frightening sound of cracking wood and collapsing plaster behind her, as though an earthquake has struck. She whirls and is appalled to see her husband breaking down the door of Martin's apartment. "I'm just in time!" Ted exclaims. "Don't move, Alice!" He reaches for her. In panic she fires without thinking. The dazzling beam catches Ted in the pit of the stomach and he goes down, gurgling in agony, clutching at his belly as he dies.

The door falls with a crash and this character in peculiar clothing materializes in a cloud of debris, looking crazier than Napoleon. It's incredible, Martin thinks. First an unknown broad rings his bell and invites herself in and takes her clothes off, and then, just as he's about to screw her, this happens. It's pure Marx Brothers, only dirty. But Martin's not going to take any crap. He pulls himself away from the panting, gasping girl on the bed, crosses the room in three quick strides, and seizes the newcomer. "Who the hell are you?" Martin demands, slamming him hard against the wall. The girl is dancing around behind him. "Don't hurt him!" she wails. "Oh, please, don't hurt him!"

Ted certainly hadn't expected to find them in bed together. He understood why she might have wanted to go back in time to murder Martin, but simply to have an affair with him, no, it didn't make sense. Of course, it was altogether likely that she had come here to kill and had paused for a little dalliance first. You never could tell about women, even your own wife. Alleycats, all of them. Well, a lucky thing for him that she had given him these few extra minutes to get here. "Okay," he says. "Get your clothes on, Alice. You're coming with me." "Just a second, mister," Martin growls. "You've got your goddamned nerve, busting in like this." Ted tries to explain, but the words won't come. It's all too complicated. He gestures mutely at Alice, at himself, at Martin. The next moment Martin jumps him and they go tumbling together to the floor.

"Who are you?" Martin yells, banging the intruder repeatedly against the wall. "You some kind of detective? You trying to work a badger game on me?" Slam. Slam. Slam. He feels the girl's small fists pounding on his own back. "Stop it!" she screams. "Let him alone, will you? He's my husband!" *"Husband!"* Martin cries. Astounded, he lets go of the stranger and swings around to face the girl. A moment later he realizes his mistake. Out of the corner of his eye he sees that the intruder has raised his fists high above his head like clubs. Martin tries to get out of the way, but no time, no time, and the fists descend with awful force against his skull.

Alice doesn't know what to do. They're rolling around on the floor, fighting like wildcats, now Martin on top, now Ted. Martin is younger and bigger and stronger, but Ted seems possessed by the strength of the insane; he's gone berserk. Both men are bloody-faced and furniture is crashing over everywhere. Her first impulse is to get between them and stop this crazy fight somehow. But then she remembers that she has come here as a killer, not as a peacemaker. She gets the laser from her purse and aims it at Martin, but then the combatants do a flip-flop and it is Ted who is in the line of fire. She hesitates. It doesn't matter which one she shoots, she realizes after a moment. They both have to die, one way or another. She takes aim. Maybe she can get them both with one bolt. But as her finger starts to tighten on the discharge stud Martin suddenly gets Ted in a bearhug and, half lifting him, throws him five feet across the room. The back of Ted's neck hits the wall and there is a loud *crack*. Ted slumps and is still. Martin gets shakily to his feet. "I think I killed him," he says. "Christ, who the hell was he?" "He was your grandson," Alice says, and begins to shriek hysterically.

Ted stares in horror at the crumpled body at his feet. His hands still tingle from the impact. The left side of Martin's head looks as though a pile-driver has crushed it. "Good God in heaven," Ted says thickly, "what have I done? I came here to protect him and I've killed him! I've killed my own grandfather!" Alice, wide-eyed, futilely trying to cover her nakedness by folding one arm across her breasts and spreading her other hand over her loins, says, "If he's dead, why are you still here? Shouldn't you have disappeared?" Ted shrugs. "Maybe I'm safe as long as I remain here in the past. But the moment I try to go back to 2006, I'll vanish as though I've never been. I don't know. I don't understand any of this. What do you think?"

Alice steps uncertainly from the machine into the Temponautics show-room. There's Friesling. There are the technicians. Friesling says, smiling, "I hope you had a very enjoyable journey, Mrs.—ah—uh—" He falters. "I'm sorry," he says, reddening, "but your name seems to have escaped me." Alice says, "It's—ah—Alice—uh—do you know, the second name escapes me too?"

The whole clan has gathered to celebrate Martin's eighty-third birthday. He cuts the cake and then one by one they go to him to kiss him. When it's Alice's turn, he deftly spins her around so that he screens her from the others, and gives her rump a good hearty pinch. "Oh, if I were only fifty years younger!" he sighs.

It's a warm springlike day. Everything has been lovely at the office—three new accounts all at once—and the trip home on the freeway was a breeze. Alice is waiting for him, dressed in her finest and most sexy outfit, all ready to go out. It's a special day. Their eleventh anniversary. How beautiful she looks! He kisses her, she kisses him, he takes the tickets from his pocket with a grand flourish. "Surprise," he says. "Two weeks in Hawaii, starting next Tuesday! Happy anniversary!" "Oh, Ted!" she cries. "How marvelous! I love you, Ted darling!" He pulls her close to him again. "I love you, Alice dear."

My Son the Murderer

BERNARD MALAMUD

One of the most famous American writers of the post–World War II period, Bernard Malamud writes of the customs and mores of American Jewry, but people of all backgrounds and nationalities have identified with his universal characters. As fine a short story writer as he is a novelist, his books include The Natural *(1952),* The Magic Barrel *(1958), the Pulitzer Prize-winning* The Fixer *(1966),* Dubin's Lives *(1979) and* Rembrandt's Hat *(1973), which contains "My Son the Murderer," a rare excursion into the realm of the criminous—and a breathtaking one.*

He wakes feeling his father is in the hallway, listening. He listens to him sleep and dream. Listening to him get up and fumble for his pants. He won't put on his shoes. To him not going to the kitchen to eat. Staring with shut eyes in the mirror. Sitting an hour on the toilet. Flipping the pages of a book he can't read. To his anguish, loneliness. The father stands in the hall. The son hears him listen.

My son the stranger, he won't tell me anything.

I open the door and see my father in the hall. Why are you standing there, why don't you go to work?

On account of I took my vacation in the winter instead of the summer like I usually do.

What the hell for if you spend it in this dark smelly hallway, watching my every move? Guessing what you can't see. Why are you always spying on me?

My father goes to the bedroom and after a while sneaks out in the hallway again, listening.

I hear him sometimes in his room but he don't talk to me and I don't know what's what. It's a terrible feeling for a father. Maybe someday he will write me a letter, My dear father . . .

My dear son Harry, open up your door. My son the prisoner.

My wife leaves in the morning to stay with my married daughter, who is expecting her fourth child. The mother cooks and cleans for her and takes care of the three children. My daughter is having a bad pregnancy, with high blood pressure, and lays in bed most of the time. This is what the doctor advised her. My wife is gone all day. She worries something is wrong with Harry. Since he graduated college last summer he is alone, nervous, in his own thoughts. If you talk to him, half the time he yells if he answers you. He reads the papers, smokes, he stays in his room. Or once in a while he goes for a walk in the street.

How was the walk, Harry?

A walk.

My wife advised him to go look for work, and a couple of times he went, but when he got some kind of an offer he didn't take the job.

It's not that I don't want to work. It's that I feel bad.

So why do you feel bad?

I feel what I feel. I feel what is.

Is it your health, sonny? Maybe you ought to go to a doctor?

I asked you not to call me by that name any more. It's not my health. Whatever it is I don't want to talk about it. The work wasn't the kind I want.

So take something temporary in the meantime, my wife said to him.

He starts to yell. Everything's temporary. Why should I add more to what's temporary? My gut feels temporary. The goddamn world is temporary. On top of that I don't want temporary work. I want the opposite of temporary, but where is it? Where do you find it?

My father listens in the kitchen.

My temporary son.

She says I'll feel better if I work. I say I won't. I'm twenty-two since December, a college graduate, and you know where you can stick that. At night I watch the news programs. I watch the war from day to day. It's a big burning war on a small screen. It rains bombs and the flames go higher. Sometimes I lean over and touch the war with the flat of my hand. I wait for my hand to die.

My son with the dead hand.

I expect to be drafted any day but it doesn't bother me the way it used to. I won't go. I'll go to Canada or somewhere I can go.

The way he is frightens my wife and she is glad to go to my daughter's house early in the morning to take care of the three children. I stay with him in the house but he don't talk to me.

You ought to call up Harry and talk to him, my wife says to my daughter.

I will sometime but don't forget there's nine years' difference between our ages. I think he thinks of me as another mother around and one is enough. I used to like him when he was a little boy but now it's hard to deal with a person who won't reciprocate to you.

She's got high blood pressure. I think she's afraid to call.

I took two weeks off from my work. I'm a clerk at the stamps window in the post office. I told the superintendent I wasn't feeling so good, which is no lie, and he said I should take sick leave. I said I wasn't that sick, I only needed a little vacation. But I told my friend Moe Berkman I was staying out because Harry has me worried.

I understand what you mean, Leo. I got my own worries and anxieties about my kids. If you got two girls growing up you got hostages to fortune. Still in all we got to live. Why don't you come to poker on this Friday night? We got a nice game going. Don't deprive yourself of a good form of relaxation.

I'll see how I feel by Friday, how everything is coming along. I can't promise you.

Try to come. These things, if you give them time, all pass away. If it looks better to you, come on over. Even if it don't look so good, come on over anyway because it might relieve your tension and worry that you're under. It's not so good for your heart at your age if you carry that much worry around.

It's the worst kind of worry. If I worry about myself I know what the worry is. What I mean, there's no mystery. I can say to myself, Leo you're a big fool, stop worrying about nothing—over what, a few bucks? Over my health that has always stood up pretty good although I have my ups and downs? Over that I'm now close to sixty and not getting any younger? Everybody that don't die by age fifty-nine gets to be sixty. You can't beat time when it runs along with you. But if the worry is about somebody else, that's the worst kind. That's the real worry because if he won't tell you, you can't get inside of the other person and find out why. You don't know where's the switch to turn off. All you do is worry more.

So I wait out in the hall.

Harry, don't worry so much about the war.

Please don't tell me what to worry about or what not to worry about.

Harry, your father loves you. When you were a little boy, every night when I came home you used to run to me. I picked you up and lifted you up to the ceiling. You liked to touch it with your small hand.

I don't want to hear about that any more. It's the very thing I don't want to hear. I don't want to hear about when I was a child.

Harry, we live like strangers. All I'm saying is I remember better days.

I remember when we weren't afraid to show we loved each other.

He says nothing.

Let me cook you an egg.

An egg is the last thing in the world I want.

So what do you want?

He put his coat on. He pulled his hat off the clothes tree and went down into the street.

Harry walked along Ocean Parkway in his long overcoat and creased brown hat. His father was following him and it filled him with rage.

He walked at a fast pace up the broad avenue. In the old days there was a bridle path at the side of the walk where the concrete bicycle path was now. And there were fewer trees, their black branches cutting the sunless sky. At the corner of Avenue X, just about where you can smell Coney Island, he crossed the street and began to walk home. He pretended not to see his father cross over, though he was infuriated. The father crossed over and followed his son home. When he got to the house he figured Harry was upstairs already. He was in his room with the door shut. Whatever he did in his room he was already doing.

Leo took out his small key and opened the mailbox. There were three letters. He looked to see if one of them was, by any chance, from his son to him. My dear father, let me explain myself. The reason I act as I do . . . There was no such letter. One of the letters was from the Post Office Clerks Benevolent Society, which he slipped into his coat pocket. The other two letters were for Harry. One was from the draft board. He brought it up to his son's room, knocked on the door and waited.

He waited for a while.

To the boy's grunt he said, There is a draft-board letter here for you. He turned the knob and entered the room. His son was lying on his bed with his eyes shut.

Leave it on the table.

Do you want me to open it for you, Harry?

No, I don't want you to open it. Leave it on the table. I know what's in it.

Did you write them another letter?

That's my goddamn business.

The father left it on the table.

The other letter to his son he took into the kitchen, shut the door, and boiled up some water in a pot. He thought he would read it quickly and seal it carefully with a little paste, then go downstairs and put it back in the mailbox. His wife would take it out with her key when she returned from their daughter's house and bring it up to Harry.

The father read the letter. It was a short letter from a girl. The girl said Harry had borrowed two of her books more than six months ago and since she valued them highly she would like him to send them back to her. Could he do that as soon as possible so that she wouldn't have to write again?

As Leo was reading the girl's letter Harry came into the kitchen and when he saw the surprised and guilty look on his father's face, he tore the letter out of his hands.

I ought to murder you the way you spy on me.

Leo turned away, looking out of the small kitchen window into the dark apartment-house courtyard. His face burned, he felt sick.

Harry read the letter at a glance and tore it up. He then tore up the envelope marked personal.

If you do this again don't be surprised if I kill you. I'm sick of you spying on me.

Harry, you are talking to your father.

He left the house.

Leo went into his room and looked around. He looked in the dresser drawers and found nothing unusual. On the desk by the window was a paper Harry had written on. It said: Dear Edith, why don't you go fuck yourself? If you write me another letter I'll murder you.

The father got his hat and coat and left the house. He ran slowly for a while, running then walking, until he saw Harry on the other side of the street. He followed him, half a block behind.

He followed Harry to Coney Island Avenue and was in time to see him board a trolley bus going to the island. Leo had to wait for the next one. He thought of taking a taxi and following the trolley bus, but no taxi came by. The next bus came by fifteen minutes later and he took it all the way to the island. It was February and Coney Island was wet, cold, and deserted. There were few cars on Surf Avenue and few people on the streets. It felt like snow. Leo walked on the boardwalk amid snow flurries, looking for his son. The gray sunless beaches were empty. The hot-dog stands, shooting galleries, and bathhouses were shuttered up. The gunmetal ocean, moving like melted lead, looked freezing. A wind blew in off the water and worked its way into his clothes so that he shivered as he walked. The wind white-capped the leaden waves and the slow surf broke on the empty beaches with a quiet roar.

He walked in the blow almost to Sea Gate, searching for his son, and then walked back again. On his way toward Brighton Beach he saw a man on the shore standing in the foaming surf. Leo hurried down the board-walk stairs and onto the ribbed-sand beach. The man on the roaring shore was Harry, standing in water to the tops of his shoes.

Leo ran to his son. Harry, it was a mistake, excuse me, I'm sorry I opened your letter.

Harry did not move. He stood in the water, his eyes on the swelling leaden waves.

Harry, I'm frightened. Tell me what's the matter. My son, have mercy on me.

I'm frightened of the world, Harry thought. It fills me with fright.

He said nothing.

A blast of wind lifted his father's hat and carried it away over the beach. It looked as though it were going to be blown into the surf, but then the wind blew it toward the boardwalk, rolling like a wheel along the wet sand. Leo chased after his hat. He chased it one way, then another, then toward the water. The wind blew the hat against his legs and he caught it. By now he was crying. Breathless, he wiped his eyes with icy fingers and returned to his son at the edge of the water.

He is a lonely man. This is the type he is. He will always be lonely.

My son who made himself into a lonely man.

Harry, what can I say to you? All I can say to you is who says life is easy? Since when? It wasn't for me and it isn't for you. It's life, that's the way it is—what more can I say? But if a person don't want to live what can he do if he's dead? Nothing. Nothing is nothing, it's better to live.

Come home, Harry, he said. It's cold here. You'll catch a cold with your feet in the water.

Harry stood motionless in the water and after a while his father left. As he was leaving, the wind plucked his hat off his head and sent it rolling along the shore.

My father listens in the hallway. He follows me in the street. We meet at the edge of the water.

He runs after his hat.

My son stands with his feet in the ocean.